THE POMEGRANATE

The Pomegranate

S. J. SCHWAIDELSON

The Pomegranate

Book Design by Danna Mathias

First Edition

Paperback ISBN: 978-1-7923-7186-8
eBook ISBN: 978-1-7923-7185-1

AUTHOR'S NOTE

The characters and events portrayed in this book are fictitious or are used fictitiously. Apart from well-known historical figures, any similarity to real persons, living or dead, is purely coincidental and not intended by the author.

Although Durham was a bishopric during that period, I have created an earldom to suit the needs of the story. And it is verifiable that Canterbury did not have an archbishop assigned at the time of the story.

ACKNOWLEDGMENTS

No novel is ever created in a vacuum, and this one is no exception. I have been gifted ample support in this endeavor and I am forever grateful to the family and friends who have graciously put up with character-speak as well as my head-elsewhere moments. From the beginning of research until the last punctuation mark, this has been a long-term labor of love.

There are a number of people who have been instrumental in getting this book written, edited, and out the door; I cannot adequately express my appreciation for their encouragement and support.

Morgan MacBain leads the pack on this one. Her copious notes, historical observations, and refusal to let me take the easy path were key to the completion of this project. I cannot thank her enough, nor can I possibly express the importance of printed out pages of notes as the first guide in cleaning up the mess. Morgan, I owe you.

Jen and Eli Tocker get a prize for putting me up and putting up with me in Israel. Being able to walk in some of the very same places Batsheva and Khalil walked was beyond thrilling. I am thankful for their hospitality, endless patience, and fine collective sense of humor.

My triumvirate of editors, Joan Naidish (copy), Eric Pasternack (continuity), and Sean Murphy (content structure), all urged me on when I was ready to give it all up. Without these three folks, my work would not have been manageable. I thank them from the bottom of my heart.

Many thanks also to Alyssa Matisec, my editorial evaluator who was instrumental in helping me pare down the book without sacrificing the story. Her input was invaluable, and her kindness much appreciated. And a shout-out in gratitude to Lisa Graham for guiding me through the jungles of blurb-writing.

Martin Jan Månsson's map of medieval trade routes was crucial to my research. I am eternally grateful to him for the additions and adjustments that created a map of Batsheva's journey for the book. Du är min hjälte!

I am indebted to Danna Mathias for humoring my quest for the perfect font and color. The cover is gorgeous, and the interior is simply beautiful. Her gracious patience and understanding was greatly appreciated.

Thanks must also go to all the volunteer readers who read, commented, and encouraged this never-ending project. Their eyes helped me to figure out what worked and what didn't. I am grateful to them all for their perseverance and willingness to be blunt.

Last, but certainly not least, thanks go to Adina and Ben who love stories, especially those about Great-Great Grandma Don't, the best story-telling actress of all time. Telling and retelling those tales to two happy faces is the greatest fun of all.

In loving memory of my grandmother

Bessie Sklar Simon
Batsheva bat Elke Chana v' David Fischel

a.k.a.

Grandma Don't

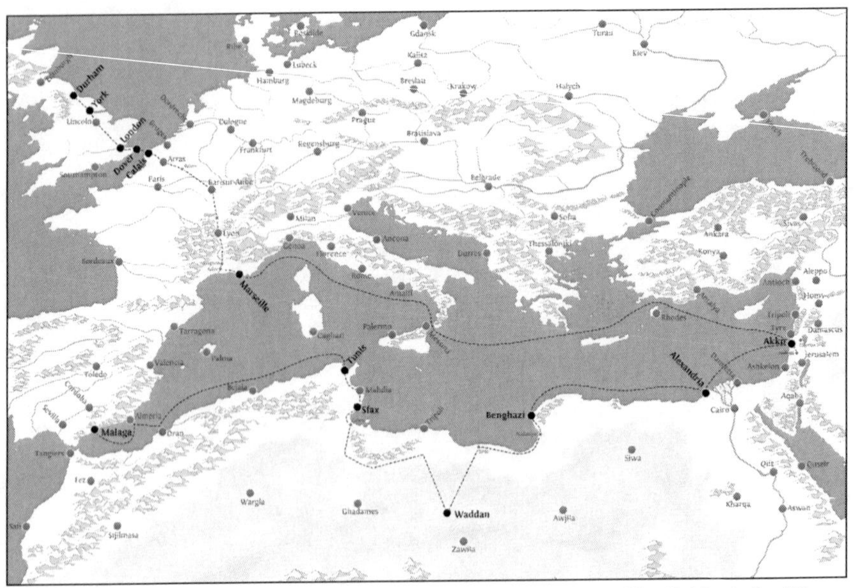

Map © Martin Jan Månsson

CAST OF CHARACTERS

Glossary found on page 547

MÁLAGA, AL-ANDALUS AND TUNIS

Batsheva Hagiz	
Miriam and Yusef Hagiz	Batsheva's parents
Farrah	Batsheva's maid
Asher and Yehuda Hagiz	Batsheva's brothers
Akiva Vital	Batsheva's betrothed
Daniel Hagiz	Batsheva's uncle
Abdul Hajji	the rug merchant in Tunis

THE MAHGREB

Khalil ibn Mahmud	Sheikh of El Ayyub Al-Andalus, son of Mahmud
Sufiye	Khalil's aunt, Mahmud's sister
Gamal	Council hothead
Kassim and Muhammed	Gamal's sons, Khalil's personal guards
Amriat Aisha	Wife of Mustapha, Amir of Alexandria

AKKO

Elena and Nikon Pappanos	Khalil's cousins, their hosts in Akko
Daud and Amina	Batsheva and Khalil's twin children
Devora Al-Fasi	wet nurse for the twins

IN THE DESERT WITH THE BEDU

Ishmael Hajji	Bedu headman
Naziah	Ishmael's daughter-in-law
Gilbert of Durham	Crusader knight
Jamie FitzHugh	Gilbert's esquire and man-at-arms

ALEXANDRIA

Mussa ibn Maimon	Moses Mainmonides - court physician

WESTMINSTER

Jane Blank	seamstress and Batsheva's dear friend
Mary	Batsheva's lady's maid
Queen Eleanor	Eleanor of Aquitaine, Queen of England
Isabella de Blois	Baroness of Lincoln
Edward of York	Gilbert's nephew, secretary to Eleanor
Lady Anne of Durham	Gilbert's daughter

YORK

The dark knight	Gaston d'Artois.
Margret	Gilbert's eldest sister, Countess of York
Henry	Gilbert's brother-in-law, Earl of York
the Jida	the old grandmother who serves the Sultan

DURHAM

Matilda	Gilbert's mother, Dowager Countess of Durham
Charles	Gilbert's uncle, Archbishop of Durham
Gwyneth	Durham's housekeeper
Isaac HaCohain	Jewish merchant in Durham
Rachel and David Vital	Isaac 's daughter and her husband
Sir Thomas	Laird of Crichton Wood
Catherine	Sir Thomas's granddaughter
Archdeacon Poore	Archdeacon of Canterbury
Father Thomas	Arcdeacon Poore's investigator

KHALIL'S MEN IN ENGLAND

Devereaux	one of Uncle Avram's factors
Yusef	Slave in the court of the sultan, English by birth
Alonso	Leader of the Jongleurs
Diego	a jongleur, Alonso's second
Rashid	Uncle Avram's factor and Khalil's man in England

PROLOGUE

Málaga

1177

"Ma ismik, ya fatah?"

A hand was touching her market basket. Turning her eyes upward, she glanced at the boy with disdain, said nothing, and went on examining the bolts of fabric on the merchant's table as if he were nothing more than an annoying fly.

"I asked your name, and I would have you answer me." His voice tightened as he tightened his grip on her basket. The girl turned again. This time, her eyes bore into his and he saw they were as grey as winter storm clouds. The way they met his, unwavering and direct, deepened his resolve to know who she was. "You will answer when I speak to you," he insisted, drawing himself up to his full height. "Do you not know who I am?"

"Unhand my sister!" Another boy, smaller than the first but wiry and ready to defend his sister's honor, pushed his way forward. This boy grabbed the offending arm and jerked it with such force that the offender landed clumsily on the ground.

Leaping up, he charged the smaller boy, ready to dispatch him into the dust. Arms entangled arms, legs flew, and a crowd of onlookers gathered to shout encouragement to the combatants. The girl dove into the fray, using her body as a fulcrum to add leverage to her brother's defense until all three tumbled into the dust. The brother, given advantage by his sister's attack, twisted around until his opponent was pinned to the ground.

"You leave my sister alone!" he shouted, waving a fist in the offender's face.

"I did nothing to your sister!"

"You talked to my sister and that is not permitted!" he countered, digging a knee into the rasping chest.

"You are a dirty boy," pronounced the girl now standing above them both, her own dress dusty, her headdress askew, tendrils of burnished copper hair falling onto her face, her hands planted defiantly on her non-existent hips. "I do not talk to dirty boys."

"Yehuda! Release him!" A richly dressed man broke through the crowd, and hauled the boy off his victim's chest. "I cannot leave you two for a moment without one of you causing one ruckus or another."

The tall boy sprang to his feet. "Your boy has no manners," he spat, "and should be beaten until he learns some." He tugged on his dusty thobe in an effort to regain his dignity. His own father would most likely take him to task for returning in this condition, but there was nothing he could do about it now. His father was striding toward him, dark eyes flashing with anger.

"What is this about?" asked the second father when he reached his son.

"This boy says I insulted his sister by speaking to her. I merely asked her name. Is this a crime in Málaga?" he demanded.

"One does not address unfamiliar women on the street." He looked about for the object of his son's attentions, but saw no woman, only a girl of no more than eight years old, her dress soiled, her headdress listing at a precarious angle. "Is that," he whispered, his voice incredulous, "her?"

Leaning close to his father's ear, the boy whispered, "Buy her for me, father. I am old enough to have a female slave of my own."

His father's laughter rang through the square. "One does not buy any female who catches one's fancy, much less a child." He saw the redness of shame staining his son's smooth cheeks and chose to ignore it as he turned to the boy who had bested his son, and his august-looking father. "Forgive my son, sir, he is young and untested. His actions were merely unwise, not meant to insult."

The other father nodded with understanding. "No offense has been taken, my lord Sheikh Mahmud. Let us both instruct our children in the proper way to behave in public."

With knowing nods and suppressed smiles, the fathers removed their children from the center of attention, and the crowd dispersed.

Whenever Khalil bin Mahmud recalled the last summer he visited the markets in Málaga, he remembered the wispy copper curls and eyes the color of the sky in winter. He did not learn her name that day, nor anything else about her, yet in the darkest part of night, when he would rise long before morning prayers, he would remember those eyes. Would that he could wipe them from his memory, the way she stared down at him when he lay foolishly beneath her brother. But he could not; they were part of his innermost history.

Now, however, he knew much more. As he watched her from across the great hall of this strange castle, he wondered if he would have been better off never having learned her name, or how her eyes danced when she laughed and flashed when she was angry, or how she smoothed Dudu's dark curls or Mina's wrinkled kaftan. But it was too late for that; he knew those things and now, he hoped with all his heart she still cherished them. Khalil watched her brush aside a coppery tendril and ached to do it for her. He knew the feel of that curl as well as he knew the texture of his own hair. Sucking in his breath, he slipped behind a pillar to wait for just the right moment.

PART I

From Málaga to the Mahgreb

1184–1185

CHAPTER 1

Málaga

APRIL 1184

"Bashi! Bashi! Put down that sword and come with me!" Farrah scurried into the courtyard, wiping pudgy fingers on her apron. "If your father sees you with that thing in your hands again, he will scold me for letting you have it. Why must you do this when you know I will be the one to catch your father's wrath?"

Jutting out her chin, Batsheva made a last parry at the fencing dummy dangling precariously from a tree limb. "I cannot feel sorry for you when you are always apologizing for me, Farrah. Why not let me take the blame? Besides, he gave me the sword." She flashed her grey eyes at the servant knowing exactly what Farrah would do.

And Farrah did exactly what was expected: she threw up her hands, shook her head, and muttered something about how difficult a headstrong fifteen-year-old could be.

Batsheva found her mother sitting beneath her favorite pomegranate tree in the corner of the inner courtyard, her fingers deftly separating strands of silk. Miriam Hagiz noticed, but did not comment on the pink flush of her daughter's face. "Come sit with me, Batsheva, and tell me of your preparations." She patted the empty space on the bench.

Batsheva took the proffered space and immediately relieved her mother of her needlework. "I wish my stitches were as fine as yours."

"Perhaps, if you spent as much time on your needlework as you did on your swordplay or your cartography, they would be." The chide was gentle, but well aimed.

"Papa says if I am to travel by caravan from Tunis to Sfax, I must know where I am going and how to defend myself," replied the girl defensively.

"I can now throw a dagger straight into a tree trunk every time. Asher says I have deadly aim. No harm will ever come to me!"

Her mother glanced from beneath lowered lashes as she threaded her needle and smiled. "I am sure you are more than able to defend yourself, my little lioness. Your brothers have sported the results of your defenses more than once, I'm afraid."

"They spend too much time with their noses in the holy books. Even the rabbi said so." Batsheva's lower lip inched forward in a pout but retracted quickly. "The preparations are going well," she said, changing the subject. "I will be ready to sail at month's end." The girl sighed and sagged. "I am very anxious to go, Mama, but I am worried."

"You are going to a place where our family is large, and there you will marry the boy you, yourself, have chosen. But for a month of travel, you will not be without people you know well, and even then, you will have Farrah with you, as well as your cousins, Yishai and Yakov." She took her daughter's hand in her own. "I am sorry your wedding will not be here, but it is more important that Akiva stay in Sfax and tend the business."

Batsheva let her mind's eye see Akiva Vital: tall, handsome Akiva with the laughing eyes and a smile that could melt even the coldest heart. When Batsheva announced she would marry no one else, neither family was surprised, for this would mean not only were they partners in business, but they would, at last, be joined as a family. That Akiva would run their business in Sfax had been planned for years; that Batsheva would join him there seemed the most sensible thing to do. Always one with an eye toward adventure, Batsheva was barely able to contain her excitement once the day of departure had been announced.

"I will miss you and Papa very much," admitted Batsheva furrowing her brow. "And I'm going to miss Asher's wedding to Esther. And it may be years before we can come home again."

"But you will be amongst family, both Papa's and mine, Batsheva; they will all be at the wedding. And you know your cousins…."

"I haven't seen them since we were children! Will they be able to teach me what I need to know about visiting the *sara'i* for Akiva? And will there be anyone there my age or will I be the youngest? And what about…."

"And, and, and!" Miriam Hagiz laughed again, taking her daughter's hands. "Just like a pomegranate, you are full of seeds of knowledge. You already know what to do and how to do it. All those hours spent at the table learning from your father will not be wasted. You will be fine, *granadita*. You will have a lovely home for as long as you are there, and when the time comes, Akiva will bring you home to us. Perhaps, God willing, with several grandchildren to dandle on my knee."

Batsheva blushed to the roots of her copper hair.

The sun was shining on the Alboran Sea the day Batsheva sailed for Tunis. Standing at the stern with her cousins and Farrah, she shut her eyes tight, trying to conjure the faces she could barely see standing at the shore waving colorful silks at the departing travelers. Too soon the ship was moving away from Málaga, leaving the familiar sights of Iberia behind, as the broad expanse of ocean loomed mysteriously ahead.

The voyage was not long; most of it spent safely hugging the Spanish coastline to Almería so they would be safe from pirates before crossing the sea. But there were no signs of pirates as the ship turned east toward Tunis where they would be welcomed by family before the caravan formed for the overland journey to Sfax. Batsheva spent most of her time on deck, perched on a trunk, out of harm's way, watching the sailors as they maneuvered the sails, their tan, muscled bodies glistening in the heat of the day. More than once Farrah scolded her for her fascination, only to be ignored. For their part, the sailors flexed a little harder, smiled a little wider in an effort to impress the daughter of the ship's owner, Yosef Hagiz. The captain, an old friend of the family, answered Batsheva's questions as she learned to read the new water compass, even though it was the coastline which served as their ultimate guide. At night, when she lay on her bunk, Batsheva would stare out her porthole at the stars. Yehuda had taught her the Latin and Greek names of the constellations, and she would fall asleep reciting all the exotic sounding words.

On the sixth day, they reached Tunis. Batsheva was dressed by dawn and stood at the rail peering into the early morning light for the first sign of the city in which her mother had been born. She was certain she would recognize the streets from the endless bedtime stories, and Abdul the rug merchant would surely recognize her when she found his rug shop in the kasbah. After all, wasn't it true that she looked exactly like her mother and Old Abdul's shop had been her mother's favorite place to hide from her maid?

Daniel Hagiz was waiting when they disembarked. "Yishai! Yakov!" He embraced his sons in his big, bearish arms. "Welcome back! Welcome home!" he cried, relieved to see them, "And just in time for Shabbat! Your mother will be so pleased!" When he saw Batsheva, however, he stopped in his tracks and bowed courteously, and, if possible, the grin grew wider. "So, this is the *kallah!* Welcome to my city, Batsheva Hagiz. I am your Uncle Daniel…in case you do not remember me."

"I remember you, Uncle," she replied formally with a little bow of her own before her enthusiasm won out. "Will I have time to see the market before Shabbat begins?"

His laughter was hearty. "Right now, we must hurry home in time to welcome the Sabbath Queen! You shall visit the market after that."

Batsheva blushed prettily and nodded. "Will I see Abdul Hadji's shop? Is it still there?"

"Just as my beard is black, the ancient Abdul is still there."

"Do you think he will know I am Miriam's own daughter?"

"How could he not? You are the vision of Miri as a young girl." With a grand sweep of his hand, he offered her the city. "It's almost Shabbat! Follow me!"

The rest of the afternoon and most of the evening passed in a blur of color and noise. As was the custom, the ladies of the house of Hagiz, joined by the ladies of Miriam's Peres family, gathered in the courtyard to welcome the bride. Dozens of female relatives floated in and out. Great-aunts poked and prodded the girl, commenting on the outrageous color of her hair and eyes, much the way they had when Miriam was a child. The younger cousins, the ones closer in age to Batsheva, hid their giggles behind their hands, rolling their eyes at the endless commentary by the old ones. Try as she could, Batsheva could barely keep their names straight and settled for calling everyone older than her mother *dodah,* aunt, for lack of anything more appropriate. When the festivities finally ended and Batsheva was led to her chamber, Farrah had not even trimmed the wicks of the lamps before her charge was fast asleep.

The caravan was to leave in four days, not nearly enough time, thought Batsheva, to see all of Tunis. Aunt Esther arranged a shopping party for the day after the sabbath, and the ladies, between bites of tajine, were eager to tell their cousin where the best bargains were to be found in the kasbah. From stall to stall they went, picking over the merchandise then bargaining professionally with the shopkeepers. Batsheva found bolts of cloth the likes of which she had never seen and was happy to let Esther haggle over the price in the language peculiar to the kasbah of Tunis.

The sun was past its zenith when they reached Abdul Hadji's shop. An old man, his face wizened into a leathery mass of wrinkles above a great white beard, grinned widely when he opened the door. "Good day to you, Esther Hagiz!" he called when the little party stopped. "Have you come for a visit?" His raspy laugh filled the air.

"Not quite, my old friend, I have brought a young lady who is anxious to meet you." She stepped aside to let Batsheva come closer.

Abdul's eyes opened wide and, again, he laughed. "This cannot be my Miri, so this must be her daughter the bride! Come closer, little lady and let an old man's eyes feast on familiar beauty."

"My mother sends her respect and affection to her friend Abdul Hadji," said Batsheva as she peered inside. "Oh, this is a beautiful place!" Her eyes took in the array of brightly colored rugs hanging from the ceiling and the walls and piled on the floor, each one different, each more exotic than the next. "I have heard so many stories, Abdul Hadji, that I cannot believe I am really here."

"Did you know your mother used to hide in my shop?" he asked and when Batsheva nodded, he clapped his hands with delight. "Did she ever tell you the tale of the monkey and the dates?"

"Is it true, Abdul Hadji? Is it really true?"

"Not only is it a true tale, daughter of Miriam, it has become legend."

"Mama said she used to go to the palace with her father to take cardamom tea with the amir and that was how she met my father."

"That, too, is true. One day, your grandfather brought gemstones for the amir and your father had come along. The minute your father saw your mother sitting with the Amir and the monkey, he fell instantly in love." Abdul Hadji sighed. "I lost my favorite visitor, but Yosef gained a wonderful bride. And the amir, so pleased with his matchmaking, proclaimed it was his plan all along that your mother would come on the same day as David Hagiz and his son." The ladies present clucked appreciatively, all of them knowing the story was quite the truth. But Abdul Hadji held up his hand for silence. "There is something else, something your mother probably never told you." He saw the grey eyes open wide and flash. "Did she tell you that Sahar the fortune-teller told her she would meet her husband at the palace long before the monkey ever appeared?"`

"No," breathed Batsheva.

"This, too, is true. Ask her. She will tell you."

It was time to end the visit, and Batsheva, although she wanted to hear more, knew she must leave with the ladies. "I do not want to go," she said sadly, hating to leave her new friend, "but I must prepare for the caravan. We leave tomorrow."

"Then you must have something to remember our time together, little bride." Abdul disappeared into the back of the shop and returned with a folded rug. With a great flourish, he spread a small rug over a pile of rugs.

The ladies, including Batsheva, gasped when they saw the unusual design. Woven into a jungle of green leaves and bright flowers were monkeys at play. Dozens of monkeys all dressed in little kaftans in a rainbow of colors. Batsheva tried to protest the richness of the gift, but Abdul waved away her words.

"I hoped," sighed the shopkeeper, his voice full of emotion, "one day to give this to Miri, when she returned to visit this old man. I think now that the daughter of Miriam will love it as much as she would." He smiled at the memory of young Miriam. "She was a child of my heart and I miss her bright laugh and sharp wit. It pleases me to see this in her own daughter."

Touched and delighted, Batsheva accepted the little rug. It was one more link to the mother she left behind in Al-Andalus.

Though the caravan would assemble early in the morning, the ladies of the Hagiz household planned an evening of entertainment for Batsheva. Musicians and dancers performed during dinner, delighting the guest of honor with their dexterity. Some of the songs were familiar to her, others strange and exotic, the haunting music of the mountains she was about to cross. Something about the melodies struck Batsheva in the core of her being, an indescribable tug to her heart. Sitting alone, off to one side, she listened to the words, searching for a clue to why the songs affected her so.

As the trays of sweet cakes were passed around, an ancient woman arrived, escorted into the room by Aunt Esther herself. The ladies twittered with delight, recognizing the well-respected seer from the kasbah. Aunt Esther clapped her hands for attention and patiently waited for the ladies to cease their chattering. "Sahar has come to tell Batsheva's fortune," she announced, "and then, if she is not too tired, to predict the babies to come." There were giggles from the corner where four pregnant women, all relatives, sat together. Esther led Sahar to Batsheva, making sure there were plenty of cushions on which the old lady could settle comfortably.

The old woman looked into the grey eyes, but did not take the place beside her, instead, she turned to Esther. "Forgive me, Lady Esther, but this is a serious matter; I would not speak with the bride in public."

There were murmurs of disappointment, but Esther knew Sahar well, and immediately suggested the little garden beside the courtyard. Leading the way, with Batsheva close behind, she saw them settled on a bench close to the garden wall, then left them alone.

"Give me your hands, little bride," said the old woman. Her grip was strong, but her hands unexpectedly warm and soft. In the torchlight, she studied the open palms carefully. "You have come a long way from your home, from your mother, the strong, beautiful Miriam, and your father, the handsome, loyal Yosef. I predicted their match long before they ever met." She saw Batsheva's eyes widen. "Your path has been easy. It will not remain so. I see two strong men. The one who now awaits your arrival is not one of them; one is dark, the other fair. The one who is right for you does not know he is waiting. You will bear children only to lose them for a time, but you will see them again, and have more." The fortune-teller stopped for a moment and sighed, a deep and lonely sound that struck fear in Batsheva's heart. "You are loved and will love, but there will be times when your heart is locked away and you cannot love. This will happen thrice. Each time, there will be great pain. You are strong; you will survive and be stronger for it. Your heart will overflow with love when you least expect it. At twilight, you will find unexpected peace and great happiness."

"I do not think I want to hear any more," murmured Batsheva.

Sahar's small smile revealed another burst of unexpected warmth. "Do not be afraid, little bride. The one who holds your heart most deeply in his will be strong like you; his love for you will know no boundaries. The fair one will need you to make him strong. They are as different as they are alike, but inside, when you search beneath the layers, you will find two good men. Never believe something is so merely because you *think* it is so. Always seek out what is hidden…in your own heart as well."

When they rejoined the others, the seer predicted three boys and a girl, much to the delight of the expectant mothers. The ladies pressed Batsheva for details of her predictions, but the bride-to-be demurred, saying only Sahar had promised her an interesting life. Only when she was alone in her bed, did Batsheva try to decipher the strange, foreboding prophecy.

Camels decked out in fanciful tassels stood calmly while nearby dozens of horses anxiously stomped their hooves. Men ran about in what seemed to the unpracticed eye complete chaos and in the middle of it all, stood Batsheva, her face aglow with expectation. The camel kneeling beside her contentedly chewing its cud, taking no notice of the girl or anything else, was saddled and ready for its young rider. Esther Hagiz had provided Batsheva with Moroccan pantaloons, more appropriate for the journey than the kaftans she usually wore and now, as she looked at the *shibreeyeh* on the camel's back, she understood why; the wide pantaloons would allow her to sit comfortably beneath the tent-like frame draped with cloth designed to keep the sun and dust off a female rider.

"Hut! Hut! Hut!" barked a driver, a long whip in his hand, as he urged one group of animals past where Batsheva stood. His bright red turban stood out amongst the dun colored beasts like a beacon. He nodded to Batsheva as he passed her, shouting "*Salaam, salaam, eurus saghira*!" *Little bride*! Batsheva could feel herself blush.

Yishai appeared out of a cloud of dust, a boy leading a horse behind him. "Are you ready, Bashi?" he asked as he relieved her of the small bag she carried and hung it from one of the camel's saddle horns. "Since we are going only as far as Sfax and won't be crossing the desert, we will ride horses. Much of our supplies are packed on mules and donkeys. They will fare better in Sfax than camels."

"Why can I not ride a horse?" demanded Batsheva. "I ride well enough to keep my seat at a gallop. Why must I ride a camel and be closed in a cage?"

"Because well-born women do not ride horses here. It's best you behave like a girl until you reach Sfax. After that, you can argue with Akiva," he laughed. "I will be riding alongside, so if you need anything, just call to me." With a lurch and a sway, the camel lumbered to its feet and began walking toward the other camels now forming two long lines.

Batsheva spent much of her time gawking at the activity around her. Even though the long lines moved in orderly fashion, outriders ran up and down, making certain everyone was going at the predetermined pace. Small problems with this camel or that donkey occasionally held things up, but generally the caravan moved steadily. On the fifth night, when Djebel Mghila Mountains were shadows in the distance, Batsheva got her first real taste of the work that went into the journey. For all her stoic resolve, Farrah was sore from the day's ride and felt unwell. Batsheva insisted that she remain in her tent and took the skin bags to the stream where others were drawing water for the evening meal. There were other women in the caravan and Batsheva soon fell into easy conversation with them, learning their names and the reasons they, too, were traveling to Sfax and points beyond. The ones returning home eagerly told Batsheva of the city, making sure to name their favorite merchants while warning her about which ones were less than honest with newcomers.

Standing at the water, Batsheva watched the women washing themselves. Pulling off her headdress and veil, she was amused by the less than subtle oohs and aahs the color of her hair elicited from the women. Several reached out to touch the waist-length burnished tresses, exclaiming with wonder at the softness of the curls. When Batsheva doubled over and wet her head, there were even more cries of delight, for when wrung out, her hair tumbled down her back in tight ringlets. Refreshed, Batsheva shouldered her water bags and went back to the camp with the women.

Farrah managed to supervise the meal for the Hagiz family from a mound of cushions brought out to ease her aching back. After the meal, several of the drivers brought out their instruments and singing followed. Batsheva stayed with the women as long as she could, but she was too exhausted to keep her eyes open any longer. Farrah was snoring softly when Batsheva came in to prepare for bed. As she laid out her clothes for the morning, she noticed her veil was missing. Without bothering to awaken Farrah, she slipped from the tent wearing nothing but a light kaftan and scurried toward the place where she was sure she had left it hanging from a bush.

The almost full moon was bright, and the light was more than enough to make the path easy to follow. The stream was not far, but in the darkness, it seemed much farther than it had during the day. Batsheva walked along the bank, letting the water tickle her bare toes as she looked for the place where she had washed with the women. Shadows danced on the water and the sand, giving the place a strange cast, sending little shivers up and down Batsheva's spine. At last, she saw her veil fluttering in a delicate breeze. She reached for the length of silk, now thoroughly tangled on a branch, and started to pull it free. She never saw the shadow moving behind her. A broad hand clamped over her mouth, stifling her scream; lights exploded in her head before the blackness consumed her completely.

CHAPTER 2

Waddan
A Saharan Oasis

MAY 1184

Trussed like an animal and stuffed in a sack, her mouth gagged, Batsheva could only conclude that she was slung over the front of a horse and that the horse was traveling at an incredible pace. Her head pounded with every hoofbeat; she fought back the desire to vomit, sure she would choke on her own bile. There was no point in struggling; her wrists and ankles were rubbed raw by the rope, and the rough material of the sack chafed her face. Drifting in and out of consciousness, Batsheva willed her brain to stay alive when every muscle in her body cried out for the simplicity of death.

She could not tell how long they rode. She was acutely aware of the hand that pinned her against the uncompromising hardness of the saddle. Once or twice she heard voices but, through the sack, the words were muffled and unintelligible. Judging by the gradual change in temperature, she decided the sun must have risen; the sack was growing warmer by the minute. She let fatigue take its course and she allowed herself to slip back into the netherworld where there was no fear.

Unseen hands grabbed Batsheva and pulled her roughly from the horse before dumping her unceremoniously on the ground. Her head still throbbed, but at least the constant jarring had ceased. She concentrated on her breathing, letting her lungs calm her beating heart while she waited for something to happen. At last, after a great deal of mumbling penetrated the rough material, the sack was pulled off. She wished she could rub her eyes, but her hands and feet remained tied. She could see her three abductors. None looked familiar or even remotely interested in her. The men went about their business, eating food taken from one of the other horses, but no one offered her anything to either eat or drink. Her parched lips cracked each time she moved them, but she refused to cry out. Batsheva knew enough not to show any weakness whatsoever. Instead, she stared up into the sky and began counting the stars.

Batsheva slept for what seemed a brief moment before she was yanked upward. The sack was discarded, and she was hoisted into the saddle. Pinned against a broad chest, her nostrils filled with the stench of unwashed man. His beard scratched her neck and Batsheva longed for at least a hand span of space between them. They rode through the night and into the morning, stopping to rest only when the horses flagged. She lost track of the days and the direction.

The three men seemed determined to ride as far as possible in as short a time as possible. Whoever they were, they were well used to the difficult trail. As if they were doing Batsheva a favor, they would allow her small amounts of food at the evening meal, and one of them, not the one she rode with, gave her a blanket as the temperature dropped in the higher elevations. Finally, they descended into the desert.

They stopped only when absolutely necessary. The men never spoke directly to her, and Batsheva never gave them any indication that she understood their language. They treated her as though she were a marginally valuable piece of goods. Any fear she had of rape dissipated after the first week; her abductors never attempted intimate contact. Her hands remained tied but, after a while, the one who rode with her, the one the others called Jamil, removed the ropes from her ankles, letting her ride astride and then walk about when they stopped to rest. Her kaftan was in tatters, yet no offer was made to replace the shreds. Her matted hair was kept out of her face with a makeshift turban with barely enough cloth to cover her face as they rode. The days were all the same; long hours of hard riding followed by brief snatches of sleep, leaving Batsheva bone-weary, hungry, and dirtier than she had ever been in her entire life.

When she thought she would rather walk away from camp to perish in the wilderness than live to see another sunrise, the leader suddenly shouted "Waddan!" as he whipped his horse, charging up a hill leaving the others to catch up. As they came over the rise, Batsheva saw an oasis surrounded by tents with clusters of sheep, goats, and camels grazing nearby.

People stopped what they were doing and ran towards them, waving their hands and shouting greetings.

Pushed off the horse into the arms of several veiled women, Batsheva was dragged, kicking and fighting with her last bit of strength, to a corner of the encampment where a pole was embedded in the ground. The women restrained her while Jamil pulled the rope that bound her hands through an iron ring, raising her arms above her head. When he bent over to spread her legs apart, Batsheva attempted to kick Jamil in the groin. He merely laughed in her face, his sour breath revolting. When he was finished tying her ankles, she was left alone except for a few curious children who came to see the captive.

Batsheva closed her eyes and feigned sleep; she could not bear to see the children staring at her. From beneath her lashes, she could see everyday life taking place in the little tent village. Women carried water from the oasis in jugs perched on hips or shoulders, chatting as they gracefully walked along. Children shouted and laughed as they played in the center of the main circle of tents. A baby cried in the distance and then stopped, most likely put to its mother's breast. Batsheva wanted to cry; she wished herself to be walking free, chatting with her friends back in Al-Andalus. She could almost hear her mother's voice calling to her, yet she knew there was no one who even knew her name. One tear slipped out, then another, then another, until she wept copiously, unable to wipe her aching eyes.

When another band of riders came racing over the hill, Batsheva's tears had dried, and her resolve to never cry again turned to steel. Straightening herself as best she could, she watched the newcomers as they wheeled their horses about and dismounted not far from where she was bound. The one wearing a bright blue turban was obviously their leader. He listened to what was being said, then looked in her direction. Entourage in tow, he strode toward Batsheva.

For a moment, her heart stopped beating. Shutting her eyes, she willed herself to breathe evenly. She could hear their voices as they approached. Only when they were close enough for her to smell the horse scent clinging to their clothes, did she lift her chin to meet his stare with her own.

The man sucked in his breath when he saw her eyes. Only once had he seen eyes that color, but that was so many years ago, he long thought the stormy stare was imagined. Reaching out, he yanked the makeshift turban from her head. Despite the layers of filth, her hair was the color of copper; her curls fell to her narrow waist. He pulled his dirk from its sheath and with a single, fluid motion, slit her kaftan and watched it slide from thin shoulders, exposing her to all those around. There were a few lewd remarks, but the man said nothing. When he spoke at last, it was a harsh sound.

"Clean her up." He spun on his heel and walked away.

The crowd dispersed but for three old crones who removed the remnants of her clothing. Silently, they went about their business, each one obviously well acquainted with what was required to make her presentable. Jugs of water were brought and Batsheva was bathed where she was tied. The dirt was washed from her hair, then the tresses braided, bound with a strip of cloth and pinned to the top of her head. While one cleaned and pared her nails, the other two began covering Batsheva from neck to toe with a muddy concoction so sweetly scented Batsheva thought she would retch. Once she was completely encased, the crones disappeared, leaving her to dry in the afternoon sun.

Sweat trickled down Batsheva's face as the mud grew hot and tight against her skin. The scent faded, but soon it was replaced by the smell of meat roasting somewhere nearby. In spite of herself, Batsheva's empty stomach growled loudly and, as if they could hear it, the crones reappeared with more jugs of warmed water. One of the women took pity on the prisoner and let her sip slowly from a ladle before she began pouring the water over her body. Gradually, with the help of constant rubbing, the mud came off. Glancing down, Batsheva almost cried out; all her body hair was gone, including the silky copper thatch between her legs.

The women seemed pleased with their work; took no notice of the two pink spots growing on Batsheva's cheeks. They dried her thoroughly, then one scurried off in the direction of the camp only to return with a small woman swathed completely in black followed by a large, swarthy man.

The old crow inspected every inch of the captive, muttering comments Batsheva could barely hear to the other crones as she poked and prodded the naked body. Batsheva held her breath as the fingers manipulated her flesh none too gently, and she bit her lip to stifle a cry when the woman inserted a bony finger into a place no one had ever touched. Satisfied with her examination, the crow woman issued a crisp string of commands and left. There was no mistaking the orders; Batsheva understood every word: she had been given to the blue turban as a tribute.

As soon as the crow woman was gone, the swarthy man pulled a knife from his sash and cut the rope that held Batsheva's feet, then her hands. The unexpected release made her crumple, but the man scooped her up in powerful arms. Too tired to bother fighting, Batsheva let herself be slung over his shoulder without a struggle.

The large tent set apart from the others was richly furnished with thick rugs, cushions, and iron-bound trunks. A drape of finely woven linen divided the space into two rooms. The first was furnished with a camp desk and low stool set to one side, yet it was large enough to seat at least 20 men in a circle, judging by the way the cushions were arranged on the floor. The second room, only slightly smaller than the first, was the sleeping chamber. A raised platform served as the bed and this was where Batsheva was deposited. Any hopes she had of fleeing into the night were dashed when the swarthy man chained one ankle to a short post. Without a second glance, he left, and the women set to work on the new acquisition.

This time, they massaged Batsheva with fragrant balms. The undeniable skill of their fingers managed to remove all vestiges of tension from her body in spite of her fear. She drifted in and out of wakefulness, opening her eyes only when moved from one position to the next. Her skin glowed pink, the chapped flesh grew tender once more. Her hair was unbound, rubbed with a silk cloth to dry it, and gentled combed. Try as she might, Batsheva could not deny it was a pleasure to be massaged by the crones who seemed intent on healing her physically. Toward the end, when Batsheva thought herself to be fashioned completely of jelly, one of the women raised her head and held a bowl to her lips.

The broth was warm and welcome. She drank slowly, savoring the rich, spicy liquid that filled her aching belly. A drowsy, lethargic feeling overtook her, and Batsheva fell into a deep, dreamless sleep.

Still damp from his bath in the oasis pool, the man entered his tent and found the three women squatting against the tent wall. Without a word, they left to await their master's call outside the tent.

He looked down at the sleeping woman. She was far more beautiful clean even than she had been filthy. Her hair shimmered in the soft light of the braziers; a glorious copper halo spread out enticingly over a pillow. He knew what was to be seen behind the closed eyelids, although he thought it odd that her lashes should be so dark when the rest of her was so fair. She was small, and skinnier than a woman should be, yet there was great strength in her arms and surprisingly long legs. Jamil said they had found her quite by accident, walking along a riverbank in the middle of nowhere. Knowing Khalil's passion for red-haired women, they had taken her for the sheikh they had offended, in hopes their gift would buy his forgiveness.

He grew hard just staring at her. Kneeling on the bed, he could not deny the burning in his blood. His hands took on a life of their own as they began to stroke the soft flesh of her belly, slowly moving upward to her small breasts. Only when his mouth closed over one impertinent nipple did her eyes fly open. Jolted into a fuzzy reality, she discovered she was bound spread-eagle to the bed.

The man did not notice the movement, so intent was he on arousing the passion he was certain lay buried within. The grey eyes watched him, nothing to be read within their stormy depths. He finally caught her stare as his tongue teased the rosy peak and it stiffened; yet she made no sound as he began to devour her with his mouth.

Through a haze, Batsheva felt herself respond. Whatever they fed her fogged her senses, leaving her vulnerable to his touch. When she strained against her bonds, he seemed only to be enflamed by her efforts. There was no escape; no way to fight him off. With his heat now spreading into her, she succumbed to her fate.

A thousand splinters shot through Batsheva when he pierced her virgin's gate, then dissipated as he moved slowly, rhythmically within her. A strange, sensual pleasure replaced the sharp pain; she could not stop her hips from moving. Sensations wrapped in a myriad of colors flashed through her brain as the man's heat consumed her. A part of her seemed to be melting into him while another part remained detached, as though she were observing herself from a safe distance. The fogginess from the broth hovered in her head, allowing this strange separation, doing nothing to either comfort or frighten her. As his relentless thrusting quickened, she could hear his ragged breath in her ear, while her own silent screams echoed through the same space.

He pushed her to the edge of an abyss; he felt her match him move for move yet he knew her eyes, unblinking, watching him dispassionately, would haunt him to the end of his days. There was no reflection of the passion her body displayed, no sign of the pleasure she obviously felt. Instead, the grey eyes were flat, lifeless. There was no spark of anger, no fire of indignation that he would have expected. Her body responded, yet there was an emptiness in the act that even he could not deny. Closing his own dark eyes against the onslaught of her cold stare, he drove deeper into the woman, letting momentum bring them both to a shattering climax.

He cried out as his seed poured into her, but the woman remained silent, her eyes wide open as one newly dead. The man rolled off her and stared at the tent wall; he could not bear to look at her face. Without a word, he left her where she lay silently staring upward.

One of the crones came rushing in as soon as the man had gone. Armed with a cloth and a bowl of warmed water, she washed away the signs of a first coupling as she checked for virgin's blood. She said nothing as she worked; her eyes, barely visible above her *hijab*, remained impassive. With brisk efficiency, she completed her task, laid a thin blanket over the girl, and went out. Instinctively, Batsheva knew the man would return to spend the night beside her.

There was nothing to do but sleep. No one came to loosen her bonds, no kindly face appeared to comfort her in her shame. Again, Batsheva wanted to cry, but she forbade herself the release. Closing her eyes, she let the broth finish its work, and she slept once more.

If there were any pattern at all to her nights, Batsheva found it in counting the number of times the man, whom she now knew was called Khalil, tortured her body with his hot hands. The broth she was given nightly made it impossible to stop responding to his caresses. Instead, she kept herself sane by staring relentlessly at him during the act. There were times he took her with tenderness and concern, but other times it was an act of unbridled passion. It didn't matter to Batsheva; she was beyond caring. Deprived of any kindness, fed food she could not taste, she wove a cocoon about herself, a protective shell to keep the pain she knew was just beneath the surface from erupting into endless screams.

Each day, in the grey hour before the sun rose over the horizon when Khalil was in prayer, she was taken from the tent and allowed to walk to the pool to bathe. There, under the watchful eyes of the three crones, a thick rope tied around her waist, the other end held by one of her guardians, she submerged her body in the water as it seemed to be required. Batsheva considered drowning herself, but there was no way to accomplish the task without being hauled from the pool by the women. Afterward, she would be returned to the tent where they would begin her daily massage and check for any hair growth.

As she lay on the bed, their fingers manipulating her flesh, Batsheva would close her eyes and imagine happier times. She could envision her mother sitting in the courtyard stitching flowers onto a Sabbath cloth, her brothers nearby, noses buried in holy books. Her father would come into the courtyard and her mother would rise to greet him. Everything in the picture was perfect, except she was missing. Batsheva wondered if her parents even knew she was missing; did they think she was dead? Tears would inevitably threaten, and she silently commanded the image to be gone.

Gradually, Batsheva was given more freedom. Instead of tying her to the bed each day, she was allowed to walk about the back half of the tent, out of view of the entry, with only a thin, symbolic rope about her waist, the other end attached to the iron post near the bed. Only at night, after the evening meal, did the crones lead her back to the bed to tie her hands and feet.

They never attempted to speak to her, nor did Batsheva speak to them. Their assumption that she did not speak their language was wrong, yet the prisoner did nothing to alter that impression. Like any proper young Jewess of Al-Andalus, she was perfectly fluent and literate in Castilian and Arabic, as well as Aramaic, Hebrew, and French. Conversant enough in Greek, Latin, Turkic, and Occitan, she could speak simply but easily, as well as read. It was, as her mother used to say, necessary to be able to communicate with everyone in his own tongue, and even more important to be able to listen without being discerned. At night, when Khalil would sit with his council, she would eavesdrop on their discussions. Usually, the men agreed with their sheikh, but she soon learned to identify the hotheads by their voices, especially the one called Gamal. Whenever Gamal raged at Khalil, she could count on him being of foul temper when he came to her.

One night, after Khalil had finished with her, Batsheva was surprised when he untied her hands and feet. Then, as if he were speaking to the air instead of her, he muttered, "There is nowhere for you to go, and I…." He paused, studying the woman as she rubbed her wrists and ankles. "Perhaps you will be comfortable…perhaps not." With an uncharacteristic sigh, he left the tent.

Khalil walked alone in the moonlight, puzzling over the woman in the tent. She accepted his caresses and responded to him, but it was without returning his passion. The mere sight of her aroused him, yet she left him feeling empty. Not that he expected her to care for him; that would not be a reasonable thing to expect from one who was a captive. Still, every night he hoped that there would be a spark in her eyes, something that would make him believe she was willing to receive him. Cursing softly in the darkness, he stood in the pool, performing the required *ghusil janabat*, then watched the reflection of the moon on the still waters. He had never been one to take unwilling women to his bed; captives were for his men after a battle. How could he, after treating the woman with such callous disregard, expect her to feel anything but contempt for him? And her contempt was nothing compared to that which he felt for himself. He couldn't very well return her to her people, whoever they were, nor could he set her free amongst his own people. Khalil's head ached with the dilemma.

Returning to his tent, he was not surprised to find her, eyes closed, curled up into a tight ball on the edge of the bed. He slipped beneath the covers beside her, wanting desperately to take her in his arms and give her comfort, but he was certain she would slide away from him.

Batsheva was not sleeping; her eyes were closed for his benefit and as soon as she heard his breathing grow even with sleep, she turned toward the man. Propped up on one elbow, she let herself examine the person beside her. She could not deny that he was handsome. His face was dominated by a square jaw, clean-shaven unlike most of the other men she had seen through the tent flap. Beneath dark arched brows, his eyes were the eyes of a gazelle, deep brown but piercing; they could be soft and kind one moment, glittery and hard the next. Between them was a straight line of a nose ending with a pair of nostrils that flared dramatically when he was angered. He was, she concluded, a man of some wisdom despite his apparent youth. Khalil, she discovered while eavesdropping, had honest concern for his people, dispensing justice with consideration and compassion. There was an element of kindness about him that Batsheva found almost fascinating when she could set aside how she arrived in his bed in the first place. When he was awake, the man Khalil was in complete control of his surroundings; now, as he slept, he looked innocent and childlike, one arm tucked beneath his head, the other draped over a plump cushion. Batsheva had, more than once, sensed an inner turmoil raging within him but she had not allowed herself to be moved.

Lying on her back, staring up at the too familiar drape of the tent, she pondered the future. What would happen to her when he tired of her? Would he leave her in the desert to die? Or would he give her to his men for their pleasure? With no way of knowing where she was or if there was a city nearby to which she could escape, Batsheva had to decide how she would end her days. In all the lessons with the rabbi who came to tutor the Hagiz children, the sanctity of life was always stressed. One could eat pig meat if there was nothing else to eat, for to observe the law and die was worse than disregarding the law to live. God was omniscient. God would know the decisions she made were ones necessary for life. She knew that atop Masada, the people chose death over slavery, *Kiddush ha-Shem*, sanctification of the Holy Name, but somehow her situation did not warrant so drastic a measure. Not that she would have been able to carry out her own death sentence. In the scheme of all things, there was no choice to be made. She would survive as his slave for that was what she was while she would pray for rescue.

Thus, the decision to live was made.

CHAPTER 3

Waddan

JUNE - AUGUST 1184

From the morning after he removed her bonds, Khalil noticed a subtle change in the woman's behavior. Instead of turning away from him, she began to meet him eye to eye. When a meal was brought to her, she nodded thanks rather than stare sullenly at the food. The women still came to massage her, but she no longer cringed when they entered the tent; the three crones stopped complaining about her; something Khalil thought would never happen.

"She will languish from boredom, if nothing else, Khalil," scolded Sufiye, the one Batsheva thought of as the black crow. "If you are going to give her a measure of freedom, you must give her something to do with her hands."

Khalil turned his palms upward in surrender; as always, his aunt was right. "But what would she do? Does she have a skill?"

"I told you the day she arrived she is a lady of quality; her hands have never known hard work. Perhaps she knows needlework...."

He did not like Sufiye's tone. "Then find her a piece of cloth and some thread," snapped Khalil impatiently. She was already walking away when he called her back. "Auntie, do you think she is mute?" he asked softly.

"No, Khalil; she is not mute nor is she deaf. She startles at noises. Surely you have noticed that?"

"Yes, but she never speaks."

"Perhaps she has lost her voice. Sometimes, after a great shock that has been known to happen."

He didn't say anything else; there was nothing to add.

While it was true that she didn't approve of what Khalil had done, Sufiye understood it. Khalil hadn't always been a solitary figure leading a small *qubila* through the desert toward the old homeland. Her brother's son succeeded his father when Sheikh Mahmud was cut down in battle by an Almohades sword. But it wasn't only Mahmud who died that summer day; Khalil's wives and son had been deliberately sought out and slaughtered in the unprovoked attack on their village. Standing over their dismembered corpses, Khalil let loose a cry so feral that the Almohades prisoners' blood froze in their veins. With an awesome coldness, Khalil beheaded them all himself, leaving their bodies to rot in the relentless Al-Andalus sun while he buried his own dead. Sufiye's husband also died that day, along with their only child, the gentle, scholarly Hamid. In the weeks to come, as they picked up the shattered pieces of their lives, Sufiye realized Khalil, who had barely known his own mother, needed a motherly hand to guide him through the fog of his grief.

The qubila remained in Al-Andalus for another year before Khalil decided to cross the straits of Maḍīq Jabal Ṭāriq to return to the banks of the Euphrates, the place they once called home. The journey was long and arduous, but it would give them time to heal their wounds and re-enter the land of the living.

Khalil did not remarry. There were women, of course, all beautiful, all willing, yet no one captured his heart the way the lost Amina had. Amina was the one to tame his temper with a smile. She was the one who found Hafsah, his second wife. Pregnant with Amahl, she worried about Khalil's comfort; when she spotted Hafsah at a slave auction, she bought her immediately. The girl turned out to be a treasure, beautiful and industrious, kind and loving to both Khalil and Amina, and devoted to their infant son. Mahmud used to tease his son that no man had the right to two such beautiful and devoted women, warning him that even the Prophet would be jealous of his happiness. When Hafsah shyly admitted she was pregnant, Khalil and Amina rejoiced with her and together asked her to be his second wife rather than a concubine. The night before that terrible day of death, they celebrated the marriage. Khalil recited his own poetry in praise of his two wives, and danced with the men long into the night, singing and laughing, not knowing the desolation morning would bring. That was the memory Khalil buried: that last night of joy before grief became his constant companion and poetry fled from his heart.

Sufiye was hopeful when Khalil kept the nameless one in his tent. To her eyes, it was a sign he was opening himself up to the possibility of another person in his life. He seemed to care, if not for her, about her. His aunt viewed it as a chance to bring him back into the world.

To procure a piece of fabric suitable for needlework in the middle of nowhere was not easy, but Sufiye managed to do it. When a caravan stopped near to their oasis, Sufiye took one of Khalil's extra camel skins and bartered for the necessary supplies. She waited for an appropriate moment to present it to the woman.

Finished with her morning massage, two of the crones had taken up their places at the entry to Khalil's tent when Sufiye shooed them away. "Come back later," she instructed, "after I have had a moment in private with the woman."

"And what can you say to a mute *majhula* that she would understand?" laughed Fatima, adjusting her hijab.

"Never mind; it is of no concern to you," Sufiye shot back as she pushed past her. Ignoring their clucks, she waited for them to leave before entering the bed chamber. "*As-'salaamu, sayidat majhula,*" she said in a respectful voice and was pleased when the nameless lady, wrapped in Khalil's burnous, looked up. She was beautiful, if perhaps still too skinny, thought Sufiye as she sat down on the cushions beside the woman, the bundle in her hands. "I have brought you something you might like." There was no response, only a look of curiosity in the steady grey eyes. She untied the strings and shook out a large square of Egyptian linen, so white it shimmered in the light of the brazier. Handing it to Batsheva, she watched the elegant fingers stroke the soft material, then skillfully test its heft and strength. Obviously, this was something the woman had done before. "This, too, is for you, *sayida*. Perhaps you are skilled with a needle; this will give you something to occupy your hands." She handed a small inlaid box to the woman and watched with relief as her eyes lit up. Inside was a rainbow of threads, a leather etui full of needles, a tiny gold thread knife, and enough space to store the cloth. "Perhaps this will help settle your mind." The nameless one looked directly at Sufiye and gave her the first tentative smile any of them had seen. Returning one in kind, Sufiye rose from the cushions and left the woman alone.

With trembling fingers, Batsheva pulled a strand of deep crimson thread from a skein and slid it through the eye of a needle. She took a deep breath, murmured a prayer appropriate to the beginning of a new project, and placed the first stitch slightly to the right of the center of the cloth. She had no idea how the picture would turn out, but she knew it would be a testament to the life she left behind, and it would begin with a pomegranate.

Except for the occasional nights he was on watch with his men, Khalil possessed the woman every night. Her eyes remained open, staring at him until the final moment of passion, only to open again to stare at the tent above. As the nights grew cool, he would awaken to find her curled up into a ball fitting neatly into the hollows of his own body. Gently he would stroke the soft skin, wishing for something he knew could never be, yet he was satisfied for the moment. Occasionally, her hands would inadvertently touch him, sending torrents of liquid fire through his veins. She tolerated him but gave no sign of coming to him willingly.

A week before they were to depart for the ingathering of the tribes, she was tormented by dreams, and he heard her voice for the first time, crying out for someone who did not come. Khalil did not know who it was, but her whimpering pierced his heart and his soul. With gentle words whispered into the shell of her ear, he tried to soothe her until she awoke with a start and a shudder. She stared at him unblinkingly, then slid out of his reach.

Khalil was angered. He left the bed and stormed from the tent, leaving the woman alone in her misery. *Why does she refuse to accept my comfort?* he asked himself over and over as he performed *ghusl janabat* in the oasis pool. *Do I not touch her with a desire to arouse her? Has that not proven I am a kind man? Does she not know that if I had it in my power, I would never have allowed what happened to have happened?* The last thought stilled him. She could not know. Never once had he tried to talk to her, to explain he had not ordered her capture. He could have refused the gift, but then what hell would her fate have been?

He remembered what it was like when he and Amina coupled. There was always joy. There was equal joy with Hafsah that, as he thought about it, must have been because she sought refuge in their household, and her initial fears were quickly dispelled. The majhula did not have even that tiny advantage.

What was it about her that drew him in? He knew nothing about her save for her steely determination to survive. She did not cower or hide;

she swathed herself in dignity and self-possession as he rarely saw in any woman, much less a captive. *You will not defeat me* could be read in her eyes whenever they met his.

The anger turned back on himself. Gritting his teeth, he returned to the tent full of good intentions, only to find the majhula asleep. As gently as he could so as not disturb her any further, Khalil slid back beneath the coverlet.

Preparations for departure were underway and, from the tent, Batsheva could see the increased activity around the camp. When the three women began taking down the tapestries and folding them into bundles, Batsheva retreated to a corner. Trunks were opened to take all the household items, braziers, lamps, and trays. Soon, only the bed was left intact. Batsheva, for the first time, was worried; she did not know what would happen to her once they all left.

When the black crow marched into the tent while Khalil was still dressing for dawn prayer, Batsheva understood departure was imminent. She listened as the older woman chided the sheikh until he, laughing, fled the tent half-dressed, his burnous in his hands. Once he was gone, Batsheva wrapped in a discarded *djellaba*, held her breath as the black crow approached and eyed her critically. Sufiye walked out of the tent to speak to one of the crones who then quickly disappeared. Sufiye returned with the other two. She removed the rope from around the Batsheva's waist.

Batsheva jumped out of the away, and stood in a corner, her little embroidery box clutched in her hands. The two women paid her no attention as they began dismantling the bed. The cushions and covers were stuffed into cloth bags with leather thongs which, once tied, served as handles. The missing woman returned and handed a bundle to Sufiye. Slowly walking toward the woman, she spoke softly, holding up a bundle of clothing.

"These are for you, sayidat majhula," she said pleasantly. "You will need to wear these as we travel." She was relieved when the majhula immediately slipped out of Khalil's burnous and into the pantaloons, tunic, and *abaya*. Sufiye helped her with the blue hijab that would mark her as member of the sheikh's household. With a quick tug, everything was in place. Sufiye took Batsheva by the arm and led her out into the dawn, in full view of everyone in the camp. "Make yourself useful, majhula; as we bring out the bundles, prepare them for loading." She had no idea how much the woman understood, but she was certain the majhula would either bolt or not remain idle for long.

When Khalil returned for the striking of the tent itself, he was astounded to see the little majhula standing in the middle of his possessions, skillfully sorting them into sensible piles. He knew it was her, even beneath the abaya and hijab, for no other woman possessed the same grace and stalwart dignity. She moved with confidence, as though she had done this all before. Walking up behind her, he placed his hands on her shoulders and was caught off guard when she spun around; her grey eyes, normally so defiant, stared brightly at him, making him wonder if she were smiling beneath her hijab. In a second, however, the wall descended, and he could read nothing new in her stare. Dropping his arms to his side, Khalil mumbled something unintelligible and left her to her work.

They broke camp as the sun rose above the horizon. Batsheva was provided a gentle mare; the black crow was visibly relieved when she mounted easily. Riding alongside the older woman, Batsheva managed, after a few unsteady moments, to gain control of the reins of a pair of donkeys laden with parts of Khalil's tent. If she thought about escape, she gave no indication to anyone around her.

And think about escape, she did. Batsheva scanned the horizon for any sign of a town to which she might flee in the night. But the sensible part of her calmed the jangled nerves, for even if she were to take flight, she knew she would be apprehended before she got very far. And even if she were to reach a town, most likely, with her coloring, she would end up in a slave market and in a worse position than she already was. She did not want him to lay with her, yet she found herself looking forward to his company. *I am lonely, that is all,* she told herself. The man treated her well and, all things considered, her life was not as horrifying as it might be. Reminding herself she had chosen to live, Batsheva settled into the new routine.

The trek was not arduous, but it took everyone's energies to make camp at dusk only to break it again at dawn. Instead of the big tent, a smaller, more easily managed affair was set up each night. Batsheva had organized the pack animals in such a way that she knew where to find necessities to be unpacked in a hurry. She was still forbidden to leave Khalil's tent once it was in place and Sufiye continued to bring her meals. More often than not, when the older woman arrived bearing bowls of hot food, she found the majhula fast asleep. Sufiye wondered if Khalil was awakening her upon his return. She suspected as much but did not dare ask.

One night, when the moon was enormous in the sky, Batsheva awoke to angry voices outside the tent flap. Peeking out, she saw Khalil sitting outside with his council, a small fire glowing in the center of the circle. The men were arguing, but Khalil seemed to be letting them argue amongst themselves.

"If we are to make an impression of strength when we arrive in Benghazi, we must have something to show for our years away! We cannot arrive empty-handed."

"And what would you have us bring, Abdullah?" asked one of the old men. "We have fine flocks to sell, a good number of hides, and a significant number of yearlings. We are not poor."

One with a strident voice, the one Batsheva recognized as the hotheaded Gamal, suddenly jumped up, waving his fist in the air. "You have become like a woman, Khalil bin Mahmud! You do not permit us to raid caravans, nor do you let us ride to the south to obtain slaves. You tell us you have lost your taste for battle because of what happened across the sea, but this has turned you into a coward! You are not your father's son, Khalil!" Shouts of anger followed Gamal's speech.

Leaning forward, Batsheva craned her neck as far as she could without being seen. She wanted to see Khalil's face and his reaction if she could, but she could only hear him.

"You prefer bloodshed over peace, Gamal?" asked Khalil in a cold, even voice.

"I prefer a life of honor!" snapped Gamal angrily. "We did not have to leave the summer camp so early; it was rumors of mountain raiders that made you change your mind!"

"Gamal," said the first old man, "we all agreed the time to return home was upon us, and the ingathering set the time. We are not looking to decimate our numbers once more; we are looking to grow in strength. If you want battle, join with those going to retake Al-Quds from the infidels."

At the word *Al-Quds* Batsheva's ears pricked up. Was it possible some were going on to Jerusalem, the holiest of holy places?

But the argument was now reaching a fevered pitch. Several more opinions were offered, none by Khalil, but all diametrically opposed to each other. Gamal was growing more vicious in his attacks, calling Khalil an unweaned calf, claiming that he was content to stay in his bed wasting his seed on a pitiful excuse for a slave. "You hide behind the skirts of a mute Christian woman!"

Christian woman, indeed! Batsheva thought with a frown. *A fat lot you know, you spawn of a mangy camel.* She snorted at her own vehemence.

"Attack my decisions, Gamal," snarled Khalil, "do not attack my household. You are crossing the narrow stream between what I will permit you to say, and what will make me kill you."

Batsheva could not believe he was defending her.

"*La kurat,* Khalil. You do not have the balls to kill me," Gamal spat in his face.

Khalil rose and stood face to face with Gamal. "With the first light of dawn, pack up your women, your children, and your tents and leave this camp. You are banished." He looked around the circle of men. "If any of you desire to go with him, do so. I will not stop you. The council is ended."

Batsheva jumped away from the flap as Khalil stormed through it. A part of her wanted to soothe his anger, but another part wanted to hide in a corner, away from his wrath. She watched him stomp around the tent, muttering to himself, ripping the clothes from his body, completely unaware of her presence until he turned and spied her beside the makeshift bed.

Naked, his muscles flexed in the dim light of the brazier, he stared at her, then, in two quick strides, reached his captive. With a single movement, he tore her light kaftan down the middle, kicking it away as he pulled her roughly toward him. "Who are you? Why will you not tell me your name?" he rasped. "I beg you; *ma ismik, ya fatah?*"

She did not answer; she braced herself for the onslaught.

His mouth bruised her lips as he took possession of them. His tongue thrust mercilessly between her teeth, a prelude to what was to come. Tumbling the woman to the few cushions that made up their camp bed, he devoured her, capturing one nipple, then the other, whipping them with his tongue until they stood taut and erect. His hands roughly manipulated her body, crushing her as the fire burned in him and transferred into her. He knew her well enough to know what movement drove her toward him and he used that knowledge to force her body to overtake her mind. When at last she arched against his assault, Khalil plunged into her, thrusting so deeply that she cried out. He did not stop; instead, he drove her further along passion's razor edge, knowing any resistance would be obliterated by animal instinct. She was, he knew by now, a passionate creature in spite of herself.

He took her with as much need as raw, pounding desire. He stopped letting her eyes torment him, choosing, instead, to believe that her steely unwavering stare was the last vestige of her dignity; he would do nothing to take that small piece away from her. He cried out at his climax; a sound so filled with anguish that Batsheva held her own breath until his breathing slowed. Finally exhausted, Khalil fell asleep, one arm draped over her, the other tucked under his pillow. It was the first time in a long time he slept with his dagger handle pressed into the palm of his hand.

Batsheva lay on her side, the weight of Khalil's arm more than a little uncomfortable. She could not move without disturbing him and, in a moment of compassion, she wished him peace after so a difficult night. Lying there, she listened for his steady breathing, hoping she could fall asleep, but every time she closed her eyes, something unseen snapped them open again.

An unbidden picture of the market in Málaga came to mind, but it was not the cherished memory of walking with her mother. This time, it was a hot summer day when a Moorish boy put his hand on her basket. "Ma ismik, ya fatah?" The dark eyes of the boy were seared into her memory. *What is your name, girl?* In that moment, as she recalled the intensity of his stare, she understood those same eyes were closed beside her. *Is this the dark one?* Batsheva stared at the man. Oddly, everything about him made new sense. Instead of feeling some relief at putting a name to that strange memory from her childhood, she suddenly felt endangered, but the danger was not from the man. It was coming from the pit of her stomach, something she could not name, but it was palpable.

A tiny movement made the brazier's shadow on the wall flicker ever so slightly. Keeping still, she focused on the black space at the flap of the tent until she was convinced someone had come in. Inching her right hand under Khalil's pillow, she felt for the dagger. Although his hand was on the hilt, she managed to slide it out far enough for her own hand to close over the top. The black-clad figure, almost invisible against the dark tent, moved stealthily along the wall, and for a moment, she hoped it might be one of the crones coming to cleanse her as they often did when Khalil went to bathe, but it was the glint of metal that told her otherwise, and she tightened her grip on the dagger.

The figure moved along the wall, nearing the bed. Batsheva had no doubt that the little flash was a blade. Counting the steps, she sucked in her breath and in a single fluid motion rolled over, sat up, and hurled the dagger with deadly accuracy. A cry split the air. Khalil flew up with a shout. He landed on his feet, momentarily confused by his empty hand. His eyes widened when he saw the body, a weapon still clutched in the assassin's hand, his own dagger protruding from the dead man's chest.

Calmly, Batsheva walked over to the body and, with her toe, pushed the hood away from the face. "Gamal," she said quietly as she bent to retrieve the dagger.

"You killed him." Khalil's eyes widened when he saw the dagger clutched in her hand. "Will you use that on me now?"

Batsheva looked at him, then at the dagger. "Do not be absurd," she replied smoothly in Arabic with a definite Al-Andalus accent. "My life would not be worth a handful of sand if you were dead. Nor would the life of your child."

Khalil stared at her. "You understand me," he sputtered. "Why did you not tell me?"

Her jaw clenched; her eyes narrowed dangerously. "You never asked." She took a step toward him and let the dagger fall at his feet. Picking up his djellaba, Batsheva slipped her arms through the enormous sleeves and pulled it over her small body. "I am going to the well," she said as she arranged the hood. "I trust you will remove this camel dung before the odor fouls our tent."

When she was gone, a slow grin split Khalil's troubled face. She may have won this battle, but he felt as though he had just won the war.

CHAPTER 4

En route to Benghazi

AUGUST – DECEMBER 1184

A crowd had gathered by the time Batsheva returned, the jug balanced comfortably on her hip. The men separated to let her pass, and when she entered the tent, she saw four men standing over the body, speaking to Khalil in intense, hushed tones. Quickly finishing their business, they hoisted the lifeless Gamal onto their shoulders and left.

"I brought water; you should wash," she said quietly.

"It was not necessary; I can go to the well." His voice was almost apologetic.

Batsheva ignored him as she poured water into a large laver. "Whatever you wish," she replied airily, "but you should know I do not speak to dirty boys."

Silence dripped between them. She dared not look at Khalil, but she could feel his eyes boring a hole into her back. When he grabbed her arm to turn her to him, the jug tumbled, and water soaked the ground beneath their feet. Batsheva jerked her arm free and bent to retrieve the jug, but his command stopped her.

"Leave it!" he roared. "What did you say?"

Batsheva casually pushed back the hood of the djellaba and met his eyes straight on. "I said I do not speak to dirty boys; not then, not now, not ever."

"*Ma ismik, ya fatah*?" he asked softly. "Please tell me, what is your name?"

"My name is of no importance, Khalil bin Mahmud. Pick one which you like and that is how I shall be known."

Although the remark was without rancor, Khalil felt the chastisement keenly. "But surely you have a name of your own, one you would want to hear spoken once more?"

Batsheva shook her head. "The name I was given is precious to me. I hear my mother calling. It would be painful for me to have you say it."

Khalil was dumbfounded; he desperately wanted a name attached to the face that danced through his dreams. For years he had applied every conceivable label to that face, but not one ever fit. Hesitantly, he touched her cheek and was amazed when she did not pull away. "Vashti. I shall call you Vashti."

This time, it was Batsheva who laughed, albeit briefly. The name was so close to her own, she wondered if perhaps those sounds made up her appearance, but it was the biblical significance which most amused her: Vashti, the discarded Queen of Persia, Queen Esther's predecessor.

"Do you not like the name? It is Persian; it means *lovely one.*"

"I know what it means, Khalil. If it pleases you, it will do."

"It would please me greatly if the mother of my child had a name," he replied gravely.

Khalil insisted on a proper burial for Gamal before the qubila broke camp. When others demanded he be left to the vultures, Khalil chided them saying Gamal's wife and children had suffered enough and to leave him exposed would cause them greater grief. When Gamal's two wives offered to separate from the qubila, Khalil would not hear of it. "Wait until we reach Benghazi," he told them gently, "then, if you choose to stay there, you will be given a share of our trade to establish yourselves in that city. To leave you behind would mean your certain death." He asked Sufiye to travel with the grieving family so that they would not be abused along the route.

Batsheva waited for a private moment to thank Khalil for his kindness to Gamal's people, but he dismissed her gratitude with a brusque reply. Still, her words strengthened his resolve not to exile them if they chose to remain; Gamal's two sons were strong young men, but old enough to develop a strong hatred for him that could be troublesome in the future. As his father had taught, kindness helps heal an aching heart with greater success than revenge. A week after the attack, Khalil asked Muhammed and Kassim to ride with his personal guard; everyone breathed a bit easier when the sons, anxious to escape their father's shame, accepted.

Khalil noticed that the woman he called Vashti was not so different from the women of his people. She took on normal responsibilities as though she were doing them for years rather than having been a prisoner in his tent, all without asking permission. Instead of weeping and bemoaning her fate, she moved with perfect ease, resting a lovely hand on her growing belly when she sat on her mare. At night, she prepared their dinner competently, although Sufiye's gentle corrections altered her combination of spices and herbs more to his liking.

Had the woman been his wife, Khalil, as was the custom of his people, would have been forbidden to touch during her pregnancy without her express permission. But with her announcement, Khalil was puzzled when she did not tell him to leave their tent, if not, at least, their bed. It was as if she had found the perfect revenge: allowing him to lie beside her without being able to take her at will. Try as he might, Khalil could not get her to say more than a few words in direct response to an ordinary, non-invasive question. She refused to speak of her past or her family, tacitly ignoring any requests he made. Still, he admitted to Sufiye that the woman had become a welcome part of his daily existence. They had settled into a routine of sorts. He liked it. He liked having her near him.

"One day, Auntie, I hope she will emerge from her cocoon."

Sufiye smiled at the image he chose. "Like a butterfly?"

He nodded. "When a butterfly emerges, she is shy. Her wings are wet. She needs a little time to become magnificent."

This was the old Khalil, the poet, the one who saw color where others saw just sand. "*Insh'Allah*, Khalil. *Insh'Allah*."

Adjusting to her new place in his world, Batsheva discovered parts of her captor she had not anticipated. She already knew he was a good leader, but once her position in his household was tacitly established, she began to study the actual man to whom she was tied. Even without his blue turban, he was unquestionably sheik of this qubila; his bearing was that of complete control. She could not deny his body was beautiful: tall, lean and well-muscled, graceful in movement. His hair curled around his ears despite Sufiye's best efforts to trim it. He was sharp, clearly well-educated. And he was unexpectedly kind. Khalil, she decided, was a conundrum.

In an off moment, Sufiye took the bold step in telling her of Amina, Hafsah, and Amahl, and how their deaths closed off Khalil to the kindness of others. That he had accepted her as a gift was a shock. He had been with other women, but never had one become attached to his household.

"I pray he was not brutal with you, Vashti," Sufiye confessed as they drew water from a traveler's well, "yet I think you would have every reason to hate him. If you can but imagine how relieved I was that he took you into his tent. I believed then, as I believe now, that he felt something he could not name when he first saw you." She reached over and grasped Batsheva's hand. "If you can find even one small corner in your heart which might feel kindness for Khalil, I would be grateful."

She did not tell Sufiye that the day she was given to him had not been their first encounter; nor did she know if Khalil had. She tried not to feel the kindness Sufiye sought for her brother's widowed son, but there was no denying that during the weeks on the road Batsheva was beginning to feel something besides indigestion and the swelling of her belly.

At night, when the camp was quiet, Khalil would sit amidst the cushions studying documents and maps while Batsheva sat nearby sewing tiny shirts and gowns. Khalil would marvel at her skill with a needle, but never once mentioned waiting for a child to be born was not new to him. Only when his work was done did he unroll his prayer rug, take the well-worn Qur'an from his leather bag, and begin his night prayers.

The soothing sound would waft through the tent; even as she was drifting off, Batsheva would rouse herself enough to listen before he brushed the corner of the bed three times as he fell wearily onto the cushions beside her. He was a good man, but he was still her captor. Had it not been for him, she would be married to the man she loved and the child she carried would have been joyous proof of that love. As the weeks went by, however, Batsheva began to question her own resolve.

Khalil showed her every kindness, seeing to her needs as she saw to his, telling funny stories and singing songs from Al-Andalus. He discovered she played *shatranj*, and the woman won more than she lost, much to Khalil's consternation. He regaled her with the history of his people carefully omitting that painful portion he could not bring himself to share. They were Ayyub, originally from Tikrit, not Imazighen as they appeared. They were in Málaga that summer, trading with the local weavers before they returned to Granada where they had built their homes, prayed in their own mosque, and increased their flocks while living quiet, peaceful lives.

On the nights when they would lie together, nearly but not touching, he told her about his childhood. As her belly grew rounder, he shyly asked to feel the movement of his child and when she took his hand and placed it on her skin, he felt not the usual flame of carnal passion, but a tender feeling, love, he supposed, for this woman who already loved this child within. Her strength, her determination, her ability to join with his people when he had been the one to separate her from her own, filled him with admiration. Khalil found himself asking her advice as though she were indeed his wife. He hoped a day would come when she would open her heart to him; until then, the more time he spent with her, the more space she took up in his heart.

Khalil's qubila was the last to reach the gathering at Benghazi and their reception was thunderous as they rode, banners flying, into the valley. Batsheva watched from her little mare as Khalil's compatriots galloped toward them at full tilt, swords in the air, ready to escort them to the place where they were to camp.

As they came over the last rise of barren desert, Batsheva gasped when she saw the sea of tents pitched in the broad valley until the land itself was all but invisible. At first, there seemed no order to the site. But, as they moved slowly toward the gathering, colored banners, each with its own design, declared each qubila's encampment. In the middle of the mass, sat the largest tent Batsheva had ever seen and over it, fairly shimmering in the sun, flew an emerald flag with a golden crescent moon, the personal standard of the sultan's envoy. Their own campsite was close to it.

In a matter of hours, tents were erected with Khalil's large one at the center of their site. Batsheva supervised the unpacking of rugs and cushions, braziers and brass trays, all the things that would make it home for the coming months. Sufiye came to help and was immediately impressed with the way Khalil's Vashti had taken over as though she were doing this all her life. The lady remained reticent around the other women, but a closeness was clearly growing between the two of them. Since Sufiye had always been responsible for Khalil's abode, she made it a point to discreetly guide the newcomer in the finer points to the sheikh's happiness. With the older woman at her side, Batsheva was introduced to everyone Sufiye thought she should know.

Her belly had grown so large on her small frame it was impossible to miss, even beneath the folds of her abaya, and Batsheva found herself the center of a certain amount of attention from the other women. As they walked to the well each morning, a veiled face would lean close and whisper one bit of advice or another to the young mother-to-be. In turn, Batsheva would graciously acknowledge the words. Soon, instead of moving alone around the camp, she was invited to join other women her own age. This pleased both Sufiye and Khalil greatly, the latter worrying less about his woman's loneliness. Gradually, as she allowed herself to be engaged in common conversation, Khalil was beside himself with hope.

Races, wrestling matches, and weaponry displays dominated the early morning hours before the sun reached its zenith. Khalil and his men participated in as many as they could, and soon his tent was surrounded by bright victory banners. As sheikh, his afternoons were spent at endless council meetings where matters of mutual concern were hashed and rehashed by leaders from across the Maghreb. Representatives of the sultan, looking for men to join in their quest to take back the holy places of Palaestina from the Crusaders, pled their case to the sheikhs.

While the men carried on, the women would ride under heavy guard into Benghazi to attend the markets. At first, Batsheva refused to go, saying she had plenty to do learning how to run a sheikh's household, but finally Sufiye dragged her along. From one shop to the next they went, finally ending at the women's baths where they washed the dust of the road from their bodies.

Batsheva, upon removing her abaya and kaftan, was the subject of many a wide-eyed stare and not just because of her advancing pregnancy. Several women approached her to ask if her hair was real. She took it with good humor, but soon word of the copper-curled woman had gossiped its way back to their camp.

"Be flattered!" Khalil laughed when he told her about it as they lay side by side. "I am the envy of every man here. The women have all run back to their men to say what a beautiful, large wife I have."

Batsheva's grey eyes widened in horror as she struggled upright. "I am *not* your wife, Khalil," she snapped. "At best, I am your concubine; at worst, your slave girl."

Khalil's face reddened. "I would prefer that you were my wife, Vashti."

"That cannot be, Khalil."

"Why not? You carry my child; you lie beside me of your own accord. You have not asked me to sleep in another bed. Why will you not agree to marry me in the eyes of Allah?"

"A man should marry a woman who loves him," she answered softly.

"You do not love me?" There was great hurt in his voice.

A long sigh escaped her lips. "I love the child I carry, your child it is true, but I am not free to choose my own way."

Khalil sat up. "But you are not a slave, Vashti! I never said you are a slave! You are free to do what you want!"

"Am I free to leave?"

This time, it was Khalil who sighed. He took a long time to compose his answer. When he finally spoke, the answer was full of pain. "If you so choose, you may leave."

"And where would I go?" She smiled sadly. "Sleep, Khalil; you will find me here in the morning." Batsheva laid down again and wished herself to sleep.

In the morning, Khalil watched her prepare to go into the city with the other women. He handed her a purse heavy with coins as she adjusted her hijab. "You are free to go wherever you wish, Vashti, but remember, with you goes my heart."

Batsheva touched his cheek. "I shall keep that in mind, Khalil," she answered, and then she was gone.

Having been in the city several times, Batsheva felt confident enough to make her own way about the market. "I have much to buy today, Sufiye," she told Khalil's aunt with as much bravado as she could muster. "I shall meet you here at midday, then we shall go to the baths."

Sufiye looked at her strangely for a moment, then sagely smiled, "You will be fine, Vashti. Enjoy your wanderings."

Completely alone for the first time since her abduction, Batsheva started her walk through the *shuk*. She did not wander aimlessly; she had a destination in mind, and it took all of her wavering courage to stroll casually through the winding lanes until she found the street of the goldsmiths. Taking a deep breath, she kept going until she saw the sign. The words *Hagiz and Sons* loomed larger than she ever expected. Through the open door, she could see several gentlemen standing in the shop laughing with a portly Jew. Racking her brains for a name, she decided the man must be her cousin Shabbatai Hagiz, the son of her grandfather's brother Moshe.

The visitors were leaving the shop and Batsheva found herself face to face with Shabbatai. With a courtly bow, he addressed her. "May I show you something special today, *ayidat*?" he asked politely, noting her bright blue hijab.

All strength drained from Batsheva, all color from her face, and she was glad for her hijab. *"La,"* she rasped in Arabic, trying not to choke, "*la shukran*!" She stared at him for a moment, then fled down the lane.

She scurried as far and as fast as she could without causing a disturbance. Down one street, then another, she kept going until she came to the street of the rug merchants. Catching her breath, she entered the first shop she saw with quality goods and proceeded to regain her wits by haggling over a large silk rug. Counting out her coins, she allowed the shopkeeper's assistant to follow her to the meeting place where one of Khalil's men waited with donkeys ready to carry their acquisitions back to camp.

While she waited for Sufiye, Batsheva treated herself to a cup of pomegranate juice. The taste took her back to her mother's garden and, for a moment, she believed she was free to return home. When she looked down at her belly, however, she realized it was nothing more than a dream; it could never be now that she carried the sheikh's heir. There was no real path to freedom, only one to more heartache than she was willing to take home to her family.

As soon as Sufiye arrived, they set off.

The baths were crowded. Sufiye tipped the attendant to secure comfortable divans near the pool and instructed the woman to take their clothing outside for a beating and airing. Batsheva went quickly into the pool, needing the coolness to soothe her after her morning's adventure. She was standing in the water with Sufiye when a dark-haired, hazel-eyed woman approached. To Batsheva, the woman looked vaguely familiar, but she decided it must be someone she had already seen at the bath. When the woman addressed her directly in accented Arabic, Batsheva grew uneasy.

"Your coloring is unique," she said with a smile. "Surely you are not from Benghazi."

When Batsheva did not answer, Sufiye did it for her. "My niece is from Algiers."

"Oh, that would explain why I have never seen you here before. You must have come for the gathering." She smiled again then swam away to the other side of the pool where she spoke to another woman who had been watching with interest.

"Do you know her, Vashti?" asked Sufiye when she was gone.

Batsheva shook her head. "I don't think so." But that wasn't completely true; the woman favored the women of her father's family.

Sufiye noticed the trembling hands and suggested they go; she was certain Batsheva recognized the woman.

The new rug was already spread when Khalil returned from the sheikhs' council. Batsheva, sitting on a cushion off to the side, put her embroidery in her lap while she watched him examine her first major acquisition.

"It is quite beautiful, Vashti," he murmured, brushing a kiss on the top knot of her hair. "Did you enjoy your day in the city?"

"Yes, I did. Did your meeting with Mustafa bin Suleiman go well?" She had decided not to mention her side trip to Hagiz and Sons, nor did the woman at the bath require comment.

"Mustafa thinks I should take my men to join the sultan in the fight for Al-Quds."

"Will you go?" Batsheva dared not ask if that included the women as well.

Khalil joined her on the cushions. "Perhaps. The men are anxious to fight, and this is a just cause." He realized that his words might stab at the woman; the battle would be between Muslim and Christian and she might not take this well.

"Fight for Al-Quds, Khalil. You are right; the cause is just."

"Are you trying to get rid of me, habibi?" he asked in a light tone.

"No."

"But you would see me go and leave you behind."

"I did not say that Khalil; you put your own meaning to my words."

"But you said I should go with Mustafa. Forgive this sunbaked brain of mine, but I do not understand."

Batsheva looked him square in the eye. "I would go with you to Palaestina."

"Ha! A woman on campaign? Impossible!"

"Did not Fatima ride with her husband?"

"That was different; she was the Prophet's own daughter."

Batsheva shrugged and resumed her needlework. After a moment of silence, she said "I think I will join Sufiye and the other women at Amira Aisha's tent this evening. She is having a banquet in honor of the birth of her first grandchild."

Her deft change of subject did not escape his notice. "I did not know you were acquainted with Mustafa's wife."

"Not officially, but we have met in passing. I received an invitation by way of courtesy for my position in your household." She did not elaborate on what position that was, but she suspected it was more out of curiosity than actual respect.

Wordlessly, Khalil rose and went to the trunk in the front room of the tent. He returned with a bundle. "I hoped for a special day to give you this, but I suppose an important woman's banquet will do."

Batsheva gasped as she unfolded the mass of fabric. Three separate garments appeared, all made of the finest materials she had ever seen. The first was a kaftan of pure Egyptian linen embroidered with deep blue-green blossoms along the hem, cuffs, and neck. Dyed to match the little flowers, the heavier silk djellaba was shot through with threads of gold, with a wide gold band running all along the edges like a large keyhole. The fasteners were miniature pomegranates, elegantly detailed, hooked with loops of beaten gold rope. The hijab was raw gossamer silk in the same shade as the kaftan with a thin line of gold woven around the edge. "Oh!" breathed Batsheva, touching the soft veil against her cheek, "I do not know what to say, Khalil. It is all so beautiful! I hope the Amirat Aisha does not take offense!"

Khalil grinned like a schoolboy who had just pleased his master. "I think not, Vashti. Sufiye knows about these things and selected the fabrics. She said the color would suit your hair. Now, close your eyes." He dug into his wide sash and withdrew something small. Taking her hand, he dropped a pair of earrings into her open palm. "These I found myself," he admitted rather proudly.

There was another gasp when she saw the matched pair of rubies set in gold with three drop pearls hanging from each earring. "This is too much, Khalil. I cannot accept these."

"You do not have a choice, Vashti. It is only fitting the mother of my child be dressed in the most beautiful adornments I can find."

Shabbatai Hagiz quizzed his daughter until she had had enough. "I would not tell you a lie, Papa," she protested one last time. "The woman at the bath was Batsheva. A very pregnant Batsheva. Of that I am certain."

"But you have not seen her since she was a babe, Rivka. How can you be so sure?"

"She looks exactly like Miriam, Papa. The hair, the eyes, the way she tilted her head when I approached. I knew Miriam well in Málaga. I was there when Batsheva was born. How much more proof do you want?"

"Did she recognize you?"

"No. Not at all."

Shabbatai leaned back on his cushion and sipped his cardamom tea slowly. He remembered the storm grey eyes staring at him from behind a hijab earlier in the day and, yes, those could be the eyes of Miri Hagiz. How could he have missed it? If indeed it was the missing Batsheva, there was no way to get to her if she was with the Imazighen gathering. Dismissing his daughter, Shabbatai summoned his sons to discuss what could be done. By morning, couriers were dispatched to Málaga, Tunis, Algiers, and Sfax.

In the weeks that followed, Batsheva's life became a round of women's parties and banquets interspersed with market days and picnics by the sea. Pleased with her early trips to the city, Khalil entrusted her with purchasing supplies. Once, when he accompanied her himself, he found her bargaining skills to be better than his own. She was shrewd of eye and judicious with his coin, both highly desirable qualities in his eyes. He took her to the street of tailors to select a long overdue wardrobe. Unlike most women presented with such choice, his woman picked only the sturdiest, most practical garments, ones best suited to her life in the desert. When Khalil pressed her to select some pretty things, she threw up her hands, told him to pick whatever he wished, and left the shop.

If the merchant was surprised, Khalil was not; he had grown used to her refusal to adorn herself. He managed to choose a few bolts of material himself and instructed the tailor on the style based on samples in the shop. When he finally caught up with her, she was standing at the bookseller's stall, arguing over a pair of volumes she wished to buy. Hiding himself, he listened to her haggle in a language sounding vaguely like his own, yet he could not understand. Whatever tongue it was, she spoke it as fluently as Arabic or, as he recalled with a twinge, Castilian. In the end, the merchant conceded victory to the veiled woman and wrapped up her books, muttering the entire time.

"You can come out now, Khalil," she called over her shoulder as she paid the shopkeeper. With a sheepish grin, Khalil stepped from the shadows and took the parcel from the bookseller.

"Now you will read books at night? Is there anything you do not know how to do?" he teased as they walked along.

Batsheva thought about it for a minute, then said, "No, I don't think so. Can you think of anything?"

"Fly." He imagined a smile beneath the hijab and wondered if she could do that, too.

The gathering was drawing to a close. No decision had been reached as to when the men would go to Al-Quds, but go they would, and under the yellow flag of Salah ad-Din. Khalil spent hours in the open field drilling his men endlessly so that, when they passed before Mustafa, they would be impressive enough to fight under their own *qubila* banner.

Tired and dirty, Khalil was pleased to find warm water and a stack of thick toweling awaiting him when he returned to the tent. "How is my son today, Vashti?" he joked as he stripped to the waist.

"Your daughter is very busy," she answered glancing up from her embroidery. Batsheva carefully tied off one strand before clipping it with the tiny thread knife.

Khalil looked at the needlework in her lap. "The pomegranate is almost done. What will you add to it?"

Batsheva looked at her work critically. "Two branches of blossoms, I suppose. I don't know."

"For you, two daggers might be more appropriate," he teased. He handed her his leather breastplate. "There is a tear on the side."

Batsheva frowned. "Were you hurt?

He shrugged. "Not really. I was distracted." He picked up his arm and showed her the bruise.

The frown deepened. "This is a simple repair, Khalil; you, injured, are not."

"Do you care so much if I am injured?"

She ignored the question. "Will there be a council tonight? I can sew this while you are with your men."

"Thank you, Vashti." He did not press his question. "The council will be a small one; we must finalize formations for tomorrow's tournament."

"Then let me bring you something to eat now before you face them," offered Batsheva, setting the armor aside. She struggled to rise from the cushions, only to fall back into their softness with a laugh. "I'm afraid my belly is getting the best of me today, Khalil."

He crossed the floor and helped her to her feet. "Be careful with my son," he chided, "it would be untoward were you to labor too early."

Batsheva was about to say something clever when, from outside their tent, they heard a commotion. "Stay here," ordered Khalil as he ran outside.

A lone horseman was tearing at breakneck speed through the camp heading directly toward Khalil's banner. Kassim bin Gamal, now one of Khalil's personal guards, leapt forward and pulled the rider from his saddle as the horse skidded to a halt. They scuffled until Khalil's sharp command stopped them.

"Release him, Kassim!" he ordered. "Who are you and what do you want?"

The man rose from the dirt to face Khalil. "I've come for the woman," he announced.

"Bring him inside." Khalil turned and went back into the tent, relieved to see Vashti had vacated the outer room. "State your business, man."

"I will pay whatever ransom you ask. I have come to take the woman back to her own people."

Khalil glanced at the closed curtain. "Who is this woman you seek?" he asked, keeping his voice as steady as possible.

The stranger stood his ground, refusing to be intimidated by the sheikh's narrowed eyes. "I demand to see Batsheva Hagiz. I know my sister is with you and by your own law you must accept *jizyah* for her."

"That name is unknown to me," he said honestly, "although I know of the House of Hagiz."

Taking a step toward Khalil, the stranger was immediately stopped by Kassim, who fastened an iron grip on his arm. "Keep your distance, stranger, lest I end your life here and now."

"Let him go, Kassim," said Batsheva as she entered the room, unveiled, her copper curls flowing freely down her back. "*Hineini, Yehuda.* "

"Bashi!" He would have pushed Kassim aside, but he saw Batsheva's condition and stopped. "It does not matter, Bashi, I have come to take you home."

"I cannot go."

"*Tahadath bialearabia*!" snapped Khalil. All eyes turned to him. "I will understand your conversation," he added more gently. Kassim left them to stand guard outside. This was now a family matter to be heard only by those directly involved.

"Surely you do not mean to stay here, Bashi?" cried Yehuda. "Your place is with your family. With Akiva."

"Look at me, Yehuda. I am not the girl who left Málaga. I carry a child who will not be one of us no matter how good the intention of our law." She was shaking. "I can no longer sit with the women and pretend I am one of them. I am tainted. I will be ostracized, an outcast. I will always be suspect."

"That is not true," shouted Yehuda. "You are the mother! Our parents are waiting for you. Akiva is waiting for you."

"He is not waiting for this." She looked down at her belly as her eyes were filling with unshed tears. She looked at Khalil. The greatest pain imaginable flickered in his eyes; he had lost his family once; she could see him preparing to lose his family again. "My place is here, with the father of my child."

"Go with him; I will not stop you." Khalil kept his eyes locked with hers.

Her heart was breaking. "No, Khalil. My place is with you."

There was a moment of terrible silence before Yehuda spoke. "What are you saying, Batsheva? That you are happy here?" he asked incredulously.

"I am content; that is all that I can ask. I am well treated; I have made a life for myself." She managed a small smile. "Are our parents well?"

"They were devastated when you were taken, Bashi, and now, our mother anxiously awaits your return. Akiva is wild with worry. We searched everywhere for you, but no trace could be found until you were seen at the baths. The father of the child in unimportant; it is your child and Akiva will accept it as his own. He has already declared it."

"This I will not permit," growled the sheikh. The statement was ridiculous, and he knew it as soon as it fell from his lips; if she left, his child would go with her.

"Nor will I, Khalil." She shot him a glance that stilled him immediately. "Will you stay and take a meal with us, 'Hudi?" asked Batsheva. "I would hear news of home."

"Not unless you are coming with me."

"Yehuda...."

"If you will not leave with me, I must return immediately to Málaga. Our mother languishes waiting to hear word of you."

"What will you tell her, 'Hudi?'"

His own grey eyes blazed with anger and hurt. "That I found you dead," spat Yehuda. "You will be dead to us, Batsheva, for you have chosen to remain amongst strangers."

"You would tell our parents that lie?"

"Yes, so they would be spared the shame of knowing you lie with a stranger. If you refuse to come home, they will observe *shiva* for you."

"So be it. May the Holy One, Blessed be the Name, go with you, 'Hudi."

Yehuda Hagiz left his sister standing in the middle of the tent. Only when hoofbeats faded in the distance did she speak again. "I am surprised, Khalil, that you did not demand to wrestle with him. I would have thought," she added rather drily, "you would want to reclaim your honor."

The old, familiar flush of shame colored his face. "We are all grown now, and you made the decision for us. Now it is for you to wrestle with yourself on the correctness of your decision, Batsheva Hagiz."

Out of a desire to respect her need for privacy, Khalil kept his distance for the next few days. He did not press her when she chose not to speak, nor did he call her by name. Vashti no longer seemed appropriate, but neither did Batsheva or Bashi. At night, he still lay with his arm around her for she seemed comforted by his touch. He heard her silent tears and was at a loss at what to do. He longed to ask a thousand questions, but suspected it was the last thing she wanted. She performed daily chores as though nothing were amiss but refrained from any more trips to the city. Because he was not convinced her brother would leave as he promised, he ordered Kassim to accompany her when she went to the well.

Eventually, life resettled itself into their customary routine. Batsheva was back to running his household with great efficiency. Khalil still had not found the courage to ask about her life, but he was certain he would find the right moment. Another fortnight passed before the decision to go to Palaestina was made. Mustafa sanctioned Khalil and his troops to fight beneath their own banner and, in a moment of understanding, suggested that Khalil take his woman with the proviso she be deposited someplace out of harm's way once they reached the Holy Land.

CHAPTER 5

Benghazi

DECEMBER 1184-JANUARY 1185

Khalil was saving that bit of news for the last night of the gathering when all decisions had been finalized and the plan ready to execute. There were a thousand details to resolve before he could tell Batsheva. He would go ahead of the others to secure a base for the men in the first wave. Arrangements had to be made for the rest of the qubila; with their best men going to Palaestina, they could hardly continue their journey. A location only a day's ride from Benghazi was chosen as the temporary camp for the women, children, and the men designated to remain behind as a ruling council. Water was plentiful, a town was nearby and, most importantly, the area was easily defendable from would-be marauders. Mustafa had already agreed to send a troop of Salah ad-Din's own guard to serve as resident defenders while training the young men who would eventually join them in Palaestina.

In honor of the last night of the gathering, Amirat Aisha hosted a women's banquet. Although tempted to go, Batsheva declined, explaining to the great lady that she wasn't feeling quite up to it.

"Is your belly that bothersome?" she asked Batsheva, a twinkle in her eye.

"I am much larger than I ever anticipated. At day's end, I am so tired I can barely keep my eyes open!" she laughed. "I don't know how I will manage to ride to the new camp without falling asleep in the saddle."

Amirat Aisha raised an elegant eyebrow. "The new camp? There won't be time my dear; we sail from Benghazi the day after tomorrow."

"Sail?"

"Yes, we are sailing from Benghazi. The ship will dock in Alexandria. Mustafa and I will go home. You and Khalil will go on to Akko. Take only the clothing you need for yourself and the baby. Everything else will be waiting for you in Akko."

Batsheva's mouth opened to protest, then closed. Making her apologies once more, she waddled back to their tent.

Sitting in the middle of the rug, maps spread around him, Khalil was finessing his *saif.* Batsheva swept past him.

"No *'a'salaam, Khalil*?'" he called after her.

"No."

He waited for a moment, then he heard a tremendous racket in the sleeping quarters. "Are you quite all right?"

"Yes."

Again, he waited for further comment. When none was forthcoming, he got up and stood at the open drape. Batsheva was emptying her trunks, dumping everything into the center of their bed. "Do you need some help?" he asked as casually as he could muster.

"No."

Daring to step into the room, he raised his arms in time to catch a flying djellaba. "Mine?"

"Yours."

"May I ask what *djinn* you are confronting?" Another garment sailed toward him.

"No."

"Shall I begin guessing?"

"Please do not bother."

Khalil laughed, but not for long. This time, a single boot whizzed past his ear. "If you were not with child, Bashi Hagiz…."

"Do not…*ever*…call…me…that!" she snarled through clenched teeth, a finger pointed at him for emphasis. "Call me anything, but never that!"

"I will call you what I wish when I wish. And you will get used to hearing your name again."

She threw up her hands. "Yes, master; whatever you say, master; your word is law, master."

The obsequious tone burned through his good intention. "You are trying my patience, Batsheva!"

"And you are trying mine, Khalil." Batsheva turned to face him, her hands planted firmly on her hips, her eyes ablaze with anger. "Just when were you going to tell me we are going to Akko? Or were you going to wait until I was halfway to the new camp? Amirat Aisha must think you treat me like a child! And honestly, Khalil, I do not like it. I do not like it one bit!"

No woman had ever spoken to him in this manner; Khalil was speechless. "I planned to tell you once all arrangements were final," he sputtered. "I did not want you to become overexcited and then crushed if permission was denied."

"But Amirat Aisha knew!"

"Amirat Aisha found out today, at the same time I was told. Have you changed your mind, Batsheva? Do you not want to go?"

"Of course, I want to go, Khalil! I want our child born in the Holy Land. If I cannot be in. . . ." Abruptly, Batsheva shut her mouth.

"Cannot be where?"

"Never mind." She started sorting through the pile of clothing on the bed.

Khalil, with a single motion, swept everything aside and pulled Batsheva into his arms. "If we are to make our lives together, Batsheva Hagiz, you will tell me who and what and where and when. I am not one of those who would have you forget your past so we can have a future. Will you not tell me these things so I might know you?"

"They are no longer important, Khalil."

"By the Prophet's beard, woman, they are!"

Looking into his eyes, Batsheva saw something new, a burning to know *about* her. Suddenly she found herself willing to tell him. *But not now.* "I will tell you, Khalil, later. I have too much to accomplish before the sun sets if we are to leave in two days."

When Batsheva did not come to the roasting pit to fetch the evening meal herself, Sufiye sent a tray, not daring to imagine what was happening inside that tent.

They ate together in the outer chamber as Khalil explained the routes and what to expect when they reached Alexandria and then Palaestina. "You will be comfortable in Akko. Until you are strong enough to travel after the babe is born, you will stay in my cousin's house."

"Will he be pleased to find himself with a Hebrew houseguest?" asked Batsheva with small alarm.

"*She* will be pleased to oversee the birth of my child. That you are a Jew will have no bearing on the matter."

"I hope you are right, Khalil. I would hate to be an unwelcome guest. I can always go to my Uncle Avram in Tiberias."

"How many uncles do you have?" groaned Khalil.

"My father has six brothers and three sisters. Each brother controls a different area of the family business. Avram is the next oldest after papa."

Hagiz and Sons was well known. They were more than just merchants; they controlled trade routes. From spices and silks to cotton and linen, from copper and brass to gold and gemstones, the Hagiz family was best known for scrupulous honesty. Khalil had done business with them in past, as recently as two months ago when he purchased the ruby earrings from Shabbatai Hagiz, never imagining that his Vashti was one of them. "Is Shabbatai your uncle?"

Batsheva shook her head. "No, just a cousin. His father was my grandfather's brother. I should have looked more closely at the earrings; I suppose I will find the Hagiz mark on the gold work." She leaned over and patted Khalil's hand. "Then the gift is all the more precious. Perhaps you can think of it as payment for me," she added without expression.

A sharp retort was about to pass his lips when the serving girl returned to reclaim the empty tray. Once she was gone, Khalil helped Batsheva to her feet and together they went into the other room. He helped her out of her heavy *abaya* and into the lighter, more comfortable night-rail. Batsheva's belly seemed to be growing at an impossible rate; never had he seen such a hugely pregnant woman. Settling beneath the covers beside her, Khalil stroked her swollen belly. "Tell me about Bashi Hagiz."

"Bashi Hagiz is dead; she died one moonlit night when she wandered too far from camp in search of her veil."

"Then tell me about Batsheva Hagiz," he gently persisted.

"What is there to tell? I just turned 15, the age my parents deemed marriageable, when I left Málaga; I was an innocent bride on my way to marry the boy I loved when my world was destroyed." Her words were soft, without malice. "I am a lifetime older now."

"You know I did not ask for this to happen."

"You favored women of my coloring. That was well known…or so I've been told. How many other red-haired women had there been?"

"The men were currying favor; they thought a woman would assuage my anger toward them."

"Did it?'

Khalil shrugged. "I never considered it could be you. I did not know if the memory was real, or I had conjured you over the years. I thought often of that day…."

"So, you honored that memory by taking the maidenhead of another girl who looked like that little girl. I was eight years old. What does that say about you, Khalil? That all those years later you were still angry with Yehuda for knocking you over?"

"Batsheva…"

She cut him off. "It no longer matters. That man, the one who lay atop me and ripped my world to shreds no longer exists the same way Bashi Hagiz no longer exists. You destroyed three souls that night."

"Three?"

"Me, the boy I was to marry, and yourself. None of us can be the people we were before that night. Your lust for that memory cost us all."

"Will you ever forgive me?'

Batsheva met his eyes with hers. "Forgive?" she echoed. "I don't know. I have set my anger aside as I have come to know you as a man and leader of your people. You are not the same man who raped me that night and all the nights after that until the night I slew Gamal."

The word *rape* stung more than if she had slapped him. "I did not wish to hurt you."

"Yes, you did. Or you would not have tied me up to force yourself into me. To you, I was nothing more than a thing, a gift, something to use in bed to satisfy…something. I do not know what to call it."

Her words infuriated him, yet he knew she was telling him the fundamental truth. "This is the way our people have taken spoils of war for generations, Batsheva." His words sounded lame, even to him.

"I was *not* a spoil of war!" she shot back. "You know better than that because you, and your father before you, forbade your men from abducting women long before I was taken. Women are targets, we are deliberately hurt. Families are intentionally destroyed." She paused for a moment. "Not unlike yours was."

He had no answer, except to whisper, "Who told you?"

"Sufiye. She thought I should know. She thought I would feel kindlier toward you if I knew about Amina, Hafsah, and Amahl."

He winced as she said their names aloud. "Did you? Do you?"

Batsheva shrugged. "In truth, Khalil, I am attached to your household, but I have no status, no voice. In the end, you will do with me what you will."

"But you do have a voice!" he protested. "And my heart, my soul, and my love. There is nothing of me that you do not hold in the palm of your hand."

"Do I?"

"Yes." He was painfully aware that no matter how their future unfolded, it began with an act of violation.

Batsheva sighed. "And you want to know if I forgive you." It was not a question. "I chose to live, Khalil. *I chose*. I could have chosen to die; there was ample opportunity. I made my choice according to the laws by which *I* live, and *I* live with that choice. I have no need to forgive you. The more difficult question, Khalil, is if one day you will be able to forgive yourself." She stared at the tent ceiling.

Khalil was silent. She had sliced into the place he refused himself permission to visit. Still, this was not the conversation he wanted to have with her.

They were both silent for a long while, but neither was asleep.

"Batsheva," Khalil prodded gently, "will you tell me about the man you were to marry?" She knew about Amina and Hafsah; he wanted to know about the man she still held in her heart.

Batsheva continued to stare at the ceiling debating with herself. She had promised Khalil she would answer his questions but now, faced with having to speak that name aloud, she was reluctant. It all seemed so long ago, but it was not even a single year. How could she tell him of her hopes and dreams when all of them died on the day she was taken? To talk about it was to remember; to remember was to mourn the loss. To share the details of her past would seal it forever as gone; yet, in some ways she knew it would free her. "His name is Akiva." Very slowly, choosing her words carefully, Batsheva told him.

"I fell in love when I was eight years old--as only a little girl can fall in love--yes, the same summer you saw me in the square pretending to be shopping for my wedding clothes. Akiva is a son of the House of Vital, another trading family. He was…is my eldest brother Asher's best friend. I can hardly remember a time when he was not running in and out of our house with Asher. But that summer," she paused again; she could suddenly see her mother's garden, the boys sitting at the old wooden table practicing their chanting for bar mitzvah, "Akiva rescued my kitten from a tree. Asher said she could get down herself but, when I began to cry, Akiva climbed up and brought her down. He was tall and strong and so handsome; when he smiled, my whole world lit up…and he smiled at me a lot. I knew we were destined for each other. Or so I thought…." Her voice trailed off as she remembered the words of the fortune teller in Tunis and shook away the memory. "On my 14th birthday, I told my father he could present me with a thousand suitors but, unless Akiva was amongst them, I would never marry."

"Your father permitted you speak to him in that manner? Khalil asked, his brow furrowed.

"He did not like it, but he is the reason I am so headstrong. He did not believe my education should end with embroidery lessons and silly stories. He made certain I read history and philosophy, that I knew math and astronomy as well."

"And your mother? What did she say?"

"She says there is nothing worse than a woman who cannot converse intelligently on any subject. We do not seclude our women as you do, Khalil. Within the family home, and we have a very big family, men and women eat together. The women are responsible for the early education of the children and the foundation of knowledge must consist of more than stories and baby songs. Akiva expected a wife who would be capable, charming, and interesting; not merely a breeder of sons."

Khalil sighed at the last remark. His wives, he thought wistfully, would have considered Batsheva too worldly, but he had to admit he found it refreshingly pleasant. "And how much do you know, Batsheva?"

"You already have seen my skill with a dagger, but I can also wield a sword with ease."

"This does not surprise me."

She turned a little, so that she could see Khalil in the glow of the braziers. "Oh, I know a great deal more than that. I know how to weigh a gemstone and how to judge its quality. I can keep an accounting ledger and I can write a contract for trade. These are things I might have been asked to do as Akiva's wife when I would be called to attend a rich man's harem." She permitted herself the smallest smile when Khalil appeared duly impressed. "And the womanly things, like running a household and supervising a kitchen. You already have seen my needlework and have eaten my cooking. Judge for yourself, Khalil."

Propping himself on his elbow, he pushed her long curls over her shoulder as he let her words sink in. "What else can you do?" he asked earnestly.

She gave him a wry grin. "Your maps are old and wrong. There are mistakes in your cartography that will cost lives in Palaestina."

He sat upright and stared at her. "You have looked at my maps?"

"I had nothing better to do when I was trapped in your tent." She took a breath and went on. "Your dispatches from Ashdod leave a great deal to be desired. They do not take into account the fortifications built by the Christians in the last 50 years. There are fortresses all over Palaestina which are not even mentioned by your friend Ali Nazim."

"How do you know this?"

"Because I read his dispatches."

"No, I mean about the fortifications."

"Our trade routes, what's left of them," she said bitterly, "must take them into account. We must know where they are and who is in control of each road. Al-Quds is closed to Jews and our Muslim trading partners. Ali Nazim says the Christians are too busy whoring to bother with defense. Think, Khalil; do you really believe such a statement?"

"No, and neither does the sultan."

"And Akko? Do you really think it is safe there? The Christians have not been kind to the people on the coast."

"*We* will land in Akko, Batsheva, not the army. We will arrive as simple people on our way home. The army will come from another direction."

Batsheva grimaced as a limb poked from within. "It seems your daughter would like to hear less heated debate, Khalil."

"Again, you are mistaken, woman; that is my son anxious to see battle." He placed his hand on her belly and was rewarded with a great deal of activity. "You see, I am right."

"And I am tired." Batsheva yawned as if to emphasize the point. Finding a comfortable position, she closed her eyes. "*Num jayidaan*, Khalil."

He turned his own body so she could sleep nestled against him as was her most recent custom. "*Num jayidaan*, Batsheva, mother of my son."

Khalil was already at pre-dawn prayer when Batsheva dressed for the journey. As efficiently as she could, she stuffed the barest necessities into the camel skin bags. The trunks would go directly into the hold onboard the ship. Everything else would be taken to the new camp to be held for their return. She had just carried out another bag when Sufiye appeared with two bags of her own and a horse in tow. "Have you come to say farewell?" asked Batsheva with a warm smile for the woman she had come to love.

"Don't be absurd, Batsheva. I have come to help you get ready lest you delay our start." She tossed her bags onto the pile and tethered the horse to a tent stake. "I am going with you. You cannot have that baby and manage everything that needs to be managed without me."

"Have you asked Khalil's permission?"

Sufiye waved her hand in the air. "I do not need my nephew's permission. I will do as I please."

In a most unexpected gesture, Batsheva hugged the old woman. "I am glad, Auntie! So very glad."

The short trip into Benghazi was made unexpectedly easy when Amirat Aisha insisted her new friend join her in her elegant litter. "Do you not think it will be too heavy?" asked Batsheva, settling back against the cushions.

"Oh, my dear, have you not seen the Amir of Benghazi?"

"Only from a distance."

"He is twice the size we are put together!" laughed the lady. "Do not worry, we are not nearly as burdensome as others."

Sharing the distance with Amirat Aisha made it all pass quickly. Housed for the night in the *sara'i* of the Amir of Benghazi, the three ladies were dining together discussing what would happen when Batsheva and Sufiye reached Akko. Sufiye, who as a young woman had traveled extensively with her husband, plied Amirat Aisha with questions about Alexandria, the city she had not seen in 30 years. As a servant cleared the last of the trays, there was a loud "ahem" at the door and the women immediately veiled themselves.

"Forgive the impropriety, my dear," said Mustafa, "but we have matters to discuss with you all." He motioned for Khalil to enter. "Sit, Khalil bin Mahmud, and let's get down to business."

Careful not to even glance in Amirat Aisha's direction, Khalil explained the latest plan to get them into Palaestina. "We will sail to Akko as we originally decided. But, instead of dressing as we do, we will appear to be Greek."

"Unveiled?" gasped Sufiye with horror.

"You will be practically covered, Auntie," replied Khalil with a chuckle. "Greek widows wear a black headdress which all but hides their faces. Unless, of course, you would prefer to remain here…."

"Not on your father's grave, Khalil bin Mahmud. Batsheva will be in need of help, and I will be there to provide it."

Amirat Aisha touched the old woman's arm. "Do not worry, Sufiye; you might find being able to breathe fresh air a most pleasant experience."

"I doubt it," she sniffed, "but I will manage."

"Good, for I did not want to leave you behind, gracious aunt." That settled, Khalil continued. "I will be a merchant bringing casks of supplies destined for places outside Akko. Each cask will have a false bottom and inside will be swords and armor for our men to reclaim before the battles begin."

"We have numerous contacts in Akko," explained Mustafa, "and they have been waiting for us to send reinforcements. With your arrival, they will know that Salah ad-Din is en route."

"Will we stay in Akko?" asked Batsheva.

"For the time being. If all goes well, that is where you will give birth to my son." Khalil allowed himself a small, self-satisfied smile. "When you are well enough to travel, I shall take you to our cousins the Benu, for that is where you will be safest and out of harm's way."

"In Akko," added Amirat Aisha, "you will be housed with a family named Pappanos. They are Greek by nationality, but they are also cousins to both Khalil and me; they are sympathetic to the cause to free Al-Quds from the invaders. Elena Pappanos is a wise woman with a good dose of common sense. She will see to your safety and your comfort."

"I will trust your judgment, Amira Aisha," said Batsheva quietly.

The next morning, as they prepared to leave for the port, Amirat Aisha suddenly switched from Arabic to Castilian. "I know you speak the language, Batsheva, and I would prefer our words not be overheard by the servants."

"*Como usted desee*," Batsheva replied in the same tongue.

"You are a Jewess, and you might not know that under our law Khalil is permitted to marry you without your embrace of Islam. The only proviso is that the children be raised in the ways of Islam."

"I am aware."

"Are you also aware that Khalil wants desperately to marry you?"

Batsheva nodded.

"I would suggest you marry Khalil before you leave for Akko."

"That cannot be, Amirat Aisha; I cannot make that promise in good faith. Let us be as we are. I am faithful to Khalil, and I have no desire to leave him."

The lady sighed with exaggeration. "He said you are stubborn."

"This is true, I'm afraid."

"And what is also true is that when you give me your word that you have no intention of leaving Khalil, that word is binding. But may I ask why? You have your own people in Palaestina, why not go back to them?"

"Perhaps you did not know my brother came to ransom me. I told him I would not go back. I cannot. My place is with Khalil."

"Then why not as his wife?"

"He deserves a wife who loves him."

"And you do not?"

"No, I do not. I care for him a great deal, but I do not love him."

Amirat Aisha shook her head. "You perplex me, Batsheva. Any woman would want a husband as handsome, strong, and kind as Khalil bin Mahmud, not to mention his family connections. Only Allah knows how many women have tried to attract his attention! You willingly share his tent and his bed, yet you refuse him."

If Batsheva fleetingly wondered about Khalil's so-called connections she did not ask. "I share a great deal more than just his tent, Amirat Aisha. I share his dream for a peaceful existence with our neighbors and I share his vision of a Holy Land freed from Christian conquest. These are things we have in common and to that end I will support Khalil. But the minute he or any of his men wantonly strikes out at a Jew defending his home, I will kill that man. Khalil knows this. Now you do, too."

The lady was silenced by the grim words. Somehow, she could envision the steel-eyed woman as warrior and did not doubt for one moment that, as she had killed Gamal when he threatened Khalil, she would kill again for what she believed to be a just cause.

No sooner had the ship left the dock in Alexandria than Batsheva pulled the hijab from her head and stood at the railing, the sun shining on her face, a steady wind whipping through her hair. From a distance, Khalil watched her, his eyes rejoicing at the sight of her turned to the sun; she was beyond beautiful in the daylight, her hair shimmering in golden waves, the sun glinting off the riot of curls tumbling all the way down her back. He caught himself wondering if it was wrong to veil women; perhaps it denied them a different kind of freedom, the type he loved best… the elements against his skin, the wind against his face, the sun narrowing his eyes against the brightness. Nearby, Sufiye stood clucking her tongue at the wanton display of flesh.

"She looks happy, Auntie," murmured Khalil, his eyes locked on the woman.

"Happy, but naked!" The sharpness of her reply was tempered with a little chuckle. "I suppose this is what she is used to."

He did not add *this is how I have always imagined her.*

PART II

AKKO

JANUARY 1185–JUNE 1189

CHAPTER 6

Akko

JANUARY-MAY 1185

The harbor was busy, but not the bustling port Khalil remembered from his last visit more than a decade ago. Evidence of war was everywhere. Instead of merchants running about arranging for cargo to be delivered, there were precious few people near the docks, mostly soldiers. Men wearing little more than tatters hovered outside the cargo houses in hopes of earning a few coins for a day's work unloading goods. Dirty, hungry-looking children waited with their hands outstretched as sailors and passengers disembarked; their cries for alms pierced the uncommonly still air. Khalil tried to put coins into every hand, but smaller ones were pushed by larger ones until a fight erupted. Three fierce looking soldiers roughly grabbed the beggar boys and hauled them away, shouting obscenities at Khalil for instigating a near riot.

For the first time in her life, Batsheva wished for a veil to shield her from the sights on the quay. The hood of her Grecian cloak could not possibly be drawn far enough along her face to hide the decay around her, and if that were not bad enough, the stench was overpowering. Holding her kerchief against her nose, Batsheva followed closely behind Khalil, hoping her enormous belly would not slow her already awkward progress. A pair of litters for hire sat at the edge of the dock and Khalil quickly signaled the master. Once inside the shabby compartment, Batsheva drew the curtains.

The house of Nikon Pappanos was far from the squalid port. Situated within the walls of the city, the unadorned stone exterior with narrow slit windows and no balconies, a foreboding presence on the street hid well the creature comforts within. The litter master held the curtain back when Khalil helped Batsheva from the conveyance. No sooner had she stepped out than the large door opened slowly.

"Greetings. Is your master at home?" Khalil asked the man who stood staring at the travelers.

The door closed again and was reopened to reveal a plump, balding gentleman. "Constantine!" he cried, "you have arrived early! Come in, come in. And this must be your lovely bride, Athena!" He extended his chubby hand to the mystified Batsheva and held hers tightly for a moment. "Elena and I were not expecting you until later in the week, but no matter, we are glad you have safely arrived." He almost pulled Batsheva into the house. She would have panicked had she not seen the twinkle in Khalil's dark eyes.

Elena Pappanos scurried toward them at great speed. "Welcome, cousins! How did you leave Athens? Is everything in order?"

All eyes turned toward Batsheva when she answered, "*Óla eínai óso kalá anaménontai, xadélfia.*"

"As good as we can hope!" Elena laughed. "Well, surely you must be hungry; come into the garden and take some refreshment while the servants see to the baggage."

"I did not know you spoke Greek," whispered Khalil, sliding his arm about her as they followed Elena.

"You never asked," Batsheva replied with a smile.

"I shall have to learn to ask better questions, Bashi." He hid his own grin when she growled at him.

The courtyard was a delightful refuge and Batsheva knew where she would spend the last days of her pregnancy: there were chairs. She had not sat in a chair since she left Tunis, and once seated, she thought she would never rise again. Khalil looked equally comfortable although she had never seen him sit in one before. With his long legs stretched out, soles of his feet still downward, one arm slung over the back he looked as though he'd never sat on anything else. Sufiye was ramrod straight, her hands firmly grasping the arms of her chair, but Batsheva noticed her ankles were crossed. With the fountain splashing merrily at the center, the occasional spray of water caught in the breeze, Batsheva almost felt normal.

Elena Pappanos kept the conversation on a casual basis until the porters had completed their task. As soon as they were shown out, the language switched to Arabic and Nikon fired off question after question while Khalil answered them just as rapidly.

"Lord Salah is satisfied with the schedule?" asked Nikon after Khalil relayed what he learned before they sailed from Alexandria.

"As satisfied as he can be from a distance. He should be in Damascus by month's end; only then we will have a more complete sense of timing." He was growing weary of the repetitious nature of Nikon's questions.

Nikon grunted as he popped a fig into his mouth. "It has not been easy here, cousin. The westerners are bent on the destruction of the city through neglect. Their health habits are non-existent, and the sewage backs up with regularity. I do not know how much longer Akko will be safe."

"Safe for whom?" Khalil snapped impatiently.

"Safe for your family, Khalil! Yes, from the Christians' standpoint, the city functions and is a great commercial success. But from our view, the city is unhealthy. Rats. Disease. Sewage. The sooner the sultan takes Akko, the better off we will be. But l tell you this, the battle will be long and hard fought. No doubt, there will be a siege and everyone within the city walls will suffer. The westerners say reinforcements are coming and, if that is indeed true, this is a most strategic location."

Batsheva put her hand on Khalil's arm to quiet him. "What is your best advice, Cousin Nikon?"

The plump man chewed deliberately on another fig as he considered his answer. "It all depends, little cousin, on what you believe to be best for you...."

His wife cut him off with a wave of her ringed fingers. "What will be best is for you to give birth and move you the south, where you will be safe with the Benu Ghassadi. They are well-hidden and the foreigners do not particularly like dealing with them."

"I have family in Tiberias..." murmured Batsheva.

Elena shook her head. "Tiberias is no safer than we are. Were it not for the network of spies in that city, we would be blind to much of what is happening to the north."

"In the meanwhile," added Nikon, "we have been laying in as many supplies as we can manage without arousing suspicion. It is a dangerous business, but we pray every day for word of the sultan and his army."

Batsheva felt as comfortable as she could possibly be, considering her girth, behind the thick walls of the Pappanos house. Elena took her on daily expeditions through the city, showing her not only the shops, but quietly pointing out the houses in which they would be safe in case of emergency. Each evening, new faces appeared at the door, faces Batsheva was told to memorize even if no names were provided. From behind a finely carved screen, the women monitored the conversations, only to spend the later hours with Nikon and Khalil discussing what had already been discussed. Crusader troops had begun a small, steady movement toward Tiberias and this reduction, the men agreed, would be good for their troops. Still, news was yet to come from either Egypt or Damascus, and both Nikon and Khalil were worried.

The baby had positioned itself in such a way as to make walking almost impossible. Early one morning on the way to the market, it was Sufiye who decided they would turn back; Batsheva looked as though she were about to faint. No sooner had they seated themselves in the garden when Batsheva suddenly felt wet. "Sufiye?" she gasped.

The pains, slow at first, continued over the course of the day until it was time to call Sarah the midwife. Only then did Nikon send a messenger to the warehouse to bring Khalil home. He ran up the stairs and found Batsheva was sitting up in bed laughing and singing songs with the midwife and Sufiye. When they saw him at the door, they shooed him away. "We will call you when your daughter is born" teased Batsheva. Nikon led the father-to-be down the stairs to the courtyard where refreshments were set out for the long wait.

The labor progressed at a good pace, and Batsheva proved to be a rather stoic patient. She followed instructions, made a variety of noises, but no-blood curdling screams brought the men running. When it was finally time to bring the babe into the world, Batsheva just smiled and got ready to push.

"Bear down, Batsheva," coaxed the midwife, "bear down and let us see the face of the babe so anxious to see the world."

Batsheva grunted and grit her teeth, holding onto Elena's hands with all her might. Her face grew red with exertion until the wave of pain passed and she fell back against the pillows. Another spasm quickly took its place, and she rose to meet it, bearing down with all her strength as each contraction worked to deliver the child.

"The head!" cried Sarah at last, "I have the head. Breathe…breathe… breathe…. Push again, Batsheva!" And Batsheva complied.

"And again!"

With a groan and a pop, the pain momentarily abated. "It's a boy! You have a fine son."

Struggling upward, Batsheva smiled broadly. "Let me see him." The tiny child was held aloft, and she saw a thatch of dark hair. Another pain gripped Batsheva and she cried out.

"Ho, ho! A foot!" chortled the midwife, "Who is this? There is another one coming!" She handed the boy, still attached to his mother, to Sufiye as she tied off and quickly cut the cord. "Batsheva, bear down gently, for this one is turned."

Batsheva could barely catch her breath; the midwife's hand pushed slowly on her belly while her other hand reached to capture the second babe's leg. Pushing against Elena, Batsheva bore down slowly while watching the midwife's face for more instruction. "Do you have it?" she rasped as she pushed.

"Keep going, Batsheva, a little more, a little more, a little…there. Stop…. Push a little…`there! It is done!" An angry squeak issued from the foot of the bed. "You are blessed with a little girl, Batsheva. A beautiful little girl." And she held up the squeaking, squirming babe for her mother's inspection.

Sufiye cleansed the little girl while Elena held the boy. Sarah tended to the afterbirth then assisted Batsheva with the necessary linen and a fresh gown. Once the afterbirth and soaked linens were removed and fresh linen spread on the bed, Batsheva settled back against the pillows and opened her arms to receive her children. With Sarah's help, the little boy was guided to one breast, and the little girl to the other.

"Two!" shouted Khalil as soon as he heard. He did not wait for anything else; he simply bounded up the stairs, three at a time, and burst into the room.

"Come see your children, Khalil," said Batsheva, exhausted but aglow with pride.

He sat on the edge of the bed and stared at the two sucking infants. "Two!" he whispered in awe. "There are two!"

"Which would account for her size, Khalil," added Sufiye. "And, nephew, it says something about you as well." Her last comment was received with indelicate snorts from the other three ladies.

"Don't puff him up any more than he already is, Auntie," chided the new mother with mock severity. "I can see he is already intolerably proud of himself." Batsheva looked at Khalil's wide eyes and laughed. With Sufiye's help, she unwrapped the babies so he might examine them.

"They are beautiful, Batsheva," he murmured as he stroked one, then the other. There was an unaccustomed dampness on his cheek when, in a fleeting moment, he recalled the day Amahl was born. Just then, the boy stopped sucking and turned his head toward his father. With trembling hands, he took the babe from Batsheva and held him against his chest. "My son," he whispered. "Another son."

Elena, Sufiye, and the midwife left them alone in the room.

"You have a daughter, too, Khalil," coaxed Batsheva.

He looked at the little girl and noticed, for the first time, the coppery fuzz on her head. "She will be like her mother; beautiful and strong…."

"And most likely spoiled silly by her doting father," finished Batsheva. "I thought we would name her Amina."

Khalil nodded. "Yes, that would be a fine name for her. Amina was a good woman; it would have pleased her." He thought his heart would burst.

"And our son, I would like him named David…Daud in Islam. David was a good king, a skilled warrior, and brilliant poet, all things we would hope for our son."

"And the name of your grandfather," Khalil managed to smile.

"And the name of my grandfather," she echoed a little sadly. "He, too, was a good and kind man."

Khalil removed a small box from beneath his sash and handed it to Batsheva. "My father gave this to my mother on the day of my birth. It was made by David Hagiz himself. I think it is appropriate for you."

Batsheva opened the box and there, nestled on a bed of silk, was an elegant, simple gold ring crowned with a delicately sculpted pomegranate. When she turned it over, her grandfather's mark was as clear as the day he had put it there. Khalil took it from her and slipped it onto her finger.

"Before she died, my mother gave it to Sufiye with the instructions it was to be given to her granddaughter if Allah willed there should ever be one. I think Amina will let you wear it for now." Khalil, still holding Daud, kissed the top of Amina's fair head, and then Batsheva's. "To say that I love you, Batsheva Hagiz, cannot make up for the pain I have caused, but perhaps, as we love our children together, you will be able to find room in your heart to love me as well." Gently, he replaced Daud in the crook of his mother's arm and left the room.

Only when he was gone, did Batsheva allow her own tears to flow free.

The sun was already streaming into Batsheva's room through the slats of the shutters when she awoke to the squirming of hungry babies. "There now, Daud, don't be greedy," she murmured to her son as she put him to breast. Amina was waving her tiny fists as she made smacking noises with her lips while she waited impatiently for her turn. No sooner than Batsheva had managed to get everything organized, did the door open and Sufiye appeared.

"It is good to see you awake in the daylight," she announced, pleased with the way Batsheva had handled the babies herself. "I trust you have all slept well?"

"So it would seem, Auntie. They slept through most of the night."

"That will change now that they have discovered hunger. I think we shall have to have a wet nurse, Batsheva, or you will spend your entire day shifting babies from breast to breast."

Batsheva wrinkled her nose at the suggestion. "Would you be terribly offended if I asked that we find a woman like myself?"

"Babies do not know the difference, Batsheva; they only know if there is not enough milk." She busied herself straightening the bedclothes and plumping the pillows. "But, since new mothers are known to be odd in their requests, I shall ask the midwife if she knows someone." Sufiye saw no reason to tell Batsheva the request had already been made.

When the wet nurse arrived at midday, Batsheva was most relieved. Instead of an older woman, Sufiye had procured the services of a girl not much older than Batsheva. Devora shyly smiled when she was introduced to the babies' mother. "I am pleased to be of service, ma'am," she said in Arabic tinged with a Maghreb accent.

Batsheva had been told Devora's own child was stillborn just two days before. As she handed Amina to her, she could see the pain of her loss, still so fresh, in Devora's beautiful dark eyes. "Your husband does not mind?" she asked the wet nurse.

"My husband was murdered on the road to Jerusalem," she whispered as she settled the little girl onto her ripe nipple. "He died with the name of the Holy One on his lips as he tried to protect me and our unborn child." She lapsed into silence. "That was five months ago. Even so, our son was stillborn."

When Sufiye had gone to fetch a light meal for Batsheva, the girl turned to her new mistress. "I hope the milk which would have nourished my son will make your children grow strong, gracious lady."

"And I hope that *Ha'Kodesh Baruch Hu* has sent you to me to be more than just a nurse to my children, but to be my friend as well."

Devora blinked at the sound of Hebrew. "Are you one of us?" she whispered.

"Yes," replied Batsheva, "so do not be afraid; you are indeed among friends here. The household is Greek, the father of the children is Ayyub; there is respect for us as we are. I am as the Holy One made me and shall continue to be so. It will be good to have a friend, for I am a stranger here."

"No, gracious lady," replied Devora, lifting her chin, "no Jew can ever be a stranger in Zion."

By dinnertime, Batsheva began to wonder where Khalil could be. He had not come to see them all day and she worried that something might have happened. When Sufiye came in with a servant carrying a large tray for her and Devora, she asked after him.

"He has gone to Tiberias," answered Sufiye a little stiffly. "He said to tell you he will return as soon as he can."

"Why Tiberias?"

Sufiye glanced at the wet nurse who sat on a cushion with Daud in her arms. "Business."

"Worry not, Sufiye; Devora will not reveal anything which takes place in this house. She is a widow thanks to the foreigners."

An eyebrow soared upward at Batsheva's remarks. Turning her piercing eyes on Devora she said, "The midwife said you were from Fez."

"This is so. My husband was from Al-Andalus. We lived first in Tz'fat, then Tiberias. We were on our way to Jerusalem when the foreign army soldiers attacked. My husband placed himself between a soldier on horseback and me. The sword went through Reuven and into me." Devora pulled open her abaya to reveal a long, ugly scar which ran from her throat and ended between her breasts." My husband died covering me with his body, and I was left for dead. In the darkness of the night, I dug my husband's grave with my bare hands and buried him outside the city of his hope. A Muslim man found me and took me to his home where his wife tended my wounds until I was well enough to return to Tiberias."

"And how did you come to Akko?" pressed Sufiye.

"I was pregnant; I had no means of support. Sarah the midwife was visiting Tiberias and offered to take me into her home here. She has been most kind and loving; without her, I would have died of grief."

Sufiye liked the strength she heard in Devora's story. If nothing else, she would make an excellent companion for Batsheva. That she hated the foreigners as much as they did was a bonus. "This house, Devora, is a house of refuge for those who would fight the invaders. If anyone is betrayed, if anything goes awry, be forewarned: you will not live."

"I have nothing left to risk, madam," said Devora quietly. "I have no home, no family, only the wish to see Jerusalem freed from the foreigners. The name for the Holy One may be different on our lips, but the Prophet himself says our God is one and the same." She looked about the room and then at Batsheva. "I would be a fool not to see this as a safe haven from what is outside the gates of Akko."

"Then you are welcome to stay here, Madam Alfasi. May Allah protect us all."

"*Insh'Allah,*" they all replied. Still, Batsheva wondered why Sufiye would say such a strange thing when, according to all reports, there was, at least for the moment, an uneasy peace in the land.

Khalil was gone almost a week. Batsheva worried about his safety and kept asking if there had been any word from him. Sufiye had relaxed considerably around Devora once it came to light that her husband had been more than just a simple student in a yeshiva; he had been an important member of the Jewish resistance, something Devora was not originally willing to discuss, although Nikon seemed to know a great deal about him. Everyone in the house was acutely aware that what had happened to her could happen to them.

The babies kept them busy. Daud was the fussier, Amina the hungrier. Daud wanted to be held constantly while his sister was perfectly content to lie in her cradle with her fist in her little rosebud mouth. Batsheva and Devora would take turns nursing each baby, sitting side by side, talking endlessly about those things they had in common. Devora was almost as well educated as Batsheva, and they both had older brothers with whom they competed as children. For the first time since her abduction, Batsheva began to feel almost whole, her old self emerging into the light.

"Do you love the sheikh?" asked Devora late one night as they nursed the twins.

Batsheva shrugged but smiled in the darkness. "I was abducted because he had a well-known preference for red-haired women; he did not ask for me to be taken. Khalil is a good man, usually very kind, and a very good leader to his people. Oh, he has his moments of bad temper, but don't all men?" she laughed lightly.

"Even Reuven had his moments," agreed Devora, "but do you love him?"

"I care for him deeply. Love?" she shrugged, "I do not know what that is anymore."

Batsheva insisted on sitting in the courtyard on the seventh day following the birth of the twins. With the help of Sufiye and Elena, she slowly negotiated the stairs. The babies were placed in their cradles and the women settled themselves, each with a tiny garment to occupy their hands. Elena marveled over the delicate precision of Batsheva's stitches. "Where did you learn to sew like that? Your work is wonderful!"

"In my mother's garden in Málaga," she admitted when pressed. "My mother was most insistent I learn fine needlework." She smiled warmly at Sufiye. "When you gave me the cloth and thread, I thought I would be unable to contain myself. It was the first time I thought my life might go on."

"I told Khalil you would die from boredom if you were not given something to do," recalled the older woman; "I did not approve of how you came to be with us in the first place."

"You approve of very little, Auntie, when it comes to the traditional ways of matchmaking," laughed Khalil as he entered the courtyard, his clothing travel stained, his face streaked with dirt.

"Khalil!" Batsheva was surprised at her own cry of relief at seeing him.

He went to her and brushed a light kiss on her upturned mouth. "I take it you are glad to see me."

"I was worried."

"My apologies." He scooped Daud from his cradle and nuzzled the sweet-smelling infant. "Are you letting your mother rest, little boy?" he cooed. Glancing up, he noticed the newcomer sitting nearby.

Batsheva hastened to make the introduction. "This is Devora Alfasi; she is helping me to nurse our demanding children," she said with a smile.

"Alfasi," Khalil echoed. "I knew of a Reuven Alfasi from Tiberias."

"My late husband."

Khalil frowned; Reuven had been an important strategist. He learned of his death only upon his arrival in that city. "My condolences, madam. Allah willing, he has gone to heaven as a warrior."

"*Insh'Allah*," murmured Elena and Sufiye.

A servant appeared bearing a tray of drinks and sweets. "Allow me to wash, then I shall tell you of my trip," said Khalil with a bow. When Batsheva rose, he offered her his arm. Neither Elena nor Sufiye missed the way they looked at each other before they left the courtyard.

"You look well, Batsheva," Khalil told her as they walked slowly up the stairs.

"Thank you; I feel well. You, on the other hand, look as though you haven't slept in several days." Her hand closed tightly over his. "I was angry when you did not tell me you were going, Khalil. And then I worried for your safety."

Khalil thought his heart would fly from his chest. Swallowing hard, he composed his reply. "It comforts me to believe you may have some kind feelings toward me."

At the top of the stairs, Batsheva turned to face him. "You are the father of our children, Khalil; it is only natural that I would be concerned." She reached up and touched his stubbly cheek. "I think, my lord, I would be most upset if anything untoward befell you."

Khalil captured her hand in his own and brought her upturned palm to his lips. "Your words give me strength," *and hope* he added silently. When she did not pull away, he put his arms around her and drew her close. "You feel so small against me, mother of our children."

Her laughter was soft. "I *am* small, Khalil; you have merely forgotten how small."

When they reached their room, Khalil closed the door behind them. "I bring you word of your family, Batsheva."

"Are they well?" she asked, keeping her voice calm.

"I went to see your uncle." Khalil put his hands on her shoulders. "When Avram Hagiz refused see me, I refused to leave his shop. Your cousin Naftali tried to throw me out, but…." He was shocked when Batsheva started to laugh.

"You are a great match for Naftali!" she laughed. "He cannot be more than 12!"

"I'm afraid I picked him up by the kaftan and threatened to drop him on his head unless his father agreed to speak with me. When your Uncle Avram finally came out of the house, he would not listen…until I told him the name of our son. He stopped shouting and stared at me, then asked me to sit with him where we could speak in private. He told me Yehuda was in Tiberias less than a month ago; he told him you were a slave in my household and died in childbirth."

"He said he would tell them I am dead."

"Your uncle has dispatched a messenger to your parents to tell them the truth."

"I did not want to believe he would hurt our parents with that terrible lie. Where is Yehuda now?" asked Batsheva.

"On his way to Constantinople." He paused for a moment, then went on. "Your uncle has made a request which we will honor, Batsheva Hagiz. It is the custom of both our peoples to circumcise our male children. My people wait until the boy is older, but Uncle Avram has asked that the ceremony take place on the eighth day. Since we are not married and since I will be leaving to join the sultan's army in two days' time, I would see my son circumcised before I go. It is a father's right. I have arranged for a *mohel* to come tomorrow morning, the eighth day."

Batsheva was speechless.

As though he could read her mind, Khalil reached out for her hand. "This is a small concession when I know there will ultimately be a battle about how the children will be raised. But I am a realist, Batsheva. If I do not return, I want you to leave Palaestina and return to your father's house. This will be told to Nikon and to Sufiye. They will honor my wishes in this matter."

"You will return, Khalil," whispered Batsheva sliding her arms about him, "and I will be happy to argue about their upbringing when Jerusalem is free."

Khalil approached his new position with fierce determination, directing much of the operation from the north, midway between Akko and Aleppo, sending messages home as often as he dared. As strategist general to the sultan's army, he structured a campaign to take back Tiberias and, after that, Akko before continuing to Al-Quds. The movements would have to be swift and decisive; nothing could be left to chance. Every town, every city had to be prepared and stocked for the armies. Reuven Alfasi's network of spies and resistance sheltered Khalil and his men when necessary. Arms flowed into Akko under the guise of Greek trade, and Nikon's establishment on the wharf was the bolthole for the resistance within the city.

Three months passed before Khalil was able to return to Akko. Sailing in on a Greek vessel, no one questioned him when he disembarked. He stopped at Nikon's warehouse long enough to see the new casks properly stored before he made his way to the stone house. His arrival sent the household into a joyous uproar.

Sitting in the courtyard, news was exchanged, and assurances given that the sultan was coming. For an instant, the world seemed to have stopped, and the family was a family for a long moment. Khalil watched the faces of those seated around him, and for the first time in a very long time, he felt he was where he truly belonged.

When Batsheva and Devora went upstairs to tend to the twins, Khalil took his aunt aside. "I look to you, Auntie, to tell me if Batsheva is adjusting to life here and with the babes. I remember…"

Sufiye held up her hand to silence him. "Batsheva is not Amina. I loved Amina as my own daughter, Khalil, but Batsheva is much stronger. They come from different worlds, and Batsheva's life has not been all gardens and pomegranates. I will tell you this much, child of my heart, she worries about you all the time. I also know she attended their ritual bath, their *mikvah*, with Devora two days ago. Go to her."

Khalil nodded and mounted the stairs. He wanted only for his aunt to be right in this.

When Khalil entered the bedroom, Devora excused herself, leaving them alone. "You work well together?" he asked softly.

"Oh, yes. I am so glad to have her help and her friendship. I think you should be, too."

Khalil sat down on the edge of the bed. "We have learned so much from her and the network in Tiberias. Reuven was central to the operation. They have saved many lives." He paused and looked at Batsheva. "But I heard something about Akko today I did not know."

"What is that, my lord general?"

He turned to face Batsheva. "That there is a Jewish bath…a mikvah… here in Akko."

Batsheva's cheeks blushed pink. "There is." With deft fingers, she loosened the fabric of his turban and unwound the length of blue until it lay on the floor in a silken puddle. Running her fingers through the dark waves, she heard him groan when she caressed his ears.

Suddenly, Khalil pulled away. He had not taken Batsheva since the night of Gamal's attack, when she told him she was with child. In the months that followed, he had sworn to himself that he would not couple with her again unless it was what she wanted. Batsheva was not his wife, nor was she his slave; she was a free woman who, according to Muslim law, had inalienable rights that he had violated.

"Are you in pain, Khalil?" Batsheva stroked his furrowed brow.

"No…Yes…" he looked up into the storm grey pools. "I want things to be different between us, Batsheva."

"How, Khalil? How would you want them to be different?"

He held her face between his hands. "I want you to come to me of your own will, not because you have the notion that I own you. I want you to…." His voice drifted off; he was unsure of how he could express what was in his heart.

"But you don't own me, Khalil. If I did not want to be here, I would have left long ago. The only bond that ties me to this house is you."

"You have said repeatedly that you do not love me," he groaned in anguish. "I cannot keep you with me if your heart is elsewhere."

"Ah, Khalil, you are so foolish." She brushed a kiss on his parted lips, stilling the incipient protest. "The minute you returned, I should have told you that I spent my nights wishing for your arms around me, that I missed you far more than I ever imagined I would."

"Yet you still refuse to marry me."

"And I will continue to refuse. I will not be married by a one-sided contract; for me, a wedding must be a sacred event according to Jewish law. I will share your joys and your sorrows, I will lie with you in the night and bear your children but please, Khalil, do not ask me to marry you according to the laws of Islam. Let this be enough." She held his face in her hands and looked deep into his eyes. "I went to the mikvah two days ago. I wanted to be ready for your homecoming."

"You come to me of your own free will?"

"Yes, Khalil."

He sighed as he pulled the pins from her hair to let the curls tumble down her back. He breathed in the scent of her. "It will have to be enough."

They undressed each other slowly, but it was only when Khalil slid her kaftan from her shoulders that Batsheva suddenly felt self-conscious. Although her body was shrinking back to its normal size, her shape was not as lean and taut as she wanted, and her breasts, heavy with milk, seemed too large and unattractive. But Khalil did not see her in that way; he saw a woman who had given him two children at once, whose breasts nourished those children, and although her belly was not so flat, the skin was soft to the touch and the thought of his seed having been nurtured within only heated his desire for her. With worshipful lips, he kissed every inch of her flesh, murmuring his love for her as he moved along the still lush curves.

Batsheva let herself be lost in his ministrations; hands made rough by weeks of battle tenderly cupped her breasts as his lips brushed against the swollen tips. Giving herself to him in this way, loosed a torrent of new sensations through her body. Arching against Khalil, Batsheva let the searing heat of his flesh consume her. When his lips traveled upward to her own, she captured his tongue and sucked it until he groaned in ecstasy. For the first time, she allowed her hands to explore the hard planes of his body, noticing the way the muscles rippled and tightened when her fingertips discovered the secret, sensual places unexplored until now.

When he entered her, Batsheva moaned, and Kahlil silenced her with his mouth. He moved slowly, letting each stroke drive deep into the core of her sex. All doubts vanished as she rose to meet him, wrapping her legs around his hips, her hands grasping his buttocks, pulling him deeper into her core. Her eyes, once always open and staring, were closed as she moved in rhythm with his thrusts. A thin sheen of perspiration made Batsheva shimmer in the moonlight, giving her an unearthly ethereal aura. He could not get enough as she tightened around him at the moment of climax. His seed poured into her as she arched against him, drawing his shaft into her own endless pool.

"I would not let myself dream of this," he told her, kissing the damp tendrils touching her face.

Batsheva smiled at Khalil, her eyes shining. "Nor would I," she answered, pressing against him. No matter what happened, she told herself, she would treasure this moment for the rest of her life. They were as one, no walls between them. Whatever happened in the weeks to come, she could recall there was once a moment when everything was right.

They slept nestled together, a tangle of arms and legs beneath a light coverlet. Only when she suddenly felt cold, did Batsheva open her eyes. The time for nursing the twins had passed and her breasts were painfully full. Turning, she saw Khalil was gone from the bed, but the door to the nursery was ajar and a pale stream of lamplight told her someone was with the twins. She slipped from the bed, wrapped a robe around her, padded over to peek in. Khalil was sitting in her chair, both babies curled neatly on his chest, softly singing a lullaby. Had the fullness in her breasts been less painful, Batsheva would have left them alone, but her need to nurse was almost as acute as their need to feed. Ever so softly, she tapped on the doorframe.

"I washed," said Khalil quietly. "Then Daud was fussing. I have taken care of those needs I could, but I am afraid I have not the proper composition to keep them happy much longer." A little awkwardly, he stood, then motioned for Batsheva to take the chair. "I think my daughter shall eat first before she consumes her entire hand." He gently slid Amina to Batsheva and watched with rapture as the tiny mouth closed firmly around the engorged nipple. Holding Daud in the crook of his arm, he let his son suck his finger while they waited for Amina to drink her fill.

While Amina nursed, Batsheva watched Khalil standing by the window looking out over the sleeping city. There was an ease about the way he held the child, and she reminded herself this was not his first-born son. Surely, he had held Amahl in the same way; she wondered if, at that moment, he was thinking of those he had lost. Were the songs he crooned the same ones he and Amina sang to Amahl? Shaking the thoughts from her head, Batsheva fingered her daughter's copper fuzz.

Amina finished and Daud took her place. Khalil loved the loud smacking noises his son made as he greedily sucked his midnight meal. An old hand at infants, he held Amina on his shoulder and lightly patted her back until a most unladylike sound erupted. Khalil took Amina into their chamber and soon the strains of the little lullaby were heard once more.

Daud was still fussing after he ate; Batsheva, too tired to pace the floor, hoped to find Khalil willing to take over. Instead, she found father and daughter curled up on the bed asleep, the baby tucked into the bend of his elbow. Batsheva allowed herself a little sigh as she started to walk. Soon, Daud was asleep and, rather than leave him alone in the nursery, she climbed into the bed and placed him beside his sister.

At dawn, a sharp cry from the nursery awakened both Batsheva and Khalil with a start. Before they could move, Sufiye came tearing into the bedroom. "The babies!" she wailed, "the babies are gone!" She practically tripped on her skirts when she saw Amina and Daud sleeping soundly between their parents. "Shame on you both," she growled with mock severity, "for frightening an old woman."

"The fault is mine, gracious Aunt, and I apologize," whispered Khalil with equally mock contriteness. "I was the scoundrel who brought Amina into our bed."

"And we could not possibly leave Daud alone."

Sufiye threw up her hands. "As long as the little monkeys are asleep, leave them be. I shall come back when they are awake." She went out through the nursery, closing the door firmly behind her.

"Do you think she was angry?" Batsheva asked Khalil.

"No, I think she was very pleased." He kissed Batsheva's mouth. "Now, lie beside me and let us enjoy the few minutes we have left."

CHAPTER 7

Akko

JUNE-AUGUST 1187

The shadow of war hovered over the city for two years, but Akko remained safe as battles raged to the north and east. Khalil came as often as he could, but sometimes months passed between visits. Everyone knew war would eventually reach them, and when it did, life in the Pappanos house would change radically.

The first change came with Salah ad-Din's siege of Tiberias. Devora's contacts sent word as soon as the siege was imminent. Forewarned, they as prepared as best they could. The sultan amassed his army at the Golan, and with their Druze allies, crossed the Jordan on June 30th. The army attacked Tiberias on July 2nd, and city fell to the sultan within a day.

The battle at the Horns of Hattin was fierce and bloody; Jews fought alongside the sultan's army using anything and everything within grasp. As one soldier fell, another man picked up the sword and continued the fight until the invaders withdrew from the Kinneret, leaving a jubilant populace to celebrate. Khalil and his men rode under the Ayyub flag, their own banner snapping in the hand of their sheikh's standard-bearer, Muhammed bin Gamal. Each evening, as they bowed toward Mecca, Khalil thanked Allah for his men's cunning; their losses had been kept to a minimum. Although few in number, Khalil's men distinguished themselves in the field and soon word of the little band and their fearsome, fearless sheikh spread through the army.

Still anxious to rid Palaestina of the foreigners, Salah ad-Din directed his forces eastward toward Akko. The invaders had been severely weakened in numbers and everyone believed Akko would be an easy victory. Khalil dispatched Kassim to the port disguised as a beggar. His message was simple: when the battle begins, fortify yourselves and stay within the walls of the house.

With Tiberias under siege, Nikon Pappanos discreetly stockpiled supplies in the house. Elena made only brief excursions to the market, often returning with messages passed from courier to courier until they were dropped surreptitiously into her basket. Twice she brought word of Khalil's continued good health, but other than that, there was nothing they could do but wait until Salah ad-Din arrived with his army.

Devora proved to be a great asset to the spy network. Her familiarity with the roads to both Tiberias and Jerusalem provided invaluable information for those who dared travel between the two cities. The underground Jewish resistance was far more extensive than Nikon realized and soon he had Devora, when she was not with the babies, teaching his men the passwords and the secret routes on which they could find friendly shelter.

The night before Salah ad-Din's army was expected to arrive outside the gates of Akko, a man in tatters, one eye patched, his right hand bandaged in rags, banged on Nikon's door.

"Alms for the poor, master. Won't you help a poor pilgrim on his way to Mecca?" He stuck out a dirty hand.

Nikon's eyes almost popped from his head. "By the Prophet's beard!" cried Nikon when he recognized Kassim beneath the grime, "what has happened to you?" He pulled him inside the house.

A lopsided smile split the thin, brown face. "Nothing you would not be proud of, Master Nikon," he laughed, pulling the ratty turban from around his head. "I can stay only long enough to eat quickly, for then I must rejoin Khalil and the others."

"Where is Khalil?" demanded Batsheva as she came tearing down the stone steps.

"He is closer than you might imagine; Salah ad-Din is but a half day's ride outside the city. Our sheikh sends greetings and reminds you to remain inside until he comes for you himself." Digging into his belt, Kassim found what he was looking for and handed a folded piece of parchment to Batsheva.

With trembling fingers, she unfolded the parchment. The message was simple: *If we fail to take Akko, take the children and go home to Al-Andalus. Do not wait for me. If I am alive, I will find you.* She handed it to Elena who read the words and nodded. "Tell Khalil I will do as he asks, but I will pray it will not be necessary."

⊛ ⊛ ⊛

Akko fell quickly. As soon as the soldiers surrendered, the people of the city ran into the streets to welcome the sultan's army with open arms. From their rooftop, the women watched soldiers streaming by, showering them with blossoms as they passed. They were about to return to the courtyard to feed the babies when Batsheva spied a familiar banner. With a cry, she ran down the stairs and pulled open the door in time to see Khalil dismount.

Tired and dirty, Khalil stayed long enough to assure everyone he was unharmed. His men were garrisoned near the docks and he needed to be with them as they finalized plans for the move on Al-Quds.

If Batsheva was content to have Khalil safe from harm for the short time the army would be in Akko, the most exciting moment of that time came late one night when Khalil returned to the house after meeting with the generals.

The women gathered on the roof where the sea breeze cooled them after a particularly hot afternoon. Stars sparkled in the black sky and the moon, a great silver disk, seemed to rival the sun for brightness that evening. The children slept on mats in a cool corner. Gentle conversation concerning everyday matters seemed almost unreal to the ladies as they enjoyed the peace that quickly settled over Akko. When the clatter of horses' hooves was heard in the courtyard below, Sufiye merely commented Nikon must be back from the wharf and perhaps they should consider going in for the evening.

"No," sighed Batsheva lazily, "let him come up here for refreshment. It is far too lovely to go inside."

Elena agreed. Pulling on a string tied to a small bell in the kitchen, she summoned a servant to the roof. "Perhaps he would like some lemonade," she wondered aloud.

"Yes, lemonade would be nice." Batsheva stretched languorously on the plump cushions.

The sound of footsteps on the stairs was not enough to make the ladies stir from their comfortable positions until they heard Khalil's voice. "Veil yourselves, women," he called softly, "we have a guest."

"This is one part of Islam I do not enjoy," complained Elena as she draped her hijab across the lower half of her face.

Batsheva helped Devora, still unaccustomed to the Muslim hijab, adjust hers. "We are veiled," she called to Khalil. "Who would he be bringing at this late hour?" she asked Sufiye as Khalil and Nikon stepped out onto the roof, a third man behind them.

The visitor, much shorter than Khalil, was an older man with a greying beard. With a graceful motion, he bowed to the ladies, touching his hand to his heart and lips. "Forgive this intrusion, ladies, but before we leave to free Al-Quds, I would see Khalil's twin blessings." When he lifted his head, Batsheva noticed one eye was clouded.

With a wry grin, Khalil introduced the high-ranking visitor as his great-uncle Yusef bin Ayyub. Sufiye stared for a moment, then moved about in a daze, keeping her comments to herself, other than vague pleasantries when addressed by the older man. That she knew him was obvious, but how well was unclear to Devora and Batsheva.

Suddenly, Elena realized who was standing on her roof and nearly toppled over as she jumped up and bowed low. The others followed. "Forgive the poverty and disrespect in thy welcome, *sayidi sultan*; we were not expecting so noble a visitor to our poor home!"

"The apologies are mine, Madame Pappanos," replied Salah ad-Din Yusef bin Ayyub graciously. "I find formal visits cause much inconvenience, and I did not wish to miss seeing Khalil's twins."

"It's time those two went to their own beds," said Batsheva as she went to wake the twins. Rubbing their eyes, they immediately ran to their *abu* who scooped them up in his arms.

The sultan laughed heartily. "These are most glorious children, Khalil. My niece, your mother, would have been overjoyed at their very existence! You are twice blessed by Allah." He pulled two coins from his sash, gave one to each child, and kissed each on the forehead.

"Excuse me, Yusef Amm, while I put them in their own beds," grinned Khalil.

"Do you need help?" Batsheva asked.

Khalil shook his head. "I shall return in a moment." Sleepy children nestled against his chest, he left the roof.

"Twice blessed," said the sultan, bowing slightly toward Batsheva. "I am sure you were told about his wives and son." He saw Batsheva's nod.

"Nothing prepares one for murder, you know. I am grateful to you for giving him new joy."

"Thank you, sayidi." She did not know what else to say. Batsheva studied the aged warrior closely. He was far more arresting than she had heard. His sharp nose and high forehead made him seem like an eagle about to take flight. His well-trimmed beard accentuated the strong jaw, and his one dark piercing eye seemed able to probe the darkest of corners. She could see why Khalil held him in such high esteem; his bearing was regal, yet the ease of his manner made one less nervous. "Would you care for some refreshment, sayidi?" Batsheva finally managed to ask as a servant, alerted by the commotion, appeared with a heavy tray laden with a pitcher, finely made glasses, and a large platter with sesame cakes, halvah, and dried fruits.

As though he were quite used to it, the sultan relieved the struggling maid of her burden and set it on the low table. "May I sit?" he asked and Elena, flustered at her own breech of hospitality, nodded, her tongue having flown from her mouth.

Yusef bin-Ayyub was a man of many graces, but he had come to the house with a greater purpose than to see the twins. Devora found herself the center of the conversation. The sultan questioned her thoroughly about her contacts and how she had come to draw her conclusions. "We owe you a great debt, Madam Alfasi, for without your intelligence, we would have lost many men unnecessarily in the days before the battle."

"We serve the same God," replied Devora firmly through her hijab, "and as you are the one who will free Al-Quds, I am compelled to assist you any way I can. Had my husband lived, sire, he would have fought alongside you."

The sultan nodded gravely. "The name of Reuven Alfasi is well respected amongst my men. Whatever reward you would name, madam, speak and it will be yours."

Devora shook her head. "The only reward I seek is to be permitted to pray at the Temple Wall in Jerusalem."

"*Insh'Allah.*" He was taken with the woman; she was as fierce in her determination as any soldier he had met yet, there was a softness about her that bespoke her devotion to her people. Over the edge of her veil, he could see a pair of luminous dark eyes boldly meet his own. Had he not known it would be the consummate insult, he would have invited her to join his household.

When Khalil returned, the sultan formally requested Khalil's permission to speak directly to Batsheva. When it was granted, he clapped his hand and a soldier stepped onto the roof carrying a small strongbox. "It is my understanding you have refused marriage to my great-nephew, Khalil bin Mahmud, son of my beloved niece Daryaa," he said gravely to Batsheva.

"This is so, sayidi," she murmured, her eyes respectfully lowered.

"Yet you acknowledge him as the father of your children."

"This, too, is so."

"Will you accept a gift to your children from me?"

"If Khalil bin Mahmud permits it." She saw Khalil's nod.

"Good, I am glad you accept on behalf of Prince Daud and Princess Amina." Batsheva's head shot up and her eyes opened wide. She was about to speak when Khalil held up his hand to silence her protests. The soldier carrying the strongbox stepped forward and placed it on the table. "The gift to the children has two purposes, Lady Batsheva Hagiz. The first is to provide them with trinkets befitting their station as children of the Amir Khalil bin Mahmud, commander general of my army. The second is to ensure that, in the event of the unforeseen, you have adequate resources to support yourself and the children until such time as they may be restored to their own people. I believe that you, Lady Batsheva, understand this."

There was no missing the underlying meaning in those quiet words. Yes, she might return to her family, but the children, most especially Daud who, *Insh'Allah*, would succeed his father as sheikh, must remain with Khalil's people. "I understand. I will see that the children are properly raised, Yusef bin Ayyub."

The sultan smiled warmly, then turned to Devora. "If your son had lived, Madam Alfasi, it might have been that you never would have come to this house. I believe in my heart it was Allah's will to take the child in exchange for the freedom of Al-Quds."

"If this is God's will, then I must share your belief that the exchange, however painful, is a fair one. May Allah ride with you when you take Al-Quds, sire."

The sultan removed a ring from his right pinky and, in a move that surprised the others, he took Devora's hand and slipped it onto her finger.

"Take this as a token of my respect, Madam Alfasi. Should you ever need help, send this to me and I shall find you. Tell your people that when we take Jerusalem, they are welcome to come home." With an appropriate embrace of Sufiye, whom he had known since they were children, he left the rooftop.

"My lord Amir," chortled Batsheva sweeping a graceful bow when the newly created amir entered their bedroom.

His own bow was just as courtly. "Lady Batsheva." He sat on the edge of the bed and began to pull off his high boots. "You could be Amirat Batsheva if you would agree to marry me."

"One princess in the family is quite enough, Khalil," laughed Batsheva as she pushed his hands away and removed the offending footwear herself.

"Have you opened the box?"

"No, I thought I would wait for you."

"The gift is for you and the children; you did not have to wait. I know how curious you must be."

Batsheva shrugged. "Not nearly as curious about the box as I am about you. What news is there from the outside world?" she asked as she started on the knot of his turban.

"Nothing you have not heard."

His hair was damp and fragrant with spices. "You went to the baths before coming home?"

"Yusef Amm insisted we all go. We were…unpleasing. Besides…."

Her mouth came down on his. "No matter what condition, my lord Amir, you are always pleasing to me."

Now when they coupled, it was with joy. Khalil took his time arousing Batsheva as her hands traversed his body arousing him beyond his wildest imaginings. Despite the long weeks apart, each time they came together it was to be as one. They talked, they laughed, they comforted each other throughout the night, and when the children stirred, it was Khalil who went to scratch backs, adjust covers, and whisper lullabies in their ears.

Through the open door, Batsheva watched tenderness flow from his entire being. She could not have imagined how this hard man, this great warrior and general, could be turned into a bowl of sweet pudding at the sight of his sleeping children. When he came back to bed, she asked him how long he would stay home.

"I planned to tell you last night, but…"

"You are leaving again." She put her finger on his lips. "I will worry until I see you home."

"*Insh'Allah*, I shall be back in a week's time." He slid into the bed beside her so she could spoon against him and buried his face in her hair. "Let us cling together until I must leave."

Khalil rose at dawn. "The battle for Al-Quds is coming closer. If anything happens to me, take the children and Devora and go to Al-Andalus." He could feel Batsheva's eyes on him as he took a clean tunic from the chest. "When the time is right, Daud shall be brought back to his people."

Which meant Amina would stay with her. She would not argue with him now. "What about Sufiye?"

"She has already decided she will go home to Aleppo."

Batsheva turned her face upward, already missing Khalil's kisses. "Do not let anything happen to you, sayidi amir."

"*Insh'Allah*, my love." He kissed her deeply, then went to the nursey to kiss their sleeping children. He returned to kiss her again. "I will see you in a week's time." And then he was gone.

Batsheva watched his departure from the window above the street then, as she went to the wardrobe to select at kaftan, she noticed the strongbox still sitting on the floor. Opening the lid, Batsheva gasped when she saw its contents. Under a rolled parchment lay a king's ransom in gold coin, enough to keep her and the children comfortably situated for the rest their lives. She took the parchment and carefully unrolled it to reveal a magnificently illuminated document written in elegant Arabic.

> *In the name of Allah the All Merciful, I, An-Nasir Salah ad-Din Yusuf bin Ayyub, known as Salah ad-Din, Sultan of Egypt to Syria, hereby grant the following to the Princess Batsheva, a Jewess of the House of Hagiz, adopted beloved daughter of Yusef bin Ayyub, mother of Prince Daud bin Khalil and Princess Aminat bnt Khalil, in accordance with the laws of Islam: a house of her own in the holy city of*

> *Al-Quds, befitting her station, to be chosen by my loyal servant and commander, the Amir Khalil bin Mahmud, son of my most beloved niece, Daryaat bnt Assad, to be held by the Princess Batsheva Hagiz and her descendants in perpetuity. Any and all children and their descendants of the Princess Batsheva Hagiz will be known as princes and princesses of Islam, in recognition of their mother's loyalty to our person.*

The signature of the sultan was strong and broad across the bottom of the parchment.

A second, smaller parchment was tucked inside the first. A small but heavy signet ring bearing the crest of Salah ad-Din was tied to the silk ribbon binding the scroll. Batsheva untied the ribbon, slid the ring on her forefinger, and read the missive. Written in his own hand, the Sultan had provided a most personal note:

> *It would please me greatly to hear of your marriage to my nephew, but I understand your hesitation in a most un-Islamic way.*

This one was simply signed *Yusef Amm.* Uncle Yusef.

Family connections indeed, laughed Batsheva as she replaced the parchments in the chest and closed the lid.

Seven days stretched into 10 before the army returned to Akko. Nikon kept the women as informed as he could, but even he was beginning to worry by the 10th day. The streets of Akko had seen a gradual decrease in the number of the sultan's men about the city, leaving the local population with a sense of foreboding. No word was issued from Salah ad-Din's commanders; no report of who was to go where, only a quiet determination that the move to free Jerusalem would happen soon. Yet by week's end, when no word had come from Khalil, any levity had ceased, and an uneasy silence hung over the house.

On the afternoon of the 10th day, horses' hooves clattered outside the Pappanos house. Batsheva and Devora were tending to the children upstairs when Elena burst into the room. "There is an emissary from the sultan in the courtyard," she said breathlessly, "and he wants to see you, Devora."

Quickly, she slipped a hijab over her face and followed Elena, leaving the mother with her children. "Do not worry, Batsheva," she called over her shoulder as she left the room, "if something had happened to the amir, they would have asked for you."

It was little comfort. Daud required her attention for the moment, and she was glad to have something else to think about.

Two men in field uniforms stood near the fountain speaking to Nikon in hushed tones. When Devora entered, they ceased their conversation and bowed courteously. "Greetings from our master, Madame Alfasi," said the taller of the two. "He hopes you are well."

"As I hope for him. How may I be of service to the sultan?" Devora was anxious but understood the need for perfect calm.

The tall man smiled at her brisk efficiency. "His Majesty is in need of your expertise, Madame Alfasi. He has asked us to escort you to his headquarters that you may instruct certain of his men on the nature of a particular route into Jerusalem."

"I have duties here, sir; how long will I be gone?"

"Only a few hours."

Devora studied them carefully. She did not recognize their clothing as that of the sultan's guard even though they wore the correct insignia, and there was an odd manner in which the shorter of the two constantly turned a ring on his finger, never allowing the top to be seen. The bottom of a cross was visible at his wrist. The tall one referred to Jerusalem as *Jerusalem*, not Al-Quds. Something was very wrong. "I am afraid, sir, that I am unable to go at this moment. If you would allow me a few minutes to finish my tasks upstairs and properly attire myself, I will be more than happy to attend to the sultan's wishes."

"We will wait, Madame Alfasi," said the tall man.

Devora swept from the courtyard, but as she went, she motioned to Nikon. After a proper time, the portly man hurried up the stairs to find Devora and Batsheva dressing the twins.

"They are dangerous," Devora whispered. "They are not from the sultan."

"Ridiculous!" snorted the Greek. "Of course, they are from the sultan!"

She did not stop moving as she explained, "The tall one is Louis Saint-Denis. He ordered the attack on the road to Jerusalem."

Sufiye arrived with the kitchen boy following behind. "Kadar knows the way, Devora, and he is fast."

Devora pulled the ring Salah ad-Din had given her from her finger and handed it to the boy. "Take this to the garrison, Kadar. Show it only to an officer with rank. Tell him to take you to the sultan immediately and, if he refuses, tell him you have been sent to return the ring by the lady from Tiberias. When you see the sultan, tell him we are in need of his strongest help; he will understand."

"There are more men outside, Madame Alfasi," whispered the boy.

"Can you get out though the kitchen gate?" she asked, relieved when he nodded.

"Take a market basket with you," added Nikon. "They will not halt a servant on the way to market; the last thing they would want to do is arouse suspicion." He took a small bag from his voluminous coat and counted out five coins. "If they give you a hard time, show them one of these, but do not show them the ring. The mint of the coin will guarantee their cooperation."

Kadar slipped the ring and the coins into a pocket beneath his sash. "I shall run as fast as I can once I am out of sight."

Sufiye and Batsheva led the children to the roof. Although it was a bit of a jump, the nimble older woman made it across to the house next door with ease, then hurried through the doorway. In a moment, she reappeared with Ali Ahmed and his wife. Using a deep basket and a rope, each twin, seeming to understand the need for silence, was passed to them. "I will come as soon as I can, Sufiye. If I am not there within an hour, hide the children. Khalil will find you."

Batsheva returned to her room. From Khalil's campaign chest, she removed the small scimitar-shaped knife she had used against Gamal and tucked it under her kaftan sleeve where she could slide it easily into her hand. Devora watched silently. Once their hijabs were in place, the only differences were height and eye color. Since the strangers had not seen them together, they hoped the men might be confused by the appearance of two women instead of one.

In the courtyard, Nikon was seated with the strangers, while Elena supervised refreshments. Batsheva, from behind her thick hijab, admired the calm with which Nikon entertained them, his own fears well-hidden as he jovially talked about the bounty of this year's olive harvest, a typical merchant's topic. At the arrival of the women, all three men stood, and the two strangers looked at each other.

"Madame Alfasi," said the tall one, not sure which was which, "it won't be necessary to take a servant with you; we will provide for your needs."

"I have no doubt, but it is not proper for a lady to travel alone," said Elena calmly. "I would prefer she take my servant along."

The short one looked decidedly nervous. "It would not be advisable, Madame."

"Then I shall not permit her to go," announced Elena with a wave of her hand. "You, of all people, should know how the sultan feels about a woman alone in the company of strangers."

"But this is on the order of our Sultan Saladin," protested the short one. He glanced at his companion who nodded almost imperceptibly.

The mispronunciation of the sultan's name caught Batsheva's ear. She curled her fingers around the knife. One look at Nikon told her he, too, was prepared. The tall one stepped to the side as the short one reached into his belt. Before he could move, Batsheva's knife flew through the air and caught him in the arm. The tall stranger, his hand already on the hilt of his scimitar, was unprepared for the lightning speed with which Batsheva charged, knocking into him as Nikon tackled the wounded man with Devora's help.

Elena fainted when she saw the sword slice into Batsheva, but Batsheva was not to be stopped by a mere cut in her own arm. Drawing her knee up, she caught him in the groin as her nails dug into his sword hand. The scimitar clattered to the ground. As she twisted to reach for the weapon, there was a great shout from within the house and Khalil tore into the courtyard followed by six soldiers. Batsheva rolled off the stranger as Kassim grabbed him by the burnous, pushed him down hard, and planted a knee on his chest. Khalil pulled Batsheva to him.

Blood was turning the sleeve of her burnous bright red; Khalil blanched at the sight. Devora stepped between them and managed to pry

Batsheva from his grasp. "I'm all right, Khalil," she said in a voice much stronger than she felt. She forced herself to walk toward the short one and calmly, to everyone's amazement, withdrew her knife from where it still stuck out of his arm.

Khalil waited for his men to haul the strangers to their feet. "Who sent you?" he demanded. When they did not answer, he aimed his scimitar, ready to kill them both with a single slice.

The tall man clamped his mouth shut, but the short one, quivering with fright, began blubbering in a language Khalil did not understand. His compatriot tried to silence him with an angry glance, but he did not shut up.

"He says their commander will punish them for failing and it is better to die here than to return to their camp or face the sultan's Saracens," translated Batsheva from the garbled French.

"Who is their commander?" demanded Khalil.

"Guy de Lusignan," Devora said with obvious distaste, "who now calls himself king of the Kingdom of Jerusalem."

Khalil turned back to Batsheva, who was now sitting on the divan while Nikon applied pressure to the wound. "Ask them if this is so."

The tall one answered before Batsheva had a chance to ask the question. "We serve the one true God and through him we will cleanse the Holy Land of the infidel!" he shouted.

"Infidel?" countered Devora hotly in French. "This is our land, and you are the invaders. How dare you come into our homes and kill our children in the name of a god you claim to be loving and merciful? Was your savior not born a Jew? Did not Jesus preach kindness, not hate?" She moved menacingly toward where Kassim held him, shaking her fist in his face. She ripped the turban from his head. "If I had a sword, I would cut you down as you stand, murdering pig!" She spat in his face. "Give me your saif," she said in Arabic, "and let me exact revenge for my husband!"

Khalil handed her the saif and stood, hands folded across his chest, watching Devora wield the cumbersome weapon with ease. She held the tip against the tall one's chest and narrowed her eyes. "Unless you want me to begin with your ears and then remove each protrusion from your worthless body piece by piece, you will tell me where you were to take me and what was to be done when I arrived."

It was the ice in her voice and the hard glint in her eyes that made him think she was not bluffing. In crude Arabic, he began slowly. "You do not recognize me? You should have died on the road with your impotent husband, infidel whore. You are known as the woman with the big mouth," he said with an unpleasant, broken-toothed grin. "You are the one who told them about the hidden fortifications. You would have been taken to de Lusignan and tortured until you revealed what you know about the plans to attack Jerusalem. And if you survived the torture, you would have been tossed to the men for their pleasure." He glanced at Khalil. "But I see, you have already spread your whore's legs."

"Have you heard enough, my lord amir?" she asked. When he nodded, she ran the saif through the man's heart, stopping before it reached Kassim. Withdrawing the blade, Devora wiped the blood on the dead man's tunic and handed it to Khalil. "His name is Louis Saint-Denis. He is known in Tiberias as a rutting pig who rapes the dead. Send him back to de Lusignan in a sack, with his cock stuffed in his mouth. Tell him the Jewess has avenged her own." Devora, her head held high, left the courtyard.

"Do as she says," ordered Khalil. Two of his men picked up the body and removed it, leaving the short one still cringing in the corner, held tightly by Khalil's guards. He faced the terrified man. "Obviously, she does not want you, or she would have killed you on the spot."

CHAPTER 8

Akko

1187-1189

Salah ad-Din held Akko for two years and Batsheva took full advantage of the lull to create a peaceful home for Khalil, a refuge from the battles raging across Palaestina. Although she had been given every opportunity to return to Alexandria, Batsheva refused, telling Khalil over and over she preferred to stay near to him.

Avram Hagiz made the trip to Akko whenever roads were passable. Each time he brought letters from Al-Andalus, Batsheva devoured them, leaving her hungry for more. Yehuda had been chastised severely by her father when he returned and, for a while, there was a rift between them. Yehuda would not speak her name, nor would he remain in the room when her mother would read her letters aloud.

Talk of marriage between Batsheva and Khalil ceased. Her refusal grated on his nerves, so she chose not to discuss it at all. Instead, she worked hard to make their time together free of worry. His devotion to the children was their strongest bond; his devotion to her was something she accepted with grace, giving him back as much as she could. There were still nights when she awoke in a cold sweat, reliving the early days of her abduction in her worst nightmares. She would lie very still beneath the covers of their large bed willing the icy finger of fear to leave her heart. When Khalil was there, she listened for his steady breathing to calm her. Batsheva would try to remember the moment she stopped hating Khalil, when the anger was replaced with this odd feeling she had for the man. His tender regard her for wellbeing had burrowed its way into her heart.

Sufiye watched them from behind her hijab, her sharp eyes missing nothing. The way they looked at each other warmed her aging heart; she wanted nothing more than for Khalil to be happy and content. Sufiye had been right in seeing the value of the red-haired woman when the other ladies of the camp dismissed her as a fleeting diversion. Sufiye, who had loved Amina as her own, believed in Allah's mercy above all else and that Allah, in His wisdom, would comfort them all. Batsheva may have been an unwilling gift for Khalil's bed, but to her ancient eyes, the copper-haired woman saved them both.

When Batsheva miscarried not once, but twice, Sufiye worried about what this would do to her, but Batsheva and Khalil never wavered in their determination to be thankful for what they had. They grieved together for the loss of a new child but stood firm to keep their family safe from the madness outside the walls.

Baron Guy de Lusignan continued his march toward Akko, but Salah ad-Din dismissed his maneuvering with nothing more than passing interest until it appeared a siege might actually take hold. At odds with his council of amirs, the sultan relied heavily on Khalil to support his desire to attack the Franks on the road rather than wait for them to take a position along the walls of Akko. The council prevailed, but it was the sultan's coolness in the face of battle that prevented the foreigners from regaining the city. When word of a fresh army coming from the sea reached Akko, the population began to worry.

At first, the rumors were dismissed with a wave of the hand, but Batsheva noticed Nikon slowly filling the storerooms beneath the house with barrels of salted fish and beef, wine, and water. Great sacks of milled wheat were also delivered, along with casks of olive oil. Dried herbs hung from the cellar rafters in huge bouquets; their aroma drifting up the stone steps. The women went about their daily business as though nothing unusual was afoot, yet there was an undercurrent none could ignore.

On a night when the moon was hidden, Khalil arrived unexpectedly. He was battle weary and the tension had etched new lines into his face. He spent the better part of the evening closeted with Nikon. Torches were burning low before Khalil went to Batsheva.

Sliding beneath the cover, he kissed her upturned mouth before he sang,

When shall I describe my feelings
To you, my delight, my torture?
When will my tongue have the pleasure

Of explaining it, instead of a letter?
Oh you temptress in consolation,
Oh you proof of a forlorn lover!
You are the sun that has hidden
Itself behind a veil from my eye.

Batsheva frowned. "You sing Ibn Zaydun's poetry to me? How could you, Khalil? They ended so badly."

He drew her close. "Yet, his words to Princess Walladah are beautiful, are they not? Can you not hear his love for her?'

"She called him a woodpecker!" laughed Batsheva. "He was unfaithful to her with anyone and everyone!"

Pushing aside the riot of her curls, he buried his face in that most sensitive spot between her ear and her shoulder, Khalil nuzzled her. "I am certain, Princess Batsheva," he breathed into her ear, "they had moments of great passion."

She pulled away, then held his face between her hands and looked deeply into his eyes.

I am my beloved's and his desire is for me alone.
Come, habibi, let us go out;
Let us live amongst the little villages.
Let us arise early and go to the vineyards;
Let us look at the vines to see if they are budded,
Whether the flowers have opened and the pomegranate is in bloom.
There I will give myself to you.
Both freshly-picked and long-stored
Have I kept, habibi, for you.

Khalil could barely breathe. Before she could say anything else, he silenced her with his lips.

When they were spent, Khalil left the bed long enough to wash before he stretched out beside her again. Now was their quiet time, those precious interludes of the mundane, when they spoke of things that mattered only to them. At Batsheva's gentle urging, he told her about the last battle.

"The Frankish knights wage war in strange ways," he said, holding her in his arms. "They fight amongst themselves as fiercely as they fight us. I have seen them kill each other in the heat of battle to advance their personal position." For a moment, he stared up at the ceiling. "There was a knight who fought with de Lusignan. Our men thought him possessed by demons the way he rode through the lines with his sword whirling so fast it could not be seen. He was fearsome in his strength, yet in the very heat of battle, I watched him come up behind another knight and run him through."

"Why?"

"I do not know. But he was strange, habibi. He slew his brother knight, then turned his sword on himself. He pierced his own foot when he thought no one would see."

"But you saw him, Khalil."

"I did, but he did not see me until I engaged him in combat. I saw his face when his helmet was thrown. It was the face of rage. He fell, but I think he fled again after I moved to the next attack. I did not understand how he could slay a brother knight. I do not understand any of them." He was quiet for a moment. "They call me the Iron Amir."

Batsheva turned to face him. "Why?"

"You ask that question too many times," he chided with a kiss. "They say I cannot be killed. That I am too fierce to fall."

"They do not know you, Khalil. You are the least fierce man in the Holy Land. You are a poet." She kissed his mouth. "You sing sweet lullabies to the children. You are a kind and gentle man."

"Not in battle, habibi. In battle, I am hard and fierce." He growled, and she laughed.

"Then there is no reason to concern yourself with these things, Khalil; they are foolish words, nothing more. You are the sultan's commander; you must be rested when you rejoin your men. Close your eyes, Khalil, and dream of the day when you can play in a peaceful garden with your children." She kissed his brow and saw him smile.

"I live for you, Batsheva, and our children. May it be Allah's will that we end this war so we may all go home."

"*Insh'Allah*, my lord amir. *Insh'Allah*."

⊛ ⊛ ⊛

Another week went by before Khalil sent Kassim back. He stayed only long enough to deliver a message. When he had gone, Nikon summoned everyone in the household to the garden. “Already there are troops amassing near the walls,” he told them in grave tones, “and the sultan has evacuated his own household. It is no longer safe to remain here in Akko.”

There was a long silence; Elena rose from her cushion and went to stand beside her husband. “I cannot speak for the others, but I shall remain here with you, Nikon. If the city falls, we shall fall with it. Akko is our home; I shall not leave.”

Nikon grasped his wife’s hand and nodded. “We shall stay,” he said grimly before he looked to Batsheva. “But you and the children must leave immediately. This is Khalil’s command. He fears for your safety should you stay.”

“Where would Khalil have us go?” asked Batsheva quietly.

“The harbor is blocked; there is no way to send you back to Alexandria. The sultan himself made arrangements for your move to the south, to a Benu Ghassani camp outside Nablus, close to Al Farisiya. They know Khalil. You will leave in two days’ time with a merchant caravan guarded by the sultan’s men.”

“If this is what Khalil wants, this is what we shall do.” Batsheva turned to Sufiye. “Will you come with us, Auntie?”

“No. I shall stay here for now, Batsheva. My bones grow brittle with age; in the desert I would be more trouble than I am worth.” She held up her hand to stop the inevitable protests. “Do not argue with me,” she insisted, “I will stay here until such time as I can join my sister in Aleppo.”

Batsheva realized arguing would be pointless and nodded her acceptance of Sufiye’s position before she turned to Devora. “And you, Devora? Will you come with us?”

Devora Alfasi shook her head. “I would go if my heart were free to go, Batsheva, but I am going up to Tz’fat. There, I can be of use.”

“But the road is lined with foreigner encampments!” cried Nikon, the ever-present worry beads clacking furiously in his hand.

“Do not worry about me,” replied Devora with a smile, “there are ways to travel which will be safe. I have known for some time that I would go; I was waiting for the right moment to tell you all.”

When the household had retired for the night, Devora and Batsheva sat on the rooftop overlooking the deserted courtyard. In hushed tones they spoke of what happened and what was to come. "Will I ever see Jerusalem?" Batsheva wondered aloud.

"One day, with God's blessing, we shall stand together at the Western Wall to thank God for restoring Jerusalem. You will see, Batsheva, this will come to pass." Devora reached for Batsheva's hands and held them tightly in hers. "I shall miss the children; although they are not mine, I feel as close to them as if my own son had lived. But now, I must go where I am much needed. Besides," she added looking down at their joined hands, "I have had an offer."

"From whom?" cried Batsheva in a whisper.

Devora blushed. "Ezra HaLevi. He sent a letter after he was here last month. I did not want to tell you until I made my decision...." her voice trailed off. Ezra was a handsome man, tall and strapping despite his years studying in a yeshiva. He had been with Devora and Reuven that fateful night. Over the course of the last year, Ezra had been a frequent visitor, ferrying messages between Tiberias and Khalil; he had earned their respect many times over.

"Devora! I'm so happy for you! When will the wedding take place?"

"As soon as we are able. He's a good man, Batsheva; a kind man. He was married, you know. His wife died of cholera three years ago. This will be a good match; we like each other, and we know each other's history. Even though I thought that part of me died with Reuven and then my son, I think I want to be a wife again." She sighed when she said, "I suppose I am a little envious when Khalil comes home. Is it so terrible to want a husband of my own?"

Batsheva understood; on the nights Khalil did not come home, she yearned for his arms about her. "You deserve a husband and children of your own, Devora," she said, hugging her friend. "It is unfair of me to want to keep you here."

"Not unfair, Batsheva. I needed time to heal my heart and you have given me that. Nursing the twins was good for me. It would have been far worse to have milk and no mouth to feed. I love the twins very much, but you are their mother; I was only their wet nurse. Ezra has two young sons who need a mother, and I would like a babe of my own one day."

Batsheva hugged her friend. "When will you go?"

"When you leave Akko. I will stay here until the wedding can be arranged."

"I wish I could be at the wedding," said Batsheva sadly, knowing it would not be possible.

"You will stand beside me in spirit, my dearest friend."

The departure was delayed when fighting erupted south of the city. Batsheva paced anxiously night after night, worrying about Khalil when he did not return home as expected. When a messenger finally arrived, it was only to tell them to wait until the battle was over. Devora sent word to Ezra in Tiberias that she would not leave Akko until Batsheva and the children were on their way south. Days dragged by as the women of the house forced their tense fingers to work needles as they sewed clothing for the children who played unusually quietly in the courtyard garden.

On the 12th night of their vigil, Ezra arrived at Nikon's door, tired and dirty from a difficult journey. Nikon immediately sent word to the garrison for a sultan's representative to come to the house. Devora and Batsheva hastily prepared a meal for the exhausted Ezra and sat on the cushions beside him as he ate. When a captain of Salah ad-Din's personal guard arrived, Ezra delivered the message he carried.

"The Frankish King has arrived with a great army and even greater treasure." Ezra told the captain.

"We know this already," he snorted impatiently, "Did you drag me from my tent in the middle of the night for old news?"

"No, sir, I did not. It is what you don't already know that is of importance." Ezra took a deep breath. "There is another king coming from the west. The English king called Richard. He has already taken Cyprus."

"That is preposterous!" bellowed the soldier.

"No, my lord, it is true. A messenger arrived at King Philippe's camp with word of the conquest. A merchant from Tiberias was in the camp and heard the news with his own ears. The English king is expected within the month."

The captain stroked his beard and considered the news carefully. Another fresh army could mean more trouble for his already beleaguered master. "If this is true, Ezra HaLevi, you will be well paid for your efforts."

"Keep your gold," spat the younger man. "Just tell your master to keep his word to my people, that we will be safe from harm when he throws the foreigners out."

"Salah ad-Din has given his word and his word is law." The captain rose and bowed graciously toward the ladies. "My master sends his warm regards to you all. He wishes you safe passage on your journey to the south." He left the house as quickly and quietly as he came.

There was no question that Batsheva and the children would leave Akko as soon as the caravan could be assembled. In the morning, Khalil sent word that they were to be ready to go on a moment's notice. Devora gathered her own few possessions, setting them in the great room beside Batsheva's own bags. There were few words said as they moved efficiently about the house. Ezra wanted Devora to go with him to Tiberias, but she argued against it, saying she could not leave before her adopted family.

"You can and you will," insisted Batsheva hotly when she heard the quiet but intense words between Devora and Ezra.

"But I cannot travel with him," Devora protested. "It would be wrong."

"Not if we were married," countered Ezra.

All eyes turned toward Ezra. "Who would marry us without *ten'aim*?" asked Devora, her eyes wide. "We do not even have a *ketuba*!"

"There are scribes in Akko," insisted Batsheva. "Surely one of them can write quickly and accurately!"

Ezra's eyes danced with joy when he saw Devora nod her head. "I will be back as soon as I can," he called before he ran out.

Devora leaned close to Batsheva and whispered something only she could hear before collapsing on a cushion, her head in her hands. "This is all too fast for me," she moaned.

"How many days?" asked Batsheva.

Devora blushed as she flashed ten fingers.

"Don't be a silly goose, Devora," chided Batsheva plopping down beside her. "You can go to the mikvah tonight. It's not as if you are a maiden beneath the canopy for the first time! You already know what happens in a marriage bed and this way I shall be there to walk you to your groom. I know this is a selfish thought, but I would leave here more peacefully if I saw you married to Ezra."

"I suppose you are right," sighed the bride-to-be.

Batsheva dropped something into Devora's hand. "Use this for a wedding ring until you can get your own. It's just a trinket I found in the market, and thought to save it for Amina, but take it. You can return it to her when we all pray together in Jerusalem."

Devora looked at the little pomegranate crest engraved on the top of the silver ring. "Oh, Batsheva!" she cried, hugging her friend. "I will keep it safe. I will never be able to look at a pomegranate without thinking of you.

PART III

From Al-Farisiya, Palaestina to Marseille

1189–1191

CHAPTER 9

Al-Farisiya

1189-1191

The Benu Ghassani encampment looked like a cluster of dark mushrooms in a place where nothing could take root. Pleased to be of service to their cousins from Damascus, the band provided whatever they could to help the newcomers meld into qubila life. The less conspicuous, reasoned Ishmael Hajji, the head of the clan, the less likely they would draw attention to themselves.

Batsheva found the women to be wary; they knew she was not *Imazighen* from her speech, if her fair skin did not convince them at first sight. They believed her to be Khalil's wife, and she saw no reason to say otherwise. Only Ishmael Hajji seemed to have some knowledge of her background and he never broached the subject. What little he told the women of his qubila allowed Batsheva to move comfortably within the camp, especially once she adopted their dress and style of hijab as her own.

Batsheva accepted an Arabian foal as a personal gift from Ishmael Hajji. "There may come a time when your ability to ride well will save your life," the chieftain told her when he introduced her to the animal. "You must give her a name and spend time with her, teaching her to trust you as you learn to trust her judgment."

Ishmael Hajji grinned as he handed her the braided leather lead. "I have trained her until now, but you must be the one to care for her going forward." Young but strong, and still dappled grey, Batsheva took the lead while she extended her other hand toward the foal's muzzle. The soft, dark nose sniffed at her open palm, then nuzzled against it.

"Oh, she is beautiful, Ishmael Hajji," sighed Batsheva, relishing the horse's gentle touch. "I am grateful to you for your kindness, and I know," she added, turning to face the horse, "we shall be great friends."

"What will you call her?" asked Ishmael Hajji.

"Yaffa. I will call her Yaffa, for she is beautiful." She looked at Ishmael. "Jamila, if you would prefer."

Ishmael Hajji chuckled. "The word does not surprise me." He stopped talking for a moment and studied Batsheva's eyes. "I bear your people no anger."

"I may be a daughter of Sarah and not Hagar," countered Batsheva, "but I have chosen to live amongst Hagar's people. If your women would be uneasy knowing I am what I am, then do not tell them. My only concern is the safety of Khalil's children, and they are safe here. I have no desire to bring strife to your household. "

"You are a wise woman, Amirat Batsheva, and a good consort to the amir. He says you are all things to him and to guard you with my life. This I shall do, not because he is the favored one of Salah ad-Din, but because he has protected us through this strife. Now that I have seen my friend with his woman, I would protect her even if the favor need not have been returned."

Khalil visited when he could. The war was taking its toll; Batsheva could see it in the hardened planes of his face and the premature gray at his temples. On the few nights he spent with her, she made certain to tell him only of pleasant things while she massaged his back and shoulders to give him a moment's peace.

"It will end," he promised her again and again, but when news of the fall of Akko reached them, Batsheva began to believe there would be no end.

Days slipped into weeks, weeks into months, and months into almost two years of desert life. The little band moved from summer camp to winter camp without giving much thought to the war raging to the north. Batsheva found life amongst them hard but full, leaving her little time to brood about her separation from Khalil. When Khalil did manage to ride south, his visits were causes for celebration. Amina and Daud searched the line of the horizon each night before going to sleep in hopes of seeing abu's silhouette outlined against the evening sky. As she tucked them in, Batsheva would remind them how much abu loved them and how he longed to be with them instead of in battle. Once she kissed them good-night, their last words were always a prayer for abu's safe return.

Daud and Amina flourished. When they ran with the other children, Batsheva could barely tell that they had not been there forever. Taller than the other boys his age, Daud was emerging as a natural leader; his opinions were delivered with a firm jut of a chin much like his father's. Ishmael Hajji's son Fayyad undertook the task of teaching Daud to ride like the desert wind, keeping the youngster with his own two sons as lessons were taught. Fayyad's wife, not to be left out, took Batsheva and Amina under her wing, teaching them Bedu customs. More than once, when they met with other qubilas, offers had been made for the grass widow, but all suitors shied away as soon as they learned the graceful figure beneath the hijab belonged to the one called the Iron Amir.

News came in spurts and not all news was good. Casualties were heavy. Khalil wrote how he was sickened by the growing number of bodies needing burial at the end of each day's battle. The foreigners had endless reinforcements and, although the sultan's progress was good, the men were growing tired. He was growing tired. On his last visit, he made love to Batsheva with such passion and ferocity that she thought she would combust in his arms. Nestled together, he warned her this would be the last visit for a while. He was moving his troops to Nablus, where the next battle would take place. Before he left, he gave her a saif. "You may need this," he said as he hung the sheath on a peg. "I know you know how to use it, but practice away from the twins."

The battle was fought and afterwards a temporary truce was drawn to allow both sides to tend to the many wounded. A messenger brought word from Khalil; he would come as soon as he could. For a fortnight Batsheva scanned the horizon searching for the telltale dust column that would be seen long before the riders. The children were equally anxious to see their father and every night they went to bed disappointed, yet hopeful abu would be there in the morning.

The weather was brutally hot, even for summer. Batsheva spent the early hours at the well with the other women. Their chatter was light-hearted as they filled goatskins with the day's water supply. Although Yaffa did not like carrying wet bags, she stood quietly as Batsheva slung as many as she could over her back, thereby saving the women an extra trip to the well. The horse followed her mistress everywhere, and after a while no one thought anything of the phantom-white beast attached to the small woman in black. Even at night, Yaffa was tethered not with the other horses, but beside Batsheva's tent. Now she pawed the ground anxiously and whinnied, as though to tell her mistress it was time to get going.

The women started the short walk back to the camp when suddenly Yaffa's head came up sharply and she stopped. "What is it?" Batsheva whispered to the horse as the other women also stopped.

Silence hung over them for a moment, then they heard what Yaffa heard first. "It's a single rider," cried Naziah, Fayyad's wife. Lifting her skirts as she balanced the heavy skin bag against her shoulder, she began running toward the tents.

The rider was half-dead when Ishmael pulled him from his horse. Naziah brought wet cloths and when they lay him on the ground, she wiped his filthy brow. Batsheva hurried the children into the tent before she went to help tend the wounded man. She gasped when she saw his face, then pushed her way toward him until she could kneel at his side.

"Do you know him?" asked Ishmael Hajji when Batsheva reached for his hand.

"He is Kassim, one of Khalil's men."

At the sound of her voice, Kassim's eyes opened. "Foreigners…" he rasped, still choking from the dust of his journey, "…moving south… Khalil…" he grimaced, his eyes closed, and his breathing grew more labored.

"What about Khalil?" urged Batsheva. "Is he coming here?"

Kassim shook his head. "Fallen…in battle…two days ago."

Beneath her hijab, Batsheva blanched. "Is he alive, Kassim? Does our master live?"

"I do not know…." His eyes rolled back into his head and his lips stopped moving. Ishmael Hajji put his head against Kassim's chest and listened for a heartbeat.

"He is alive, but barely." The chieftain stood, then summoned Fayyad. "Take the women and children to the Well of Tears and hide them. Then return to me and we will plan our next move."

Immediately, the women began gathering what they would need. The large tents were left intact, but the smaller travel tents were slung onto animals' backs along with water skins, food bags, and bedrolls. Whatever else they needed could be improvised. Batsheva instructed Fayyad to take Kassim, now semi-conscious but in great pain, to the well with the children.

Batsheva saw the children safely mounted with Naziah's own, before she drew the other woman aside. "Take the children now, my friend, and I will join you later. Keep them well hidden and safe."

"Where are you going?" whispered the Bedouin woman, her eyes wide with fright.

"To Nablus. I will return in three days' time. If I do not, take the children and go to Akko. Bedouins still have access to the city. From there," she said, "Nikon Pappanos will care for the children. They must return to their father's people. He will know what to do."

Once the horses and camels disappeared over the hill, Batsheva went into her tent and quickly shed her voluminous *madraga* and thobe, replacing them with clothes more suitable for a young man: cotton *sirwal*, sash and shirt under a thobe and striped abaya. Her own soft boots were plain enough to pass as a man's boots. Using a strip of linen to bind her breasts flat, she set to work braiding her hair as tightly as she could. Despite the effort, she could not make the thick tresses lay flat enough. Pulling her knife from its sheath, Batsheva hacked off her long braid. "It will grow back," she muttered as she tossed the mass of hair onto the ground. Without benefit of a mirror, she chopped at the rest her hair until nothing remained but a hint of short curls. That done, she opened the small chest she brought from Akko and sifted through the contents until she found a small leather bag. In it she placed fifty gold coins and the earrings Khalil had given her, then tucked it securely into the inner folds of her sash. She removed the sultan's ring from her finger and slipped it onto a heavy gold chain and dropped it over her head. The cool gold made her shudder when she stuffed the ring beneath the binder and between her flattened breasts. The pomegranate ring Khalil had given her, the one made her own grandfather, went into her embroidery box; it was not hers to take. She closed the chest but kept the box with her.

Ishmael Hajji was horrified when he saw her emerge bareheaded from the tent. "What have you done?" he cried, "Khalil will kill us both!"

"Do not concern yourself with me, Ishmael Hajji. I must do what is right. I will wait until the moon has risen before I ride."

"I will go with you."

"You will do no such thing. You must stay to protect the others. The ride to Nablus is easy and I will be careful. How do I look?"

"Like a beardless boy, lady. A very pretty, beardless boy. You need a *kufiya*," he said.

"Here," she said, handing him her blue hijab. "We can cut this. Do you have an *agal* I can use?"

"You must take your saif," Ishmael called over his shoulder as he walked back to his tent and returned with a child-sized agal. He adjusted the kufiya, then helped her anchor it with the agal. He shook his head sadly. "I fear for your safety. Take two men when you go."

"No. I will be fine. Three men will draw unwanted attention." She thrust the embroidery box into his hands. "Give this to one of the boys going to the well. Tell him to give it to Naziah for Amina."

The day was fading when Batsheva finished helping with the livestock. The last of the sheep had been herded to the well, but most of the horses and camels were returned to the camp. Working swiftly and quietly, the animals were tethered securely to posts hammered into the desert floor. Batsheva led Yaffa to the rail closest to her tent and threw her saddle over the horse's back, leaving the girth loose; it was too early to prepare her for travel. "Wait, wait," crooned Batsheva as she brought the silken muzzle to her own cheek. "Soon enough, we will fly to Khalil." She went back into the tent; there was time to lay down for a little while before they left.

Batsheva dozed on her pallet until the thunder of hoofbeats and shouts of alarm made her bolt upright. Grabbing her saif she raced through the tent flap. A cloud of dust was bearing down on the encampment. She could not tell how many horsemen there were, but the thick, dull pounding that vibrated the ground beneath her feet told Batsheva they were not Arabs; they were heavily armored foreigners. Ishmael Hajji shouted to her to flee, but there was not time enough to cinch the girth. Instead, as the foreigners charged the encampment, Batsheva tightened her grip on her scimitar and ran towards where men prepared to defend themselves.

They were no match for the riders. Outnumbered three to one, the Bedu fought bravely yet fell covered in the blood of their enemy. Batsheva fought beside Fayyad when the biggest horse she had ever seen mowed him down; only her agility in boy's clothing kept her from sharing his fate. Swinging the saif with all her might, she managed to cut into the leg of the rider. He screamed in pain and jerked hard on the reins of his mount. The horse reared, pitching his rider into the dust. As the animal crashed to the ground atop the knight, Batsheva leapt to the side, only to be caught in the path of another horse. She fell and rolled away, then jumped up and charged the knight on horseback. Saif raised, a blood-curdling scream came out of her mouth as she swung, catching the knight midsection. The knight, bleeding profusely, managed to swing his shield around as he fell, hitting Batsheva on the side of the head. The blow sent her reeling. She felt something else hit her just before the blackness swallowed her whole.

CHAPTER 10

Al Farisiya

JULY 1191

Sir Gilbert of Durham surveyed the wreckage and felt the bile rise in his throat. Body parts were strewn about like so many pieces of broken statues. His horse picked its way around the corpses; the smell of blood and death made the animal skittish despite the weight of his armored master. Even at dusk there was no way to mask what happened. Fury rose in him as bitter as the taste in his mouth; his knuckles, white with anger, gripped the reins. Riding slowly to where the troops now stood silent, still stained with blood, Durham stood in his stirrups. "Who ordered this?" he bellowed. "What man dared counter my order of peaceful march?" No voice was heard; Durham's wrath was well known amongst his men, and no one dared to stir it more. "Where's Hal?"

"Dead, my lord," answered one of the soldiers. He pointed to where a knight stared sightless into the sky.

"And Peter Kydd?"

Another soldier pointed at a body lying near a dead horse. "A boy slew him and his horse."

"Bury the dead," he roared, "if it takes all night. *All* the dead. These people were not the enemy, they were not warriors. We will not shame them by leaving them to the beasts of this God-forsaken land." He threw the reins to his squire and slid from the horse.

Durham was disgusted as he walked back to the encampment. In the dying rays of light, he saw not only his own who had fallen, but also the faces of the so-called enemy. Old men, mostly, and a few youths barely old enough to be called men. He poked around the remains of tents and noticed there were no women or small children amongst the dead; he wondered where they had hidden. Using the tip of his sword, he pushed aside the flap of the only tent left intact. It was empty save for a few personal possessions. A trunk stood off to the side. He opened it, expecting to find household goods, but instead, there were several books on top. He picked one up and opened it, only to discover the marks were strange and indecipherable. A small dagger lay near the trunk, beside it what seemed to be a pile of red hair, obviously long and curly. He did not want to think who had committed so heinous an act as to cut a woman's hair, much less what had happened to its owner. Durham swallowed back the vomit as he left the tent. He scanned the faces until he found the one he was looking for. "Philippe d'Anjou, did you lead this charge?"

A knight wearing a surcote with the arms of the King of Jerusalem dismounted and walked toward Durham. "I told the men to scatter them and take the sheep."

"Know you damn well that was not my order."

"We need food, my lord. We cannot continue patrols if the men are hungry."

"And where are the sheep now?"

"There were none."

"So, you turned your men loose on a peaceable encampment?"

"I told them to scatter the people and take what they could."

Durham was livid. "This is not what was ordered!" He thundered. "Bury them all, d'Anjou. Do you understand? All of them, ours and theirs. In proper graves now. Not tomorrow. Now."

A commotion caught his ear. Durham saw three of his men trying to subdue a magnificent white horse. The animal stood over a small body, face down in the sand, and all efforts to approach caused the horse to kick and rear dangerously. He waved his men back before slowly inching toward the animal. He watched the mighty hooves stomp the ground close to the body, but something told Durham the animal was protecting its master. Clucking softly, he removed his gauntlet and extended his hand, palm upward. He squatted several feet from the horse and waited for it to quiet before he crept close enough to see the slightest motion in the fallen Bedouin. Still low to the ground, he moved slowly, talking softly until he was within a hand's breadth of the body. The horse seemed to understand he meant no harm and allowed the stranger to touch the hand outstretched in the sand. Now, Durham was beside the animal and the body. Sliding his own body between the hooves, he held his fingers beneath the small nose. He felt the warmth of shallow breathing. "Let me help," he murmured to the horse, praying the animal would not rear when he tried to move the child.

Yaffa stepped to the side as if to give her consent and watched closely as the stranger scooped the limp form into his arms. Durham rose slowly and started to walk; the horse followed. He looked down into the face of a young boy, not yet old enough to grow whiskers and he was sickened; he did not make war on children and old men. As gently as he could, he lay the body over the saddle and then tightened the loose cinch straps. Durham walked away. The horse remained still. When he reached his men, he repeated his order to bury all the corpses, adding that if a single possession was removed from a tent, he would execute the thief himself. "John," he said to his second in command, "you will bring the men of Durham to the king's camp in the morning. I will ride tonight. D'Anjou, when you are finished here, take your men and return to Jerusalem. Directly. If I hear of another raid, you will pay the price with your head."

"What about that horse?" asked John.

"I will take the horse and the boy. If we leave the boy, he will die." He scanned his troops with narrowed eyes. "William, you ride with me. Jamie, help me with this and pack it on my saddle. Ride my destrier."

The knight's squire hurried forward to remove the helmet and breastplate from his master. "Are you to ride unarmed, my lord?"

"No one will molest us in the night." Durham handed over his shield and mace; he retained his broadsword and dagger. Taking his cloak from his squire and feeling freer than he had in months, Durham swung unaided into the strange saddle behind the boy.

Their progress was steady but slow as they made their way toward Akko. Just as the dawn was creeping over the eastern horizon behind them, they reached the king's encampment. Too tired to do more than collapse, Gilbert of Durham sent word to his king that he would join him at midday. He would not let anyone take the unconscious boy from his arms as he carried him into the tent. When he laid the body on a pallet of pelts and wool, he thought he saw the eyelids flutter slightly. He left the boy there and went to stretch out on his own pallet.

❁ ❁ ❁

The sun was almost to its zenith when Durham awoke. He splashed his face with water from a bucket left by his squire, then quickly pulled on his mail and tabard. As he belted his sword about his waist, he noticed the body had not changed positions. Leaning over, he checked for breathing and was relieved when he saw the narrow chest rise and fall. Outside his tent, he found Jamie asleep across the threshold. Gruffly, he shook the man awake. "Keep watch on the boy; do not let him leave. Should he rouse, send word and I will come." Without waiting for a reply, Durham headed toward the king's tent.

King Richard's banner snapped in the stiff sea breeze. Soldiers milling about the area cleared a path for the knight. Two guards in full battle gear stood at attention outside. Another knight was standing in the doorway.

"Welcome back, Gilbert of Durham! We did not expect to see you so soon." Guy de Lusignan extended his arm to his fellow knight.

Durham did not take the proffered hand. "Nor did I expect to be here. How is the king?"

"Tired but flush with recent victory. He has been patiently awaiting you. We heard you rode through the night with a prisoner strapped to a fine Arabian. Of what value is this boy you have brought into camp?"

"Of no value, Guy. He was wounded and too young to be left to die in the desert. It was an act of Christian charity."

"To bring the enemy into camp? Have you grown soft, Durham?"

"Not as soft as you would have me, Guy." He narrowed his eyes. "Am I to keep his majesty waiting?"

The knight stepped aside. It took a moment for Durham's eyes to adjust to the darkness of the tent. King Richard sat behind a table, several men surrounding him as he poured over a map. No sooner had his feet touched the thick rug than the king looked up and Durham dropped to one knee. "Greetings, Your Majesty."

"Welcome, cousin." The king rose from his seat. "Leave us." The other men quickly left the two men alone. The king poured wine into two goblets and handed one to Durham. "What news, Gil?"

"The roads to the south are clear, but there is nothing worth pursuing. Just as we anticipated." He waited until the king drank before he touched the goblet to his own lips. "And from England, sire?"

"Sit down, cousin, and I will tell you the news. 'Tis not good." He sat on a nearby chair and waited for Durham to sit. "It grieves me to tell you, Gil, your father is dead."

Durham was shaken to the core of his soul. "How, sire?"

"A winter ague right before Lent."

"And my lady mother?"

"At last word, she was well. She has asked that you be allowed to return to England with haste. She fears for your lands should you remain away much longer."

"'Tis just as well," sighed Durham, "I've had my fill of war."

The king nodded. "'Tis a gruesome business, cousin. We have lost too many in this last campaign."

Durham studied his cousin Richard and saw the hard lines around the deep-set eyes. A new scar was visible above his left cheek. Although they were only eight years apart in age, Richard looked decades older; the weight of the crown had taken its toll. "May I speak frankly, cousin?" The king nodded. "Yesterday, against my orders for peaceful march, Philippe d'Anjou destroyed an encampment."

"There was no provocation?"

"None. They were shepherds: old men and young boys. No women or children."

"And your men?" asked the king, unwilling to believe they were completely innocent.

"Anjou and his men were scouting ahead; my men joined the fray when they arrived." Durham repeated the story about the sheep. "The Bedouin defended themselves as best they could, but they were slaughtered, all save one…a child."

"Ah, the one on your saddle. What will you do with him?"

"There were no others left alive. Perhaps I will take him with me. I am in need of a page."

"But he is the enemy, Gil."

"A youth of such tender years cannot be an enemy, nor can he be left to perish in the desert." Durham paused, then nearly shouted, "What we are doing is wrong, Richard. We are the invaders. We are the enemy. If foreign armies were to attack England, would we not fight with our last breath to save her? To what end is this crusade? Is any city worth the blood price we have already paid?"

"You are speaking heresy, Gil."

"I am speaking sanity, Richard. What will England have gained should you be slain on the battlefield? Lackland, your brother, will be king. Will that benefit England? I should think not!"

The king chuckled softly. "You have never been overly fond of any of my brothers. Would you serve him in my stead?"

"I would be tempted," snorted Durham, "to join with the Scots."

"That," chortled the king, "certainly is treason!"

Durham did not understand his levity. "Do you make light of this, Richard?"

"No, Gil, I do not. I ask myself the same questions, yet my soul yearns to free Jerusalem in the name of our Lord. This is a holy task we have undertaken, and we will see it through no matter the cost."

"Beware the cost, sire. I have found it is far greater than simply dying…it is living with the knowledge that I have broken God's law. I have murdered when I should have turned the other cheek."

The king rose and clapped Durham on the shoulder. "Make your confession on holy soil before you leave for England, Gil. Cleanse your soul before you depart this sacred place."

Durham dropped to one knee. "I will serve you, my liege lord, until my dying breath. My oath of fealty remains with you."

"But not with my brother?"

"I will serve the Crown so long as the Crown serves England, Your Majesty."

"That is all we can ask." Richard embraced his younger cousin. "If you leave on the evening tide, you can be in England before Christmas. A ship lies at anchor awaiting dispatches. You shall be my courier. Take the remaining men of Durham home." Richard removed a ring from his finger and dropped it into Durham's hand. It was the signet of the late earl, Gilbert's father. "Godspeed, Gilbert, Earl of Durham."

"You cannot take him, my lord!" cried the priest when he saw Durham carrying the limp body over his shoulder like a sack of so much threshed wheat.

"I will not leave him here."

"You carry with you an enemy, Gilbert of Dunham. I cannot condone your act of wanton disregard for the safety of this ship's company." The priest's face was mottled with rage.

Durham strode past him up the gangway, the horse behind him. "Keep to your cabin, priest," he growled dangerously, "and you shall not be offended by the sight of him. I will take him with me." He turned to glare down at the priest. "And while you are in your cabin, meditate on the principles of Christian charity and pray that our Lord Jesus Christ can forgive you your lack of them!" He handed Yaffa's reins to Jamie before he bore the featherweight easily to his cabin and laid his burden on the bunk. Durham pulled the rope of the blood-stained kufiya, and the fabric fell away, revealing a head not of black, Saracen hair, but soft reddish curls He stared at the face, then ran his hand over the thin body. Some sort of binding had been wrapped tightly about the upper torso. Something was hanging from a chain and tucked inside; as Durham felt around the shape, he felt something else, and jerked his hand away as if burned. "Mother of Christ!" he swore, "you're a girl!"

Since he had taken the child from the camp, Durham had tended her himself. Now, he was loath to let anyone else know the boy's secret. He was certain she was not Bedouin. Not only was her hair as the color of a copper coin, but the skin beneath her tunic was most fair. Her eyes, he noticed when they fluttered on rare occasions, were not dark; they were as grey as London's fog. Durham vowed he would find out from whence she came and return her to her own people for, surely, she was a captive slave. He denied that he longed to see her return to the world of the living so that she might think kindly of his rescue. He bathed her face and her arms, but that was all. Now that they were aboard the ship that would carry them westward, he prayed to the Blessed Virgin that she would heal.

CHAPTER 11

On the Mediterranean

JULY-SEPTEMBER 1191

The first night at sea, Batsheva fully awoke. Clutching the sides of the bunk, she stared at the lantern swinging from the ceiling. Her head ached and her mouth was dry, but she lay still, too frightened to move. There was no light coming in through the tiny window opposite where she lay, and she decided it was night. The creaking of timbers told her she was aboard a ship and she hoped against hope she was on her way to Alexandria. A muffled snort frightened her and, slowly, she dared to look over the edge of the bunk. A strange man was asleep on the floor, snoring softly. In the dim light she could see his hair was fair in color and long enough to curl against his forehead and neck. His flesh was tan where the sun had touched him, but his upper arm cast over a blanket, was pale. A gold signet ring circled the fourth finger of his right hand. Instinctively, her hand touched her chest; she was relieved to feel the binder still in place. Letting her fingers creep along the edge of the fabric, she sighed with relief when she felt the sultan's ring wedged between her breasts. Moving her hand lower, she felt the lump that was her pouch still tucked into her sash.

Batsheva rubbed her temples and lay back down. Staring at the ceiling, she tried to picture the last thing she remembered. The pounding in her head matched the image of horses' hooves pounding against the desert floor. She remembered seeing Fayyad fall. She had seen Ishmael slaughtered. Involuntarily, she cried out, "Laaaaa!" and shut her eyes against the memory. Then she heard a voice speak in a strange tongue. She opened her eyes just a crack and saw his face level with hers.

"Praise God, you're awake." Durham sucked in his breath when he saw her stormy eyes. They were magnificent, ringed with thick lashes, and perfectly clear. "You cannot understand me, can you?" He managed a small smile. "I mean you no harm. You are safe with me." He turned his palms upward, hoping she would understand the gesture.

Batsheva stared into his blue eyes and tried to take a measure of the man. His voice was gentle and kind; he made no move toward her. Batsheva had to admit he was a handsome, if not fierce-looking man. She wondered if he knew she was not a boy. Since he had not raped her, she hoped that, for the moment, she was safe. Closing her eyes against the incessant pounding in her head, she turned her back to him and let herself drift back to sleep. The last thing she heard was a soft, unexpected chuckle.

When she awoke again, Batsheva realized the noise that awakened her was of her own making. The man was holding her; his voice like that of a father trying to sooth a frightened child. The terror gripping her bowels receded in the faint morning light and she stopped screaming. The man did not release her; he continued to stroke her head and whisper strange-sounding words into her ear. Finally, her breathing began to slow.

Durham released his hold. Reaching over, he filled a goblet and offered it to her. Batsheva sipped it slowly. When he offered her a piece of bread, she accepted that, too. Looking up at him, she cleared her throat and, in a voice as low as she could manage, she murmured, "*Merci, monsieur.*"

She did not expect to see his face light up with pleasure. "*¿Parlez-vous français?*"

"*Oui, monsieur.*"

"Are you Norman? Frankish?" he asked.

"*Non.*"

"Yet you speak French." He grinned boyishly at her. "My name is Gilbert." She did not respond. "Do you have a name?" he prodded.

"My name is of no importance." Emboldened by the wine, she asked a different question. "Where are you taking me, monsieur?"

"I would take you to England as my ward…if that is acceptable to you. Or do you have a family awaiting your safe return?"

"Return me to Akko."

"That is not possible."

"Then I am your prisoner."

Durham shook his head. "If you are without family, I would adopt you."

Her bitter laughter took him by surprise. "That would not be possible, monsieur. I already have parents." She glanced around the cabin. "With your permission, monsieur, I would…wash."

Durham stood and pointed to the pitcher and basin on the table. "I shall leave you to your ablutions, young sir." He bowed gravely and left her alone in the cabin.

Batsheva slipped off the bunk and promptly grabbed the edge for support; she had overestimated her strength. Steadying herself against the roll of the ship, she reached the cabin door and dropped the bar. It would not do to have him walk in on her. She removed her soiled clothes; they were filthy and odiferous. Tossing them in the corner, she spotted a chamber pot and availed herself of its presence. A shirt was lying on a sea chest; that would do once she was cleaned up. She unwound the binding around her chest breathing deeply for the first time. A sharp pain tore through her chest and she collapsed in the chair. The throbbing subsided; gently she washed her sore body as best she could before drying herself with a cloth she found hanging from a peg. There was enough water to rinse her hair and she silently thanked God she had cut it short. At least one rib, she decided, was broken; she rebound her chest as much for the support the bandeau offered as for flattening her breasts. She slipped the shirt over her head, thankful that it covered her to her knees. She removed the bar from the door before she slipped back into the bunk.

The effort had taken its toll and Batsheva slept. When she next awoke, the man was sitting at the table, two bowls of steaming broth set before him. "Are you strong enough to eat?" he asked.

As good as it smelled, the thought of eating was not nearly as appealing. "Perhaps later."

"If you do not eat, you will fade into nothing. I have not brought you this far to have you perish from starvation."

Batsheva shrugged her thin shoulders. "If you will not return me to Akko, then it is of no consequence whether I live or die."

"It is to me. I am not a barbarian that I would allow you to die in my custody."

She regarded him suspiciously before she asked, "*Votre garde, monsieur*? That implies I am your prisoner although you have already denied that. Are you hoping to gain something from my ransom?"

His eyebrows knit themselves into a single line across his forehead. "I had not considered ransom. Would someone pay for your release?"

She shook her head. There was no way to send word to Khalil's men without risking their lives. Suggesting Nikon would compromise the safety of those in Akko. Considering her options, Batsheva decided the best would be to allow him to take her to England with the hopes she could contact a member of Akiva's family in York. "Non, monsieur, there is no one who could pay."

"Perhaps, then, it is better if you eat and regain your strength. I have need of a page in my household," he said seriously.

Batsheva was about to swing her legs over the side of the bunk but stopped. Her legs would surely give her sex away. Clutching the blanket around her, she maneuvered herself out of the bed and hobbled to the table. "I lack sirwal," she admitted when she saw him closely watching her.

Without comment, Durham opened his sea trunk, removed a pair of breeches, and tossed them to her. Folding his arms against his chest, he waited to see what the girl would do next. Batsheva murmured "Merci," then turned her back and slid the breeches under the blanket. They were far too big for her; she used the excess fabric to tie a knot at her waist. The shirt, left hanging, still covered her curves. Dropping the blanket, she walked unsteadily to the table.

"Your sea legs will come now that you are moving about," he said when she sat down. "You need food and exercise."

"May I have your permission to walk on deck?"

"No." He saw her face fall and quickly added, "For your own protection. The men are rough and would not take kindly to a Saracen boy amongst them."

She did not correct him although she knew he knew her hair belied his last statement. Silently, she tasted the broth; the seasonings were strange to her palate, but her stomach welcomed the nourishment. She ate as much as she dared; she was still nauseated, and her head throbbed. When she could tolerate no more, she pushed the bowl away.

Durham was concerned by the pallor of her cheeks. He had expected her to devour the broth and was concerned when she barely managed to swallow a few spoonsful. "Are you not well?"

Batsheva tried to stand. Suddenly, the room swam; she lurched for the table, but Durham was quicker. Grabbing her by the waist, he turned her just in time to reach the bucket near the door. She vomited the broth as he held her. Without asking, he lifted Batsheva and carried her back to the bunk. "Perhaps later you will feel more like eating," he said softly as he tucked her in. He watched her eyes close once more, then sat on the edge of the bunk until he was certain the crisis had passed.

This time, when Batsheva awoke, it was night. Her captor sat at his table, a map unrolled before him, snoring softly in his chair. A loaf of bread and a basket of dried fruit sat at the edge of the table. Had not hunger gnawed at her belly, Batsheva would have gone back to sleep, but the sight of food made her rise from the bed. Without disturbing him, she sat down and took a fig. As she chewed slowly, she considered the man before her. He was not at all like her image of a Crusader. The ones she had seen were hard, cruel men with a love of killing and destruction. This one was kind, gentle in his conversation, and almost tender in his regard for his captive. She found his fair hair strange, but it was the deep, dark blue of his eyes that she thought almost unnatural. She had seen blue eyes before, but none quite like his. He insisted she was not a prisoner, yet he refused to return her to Akko. He had carried her to this ship, yet he referred to her as a boy. Was he toying with her, or did he honestly think her to be a male? She smiled at the thought. No, he was not stupid; he was decidedly cagey.

Sitting up a little straighter, she took another fig, then leaned forward to study the map. It was not the drawing of a place she recognized, although she had seen many foreign maps before this. The words were written in the same characters as French and Castilian, but the names seemed unpronounceable. Moving her lips, she tried to sound out one of the words.

"Yorkshire," said Durham, opening one eye. He pointed to an area not far to the north. "These are my lands."

"They are near to York?" she asked.

"Not too distant. Do you know York?"

"*Non*," she lied, but she would give him no more information than necessary. "I have but heard the name before."

"Where are you from?" he asked gently.

"Akko."

He smiled slowly and shook his head. "I think not, little girl." Batsheva choked on the fruit in her mouth. Durham was up in a flash to pound her back. "Are you all right?" he asked when the coughing subsided.

She nodded, then frowned. "Hardly a little girl, monsieur. A young woman, perhaps. A mother of twins. Not a little girl."

His laughter rang out; it was a rich sound which took her by surprise. "A mother! You are hardly past your 12th birthday!"

Batsheva's laugh was harsh. "Well past, monsieur." Her brief, sardonic smile turned downward. "But do not think I am an unschooled maid who will allow you your freedom with her. I have killed with my sword, and with a single throw of a dagger." Her eyes narrowed dangerously. "I have tasted death; it does not frighten me."

Durham sobered quickly. "I would hope I give you no cause to kill me, my lady; I did naught but rescue you from the arms of death."

"You are the one who took me from the camp?" She saw him nod. "Was it your men who slaughtered my people?" Again, he nodded. "Then I should kill you. Does not your Bible say a life for a life?"

"We are at war, but I will tell you this, madame, the attack on your camp was unwarranted. I did not order it."

"You now feel an obligation toward me."

"Yes."

Batsheva rose to her feet. "Don't. Leave me at the nearest port and I will find my own way home. I have obligations you cannot imagine."

"You are without resource, little girl. You cannot make your way back to Akko without the protection of a powerful lord. Your disguise would serve only so long before your gender would become your downfall." He regarded her carefully. "No, I will not leave you in a strange port. You will return to England with me. If you choose, you may send word to your family that you are out of harm's way." Batsheva was about to launch another argument when a sharp knock sounded against the door. Durham waved her to remain seated, then called "What is it?"

"My lord," shouted his squire through the oak door, "the white is rearing in her stall again. She is endangering the other horses and the ship."

Durham got up, grabbed a tabard from his sea chest and tossed it to Batsheva. "Cover yourself and come with me."

"Yaffa!" she cried, and did as she was told, pausing only to wind her kufiya around her head to hide her hair. She scurried to keep up with his long-legged stride as he left the cabin.

Salty wind caught Batsheva full face, and she took a deep breath. Despite the pain in her side, she relished filling her lungs with fresh air. Above her, the sky was studded with twinkling diamonds. As much as she longed to stare at them, she followed Durham down another ladder into the hold of the ship. The sea air was replaced with the sharp odor of animals. An angry, indignant shriek split the air. Batsheva's head snapped up and she pushed past her captor, running toward the noise. As soon as she cried "Yaffa, a*na huna*!" the noise ceased, and the rearing stopped.

The sailors assigned to the horses watched in silent amazement as the small boy dashed under the rope and threw himself at the white mare. They could not hear what the boy said, but the horse turned from demonic to docile in a heartbeat. The boy took a handful of feed from the bag hanging on the hull and the sailors were amazed when the horse ate placidly from his hand.

"Obviously the master," grumbled Durham. He stood in silence as Batsheva reassured the horse. When the boy was satisfied the horse would go on eating, he crawled back out of the stall. Durham watched how the men cleared a path for their enemy and saw her chin tilt ever so slightly upward. It was over in a matter of minutes, but Durham grudgingly admitted to himself that his ward had just earned the respect of the crew. He knew the mysterious youth would be the talk of the ship by dawn.

She was sitting at the table when Durham returned. "Very impressive. You wind a turban efficiently. What else can you do?" he teased as he sat across from her.

"More than most of your northern women, I am certain," she snapped. "Where I come from, women do not sit idle."

"And where exactly do you come from, my lady?"

"That is none of your concern, monsieur. That I must return to Akko is all you need to know." She pulled the pouch from within her shirt and counted out coins. "Here are 20 gold pieces. You may have this and the rest I will keep for my journey homeward. You may have the earbobs… they are quite valuable."

"And the ring, my lady; the one on the chain? That is worth far more than double…nay, triple what you offer me."

If he sought to frighten her, it did not work. Batsheva did not move a muscle when she replied, "The ring is for me alone; it is not a bargaining chip. Should you be found with it, sir, you would be slain on the spot."

"Assuming it was a Saracen who found it on me."

A cold smile crossed her lips. "Not all Muslims are, as you appear to think, what you call Saracens. Would you take that chance?"

"Perhaps I would. What will you give me for its safety?"

Batsheva felt herself redden under his sapphire stare. "Would you touch a woman who carries another man's child?" If she hadn't been completely sure before, Batsheva was certain now Khalil's child was safe within.

His mouth fell open then snapped shut. Durham regarded her in silence for a moment. "I do not believe you, little girl," he pronounced with more conviction than he felt.

"Whether you do or not is unimportant, monsieur. Time will prove me right."

"Who is your husband that he would abandon you in the desert?"

"You have kidnapped no unimportant chatelaine, monsieur. I am the sole consort of the Amir Khalil bin Mahmud." Batsheva sat back and let the impact of her words sink in.

The Iron Amir was a formidable foe; his men cheered when he fell. Durham spoke again; his voice was as soft and gentle as he could make it. "You are a widow, my lady. Your husband fell in battle."

Her eyes closed. "I heard only he had been struck down on the day your men attacked our camp. I was preparing to ride to him."

"That was your hair in the tent. Those were your books in the trunk."

She nodded. "Is he truly dead?"

"I saw him fall. He did not rise again." Durham paused. "He was a courageous man, my lady. He fought with fury and died with his sword in his hand."

"Did *you* kill my lord Khalil?"

"No, I did not. He was slain in hand-to-hand combat by another knight, Raymond de Normandie."

The grey eyes opened again. "The attack on the desert camp…did it stop after I had fallen?" She saw him nod. "And did you go further…to the Well of Tears?"

"No. We did not go there."

Relieved, Batsheva pushed the pouch toward him, then slumped in her chair. "Take it all, monsieur, save the ring. Leave me that, for it is of personal importance. If you will not return me to Akko, the rest is inconsequential. Do with me as you will." She had to believe the women and children were safe if his men did not find their hiding place.

Durham pushed the pouch and all the coins back across the table. "I will leave you to your grief, my lady." With a deep bow, he left the cabin.

Durham returned to the cabin each evening for his meal, but where he spent the remainder of his time, Batsheva neither knew nor cared. He would watch her eat sparingly of the foods placed before her. Other than an occasional polite *merci*, she uttered not a word. Although he never saw her eyes red with weeping, he was certain she wept in the privacy he afforded her. Durham avoided all curious questions about the youth hidden away in his cabin save for the daily visits to the mare. Because the earl slept on deck, there were no questions of impropriety, but Durham was aware of whispers behind his back. Only the priest had dared broach the subject of the boy and Durham made it very clear to the cleric that it was none of his business.

As the ship neared Marseille, Durham found himself reviewing options. He was needed at home; he could not very well turn around to take the lady back to Akko. He had no desire to leave her in France alone and unescorted. The only reasonable thing to do was to take her to England. He decided that once in port, he would dispatch a messenger to the Holy Land with instructions to reply to Durham Castle.

The night before landfall, Durham told her of his plan and was puzzled when she laughed at him. "To whom will you address such a message, monsieur? And what would you say? That you have kidnapped the Iron Amir's widow? I assure you, you will receive no reply."

"Surely," he protested, "someone would want to know you are safe, my lady."

"Do what you will, monsieur; it's of no concern to me." Batsheva lapsed back into her customary silence.

Marseille's harbor was jammed with incoming and outgoing ships. Trading vessels awaiting berths bobbed in the outer ring while other ships loaded and unloaded endless barrels, casks, and crates dockside. A cacophony of languages caught the wind, like Babel after the Tower. Whitewashed buildings topped with red tiles lined the dock, each with a bright sign declaring ownership of each warehouse. Huge, brawny men carried enormous burdens down gangplanks only to be redirected by some somber harbor official or strangely clad captain. Pens of restless horses destined for the Holy Land were guarded by men in warrior garb: white tabards bearing bold crosses distinguished them from all others. Nearby, troops sat on the ground waiting for the order to board ship. A group of knights, broadswords hanging from their belts, stood together observing the activity with interest. In particular, they watched the ship flying King Richard's standard. This would be fresh word from the Holy Land.

On deck, Durham, his accidental captive at his side, scanned the dock looking for a familiar banner, the recipient of the first dispatch he carried from his king. His face became a grim portrait carved in stone as he saw fresh troops preparing to take up the sword. He wished with all his heart he could tell them to go home to their families and forget this crusade. But they would go and precious few, he knew, would return.

The ship bumped hard against the dock. New shouts arose from land to be answered by calls from the ship as ropes were tossed to tie off the vessel. Immediately, the stevedores boarded and began removing cargo from the hold. Batsheva watched the procedure with a practiced eye; she had seen all this before…in another lifetime.

And Durham watched her. He saw the way her eyes followed the barrels being off-loaded and he saw her wince when one was almost dropped. There was something about the way she observed the procedure; this was nothing new to her. Only when the first horses were led from the hold did she perk up.

Durham's destrier came out first. His great hooves stomped the gangplank as if testing its strength. The handler coaxed him onto the ramp and was almost pushed off when the horse lunged toward land. Yaffa was less cooperative, balking at each step. She refused to set hoof to ramp and reared in protest. Only when she threatened to trample her handler, did Durham allow Batsheva to lead the mare to land. Once on solid ground, the Arabian quieted and let herself be tied to a rail. Durham ordered his squire to saddle the horses.

"Can you ride?" he asked her gruffly. His brow was furrowed, and he did not look happy.

She wondered what was wrong but dared not ask. "Of course," she answered evenly.

"Wait here; I have business for the king. I shall return for you shortly." As he strode down the dock toward the congregation of knights, he wondered if she would be there when he got back.

Batsheva leaned against the rail and rested her head on Yaffa's snowy shoulder. Through half-closed eyes, she watched the activity around her and beyond that, her eyes scanned the buildings along the quay, looking for a familiar name. She would not leave without Yaffa and she could not take Yaffa without her saddle. Riding a horse like this bareback would cause too much attention to be paid to her and she could easily be marked as a thief. No, she had to wait for her saddle.

"I know what you're thinking," said a soft voice cutting into her reverie, "and I will not tell you not to do it. If you run now, you'll be caught in faster than a blink."

Batsheva looked up into the squire's steady brown eyes. "Are you a mind reader?" she asked flatly. She saw he had her saddle in his hands.

"No, but I have been taken in battle. Bide your time, boy; you could have done worse than to be rescued by this knight. He will treat you well. Has he not already?"

"He has acted with honor, if that is what you ask."

"Then accept his protection for now. He is of a mind to send you home."

"He has told me he cannot."

Jamie shrugged his wide shoulders. "You've a pretty face, boy; alone in a place like this it would not remain pretty for long. There are slave traders here. Do not risk a second capture."

Batsheva listened to his warning and knew he was telling the truth. "Perhaps you are right, squire. In truth, I have nowhere to go." She relieved him of her saddle. "I can tend the mare myself. Go about your master's bidding; I will be here when you return."

Durham returned with his mouth set in the same grim line it had been when he left them. He mounted, then waited for Batsheva to do the same. With the squire walking ahead to clear the way, they made their way through the town past the shops and the lesser houses until they came to an inn familiar to the knight. The squire secured a room for his master and his captive, camp space for the remaining men of Durham, then arranged for stable space for the horses.

"Stay with the animals, Jamie, lest someone try to steal the white." He turned to Batsheva. "You will need clothing of your own. Let us attend to that now."

"I prefer the garments of a boy, monsieur," whispered Batsheva.

Durham frowned, but nodded. "Come with me." He led her back through the labyrinth of the port town to where he knew merchants would have the supplies necessary for the coming journey. He refused to let Batsheva pay for anything despite her protests that she could well afford her own clothes. Under her watchful eye, he chose a few sturdy garments that would serve her well during the ride north. They were making their way back toward the inn when Batsheva suddenly stopped before a goldsmith's shop.

"I need to stop here," she told him bluntly.

"To sell your earbobs?"

"No."

Durham stared at her for a moment, then shrugged. He glanced up at the sign over the door and noted the name of the merchant. The name *Hagiz* was not unknown to him; he wondered if it was known to this woman as well.

The interior of the shop was dark, but the glint of gold work was unmistakable. A strangely clad young man approached him. "May I be of service, my lord?" he asked in impeccable French.

"My page would speak with you."

Batsheva stepped forward. "Are you Hagiz?" she asked suspiciously. She did not recognize the man at all and the thin wisp of hope that flooded through her breast at the sight of the sign quickly dissipated.

"No, I am Moises Luria."

"But this is the shop of Hagiz," she said cautiously.

"The master is away. Perhaps I can help you."

She could not ask this stranger for asylum; it would endanger his life in a place where Jews were not particularly welcome. If Durham protested, the authorities would come and she risked not only her own life, but Luria's as well. Thinking swiftly, she switched into Castilian and said, "Send a message to Yosef Hagiz in Málaga. Tell him his daughter is safe."

The man's eyes flared, and he frowned. The House of Hagiz seemed to be in mourning more often than not these days. "Everyone knows she is dead."

"Who told you that?" demanded Batsheva as calmly as she could. "Who told you the daughter was dead?"

"The House of Hagiz grieved for the daughter lost to them on the road to Sfax." He eyed the youth in white suspiciously. "Why would you send such a message to that family when they know such recent grief?"

"Recent grief? What has happened?"

There was something compelling about the boy, thought Luria. Against his better judgment, he answered, "Yosef Hagiz died not three months ago. His wife followed him to the grave." He saw the youth turn white.

"How?"

Moses Luria glanced at the knight standing beside the entrance to his shop, then looked at the youth. "A plague. Cholera."

"And Asher? Yehuda?"

"Asher was in Córdoba and was spared. We are not certain where Yehuda is."

"*Baruch Dayan ha'Emet*," she whispered. Then she looked up at Moses Luria. "Send the message. Asher will understand."

"Boy, I know not what game you play, but I will be no party to it!"

"This is no game, Moises Luria; send the message."

"But I would need proof! You cannot expect me to add to their misfortune."

Batsheva met his stare with one of her own. She hoped he was well acquainted with enough members of her family to recognize the unusual color of her eyes. There was no flicker of recognition. Quickly, she tore the neckline of her tunic, then set a gold piece on the counter. "I promise you, Moises Luria, you will not add to their grief; if you are unsure, send the message to Avram Hagiz in Tiberias. Yes, send the message there. That would be best. He will know what to do."

When Luria saw her action, a traditional sign of mourning a death in the immediate family, he ceased his protests. "As you wish."

"Thank you, Moises Luria." Batsheva turned and fled the shop.

Luria stared at the gold piece left on the counter. A portrait of the Sultan stared up at him, and in that moment, he knew he was sending the message that the daughter was safe, and he was sure she had just been standing in the shop.

By the time Durham caught up with her, Batsheva was halfway down the narrow street. "What manner of language was that?" he growled, grabbing her arm.

"My language, monsieur. Do not worry, I have done nothing to cause you harm."

"Why did you tear your shirt?" He demanded. "I have a right to know!"

Batsheva looked at him oddly. "You do? I am sorry; I mistakenly thought I was not your prisoner, monsieur. Do you often ask prying questions of your traveling companions?"

Had he not been so angry, he would have seen the shimmer of tears in her eyes. "I will ask what I want as I see fit!" he bellowed at the slight figure before him. "Did you ask him for ransom?"

She shook her head slowly. "There would be no point. I do not know him; he does not know me. I did not even tell him my name, if that calms your vapors."

"Is your name so notorious that you share it with no one?" he asked demanded.

"My name belongs only to me; I share it with whom I see fit." She wrenched her arm from his grasp. "I am tired, monsieur. I would return to the inn."

Batsheva silently picked at her food. But once she was on the pallet in the room they shared, Durham could hear her muffled sobs. It was a pitiful sound and he yearned to reach out and hold her. But her rigid posture throughout the evening convinced him it would be a mistake to take her into his arms. She would misread his intentions, however chivalrous his motive. Turning his back to her, he willed himself to sleep.

In the early morning light, Batsheva rose before Durham, washed with the water left in basin, and dressed for the journey. She bound her breasts, although not as tightly as she had been, then slid into the new clothes. She was thankful for the longer chemise; with it, she was able to keep the ties of the breeches comfortably loose. Although her belly was still flat, she was loath to tighten the laces over much. As she pulled on her soft boots, she noticed Durham watching her. "I am ready to travel," she said with perfect calm.

Her eyes were unnaturally bright. For a moment, Durham wondered if she had a fever, but instead, he decided it was from lack of sleep. "Turn around," he muttered as he slid from the bed. He dressed quickly. "We will go down to break our fast and then we shall leave this place." He stuffed his few possessions into his sack while Batsheva did the same. He was about to open the door, when suddenly he stopped and faced her. She looked like any other page; clear skinned, thin, young. Digging into his sack, he pulled out a folded piece of fabric. "If you are to play at being my page, you must dress like him." He tossed her the bundle. "Put that on; it belonged to my last while he served me."

Surprised by the weight, Batsheva unfurled the cloth carefully, revealing a child's sized mail hauberk and a tabard. She shot him a wry smile. "Now we shall look like twins," she commented dryly as she saw the image of a lion rampant on the front of the tabard. Batsheva slipped it over her head. The weight of the mail felt odd, but Batsheva had to admit she was glad to have it. "There, are you less afraid to be seen with me, monsieur?"

"Decidedly, my lady." He picked up his bag. "We travel light, little girl. We should make Calais in a fortnight."

"And from Calais?"

"Home. To England. I would cross the Channel before the weather turns foul," he answered. This was the first time she had expressed any interest in their final destination, and he was relieved. Perhaps she had resigned herself to the journey. "We will stay in London over the winter, then travel north come the spring."

Batsheva slowly picked up her own little bag. "And what of me, monsieur? When I am ripe with child, how shall you explain me?"

"I shall tell any who dare ask that the child is mine. What we do behind the curtain is no one's business but our own." He looked at her. "When will the child be born?"

"In late winter, monsieur," she replied, "in the month you call *février*."

"Then it is well we shall be in London. I would not have you give birth on the road." Durham swung his bag over his shoulder. "There is one last thing I would ask of you, my lady." She did not reply, but he noticed one copper eyebrow slide upward. "If you will not tell me your name, tell me what I should call you."

Batsheva shrugged. "Choose a name for me, monsieur, and that is how I shall be known." She felt a small tug at her heart; the last time she said that Khalil had called her *Vashti.* Suddenly, she didn't want him to choose a name for her. "For now, call me *boy.* No one will notice."

He did not like it, but he nodded. "By the time we reach England, my lady, you will have to provide me with something more appropriate to your condition," he warned.

Her shoulders rose and fell once more. "We shall see."

They rode as fast as they dared, but rain made the roads muddy and slow. By the time they reached Calais three weeks later, Batsheva was exhausted. Durham left her asleep in an inn while he went in search of ferries that would take the company and the horses across the Channel. Storms delayed their departure for another week, but when the weather finally broke, even Batsheva was anxious to travel again. Standing on the prow of the ferry, Yaffa's bridle clutched in her hand, she peered westward until at last, the chalky cliffs of Dover could be seen in the distance.

PART IV

London 1191

CHAPTER 12

London

OCTOBER 1191

Nothing in her wildest imagination could have prepared Batsheva for England. Conditions were primitive; even in the brisk autumn weather, children ran about near naked. The sound of their language assaulted Batsheva's ears; it was harsh, guttural compared with the languages she spoke. The towns were hardly more than haphazard collections of mud-walled huts with thatched roofs. Despite a rich-looking harvest, the people appeared poor and malnourished.

"Are they not protected by a powerful lord?" she asked Durham when they rode past yet another poor hamlet.

"Not all lords tend to their people with kindness," he replied grimly. "And not all villages look like these." He thought of his own land and hoped that in his absence they had fared better. He could understand the disgust mirrored in her eyes.

When they bedded down for the night at a roadside inn, Batsheva was loath to lay on the pallet. One whiff of the foul-smelling straw on the bed made her wrinkle her nose in disgust. "Monsieur, I think the horses fare better in the stable," she frowned. "Perhaps we should lie there."

He laughed but shook his head. "We will manage, my lady." He was not surprised when she wrapped herself in her cloak and curled up on the wooden bench beneath the shutters.

In the morning, Durham took her to the common room for breakfast. A slovenly maid with stringy hair and a filthy apron slapped a trencher before them. Durham pulled his knife from his belt, sliced a piece of meat from the slab, and handed it to her.

Batsheva stared at the oddly colored meat. Until now, she had managed to eat mostly cheese and bread while they traveled, occasionally allowing herself a piece of recognizable poultry. "Is there no bread?" she whispered.

"Apparently not," replied Durham, popping a piece of meat into his mouth. "You'd better eat this, for it is all they will provide."

Cautiously, Batsheva tore a small piece with her fingers and tasted it. The flavor was foreign and had the distinct taste of rancid fat. "What manner of beef is this?" she asked, forcing herself to swallow.

"*De boeuf? Ce n'est pas de bœuf, mon garçon.* This is good English ham!" He joyously cut another, bigger slice.

"Ham?" She repeated the English word. "*Qu'est-ce que c'est*…ham?"

He laughed heartily. "*Jambon*!"

Batsheva turned white and began to choke. Durham turned to slap her back, but she was already up from the table and halfway to the door. He ran after her in time to see her retching in the yard. He held her head as she emptied the meager contents of her stomach into the dirt. "Are you alright?" he asked when she finally stopped.

"You fed me pig meat! Barbarian! How could you do such a thing?" she railed "No civilized person eats swine! 'Tis an unclean animal. I shall surely die!" She retched again.

Durham stared at her in disbelief. "I am sorry, I did not know."

"Barbarian," she growled, her eyes flashing with anger. "No wonder these people look the way they do. They eat pig meat!" Tossing her head, she marched toward the stable.

Durham watched her storm away and stifled a laugh. It was the first sign of life he had seen in her since the night she threatened his life, and he was glad for it. He returned to the common room to finish his breakfast.

London, in Batsheva's opinion, was simply a bigger sewer. The streets reeked of excrement and the rats were fearless, darting between horses' hooves with impunity. When Durham announced they would seek shelter with his cousins in the city, Batsheva provided him with another display of temper. "You, monsieur, may find solace in this city, but I will not. I will not give birth to my child in this disease-infested hole!" she demanded with much more bravado in her voice than she was feeling in her head.

"Have you another suggestion, boy?" he growled.

"Let us go straight to your lands as your men have gone. Perhaps there I will find a place clean enough for people to inhabit."

Durham sighed loudly but said nothing. He secretly wondered if his page's recent thickening around the waist had added to her ferocity. He could not help but notice she was no longer tightening the laces of her breeches when she dressed, and he was thankful the tabard hid her swelling belly.

Batsheva saw nothing in London that looked tolerable as even a temporary residence. Although she said little, her steely glance told Durham all he needed to know. When they reached the bridge across the Thames, it was Jamie who suggested they cross over and ride to Westminster where better accommodations could be secured. There, they found a reasonably clean inn in which Durham could deposit his page and his squire before he went in search of available lodgings. Batsheva agreed to this and when he left her, she seemed relieved.

Jamie was waiting outside the inn for his master. Somewhere in France, the squire had finally told his master he knew the page was a girl. When Durham admitted as much, he assured his master the secret was safe. But the bigger secret, that she was with child, was not revealed until they had reached Calais. Durham had carefully explained that the child was that of her late lord, but he would claim paternity. Now that they were to be settled for the winter, Jamie was sure there would be a transformation. Surely, she could not go on in men's clothing for much longer. "How is she?" he asked.

"Resting," said Durham. "For now, I would leave her to sleep, but while she does, we need to find a dressmaker…a discreet dressmaker. Look about, Jamie, and see who you can find. Arrange for her to come when summoned; tell her she will be well paid. For now," he said with great resolve, "I am off in search of proper accommodations for my lady."

Jamie watched his master swing into the saddle. It came as no surprise that Durham would do as the lady bid; he wondered if it had occurred to his lordship that this was the beginning, if not the middle, of love. There was just something about the girl that even drew him in. Had she not been a lady of high birth, he might have attempted to court her himself because when they returned to Durham it would be long past time for him to find a wife of his own. Shaking his head, Jamie set off in the opposite direction, to where he knew the shops were to be found.

"I have secured adequate lodgings, my lady," announced Durham with a courtly bow when he returned to the inn, "within the walls of Westminster Palace."

Batsheva's eyes flicked momentarily but she sighed, "Perhaps there is hope. When do we go?"

"When you are properly attired," he replied solemnly but with a faint twinkle in his eye. "I would not enter at evening with a page only to have a lady mysteriously appear in the daylight. No, that would be most peculiar." He would have continued his teasing had a knock at the door not interrupted him.

Jamie arrived, flush with success. "I have found a woman to make the clothes," he sputtered. "She is kind and patient."

Durham studied a newly acquired gravy stain on his squire's tunic and laughed, "No doubt, she is also a fine cook!"

The squire reddened but nodded. "Oh, my lord, that she is! When I told her we were recently returned from the Holy Land, she couldn't help but stuff me full of her good kidney pie. She said "'twas her Christian duty to feed a soldier of Christ." He fairly beamed at Durham and Batsheva. "But there is one thing, my lord."

"And that is?"

"We should attend her shop tomorrow to select the cloth. Mistress Blank has much to show; she could not possibly bring her wares to us, considering how much we need." His dark brow furrowed seriously.

"How came you to find this paragon of womanhood, Jamie?" asked Durham.

A wide smile split his face in two. "I was very careful, my lord. I went 'round to the shops and spoke with many people. Discreetly, of course. At last, I found a fine-looking lady, begged her forgiveness, and explained my lord needed a special gift for a special lady. She was most kind, this lady, and she directed me to Mistress Blank's door all the while assuring me the seamstress was the most discreet in London." His chest puffed out just a bit. "Mistress Blank assured me she made special gifts for many ladies…but their names would be forever locked in her heart. She's a great romantic, that one. And she speaks French." Then he sighed rather loudly.

Batsheva stifled a laugh. In the months she had been with the knight and his squire, she had never seen Jamie so effusive. "I think, monsieur, we have a seamstress."

The shop was not difficult to find, but neither was it open when Jamie arrived with Durham and Batsheva in tow. He rapped softly at the shutters until a voice called from within, "Who bangs at my window at this hour?"

"'Tis I, good mistress, and I have brought my master." The shutter opened a crack and a pair of blue eyes tucked in a round face appeared. "Good day to you, Mistress Blank," grinned Jamie.

"And good day to you, squire." The shutter closed and, in a moment, the door opened. "Come in, come in," she bustled. When she saw Durham, she dipped a quick curtsy; on sight, she knew she had a member of the nobility in her shop. "Your squire, my lord, says there is a need for discretion. That is why my shop remains closed this morning."

"Thank you, mistress," replied Durham easily. "I would not usually be seen in a ladies' shop. And, yes, there is a need for discretion." He took a measure of the woman and knew at once why Jamie was so smitten. She was pretty, with clear peaches-and-cream skin and merry blue eyes. Her thick brown hair was neatly plaited into a long braid hanging down her back over which was tied a crisp, white scarf. Her own dress bespoke her skill with a needle; although plain, it was well cut and expertly sewn. *Yes,* thought Durham, *this is the woman we need.*

Jane Blank eyed them just as carefully. Despite the travel-stained clothing, she could see a nobleman of means standing before her. He was almost as tall as the shop was high, and his legs looked to be as big as tree trunks. Despite the strong planes of his face, his blue eyes were warm and kind, not hard and cold like so many of his peers. Any woman he favored, she decided, must certainly consider herself lucky. The page, however, was another matter. One glance at the face and Mistress Blank knew this was no boy. No male child could possibly be so pretty. "How may I serve your lordship?" she asked, keeping one eye on the boy.

"I am in need of a woman's wardrobe, Mistress Blank. Quickly."

"A wardrobe is a quite an undertaking, my lord, and requires time if it is to be made well. How quickly?"

"A garment or two right away, and then you will have the winter to sew. We do not leave until spring."

"I see. And the lady? Will she be available for me to measure?"

"You may measure the boy, here. They are the same size," he answered smoothly. "He speaks only French."

Jane pointed to a set table near the hearth. "Sit yourself down, my lord. There is bread and cheese and ale for you. Since your squire said you would come early, you will need to break your fast." Her eyes twinkled when she looked at the squire who now blushed furiously. She turned to Batsheva. "*Petit garçon; viens ici.*"

Batsheva did as she was told and followed the seamstress through a curtain in a separate workroom. Bolts of cloth were neatly stacked on shelves. A large oak table dominated the space and on it were the tools of Mistress Blank's trade. When the lady pointed to a block of wood off to one side, Batsheva dutifully stepped onto its worn surface and automatically held her arms out.

Obviously, you have done this before, thought Jane as she prepared a length of yarn with which to measure. Wordlessly, she began the process and would have remained silent until she slipped the yarn about Batsheva's waist. "Oh, Holy Mother!" she yelped, and, within seconds, Durham rushed through the curtain followed immediately by Jamie.

"What is the matter?" he demanded, wiping crumbs from his mouth.

"Milord, this *boy* is with child!"

Batsheva snorted indelicately. "Did you think she would not notice, monsieur?"

Durham was a fine shade of pink from his chin to his hairline. "Yes, Mistress, the lady is with child."

She turned to Batsheva and addressed her in French. "How far along are you, madam?"

"Four months, nearing five. I think."

Mistress Blank clucked her tongue. "'Tis unnatural to keep yourself so bound. You must have a dress immediately!" She shooed the men from the workroom. When they were gone, she turned to Batsheva. "What happened to your hair? Surely that is not the fashion elsewhere!"

"I cut it off to be a boy," answered Batsheva.

"How is it you came to be a boy?"

"My home was destroyed. The kind monsieur rescued me. These were the only clothes available at the time."

"But surely there were towns where you could have bought something!" She began measuring again.

Batsheva shrugged, "Yes, but for the sake of travel, we thought this best."

"And how did you travel, madam?"

"On horseback." When she saw the look of horror on Jane's face, she smiled. "I am used to riding; there was no hardship."

The plump woman clucked her tongue again. "He should have found you a wagon at least."

Batsheva found herself liking this bustling woman. There was something so pleasant about her, so kind, that she couldn't help but relax her stance. "Tell me, madame, how come you to speak French?"

"My mother was from Brittany; she never did learn proper English. My husband, God assoil him, was Norman. His name was Pierre LeBlanc, but here, he was called Peter Blank. My given name was Jeanne, but everyone calls me Jane." She smiled warmly at Batsheva. "From where do you hail?"

"I was born in Al-Andalus, but I have lived elsewhere these last years. My mother insisted that I know several languages, but English was not amongst them."

"'Tis a difficult language to learn, I've been told, but if you speak others, you should have no trouble learning this one." She patted Batsheva's leg and the girl automatically turned. "Let me teach you your first words. *Thank you*. It means *merci*."

"Thank you," repeated Batsheva with a smile. "Thank you beaucoup?"

"Very much," laughed Jane.

"Thank you very much," repeated Batsheva slowly. Then they both laughed.

The sound of their laughter drifted through the curtain and Durham was relieved to hear it. It was not the bitter laugh from the recent past; this was a happier sound.

Jamie noticed it, too. "They're getting on," he whispered to the earl.

"You have done well, Jamie. 'Tis what she needed." Leaning back against the hearth wall, Durham closed his eyes. Perhaps now the healing would begin in earnest.

When Batsheva emerged from the workroom, Durham jumped up. Gone was the imp in page's clothing, replaced by a small, slender woman wearing a simple linen chemise and hunter green cote. On her head, a bleached linen wimple disguised her lack of hair. Her mantle was of soft grey wool. She stopped and looked at Durham. "Are you happier now, my lord?" she asked haltingly in English.

"Yes, yes!" he cried, then stopped. "What did you say?"

She repeated the question, then dissolved into giggles, joined by Jane. She took the seamstresses hand in her own. "Jane will teach me to speak in your tongue," she announced in French, "since you have not bothered to prepare me for this. I have engaged her services and will pay her myself."

"*Vous ne ferez rien de tel, garçon!"* roared the earl.

"*Mon nom ce n'est pas 'garçon!'*" she shot back. "*Je suis*...Elizabeth!"

The apartment at Westminster were spacious and in dire need of cleaning. As soon as Batsheva walked through the door, she wrinkled her nose in distaste. "Is this how your people live?" she asked with disdain.

Durham shrugged, "The rooms have not been in use of late."

"I shall need help. Are servants available for hire?"

"Demanding, aren't you?" chuckled the earl. A single glance at Jamie and the squire was off on his next mission. While he was gone, Batsheva ordered Durham to open the few shutters there were. Obediently, he did as he was told.

"This will help," she said as she began a closer inspection of the premises. She dragged old straw bedding into the salon and started a pile in the center of the floor. "We will need fresh bedding...and rugs."

"Rugs?" echoed Durham.

"Rugs, monsieur. For warmth." She saw the puzzled look on his face. "Do people not put rugs on the stones in England?" He shook his head. "Visigoths," muttered Batsheva, "and a miracle everyone hasn't died from the cholera."

Jamie arrived with three stout women and a rather elderly man carrying twin buckets. "This is the best I could do, my lord. Servants are difficult to find."

Durham asked Batsheva what she wanted done and then he translated the commands into English for the benefit of the newcomers. "My lady does not speak English," he explained when he was done. "If you have need of further explanation, you may ask me or my squire."

The three charwomen curtsied and set to work. "What is that little thing they do?" Batsheva asked when they were alone in the outer chamber.

"'Tis a bow ladies make to a person of higher rank."

"Oh."

"You will need to learn to do that, Elizabeth." He used the name for the first time.

"To whom would I curtsey, monsieur?" she asked.

"To anyone who outranks you."

"But no one here does," she countered with feigned innocence, her chin jutting out.

"Oh?"

She nodded, then smiled slyly. "The queen is not here. Who would outrank me, a princess?"

"You're a what?" bellowed Durham.

The smile broadened just a little. "Do you still think you kidnapped a simple little concubine, monsieur?" She laughed at his building outrage and pulled the sultan's ring from beneath her chemise and dangled it on its chain before him. "This, monsieur, is worth more than all your lands, your houses, and your fields. My rank is not merely that of Amira to my lord; my rank is my own." Durham sat down with a thud. "Did I tell you that you may sit, monsieur?" she asked sweetly.

Durham slowly rose, towering menacingly over Batsheva. "Who *are* you?" he demanded between clenched teeth.

"Later," she answered with a delicate wave of her hand. "Right now, monsieur, I have work to do." She left him standing in the middle of the room.

Sleeves rolled back, Batsheva set to work with servants who could not understand why a noblewoman would be scrubbing alongside them. They thought her a bit odd, but she quickly earned their respect. Jamie was kept busy running errands assigned by Batsheva while Durham sat in the salon translating whenever necessary. By the time more servants arrived from the kitchen bearing their supper, the rooms were clean enough to install fresh rushes and clean bedding. Fires were lit in swept-out hearths, and the rooms gradually warmed.

Although she was hungry, Batsheva ate modestly of the food laid on the table. After learning pork was commonly served, she questioned Durham about each dish. He noticed she avoided the meats but ate the fish and vegetables. When he asked her about it, she yawned, "Later."

"Tomorrow," began Batsheva when the last remnants of the meal were cleared by a servant sent from the kitchen, "I will buy what we need for proper living."

"I will accompany you, madam," countered Durham. "And I will provide payment for the goods. You are not to touch your gold pieces; their mint will raise suspicion." He braced himself for an argument, but none was forthcoming. Pressing her, he asked what she required.

"Proper bedding, linen, cups and plates," she replied. "If we are to live in this place, we will be expected to participate in society. It is unbefitting your rank to live poorly."

"And what is my rank, *Votre Altesse*?"

"You, monsieur, are an earl, are you not? And is that not a noble rank?"

"*Oui.*"

"Then you should know what to expect," she added airily. "This place is full of people and already there is talk. You will be expected to attend the queen once she is in residence.

"How is it, madam, that in so short a time, you have learned so much?" he asked with unabashed amazement.

"Servants, monsieur, usually know more about what takes place within the walls than the high born." Although she had never lived in a palace, she knew servants the world over were the same. "There is enough French spoken here; they are eager to talk. Do you doubt me?"

"*Mon Dieu, non!*" laughed Durham. "I fear, Elizabeth, you already know more than I!" He studied her for a moment. "I think," he said slowly, "that Elizabeth is too long a name for you. I shall call you Bess if, of course, Your Highness has no objections."

Batsheva shrugged. "Whatever you wish, monsieur. I am still your prisoner." Without waiting for a response, she rose from her seat and retired to the bedroom, closing the door firmly behind her.

With a sigh of resignation, Durham realized the bedding laid out on the wide window bench was for him. He would have to requisition a bedframe for the other bedchamber.

Free of restraining breeches and without the benefit of hard exercise, Batsheva's belly grew visibly rounder, although she was relieved that it was not growing at the same furious rate as her first pregnancy. Jane Blank's nimble fingers rapidly produced a wardrobe befitting Batsheva's rank, while her equally nimble tongue taught the lady the rudiments of English. Each morning the seamstress arrived with her workbasket to keep sewing while she drilled Batsheva. In the afternoons, with Jamie dutifully close behind, they would scour the city of Westminster for those things Batsheva declared too important to live without. Tapestries, crockery, and bedding began arriving at Westminster Palace with uncommon haste. Dried fruits and other delicacies were procured and carried back in baskets.

Rumors raced through the corridors of the Westminster as quickly as a brushfire in the heat of a dry summer as thick tapestries were placed on floors instead of hung on walls. Servants who had been in the apartments were quizzed by those who had yet to see the transformation. But it was not until an enormous copper tub was delivered to the suite that Gilbert of Durham found himself summoned before newly arrived Queen Eleanor, the king's ageless mother.

When he knelt before her, he immediately acknowledged the death of King Henry. "My condolences, Your Majesty. Long live King Richard."

Eleanor waved the courtiers from the room. When they were alone, she clucked at him. "No great loss, Gil. The loss of your father is a far greater tragedy. He was a good man, and we already miss his good counsel and fine humor," she said, extending her elegantly ringed hand to him. "I trust you found your mother's chambers to be in good order."

"Thank you, Your Majesty; 'tis good to be home. I bring you warm tidings from His Majesty in the Holy Land," replied Durham, touching his lips to her fingers. "His Majesty's fame in battle is justified with the taking of Akko."

So we have heard." The old queen smiled sadly. "We pray for his safety and safe return."

"As do I, Your Majesty."

"Dispense with the formalities, Gil," said the queen, "and tell me why my palace is rife with rumors about you…and why you, you who have always been above reproach, are suddenly the latest topic for the local gossips." She pointed to the other chair at the table.

"I cannot imagine why, ma'am," Durham replied as he sat down.

"Surely, Gilbert," she said with a disappointed frown, "you do not consider me to be so old and feeble that I have grown deaf and addled? No, I think not." She waited for him to say something. When he remained silent, she continued. "Nor do I think you were the one to put tapestries on the floor…or bring a polished copper horse trough into your chamber." His face reddened and she knew she hit the mark. She poured two goblets of wine and handed one to Durham. "Is there something you would like to tell your old auntie?"

Durham accepted the cup and drank only after Eleanor sipped from hers. "I did not return from the Holy Land alone, ma'am."

"I have heard," she said dryly.

"Dare I ask what else you have heard?"

"That she is quite lovely, speaks excellent French, and has a somewhat…rounded shape at present."

"Aye, ma'am; 'tis all true."

"Are you married to the lady, Gilbert?"

There was a prolonged silence as Durham considered his answer. "Not," he said slowly, "in the eyes of our church." It was as close to the truth as he dared.

"Will you acknowledge the child?" she asked.

"Yes."

"Then what are you waiting for, Gilbert? Is there an unspeakable obstacle that prevents your churching? Or are you waiting for my permission?"

Durham felt himself at the edge of a deep precipice, but he could not explain further without compromising the lady's position. "The lady has not agreed to marry me in our church."

Eleanor laughed heartily at the revelation. When she was able to compose her thoughts, she asked Durham why. "I have only heard the most glowing reports of your misadventures, Gilbert. There must be a dozen ladies who would gladly plight you their troth, given the opportunity. How is it this lady refuses?"

"The lady is recently widowed and…her rite is not our rite."

"Yet, she willingly shares your bed." The queen's eyes pierced Durham's. "Or does she?" When Durham maintained his silence, Eleanor laughed again. "Your secret is safe with me, Gil, although I cannot fathom why you are doing this. But, as the mother of several sons, I am well aware young men rarely make sense when it comes to a beautiful lady in distress."

"The child is mine, Aunt Eleanor. Should she bear a son, he will be my heir."

"That choice is yours, Gil, but it's high time you were wed…in church…once more. Know that you have our blessings to summon a priest."

"Thank you, Your Majesty."

"Bring her to dine with us tonight, Gilbert. I would meet this charming creature." She rose and extended her hands to him. "Come, nephew, give me a proper, filial kiss and be on your way to your lady."

Dutifully, Durham touched his lips to one cheek, then the other. He bowed deeply from the waist and took his leave of his royal aunt.

Outside the queen's chamber, a lanky, well-dressed nobleman stood deep in conversation with a particularly lovely lady. Durham was about to pass him when he suddenly stopped, stared, and started laughing. "God's bones!" he cried, grabbing the man by the shoulders. "I'd have not recognized you, Edward! You've grown up!"

The young man looked puzzled for a moment before his eyes opened wide. "Uncle?"

"In the flesh, Edward. What are you doing in London? I thought you were at Oxford up to your nose buried in parchment."

"I was, but I was just summoned to court when Eleanor returned from Sicily." His chest puffed out a bit. "I am to scribe for Her Majesty. Walter de Coutances is Richard's justiciar this time, and she believes he needs watching.

Durham frowned, then glanced at the lady who giggled before disappearing into the queen's chamber. "More like you're writing your own romance. Who is she and does my sister know of your liaison?"

"She is Rochford's daughter, Alice," sighed Edward of York, eldest son of Durham's eldest sister. "She is more intent on me than I am on her."

"Is there an impediment?" Durham inquired again.

The younger man shrugged. "Her father is disposed to the match although her mother has an eye for Geoffrey Spencer. But Spencer is not so rich as York."

"And not as handsome, I wager," chuckled Durham, "but I sense there is something else afoot."

Edward looked down at the ground. "'Tis true, but not something I would speak of here."

"Oh?"

"Let it be, Uncle."

Durham realized he had hit a wall with his nephew. "Tell me, how fares my sister?"

"Mother is feisty as ever, perhaps more so now that she is to be a grandmother before Christmas," Edward suddenly grinned. "Rosalind and Robbie were wed right after Easter. But I suppose this comes as no surprise."

"The surprise is that the babe was not born at Pentecost last. She is hot-blooded and hot-headed. I pity poor Robbie; she must lead him about by the reins."

"And willingly he goes. I've not seen so moon-faced a man as he. But if the moans in the night continue, he'll die happy," Edward guffawed. "But what of you, Uncle Gil? Rumor says you have brought home a wife."

"A lady has indeed accompanied me."

He raised an eyebrow in question. "Are you wed?" He saw his uncle stiffen and immediately regretted the question. Reaching out, he grasped his uncle's arm. "I know there are years between us, but I am not so young as to have forgotten."

It was the second time in less than an hour that he had been reminded. A wave of sadness washed over him. "Nor have I, Edward," sighed Durham, "nor have I."

"She is buried a long time; even mother speaks aloud of her desire to see you wed again." Edward paused to consider his next words carefully before he spoke them. "My cousin needs a mother, Uncle. And she needs you."

"Have you seen my little Anne?" he asked, his voice so soft as to almost disappear.

"Hardly little anymore. She is the image of Joan, but she has your temperament. Grandmother says she will make her old before her time."

Durham snorted at the remark. "I will return home in the spring," he told Edward, "to rescue my mother from her own granddaughter. 'Tis past time Anne had a father."

The Rochford girl poked her head out of the door and beckoned to Edward. "Her Majesty is ready for you, my lord."

"I must attend Her Majesty," groaned Edward. "When shall we have the pleasure of your company at the board?"

"We dine with Her Majesty this eve."

"Good. I shall look forward to meeting the mysterious lady."

When Durham returned to their chambers, he found Jamie, in his stocking feet, sitting outside the door. "Remove your boots before you go in there," he grumbled and then helped the earl to comply with the new edict. "And be careful when you enter; the lady is in the bath."

Cautiously, Durham opened the door a crack and peered in. The outer chamber was empty, but the door to the bedroom was closed. He took a step onto the newly laid tapestry and sighed at the warmth. It was a good idea, he decided, especially since he hated the cold stone floors in winter, even if they were covered with rush. Shucking his cloak, he poured himself a cup of wine from the pitcher on the table then sat down in the chair before the hearth. No sooner had he stretched out his feet than Jane appeared at the door.

"Do not come in here; the...," she warned, but before she could finish, Durham did it for her.

"...lady is in the bath. I know. 'Tis just as well; we take supper with the queen this evening."

Jane's hands flew to her face. "Her Majesty! Mother of God, my lord, you've not given us time to prepare!"

"What is there to prepare?" he asked innocently. "Does she not already have a frock that would suit?"

"Men!" grumbled Jane as she gathered up a basket of sewing from the seat beneath the window. She disappeared into the bedroom only to return again with a neatly folded bundle. "You'll need these," she said handing it to him. "And there's hot water by the fire for your washing."

"Washing! What need have I of washing?" roared Durham.

"Men!" muttered the seamstress again before she closed the door.

Batsheva was sitting in the copper tub humming to herself as she luxuriated in the warm, scented water. Jane had provided a few drops of precious lavender oil from her own private stock. The scented soap had come from a Spanish peddler the seamstress encountered in the marketplace the month before and she was more than happy to share her bounty with her friend. Rolling up her sleeves, Jane helped Batsheva to rinse the soap from her hair.

"'Tis not long yet, Bess, but 'tis nicely curly. With a barbette and veil or a pretty wimple to hide your shortcoming, no one will guess."

"Did I hear Durham?" asked Batsheva, closing her eyes against the water being poured over her.

"Yes." Jane took a deep breath. "You are to dine with Her Majesty tonight!"

"*Non!*"

"*Oui!*"

Batsheva slid deeper into the water. "I had not expected this so soon, Jane. What shall I do? I'm not ready."

"You're ready enough, Bess. The queen is Aquitaine born; you'll have no trouble conversing with her. Simply answer her questions and remember to smile."

"But what shall I wear? And I have no proper shoes!"

"No one will notice your boots, Bess. Wear the blue woolen cote over the ivory chemise," replied Jane almost immediately. "Yes, that is the most fashionable and the most comfortable for the long supper hour. And the warmest." She dried her hands on her apron and went to the wardrobe chest. Pulling out the deep blue cote, she held it up for Batsheva's inspection. "'Tis modest, yet stylish. And of course," she added with a giggle, "well made."

"Then I shall wear the blue and pray to God I can keep smiling!"

Batsheva was wrapped in warmed toweling when Durham banged on the door. "I would have a rest, my lady!" he called through the heavy oak door. Without waiting for a response, he pushed the door open and walked in. He made a courtly bow from the waist, then picked his head up. "I hope I have not inconvenienced you, my lady."

"You are being rude, monsieur," wasped Batsheva. "I shall leave you to your toilette."

He watched the tiny figure in its newly rounded glory sweep regally from the room. Durham quickly stripped off his clothing, dropped them unceremoniously in a heap. Taking advantage of the warmth of the room, he stretched out on the bed he was being denied while his own bed had yet to appear.

He had almost fallen asleep when a resounding thud of wood against stone caused him to startle. He jumped up and was reaching for a cushion when Batsheva, clad in a simple ivory chemise, sailed into the room. At first, his hands flew to his groin, but then they dropped, leaving himself exposed to her examination.

Batsheva stopped in her tracks and stared at him. For a long moment, no words passed between them. Finally, Durham spoke, "Well, my lady?"

Her grey eyes traveled critically from his head down the length of his naked body. Whereas Khalil was darker, taller, leaner, hard-muscled, and long of leg, Durham was broader across the chest and his legs were shorter, but powerfully made. *Tree trunks,* she thought, recalling Jane's description. His body sported battle scars, some obviously newer than others. She could almost imagine Khalil and Durham side-by-side, then shook the image from her head. Batsheva's perusal paused briefly at the sight of his thick, stiffened shaft, then back up again. She raised a single eyebrow. "That you are a man," she commented dryly, "comes as no surprise to me, a widow. That you are uncircumcised I find rather…," she was thoughtful a moment before she concluded, "*sauvage*." Batsheva brushed past him to get to the chest against the wall, opened it, removed her pouch, then sailed back out of the room, slamming the door behind her.

Durham did not know whether to laugh or to throttle her. He settled for a nap.

A fire burned brightly in the hearth when Durham opened his eyes. Adjusting to the light, he struggled to right himself when he realized he was not alone in the room. It took a moment to realize the woman sitting on his mother's chair was neither his mother nor one of his sisters. "Good evening, Elizabeth," he pronounced gravely, pulling a cover over his bare limbs. Batsheva rose from the cushioned seat and stood beside the bed. Gone was the simply clad maid he had grown accustomed to seeing. The folds of the soft woolen cote accentuated the slight bulge of her belly. Her short hair was skillfully hidden beneath a wimple of fine linen and on the lobes of her tiny ears hung the ruby earrings. He fumbled for the right words. The result was lame. "I see you are already dressed to meet Her Majesty."

"You would do well to do the same, monsieur, lest we be late." She tilted her chin toward the table near the fire. "Your clothes are brushed and laid out. I will send in your squire." Then she left him.

Even after she was gone, the fresh scent of her remained in the room and Durham breathed deeply as if that would capture her essence and keep her within him. Sighing, he forced himself to rise from the bed to prepare himself for the evening to come.

CHAPTER 13

Westminster

OCTOBER 1191

The thin sound of reed and drum drifted into the gallery directly above the hall. Laughter could be heard, as well as the muted tones of conversation. As they approached the stairway, Batsheva touched his arm. "With whom shall I be seated?" she whispered, suddenly nervous.

"With me, of course," he laughed softly. "Do not fret, Bess. I shall be at your side throughout the evening."

"I hope so, monsieur," she whispered.

"Just smile and speak cautiously. Court in England is as intriguing as court anywhere else."

"I'm afraid I know little of court life, monsieur," she admitted, knitting her eyebrows into a line above her grey eyes.

Durham raised his own eyebrow; this was the most information she had given him about her life to date. He was not about to let the moment slip quickly away. "Did you not live in a harem?" he asked.

The frown deepened. "Never!" she whispered. "In ladies' quarters for visiting, of course, but not in a harem! I am a freewoman."

From what little he knew about life in the Holy Land, this did not make sense if she was, as she claimed, a princess in her own right. Surely a princess would have lived her early life in a palace. As much as he wanted to ask, he realized this was neither the time nor the place to engage her in this conversation. He settled for grasping her hand firmly in his. "Anyone of any consequence will address you in French, Bess, 'tis the language the queen prefers. You will have no trouble in that quarter." He squeezed the little hand in his. "Smile and let us go in."

The queen had yet to make her appearance, but her ladies were there, anxiously awaiting the arrival of Durham and his lady. All conversation ceased and all eyes turned toward the archway as they made their entrance.

The majordomo led them to the dais where two empty chairs awaited them at the high board. Durham waited until the lady was seated before he took his own. He watched the men in the room appraise his lady as openly as the women. She, however, seemed rooted to her seat, a perfectly polite smile frozen on her lips. She looked more like a doe caught in the sights of a bowman than a gracious lady at ease with her surroundings. Quickly, he leaned close to her and began naming those already gathered.

This was the perfect distraction. She listened attentively, following his descriptions with her eyes, trying to memorize faces with names. Without turning her eyes away from the others seated below them, she asked, "Why are we seated here and not with the others, monsieur?"

"Because I outrank them, Bess," he grinned. "'Tis my right."

"Why is the seat beside me empty, monsieur?"

"'Tis her majesty's seat. She is most anxious to meet you."

Her eyes flared wide, but she retained her composure. "How shall I converse with her?" she asked hoarsely.

"You are a princess, Bess; you should have no trouble."

Batsheva swallowed. She was sorry she ever told him she was a princess; it was a foolish remark even if it were technically correct. True, she was the consort of an amir, and true, she had spent much time with great ladies of her world, but this was a queen! As for the ladies already present, Batsheva thought they must all be wantons; they allowed men to touch them in ways she thought far too intimate for public display. Although their clothing completely covered them in length, it was form-fitting, revealing the shapes of intimate parts. Somehow, she had thought that women of breeding would behave more discreetly than those she saw on the streets of London. Batsheva was about to comment when a fanfare of trumpets sounded, and everyone rose. Batsheva decided this must be the entrance of Queen Eleanor and her retinue.

Eleanor of Aquitaine was old, but even at seventy she was the dominating presence from the moment she entered the hall. She had outlived her husband despite his attempts to rid himself of her, and now, with her son Richard on crusade, she ruled England as the king's designated regent. There was no masking the awe the woman commanded as she swept through the room. Swathed in the most exquisite fabrics available, and on the arm of her justiciar, Walter de Coutances, Eleanor was every inch a queen. When she reached her seat at the high board, she stood for a moment looking out over the silent assembly. "My lords and ladies, we are most happy to celebrate the return our beloved great-nephew Gilbert, Earl of Durham, and his Countess, Elizabeth. Let us raise a cup to their happiness!" All hands reached for and raised goblets. "To the earl and his countess!" led the queen. The others echoed her. She then took her seat.

"*Comtesse*?" gasped Batsheva as quietly as she could when she really wanted to scream.

"Hush, I shall explain later." He knew this would hardly mollify her, but it would have to do for the moment.

There was a ferocious scraping of chairs as the others regained their seats. Immediately, the queen turned to the stranger beside her. "Welcome to our table and our home, Lady Elizabeth," she said, her voice filled with genuine warmth. "We are pleased our nephew has at last found a companion."

Batsheva's head swiveled momentarily toward Durham and she saw him pursing his lips like an errant child. Turning back to the queen, she dipped her head. "I am pleased to be here, Your Majesty. Your kindness in letting us lodge with you is most appreciated."

"We hope you have found Durham's chambers to your liking. They've been long empty, and we have missed his company."

Again, she turned briefly to Durham and again she saw a more somber face. "The chambers, Madame, are clean and warm. I could not ask for more."

The queen smiled and patted Batsheva's hand. "And we have heard the improvements you have made are quite…spectacular. We should enjoy seeing what you have done."

Batsheva turned red from the tip of her chin to the edge of her wimple. "Of course, Madame, I would be pleased to show you the apartments, but I am afraid you'd be disappointed. I have only added rudimentary comforts, nothing of extravagance."

"Perhaps rudimentary to you, Lady Elizabeth, but to us, tapestries spread upon the floor are quite revolutionary. Is this the custom of your people?"

"Yes, Madame, it is." She glanced at Durham again and saw him nod.

The queen regarded her carefully for a moment. "Although your French is nearly perfect, do we detect a small accent in your pronunciation?"

"I was born in Al-Andalus, Madame," she replied steadily. "French is not my mother tongue."

"Yet, you have lived in the Holy Land. T'would seem, Lady Elizabeth, you are widely traveled," smiled Eleanor. "Perhaps we should compare our sojourns to see if we have crossed paths before this."

"I am certain I would recall so momentous an occasion, Madame."

"But your late husband," pressed the queen, her curiosity now piqued, "must have served one of our cousins on crusade. How else would you have come to be in the Holy Land?"

Durham quietly took Batsheva's hand and held it firmly. He had no idea how she was going to respond, but he wanted her to feel his support. "Perhaps," he offered, trying to ward off disaster, "my lady finds the subject too painful to discuss in such festive surroundings."

The queen smiled and accepted the chastisement graciously. "As usual, Gilbert, you are kindly. We are anxious to know your countess as well as we know you." She swept her ringed fingers in the air. "Let us enjoy this evening's amusements and leave the serious conversation until we can be closeted in private chambers." Eleanor turned to de Coutances on her other side.

"Comtesse?" hissed Batsheva. "What did you tell her?"

Keeping his lips to her ear, he replied, "I told her we wed, but not in church. She may press for a church wedding before we leave, but I will not agree. This is as much to protect you as the child."

"Do I thank you now, here on the high board, or would you prefer to wait until we are in chambers?" she countered, her eyes flashing in anger.

"Do not judge until you've heard me out, Bess."

She managed to glare at him even with her smile still in place. "I am anxious to hear this explanation."

The banquet passed in a blur of color and noise for Batsheva. The evening's entertainment consisted of skilled jugglers and acrobats from somewhere in middle Europe. Their colorful costumes were a delight to the eye, but Batsheva barely noticed. She was preoccupied with trying to keep up with the conversations around her. When a troubadour offered a local song, she thought the melody haunting and beautiful, but she understood not a single word. The wine made her sleepy; she could barely keep her eyes open. Just when it looked as though Queen Eleanor was preparing to end the evening, there was a commotion outside the hall.

A page approached the high board and spoke privately to the queen. She grimaced, nodded to the page, and then leaned toward Batsheva.

"We are afraid, Lady Elizabeth," she said dryly, "the true entertainment is about to begin." She leaned back, her bejeweled fingers resting lightly on the arms of her chair and smiled.

A woman swathed in a fur cloak flew into the room and made her way directly to the queen. She dropped into a low curtsey and remained there until Eleanor addressed her. "Welcome to court, Isabella. 'Tis too long since we have seen you." There were several guffaws from the lower tables, but the queen raised a single finger and they immediately ceased.

The woman rose and as she did, her hood slipped her from head, revealing two long, blonde braids beneath a circlet of gold with numerous cabochon stones. "Forgive me, Your Majesty," she breathed, "I came the moment I heard the news."

"And what news was that?" asked Eleanor.

"That Prince John has gone to France, ma'am!"

"And *that* has brought you back to court, Isabella?" asked Eleanor with an unmistakable edge of skepticism. "We think not." She glanced at Durham.

Isabella's large, blue eyes followed the glance and her thick lashes fluttered. She turned slightly and looked at Durham. "My lord, 'tis good to see you home again." She faced the queen once more. "How well you know me, Your Majesty," she chirped despite her blush. She turned her gaze back to Durham. "My heartfelt condolences on the passing of the earl, your father. He was a great man."

The queen raised her hand to prevent him from replying. "Heard you, then, that our handsome earl has brought a beautiful countess to court?"

Her eyes flickered her shock as they moved again, but this time they came to rest on Batsheva's face. "Congratulations and felicitations to you both," she said, sweeping into another deep curtsey, this one directed at Durham and Batsheva. When she tilted her eyes upward, she examined Batsheva with undisguised hostility. She noticed the twin rubies in her ears and the richness of her garments. She immediately noted the way the lady's hands rested protectively on her belly.

The queen turned to Batsheva. "Elizabeth, my dear, you must forgive us; I'm afraid we've kept you at the board overlong for your delicate condition." She rose and bid the assembly good night. As she left the high board, she called to Isabella. "Come, walk with us to our chamber door. We would hear news of your charming brother-in-law."

Isabella looked from the queen to Durham, sighed, and followed the old queen as she swept from the room.

In their receiving chamber, Batsheva stood tapping her foot as Durham played lady's maid, unlacing her tight sleeves. Her mouth was set in a straight line to match her narrowed, angry eyes. When he finished, she marched into the bedchamber and slammed the door.

Durham, however, was not about to rest without setting her straight. He jerked the heavy oaken door and bellowed, "You will hear me out, madam!"

"You will wait until I am finished with my toilette, monsieur!" she shouted in kind. She showed him her back.

Stomping back into the other room, he paced until he heard the door open once more. She was standing in the doorway wrapped in a grey woolen robe, her copper curls glinting in the torchlight. "Sit," he commanded and was genuinely surprised when she complied. "I told the queen we were wed, but not in church," he began slowly. "Otherwise, she may not have allowed us to remain at court."

"How kind of your *aunt* to give us shelter," sniped Batsheva, "in *your* own chambers. You neither told me these were your apartments, nor did you tell me she is your aunt!"

"Great-aunt, Bess. My mother's aunt, although they are close in age."

"And these chambers?"

"My mother's. She has not used them in years."

"And you have?"

"Yes, by God's bones, I must sleep somewhere when I am at court."

"Surely the Lady Isabella has comfortable apartments here?"

Durham's face flushed red. "Isabella has nothing to do with this."

"*Au contraire, monsieur*," said Batsheva, jumping to her feet. "She seems to think she has a great deal to do with this."

He could not help but laugh at the righteous indignation in Batsheva's stance. Her hands, balled in tight fists, rested on her hips and her belly clearly protruded beneath the material of her robe. "Do I detect jealousy in your voice, my lady?"

"Ha!"

"Oh?" he drawled.

"If I am to play at being your wife, *monsieur le comte*, I will expect you to behave as a proper husband. I will not be shamed in this place. Not by you…not by her!"

He chuckled as the grey eyes flared with fury. "All this from a single greeting? Are you a seer, my lady?"

"I am a woman who understands the way of other women. You have created this…this…situation and you will live by its rules. We are not in Islam, and I will not tolerate a concubine."

"Who are you to tell me what you will and will not tolerate?" demanded Durham, suddenly angry himself. "You, who are safe by my mercy, have not the right to issue me commands."

"I have every right. I am not your slave," Batsheva shouted, "I was kidnapped…taken from my home and my children, by a man who would not return me when given the opportunity. I did not know Christians took slaves in that manner." She pointed a finger at him. "What would your royal aunt think of a nephew who took a woman against her will? Shall I tell her how I came to be in your tender care? Shall I recount for her the number of Christians I slew with my own sword that day? I am not one of your delicate little Christian flowers, monsieur, and frankly, I'd rather be dead than be one of them! At least then my orphaned children would be spared their mother's humiliation!" Spinning on her heel, she flew into the bedchamber and slammed the door behind her.

From behind the door, he thought he heard sobs muffled by her pillow. *Children*. She had said she was the mother of twins, but until that moment, he had not thought of them as orphans and suddenly he was awash with guilt. She was right; as goodly as his intentions, he had, in effect, kidnapped the lady. Somewhere in the Holy Land, there were people who grieved for her believing she was dead. The depth of her inner strength convinced him she must have loved that fierce warrior greatly, yet, she did not look like any Saracen woman he had ever seen. Tonight, he learned she had been born in Al-Andalus, but how did she come to be with the amir? He had no answers to a thousand questions now racing through his mind. Durham no longer felt the merciful Christian; he felt ashamed, and he knew not how to rectify his error.

CHAPTER 14

Westminster

NOVEMBER 1191

Batsheva awoke to howling winds banging noisily against the shutters. Creeping from beneath the heavy bedclothes, she hurried to the window and peered through a crack in the wood. She could see nothing but swirls of white. She wrapped herself in a wool shawl before she ran into the chamber where Durham was snoring softly on his makeshift pallet; it did not stop her from shaking him awake.

"What?" he grumbled, trying to pull the covers over his head.

"I cannot see outside! Something strange blocks my view!" she cried with alarm.

"Is it white?" came the voice from under the blankets.

"Yes! And very noisy."

"'Tis snow, Bess, and wind. Nothing more than snow and wind. Go back to bed."

With a gasp of delight, Batsheva ran to the window and stood on the window seat. She unlatched the shutter and pushed hard until it opened. There was a rush of cold air as a small drift of snow that had gathered on the outside ledge blew inward. She shrieked at the shock but scooped up the fluffy white precipitation only to watch it dissolved from the warmth of her hands.

Durham shivered and poked his head out of his cocoon. "God's bones, woman, close the shutter!" he roared, but he could not help smiling at the sight of her in her night rail with her bare feet dancing against the cold stone of the ledge. When she ignored his request, he rose from the bed and joined her at the window. "You've not seen snow before?" he asked as he pulled the shutter back into place.

"I've seen snow on the mountains, but I've never touched it. Look, it disappears!" She shook the last drops of water into his face. "It sits on my hand then disappears! Why does it not stay?"

"Because, my lady," he laughed as he took her cold hands in his, "you are warm. Just as the sun melts the snow in the spring, your hands do the same."

"But I want it to stay," she frowned. "Will it now snow until spring?"

"It will come and go like the rain. Here, in England, we have snow in the winter. When you go outside, you will walk on it until you can no longer bear the sight of it."

"Does it snow, too, in Durham?"

"Yes, much more and much harder. There are often weeks on end when travel is impossible. The rivers freeze so hard that you can walk on the water."

"Oh, I should like to do that!" she breathed.

"I shall make sure that you do." Boldly, he slid his arm around her waist, lifted her, then set her on the floor. He felt her stiffen; yet she did not shake him off. "Now, get back to bed. Jane shall not come today, I warrant," as he pulled the shutter closed. Batsheva frowned again but allowed him to escort her back to bed. Like a parent with an excited child, he tucked the covers around her. "Should you be cold, Bess, I would gladly warm you," he said with mock seriousness.

She rewarded him with a wry smile of her own. "I shall lie here and think about hard water, monsieur. I shall be just fine."

"As my lady wishes, but that is not the only thing here that is hard," he grumbled. With a long, exaggerated sigh, he left her alone in the bed chamber.

The snow had ceased, and the wind gone when Durham rose. He performed his morning ablutions and quickly dressed. Mary, the maid assigned to them by the master of the queen's household, arrived with a timid knock and a basket filled with bread and cheese. Jamie followed, wrapped in his warmest cloak. "Are the roads passable?" asked Durham, as he broke off a piece of bread still warm from the ovens.

"Commerce is slow this morning, my lord," he replied with a frown, "but the roads can be crossed."

"As you have done," Durham chuckled. "And how is Mistress Jane Blank on this snowy morning."

"Warm and pleasing," replied Jamie with a dramatic sigh. "She is a wonderful woman."

Mary stood quietly near the table. "My lord?" she asked timidly.

"Yes?"

"The master of the household thought your lady might require a maid." Her hands twisted the end of her apron. "I could, my lord, I mean I've had some experience…I thought I…." Her voice tapered off.

Durham regarded the girl seriously while he considered the application. It was true that Bess needed a lady's maid and to date, when Jane was not present, he had served rather poorly in the job. "Go in to the Lady Elizabeth and make your proposal. I think you would find her favorably disposed to the idea." Durham liked the way the girl's eyes sparkled when she looked up at him. "Oh, do you speak French, Mary?"

"*Mais oui, monsieur!*" She blushed a pleasant pink. "At least enough to understand my lady's needs."

"*Très bien*, Mary," smiled the earl. He watched as she knocked softly at the chamber door, then went in, closing it just as softly behind her. He turned his attention back to Jamie. "I have the queen's business at the Tower this morning. Will you attend me or am I forced to ride alone?"

"Let us go now, and we should return before nightfall."

Durham braved the bedroom door and found the lady sitting up in bed with Mary at the wardrobe brushing out her gown. He told her he was leaving for the day but would return in time to take supper with her. "May I bring you something from the City?" he asked.

"Oh," sighed Batsheva unexpectedly, "to see an orange again."

"An orange!" cried Durham, half laughing. "You might as well ask for the moon on a tray."

"Or a fig or a date. Or cinnamon! Or cardamom! The food here is so bland."

"I fear it is your condition speaking, not your head," he answered, not at all unhappy to hear her jest. "I will see what I can find to make your meals more palatable, Bess." Impulsively, he brushed a kiss on her brow. "Stay inside, my lady, and stay warm. No visiting your horse today. I would not have you coming down with a fever."

"Yes, my lord," she answered dutifully, but she did not shy away from his touch.

By midmorning, it was obvious to Batsheva that Jane indeed would not be coming. Picking up her needlework, she sat by the fire to continue work on a decorative border for one of the new gowns. The fire was warm and her mood pensive as she stitched. In her mind, she tried to picture what the twins were doing at that very moment. She missed them terribly, but she was certain they were safe; most probably they had been rescued and taken back to Khalil's people. But to attempt to send a message to them could jeopardize their safety. Her lips moved as she murmured a prayer for their safekeeping. Then she added a prayer for Khalil. Although she had been twice told he was dead, Batsheva could not quite believe it. "I would know," she suddenly said aloud. Then there was silence, save the crackling of the logs in the hearth. Closing her eyes for a moment, she could see his face, his smile white against his dark skin, his dark eyes sparkling as his mouth moved silently as though talking to her. Batsheva let herself be comforted by the image.

Her eyes were still closed, but she heard a soft footfall on the rug. "Madame?" asked Mary, "are you awake?"

"Yes."

"You have a visitor, Madame."

Batsheva opened her eyes and saw Lady Isabella standing in the doorway. She took a measure of the woman; she was, in Batsheva's opinion, over-dressed for a morning visit. Her blue cote was highly decorated with threads of gold and silver and around her throat she wore a heavily jeweled collar. Her blonde hair was plaited over her shoulder without benefit of a wimple. Batsheva wondered if this was considered proper for a lady and made a mental note to ask Jane. "How kind of you to come," she managed in English after she sat up straight in her chair. "Would you sit?"

Isabella had expected her to rise, but when the younger woman did not, she replied in French, "*Merci*, Madame la Comtesse." She waited until Mary brought the other chair close to the fire. "Forgive me for coming uninvited, but I thought you might enjoy the company. I hear you prefer to remain in chambers and have not ventured out at all."

"I have ventured out to the shops, Lady Isabella, but I am certain there is more to see." She put her sewing aside and folded her hands against her blossoming belly.

"You must tell me about yourself," Isabella announced with what was meant to be a friendly smile. "I've heard such wicked rumors about you that I cannot believe any of them are true!"

Batsheva was curious about what was being said. "Tell me what you've heard, I shall tell you if it's true."

Isabella settled herself into the chair and prepared for a long, intimate chat. "You know how gossip flies in a household, and the gossip about you is most…unique. They say you are a princess, but no one knows of what kingdom. They say your late husband was commander in the Holy Land, yet no name, other than yours, has been mentioned." She paused, waiting for a reaction, but when none came, she continued. "The gossips say you came back wed with Gilbert from the Holy Land, but you told Her Majesty you were from Al-Andalus. So, you see, there are so many tales afoot that no one knows what truth there is in any of them."

"And you have come to find out?" asked Batsheva pleasantly. "How kind of you to be concerned about a newcomer to court."

Isabella laughed lightly as she nodded. "I have always found truth is far more intriguing than rumor."

"I was, as I told Her Majesty, born in Al-Andalus, but it is also true I lived in the Holy Land for a time. My late lord was indeed a commander, but I assure you, his name would be unfamiliar to you. My title is not tied to his; I am a princess in my own right. These things, too, would be most unfamiliar," she waved a casual hand, "and therefore of no importance."

"And Gilbert?"

"My lord rescued me from the site of a battle. I am indebted to him for his kindness," Batsheva said smoothly. She patted her stomach. "Gilbert anxiously awaits the birth of his heir."

Stymied, Isabella realized the woman had told her practically nothing. Forcing a smile, she asked when they would leave for Durham. "You must be anxious to meet Anne."

"Anne?" echoed Batsheva.

"He did not tell you, did he?"

"Tell me what, Lady Isabella?"

"How like a man!" Isabella laughed then leaned forward, closer to Batsheva. "Gilbert is widowed, Lady Elizabeth. Anne is his daughter."

Fighting the redness inching over her cheeks, Batsheva maintained her composure. "You are right, Lady Isabella, he has not told me. How like a man, indeed! I am certain if it were a son, I would know."

"He married quite young, and she died in childbed along with their second babe, a son. Anne lost more than her mother on that day; she lost her father as well. Gilbert left Durham; save for a few brief visits, has paid scant attention to the child."

"Who tends her now?" asked Batsheva.

"Her grandmother, the Dowager Countess Matilda." Isabella sat back in her chair and allowed herself a small, sad smile. "The child is lovely, but alas, she does not even know her sire." She pressed an elegant hand across her breast. "Of course, I have tried to see to her needs as best I can, but my duties at court do not allow me to be at Durham as often as I would like." She sighed dramatically.

Batsheva did not know what to make of the revelation. True, she had never asked Durham about his own family, but then, they rarely had conversation of more than a word or two unless one was shouting at the other. "How kind of you to tell me, Lady Isabella. You may rest comfortably knowing I will treat Anne as one of my own." *As I hope whoever cares for my twins are treating them,* she thought sadly. "But tell me, how came you to care so tenderly for the child?"

"I have known Gilbert," she cooed, "since we were children. Long we have been close, but his father had arranged a marriage for him while he was still in the cradle. Joan," she sighed dramatically, "was beautiful, but frail. When she died, I did my best to comfort him in his grief."

I am certain you did, and would like another chance to do the same, thought Batsheva. Casually, she redirected the subject to Isabella. "And you, Madame? What of your own family? Have you children?"

"A daughter and a son, Lady Elizabeth," she replied proudly. "He is a fine, strapping boy of five, the very image of his late father." There was yet another sad sigh. "My husband died on campaign in France whilst serving the king."

"My sympathies are with you, Lady Isabella."

Isabella suddenly grasped Batsheva's hand in her own and gushed, "You see, Lady Elizabeth, already we share much in common. We should be fast friends. Do me the honor of allowing me to be your guide in our little society."

"That is most kind, Lady Isabella," she replied. As quickly as she could without seeming repulsed, Batsheva extricated her hand. "But it is too much to ask when your duties to her gracious majesty take so much of your time."

"Oh, do not concern yourself with *that,*" she breezed, "'tis imperative you have a friend at court, one who can tell you who is who and worth… cultivating. Gilbert is hardly aware of his own surroundings. Joan never spent time at court, so he has not even her memory of such things to guide him in your education."

Before Batsheva could answer, the door opened, and Jane bustled into the room. "Oh, 'tis bitter out…." She stopped as soon as she realized Batsheva was not alone. "Forgive my intrusion, my lady," she said and, bobbing a curtsey, she quietly deposited her basket on the table before disappearing into the bedroom with the bundle in her arms.

"You must teach servants their place," said Isabella in a voice loud enough for Jane to hear. "They must learn to enter the room silently and wait until spoken to before speaking, and even then, they must not engage you in idle chatter."

"Mistress Blank is not my servant," replied Batsheva calmly, "she is my tutor."

"Your tutor? What does she profess?"

"The lady teaches me English. If I am to live at Durham, I must speak the language."

"Oh, my dear," laughed Isabella, "'tis hardly necessary; everyone of importance speaks French!"

"I was taught by my lady mother," countered Batsheva with a serene smile, "the more one understands the language of servants, the easier it becomes to have them do one's bidding without rancor. It has always seemed to me to be sage advice." She paused, and added in a puzzled voice, "In my land, ladies of quality not only speak several languages, they are expected to read and write in them as well. Is that not true for English ladies of noble birth?"

"Hardly, Lady Elizabeth. "Twas Eve's desire for knowledge that expelled her from the Garden of Eden, was it not? Too much learning is poison to a lady's position."

"I am sorry to hear that, Lady Isabella. I have always thought of learning much the same way I think of breathing. One does it naturally…like a babe learns to walk and talk."

Isabella stared at her for a long moment. "I'm afraid I've tired you, Lady Elizabeth. Please, do me the honor taking supper with me Sunday; I host a small gathering after None."

"Thank you for the kind invitation. I will speak with my lord when he returns." She managed a small laugh. "I am hesitant to accept any invitation, no matter how kind and generous, until I speak with him. I am unfamiliar with his duties here at court."

"I'm certain Gilbert will be delighted. Until Sunday, then." She rose to leave, but as she swept through the door, Isabella collided with a man coming through it. "Edward!" she cried, regaining her footing. "I would have thought your time at court would have taught you better manners."

Edward bowed low from the waist. "Forgive me, Lady Isabella. I did not know you were visiting." His face was grave, but his eyes twinkled mischievously.

"You are forgiven, Edward," she replied. Then she was gone.

Edward grinned at Batsheva. "Whatever you have done to the Lady Isabella, I congratulate you. I am unaccustomed to seeing her so...so polite."

"*Pardonnez-moi, monsieur,* but I do not understand." Batsheva furrowed her brow in confusion. "Who are you?"

In several long strides, he crossed the room, took Batsheva's hand, and raised it to his lips. "Allow me to introduce myself, *ma belle tante.* I am Edward of York, eldest son of Margaret, formerly of Durham, and her husband, Henry. In other words, my lady, I am your nephew."

Batsheva could not help but smile at the young man who seemed so close to her own age. "*Enchantée*, Edward of York. Did I not see you at the banquet last night?"

"I confess I was there, but much preoccupied," he admitted.

"With a lovely young lady, if I correctly recall." Batsheva frowned as she thought. "Rosalind, I believe was the lady's name. Am I right?"

"I am duly impressed, Tante Elizabeth." Without being asked, he took the seat Isabella had vacated. "Tell me, gracious lady, did Isabella do anything to cause you discomfort?"

"She offered her friendship and her good counsel, although I cannot say I would readily avail myself of either. She seems...frivolous."

"Aye, that she is!" laughed Edward. "What a treasure my uncle has brought back from his travels. I can well see why he finds you so fascinating."

"I am afraid, Edward, you assume too much. I think before this conversation goes continues, I must speak with my lord earl."

"As must I. Is he here?"

Batsheva shook her head. "He had business in the City but said he would return in time to take supper with me. Perhaps you would join us?"

"T'would be my pleasure, but alas, I am committed to her majesty this evening."

Batsheva was disappointed; she liked this ebullient young man with his merry blue eyes and sandy colored curls. "Perhaps another time, then."

"I would be delighted to attend you and my august uncle, Tante Elizabeth." He took her hand and pressed her fingers to his lips. "Speaking of my uncle, would you tell him I would have a word with him at his earliest convenience?"

"I shall be happy to, Edward of York."

He rose and bowed gracefully. "I look forward to our next meeting, my lady." He went to the door. "Be wary of Isabella, Tante Elizabeth. You are new to court and do not know the intrigue which haunts our corridors. I cannot imagine t'would be different anywhere else, but…."

Batsheva nodded. "Thank you for your warning, Edward, but you need not worry; I am not so inexperienced that I would be foolish."

"You are exactly what my uncle needs." And with that, he was gone.

When the door closed, Batsheva called to Jane. "You can come out, *Professeure* Blanc," she laughed.

Jane poked her head out the door. "The young man was right, Bess," she said as she carried several frocks from the bedroom; "Lady Isabella is well known for her sharp tongue and designing ways. No respectable dressmaker will attend her without payment in advance. She is notorious for not paying her bills."

She told Jane about their conversation. "I'm afraid," sighed Batsheva, "she may be notorious for other things as well. I would do well not to trust her."

"She has something else on her mind besides your welfare…and I am sure he is quite tall."

Their day was spent sewing and practicing English. As dusk fell, Mary arrived to stoke the fire in the hearth as well as tell Batsheva the earl had returned. "He is with her majesty now," she dutifully reported, "and asks that you wait supper for him."

"Which means Jamie is also back and will be wanting his supper," added Jane as she folded the chemise she was sewing. "I daresay, Bess, 'twas a lucky day for me when his lordship decided you needed frocks."

"Does he treat you well?" asked Batsheva.

"Aye, that he does. He's more than just warmth in my bed, forgive my boldness; he is good company and salve for my grieving heart."

"Then I am truly happy for you, Jane," smiled Batsheva.

"One day," sighed the plump seamstress, "you shall tell me the earl does the same for you and I will be just as happy for you."

"Jane," she asked as casually as she could before her friend could leave, "has Jamie ever mentioned the earl is widowed and has a daughter?"

Jane stared at the floor for a long, silent moment. "Yes. He wondered if you knew."

"Why did you not tell me?" Batsheva's voice was pained. "Why would he think I would not want to know?"

Shaking her head, Jane put the chemise in the basket. "Jamie says he does not know how to tell you."

"Men!" snorted Batsheva. "They have no sense whatsoever when it comes to family matters. This will be remedied today."

CHAPTER 15

Alexandria

NOVEMBER 1191

Amidst a sea of silken cushions, Khalil watched Amina play with her latest acquisition: a doll dressed in garments identical to her own. Her copper curls bounced as she instructed the doll in proper deportment. The child's voice drifted across the short distance between them and for a moment, Khalil imagined it was Batsheva that he heard. The pain in his heart was unbearable, even in comparison to the pain from his healing body. Shifting his weight, he gritted his teeth as he slowly bent his right leg at the knee. Knives thrust into the center of the joint with each motion, but he persisted. The physician assured him the pain was a good sign; the nerves were healing and that soon the sharp jabs would diminish. When he reached the point where the pain became too great, he involuntarily grunted, causing Amina to look up.

Silently, the doll tucked under her arm, she rose gracefully from her own little bank of cushions and approached her father. "Now, Abu," she said in a most patient voice, "Mussa bin Maymon says not to work too hard, lest you tear the muscles." Her grey eyes were as solemn as her words.

"Come, little mother, give your abu a kiss to make the pain go away." He opened his arms to her, and the little girl dropped down beside him, being careful not to jostle him too much. She planted a kiss on his bearded cheek, then frowned.

"Are you going to make the beard go away, Abu? I don't like it; it scratches me fiercely." She rubbed her tender cheek.

Khalil smiled, "One day, *Insh'Allah,* your mother will make me scrape it off. Only then, little djinn, will it go away."

"Then you must find Mama and bring her home. Daud doesn't like the beard either." She snuggled into the crook of his arm. "Will Mama come home soon?"

Before he could answer, a slave entered and bowed low. "Forgive my intrusion, my lord, but the physician has arrived."

"Show him in." Khalil smiled broadly when the old man entered his chamber. *"As-salāmu 'alaykum*, Mussa bin Maymon!"

"And *wa-'alaykum salaam* to you, my lord Amir," replied the old man with a smile almost as wide. "You look most comfortable today."

"Every day, Mussa, I feel myself grow stronger. I am grateful to you, my friend."

"Healing is in the mind of the sick man," the physician admonished his patient. "And you? You are already well."

"Not well enough to sit astride a horse."

"Perhaps not today, but perhaps tomorrow." He sat on a low stool provided by the slave. Moving the folds of Khalil's djellaba without risking the amir's modesty before his daughter, the physician examined the ugly, jagged scar running the length of his left thigh. "Good, good," murmured Mussa bin Maymon, "there is no sign of new infection." He prodded the wound gently but firmly. "This is good, Khalil." He rearranged the djellaba to allow examination of a second, equally vicious wound on the amir's right leg. Now, if you would bend the knee." He watched as Khalil slowly moved the joint. "Good! Good! You see, there is more range today." He turned to Amina. "Has he been working too hard, little one?"

"Yes, I think so. He grumbles a lot."

"That is to be expected. Now, tell me what you see."

Amina pointed to the widest part of the scar. "Abu's gash is less red, Mussa bin Maymon. The medicine has worked."

"And what does that tell you?" prodded the physician.

"That keeping it clean is important," recited Amina with great conviction. "When the wound became dirty, it got red. And ugly. Only a good, strong dose of chamomile, yarrow, and nettle poultice will keep the evil spirits away."

Mussa bin Maymon clapped his hands with delight. "Such a bright child. She will make a good wife and mother. She learns well what she is taught."

"She forgets nothing," added the proud father. "Already she is reading Arabic."

"I can read the Qur'an," she said just as proudly. "Abu says my mother can read many languages, including yours."

For a moment, Mussa bin Maymon's face clouded. "Where is your brother, little girl?" he asked, changing the subject.

"In the garden with his maps."

Khalil saw the change in his physician. "Go find Dudu, little mother, and make certain he is staying out of trouble."

Amina knew she was being sent away on purpose and frowned but did not contradict her father. With a long, dramatic sigh, she left the two men alone. Her personal attendant materialized and followed her out.

"What is wrong, Mussa?" asked Khalil as soon as the child left the room.

"News from Marseille, my young friend." He removed a parchment from his robe and handed it Khalil. "A knight was seen in the port city and with him, a young page. They stayed in Marseille briefly, but long enough to stop in a jeweler's shop. According to my friends in Marseille, the page inquired about the house of Hagiz."

"What was said, Mussa?"

"That I do not know. But what I have learned is that the page had eyes of the most unusual grey…and his curls were the color of copper."

Khalil almost leapt from the divan. "Batsheva?" he cried. "Was it Batsheva? Where were they going?"

"To the north, Khalil. Beyond that, we know nothing."

"And the knight? What was his insignia?"

"A lion rampant with a plant in its hind claws; perhaps Saxon or Norman, but from where, we do not know." Mussa bin Maymon pointed to the parchment "That is a drawing of the design; perhaps someone will recognize it."

Khalil unfurled the parchment and studied the crude drawing. "I am in your debt once again, Mussa."

The old man shrugged. "There is no debt here, Khalil; I am doing what I believe to be best for the lady."

"I thought you disapproved," admitted Khalil. Although the physician had never come out and said it, he knew the physician did not believe a Jewess should be with a Muslim man. "What has made you change your mind?"

"Devora Alfasi has written to me of this…situation, but even her words were not enough to convince me."

"Then who did?"

"Amina."

"Amina?" chuckled Khalil. "How did my little djinn change your mind?"

"One night, when you lay deep in unnatural slumber, Amina crept into the room. I began to scold her, but she stood her ground and told me I could not keep her from her abu. She is a remarkable child, Khalil, with an excellent memory for detail. She told me a tale of love and devotion between her mama and abu that brought tears to even these ancient eyes. She knows her mother is a Jew. And she knows that you will move heaven and earth to find her."

"I am not without eyes, Mussa," smiled Khalil his own eyes soft with undisguised love for the little girl. "She is the image of her mother. And she has her temperament as well."

"God be kind to the man who eventually weds her," laughed the physician. "But tell me, Khalil, what will you do now? Will you search for her?"

"Am I able?" he asked in return.

"If you follow my advice assiduously, there is no reason why, when winter is past and the leg is stronger, you cannot travel. But what of your people here?"

"They are safe and well-managed without me." He paused for a moment to consider the intelligence of sharing his recent news with the physician. He knew the old physician was well trusted by the sultan himself and had counseled him many times. In fact, he suspected the old man already knew what he was about to tell him. "When you pronounce me well enough, I will succeed Mustafa as amir here in Alexandria. You know he is dying, Mussa, and he has no son worthy of the title. The sultan will settle a small governorship on Selim, for that is all he wants. Now," scowled Khalil, "I must learn the art and craft of serious government. A simple desert sheikh is a far cry from an amir with ministers and a court.

"Times are changing for us, Mussa; we must learn to live together, united under a single sultan. Islam has united us in spirit, but now it is up to us to unite ourselves as a nation. We have splintered factions amongst us. We can learn much from your people."

"We are not without our fractures," frowned the physician. "Although we do not wage war amongst ourselves, we have our differences. Perhaps our lack of a home to call our own has served to strengthen our resolve to remain a single people under many flags. Like Islam, we are of a singular faith. Would that more feel the way you do, my young, idealistic friend." The physician fell silent for a moment, then turned back to the injured limb. "Have you been walking?" he asked.

"With difficulty. I lean heavily on the cane." He clapped his hands and a slave appeared to help his master rise. Khalil took the cane and took several steps. "The pain diminishes each day, but I have no stamina."

"This will come," nodded the physician as he, too, was gently helped to his feet by the slave. "Now, let me have the cane."

Khalil did as he was told and slowly walked across the room. His face grew taut as the pain shot up his thigh and into his belly. "Will this ever heal?" he growled through clenched teeth.

"In time, but you will always feel fatigue in the legs before the rest of your body feels it. Still, your progress is good, very good; you must work hard to increase your endurance."

"What about riding, Mussa?" pressed Khalil. "I am worthless if I cannot sit upon a horse."

"Tomorrow, Khalil, you may sit upon a quiet mare. Use a mounting block. This means sit. It does not mean walk the beast, or God forbid, trot. Sit in the saddle and allow your legs to become reacquainted with the position." The amir beamed like a schoolboy. "I will come again after the Sabbath and examine your leg. Be warned, though, do not tire yourself; you are still weak and susceptible to infection." Gently, Mussa parted the folds of the amir's djellaba at the waist and studied the wounds on the amir's chest and stomach. "Does this hurt?" he asked as he pressed against a still livid sword cut on Khalil's left side.

"Yes, but not terribly. It is more sore than painful."

"Good," murmured the physician. "And this?" He prodded another spot.

"Tolerable."

"And your bowels? Your stream?" Mussa bin Maymud raised a delicate eyebrow.

"They *all* seem to work well enough," chuckled Khalil.

The physician let the djellaba fall. "Continue eating mostly fruits and vegetables, do not strain. The sword missed your vitals by a hair's breadth;

what you feel is good pain; it tells me you are healing inside. There is no evidence of infection but continue to cleanse the area and apply the ointments I have provided. In a week, you may be ready to soak in a real bath."

"I cannot think which is better, Mussa, to be allowed to sit on a horse or to sit in a bath."

"That, Khalil, is for you to decide."

CHAPTER 16

Westminster

NOVEMBER 1191

"The queen goes to Normandy for Christmas," announced Durham as he pulled off his boots. "She invited us to attend, but I declined, stating your condition did not warrant another long journey."

"Thank you, my lord. I have no desire to cross the Channel again so soon." Batsheva poured a cup of hot mulled wine and handed it to Durham.

He raised a questioning eyebrow as he accepted the goblet. "I thought you would have argued the point, Bess. Crossing the Channel would take you closer to Al-Andalus." He did not add that he thought she would continue south if given the opportunity.

She shook her head. "There is no point," she said softly, "there is nothing for me there. Besides, you are right when you say my condition does not warrant the journey. I am already cumbersome." She allowed herself a wry grin.

She was far from cumbersome, considered Durham as he watched her glide across the room, his boots in her hands. Despite her pregnancy, she moved with uncommon grace. "Did you pass the day pleasantly?"

"Oh, yes. Jane did come, but I also had visitors! Two most fascinating people." She told him about Edward's call and gave him the message. "He is a charming young man," she added.

"Too charming," grunted Durham. "Who else?"

"Lady Isabella."

This time, Durham simply groaned. "And what poison did she pour in your ear?"

"Not poison, my lord." She faced him with her hands planted firmly on her hips. "It would seem the lady provided me with information I was lacking." She thought she noticed him blanch ever so slightly. "Your daughter, my lord, is in need of her father."

"I have been made aware," he mumbled, his face reddening.

Any anger she had toward him because of his apparent desertion of his child melted into compassion when she saw the sadness in his eyes. She softened her voice immediately. "Why did you not tell me about Anne, my lord? Surely we could have sent for the child upon our arrival."

"I hardly know her, Bess; she is with my family at Durham. To wrench her away from those she knows and loves would be cruel."

"Is it too late to go to Durham now? Can we not travel northward before the hard winter sets in?"

Durham shook his head. "There is mischief afoot here, in Westminster. The queen has asked me to sit in council until it is put down."

Batsheva refilled his goblet. "Am I wrong to ask what is this mischief?" Unskilled in court ways, she was unsure of her role as his so-called wife.

"Lackland would usurp the throne. With the king in the Holy Land, Prince John believes he can take the seat without difficultly. Eleanor will see him dead before she allows that to happen."

"Her own son?" gasped Batsheva.

"Her own son has been plotting treason against the Crown for well over two years and she knows it. The Archbishop of Rouen is holding the kingdom for Richard, and although John is quiet for the moment, the queen wants consolidation in the Privy Council."

"So, you must remain here," murmured Batsheva, beginning to understand. "Is that why Edward seeks you out?"

He nodded. "He will go with her to Normandy." He swallowed hard before he added, "And the queen will call on you tomorrow."

"Here?"

He nodded again. "She would see what you have done to my mother's apartments."

Batsheva's eyes widened. "What shall I do? How should I entertain her?"

"Serve a light repast when she arrives at noon; Eleanor is not one for a heavy meal at midday. Your conversation with her will be enough of an amusement."

"But what should I serve? I have no experience with English cuisine!"

Durham held up his hand to still her and went to pick up the sack he had brought with him. "Perhaps this will help ease your mind." He untied the strings and dumped the contents onto the table. A unique aroma filled the room.

With a squeal of delight so unlike her, Batsheva began sorting through the little packets and parcels. "Cinnamon! Cardamom and cloves! How did you find them!" She held twin bags to her nose. "Saffron and turmeric!" She replaced those and picked up a small, wrapped box. Quickly opening it, she groaned. "Dried dates. Beautiful, beautiful dates!"

Durham handed her another box. "And figs."

"Oh, my lord, this is too much! I should die happy!" she laughed as she popped a dried fig into her mouth. "I must have Mary find a cook!"

As if she were clairvoyant, Mary appeared at the door with two servants bearing supper trays and another man whom Batsheva did not recognize. "Forgive me, my lady," she said as she bobbed a curtsey, "but Her Majesty's cook wishes a word with you."

Batsheva smiled at the portly man delivering a sweeping bow. "I am glad you have come before I could even call on you!" she said excitedly. "The queen will take her midday meal with me tomorrow and I need your help."

"That is why I have come, my lady. Her Majesty, in all kindness, has already sent word to the kitchens. I am at your service."

The conversation began in earnest and Durham chose that moment to take a plate into the bedchamber. He had no desire to learn how his meals came to appear on his table; his only concern was that they did. On time.

Batsheva rose at dawn, dressed in her sturdiest clothing, and asked Mary to take her to the kitchens. In her arms, she carried a basket filled with the spices and fruits Durham brought the day before. The cook and his staff were already gathered when she arrived and if any were surprised at the appearance of the earl's lady, they had the good graces to say nothing. Pushing her up sleeves, Batsheva began instructing them on how to prepare the dishes she wanted served.

If Batsheva found the conditions in the palace kitchen less than satisfactory she had the good sense to refrain from comment. Instead, she asked for and received several copper bowls that she immediately instructed the scullery maid to scrub until they shone. Turning her attention to the pantries, she poked through the baskets and barrels until she found things familiar to her. "This, this, and this," she commanded the porters who picked up the items and carried them to the work area. When everything was assembled, she began explaining the process.

Soon, a large salmon, expertly filleted by the fish monger, was poaching gently in a long pan half-filled with consommé of wine, herbs, and vegetables. Nearby, sweetened dough rose in a copper pot, waiting to be punched down and shaped before baking. Using honey and cinnamon, Batsheva showed the cook how to simmer the dates and figs for a few moments before spreading them on a clean marble slab to cool before chopping. In another pot, bulgur wheat steamed above a broth made of vegetables and saffron. Familiar aromas soon filled the corner of the kitchen where she worked, comforting Batsheva in a way she did not anticipate: they were the scents of home. For a moment, she could almost hear the chatter in her mother's kitchen.

"Will you serve a sweet, my lady?" asked the cook, disturbing her reverie. "The queen is fond of sweets."

"Let us make a flan."

"Flan? What is flan?" he asked.

Batsheva shook her head; she did not know how to describe it. Instead, she asked for a dozen eggs and another copper bowl. Carefully, she broke the eggs and examined each yolk before dropping it into the bowl. With a practiced hand, she began mixing.

"Why do you look at the eggs?" asked the cook, rather stymied at the process.

"To check for blood spots. Those eggs are discarded."

"But why, my lady? Of what harm are blood spots?"

Batsheva was about to tell him a spotted egg was unclean, but she caught herself. Thinking quickly, she replied, "The spots would pollute the color of the flan. 'Tis better not to use them. Do you have *sucre* in your stores?"

"*Mais bien sûr!* We are never without for her majesty does love her sweets!"

"Then let us prepare the milk and we will begin," announced Batsheva with a huge smile.

When the last loaves were in the oven and flan was cooling on the long trestle, Batsheva reviewed the instructions for presentation of the meal. "The sauce must be warm, not hot," she warned the cook, "and should not be poured until you are outside my door, lest it cool too soon. The couscous, for that is the name of the wheat dish, must remain covered until it is served; the roasted almonds must be set it in a bowl apart or they will grow soft from the steam. She furrowed her brow. "Have I forgotten anything?"

"No, my lady, I think not." The cook bowed gravely from the waist. "It has been my pleasure to work beside you, my lady. I have learned much today." He offered a tentative smile.

Batsheva thanked them all before she hurried back to her chamber to prepare herself for the queen's visit.

"I only tell you what I've heard, Your Majesty," sighed Isabella as she sat beside the queen in her chambers. "My own maid has seen the uproar in the kitchen."

"And you think this is cause for concern?" languidly asked the queen.

"If she is planning to serve you strange food, would not a taster be in order?"

"Are you volunteering, Isabella?" Eleanor laughed gently. "The lady has no reason to poison us, child. We would prefer to think the lady's actions are simply with the best of intentions. We have eaten many strange things in our travels and doubt if anything she will serve shall seem strange at all. Do not concern yourself, Isabella. Instead, confine your attentions to a renewed search for a husband. 'Tis high time you married again."

"I had hoped this would be settled when Gilbert returned, Your Majesty," she pouted.

"We would say it is well settled," replied the queen, "just not the way you had hoped. You had no agreement with the earl."

"True, but…."

"The ways of the heart should be more familiar to you, Isabella. There is no point dwelling on what cannot be."

"I suppose not," she grumbled, less than satisfied. Since it was common knowledge the marriage had not been recorded in church, Isabella had hoped Eleanor would demand the little foreigner be set aside. But like everyone else who had encountered this upstart, the queen seemed besotted by her. "Would you like me to accompany you to Durham's apartments, Your Majesty?"

Eleanor shook her head. “This will be a private meeting, Isabella. I have no wish to populate it with additional ears.”

“Then with your permission, I shall retire; I fear I am experiencing a headache.” When the queen nodded, Isabella rose, curtsied, and left.

Wearing the simple hunter green cote over an ivory chemise, Batsheva stood perfectly still while Jane laced the long, tight fitting sleeves with darker green ribbon. On her head sat a barbette and veil, over which Batsheva wore a narrow circlet of fine, beaten gold leaves. At the center was a single thistle blossom. The circlet had belonged to Durham’s grandmother, the late Countess of Durham, and Durham had retrieved it from the treasury at the Tower where his mother stored her court jewels. At first, Batsheva refused the gift but Durham insisted. After all, he pointed out, she was considered Countess of Durham and appearances did matter. Now the circlet was firmly in place and although the piece was delicately wrought, Batsheva could feel the weight as if it were made of lead. Other than the circlet, she wore no jewels, save a small gold ring Durham urged her to wear to ward off the gossips.

Jane tied the last bow. “There, Bess, ‘tis done. How does it all feel?”

“Heavy,” she replied, taking a few steps. “But it moves well. Must the sleeves be so tight?”

“Yes; do not toy with the laces. It would not do to have your ribbons dragging across the table. What about the slippers?”

Batsheva glanced down at her feet. Instead of the red Morocco boots she had been wearing since the day Durham found her, her feet were clad in soft, embroidered French slippers. “They are comfortable enough,” she admitted, “but they feel strange. Not at all what I am used to wearing.”

“You are used to wearing those boots…or going about in stockinged feet, my dear Lady Elizabeth,” wagged the seamstress. “These are slippers for a proper lady, so you’d best get used to them.” Jane swung her heavy woolen cloak over her shoulders. “Now, rest until the queen arrives, Bess. I must be off to my shop. I’ve been away far too often, and I do have other ladies in need of my skill.” She scurried out the door, the ever-present sewing basket tucked under her arm.

Batsheva had just dozed off when Mary was gently shaking her. "'Tis time, my lady; the queen is on her way."

Pushing herself out of the chair, Batsheva smoothed her dress. She took a quick look around the room and smiled. "You've done well, Mary," she beamed at the servant. "Would you like to serve the queen?"

"Oh, my lady! I would like that very much!" gushed the girl.

"Good, then you shall serve Her Majesty and let your friend Agnes serve me. Present the meal, then withdraw. I will serve personally during the meal. I know this is unusual, but this is how it would be done in my homeland. I will summon you and the footmen when I need you."

Mary bobbed a quick curtsey as she thanked Batsheva for the honor of serving Queen Eleanor just as the queen's guard arrived.

"Welcome to our chambers, Your Majesty," murmured Batsheva from her deep curtsey. "You honor us with your presence."

"And you, my dear child, honor us with the effort that has gone into the preparation of this feast. Word has flown about the palace of your morning's adventures." Eleanor extended her hand to Batsheva, who touched it with her own before rising.

"They were hardly adventures," she murmured, "I was happy to have some useful task to occupy my time."

Eleanor sat in the chair her servants had delivered to the apartments earlier in the day. "Come, Comtesse Durham, let us sit together. We are anxious to sample the savories you have created."

The meal moved smoothly from first course to last. Batsheva was amazed at the queen's prodigious appetite; it seemed the old woman devoured everything set before her with great relish, and even helped herself to more of the couscous with figs and dates. She asked about seasonings with the expert sense of one whose palate had experienced a wide array of flavors. The queen denoted the note of cloves in the sauce accompanying the fish as well as the faintest hint of cinnamon in the rich, brioche. Instead of being flustered by the royal presence, Batsheva found herself unexpectedly relaxed.

"Tell me, Lady Elizabeth, about the needlework on your cote. It is exquisite. Is your seamstress so skilled?" asked the queen as the flan was served.

Batsheva blushed prettily when she answered, "No, Your Majesty, this work is mine."

"And what are the fruits and flowers?"

"Pomegranates, Madame, and pomegranate blossoms. They remind me of my home."

Eleanor was delighted. "I have had pomegranate seeds and juice in Sicily!" she laughed. "There is nothing more refreshing. Would that we could grow them here. I shall declare the pomegranate to be your personal emblem, Elizabeth. Gil will be delighted."

When the dessert had been cleared, Batsheva refilled their goblets with mulled wine, taken directly from a kettle simmering in the hearth. The queen unfastened the clasp that held her blue woolen mantle. "I fear I grow warm from the meal," she said as she accepted the goblet from Batsheva. "Never have I been so warm in Westminster in the dead of winter!"

"'Tis the tapestry on the floor, madame," explained her hostess. "The tapestry keeps one's feet warm while helping to stay the drafts. I will move the tapestries onto the walls when I can find proper rugs."

"I daresay I shall look into putting tapestries on my floor!" she laughed. "Although I've seen rugs in France and in Italy, I've never thought to bring one to England." Then, the queen noticed Batsheva was staring at her. "Are you unwell?" she asked gently.

Batsheva shook her head. "Your brooch, Your Majesty" she said as she continued to stare at the brooch the queen wore on her left shoulder. "'Tis a most unusual piece."

The queen glanced down at the ornament. "'Twas a gift, Lady Elizabeth, from Geoffrey, the Archbishop of York." Eleanor frowned as she said the name. "Of course, you would not know Geoffrey; he is a horrid little by-blow of one of my late husband's affairs. 'Tis of no importance, my dear; he is safely tucked away in his Episcopal palace and shall remain there. The brooch, however, was part of an apology." She unclipped the brooch and studied it for a moment. "He says the markings have meaning, but he did not tell me what they meant. Knowing him, 'tis an incantation for summoning the devil." She laughed again, but it was a harsher sound. "Here, look for yourself."

Batsheva accepted the brooch from her outstretched hand. She did not have to study it to know what the words said, but she looked down at it. A shiver ran through her. Her mother wore one just like it. Had she married as planned, she would have been given one on the day of her wedding, a symbol of her marriage within the community. "'Tis a line from Scripture, madame," she said softly, "it means, *I am my beloved's, and my beloved is mine;* 'tis from the Song of Solomon."

"I had heard you were learned, Lady Elizabeth, but I am amazed. What letters are these?"

"Hebrew, madame."

"Your father must be a remarkable man to allow his daughter to study such an archaic tongue. I thought Hebrew to be reserved for monks and scholars."

This was a subject Batsheva did not want to pursue. "If I might be permitted, madame, may I ask how this Geoffrey came to be in possession of this brooch?"

The queen looked at Batsheva quizzically, then answered, "On the day my son was crowned King, there was an incident involving the Jews of London. Since we had no quarrel with them, Richard put down the rabble and hanged the instigators. Shortly thereafter, when Richard left England for the Holy Land, more trouble erupted for the Jews of York. There are many tales of the event, but the ending is the same. They took refuge in the castle keep, but their lives were in peril. Many chose suicide, or so I am told. The keep was burned. Anyone left alive perished."

Batsheva felt faint; she gripped the arm of her chair until her knuckles turned white. The Vitals were in York; Akiva's sister was in York. "All of them?" she asked, her voice barely above a whisper.

"All of them," replied the queen. "Do you know someone there?"

"No," she lied. She willed herself not to let tears forming in the corners of her eyes spill down her cheeks. "It just seems so sad," she managed to say.

"'Twas more than sad," said the queen emphatically. "'Twas a tragedy of the worst kind. I have no love of Jews, of course, but those people were loyal to the Crown and did not warrant the price they paid for trading in England. We strive for peace in our land, for a good economy, and this is a black mark against us. Will those who brave the outer reaches of the world want to bring their wares to us if we murder traders within our borders? This act has wider ramifications than Geoffrey considered when he permitted the massacre to occur." She pointed to the brooch. "This was part of what was found amongst those poor souls. I wear it as a reminder; I have a personal obligation to hold the kingdom in safekeeping for my son."

"Your words are just, madam; may God keep you and the kingdom safely in His care." She returned the brooch to the queen.

Eleanor refastened the ornament to her shoulder. "I fear I have tired you, my dear; 'tis long past the hour when you should be taking your rest. After all, you are carrying the heir to Durham."

"Thank you, Your Majesty, for your concern. 'Tis true; I am tired."

The queen rose and Batsheva did the same. She curtsied to the queen, but when she stood, Eleanor embraced her, kissing her on both cheeks. "Your hospitality, Elizabeth, does your husband proud. Would that you were well enough to cross to Normandy with me, but perhaps, after the babe is born, you will come to us at our home in the Aquitaine. You are most delightful company, child."

Batsheva curtsied again. "Thank you, madame; you are most kind."

No sooner had the door closed behind the queen than Batsheva fled into the bedchamber. She tore the circlet and veil from her head and let them fall to the floor before she threw herself onto the bed, She wept copiously until she finally cried herself to sleep.

"I do not know what happened, my lord," quivered Mary when the earl returned to the apartments. "All seemed to go quite well, and when the queen left, she gave us each a coin. We came in to clear the rest of the dishes and I heard my lady weeping in the bedchamber. Perhaps 'tis her condition."

Durham crossed the room and quietly pushed open the bedroom door. Even in the dim light he could see her curled up in a little ball on the wide bed; the circlet and veil laying on the floor. Taking a fur coverlet from wardrobe, he gently laid it over her and left.

CHAPTER 17

Westminster

NOVEMBER 1191

No light filtered through the shutters of the narrow window when Batsheva opened her eyes. Struggling to sit up, she drew the pelt around her cold body and listened closely to the dull rhythm of voices outside her door. She slipped from the bed and padded toward the half-open door. Durham sat near the fire with another man, deep in conversation. It took her only a moment to realize the other man was Edward, his nephew from York. Rage boiled up from the very bottom of her soul until she saw nothing but blood through burning eyes. Unable to control either, she launched herself at Edward, nails arched into claws, the vilest Arabic epithets spewing from her mouth.

Durham leapt up, knocking over the chair as he grabbed Batsheva. "Have you gone mad?" he shouted as he pulled her off Edward.

"*Meurtrier!*" she shrieked in French. "You murdered them all, Edward of York! How dare you play the gentleman when you are naught but a filthy, lying murderer!

"What is she raving about?" yelled Gilbert as he restrained her. "What in sweet Jesus' name is she raving about?" Durham pinned her arms until she stopped struggling, only to have her renew her vigor when his grip loosened. "Enough!" he roared, grabbing her again. "Control yourself, Bess, and explain!"

Batsheva stopped squirming and stood rigid against Durham's broad chest. "He killed them all. Yoav, Eli, Samuel, David…all of them are dead. He killed them; he burned them alive." She shook off his grasp. "Kill him, Durham; kill him for me or I will do it myself." Her voice was cold as ice.

Edward fell into his chair and stared down at the floor. "I didn't kill them, my lady. I tried to stop it." He took his dagger from his belt and slit the laces of his sleeve to reveal an ugly scar covering his upper arm and shoulder. "Here are the burns to prove it."

"They prove nothing," spat Batsheva. "You might have burned starting the fire, not trying to stop it."

"But I did try to stop them, my lady. I never would have hurt any of them. They were kind and good to me and…and…and…," his voice disappeared.

"And what?" prodded Durham.

Edward looked up; tears were streaming down his face. "The woman I loved was in there. I would have done anything to stop it and I couldn't. We couldn't. They stopped us, Geoffrey's men. They held back those of us who would stop it. And we watched. We watched and we heard their screams." Edward wept openly now, the pain he relived etched on his face, the anguish in his voice. "Hannah was in there. I heard her screaming my name…and I could not reach her."

"Hannah?" whispered Batsheva. "Hannah who?"

"Hannah Vital. The most beautiful maid who ever graced this earth. We loved each other."

The anger melted, replaced by terrible sadness and compassion for the man whose eyes were now red with weeping. Batsheva walked slowly to him and knelt beside the chair. "Edward, tell me. Tell me everything."

"I met Hannah in her uncle's shop. We spoke and I was lost in her eyes. They were as green as her hair was black. Her voice was as soft as the dawn. We met again in the town square, by accident. And then we met, again and again. We wanted to marry, but our parents would not permit such a union. We spoke of running away together, but…."

Durham was stunned; he could not imagine his nephew in love with anyone but a lady of means. "Who is this Hannah to you, Bess?"

"She would have been my sister-in-law. She was the sister of my betrothed."

"Your betrothed? I do not understand."

Batsheva took Edward's hand in hers and held it tightly as she looked at Durham. "I am a Jewess, Gilbert of Durham. I was kidnapped from my caravan en route to my wedding and given to Khalil bin Mahmud as… tribute."

"You were his slave?" asked Durham, stunned.

"No…perhaps in the beginning, but not in the end."

"Yet you are a princess?"

"I am," replied Batsheva with a small, sad smile. "I am the adopted daughter of Sultan Salah ad-Din."

"Holy Mother of God!" cried Durham as he fell with a thud onto his chair.

"Khalil is the sultan's great-nephew as you are Queen Eleanor's. Because I refused to marry Khalil in Islam, my lord's Uncle Yusef entitled me for the sake of my children." She looked up at Edward. "I knew Hannah well, Edward. She was my friend. She, her brother, and her cousin David Vital lived beside us in Málaga."

"She spoke often of her time in Al-Andalus, my lady. She lived at a villa in Málaga with…." Suddenly, he stared at the woman kneeling beside him. "Batsheva? Are you Batsheva Hagiz? I should have known you by your eyes…and your hair. She was inconsolable when you were lost. Then, there were strange tidings from the east. They said you were alive, but others insisted you were not. Obviously, you *are* alive. And here! How is it so?"

"'Tis my fault," muttered Durham. "My men attacked the camp where she was hidden. But she was dressed as a boy. When I found her to be the only one left alive, I took her with me; I thought to make *him* my page."

"I was unconscious," added Batsheva. "I was not asked."

"But you must return her, Uncle! You cannot keep her. That would make you no better than…."

"Better than who, Edward?" she asked softly. "There was no one greater than my lord Khalil. He was a kind, brilliant man. I grieve for him greatly."

"But he kidnapped you!" cried Edward.

"That is not true. I was kidnapped by two men who would curry favor with their sheikh."

"Yet you are with my uncle now."

Batsheva touched her belly. "The child I carry is Khalil's. Your uncle has never touched me in that way."

"Regardless, I will acknowledge the child as my own," said Durham emphatically. "That child will have a father."

Batsheva sighed. "I never asked him to do that, Edward. If it were up to me, I would return to Khalil's people."

"You are not his slave," Edward protested. "Surely, you can leave if you choose."

"I am not exactly in a condition to undertake a long journey right now."

"Then I will escort you to wherever it is you wish to go after the babe is birthed."

"You will do no such thing!" growled Durham. "I will not have her trotting off with an inexperienced puppy!"

"Will you take her, then, Uncle? Will you return her to her own people?"

"I will do what is right for the lady when the time comes."

"Does that include locking her in Durham Castle if she chooses something other than to stay bound to you?"

Batsheva stood and held up her hands to silence them. "I think, gentlemen, that I am capable of making my own decisions. I would have you cease arguing over me as if I were a mindless child." She turned to Edward. "Forgive my rash judgment, Edward of York. I am aggrieved to learn of my people's fate, but my grief is lessened knowing Hannah had someone in her life whom she loved dearly. Now, if you would forgive me once more, I would seek my bed."

Both uncle and nephew were silent for a long time; the only sound in the room was the crackling of dry logs on the fire. When Durham finally spoke, his words were without rancor. "I now understand why you were sent down from York. Where stood your father in this matter?"

"He is no friend of Geoffrey's if that is what you ask. But he did not move to stop the riots. For this, Uncle, I will never forgive him."

"And your lady mother?"

Edward shrugged. "She is not one to go against her husband's wishes. I have little patience for a woman who has no ability to think for herself."

Durham laughed mirthlessly. "Be warned, Edward, a woman with a mind of her own is far more difficult than she may be worth."

"Is Batsheva?"

Durham frowned at the use of Bess's given name. He thought she was merely a woman who had landed in the amir's harem; that in time she would come to love him as he already loved her. What he learned did not ease his conscience; the woman was far more complex and complicated than he ever imagined. Khalil was dead and despite the children left behind, who might very well be dead, he hoped beyond all reason that she would ultimately choose to stay with him and be his wife. As to the matter of religion, that could be remedied.

Edward's mouth curved into a wry smile when he said, "The question remains, Uncle: is that what the lady wants? Be fairly warned, I will champion her cause against you if it comes to that."

Durham regarded his nephew carefully for a long moment. "I have no doubt in all heaven and on earth that you would."

When Edward had gone, Durham went softly into the bedchamber. Instead of finding the lady sleeping soundly beneath the thick covers, he saw she was sitting up, awake, staring into the fire. "Talk to me, Bess," he urged as he sat on the edge of the bed.

Unexpectedly, Batsheva reached out and touched Durham's cheek. "There is so much I might have told you before this, but I chose not to." She smiled sadly. "My reasons…are my own."

"But now…now that I know…what do I do? Can you not be honest with me?"

She sighed and shook her head. "I would not put you in jeopardy."

"How could knowing the truth be of any danger to me?"

"Would the consort of your adversary, the adopted daughter of your enemy, be welcomed in this court with songs of joy? I think not. More likely, I would be imprisoned as a spy. And your own loyalty would be questioned as well. "

"I would not permit that to happen."

"You have no guarantee that it would not, despite your good intentions, Gilbert," Batsheva countered, using his name for the first time. "I will give birth to this babe and then I will conveniently die in childbed. With Edward's help, if not yours, I will leave England and go home to my people."

"And if I do not want you to leave?"

"'Tis a sweet sentiment, but not one founded on good counsel."

He captured her hand in his and pressed it to his heart. "Every day I wake with the thought that I will see your face in morning's light. At night, my last thought is of you. I would do whatever is in my power… and then some, to make you content in my world. Would you retire behind the walls of Saladin's harem to live out your days alone? What is left for you in the Holy Land?"

"My children…."

"You know not if your children are even alive, Bess. Would you sacrifice this babe as well?"

"My children are alive, Gilbert. They need me." She managed a smile. "I need them. I need to live in a world with warmth and sunshine and hot desert winds. England will kill me in the end."

"Then we shall go to the south of France. Or Al-Andalus. But God's bones, Bess, let us be together!"

Her laugh was gentle, not mocking, but warm and endearing to Durham's ears. "Let us pass the winter together, my lord earl, and when the babe is ready to be born perhaps then we will have a better sense of what is to be done. I make no promises, Gilbert of Durham."

He kissed her hand. "'Tis all I can ask, my lady. For now, let them think we are husband and wife." His thumb rubbed the gold band she wore. "Come the spring, we will decide together how to proceed." He helped her slide down into the warm nest of the bed, then kissed her chastely on the forehead. "Sleep well, Batsheva Hagiz, Princess of Islam."

CHAPTER 18

Westminster

DECEMBER 1191–JANUARY 1192

Christmas court convened in Normandy, leaving Westminster to celebrate quietly. Batsheva was not sorry for the solitude; she preferred to spend her days with Jane, sewing not only the remainder of her own wardrobe, but a smaller, more delicate one for the child she carried. During the short winter days, Durham busied himself with the business of government charged to him by Eleanor who was glad to have his eyes and ears in place while she was gone.

Batsheva found a chessboard and pieces in Durham's trunk. He howled with delight when he saw the carved ivory and onyx figurines set out beside the board, and declared enthusiastically, "I shall teach you to play!"

Batsheva had not the heart to tell him she already knew the game well. Instead, she listened patiently as he demonstrated the movement of each piece with great deliberation. That done, Batsheva settled back in her chair and let him take the white. She watched his opening gambit and then, after a dramatic pause during which she chewed her lip thoughtfully, she proceeded to take his king in eight moves. Batsheva clapped her hands with delight as she moved her queen into position. "Shatranj!!" she declared with great satisfaction.

Durham stared at the board, not quite believing what he saw and cried, "I have been had!"

"Do you yield, Durham?" she laughed.

"Yield? What choice do I have? You know the game better than I!"

"That, my lord, is obvious. I hope you were playing easily with me, lest I think you a poor strategist."

With a vengeance, Durham began resetting the pieces. "*En garde*, madame. This time, I shall not fall into your trap!"

Batsheva grabbed a white pawn and a black pawn, hid them behind her back, then produced two closed fists. "Choose, sir knight." He tapped her left hand. It opened to reveal the black. "I shall open…and beware, my lord, I toyed easily with you last time."

Edward returned from Normandy ahead of the court. "I am to York," he told them at supper the night he arrived. "I leave tomorrow."

"What is afoot that you are here and gone so quickly?" asked his uncle. "'Tis the queen's business?"

"Aye, that it is. She will cross the Channel at month's end and will summon a Great Council at Windsor. Word is Philippe of France is aiding Lackland to mount an army."

At the mention of Richard's younger brother, Durham shuddered. "Would that she would imprison him," he muttered, "so the rest of us could tend to England."

"That she will not do…at least not yet. She has ordered her bailiffs to be alert. You would do well to keep your ears open here at Westminster."

Batsheva, sitting beside Durham, was confused by their talk. "This Lackland, he would overthrow his brother?"

"In a blink of an eye, Bess," replied Durham.

"And he has tried this before?" Both men nodded. "I do not understand why your Richard allows him to live. The sultan would have fed him to the dogs the first time!"

"This is not Islam," explained Durham. "Richard cares much for his brothers as well he should. The king has no issue or, rather, legitimate issue; John is his heir."

"But the king is married, is he not?"

"To the fair Berengaria of Navarre," said Edward, "but she has not yet produced a child."

"It would seem to me, a mere woman, that your king would do better fighting his own battles at home rather than attempting to wrest homes from the innocents of Palaestina," she sniffed. "Quite obviously, your governance is unstable."

"Aye," laughed Edward, "they are that and more. I thank God we have old Eleanor to guard our safety; she is a great and wise governor." He stood up and stretched. “I must bid you both good night; I’ve a long journey ahead in the morning.”

Durham rose to walk his nephew to the door. “Take regards to my sister,” he said, “and tell her I hope to see her soon.”

“I will, Uncle.” The men embraced.

Durham rejoined Batsheva at the hearth. “Maggie is a levelheaded woman who may provide good counsel to you if you let her.”

“You say that now, but you and Edward concur she is subjugated by her husband to the detriment of their people,” Batsheva shrugged. “‘Tis a pity the world is in such a poor state, Gilbert, for I am just as certain you and Khalil would be fast friends.”

“You speak of him as though he were still alive,” frowned the earl.

“My heart tells me that he is. Were he truly gone from this earth, I think I would know it.”

Durham shook his head sadly. “He is dead, Bess. Too many saw him fall. No one saw him rise again.”

“Until I have proof, I shall continue to hope against hope that he is alive.”

Near the end of January, Durham went to Southampton to view the army Prince John claimed was for defense of England. Although he traveled well-guarded with a cadre of 50 men, Batsheva was anxious. Pacing the chambers endlessly, she awaited his return. Mary and Jane did their best to keep her occupied, but their efforts fell short. Batsheva was a caged tigress, short in temper, and restless.

Mary, on Jane’s instruction, left the palace early one morning to go in search of figs for the lady. Armed with coins and the name of a shop, she bundled herself against the elements and set off with a footman for protection. She found the shop easily enough, made her purchase and was about to start back to the palace when a commotion caught her attention. Several heavily-armed guards thundered down the snow-covered street, followed by a closed box coach. She would not have thought anything of it, but when the carriage passed, she noticed the Durham crest on the door. “Hurry,” she said to her companion, “’tis a Durham coach!” Wending their way through the back streets of Westminster, they reached the palace gates just as the coach did. Mary pushed the footman ahead.

"Go to my lady's chambers and tell her the earl has arrived." As the footman raced off, Mary hurried to where the coach now stood in the yard.

Instead of the earl, Mary saw Edward step from the conveyance. She curtsied as he approached her. "I'm glad you're here, Mary," grinned the young man. "I've brought a surprise for my uncle."

"He's not here," she said, "he's gone to Southampton."

"No matter, 'tis the Lady Elizabeth who is required." As he spoke her name, Batsheva came through the great oak doors wrapped in a heavy cloak.

"Edward!" she cried, "I thought your uncle had returned."

"Are you disappointed?" he asked.

"A bit, but I am glad to see you." She looked at the box coach. "Have you given up your mount? Are you injured?" she asked with sudden concern.

He laughed heartily and assured her he was not. "I borrowed my grandmother's box; I have brought someone in need of your attention, my lady." He opened the door of the coach and extended his arms to the occupant. "May I present," he said as he lifted a child from within the coach and set her down before Batsheva, "Lady Anne of Durham."

Batsheva's eyes opened wide, and she immediately bent to greet the young traveler. Taking the smaller hand in her own, she held it tightly. "Welcome to Westminster, Lady Anne," she said warmly, "I am so happy to meet you at last." She caught a nervous glance between the two cousins and saw Edward nod slightly.

The little girl nodded back, then curtsied. "And I you, madam," she answered in French, her voice barely above a whisper.

"Come, Lady Anne, let us get out of the cold. Our apartments are warm, and you probably could stand some nice, hot broth to warm you after your journey." Still holding the hand fast, she led the child into the palace.

Anne of Durham was a slender child of 10, with great blue eyes and fair hair like her father's. But that was where the similarity ended. Where her father was open and curious, Anne was reticent and withdrawn. She dutifully accompanied the lady up the great stone stairs to her new home. She sat where she was told, her hands folded primly in her lap, her feet barely touching the floor. She answered each question the lady asked in soft, barely audible French. Her eyes were open, but nothing could be read in their blue-violet depths.

They took supper alone, but Edward joined them briefly when a bed for Anne was hauled into the apartment by two brawny men. The frame was placed in the small chamber, between Batsheva's bedchamber and Gilbert's. and Mary hurried about preparing the fresh bedding. Through it all, Anne stood silently staring into the fire; showing no interest in the bustle about her. While Mary unpacked her trunk into a small wardrobe Edward had sent up from the palace storeroom, the little girl maintained her silence. But when Mary removed a doll from the trunk, Anne's hand shot out and grabbed the beautifully clothed plaything. "'Tis mine!" she snapped in English.

"I'm sure it is," replied the maid with a kind smile. "Tis a lovely doll. Has she a name?"

The child lapsed back into silence, clutching the doll to her chest.

The exchange disturbed Batsheva, but she said nothing. Obviously, the child was unhappy, and she understood the pain at being wrenched from one's home. Still, she could not understand why Anne showed no interest in news of her father. Drawing Edward into the outer chamber, away from the child, Batsheva asked why he had brought her.

Edward closed the door between the two chambers. "My grandmother is not well. She and Anne traveled down to York for the holiday, but I think it was really because she is failing. My own family is a noisy, boisterous crew and Anne simply refused to join in. She sat for hours near the hearth in the great hall in silence. Neither my mother nor my sisters could coax her. 'Twas my grandmother's decision to send her to you…not to her father; I told her about you. She thought Anne could benefit by your gentle counsel."

"How much," asked Batsheva with some alarm, "did you tell her?"

"Not everything, but enough to convince her that you may be the one to help Anne. We are all worried about the child."

"I can see why," she responded with a frown. "What do you know of her?"

"She has been lonely in Durham. 'Tis a great, empty space with naught for a child to do. She's the only child there and isolated by it. She needs a mother's guidance."

"I will try, Edward," sighed Batsheva, thinking of her own Amina.

"That is all I can ask." He started to leave.

"Edward, wait!" she called before he reached the door. "How will the earl take this?"

"Well, I hope," he swallowed. "You will manage him."

Batsheva laughed with more confidence than she felt. "I suppose I will have to."

Only when Anne was tucked beneath thick down and fur covers did Batsheva take a few moments to stare into the hearth, herself, and consider her new project. Anne was Amina's age when her mother died. Was Amina doing the same thing wherever she was? Batsheva closed her eyes and tried to conjure up the faces of her twins. Only six months had passed since she saw them ride off to the Well of Tears with the other children, yet it seemed years had passed. *Does she miss me? Does Daud ask for me when he awakens in the night?* She refused to consider the twins as anything but safely tucked away somewhere with Sufiye and Khalil's people.

Fighting off her own desire to weep, Batsheva dragged herself into the bedchamber and allowed Mary to help her undress. After she dismissed her maid, she stole into the other chamber and stood over Anne's bed, watching the sleeping child. Concern and pity welled up in her heart. Softly, she brushed away a lock of flaxen hair that had fallen across Anne's face. The child stirred but did not awaken. Bending over, she kissed the pale forehead. "Sleep well, little girl," she whispered against the small shell of her ear. "Sleep well and we shall begin anew in the morning."

But the morning was no better. Anne ate her breakfast in stoic silence. She allowed Mary to help her dress but refused to talk. When Batsheva asked her how she spent her days, the child merely shrugged.

Batsheva was stymied by the sullen silence of the girl. Even Amina, who more often than not hid behind her mother's burnous, was more openly curious than Anne. Batsheva chided herself at the comparison, then concentrated on trying to draw the child into conversation. To each question came a two-word reply: *Oui, Madame; non, Madame; merci, Madame,* until Batsheva thought she would scream. Out of desperation, she tried another tack. "The weather is not so cold today. Would you like to see the shops?"

The girl shrugged again, then nodded. Anything was better than staying indoors. Once again, she let Mary help her get ready.

Outside, the sun was shining in a perfectly blue sky and the air was crisp. Accompanied by two footmen and Mary, they set off across still frozen streets.

Their first stop was at Jane's shop. The seamstress was quite surprised when Batsheva came through the door with a child. "What have we here?" she asked in her jovial, lilting voice.

"Allow me to introduce my lord earl's daughter, the Lady Anne of Durham. Lady Anne, this is my friend, Jane Blank." Batsheva frowned when the girl remained silent. "I'm afraid Lady Anne is rather shy, Jane. I thought perhaps you might have something which would be suitable for a young lady."

Jane smiled at the pink-cheeked Anne. "I think I have just the right material to bring a smile to those great blue eyes." She bustled into the back room and emerged a moment later with a bolt of cloth wrapped in muslin. "This just arrived," she explained as she lay the parcel on the table and began untying the strings. "'Tis small, short in length, but just enough for a young lady's cote." A bolt of bright blue silk appeared from beneath the plain white cloth. "What think you of this, my lady?" Jane held up the cloth for Batsheva's inspection.

Batsheva gasped when she saw the cloth. It was finely woven silk samite with threads of silver shot through the fabric. It was so like fabric she had purchased in Benghazi that she was stunned at the sight of it. "How came you by this, Jane?" she asked.

"A merchant brought it directly to me," said Jane, "with many stories, but I bought it because it was so beautiful." She stared hard at Batsheva.

Anne stepped forward and fingered the fine material. "'Tis not practical. It would not suit me at all."

This was the longest sentence the child had yet to utter and its content disappointed Batsheva. "But do you not think a new frock is in order, Anne?"

"My garments are adequate, Madame," she answered.

"Adequate for Durham," Mary stated bluntly, "but not for Westminster." The maid turned to Batsheva. "My lady, when the queen returns, she will expect to meet the Lady Anne. The frocks she brought are serviceable garments, but hardly suited to meet her majesty."

Jane unrolled the bolt and held the end up across Anne's body. "With a white chemise and a narrow girdle, she would most certainly be presentable."

"Yes," agreed Batsheva, "I think you are right. Mary, please take Anne into the back. Jane will need to take measurements." With a firm hand,

Mary did as she was told. When the curtain closed behind them, Batsheva turned to Jane. "What stories?"

"'Twas a strange thing, Bess," said the seamstress, "a swarthy man came to my shop. He asked if I was the one who sewed for the copper-haired countess. I was very cagey and said I might, but I might not be that one. He showed me the cloth and bade me show it to you. I said there was not enough to make a lady's frock and he said it was of no matter. You would recognize such fine cloth when you saw it."

"This man, Jane, did he speak English or French?"

"French, with a strange accent."

"What did he look like?"

"Oh, he was fierce looking, like a Spaniard. He had dark eyes and a dark beard. A pointy dark beard." She thought for a moment. "He was well dressed, but his clothing was odd. He wore a strange cape."

"How was it strange?" Batsheva knew Jane would notice something like that.

"It was sewn in layers, four that I could count, each one a different shade of grey, the darkest on the outside, the lightest inside. The clasp was twisted brass…or perhaps old gold, I could not tell which, and at the center of it was a brown stone."

The cape was not strange to Batsheva; it was a burnous from Al-Andalus. "Did he wear a ring?" pressed Batsheva.

"Yes," Jane whispered, "he wore a ring on his forefinger, with another brown stone like the one on his cape."

Batsheva sat down with a thump. Jane had just described one of her father's emissaries on the continent, a fellow named Ezra. "Did he say anything else?"

"When I paid him for the cloth, he would not take as much as it was worth. He said it was enough to know that the cloth would find its proper owner. He meant you, didn't he?"

"The cloth is mine." whispered Batsheva, fighting back tears, "some-one knows I'm alive."

CHAPTER 19

Westminster

JANUARY 1192

"Anne," Batsheva asked slowly, "do you know why Edward brought you here?" Servants had cleared the supper dishes, Mary had been dismissed for the night, and now Batsheva and Anne sat alone in the outer chamber. After three days of foul weather made worse by Anne's sullenness, Batsheva was at her wits' end with the girl. Sooner or later Durham would be back from Southampton, and this was not how the earl should encounter his daughter.

"Non, Madame."

"Do you think we might guess the reason?" Batsheva prodded gently.

The girl frowned. "*Non, Madame.*"

"Do you think Edward brought you to Westminster to be my serving girl?"

The frown deepened but she straightened just a little. "*Non, Madame,*" she replied almost emphatically.

"Do you think he brought you here to be an ornament in these chambers?"

"*Non, Madame.*"

"Or, perhaps, he brought you here because he thought you might like to see your father."

There was a brief pause before she said, "*Non, Madame.*"

"Do you want to see your father?" Batsheva asked gently.

This time, the girl stared not at Batsheva, but at her hands. "*Non, Madame.*"

She was not surprised by the answer. "Perhaps he thought your father would want to see you?"

Slowly, the blue eyes rose. "Why would he want to see me now, Madame? He has never wanted to see me before."

There was undoubtedly great pain behind the icy stare and Batsheva felt great empathy for the child. Did Daud or Amina think the same thing of her? Batsheva drew a footstool close to Anne's chair and sat down so she could look up at the child, rather than down. Taking the small hands in her own, she spoke softly. "Sometimes, Anne, parents cannot do what they know is right for their children. Sometimes, a mother or a father must be separated from the ones they love most even if they truly want to be there." There was no change in Anne's expression, but Batsheva pressed on. "I know you have been without your father for a very long time, but what I think you do not know is that your father cares deeply for you."

"You are wrong, Madame," said Anne suddenly. "My father went away because he could not bear to be near me. I know this to be true."

Batsheva was puzzled. Edward assured her that she was well-loved at home and she could not imagine someone pouring such nonsense in the child's ear. "Who told you such a thing, Anne?"

"Charlotte de Blois," she whispered.

"And who is Charlotte de Blois?" asked Batsheva.

"Lady Isabella's daughter. Her father is dead."

"Oh, I see. Is she much older than you?"

The little girl shook her head. "We are the same age."

"And did she tell you how she came by this knowledge?"

The little voice grew hard when she said, "Her mother told her. She told her my father ran away from me because I remind him of my dead mother." Her lower lip quivered just a little, giving away the pain and anger she was so obviously feeling.

"And you believed her, Anne?" The fair head nodded slowly. "Did you ever ask anyone about this?" This time, the head moved from side to side. "You know, Anne, there may be a tiny bit of truth in what Charlotte told you, but I think it is not the whole truth."

"But it is!" she cried, "Papa never comes to Durham to stay. He just comes, then goes away again for a very long time."

"Perhaps that is because he does the king's bidding," suggested Batsheva.

The head shook firmly from side to side. "He did not have to go to the Holy Land. He went because he wanted to get away from England. From me. Charlotte says he knows I killed my mother because I did not love her; I did not pray hard enough for her when the babe was being born. She told me I was going to hell because I didn't want a new brother!" Tears slid slowly down the pale cheeks. "'Twas my fault they died."

"How could it be your fault, Anne?" gently asked Batsheva. "You could not have prevented what happened to your mother and brother."

"I could have prayed harder. I know I could have. But I did not. I did not want the babe."

"Oh, sweetheart," cried Batsheva, gathering the child into her arms. "Of course you didn't. 'Tis always hard for a little one when a new babe is expected! You did nothing wrong! You were a babe yourself." The flood-gates were opened, and they were both weeping. "Your mother knew you loved her and I'm sure she told you that over and over."

"I don't remember," lisped Anne.

"And your father loves you so much that he cannot bear to be sad when he is near you. He is not running away from you, dearest Anne; he is running away from himself."

The blue eyes bore into hers. "How can you be so certain, Madame?"

"'Tis the way of men; they do not understand the heart as we women do; we must help him to stop being afraid. He loved your mother very much and her death hurt him gravely; he still grieves for her. But," added Batsheva with a hint of a smile as she wiped Anne's eyes with her hand, "you are alive and well and healthy and beautiful, and he needs to know you so very much."

Anne thought about all this for a long moment. "I am not so certain, Madame. I have been told so many different things and I am not so certain about any of them."

"What have you been told, Anne?" Batsheva prodded. "Perhaps if you told me about them, I could help you understand."

The pink lips turned downward. "None of it was very nice," she murmured.

"Well," sighed the lady, "there's not much we can do about that, save talk about it." The weight of Anne against her belly was becoming uncomfortable. Shifting her position, she helped Anne to perch on what was left of her lap. "There, that's a little better, do you not think so?"

Anne smiled tentatively. "'Tis comfortable, Madame."

"And that's another thing, Anne. You must not call me *Madame.* It makes me feel quite old. Call me Bess, for that is what your father calls me."

The little girl was surprised at the remark. "How old are you?" she asked boldly.

Batsheva sighed, but smiled when she answered, "To you, I must seem very old, but come the spring, I will be 22."

"Oooh, that's not old at all! Lady Isabella says she is twenty-eight, but she is really older. She has set her eyes on my father. Charlotte says her mother thinks he is lusty." Anne realized what she said and clapped her hands over her mouth.

But Batsheva only laughed. "I have met the lady, and you tell me nothing I do not already know."

"Charlotte told me her mother encountered you here, at Westminster." The little girl leaned forward and spoke in hushed, conspiratorial tones. "When the lady heard my father had arrived from the Holy Land, she left her home the same day. But when she returned, Charlotte said she was quite angry."

"Is that when you heard things that were not nice?"

"They came to York at Christmas," Anne nodded. "Charlotte said you were fat. And unpleasant. And homely. And that there was something terribly wrong with your hair."

"I *am* fat!" laughed Batsheva. "I am with child. And as for my hair," she pulled her wimple from her head and shook out her short curls, "I suppose it is rather odd."

"'Tis so short! Like a boy's!" Suddenly, Anne giggled. "Is this the style in the Holy Land?"

"No," Batsheva replied adding her own giggle. "I cut off my hair."

"Why?"

She debated telling Anne the truth and decided on a modified version of the tale. "I wanted to join my lord. To do so, I dressed as a boy. No proper boy would have waist-length hair, so I chopped it off with a knife!"

"Was my father angry?"

Batsheva chewed her lip for a moment. "'Twas not your father I planned to meet. 'Twas my late lord."

"Oh, you are widowed." Her voice was very soft again.

Nodding, Batsheva told her that she was. "He fell in battle," she said, careful not to say *died*. "Your father rescued me from another battle. He thought I was a boy and thought to make me his page."

"And then he found you were a lady and fell madly in love with you?"

She hugged the girl tightly. "Not quite like that, but that will do for now. Perhaps when you are older I will be able to better explain."

Anne frowned just a little. "I hear that often enough."

Batsheva felt she was moving into dangerous territory and opted to change the subject. "Charlotte sounds like a fascinating child," she said. Somehow, from Isabella's brief mention of her children, she had assumed, wrongly, that they were quite young. Obviously, Charlotte was old enough to participate in rather adult conversations. "Tell me more about her."

This is a subject Anne was more comfortable with. "She's bigger than I am, even though we are the same age. Charlotte likes to wear very fancy frocks and she never gets dirty."

"Do you like to get dirty, Anne?"

An impish smile played on her rosebud mouth. "Well, sometimes," she drawled.

"When I was your age, I loved to get very dirty. I played with my brothers when we weren't studying our lessons. I even learned to fight with a sword."

"A real sword?" gasped Anne.

"A real sword." Batsheva untied the ribbon on her left sleeve and pushed up the fabric. "This," she said, pointing to a thin white scar, barely visible, about two inches long, "is from a duel I won in my mother's rose garden. My brother drew first blood. But I got him back; I flipped the sword right out of his hand."

"What did your mother do?" gasped Anne with eyes as wide as dinner plates.

"She scolded us severely, but my father gave me a prize for winning."

"What did he give you?"

"My own sword!" The two dissolved into a fit of giggles.

Anne rested her head against Batsheva's breast and yawned. "Charlotte said you are from Al-Andalus. Would you tell me about Al-Andalus? They say it is always warm there."

"I will tell you about my home," replied Batsheva as she brushed a kiss on Anne's forehead, "if you get into your nightgown and let me help you get ready for bed."

Anne slipped from the sheltering safety of Batsheva's arm and padded across the thick tapestry to the bedchamber door. "You should rest," said the girl with her chin jutting out ever so slightly, "'tis been a long day and you must be so very tired. I can manage myself."

"Will you call me when you are ready to hear a story?"

"Most assuredly...Bess." The child disappeared behind the oak door only to reappear a scant moment later in her nightclothes. "My frock is folded and I have washed. I am ready."

Batsheva looked at the fresh-scrubbed face and marveled at the difference a few words could make. "Come here and let me tie your ribbons and brush out your hair." Anne scampered to Batsheva and stood with her back to the lady. "Let me know if I hurt you, for I shouldn't want to do that."

Anne was about to say something when there was a loud commotion in the corridor. The door flew open and Durham clattered into the room. His cape was gone, but the tabard over his mail shirt with spattered with mud. His face, still red from cold, was just as filthy. He had remembered to remove his boots, but his chausses were dirty and torn. When he saw Anne standing in front of Batsheva, before she dashed behind the lady's chair, he stopped dead in his tracks. "Anne?" he called softly.

Batsheva stood and took Anne's hand in hers to draw the girl forward. "Good evening, my lord. Anne," she whispered, leaning close, "can you greet your father?"

Two blue eyes stared up at the tall, fair-haired man with eyes that matched her own. Her father, even in half-armor, was an awesome, frightening sight. Licking her lips nervously, she dipped a little curtsey and said, "*Bonsoir, Papa.* "

Durham stared back at the child he had not seen in years. She was a miniature Joan, right down to the way her lashes fluttered against her pale cheek when she was nervous. Dropping down to one knee, he opened his arms to her. "I am so very, very glad to see you," he said.

The girl looked from her father to Batsheva and saw the lady nod. She took two hesitant steps toward Durham, then launched herself into his arms. He almost crushed her in his embrace as he buried his face in the flaxen hair, murmuring her name over and over.

From where she stood, Batsheva could see Durham weep and she could not help the tears that trickled from her own eyes. The sight of father and daughter warmed her soul, yet a sharp stab of pain tore through her heart; would that it was Khalil holding Amina!

Then, Durham pushed the child back, still holding her arms. "Let me look at you, my sweet babe!" he laughed against his tears. "You are not a babe at all! You're but a grown woman! And I've made you dirty with travel mud!"

"I do not care, Papa," she smiled shyly.

"You will in the morning," chuckled the earl, kissing the tip of her nose. He scooped her up into his arms and the widest smile Batsheva had ever seen split his face in two when Anne began to giggle. "But right now, you are still my little girl. Why, you weigh less than a feather!" He danced around the room with the child pressed against him.

Batsheva let them dance for the moment, relieved that Durham was happy to find his daughter at Westminster. Finally, when he slowed his pace, she took on the role of mother. "There will be endless time for you two to play, but right now, Anne needs a clean nightgown to replace the one you have muddied," she said in her best maternal voice. The sound of it caught in her ears; she winced at her own brief pain, then pushed it aside.

Durham frowned and pouted but carried Anne into the bedchamber and deposited her on her bed. "I am glad you have come, Annie Lamb," he said as he untied her ribbons.

"Are you, Papa? Are you really?"

"Of course, I am, little goose. Did you think I would not be?" He kissed her cheeks with big, smacking kisses.

Anne sighed as she touched his rough, bearded cheek. "I did not know, Papa. Edward said you would be happy, but…."

"Someone told you I would not be? Should I guess who the someone was?"

"Oh, I should not think you would know, Papa," Anne giggled.

Durham perched on the edge of the bed. "It was not my mother, your grandmother," he began slowly, "and it certainly was not your Aunt Maggie, I'll wager. So," he drawled the last word slowly, "I would guess that you had conversation with Charlotte de Blois."

The little girl nodded very slowly. "She told me terrible things and none of them, not even one, was true, Papa."

"Turn around," Batsheva instructed Durham. Quickly, she removed Anne's muddied gown and replaced it with a new one, using a clean corner of the old one to wipe the child's face. "You may turn around, my lord."

Durham was careful not to hug Anne again as he helped her into the bed. "You will sleep soundly knowing you are safe, and there is naught to worry about." He tucked the bedclothes around her slender form and gave her one last kiss. "In the morning, I will answer all your questions and you will answer all of mine. Until then, *ma chère petite*, sleep well."

"Is she not beautiful?" sighed Durham when the door to the bedchamber was shut.

"Beautiful, yes, and quite stubborn. Be thankful you did not arrive sooner, monsieur. You would have encountered a very different scene," she told him sternly.

"Oh?" Durham began stripping off his armor, automatically handing each piece to Batsheva who piled them in the corner where Jamie would retrieve them in the morning.

"Edward brought her here without warning three days ago," she explained. "She was frightened and completely unprepared for this change of venue. Your dear friend Isabella managed to pass a good deal of damaging information about you *and* me to Anne through her own daughter... as you had guessed."

"'Twas no guess, Bess. Edward warned me. He said they had been to York at Christmas."

"Well, Edward did not warn me," snapped Batsheva, suddenly angry at them all. "Anne was sullen and silent for three days, Durham. She was angry at being taken away from York, although she was not happy there either. Your mother is not well, and your sister was not prepared to provide Anne with the time and the comfort she needed. Instead, the child was exposed to that horrid Charlotte and damage was done."

"You seem to have undone it," said Durham somewhat dryly. Wearing only his braies he went to the basin and began washing the dirt from his body.

"On the surface, Durham, *only* on the surface," she argued. "The child is hurt by your lack of attention and while tonight is sweet, you must realize that she does not completely trust you. She wants to trust you but has no history with you. If you want to be her parent, then be one. Do not expect me to take your place!"

Durham looked up, confused. "But you seem to like Anne?"

Batsheva sighed with exasperation. "She's lovely, but I am afraid to let her think of me as mother. I will leave here, Durham. She will have to know and understand that. My own children need their mother."

"I do not want you to leave, Bess," he said softly.

"'Tis not your decision." She saw the pain etched in his face and her heart ached for him. "You need a wife, Gilbert; a real wife; one who will bear your children and be a mother to Anne. I cannot be that woman."

"But the amir is dead," he protested. "You are free to marry."

"I have no proof." She debated telling him about the bolt of blue silk but decided against it. "Until I have proof that he is dead, I cannot help but hope he is alive."

"What proof do you want, Bess?" Durham asked angrily, mindful to keep his voice down. "Do you want his corpse? Shall I send a messenger to Akko to bring it back for you?"

"I do not know!" cried Batsheva, suddenly feeling desperately alone. She fled the sitting room for the dark safety of her bed.

She wept silently for hours, but in the dark hour before the dawn, she began a practical examination of her options. Return to Alexandria, for that would be the likely place to go, was not an immediate possibility. The real problem, decided Batsheva as she lay in her bed that night, was that she knew she could love Gilbert of Durham if she allowed herself to. The strength of his arms, the twinkle in his eyes, his unyielding sense of honor were all things that appealed to her. She believed him when he said he was not the one who killed Khalil. Still, a niggling, nagging corner of her heart warned her against loving him; there was a portion of her left behind in that other part of the world and she needed to return there to be complete. Part of her was convinced Khalil was dead, yet she cherished an ember of hope he was not, and that she would be reunited with her children. Torn and upset, she tossed beneath the down covers until exhaustion, pure and simple, forced her to sleep.

In the morning, she found Durham and Anne sitting at the table speaking in hushed tones. As soon as they saw her, twin smiles graced their faces and Durham rose from his chair. "Come eat, Bess; 'tis late and you must be starved!"

She let Durham hold her chair. "I apologize for being so long abed," she said between bites of cheese and bread. "Already I have missed my morning exercise."

"Do not apologize," said a subdued Durham, "for I was the one who sent Mary away when she would have awakened you." He glanced conspiratorially at Anne. "'Tis a beautiful day, Bess; Annie and I have already been out for a ride."

"Have you?" asked Batsheva. "And what great wonders did you see, Anne?"

The child giggled before she answered, "Oh, Bess, I saw a wonderful sight we think you should see, too. Please say you'll come with us!"

Batsheva chewed a slice of cheese slowly, as though she were thinking it over. "I suppose I have no choice," she said slowly, glancing up at Durham.

The double meaning was not lost on Durham. "I've business with the king's chamberlain. Be dressed when I return, and we shall go." He kissed Anne's forehead, then left the apartments.

Wherever Durham was taking her, it seemed Batsheva was the only one who didn't know about it. Sighing, she lowered herself into the chair and let Mary brush out her short curls. Her hair was growing quickly now, but it was not fast enough to repair the damage she had done when she lopped off her long tresses.

Mary's skilled fingers managed to braid the sides flat against her head while leaving the back alone. Using a wide ribbon of ivory linen, she tied off a headband over Batsheva's ears. Over this, she dropped a wimple that wrapped around the throat before being dropped behind the shoulders. "There, that should keep your ears from freezing, my lady," announced Mary with satisfaction. "'Tis odd, but I wager you'll be setting the new fashion by spring."

Mary handed Batsheva a round fur cap. "This should sit atop it all, my lady. It matches the fur of your peliçon."

"Did Jane send this?" she asked as she carefully examined the hat.

"No, his lordship did."

Batsheva set the hat on her head and admired the way it framed her face. "I like it," she commented as she adjusted the rim. Taking the cloak from Mary, she went into the outer chamber.

Anne was sitting at the table staring at a piece of parchment her father left behind. "Papa says you can read this," she said when Batsheva joined her at the table.

"This and much more. I read and write in several languages."

The girl looked quite surprised. "Does my father think it strange?"

"A bit," shrugged Batsheva, "but there is nothing he can do about it; I am already more learned than he."

"Would you teach me to read and write?"

This time, it was Batsheva who looked shocked. "You do not know your letters?" The girl shook her head. "Then you shall learn them! Both French and English. It is not proper for a lady to be unschooled. How is it your grandmother has neglected your education?"

"Our confessor says a woman with learning will not be content to be a wife; she will want more."

"Nonsense," Batsheva shot back. "Not even your father believes that! We shall begin this afternoon when we return from our excursion."

A shiny new box coach was waiting for the earl, his lady, and his daughter. Durham lifted Anne into the conveyance and was about to offer his arm to Batsheva when she took a step backward to study the new acquisition. The outside was black, but inside, she could see thick, padded cushions and fox lap robes folded neatly on the seats. His personal crest was painted on the door. "I ordered it be fitted for you the day we arrived in Westminster."

"Do you like it, Bess?" gushed Anne. "Please say that you like it!"

"I do. It is very beautiful," Batsheva turned to the earl. "A costly piece of work, my lord," she commented.

"Nothing but the best for Bess and Anne. Are you pleased?"

"This will give me more freedom. I must confess, monsieur, I was beginning to feel somewhat chained to the palace. Walking to the mews and back for exercise is all well and good, but the scenery never changes."

"Why do you walk only to the mews," asked Anne.

Batsheva smiled. "I go to see Yaffa. She is so unhappy but there is little I can do about it."

"Yaffa?" asked Anne. "Who is Yaffa?'

The adults both laughed. "My horse, "admitted Batsheva. "She came with me from the Holy Land."

"May I see her?"

"Of course! You shall come with me on my daily exercise to the mews. Perhaps you can sit upon her and walk with us. That might liven her spirits."

"Oh, I would like that so very much."

"Then consider it done," Batsheva grinned.

Durham's eyebrows came together. "I had not reckoned you would want to keep up your furious pace once we settled in," he admitted rather sheepishly.

Unexpectedly, Batsheva touched his cheek with her gloved hand. "My lord earl, I am used to a nomadic life. 'Twas nothing to awaken at dawn, strike camp and move on, only to set up camp at dusk. Even when I was with child, I rode every day until the very size of me prevented my mounting a horse." She smiled at him. 'Tis a wonderful conveyance, though. Thank you, my lord."

He swept a deep, courtly bow. "'Twas my pleasure, my lady." He proffered his arm and helped her into the box.

After a long drive through the city and its environs, Batsheva was ready to return to Westminster. Much of what she saw amazed her; the grand houses, the frozen river, and the market that bustled in spite of the cold weather. Durham played footman while Batsheva and Anne investigated some of the stalls. The ladies made several purchases, for all of which Durham insisted on paying.

Her head was full of ideas during the ride back to Westminster. "I expect the rugs we ordered to arrive soon," she said, furrowing her brows in thought, "we shall be far more comfortable once proper rugs are on the floors instead of what we have now."

"I much prefer the tapestries on the walls where they belong," admitted Durham, "but no one has seen rugs in London. Did the merchant know what it is you seek?"

"Oh, yes, he understood completely. T'would seem the queen is planning to bring rugs when she returns from Normandy."

Durham winced at the mention of Eleanor's return. He knew that, as soon as she set foot on English soil, the great councils would be convened, and he would be forced to leave Batsheva's side once more. Suddenly, he was glad for Anne's company; at least she would keep Batsheva busy with the art and craft of mothering.

Batsheva was still talking to him. "Jane says that the cloth I want from France should be here soon, too. We will be very busy sewing for the babe." She patted her stomach.

"Jamie wants to marry her," Durham blurted out.

Batsheva stopped talking and stared at him. "Truly?"

"Truly. He will ask her this week," he said, happy to tell her something she did not already know. "It makes a great good sense. He needs a wife and she needs a man."

"She does quite well on her own," countered Batsheva. "She has a good business."

"That she would give up gladly if she had a husband."

"Not every woman needs a husband, monsieur," she replied, annoyed. "There are times a husband is a greater inconvenience than a convenience."

"Oh? Are you of that mind, my lady?"

Batsheva glanced at Anne who had fallen asleep leaning against the side of the coach, wrapped in a lap robe. Keeping her voice low, she countered, "Yes, I am. I, for one, am well aware of the inconvenience of being tied to a man."

"I did not mean it in that way, Bess. I only meant…."

She cut him off before he could answer. "What you meant is that a woman requires the presence of a man…a protector. I was managing perfectly well before you swept me off to sea."

"As I recall," groused Durham, "I found you lying face down in the sand."

"*That*," she snapped, still whispering, "was because *you* had no control over *your* troops. Khalil's men would never have disobeyed him in that manner."

"And I would never have left my wife and children in so unprotected a location."

Batsheva's hands were clenched into tight-fisted balls. "Do not presume…."

"'Tis done, Bess!" hissed Durham, "'tis over. What was done is done. You are here, not in Palaestina or Alexandria or anywhere else you may want to be. You are heavy with child and under *my* protection. And you should thank your God that I was the one who found you. Heaven only knows how you would have met your end had a less chivalrous knight discovered your *hidden* charms."

"My God? *My* God? How dare you? Or perhaps you've forgotten your precious savior was one of us!" Her eyes narrowed into dark grey slits. "Remember this, Christian, we…came…first!" She clamped her mouth shut, signaling the end of the conversation.

Durham glowered at her from across the coach. When she should have been grateful for his protection, she flung it in his face. Instead of thanking him for her rescue, she cursed him for his chivalry. Any other woman would have bent a knee in thanksgiving for his generosity, yet she refused to acknowledge his good intention. Her anger was palpable, and it angered him in turn. Finally, turning his face away from her, he closed his eyes and feigned sleep.

CHAPTER 20

Westminster

JANUARY 1192

For Anne's sake, Batsheva and Durham behaved well in public, but at night, when the child was tucked in, they barely spoke. She busied herself with tasks for the forthcoming birth while he went about the business of government. The queen's expected arrival, coupled with increasingly bad news from Southampton, kept the earl closeted with the queen's counselors who remained in London. Word had come from Normandy that full councils were to be convened as soon as Eleanor set foot on English soil.

Added to that, much to Durham's annoyance, were the upcoming nuptials for his squire and the dressmaker. They were to be married on Thursday with Durham and Batsheva as their witnesses.

Batsheva was nervous about the ceremony, but Edward explained what would occur in the mass and prepared her as best he could. "The Archbishop will be too preoccupied to notice you," he promised, "so watch Gilbert; do as he does. I will make certain he does not make confession beforehand, so you will be spared the need to take Holy Communion. No one will question this."

"What if he asks me if I have made confession?" asked Batsheva with concern. "What shall I say?"

"Simply smile down at your belly and sigh. That should be enough of an excuse."

The wedding day dawned bright and, with the rising sun, Batsheva began preparations for the wedding luncheon to be served after the mass. The kitchen staff was by now used to her forays into their domain and they greeted her with pleasure as she checked the menu one last time with the cook.

At the appointed hour, Batsheva and Anne led a blushing Jane to the queen's chapel. Jamie awaited her at the altar, his face pink from a scrubbing, his new clothes shining like a beacon amid the flickering light of dozens of candles. Durham stood beside him wearing a hauberk Batsheva had not seen, looking uncommonly handsome but as nervous as the groom. From her place at the side of the altar, Batsheva watched him from beneath half-closed eyes and wondered what he was thinking.

Durham barely listened to the service. He was keenly aware of Batsheva's proximity; he longed to touch her hand. Almost as sharp was his desire to be the one standing before the Archbishop. As the Frenchman droned on, he felt himself wishing the mass were ended. If Batsheva's refusal to marry him continued, he thought he would go mad.

The wedding feast passed in a haze of muted color for both Batsheva and Durham. They sat smiling at the festivities, participating as best they could. Only Anne seemed oblivious to impending upheaval as she sat at the high board between her father and Jane.

The newlyweds returned to Westminster from Jane's house the next afternoon. Jane, bundled against the cold in a cocoon of grey wool, bustled in chamber. "'Tis bitter cold outside," she complained as she unwound her wraps. "I would not have come had you not sent your carriage, my lord."

"What!" cried Durham, "Jamie isn't keeping you warm enough? I should have a word with him."

"Have all the words you like, my lord. It will not change the weather."

"You did bring him with you, did you not? Or have you killed him with loving, Mistress FitzHugh?"

"More like he tried to kill me, my lord. 'Twas a grand wedding night," Jane sighed. "Aye, I brought him. Not that he wanted to leave the warmth of our bed! You'll find him recovering in the stables."

It was Durham who blushed this time. "Come, Annie, let us find poor Jamie!"

No sooner had Durham and Anne left, a commotion was heard outside the door. They could hear Mary's exasperation, and ran to see what was amiss. "Carpets" cried Batsheva.

Mary was directing three men up the stairs, large rolls perched on their shoulders. "These have just arrived, my lady."

Batsheva stepped aside to let them pass, and told them where to place the rolls. "If you would be so kind as to take these tapestries for a beating," she said, pointing to the ones on the floor, "and then return them for hanging. And Mary, the stones must be swept and swabbed."

The men set to work on their task while the ladies waited patiently nearby. Finally, the last tapestry was carried from the apartment. Mary returned with two charwomen and soon the stone floors were near to sparkling.

Once the charwomen were gone, Batsheva turned her attention to the bundles near the door. "Shall we see how I've spent the good earl's coin?"

Mary cut the cord on the first rug and unrolled the corner. "'Tis beautiful!" she cried as the deep red appeared. "Are they all like this?"

"I do not know, Mary," laughed Batsheva. "I simply said find six rugs and bring them to me."

"Six? There are seven."

One by one, they cut the thick twine to expose the rugs. The first two seemed to be well matched with a field of deep red into which a fantasy of flowers had been woven. The third and fourth rugs were similar, but the decoration was more subdued. The next two were more masculine; instead of flowers, Moorish swirls and arches dominated over a center field of dark, dark blue. "These last two," announced Batsheva, pleased with the rugs, "are for my lord's chamber."

"And what about this little one?" asked Mary, pointing to the last bundle "'Tis much smaller than the others."

"Perhaps it will lay well before the hearth," suggested Jane. The porter did as he was told and put it before the enormous mantle.

Batsheva took the knife from Mary and slashed the cord. As if it had a life of its own, the little rug unrolled. Jane and Mary gasped at the vivid picture before them, but Batsheva reached for something to support her.

"Bess? Bess, are you all right?" cried Jane and she hurried to Batsheva's side.

The lady was speechless. There, on the floor at her feet, lay the rug covered with monkeys. She stared at it while tears burned her eyes. She was unable to speak.

"Mary, go to the kitchen," ordered the seamstress as she pulled a stool over for Batsheva, "and fetch some mulled wine for the lady." The maid did as she was told, and Jane closed the door. "What is it, Bess? Shall I call the earl?"

"No," she cried sharply.

"Let me roll this up."

"No! Leave it." She slipped off the stool and knelt on the rug, letting her hands run slowly over the thick wool. "'Tis from Abdul Hadji," she whispered. She looked up at Jane, her face stricken with pain. "'Tis *my* rug, Jane. 'Twas a wedding gift to me."

Jane knelt down beside her. "When you wed your late lord?"

Batsheva shook her head. She had never told Jane the whole story, fearing what her friend would think if she knew. She had the sudden need to speak the names, to recount the tale, but she knew this was not the time.

There was a clatter outside the room before Durham burst in. "Mary said you were faint. Is it the babe?"

"No," she answered as she struggled to her feet. When Durham extended his hand to her, she refused it. "I am all right."

Jane quietly left the room. Whatever meaning this rug had for her friend, she would find out later. For now, the earl was there, and all conversation would cease.

Durham stared down at the strange little rug. "Does this displease you, Bess?"

She shook her head. "In too many ways, it pleases me greatly."

Despite her refusal, he took her elbow and guided her to the bedchamber. "Lie down for a while, Bess," he said softly. "I shall have supper brought to you later. I fear the day has been tiresome for you."

She did not argue. Instead, she let him tuck a cover around her and closed her eyes. Someone knew where she was; if she had any doubts when the bolt of cloth appeared, she had none now. The only question she had was *who*?

CHAPTER 21

Alexandria

JANUARY 1192

Avram Hagiz was ushered into the chamber by a guard with a wide scimitar at his waist, yet he felt no fear as he awaited the return of the amir. He glanced around the well-appointed room and spotted evidence of children scattered in one corner. He could not help but smile; children were children wherever they were, even in this secluded wing of the sultan's Alexandria palace.

The amir entered from the garden. Khalil's face no longer matched the color of his fine linen kaftan; his skin had resumed its healthy deep tan. Still, the first thing Avram noticed was the limp although it was much improved from the last time be had visited. He did not bow when Khalil approached; the amir would not have expected him to. "Welcome back, Uncle Avram. I hope your news is good today," he grinned as he embraced the older man.

"Both good and bad, Khalil. The sultan continues to hold Jerusalem, but the war goes badly for all involved."

"It is to be expected," grunted Khalil as he lowered himself onto the cushions of his divan. "If the Christians had any sense at all, they would quit this endeavor and go home."

The older man joined him. "But they do not, so they fight on. Malik Rik, however, has troubles of his own in England and has been summoned to return. His brother threatens his throne."

Malik Rik was feared by most of the Muslim forces as a man enchanted in battle. He was, to their eyes, indestructible. "Has he gone?"

The old man shook his head. "Not yet. They say he will leave in the spring."

"And what of our other affairs, Avram?" asked Khalil, almost afraid of the answer.

"She is most definitely in England, under the protection of the Earl of Durham as we suspected. Some say she is his wife."

"His wife?" choked Khalil. "That is not possible!"

"You know Batsheva better than I," shrugged Avram. "I cannot believe she would wed with a Christian by her own will."

"Let us hope you are right, or I will kill them both," he growled.

Avram frowned at Khalil. "I think it unlikely she is married, but remember, she has no reason to believe you are alive. Kassim himself told her you fell in battle. If she believes she is a widow, then…."

"Do we know this for certain?" he asked through clenched teeth.

"Ezra Torres has been dispatched from Málaga, my lord, with an item she will recognize: the blue silk cloth we found in her trunk. You, yourself, said she was saving it for Amina."

"But will she understand how this comes to be with her?"

"This I cannot say, but Batsheva is sharp. At the very least, she will know that she has been found."

But does she want to be found? Khalil furrowed his brow. "I will leave for England as soon as travel is possible."

"Khalil, no Muslim has ever made the trip!" protested Avram. "Please, let us handle this within the family. We have people we trust in England."

"No," the amir snapped, "and risk Yehuda slitting her throat while she sleeps?"

"It is true Yehuda remains angry, but he is a rash young man and given to passing fits of temper." An uneasy silence hung between them for several long moments. At last, Avram said, "Do not let yourself be rash when you find her; hear her out before you do anything to jeopardize her safety or your own. You have more to take into account now than ever before. In a month's time, you will be named successor in Alexandria."

Khalil nodded slowly. "Your council is good, Uncle Avram. I will make the necessary provisions with Mustafa before I undertake the journey, but I will go to England. I will bring her home."

Avram Hagiz stayed long enough to take refreshment with the children before he left. Torn between wanting to sail to Venice, where he believed Yehuda resided for the moment and wanting to go home to Tiberias, he chose home. To go to Venice would give Yehuda more information than he wanted his nephew to have. The less he knew, the better.

PART V

London to York, 1192
The Progress North

CHAPTER 22

Westminster

JANUARY 1192

Queen Eleanor descended on England with the wrath of an avenging angel. She summoned councils at Windsor, Oxford, Winchester, and London, finally putting to rest her wayward youngest son's rebellion against his brother, King Richard. Despite her entreaties to her son the king, Richard remained in the Holy Land fighting a losing battle to take Jerusalem. Word from there had not been good and she was annoyed with his reluctance to return to his kingdom.

"We can hardly keep on like this, Gilbert," stormed the queen after the last messenger from Richard arrived empty handed. "Surely he was taught better than this. Let us hope he receives this last epistle with the gravity it deserves," she said, her voice filled with fatigue. "We are far too old to be playing at this game."

Durham could not help but chuckle, "Your Majesty will never grow too old to practice politics. I think it keeps ye fit."

"Fit?" echoed the queen with a small smile. "Perhaps but exhausted as well. Tell us, Gilbert, how fares the lady?"

"Big as a house and ornery as a wet hen," grinned the earl. "This pregnancy weighs heavy on her; she is more than ready to deliver the babe."

"Are you ready to receive it?" countered Eleanor.

"Aye; that I am. I do not enjoy the mercurial moods, nor the forays into London to find dates in winter."

"Poor, poor Gilbert," teased the queen. "Her time draws near. It will be soon."

"Not soon enough," he grumbled.

Despite the bone-chilling cold and Durham's absence, Batsheva kept busy sewing dozens of shirts, gowns, and nappies. Anne sat nearby, working her letters and numbers on a large piece of slate. When she grew tired of writing, the girl would read from books Batsheva borrowed from the queen's meager library.

At Batsheva's request, Jane found a midwife. The seamstress made discreet inquiries about the services of a woman whose reputation was well known in foreign circles. At first, the lady had been hesitant to come to Westminster Palace but, upon her arrival, she took a private interview with Batsheva. Adèle left convinced she could be of service to the lady. Now that the lady's pregnancy was drawing to a close, the midwife was a frequent visitor to the palace.

Near the end of January, Durham returned to Westminster. Dismissed by the queen to await the birth of the child, he arrived just as a blizzard bore down on England. Howling winds and heavy snows lasted for three days, keeping everyone indoors. Durham spent the time reading documents recently delivered from his lands to the north. His mother had returned to Durham despite the cold weather, but her health, according to his Uncle Charles, was precarious. Jamie's own visit to Durham did nothing to alleviate his worries.

"Play Shatranj with me," said Durham on the third night of the storm. "I am weary of these missives and would not mind a challenging diversion."

Batsheva glanced up from her embroidery. It was the first time in almost two months he had asked her to play. "I shall get the pieces," she said hoisting herself up. A sudden pain gripped her and she grabbed the arm of the chair.

"What is it?" asked Durham.

"Nothing to worry about," she answered with a smile. Waddling to the chest, she retrieved the bag of chessmen and joined the earl at the table where the board sat long unused.

She had him on the run. As usual, Batsheva had cunningly set a trap using her rooks and bishops to force the sacrifice of Durham's queen. He scowled when he realized what she had done and growled when she laughed at his dilemma. "God's bones, woman!" he grumbled, "how is it that you always bring me to this?"

"God's bones have nothing to do with it, my lord earl," she scolded. "'Tis more a case of not seeing what is before you. Jamie tells me you are a fine strategist in the field; still, you manage your army poorly on the board. I think…" her voice stopped as another pain gripped her middle. It passed, but not before Durham blanched with fear. "Pay heed to the board, my lord, not me," she teased as she turned her attention back to the game.

The game continued, with Durham moving a little more skillfully while at the same time keeping one eye on Batsheva. Each cautious move he made, she countered with an equally aggressive one of her own. When it appeared as though he would lose within the space of three more moves, Batsheva suddenly looked down at her lap. The cloth of her gown was quickly growing damp. "'Tis time, my lord, to end the game," she said with a smile.

Durham leapt up so fast his chair tipped over behind him. "Are you in pain, Bess?"

"Get Jane and send Jamie for Adèle. Then take yourself away from here and do not return until the child is born. I would not have you hovering whilst I labor."

He did as he was told and, in short order, Jane and Mary had the lady in bed while Jamie rode for the midwife.

Throughout the long night, Durham paced the rush covered floor of the queen's chapel awaiting word from above. So far from the bedroom, he could not hear what was going on, but his imagination supplied the cries and screams from his memory of Joan's difficult births. He drank liberally of the mulled wine a footman had delivered, but not enough to force his overactive imagination into submission.

Batsheva labored easily. Sitting propped up in bed, she chatted with her companions, pausing only when the contractions forced her to stop talking. Mary was sent to her bed near dawn when, despite her protest, the other women could see she was falling asleep on her feet. Batsheva assured the little maid there would be more than enough to do in the morning and she needed her to be fresh and ready to take care of Anne once she awoke.

When the pains increased in severity, Jane kept Batsheva sitting upright while Adèle urged her to breathe steadily and evenly. The midwife kept a careful eye on the progress, pleased that this lady did not quail in the face of labor. She encouraged her charge to rest between contractions whenever she could, and let Jane continue her role as comforter. Finally, Batsheva announced she felt the need to bear down.

Adèle pulled back the covers and checked Batsheva one last time. "It is time for the stool." She helped Batsheva move to the birthing stool. "When you are ready, my lady," she said, laying out the swaddling at the end of the bed.

"Now," cried Batsheva as a fierce wave of pain swept over her. Grunting, she pressed as hard as she could while the pain helped push the child through the birth canal. As soon as it diminished, she panted in preparation for the next pain. As it rose again from the depths of her belly, she gripped Jane's hand. "Again," she groaned as she worked to give birth.

The process was repeated over and over until Adèle cried with delight, "What a fine head of red that I see! Again, my lady!"

Batsheva bore down with all her might as she felt the babe slide from her body. "'Tis a girl?" she asked, catching her breath. The babe cried forcefully in protest as she was pulled from her warm hiding place.

"'Tis a beautiful girl, Bess," sighed Jane as she took the babe, the cord still attached, and handed her to the mother.

"And there is not another one hiding inside?" she laughed, sure there was not.

"Only one, madame," smiled Adèle.

Batsheva stared down at her daughter and began to weep, "*Habibi,* we have another daughter." She touched the thatch of copper hair matching her own in color and then kissed the squalling infant. The new eyes opened and seemed to stare up at her mother. "Her eyes are blue now, but they are dark. They will be his eyes," she sniffled. The shape of those eyes tilted upward just as Khalil's did, and the tiny mouth had his full lower lip. Closing her own eyes, Batsheva murmured a prayer of thanksgiving to God for letting her have a girl; now there would be no question of succession in Durham's mind. Quickly the cord was cut, the afterbirth expelled, and the babe washed clean. Jane helped Batsheva to change her nightdress while Adèle removed the soiled bedclothes. Once tucked back into her bed, she put the child to her breast and told Jane to fetch the earl.

Durham stood frozen in the doorway. "May I enter?" he asked in a whisper.

"Of course, my lord," replied Adèle as she gathered up the last of her supplies. With a quick curtsey, she left the earl alone with his lady.

Slowly, Durham approached the bed where Batsheva sat with the babe in her arms. He looked at the sleeping pink face and gently touched it with his finger. "She is so tiny," he murmured.

"She is a little early, but not too much," smiled Batsheva. "I am glad for a girl, my lord. T'would be complicated had she been a boy."

He noticed she used neither son nor daughter to describe the child. He was painfully aware she did not consider the child his; now that she birthed a girl, she would surely leave him. Pushing the thought away, he leaned over and kissed Batsheva's forehead. "She resembles you greatly, Bess. For this I am thankful."

She nodded, fully understanding his intent. "Had you known her father you would see the strong resemblance between them." She smiled down at the sleeping infant. "She has his stubborn mouth, you see, and square chin. I fear her temper will be like his if her entry into the world is an indication."

"I will love her as my own, and will dower her richly when the time comes, Bess."

Batsheva sighed. "You are a kind and generous man, Gilbert of Durham, and I thank you. But God willing, her own people will dower her when the time comes."

"Stay here, Bess. Stay here with me and be my wife. My name is yours already…and my heart."

She looked up and saw the love mingled with pain mirrored in his eyes. "I need time to decide now that my daughter is born."

"I will give you all the time you need, my heart." He kissed her brow once more.

She sighed again. "I am tired, Gilbert. I think I would sleep now."

Gently, he took the babe from her arms and held it close against him. He could smell the sweetness of her skin, so new from the womb. Gingerly, he touched her cheek and smiled when the little mouth opened and closed several times. "What would you call her, Bess?"

"Maryam…Miriam," she murmured as her eyes closed. "I would call her Miriam for my mother."

❁ ❁ ❁

Durham remained at Westminster for a fortnight until summoned back to Windsor. Despite the defeat of John's rebellion, the people were grim. There was no evidence King Richard was soon to return and even the lowest born of his faithful subjects began to doubt that he would return at all. Durham made up his mind to ask the queen's permission to return to Durham as soon as his lady was able to travel. Even so, he was uncomfortable leaving Batsheva and the children at Westminster.

"Windsor is but a short ride, my lord," Jane assured him for the one-hundredth time. "Bess will be fine here; there is no reason to drag her to court. She's newly delivered and needs her rest."

Durham could find no argument with the lady's logic, but he remained concerned about the wisdom of leaving Bess alone. It was more than just her safety; he wondered if she would still be there when he returned. "Send a rider should there be anything amiss," he grumbled as Jamie helped him with his mail.

"Nothing will be amiss, my lord," said Batsheva as she swept into the room, the babe asleep in her arms, Anne beside her. "But do give my thanks to her majesty for the generous gifts she has sent Miriam." She looked him over and smiled, "You look most fearsome in your armor. I certainly would not cross swords with you."

"And if you did," he answered dryly, "I would have reason to doubt the outcome. I have seen your skill with the weapon, my lady."

She laughed although she sensed the seriousness of his comment. "You would do well to remember that; I am more than capable in battle."

"Oh, Papa, Bess is fearsome with a sword! She has a scar to prove it!"

Jamie snickered, but Jane had the distinct impression her friend was not joking at all. "Let us get your Papa's cloak," she said, taking Anne's hand in hers, then motioned for Jamie to follow her out of the chamber.

"We'll leave for Durham when I return, Bess," he told her.

"So soon?" asked Batsheva. "Are the roads passable?"

"Soon they will be. I think it wise if Jamie rides on ahead." He paused and his brows came together. "Will you come with me?"

The question surprised Batsheva. Before this, he spoke and acted as though her presence on the long journey north were a *fait accompli*. "What are my choices, my lord? Can I remain here?"

He shook his head. "The queen would find it odd; you would not have my protection."

"Where would I go? I cannot very well take myself to board a ship, as you have often pointed out. 'Tis true, I would rather go home."

"And I would take you if I could, Bess. But I cannot. I must return to Durham as soon as possible. My lands are unsecured without my presence."

"Yet you saw fit to go on crusade, my lord."

"My father was alive. While he lived, I was not earl."

Batsheva was silent. Until this moment, she hadn't considered when the departure would occur. Until now, it was in the future. Now, however, the moment had arrived, and she had neither a plan nor an answer. "Let me think on this, my lord. I will give you my answer when you return."

"I will respect your wishes, Bess, but I will not allow you to put yourself and the babe in jeopardy." He brushed a chaste kiss against her cheek.

"Be careful, Gil; Jamie says the roads are rife with highwaymen." She leaned forward to touch her lips to his cheek.

Durham savored the warmth of her lips against his face. It was a good feeling and even beneath his mail, he felt an unexpected warmth. "I will return before you have a chance to notice I was gone."

Eleanor kept Durham with her as she visited her councils. A week turned into a fortnight, and the fortnight was approaching a month. Batsheva did notice he was gone, but she busied herself with preparations for the coming journey. Whether or not she decided to go, the household was still going to move, with or without her. She kept her spirits up despite the confusion she felt, and only when the candle burned low beside the bed, did she allow herself to consider her decision.

Daily visits to Yaffa had resumed. The horse seemed glad for her mistress's company and Batsheva was happy to sit upon a hay bale and talk to the horse while Anne sat astride her bare back. Worried that her own languages were disappearing amid the French and English, Batsheva found a willing listener in Anne. The girl loved to hear the different languages, and Batsheva happily chattered and translated for her. If Yaffa found this strange, who could tell? The horse was, however, content to have Anne on her back. This daily diversion brought welcome relief from the problems Batsheva still faced.

She knew she could not travel alone. Had Jane not wed Jamie, she would have asked her friend to go; there was more than enough gold to support them both. Mary was too young to be of much use, but Batsheva suspected that if asked, the little maid would gladly go despite her budding romance with one of the grooms. *Go to what? Go to where?* Going to Málaga was pointless. If Yehuda was there, he would surely lock her away if he even let her in the house. And Akko? If Nikon and Elena remained in Akko, she might not be able to reach them if indeed, as she heard, the city had fallen to the crusaders. That left Alexandria or perhaps Benghazi. Getting there would be a problem; ships were too often attacked by pirates and female passengers usually found themselves sold into slavery. No matter how much gold or how important the ring she wore, these things would not guarantee her safety, let alone Miriam's. Durham was right about one thing…she needed an armed escort. Edward said he would take her if his uncle refused, but Edward was inexperienced in battle. How much protection could an untested youth provide?

She had no idea where her children were to be found. And once found, would Khalil's people allow her to join them? She was, after all, nothing more in their eyes than a captive slave, at best a concubine. Whatever their feelings were for Khalil, she had no standing with them. *Daud and Amina are young,* she admitted painfully, *in a year or so, I will be nothing but a fleeting memory to them both.* She knew they would be well cared for by Sufiye, and if not Sufiye, one of the other women. And what about Anne? She would hurt Anne terribly if she just disappeared. The child was so excited to be a big sister, and she was proving to be a fine one. Batsheva's love for the little girl grew more and more each day; she already felt like her mother.

If Khalil were indeed dead, Daud was their sheikh. A shudder racked Batsheva each time she allowed that thought to cross her mind. A part of her was certain Khalil was alive, but another part, a more rational, practical part, told her it was not possible. Too many saw him fall. Even Kassim said he was dead. There was no reason for her to believe otherwise. Kassim would never have left Khalil if there were the shallowest of breath left in his body. *He must be dead,* she told herself over and over. And every time she formed the words, the tears would come. *Life is precious,* she finally decided; *I cannot risk Miriam's when she is all I have left.* In the end, she knew she would go to Durham.

A messenger from Durham Castle brought less than good tidings. The dowager countess was gravely ill. Although the missive did not specifically ask that her son hasten his trip north, it was clear from the letter that the populace was in dire need of their earl. Twice the Scots had raided the northern most borderlands and the people were ill equipped to defend their lands and their animals. Batsheva sent the messenger on to Oxford where the latest council was taking place. Durham sent word back to Westminster that the queen gave her blessings to begin the journey home immediately after Easter, just two weeks away.

Now she sat in the middle of her bedchamber as Mary sorted through the earl's clothing. "Jamie should be doing this," complained the maid as she folded linen shirts. "I hope the earl can find a proper manservant for himself in Durham."

"He has one," answered Batsheva. "Jamie tells me he will keep his late father's valet in service." She continued separating ruined hose from good ones.

"'Tis high time, my lady. I am not a manservant and feel odd tending his lordship."

"As well you should," snapped a sharp voice from the doorway. Isabella rapped belatedly at the open door. "I hope I have not come at an inopportune time, Lady Elizabeth."

Batsheva stared at the woman's audacity at entering the apartment without invitation. Pasting a smile on her face, she said, "Why, Lady Isabella, what a lovely surprise!" She dropped the hose into a basket and quickly led the woman from the room. "To what do I owe the honor of this visit?"

"My daughter expressed a desire to visit with Anne," replied Isabella. "I thought it would be a nice change for the children. Life is so dreary in the country these days."

"We are delighted to have the company," replied Batsheva with a forced smile. "Will you join us for supper?"

"That would be lovely, Lady Elizabeth. Charlotte is with Anne, which leaves us to have a private visit." She glanced around the room. "You've done even greater wonders since last I was here. I do not see how you can leave this for that drafty castle in the north."

"I am sure I will find Durham lovely in the spring," replied Batsheva, mindful to keep her smile in place.

Before Isabella could comment, a maid appeared bearing a tray of refreshments. She curtsied deeply to the ladies before setting it on the table before their chairs, then silently withdrew. Isabella seemed to settle herself in her chair. "So, Lady Elizabeth, where is your new daughter?"

As if on cue, Mary entered the chamber with a fussy Miriam in her arms. "Excuse me, my lady, but she is…restless."

Batsheva extended her arms to take the child. Mary handed her the babe, then dropped a shawl over Batsheva's shoulder. "If you would not be made uncomfortable, Lady Isabella, I would nurse my daughter."

"Have you no wet nurse?" She was shocked at the very thought.

"No; a child thrives best on her own mother's milk." She discreetly opened her gown beneath the shawl and helped guide Miriam to the rosy nipple. The infant's loud sucking noises caused Batsheva to smile serenely.

Isabella was nonplussed at the performance. "I shall give you your privacy, Lady Elizabeth," she said as she rose from her seat.

"As you wish, Lady Isabella." She stifled a laugh until Isabella had gone.

CHAPTER 23

Westminster to York

APRIL 1192

An uncommon spring settled over the English countryside, bringing warmth and sunshine after the particularly dreary winter. Tender shoots broke through the earth, quickly changing the landscape from dull brown to bright green. Even the herbs in the kitchen garden poked out their leafy heads to gaze at the sun.

Batsheva was acutely aware of the week of Passover and refrained from eating bread. If Durham noticed, he said nothing, already used to her picky ways at table. It was a small concession to the isolation she was feeling at this time of year, when holy days collided, and she felt so alone. Observance of at least some holy days had been easier in Akko, where she and Devora could observe together, and no one thought anything of it. Here, however, any observance would be suspect.

The court returned to Westminster just in time for Holy Week. Jollier than Batsheva had ever seen him, Durham spent his days riding, Anne beside him on a new pony, Batsheva would watch them trot off, envious that she was still unable to join them. But she knew how important it was to Durham that his daughter ride well and she did not begrudge them their time together. While they were away from the hall, she saw to the final stages of packing. Jane and Jamie had gone on ahead as soon as he had returned, but Durham planned their departure for Wednesday morning after Easter.

There was no possible excuse Batsheva could invent that would allow her to miss mass during Holy Week. Durham arranged private services for his household in the queen's small chapel, sparing the lady the need to appear in public. But on Easter, her presence would be required at the cathedral.

"What do I do?" she asked him in a private moment.

"Sit, stand, and kneel as the others do," he instructed, "and when the time comes to take communion, approach the rail with me. Just do as I do."

"I cannot," she protested. "I cannot possibly do that!"

"You must, Bess. Otherwise, it would cast suspicion on you."

"Surely there must be some way around this."

Easter Sunday dawned sunny and bright, with the heady scent of fresh-turned earth hovering in the air. Mary helped Batsheva to dress in a light wool cote of spring green, with a buttery yellow chemise showing at the throat and sleeves. A bleached wimple floated over her shoulders, held in place by the circlet of golden thistle leaves.

Anne stood perfectly still as Batsheva adjusted the line of her sleeves. "Do my ribbons show, Bess?" she asked.

"Yes, your ribbons show," laughed Batsheva. She stood back to take a last look before they were to meet Durham downstairs. "Do you like the cote?"

"Oh, yes," gushed Anne. "I am so glad Mistress Jane made it for me." She twirled slowly around; the silver threads in the blue samite shimmered in the sunlight. "Tell me about silk again, Bess."

"I've told you one hundred times how silk is spun from the cocoons of little worms," she grinned. "Is it that you do not believe me and hope the story will change?"

"No, not truly, Bess," replied Anne. "'Tis just that you seem to know so much, and I know so little. I do not think you were as dull as I am when you were my age." She turned around to allow Batsheva to plait her long, flaxen hair.

"You are hardly dull, sweetheart; I fancy you are as bright as a newly-minted coin. After all, Anne, if you were dull, you would not have mastered your letters as quickly as you have."

"But at my age, you spoke several languages!"

"At your age, I was living in a place where many worlds seem to come together. 'Twas a necessity that a lady be educated in several tongues."

Anne's brows knit into a single golden line. "Charlotte says you do me a disservice by filling my head with learning, Bess."

"Do not listen to Charlotte, sweet child; she is the one who will be poorer for lacking knowledge. No one has ever died from knowing too much, whereas a lack can, indeed, kill." Batsheva finished off the braid with a ribbon and turned the child to face her. "A woman well versed in practical knowledge is a valuable helpmate to her husband, Anne. When the time comes for your father to find your spouse, I am certain he will seek one out who will appreciate all of your skills, not simply your dowry."

"Are the ladies ready?" called Durham from the doorway.

"We are ready, Papa!" answered Anne. Slowly, she walked toward Durham, taking special care not to step on her hem. "Is this not the most beautiful cote you have ever seen?"

Durham clutched his hands to his breast and dropped to one black-hosed knee. "My lady, you all but take my breath away! Come give your papa a kiss!" The little girl flew giggling into his arms. He hugged her tightly, then held her at arm's length. "'Tis hard to believe such a grown lady is my young daughter. You do me proud, Annie lamb."

From her seat, Batsheva watched the tender exchange. Was there someone to tell Amina she was beautiful? And her Daud; did someone help him to tuck in the end of his sash when he dressed in the morning? Tears prickled the back of her eyes. *Yes!* she shouted inside, *they are lovingly tended wherever they are.*

Durham looked beyond his daughter and caught the wrench in Batsheva's eyes. She did not have to tell him what she was thinking; he instinctively knew. Rising, he extended his hand to her. "Come, Bess, let us go to church." When she was at his side, he added in a whisper, "Follow my lead and you shall be fine."

She nodded, placed her hand on his arm, and took Anne's small hand. "Remember, dearest Anne, keep your head up and your back straight. You are an earl's daughter."

The heavy scent of incense and the drone of the mass provided Batsheva with a pounding headache. When the moment came for them to approach the altar rail, Batsheva stood rooted to the spot. She glanced around and saw others kneeling in prayer. She turned her eyes beseechingly on Durham, then dropped to her knees. "Pass by me," she whispered.

Gilbert moved around her and hoped no one would notice he went to take communion with only Anne at his side. Kneeling at the rail beside his daughter, he closed his eyes and hoped against hope the lady would come to understand the danger around her refusals. When the priest approached with the wafer, he opened his mouth to accept the gift, then wondered why he felt less shriven now than he did before he went on crusade. Holding Anne's hand tightly in his, they returned to the pew.

Once outside the cathedral and in fresh air, Batsheva managed to hold herself together as the crowds cheered for the queen. Holding fast to Durham's arm, she walked in procession behind Eleanor and her ladies. Anne tightly held her other hand, more than a little afraid she would be separated from them in the crowd and lost.

The queen's Easter banquet immediately followed the mass. At the high board, Batsheva was stunned when the steward showed her to the seat on Eleanor's left. Durham, also surprised by the honor, was less pleased when Isabella took her place to his left.

"I noticed Lady Elizabeth did not take communion," she said with an odd look. "Is she not shriven?"

"My lady prefers not to make a show of her devotion in public," he answered quickly. "She is most modest in these matters."

"It must be the Spanish way," she mused; "I confess I've heard they take the sacraments quite seriously. Perhaps you should arrange for a priest to attend her in your apartments."

"I will give it due consideration, Isabella; thank you for taking such an interest in my lady." He waited for Isabella's attention to be drawn to her other dinner partner before he told Batsheva what he had said. She nodded and relief flooded her face.

From the high board, Batsheva could see Anne and Charlotte seated at a table with several other children of the nobility. Judging by the way the little girl cocked her head to hear Charlotte's conversation and the composure which kept her erect on her bench, Batsheva could only hope Anne was now capable of fending off the other girl's spiteful remarks.

Durham noticed the same thing. "She's grown since she's been under your wing, Bess. I do not think the little snip will rattle her as she used to."

"I hope you are right," she sighed. "I can only imagine what poison she pours this time." Before she could add anything else, the queen turned to engage her in conversation.

She, too, had noticed the lady eschewed communion. "Do you prefer to take your sacraments privately?" she asked in a kindly tone.

Batsheva was prepared. "I am not yet comfortable with your customs, Madame; in our rite, ladies do these things away from men." It was not so far from the truth.

"Are your men so distracting?"

"Yes," she laughed lightly, "they are. We are taught one must concentrate fully on prayer while not allowing temporal matters to take our minds from holy thoughts. I need not say how flighty a lady might be in the presence of so many handsome knights!"

"Not the least of which is my nephew," added Eleanor with a wicked grin. "I fear he has distracted Isabella from her plate."

Batsheva followed the queen's glance and saw Isabella's jaw moving rapidly as she spoke to Durham. The bored glaze over his blue eyes was not missed by either Batsheva or the queen. "Are you certain, Madame? Perhaps 'tis the other way around."

Eleanor's sharp laugh caused others to look in their direction momentarily. "You *are* sure of yourself, are you not, Lady Elizabeth?"

"As sure as I need to be, Your Majesty."

"As well you should. You have my nephew wrapped tightly around your little finger and he is no worse off for it. Nay, 'tis a good thing for Gilbert; he was too serious for too long. Even in council, he urged speed so that he might return to your side. That is hardly the man who left England to join the crusade. I fear, Bess, you've turned him into a homebody!"

"Only when he returns to his own lands, madame, will he truly be home."

The queen smiled at Batsheva. "You are wise beyond your young years, Bess. Would that other wives knew their men as well as you know yours. I think you will make a grand addition to Durham. 'Tis time Gilbert went home."

The queen kept Batsheva occupied through most of the meal. She ate as much as she dared, careful to avoid anything that looked the least bit unfamiliar. When Eleanor questioned her about that, she replied that her constitution remained somewhat delicate after the birth of her daughter. The queen accepted the answer but urged the lady to find a wet nurse. "It is not the way of my people," Batsheva explained; "I would not deny myself the joy of nursing my own child."

And when her breasts became too full to ignore, it was that very excuse she used to beg the queen's indulgence to allow her to leave the high board. She insisted Durham stay on, but Isabella's feline smile made her almost regret the decision. As discreetly as she could, Batsheva slipped quietly from the hall and returned to their chambers.

She was standing at the edge of an oasis with Miriam. As in all the other dreams, she saw Amina and Daud at the water. This time, however, Khalil was not with them. Batsheva called to the twins who simply laughed and pointed at the water. Miriam's hand in hers, she saw herself walk to the water's edge. A body seemed to be floating in pool, face down. She heard herself cry out. Suddenly, the body flipped over and began swimming toward the shore. When he reached the sandy beach, Khalil rose, shaking the water from his hair and beard. "Beard!" thought Batsheva in the dream. "You've grown a beard, habibi" she said aloud. Then she began shaking.

Batsheva's eyes fluttered open. She was shaking. She was being shaken. Focusing, she saw Durham standing above her, a sleeping Miriam in his arms. She heard him call her name, but when she opened her mouth, no words came out.

"Are you all right?" he asked, touching her face. "You cried out in your sleep, but I could not understand what you said." He sat down beside her.

"A beard," she said softly. "He grew a beard."

"Who?"

"Khalil."

"He did not wear a beard?" asked Durham, puzzled. "I thought all Moorish men wore beards."

She shook her head. "Ayyub do not. But in the dream, I saw him. He has a beard."

Without asking her permission, he slid his free arm about her and drew her close. "'Twas but a dream, Bess. Only a dream."

"But it was so real, Gilbert. It was as if I were there. With the children."

He kissed her face where tears had slid down her cheeks as he held her close. "'Twas only your heart telling you the children are safe, my love. Please, do not fret."

Batsheva was trembling. "I pray you are right, Gilbert."

He wanted to tell her that night they arrived in Westminster he dispatched two messengers with missives to the king asking his aid in locating the children. He had learned enough about them from her to know they were twins, that Saladin most likely knew where they had gone when they left Akko, and that they had been hidden at the Well of Tears when the attack came. Surely, someone would know something. Perhaps, when King Richard returned, he would bring news of the search and then he would find a way to bring them to their mother. To tell her now might raise hopes that would be dashed with lack of news; in the end, he decided to keep this to himself.

Twenty men-at-arms from Queen Eleanor's personal guard thundered into the courtyard on the third day after Easter. Durham had been up before sunrise, but Batsheva felt she had not slept at all. Between Miriam's need to nurse and her own nervousness at beginning the journey, she lay awake most of the night staring at the whitewashed ceiling. She wished Jane were with her, but Mary had proven herself most able in sharing the burden of final preparation with her mistress. Batsheva was greatly relieved when the little maid offered to go with them. Even Anne, who had expressed a desire to stay at Westminster rather than return to Durham Castle, had thrown her little self into the work. Now the carts were loaded and all that was left were the few small trunks they would require for the journey.

Taking a last look about her chamber, Batsheva tossed her cape over her shoulders and picked up her embroidery bag. When Durham rapped smartly at the door, she was surprised to see Miriam in his arms. "Is she fussing?"

"No," he grinned, "simply in need of portage. The coach is ready, my lady."

"Then let us go." She managed a small smile but wondered if Durham saw through it to the jumble within.

In the courtyard, Batsheva stopped to talk softly to Yaffa. The grey nose nuzzled against her shoulder, its velvety smoothness tickling her. Batsheva checked the reins hitched to coach and with a last kiss to the horse's muzzle, she let Durham help her into the box took the babe. Anne was already tucked inside. "Are you warm enough?" she asked the girl.

"Papa says we are stopping at York." she grumbled with a decided frown.

"It would be wrong not to stop there, Anne," replied Batsheva gently. "Your aunt is expecting us."

Anne's little nose wrinkled. "I do not like York. 'Tis a cold and unfriendly place."

Batsheva was surprised and said so. "I thought you liked your cousins."

"They are rough and ill mannered."

"That is only because you did not want to be there. I think this time you will find them far more palatable."

"I shouldn't think so," Anne sniffed. "I much prefer gentle company to their silly games."

Batsheva stifled a laugh. "Then you shall sit and embroider with the ladies while we visit. You may find the conversation stimulating." She settled Miriam into the basket Mary had earlier put in the coach. "For right now, however, I would suggest we both close our eyes and take advantage of little Miri's nap with one of our own." Then she arranged her own lap robes and closed her eyes.

They stopped when the sun was at its highest point in the sky to take refreshment, then continued on their way to the next destination. Thus, a pattern to the days was set, the only variable being where they spent the night. Whenever possible, they stayed with noble families, long used to the unexpected guest putting in for the night. It was, as Durham explained, one way of gathering news and visiting old friends and, in some cases, family. Batsheva found the custom to be remarkably like the one in Al-Andalus; she took full advantage of the experience.

Batsheva made certain Anne carried her slate and the hours in the coach were quickened with little lessons despite the bumpy ride. Only Miriam seemed untroubled by the constant bouncing. Even Mary preferred to sit on the buckboard of one of the carts with the other servants to riding in their conveyance. That a certain groom from the palace traveled with them was simply, according to the blushing little maid, a pleasant diversion.

Durham took his meals with Batsheva and Anne, but during the day, he rode with the men. Along with the 20 guards and men of Durham, 10 new recruits rode with them. Whether it was the imposing presence of armed men or by sheer luck, they met with no resistance on the road.

On the day they were to reach York, the party stopped to take lunch on the banks of the River Ouse. Durham found a spot overlooking the river where he instructed the servants to arrange the meal. Leading Batsheva and Anne to the place, he saw them settled before going off to see to the horses. Batsheva, Miriam at her breast, kept a careful eye on Anne who had shed her hose to dip her toes in the water. "Stay within my sight, Anne," she called when the girl began to wander. And then she chided herself; this was not the road to Sfax and there were no kidnappers lurking behind the bushes. But when a heavy footfall approached, Batsheva nearly leapt out of her skin. Durham dropped down beside her. "Must you sneak up on us?" she asked, annoyed.

He looked perplexed. "I did not mean to startle you, Bess. 'Twas not my wish."

"Hell, monsieur," she snapped, "is full of good wishes."

He laughed at her frown and saw it deepen. "You worry too much, my sweet," he waved his arm in the air. "There is no greater place on earth than England in her springtime finery."

Batsheva looked about her and could not disagree. The earth was lush green with new growth beneath a perfect azure sky. "'Tis lovely," she admitted.

"Almost as lovely as you, Bess. Even when you frown, you eclipse the sun."

She laughed lightly. "I fear, monsieur, the heat of the day has addled your brain beneath your helmet. Look toward the river if you wish to see true beauty."

For a long moment, he watched his daughter at play. Gone was the chubby babe he barely remembered, replaced by a slender girl fast approaching young womanhood. Her resemblance to Joan was uncanny and, for a moment, he recalled his late wife when she was little older than Anne. He had known her since they were children; he had watched her blossom into a magnificent woman who held his heart tenderly in her slim, elegant hands. For a moment, he saw Joan in her wedding finery, her blue eyes looking lovingly up at him as they stood before the priest. And his heart ached. She died too young, and he missed her sorely. Even now, years later.

Batsheva turned her eyes toward Durham. Reaching out, she touched his hand. "Sometimes, Gilbert, we share a similar pain," she said softly.

His sapphire eyes captured her grey ones and held them locked in his gaze. "The heart remembers, Bess, but we go on. We make new lives where once the old ones turned to ashes." He closed his hand over hers and drew her to him. His lips met her lips. He tasted the sweetness of a kiss returned and his heart broke free and soared.

From the riverbank, Anne saw her father kiss Batsheva. It was the first time she had seen any outward display of affection between them, and while it pleased her, she was confused by it. She knew they did not share a bed, even now, after Miriam was born. Anne knew enough about marriage to know her aunt and uncle slept together, and while her grandfather was alive, he often shared her grandmother's bed. Whatever was between her father and his lady, she was not privy to the details, but she thought, in her childish way, that this was a good thing to see. But the cool water against her bare feet was more a distraction than Anne could ignore. Turning her attention back to the river, she waded along the shore where, beneath the crystalline water, she could see minnows and tadpoles swimming between her toes. Wading a little deeper, she held up her skirts as she bent to capture one of the silvery fish.

On the hill, a loud splash made both Batsheva and Durham snap up. "Oh, merciful God!" cried Batsheva when she saw Anne flailing in the water. Durham was already clambering to his feet, the weight of his mail and light armor hampering his motion. Batsheva was faster and she thrust Miriam toward him. "Take her," she ordered as she tore her wimple from her head. She raced down the steep bank and plowed into the water.

Anne's cries and her waving hands provided Batsheva with enough focus to reach her in a matter of seconds. Despite her own long skirts, she was able to kick around the child as she grabbed her from behind. "You're safe, Annie; just hold on to me." For a moment, the child continued to flail against the water, but Batsheva's iron grip around her middle seemed to calm her. Treading water, Batsheva adjusted her hold on Anne, then swam the short distance to shore where Durham stood helplessly by, Miriam still fast asleep in his arms. "Put your feet down," urged Batsheva when her own feet touched the sandy bottom. The girl did as she was told, smiled, and marched herself from the water. Batsheva pushed the hair out of Anne's eyes. "Has no one taught you to swim?" The girl shook her head. "Well," she grinned, "one more thing I must teach you. Now, run up to the coach and ask Mary to fetch dry clothes for us both."

"You are a wonder, Bess," said Durham with awe. "I know no other woman who can swim."

"And you would drown in your armor, my lord," she frowned. "'Twas a good thing I was here." She started to take Miriam from him, then thought better of it. "'Tis another good thing the weather is warm," she muttered as she wrung out her skirt.

Durham chuckled at her predicament but dared not laugh. Instead, he put his arm around her. "Still, you are chilled, Bess. Warm yourself against me."

She gave him a rather withering look and kept twisting the light blue wool of her dress. "You would do better to keep at rocking Miriam. Should she awaken, she will not like a clammy breast."

Reluctantly, he released his hold on Batsheva and returned to the blanket on the grass.

Six riders came thundering down the road to where Durham and Batsheva were about to continue to York. A knight in dark armor and tabard led the band and the lack of a crest caused Durham to lay his hand on his sword.

"Identify yourself!" called the knight as he wheeled his horse to an abrupt stop.

Durham, astride his horse, stood his ground. "Identify yourself, sir knight."

"This district is closed to travel. There are highwaymen afoot."

The muscle in Durham's jaw twitched dangerously. "We are on our way to York on the queen's business. Do you challenge the queen's men?"

"There is no queen. Only an absent king and his aged mother. Are you sworn to Richard?"

""I am Gilbert, Earl of Durham." His fingers tightened around the hilt. "My oath is to England. Stand aside."

The dark knight rode close to Durham. "You say you are Gilbert of Durham. Have you proof?"

"My shield is my proof. You," said the earl through clenched teeth, "have yet to identify yourself, sir. Will you do so now, or would you prefer to face my men?"

Tense silence blotted out the sound of the birds in nearby trees. Not even the horses snorted as the two knights clashed stares. Durham took close measure of the man, carefully watching the way his fist opened and closed on the hilt of his sword. Tightening his own grip, he prepared to draw his weapon at the first sign of movement from either the knight or his men. Finally, the dark knight jerked the reins of his horse and wheeled around again.

"Be warned, Gilbert of Durham, you ride Prince John's lands," he shouted. Without waiting for a response, he galloped off, his men close at his heels.

Durham watched him go, then signaled his own men. "Let us make haste to York," he called. The troops positioned themselves strategically around the coach and carts before they started toward the city with increased speed.

Margaret of York greeted her brother with what he thought was almost excessive joy. She flew down the steps of their Norman castle and into her younger brother's open arms. More decorously, Henry descended the stairs to greet his brother-in-law. Batsheva stood nearby with Anne, who was less than happy to be back.

"You must be exhausted, Lady Elizabeth," pronounced Margaret, taking the much younger woman's arm. "Let me show you to your chambers where I've laid refreshments for you all." She led Batsheva inside before she turned to Anne. "Your very own chamber is awaiting you, Annie. Would you like to join Genevieve and Helen in the garden? They are anxious to see you."

Anne knew when she was being dismissed and nodded, "Yes, Aunt Margaret." With a bobbed curtsey and her chin held high, she marched herself through the great hall and out to the kitchen garden where the other children were playing.

When she was gone, Margaret turned to Batsheva. "I'm afraid Anne is not particularly pleased to be here."

"So she has said," replied Batsheva, unsure of how to proceed. At the forefront of her mind was the massacre at the keep. Still, there was a need to set that aside while she was York's guest.

"Anne is a bright, lovely child, but she is unused to the bustle of York. Since her mother died, she has lived in virtual isolation with my own mother who is far too old to be raising a child. Instead of a child who loves to play, she has raised a little old maid."

"I hope not, Lady Margaret," said Batsheva, finding the frankness of Durham's sister to be refreshing. But as long as Margaret was going to be honest, she felt obliged to follow her example. "Anne is indeed a bright child, and you are right, she had been left to her own devices far too long. Since she arrived in Westminster, however, she has turned from a silent, sullen child into a happier little girl. Although she was slow to join others at play, she was beginning to make friends amongst the children at the palace."

"And perhaps they will be better friends to our little angel than Charlotte de Blois."

Batsheva snorted. "I fear Charlotte is her own best friend. What little contact I had with that child during a brief visit left me with a certain distaste."

"My, how kind!" laughed Margaret. "I would have said the child is positively evil. I daresay I did my best to keep them apart!"

"'Tis not the child who is evil, Lady Margaret," added Batsheva drily.

"As they say, the apple falls not far from the tree. I'll wager Isabella was most unhappy to see you at court with Gil."

"An understatement, to say the least."

"Then you will be as distressed as I was to learn she is en route to York as we speak. Isabella has sent word to expect her arrival."

"I cannot tell you," Batsheva said with a cold smile, "how pleased I am to hear that."

"God's bones!" roared Margaret in a most unladylike manner, "has the Holy Mother finally taken pity on my wayward brother and sent a woman worthy of his drollness?"

In the courtyard, Durham dismissed his men, then told his brother-in-law of the stranger they met on the road. "What manner of knight is this to be allowed free rein in your county, Henry?"

The older man frowned. "He is one of Prince John's lackeys. A bailiff of some sort. They say he is Norman, but I am not certain. I've seen him but once, at a tournament in Nottingham; he is a strong jouster."

"Does that give him leave to terrorize travelers?" asked Durham. "And why did he say these are John's lands? Are you not earl here?"

"Aye, but these are troubled times, Gil. Some would see Richard overthrown by his brother; Geoffrey may be archbishop of York by the grace of God and the king, yet he holds no fealty to Richard."

"This is not news, Henry," Durham retorted. "Geoffrey has long been a thorn in the king's side. Eleanor has no love for him, either. She would sooner see him in his grave than take Holy Communion from his hand."

"What, and have the blood of another Beckett on Angevin hands? I think not, brother. Distancing myself from the bastard has endeared me to my people, and for that I am thankful. In the end, we are who we are by their consent, and I would not risk their good thoughts of me." He frowned at Gilbert. "As lords, we have an obligation to see to the welfare of our vassals; he who forgets that duty will find himself without a head on his shoulders."

Durham nodded; he knew not all lords shared Henry's concerns. "I fear I shall have a time re-insinuating myself to the people of Durham."

"They've gone too long with an absent lord," Henry agreed, "but they know you have returned. Your father was a good earl, and so will you be… if you tend to your lands and keep your sword handy."

"There are troubles in Durham as well?" he asked.

"There are troubles everywhere, my young brother." He clapped Durham heartily on the back. "Come, let us raise a cup and solve all the ills of England."

Henry motioned for Durham to follow up the stairs at the rear of the great hall. Durham obliged, cup in hand, and soon found himself standing on the crenellated battlement overlooking the whole of York. "This new castle was worth the effort. From here," he said, sweeping his arm across the panorama, "I can see who, what, and where."

"'Tis a handsome place, Henry." He slapped his hand against the stone parapet. "And stronger than any I've seen."

"'Tis concentric, not unlike Durham. The best there is." He smiled grimly. "'Twas costly but 'tis worth it. I would have my folk safe against whatever comes." He waited for Durham to comment, but when he was silent, Henry walked to the other side of the parapet and pointed downward. "There is room enough for 500 to take shelter in battle, and stores beneath to feed them. We have taken the story of Joseph in Egypt to heart and have prepared for the worst."

"Famine? In England?"

"War, Gil. Should Lackland rise again, there will be war. My oath was to Richard and to his father before him. I will not join with John. I've been to councils where others chafe at serving a king who refuses to remain in his country. There is dissatisfaction that must be addressed. And soon, too. Tell me, you've served Eleanor at the Great Councils; what is the word?"

"The word remains Richard is king, but John will succeed his brother if Richard dies without issue. But as we stand now, we stand with Richard."

For all his travels and adventures, Henry thought his brother-in-law naive, yet refrained from saying so. Instead, he reaffirmed his own support of the king. "I pray he has the good sense to return soon."

"He will, brother; he has no choice."

Henry laughed when he countered, "Kings always have choices, Gil. That is what makes them kings. Let us hope Richard makes wise choices."

The chambers Margaret assigned to Batsheva were not as spacious as Westminster's, but neither were they spartan. A large, heavily curtained bed dominated the room, with sturdy cradle and table nearby. A beautifully carved chest served as a seat beneath the wide window. The fireplace, unlit because of the warm weather, boasted a fine stone mantle. A wide cupboard dominated the opposite wall.

"I have not yet adopted your practice of tapestries on the floor," said Margaret, "but perhaps you will convince me."

Batsheva blushed; she was more than a little surprised that word of her peculiarity had reached Margaret's ears. "'Tis merely old habit," she offered in way of an apology, "for one used to warmer climes."

"And a good habit, too, I think. But tapestries, not to mention rugs, are hard to come by outside London."

Batsheva made up her mind to order rugs for Margaret when Durham eventually returned to Westminster; she was certain he would not object now that he had lived with them in the hall. "May I ask where Anne will sleep?"

"Down the corridor, in the next chamber," replied Margaret, pleased that she asked. "Anne seems very fond of you."

"And I of her. She is a lovely child."

"And this one?" she asked, taking Miriam from her mother's arms. "Is this little flower a good babe?"

"When she is not hungry. When her belly rumbles, she is as fierce as any lion," sighed Batsheva.

Margaret adjusted the swaddling to look at the tiny face. "She favors her mother, I see. Perhaps the next will be a boy."

"Perhaps," echoed Batsheva. She was not at all certain there would be another child. A knock at the door broke her train of thought.

Mary entered and curtsied to the ladies. "My lady," she said, addressing Margaret, "there is a young woman outside who says she is to be Lady Miriam's nurse."

"Oh, I had almost forgotten." She turned to Batsheva. "I heard you had no nurse for the babe, so I thought to recommend one from my household. She lost her own and is still wet."

"I nurse Miriam myself and would continue; 'tis the custom in my home. But I thank you for the kind thought."

Margaret furrowed her brow thoughtfully. "I daresay she will be disappointed, but perhaps you could use an extra maid. The girl is without a husband and there is no need for her services in my household. Would you care to meet her?"

There was a certain amount of wisdom in Margaret's suggestion; Batsheva felt Mary was already overburdened. "Yes," she answered slowly, "I would meet her."

Mary left and returned a moment later with a slender young girl. "This is Lydia, my lady."

The girl curtsied gracefully and when she rose, Batsheva saw an attractive yet sad face with dark eyes and dark hair. "I would be most grateful for the work, my lady," she murmured in soft English.

"She does not speak French," added Mary with a touch of haughtiness in her own voice.

Batsheva shot the maid a disapproving glance, then addressed Lydia in her own language. "My English is slow, Lydia, but if you would be patient with me, perhaps we can get on. Do you like small children?"

"Very much, my lady. I am the eldest of six and have always helped my mother."

"There is another child as well: Lady Anne."

Lydia's face brightened. "I know Lady Anne well, ma'am. She is a goodly little girl."

"Then 'tis settled," Margaret breathed with relief. "You shall sleep in Lady Anne's chamber at night to see to her needs as well as those of Lady Miriam during the day."

Lady Miriam. The words struck Batsheva as if she had been slapped. Miriam was *Princess* Miriam, yet she could not tell that to Margaret. The old pain suddenly sliced through her heart, but rather than give in to it, she pushed it aside.

Margaret noticed Batsheva's sudden whitening and hurriedly spoke. "I fear you must be terribly tired, my dear. Why not lie down until supper? I shall send Mary back to you in plenty of time to dress."

Batsheva nodded. "Yes, that would be nice. I am fatigued."

Handing Miriam to Lydia, Margaret went to the door. "Sleep well and we shall visit again at the high board." Softly, she closed the door behind her.

Margaret hurried up the stairs to where she was sure to find her husband and brother. Pausing at the top to catch her breath, she caught sight of them at the end of the rampart and smiled to herself. Of all her siblings, Gilbert was her favorite. As a child, he was all light and joy, always ready to join the game or lend a helping hand to a struggling farmer. He was the apple of their mother's eye, yet no one begrudged him the place. He was, after all, the long-awaited son born after three daughters! Now he stood tall and strong beside the other man in her life and, for once, she did not murmur her prayer for his continued safety. At least for a few days, she would have him within eyeshot.

They were deep in conversation and did not see Margaret approach until she was almost upon them. A wide smile split the earl's face as he dropped an arm over his sister's shoulder. "How fares my lady, Maggie?"

"Sleeping, I hope," she answered with no small amount of rebuke. "She is a tiny thing, Gil, and I fear you've exhausted her."

His hearty laughed took her by surprise. "'Tis true, she is a mite, but do not underestimate that spine of tempered steel running through her. I've seen her pick up a sword and she knows how to wield it."

"Gilbert!" cried Margaret, shocked to the bones. "No lady of her breeding would have cause to know such a thing. I think you tease me."

"I do not, Maggie; on the soul of our father. She is as tough as any man I have known," he admitted, "and I have the bruises to prove it."

Henry chuckled as he watched his wife prepare to fence words with her brother. "Beware, Margaret, he is not a little boy you can bully."

Margaret drew herself up to her full height and although it was less than Durham's, she was no weak contender. "Did you receive those same bruises in a battle off the battlefield?" she asked sharply.

"Aye, that I did."

"And how did you receive them? Was she unwilling to have you in all your armored glory?"

"Margaret," warned Henry.

"She is here of her own choosing, Maggie. No one has forced her."

"Perhaps not now, but I have the strangest sensation that was not always the case."

Durham wondered if his sister was fey. Certainly, there were times when he was growing up that he was certain she had the second sight. Now, however, it wasn't nearly as amusing as it was then. "Bess will tell you whatever she sees fit, Margaret," he growled, unwilling to speak without her express permission. "Ask her, if you would dare be so bold."

"I think," she sniffed, "I will." Two pair of sapphire blue eyes were deadlocked in a stare.

Henry gently put his arm around his lady and turned her back toward the stone staircase. "See to our supper, Maggie."

With a last, indelicate snort, she left them on the battlement.

Durham held his chuckle until she was gone. "You should be canonized simply for living with my sister."

"Probably, but she has her good points, too. I could think of no other woman in whose bed I would wish to sleep…even after all these years together."

"She always was hot-blooded."

Henry nodded, his eyes soft. "Aye, 'twas a miracle Edward was birthed as late as he was…but of course, you were too young to take note of all the fingers being counted."

CHAPTER 24

York

APRIL 1192

All of York's society turned out to greet the Earl of Durham and his entourage. The great hall was filled to capacity with the finest of the city's gentlefolk as well as the local nobles, happy to have another occasion to gather in the new castle. A hundred torches burned brightly against the walls, giving the hall a rich golden glow. The high vaulted ceiling boasted a huge wrought iron chandelier and that, too, was ablaze with beeswax candles. Elegant women in fine wools and linens in every color of the rainbow gossiped happily at the tables while the men, in more somber tones but no less richly attired, discussed more pressing topics.

At the high board, Margaret sat Batsheva beside her to facilitate the identification of the ladies in the hall. In dark blue samite, her bliaut was just a little richer, a little more highly decorated than those of her guests. Her hair, darker than her brother's, was hidden beneath a linen veil, the same color as her gown, kept in place by a crenellated circlet of gold, with rubies centered in each panel. Around her waist, she wore a girdle of gold cloth and from it dangled a chatelaine and a gold pomander filled with cloves and cinnamon. She glowed as she introduced her friends and neighbors to Lady Elizabeth.

And Batsheva, a smile pasted on her face, managed to say a few words to each one. She could feel their eyes on her as she sat on the dais; she wondered if her dress was incorrect, or perhaps her circlet was askew. More than once, she surreptitiously reached up to check her own plain gold circlet Finally, when she could stand it no longer, she asked Margaret what was wrong with her appearance.

"Wrong?" asked Margaret. Then she laughed. "I would hardly call it wrong, Bess. I would think the ladies are jealous and the men, envious!"

Batsheva chewed her lower lip thoughtfully. "I would not like to earn their disapproval. Perhaps I have overdressed."

Scooting back in her chair, Margaret studied Batsheva's attire critically. The deep claret of her cote was simple and unadorned save for a narrow gold pipe around the square-cut neckline. Her ivory chemise was just the right shade to compliment both her cote and her skin. Her mantle, made of samite a shade darker than her gown, lay perfectly across her shoulders and the gold clasp was a simple, sculpted pomegranate clasp. "Overdressed?" repeated Margaret, "I think not. If anything, Bess, you've shamed us with your simplicity. There is a tendency to show our wealth in our clothes here."

Batsheva sighed, somewhat relieved. "'Tis true all over the world, my lady. Ladies are ladies the same no matter where they call home."

From his seat on the other side of Henry, Durham watched the exchange. He was somewhat concerned about Bess; she was nervous before they descended to the hall and he could see her hands smoothing and re-smoothing the folds of her gown. Glancing out over the sea of faces, he thought himself the most fortunate of men; his Bess outshone every woman in the room. It wasn't simply her face; it was her presence. She appeared to all as serene as a moonlit lake at midsummer and just as bright. Just then, he saw her look up and met her eyes with his. He smiled and was rewarded with the slightest tug upward of her full lips. When she turned back to Margaret, he felt as if the sun had withdrawn. *If only*, he thought as he resumed his conversation with Henry.

"I thought you said Isabella was coming," whispered Batsheva to Margaret when the first course was served.

Margaret put her hand over Batsheva's and said, "Isabella always arrives late and makes an entrance. She will arrive, I predict, between the third and fourth course."

"Tell me about her."

"What's there to tell?" answered Margaret with a shrug. "She is the daughter of a minor baron who earned his wealth in trade and married above his station. Her mother was the heir to a small estate in Gloucestershire and when they married, he got the land. Old Henry gave him the title for services to the crown."

"What does that mean?"

"He lent him money," Margaret laughed. "A considerable amount, I should think. Isabella has only an elder sister, so her father offered fat dowries for his daughters. He married them off to the highest bidders, or so it was said. Not only did he ensnare an earl for his elder daughter, he received, in return, additional lands in Gloucestershire. As for Isabella, she went to a fat, old baron from Lincoln who needed money to keep his lands together."

"What could he possibly have given her father?"

"His widowed sister to wife. With his own wife dead and growing longer in the tooth himself, he wanted a proven breeder. The lady was exactly that and she gave him the son he wanted a year before he died."

"That could not have sat well with Isabella," Batsheva said dryly.

"It did not, but what could she do? She wanted Gil, but my brother was promised to Joan when they were in nappies." Margaret smiled sadly at the mention of her late sister-in-law. "You would have liked Joan. She was a lovely girl with great good sense. In many ways, she was much like you." She waited to see if Batsheva would respond, but when she remained silent, Margaret continued. "She was forthright and honest, sharp in observation and a good match for Gil. Joan brooked no nonsense from my brother…and he was prone to nonsense, but she loved him tenderly and he worshipped her. We all grieved when she died."

Surreptitiously, Batsheva stole a glance at Durham. He seemed relaxed and happy to be amongst his family and friends. It was obvious that he knew most of those gathered. His booming laugh, a sound she rarely heard, often carried over the noise of the hall. "He is happy here," she said to Margaret.

The older woman smiled as she looked at her brother. "As well he should be. Gil has spent a great part of his life here. He was page, then squire to Henry before he earned his own knighthood. My father was against sending him here; he felt Gil would be favored over the other boys, but his fears were groundless." She laughed at the memory. "I think Henry rode him harder than the others under his tutelage; he made Gil kneel in the old chapel from night to dawn every time his tongue got the better of him."

"Was he a sassy lad?" asked Batsheva, honestly curious about the boy who had become the man.

"Oh, my word, yes! He could not keep his comments to himself and often paid the price. At the same time, he worked harder than the others; Gilbert had something to prove."

Batsheva thought of Daud. Even in the Bedouin camp, he had the need to do everything himself rather than rely on others. "This grows strength in a man," she said, "and character."

"Inner fortitude, I'm afraid, is a Durham family weakness. I swear, the men are bred to oaken-spines and iron-wills. This does not always make them easy to live with."

"I know something of rigidity," admitted Batsheva; "he is no better… or worse than others I have known."

Margaret was about to add something to the conversation when a flurry of movement at the end of the hall caught her attention. Batsheva followed her gaze and saw, just as she had the night she dined with Queen Eleanor, Isabella making her grand entrance.

With the aplomb of a seasoned diplomat, Margaret welcomed Isabella and saw her seated amidst her peers. If she was annoyed at not being seated at the high board, she had the good grace to hold her tongue. But for Batsheva, the remainder of the feast was an uncomfortable exercise in dodging the lady's persistent stare. Afterward, when the last course was cleared, the guests took air in the courtyard while the hall was prepared for the evening's entertainment.

A troop of jongleurs, traveling through the countryside, had been engaged. Dressed in colorful, fanciful costume, they began their performance in the courtyard skillfully tumbling about the guests. Batsheva, Anne at her side, clapped in delight at their antics. Anne was especially pleased when a young magician caused a copper to pop from her ear. In another corner, a handsome minstrel sang the latest ballads from the Aquitaine while a bevy of local beauties sighed at his romantic lyrics.

As the wanderers led the way back into the hall, Isabella caught up with Batsheva. "I am glad to see you looking so well, Lady Elizabeth," she crooned. "You looked so peaked at Easter."

Biting back the sharp retort at the tip of her tongue, Batsheva forced a smile and thanked her for the compliment. "The children keep me quite busy; I have no choice but to be well."

With a smile returned, Isabella turned her attention to Anne. "Charlotte is just over there," she said, pointing a finger toward the minstrel. "Perhaps you could join her."

The girl glanced up at Batsheva hopefully, but the lady simply nodded. "Go on, Anne. Join me again when we take our seats. Anne frowned, but went anyway. "Is there some reason you would speak to me privately Lady Isabella?" she asked rather stiffly, the smile still intact.

Isabella played with the knot of her girdle, inspecting it in silence, her eyes cast to the stone cobbles of the courtyard. "I would not mention this odd event, Lady Elizabeth, had I not heard it from a most reliable source."

"You have me at a disadvantage."

She dropped the cloth and looked up. "There was some talk, Madame, that you are not quite what you say you are."

"And that is?" inquired Batsheva as politely as possible.

"Spanish. It is rumored at court that you are…the daughter of a Saracen."

The news did not elicit the reaction Isabella expected. Instead, the lady laughed softly. "I can assure you I am not the daughter of a Saracen."

"But it is said you lived in the desert outside the Holy City!"

"That much is true." She was not about to tell her anything more. She swept up the hem of her gown. "'Tis time we joined the others, Lady Isabella." Without waiting for her, Batsheva walked, head erect, through the archway.

Ablaze with freshened torches, the great hall had been transformed into a veritable carnival of colors. Rainbow banners on poles were held by members of the troop while others performed feats of agility and daring in the center of the room. No less than 20 young men cavorted through the hall, their parti-colored costumes becoming blurs in the speed of their motion. In a corner, a little band of musicians played lively tunes, while several dark-haired unveiled women kept time on tambourines with bright ribbons flying in all directions.

Batsheva spotted Anne sitting on Durham's lap at the high board, her seat beside him vacant. Hurrying to join them, she scurried around the perimeter of the hall. Several new acquaintances stopped her progress for a word or two, but she was determined to reach Durham and allowed for only the briefest of pauses. As she neared the dais, a wrinkled hand grasped her arm. Batsheva turned to look into a pair of dark, aged eyes. Frozen, she was caught in an ancient gaze.

"You are the lady who traveled far?" croaked the old woman. She did not wait for a response. "I would tell your fortune."

"No," she replied sharply, then added, "but thank you."

The old crone revealed toothless gums when she smiled. "*Es muy importante, Infanta,"* she crooned in Castilian.

Batsheva recoiled; there was no one here who would call her *Infanta.* "*¿Por qué?*"

"You are sought in many corners, Madonna," she told her in the same language.

"Who looks for me, old mother?"

The woman shrugged her bony shoulders. "*No es importante.* Once you were told of three men but it is the dark one you hold deepest in your heart."

Her heart beat furiously in her chest and her breath came in short gasps. Batsheva's lips were dry; she licked them as she tried to put words to her fears. "Who told you this?" she rasped.

The old woman cackled, "You ask too many questions for a woman who needs fewer answers. I will tell you but one answer. Ask the right question and the answer is yours."

A thousand questions welled up in her brain, but there was only one that must be asked. Leaning close to the crone, she whispered, "Are they safe?"

"*Bueno, bueno, mamacita;* you ask the right one. They are safe in the bosom of their family. Worry not about them, the lost are always found, even when hidden behind a well of tears." With a gnarled finger, the old woman reached up and wiped away a tear from Batsheva's eye. "A mother's tears," she murmured gently, "a mother's tears for her twin children who are safe."

Batsheva's heart felt as though it would burst. "Will I see them? Where are they now? And their…."

The old woman cackled again and held up her hand. "*No más, no más.* You know what you need to know. Hold it in your heart and be strong. There is no more I can tell you." She patted Batsheva's cheek and disappeared into the crowd.

Batsheva sagged against the cold, stone wall, her face white, her breath coming in ragged gasps. Suddenly, the noise in the room was deafening; the laughter sounded harsh and unpleasant, the smells of rushes and herbs, overpowering. She fought back the urge to retch. Digging her fingers into the unrelenting stone, she tried to calm herself, to will herself to composure. Her mind filled with the fog of worry.

Then two hands grabbed her by the shoulders.

"What's wrong?" Durham's voice pierced the clouds, bringing her back. She opened her eyes and stared blankly up at him. He did not wait for an answer. Scooping her up, he quickly carried her out of the hall.

From the dais, Margaret saw her brother leave, his lady in his arms. She would have followed, but Henry's hand stayed her. "Let them go, Maggie," he told her quietly. "His lady must be tired." He did not believe that was the case; he had watched her exchange with the old woman from the high board.

"Perhaps you're right," Margaret replied, leaning back against her chair. "Perhaps this is too much after so long a journey. After all, she is recently out of childbed."

Henry watched his brother-in-law go through the door and silently prayed nothing was wrong.

The chamber was empty when Durham kicked open the door. Kicking it closed behind him, he carried Batsheva to the bed. He lay her down, then deftly untied the laces of her gown. "Here, sit up," he ordered softly, and was surprised when she did as she was told. He removed the heavy mantle first, then tried to pull the gown over her.

From beneath the heavy folds of cloth came an unexpected snort. "Wait," she laughed, her words muffled by the cloth. He released the fabric. Her head popped out and she removed her circlet and veil. Sliding her legs over the side, she stood up. "Now you may assist me, my lord."

He helped her shed the heavy cote, then stared at her in her ivory chemise. "'Tis odd to see you slender again, Bess," he said, "I'd grown used to your rounded belly."

"And you doubted I was old enough to bear a child!" She eyed him suspiciously, and then laughed gently. "I, for one, am not sorry to be flat once more. I grew weary of trying to sleep on my side."

Durham watched her as she retrieved her chamber robe from the wardrobe and wrapped it about herself. "What happened in the hall, Bess?" he asked slowly.

For a moment, she considered whether or not to tell him the truth. He had, in the past, been patient and understanding when the specter of the children arose to haunt her. As much as she knew about him, she did not know if he put much stock in fortune-tellers, but the old crone wasn't so much a seer as she was the holder of some knowledge. How she gained her knowledge, Batsheva did not know, nor did she think the woman would tell her. Carefully tying a knot in her sash, she formed an answer to his question. "There was an old woman," she started slowly, "who spoke to me."

"Did she frighten you, Bess?"

"No."

"Then what did she say to you?"

"She…" Batsheva's voice grew very soft, "told me my children are safe with their father's family."

Durham sat down on the bed with a thump. Was this the moment she would tell him she was leaving him? The pain he felt was mirrored in his eyes when he asked, "How did she come to know this?" He thought of his own search for the children.

Batsheva crossed the room to him and sat beside him, taking his hands in hers. "I did not ask, for I doubt she would tell me. But know this, Gilbert, she called them twins. I do not doubt her words."

"Did she say where?"

Batsheva shook her head. "'Tis enough that I know they are safe." *For now*, she added silently. "I've Miriam to care for, Gilbert; I'll not risk her safety with foolish actions."

If he felt a certain twinge of relief, Durham feared it would be short lived. "I love the child, Bess; she is a miniature of her mother. Anne thinks of her as her sister."

"She has no reason to think otherwise, my lord," smiled Batsheva sadly. "I've told her nothing."

"Nor have I." He pressed her fingers to his lips. "Marry me, Bess. Marry me in whatever way you will, but marry me and be my wife."

She sighed as she leaned against him. When she glanced up again, she saw the intensity in his eyes and wondered why she continued to say *no*. Khalil was dead; Durham had seen him fall with his own eyes. He loved her, yet she was unsure. If the world were perfect, she would return to Málaga or one of the Hagiz households and, from there, either seek out Khalil's people or perhaps marry from within her own community. But the world was not perfect. No matter where she looked, she found herself surrounded by people so different that there was no commonality, no congruence of background or experience. It would be easy, she knew, to pretend she was a Christian, take their sacraments, and slide into a comfortable life as Countess Durham. Yet something prevented her from giving up the hope she could return to her own world. Each time she had asked for more time, Gilbert had given it, but how much longer would he be willing to give? She did not know the answer and, truthfully, she was loath to ask. "Let us not discuss this now," she said finally, "let us wait until we are at Durham."

At least she did not say no. His heart leapt with hope and he kissed her hand once more. "I love you, Batsheva," he murmured softly against the fingers, using the name he rarely spoke. "I will wait for however long you would have me wait."

Slowly, Batsheva rose and stood before him. "My lord, you have shown me more kindness than I would have dared ask. I am forever grateful to you for that."

"Do you forgive me for taking you away from the camp?" he asked seriously.

Batsheva flashed on another time when she was asked the same question, but this one needed a much different answer. She replied with equal gravity, "Forgive? No, that is not the right word. Understand, yes. Accept that you performed what you thought to be an act of charity, yes. But forgive? That is not necessary. There is nothing to forgive." She slipped her hands from his grasp. "I am bursting with milk for Miriam. I should get her."

Used to seeing her in the cot near the lady's bed, Durham glanced around the room. "Where could she be?"

Batsheva laughed lightly. "I am certain, monsieur, if you were to look at the railing above the hall, you will find Mary, along with Lydia and Miriam."

"A mother's second sense?"

"No, simply a sharp eye. I saw them from the hall. Take the babe from Lydia, please. I would not wish them to miss the entertainment."

Durham bowed gallantly from the waist. "As you wish, my lady."

He was gone, then back in a matter of moments with Miriam nestled comfortably in the crook of his arm. "I am loath to give her to you, Bess," he whispered. "She sleeps so well against me."

"You say that now," she teased in kind, "wait until she screws up that little face and wails. Then you, my lord, will change your mind."

"I think I shall hold her for a moment. I find I like the feeling." He sat on the edge of the bed.

Batsheva sighed as she watched him softly touch Miriam's cheek. For a brief moment, she recalled Khalil holding Amina in much the same way. There was an indefinable bond between a father and his daughter; Batsheva shivered knowing Miriam would never know her father. *But Amina and Daud did,* she thought suddenly. *And they must remember me!* Silently, she went to her trunk and pulled out her pouch. From it, she took a single gold piece, one of the coins Saladin had given her. "Gilbert," she said slowly, placing the coin in his hand, "find the old woman and give her this."

"'Tis a foreign coin, Bess! And in the realm, it would be suspect."

Batsheva closed his fingers over the coin. "Give her *this* coin, my lord. 'Tis important to me."

"If you insist."

"I do."

Miriam began to stir; her little rosebud mouth opened and closed several times. At last, her eyes opened and she seemed to stare up at Durham before she let loose with a squeaky cry. Reluctantly, he handed her to her mother. "I think she has need of that which you alone can supply," he said somberly.

"That, and a dry nappy."

Durham laughed aloud, then kissed Batsheva's cheek. "I will do your errand, Madame. Then I shall return."

"Do not hurry, my lord. Enjoy the entertainment." Before she was settled on the bed with Miriam, he was gone.

Six women in fancy slash costumes were whirling, tambourines flying, in the center of the hall when Durham slipped inside the door. No one seemed to take any notice of the earl as he moved around the room in search of the old crone he had seen talking with Batsheva. He was about to give up the search when he spotted her sitting on a stool beside the enormous hearth. Quickly maneuvering through the crowd, he reached her just as she popped a piece of bread into her mouth. She started to rise, but his hand stayed her as he knelt down to speak. "Sit, old mother. The lady has sent you a coin for your troubles."

"The lady's coin is no good with me," she cackled. "Tell her to keep it."

"She will insist, old mother," replied Durham. He took her gnarled hand in his own and dropped the gold piece into the open palm.

"Aieee!" cried the old woman. "This is what she sends me?" She saw Durham nod. Turning the coin over and over, she examined it carefully. "She is a cunning one, the lady. She asks without asking. She tells without telling."

Digging into his purse, Durham withdrew a handful silver coins of the realm and gave them to the old woman. "This will buy you plenty of bread. Take them as thanks for your good news."

She wheedled a bony finger into the hard muscles of his chest. "You cannot buy me, little man, but she…she is the one whose bidding I do. You tell her this. Tell her the coin will be returned to its master. Tell her that, little man. It will make her happy."

"To whom will it be returned, old woman?" pushed Durham.

"If you do not know, it is not for me to tell you. Women's secrets… women's secrets. Not for little boys." She slipped the coins into a ragged purse dangling from her waist and cackled, her dark, dark eyes alive with merry lights. "Yes, yes, the coin shall go home. You tell her that." Without a second glance at Durham, she scurried away from the fireplace and through the side archway.

Durham considered following her, but before he could move a foot in that direction, Isabella sidled up to him and slid her arm into his. "Gil," she cooed, "is your lady unwell?"

"She is tired after the journey," he replied, his eyes still on the door, "and the babe needs her."

"Strange that she would nurse the child herself."

"Hardly strange, Isabella. 'Tis a proper thing for a mother to do."

Isabella took the rebuke in stride. "Well, while the lady is engaged, come sit with me and tell me the news. I hear you were late with Eleanor."

By now, the old woman would be gone from the castle; there was no point in trying to find her in the darkness. Sighing, he let Isabella draw him deeper into the hall.

Her tattered cloak drawn around her, the old woman scuttled across the courtyard to the place where the jongleurs' wagons sat all but deserted. She opened the tailgate of the cart she called home and slipped inside.

"*Kli shay' ealaa ma yaram, kulu hsay' ealaa ma yaram,*" she cackled into the darkness. "All is better than well."

A deep whisper answered her. "You are certain?"

"More certain than you are of your name," she snapped. Pulling the gold coin from her purse, she handed it to the man. "See. See for yourself. The lady is the lady. When you give this to our master, tell him she weeps for her children. Now she knows they are safe."

Emerging from the shadows, Kassim took the coin and held it up in the moonlight. He studied the strikes on both sides and smiled, his teeth white against the night. "You have done well, old mother," he said, sliding it into his sash. Tossing a bag of useful coins on the pallet and his cloak over his shoulder, he left the wagon. It was a long walk to where his horse was tethered in the woods and an even longer journey home.

The hour was late when Durham returned to the chamber where Batsheva sat reading a thick volume by candlelight. Quietly, he closed the door behind him, and he saw her glance up. "Forgive the intrusion, Bess," he softly called, "but the other chambers are filled. My sister assumed I would sleep here so my chamber could be used by other guests."

"I cannot imagine why she would think such a thing, Gilbert." She let the corners of her mouth turn upward.

He joined her at the table. "What is it that keeps you awake so late?"

She closed the book, leaving the ribbon marker at her page. "'Tis the *Book of Psalms*, in French. I had not known such things were translated."

"Some are, I suppose. Where did you find it?"

"Margaret's maid brought it for me. I had asked your sister if there were books in the castle and she admitted there were a few. She thought I might enjoy the poetry."

"And do you?"

She smiled again, this time wryly. "'Tis interesting, the choice of words. Several of these I know well in their true language. The translation seems to be…" she chewed her lip thoughtfully, "dull, lacking in passion." She noted the look of surprise on his face and continued. "The original is much more beautiful."

He stared at her. The grey eyes were especially intense, the creamy ivory of her skin took on an ethereal glow from the candle. The column of her throat ended at a place where he could see a pulse point above the square neckline of her night rail. And beneath that, he could see the swell of her breasts, full of milk, firm and rounded like twin melons. He longed to touch her, but without her permission, he would not. Instead, he continued to stare.

"Are you not well, Gilbert?" she asked after a long silence.

He brought his face close to hers until she could smell the strong scent of wine on his warm breath. "'Tis you, Bess, who make me feel jelly where my innards are kept." Abruptly, he rose and walked to the open window. He breathed deeply of the cool night air, letting its freshness clear his head. "I cannot do this," he rasped, his back still to her. "I cannot go on pretending to be your husband when, in truth, I am not."

"You've had too much to drink, my lord. Leave this for another time."

"I cannot." He spun around and faced her. "Do you find me so monstrous that you would not have me?"

Suddenly, Batsheva's composure snapped. "What would you have me do, my lord? Spread my legs because you wish it? A marriage should be more than that!" Her voice rose, then she lowered it when Miriam stirred in the cradle. "You know I never married Khalil. I could not marry him anymore than I can marry you. It would be wrong, terribly wrong. I would be forced to make vows I cannot keep. Now, let me be."

"I shall let you be, madam," he snarled, "if *that* is what pleases you!" He stormed from the chamber, slamming the door as he went.

From the cradle, Miriam let out a yelp and a wail. Batsheva scooped her up and snuggled the startled infant against her breast. "*No llores, mi pequeño tesoro*," she cooed in her native tongue, "*no llores*." And although she told her daughter not to cry, there was little she could do to stop the tears starting to trickle down her own cheeks.

CHAPTER 25

York

APRIL 1192

Batsheva did not know where Durham slept that night; it was enough to know he slept somewhere other than her chamber. When Lydia arrived to tend to Miriam, Batsheva handed over the child without objection, rolled over and went back to sleep. She had no stomach for confrontations and even less tolerance for Margaret's questions.

My children are safe, she thought as she buried her face in the pillow, *why not stay here and raise Miriam as his daughter? What future is there for me if I return to Khalil's people?* The same thoughts rolled around in her head, growing louder and louder until she wanted to shout them away. But they would not go away and, in the end, she threw back the covers and stormed out of the nest she had created between the heavy bed curtains.

Without Mary's help, she dressed herself in a simple gown of grey wool and shoved her hoseless feet into a pair of slippers. She paced the chamber several times and, realizing that was a useless exercise, she kicked off her slippers exchanging them for hose and her red leather boots. Grabbing a light woolen mantle from the wardrobe, she marched herself out of the chamber and down the stairs.

In the solar Batsheva had seen the night before, Margaret was sewing with a group of ladies. "Come in, Lady Elizabeth, come join us."

Batsheva spied Isabella amongst the ladies and realized she had no desire whatsoever to join them. She wanted to be outside, in the sunshine, feeling the wind on her face. "Thank you, Lady Margaret, but I must decline."

"Where are you going?" asked Isabella with a bright smile.

"Out," Batsheva replied shortly. She saw the shocked look on the faces of the other ladies. "I need some fresh air, Lady Margaret. Where are the stables?"

"On the far side of the courtyard. You are not planning to ride alone, are you?"

"I shall take a groom, if that is all right. I simply need exercise."

Margaret eyed her suspiciously but held her tongue. She had already found her brother asleep in the great hall, lying on a bench near the fireplace. Whatever took place between them was none of her business no matter how curious she was. "Ask for John. He'll lead you on a pleasant ride."

"She is an odd duck, isn't she?" said Isabella when she was gone.

Margaret shot the woman a hostile look. "I think, Isabella, that my brother's lady has managed remarkably well, considering everything she has gone through."

"And what exactly is that?" Isabella pressed.

None of your business, thought Margaret, but she replied, "The lady was recently widowed; she has left her homeland for a strange place where the language is nothing like her own. She has been thrust into our society without the benefit of a mother's guidance, and she is joined to a man who is about to assume the responsibility of an earldom. All things considered she is remarkably poised."

"Did you mean wed?" Isabella inquired with exaggerated politeness. She did not wait for Margaret to respond. "When they left Westminster, Eleanor was quite upset with them both; it seems Lady Elizabeth has refused to marry Gilbert in church."

Yaffa was in a stall near the front of the stable. No sooner had Batsheva crossed the threshold than the horse snorted and whinnied. A boy was pitching hay nearby and she called to him. "Where is Earl Durham's tack?" she inquired politely.

"Both lords are out, my lady," he replied, wiping the sweat from his face with his sleeve.

"My saddle should be with our tack wagon. Can you find it? 'Tis a strange looking saddle, easy to see." She did not want to say it was a Saracen saddle; it might frighten the boy.

The groom bowed and hurried away. Batsheva unlatched the gate and led Yaffa out without benefit of a lead. She systematically began checking over the animal. Satisfied that Yaffa was sound, she stroked the velvet nose until the groom returned. She frowned, "It was not there?"

"No, my lady, just the bridle."

She took the leathers and slipped the bit easily into Yaffa's mouth. "Can you find me a blanket?"

He nodded, puzzled by the request, and went to fetch one. When he brought it to her, he watched with amazement as she threw it over the mare's back, then swung on. "My lady!" he cried in protest.

"Go find John, boy. Lady Margaret said he would ride with me."

"He's not here, my lady. He's out with the master."

She looked down at him critically, taking in his small size and wiry frame. "What is your name?"

"Kip, ma'am."

"Can you ride, Kip?"

"Yes, ma'am!"

"Then find a mount and we shall ride."

Durham and York rode in the company of 30 men to where the dark knight had been encountered. When Durham had shown him the place, Henry waved the men to follow him and they raced over open fields to where the burned-out shell of a village stood like a blot against the verdant countryside. The soldiers remained at a distance while the two noblemen picked their way through the remains.

Not even the small church had escaped the conflagration. Charred timbers littered the churchyard where even the crude headstones were lying flat against the black earth. Of the houses, nothing was left except the burned-out footprints of their locations. An overturned cart sat deserted in the middle of what had once been the village square, a single wheel turning eerily in the breeze. Somewhere in the distance, a single sheep bleated, but it was the only sound.

Durham was thoroughly disgusted by what he observed. "Where are the people?"

"They've taken shelter where they could find it. Some are staying within the walls of the castle, some in the city with kinfolk, and some have found shelter at Swine. But they will come back; they are tied to the land as much as I am."

"Why was it burned, Henry?" asked Durham bitterly, "Who benefits?"

Henry frowned as he picked up a piece of crockery and threw it away. "It was a warning, Gil, not from me, but from Lackland. The men of Chatterham, for that was this place's name, refused to send aid to Lackland."

Durham narrowed his eyes at Henry, until they were nothing but hard blue slits. "Where were you, Henry? Why didn't you stop this?"

"Leeds," he answered bitterly. "I was in Leeds with the others."

"And where were you when they burned your keep with the Jews inside?"

Henry stared at him; his mouth moved, but nothing came out.

"Could you not avert that tragedy either? Those people were as innocent as these."

"Edward told you that," he murmured, his face turned away. "What happened with the Jews was an ugly thing. I did try to stop it."

"Obviously not hard enough. They burned."

Henry shielded his eyes against the sun and stared off in the direction of the city. "They paid taxes; they were good citizens."

"They lent you money, Henry. How else could you afford your castle?"

"I paid my debts to them," he shouted into the silent air, "in full!" He faced Durham again. "My influence is sorely corrupted by an archbishop who serves not God, but himself. He seeks profit from whatever opportunity avails itself, regardless of the moral imperative."

"And you do not."

"No, I do not. My charge is greater than that, Gil, and you know it. I would not be harboring half the county behind the walls of my castle if I did not believe it were so. As earl, I have responsibilities tearing me down the middle. My presence is required here at the same time it is required by the councils. I cannot be in two places at once."

"They waited until you were gone."

"That was obvious." He kicked at a stone with his boot. "Did not Edward tell you any of this?"

"Did he know?"

"Yes. And he blamed me for this, too, until he spoke to their reeve. Thomas Crane lost his hand in the battle, but he lost far more. His wife and sons were murdered. They were Saxons, Gil, like me, and they stood their ground against another Norman invasion, however small it was. They're Normans, you know. All of them. Every last one of the bastards John has riding about the country…all Norman. I've petitioned the old queen more than once, but she remains silent…and in France."

"She's here now," countered Durham, his voice still bitter. "She may not be English born, but she knows what is good for this country. Otherwise, why would she banish her own son?"

"Because if she didn't, she would lose England for Richard. You've been with him, Gil. Why doesn't he come back for the sake of his country? We are eaten alive by civil strife, yet he remains in the Holy Land fighting a war which isn't ours."

"'Tis God's war," answered Durham although he knew the defense was untrue. He had put the question to Richard himself before he left for home. The king no more recognized the need for his presence in England than he understood why the sun rose and set.

"Nonsense; 'tis no more God's war than this is. The crusade is bleeding the country dry, and it will only get worse. I am no more able to prevent this," he gestured with a sweeping hand, "than he will aid in the Second Coming of Christ. The care of my people and my lands is infinitely more important to me than the walls of the Holy Sepulcher."

Durham laughed, but it was a harsh sound. "Blasphemy, brother?" He did not admit he had said as much to the king.

"Nay, not blasphemy. Reality. I am faced with the very survival of my vassals, and so are you. Your talk will change when you reach Durham and learn what it means to be earl."

The words stung Durham harder than if Henry had slapped him. *What it means to be earl.* He had not considered that when he returned it would not be to his father's presence. Robert, Earl of Durham, was dead and he, Gilbert, now bore the title and the responsibility. He had already been recognized as earl in Westminster and at the councils when, in fact, he felt as if he played the role as surrogate for the man he admired most on this earth. His father had been an exemplary noble, fighting for the good of his vassals, serving as a fair judge and strong leader. He had earned the respect of the people of Durham and he cherished their loyalty. More than once he told his son that, without the goodwill of the people, a noble was no more than a millstone around their necks. Not everyone appreciated old Durham's diligence; his son, however, valued it above all else. Now he would fill his father's enormous boots. *Am I equal to the task?* he repeatedly asked himself.

As if he could read the younger man's mind, Henry placed his hand on Durham's shoulder. "Robert was my teacher when my own father was unable to fulfill the role, Gil. I learned from him what it meant to be a leader of men and I think you learned the same lessons. Did not the men follow you on crusade willingly, without question?"

"And most of them died," snorted Durham. "I bring back not glory, but pain for too many families."

"They knew the price before they went."

"It does not matter."

Henry waited for him to say something else, but when the silence became oppressive, he added, "Go home, Gil. 'Tis time you took your place at your own high board."

Kip watched with awe as the lady charged up the first hill. Her horse was surely the most magnificent he had ever seen, and it was obvious the mare was devoted to her mistress. Despite the lack of saddle, the lady was easy in her seat and seemed to barely touch the reins as the horse flew over the hard-packed dirt of the road.

An open field lay to Batsheva's left and she called to her escort. "Can we ride there?"

"Yes, my lady," he shouted back. He could barely keep up with her as she tore across the grassy slope. He had never seen anyone ride quite like she did. He was used to seeing ladies sit daintily on their saddles, delicately holding the reins of some gentle palfrey trained to nothing more than a spirited trot. Oh, he had heard about ladies who rode like men, and had even seen some of the young noblewomen attempt to do just that, but this lady was at home on the horse's bare back. Kicking his own horse, he leaned as far as he dared over the animal's thick shoulders and pressed himself against the sweating body, cursing himself for thinking he could ride as well without benefit of a proper seat.

Batsheva reined in Yaffa at the top of the knoll and looked out over the lush countryside. The cultivated fields were rich with new green growth contrasting against the dark brown of the earth. She could see sheep dotting the far hillside, their shepherds standing nearby, cutting dark figures against the outrageous blue of the English sky. She laughed aloud, thinking how amazed Khalil's people would be to see a place so green, so full of water that no one thought about spilling precious drops on the ground.

Kip joined the lady on the knoll. "My family lives over there," he said pointing down the road. "I am a page to his lordship because I want to be a knight."

"A knight?" asked Batsheva. She thought all the knights were of noble birth and said so.

"Oh, no, my lady. Some have earned their knighthood in battle. That is what I want to do. I am good with a sword. I want to be a soldier and go on crusade with the king. I want to wrest Jerusalem from the infidels!"

Inwardly, Batsheva shuddered. This was how hatred was bred, in stories to children who knew nothing more than what they were told by their elders. "Infidels," she said slowly, "are flesh and blood, just like you. Are you so anxious to see the gore of battle?"

"God protects His own, my lady," he replied gravely. "Every good Christian wants to see the Holy Sepulcher in Christian hands."

"Are you willing to die for it, too?"

"Yes, my lady, most willing. Then I would be assured of a place in the Kingdom of Heaven." His voice swelled with great pride. "You see, my lady, Lord Henry says if I keep working hard, he'll let me go with Charles when he goes on crusade."

Batsheva tried to remember the name Charles, then recalled he was Margaret's third son. "Is he older than you?"

"Yes, my lady, but not very much. We practice our swords together and he teaches me whatever he learns from his lordship." He puffed out a little, "Me and Charley, that's what we call him, we're good friends."

"How old are you, Kip?"

"I'll be fourteen near midsummer…old enough to squire.

"And your father, what does he say?"

"He wants me to seek my fortune away from here, my lady. If I stay, I will be nothing more than a groom or perhaps, if I am lucky, a stable master. But I want more than that. I want to use my good right arm to serve my king and God. And I will. Lord Henry says I am strong enough to send with his own men."

Something in Batsheva snapped and she shouted at the boy, "You are young and green and full of silly dreams! Men die on crusade, even the best of the best. My own late lord was a great warrior and he fell in battle. Stay here, little boy; stay here and grow old serving your lord in his castle. Do not risk yourself for an old man's foolish dreams!" She kicked Yaffa hard in the side and galloped off leaving Kip, red with shame, sitting atop the hill.

The pounding of hooves against the hard road sent tremors up Batsheva's spine, but she did not care. It felt good to ride hard in safety although she could almost hear the sounds of battle echoing in her ears. Ignoring the countryside around her, she urged Yaffa on, away from the castle.

York and Durham rode abreast in silence, each one deep in private thought. The men trailed at a slight distance behind them, leaving the lords enough space for private conversation. Neither lord seemed to be taking much notice of the other or of anything else, for it was the captain of the guard who shouted, "Look, my lords; a rider is coming."

The two men looked up. Tearing down the road at breakneck speed was a single rider. "What in hell comes here?" cried Henry as he halted.

But Durham recognized the rider bent low over a white horse and spurred his mount. Charging hard, he galloped toward Batsheva.

She saw the single rider and suddenly wheeled her horse around. Glancing over her shoulder, her pursuer gaining ground, she shouted for Yaffa to go faster. Now she could hear the hoof beats, as did Yaffa, and the horse picked up speed. Through the pounding, she thought she heard her name, but she decided that could not be. Yaffa reached a rise in the road and Batsheva saw Kip coming toward her. "Go back!" she shouted, "Go back!"

Confused, Kip halted his mount and paused. Then he saw the other rider. Quickly, he turned his horse and as soon as Batsheva reached him, he took off beside her. "'Tis Durham!" he shouted over the din. As suddenly as she began, Batsheva reined in Yaffa and brought her to a halt. Kip did the same.

Durham, breathless from shouting, wheeled his mount around when he reached the twosome at the top of the rise. "Are you mad?" he shouted, his face flush with anger. "You'll kill yourself and the horse!"

She couldn't help herself; she laughed. "You would not have caught me had I not stopped, my lord," she announced. "You never knew how to be one with your mount."

Durham trotted close to her and glared, his eyes dangerously narrow, the small muscle in his jaw twitching with anger. "Have you no sense, Bess, to be out on the road alone?"

"I am not alone; Kip is with me."

"Idiot!" he snarled. "Even we took armed men. The roads are full of highwaymen and thieves who would sooner rape you as they slit your throat."

Batsheva sat back and frowned at him. "And you think I cannot care for myself?" she asked with an arched eyebrow. "I, who have killed when necessary? Remember, my lord, it is at *my* will that you enjoy continued good health." She tapped Yaffa in the side with her heel and the horse trotted toward the castle at an easy gait. Batsheva did not bother to look to see if Durham and the others followed.

Henry reached Durham first. "Was that your lady?"

"Yes," answered Durham between clenched teeth.

"She rides without benefit of a saddle?"

"She rides like a madwoman."

Henry's head tilted backward as he laughed heartily. "She's a fine one, Gil; you deserve each other."

Durham growled. He was in no mood to tolerate Henry's barbs as he followed Batsheva's dust back to the castle walls.

In her chamber, Batsheva was sitting near the open window contentedly nursing Miriam when Durham slammed open the door. "Out! he roared at the startled Lydia. The maid scrambled up from where she sat amid freshly laundered nappies and scurried out the door as fast as her legs could carry her. "You are a madwoman!" he shouted as soon as the door closed. "Do you not know the risk you took dragging that boy out of the castle for your bolt? Or perhaps motherhood has addled your brain and you do not recall the dark knight we met on the road just two days ago!"

Batsheva took no notice of him; she adjusted Miriam in her arms, then paid attention to the drape of the babe's little gown. Humming quietly, she stroked Miriam's cheek as she nursed.

Durham was incensed. He could not abide the silence. "Say something, damn you!" he shouted at her.

Batsheva glanced up and met his angry stare with a placid one. "What would you have me say, my lord?"

He was gnashing his teeth. The muscle in his jaw twitched visibly. "You, madam," he said through clenched teeth, "are the most thoughtless, careless, infuriating woman I have ever had the misfortune to know."

"Then let me go home."

"And where, pray tell, is that? Shall I ship you off to the Saracens? Or perhaps you would prefer to return to that piteous excuse for a camp where I found you?"

"Where I go, monsieur," shrugged Batsheva, "is of no concern to you."

"*Monsieur*? I thought we were past that."

Her shoulders rose and fell once more. "What you think is of no concern to me."

He stared at her for a long time before he spoke again. When he did, his voice was low and ragged with pain. "What has brought this on, Bess?" he asked. "You seemed to be happier of late."

Miriam had fallen asleep at the breast. Batsheva lifted her gently, drew her gown over her exposed flesh, and placed the babe in the cradle. She stood, smoothed the fabric of her frock, then faced Durham. "I am not suited for this life, my lord. I cannot live locked away in a castle. Today, as I rode Yaffa, I wanted to ride south until I reached the sea. Had Miriam not been here, neither would I."

"I suppose a harem would be better."

"This," she spread her arms wide, "is the same prison for your womenfolk. They have no freedom. They cannot read. They cannot think for themselves. They are ignorant of anything other than the pabulum their mothers taught them before they were six years old! Their conversation is stilted and centers on idle gossip."

"And in a harem it is different?"

"I would not know," she snapped, "never having lived in one."

His hand slammed against the wall. "You say you are the adopted daughter of Saladin; you say you were the consort of an amir," he bellowed in anger and frustration. "If you've not been kept hidden away in a harem, how can you be these things?"

"Lower your voice, my lord," she hissed, "and listen carefully. I will say this but one more time and then I will say it no more. I am not a Muslim woman. I was raised in a free home. My time with my lord Khalil was spent in the desert, not in a palace. The sultan came to me, not me to him.

I am everything I say I am and more, more than you can ever imagine. If that, my lord Earl, makes me less of a woman in your eyes, then so be it. *I am who I am*!" Miriam wailed in her cradle, causing Batsheva to glance at Durham with pure disgust in her ice grey eyes. "You bring out the worst part of me," she sniped as she rescued the crying child.

Durham did not know how to respond. It was true, he never really paid much attention to how she might be feeling beneath the obvious. He never asked her about her life; he assumed it was something she chose not to discuss, and he was reluctant to pry, lest it cause her undue pain. What little he knew was because she spoke freely with Edward. Suddenly, he wished Edward were at York; his nephew had an easy way with her, something he had been unable to develop despite their time together. And in that thought, Durham discovered he was jealous of the young man. "We leave for Durham on the morrow, Bess," he announced gruffly; "'tis time I went home."

She wanted to tell him he could go without her, but she bit back the words, answering instead, "Yes, my lord."

He stared at her, his eyes narrow blue slits. "You will ride in the coach with Anne, Miriam, and Mary."

That was too much. "I will ride Yaffa, my lord. We are both in need of exercise."

"I said you *will* ride in the coach."

"And I said I will not." She positioned herself with her feet apart, one hand on her hip, the other holding Miriam against her shoulder. Her eyes met his steadily and they did not waiver.

Durham opened his mouth, but before anything could come out, someone banged on the door. "Leave!" he shouted at the oak.

"I will not," replied Margaret as she sailed into the room. "Gilbert! Go outside and take a walk to cool your temper. Half of York hears your shouting." His hard glare flew from Margaret to Batsheva and back to Margaret before he stomped from the room, slamming the door behind him. Miriam howled in her mother's arms and Batsheva did what she could to calm her. Over the wailing, Margaret ordered Batsheva to sit, then took the other chair, dragged it over close to Batsheva, and did the same. "Now," began Margaret in a voice which brooked no nonsense, "you and I have a great deal to discuss, especially if you are to leave for Durham in the morning."

Batsheva regarded her with suspicion. Although she liked Margaret, she knew her to be Isabella's friend and she had no reason to believe anything said between them would not be repeated to Isabella. "Forgive me, my lady, for I mean no disrespect; but I choose to keep my own counsel."

Margaret frowned and then stood up. Without asking, she removed Miriam, now calm, from her mother's arms and walked to the door. Opening it, she called for Lydia and handed the child to the nursemaid. "Now, Lady Elizabeth, you and I are going for a walk. Do take a mantle; there is a chill in the air."

Outside, Margaret silently marched Batsheva through the gardens to a secluded area where a small gazebo stood near the outer wall of the castle. Two rough-hewn chairs sat in the center, with a small table between them. Surrounded by trees, it looked as though the wall had been skirted around the miniature copse intentionally, providing a place for quiet meditation and reflection. Beside the gazebo, lilies of the valley bloomed in profusion, their gentle scent filling the light breeze.

Margaret led Batsheva into the little shelter and pointed at the chairs. "Let us sit and enjoy the day, Lady Elizabeth." She waited until Batsheva was seated, then took the other chair. "You are about to leave for Durham and I would speak with you privately. There are disturbing rumors afoot which I would have you dispel now, before I hear them from other sources." Batsheva remained silent, trying the older woman's patience to the limit. "I would strongly suggest that you find your tongue," she said, keeping her voice as calm and even as possible, "before you find yourself in grave danger. I am your ally, whether you admit it to yourself or not. I will not have Gilbert the subject of idle gossip when the root of that gossip has been in my home."

In the shade of the gazebo, the air was cool and Batsheva drew her mantle close around her. "I'm afraid, Lady Margaret, I have no idea what you mean."

"Never bluff when you do not know the stakes, Elizabeth. Let me assure you, the stakes are high."

"How high?"

"High enough to burn you for a witch, for that is part of the gossip."

"Oh, no! 'Tis not true!"

Margaret was relieved she finally had the lady's full attention. "I know that, Elizabeth, but there are others who would believe whatever nonsense is told to them. You have made a powerful and ruthless enemy, child, who would see you burned if necessary."

She did not need to be told it was Isabella. "She is nothing more than a simpering gossip. Queen Eleanor gives no credence to her words."

"A gossip with the ear of an archbishop!" Margaret leaned forward and drew Batsheva's hand into her own. "Begin at the beginning, Elizabeth, and tell me your story from start to finish. Only then we will be able to still the wagging tongues together."

Margaret was asking for her trust, but Batsheva was not certain she could give it. She trusted Jane, yet she had never told more than bits and pieces. To unburden herself might be cleansing, but how prepared was Margaret for the truth? Isabella obviously counted Margaret as her friend, yet the lady seemed to take a dismissive attitude when her name was mentioned. Durham had told her his sister was a practical, down-to-earth woman who judged people on merit, not on birth. He had assured her she would be welcomed with open arms and, indeed, she was. Still, Margaret was unknown to Batsheva and she hesitated.

Seeing her discomfiture, Margaret leapt into the gap. "I know more about you, Elizabeth, than you might think. Edward told me of your connection to Hannah."

Batsheva felt herself shiver. "Did he tell you that I, too, am a Jewess?"

"Yes. And he also told me you are a most honorable lady. It is obvious to me that you are no fortune hunter seeking to snare an earl for a husband. Gilbert introduces you as his wife and the child as his daughter, yet Isabella claims you have refused to wed him in church. I do not doubt Isabella's word on this, Elizabeth; what I doubt is your ability to continue the charade without someone to help you manage it." She did not smile when she added, "Can you see my point?"

"I can see you have decided I should open myself up to your scrutiny, my lady," replied Batsheva, somewhat waspish in her tone.

Margaret was not put off. "Think what you will, but let me assure you, this is for your own good, Elizabeth. I am offering you safe haven, a port in this tempest that I think you sorely need. You will require allies if you are to survive in England."

Batsheva was suspicious. "Why, Lady Margaret, if I might be blunt, are you willing to do this for me?"

"Because my brother loves you and I love my brother. 'Tis that simple."

"Your brother," snapped Batsheva jumping up from her seat and pacing angrily, "is in love with an icon. He knows little about me, save how he found me, and a few minor details of my life. He neither knows me nor has ever expressed any interest in knowing *me*. He is a knight, like all other Frankish knights, living for some bizarre ideal that I cannot possibly fathom. He serves his king by dancing attendance on the old queen, not by leading his people. He delays his journey home because he is no more prepared to be their earl than he is to…to…to sprout wings and fly!"

Margaret's laughter caused Batsheva to stop pacing and stare. "I see you know my brother well, Elizabeth. You are right and I shall not argue these points with you. However, do not doubt for a single moment that he loves you as best he can. For now. Given the opportunity, I think he could grow to love you as a living being instead of this icon, as you call it. He idolized Joan while she lived, and when she died, it grew worse. Is it any wonder he fled Anne, lest she learn he was not as perfect as her mother had been? You cannot imagine how thrilled I was to learn he brought a woman home! And not some shrinking flower who simpers her way through a room! You, my dear, will make a fine countess to his earl."

"I am not for sale, Lady Margaret."

"I did not imply that you are."

"In the past, decisions have been made for me without my consent. I will not permit that to continue."

"Then make your own. No one will force you to do anything," smiled Margaret. "I, for one, will not permit that."

Sitting down again, Batsheva considered what Margaret had said. "You make it sound easy," she admitted, "yet I cannot believe it is so."

Margaret patted her hand. "You will find it easier once you have sorted the past from the present. Tell me your history, Elizabeth, and I will listen without complaint or comment. When you are finished, you will have gained a true friend as well as a knowledgeable ally. Together, we can set you on a path *you* want to follow, one of your own choosing."

For the next hour, Batsheva told her everything, for she did not doubt Margaret's good intentions. She began with the summer Khalil tried to buy her in Málaga, sailing to Africa, the wedding rug Abdul had given her, the caravan, the kidnapping, Gamal's attempt to kill them, and how she came to care for Khalil. Tears streaming down her face, she spoke of Yehuda's repudiation at Benghazi, and how her uncle Avram had tried to help from Tiberias. She managed to smile when she described Amina and Daud, and laughed when she described how the sultan came to see her incognito. She showed her the ring and told her about his note. With shudders she told of the attempted assassination in Nikon's house, the other scar on her arm, and the subsequent departure from Akko. And with little emotion left to expend, she recounted the attack on the Bedouin camp by Durham's company. "I was 15 when I left my father's house," she said when she concluded her tale with the morning's adventure, "but now I am an old woman of almost 22. I feel as if I have lived a thousand lifetimes and have died a thousand deaths. There are times I believe I will simply die from the pain, yet I force myself to go on because of Miriam. She must be returned to her father's house."

Margaret, who had wept and laughed with her, felt drained as she tried to find the words to comfort the woman she now knew was Batsheva Hagiz. In all her wildest imaginings, as she had listened to Isabella's lies in the morning, could she have conjured up the tale this young woman told. She had endured more than anyone should have to and lived to tell the tale. She was stronger, more resilient, more courageous than any man Margaret had ever known. To have experienced the depth of passion she had with her Khalil, Margaret would have sacrificed much. She loved Henry, of course, but not with the same fervor this woman had for the man for whom she risked her life. At the same time, she was incredibly angry at her brother for carrying Batsheva off when he could have easily returned her to her own people. "If it were in my power to return you to Akko or Alexandria, I would," she admitted, "but we both know that at this moment, it is impossible. For now, you are committed to playing the part of Countess Durham whether you like it or not. How you break free from that," sighed Margaret, "will take a great deal of planning and forethought."

"Do you think it can be done?" asked Batsheva with a faint glimmer of hope rising in her breast. "If the old woman knew where to find me, Lady Margaret, surely someone else knows. I want to believe that. I must believe that."

Margaret nodded slowly. "You must continue the charade for now. Yes, go to Durham; we will ultimately need help in this. What help and from whom, I do not know."

"And Gilbert?"

"Leave him to me. I am still his eldest sister and he will be brought around to our plans in due time. As for Isabella..."

Just the name made Batsheva shudder. "Can she be manipulated?" she asked softly.

"Aye, Isabella can be handled. Not easily, but it can be done. She has more than her fair share of skeletons to hide and I am privy to many of her secrets. She can be dealt with in a way she will understand."

Durham sat glowering in the solar. Two men, still dusty from the road, stood before him, awaiting his next order. Henry watched the exchange from the doorway, his face etched with anger. The men had arrived from London just moments before, and their news was not good. "And the king has made no move?" demanded Durham.

"None, my lord. He knows and remains mute. What of Queen Eleanor? We heard nothing."

"She is angry no doubt, but this will pass," replied the earl. "She will not give Lackland her support. Richard is rightful king and, until he dies without heir, she will not turn." He fell silent for a moment then asked, "What of the amir?"

"Some say the Iron Amir lives, my lord, but we could find no one who saw him after the battle. No one saw him buried, but 'tis possible the body was buried with the other infidels."

One of the men presented Durham with a bundle tied with cord. "We have brought you this, my lord. Lord Warwick claims it belonged to him."

Durham accepted the parcel and was surprised by its weight. "What is inside?"

"A sword, my lord. His sword."

"Are you certain?" He saw them both nod. "What of the children?"

The two men exchanged nervous glances. "They have disappeared. We learned of twins near Nablus, but they were boys and not of the right age. We could find no children to match your description."

"Damn them all," swore Durham, "I'd hoped for better news."

One of the soldiers cleared his throat. "My lord?"

"Yes, Will?"

"We did learn one thing. We learned Saladin looked for twins. He sent an entire army to the south to find them."

"And?"

"We do not know, my lord. But we do know he dispatched three ships September last, under heavy guard, carrying members of his household."

"For where were the ships bound?"

"Egypt…perhaps Alexandria. It was said his greatest treasures were aboard those ships."

Durham scowled. It was highly unlikely Saladin would be transporting coin back to Egypt; he would need whatever he had to wage the war. Whatever was on those ships had to have been of personal value. "You've done well," said Durham suddenly. "Stay the night and you will ride home with me tomorrow."

The two men breathed easily as they thanked their earl. They had been gone from Durham for almost five years and they were glad to be heading home at last. Had the earl ordered them back to the Holy Land, however, they would have gone without protest. Fiercely loyal to Durham, they had sworn their allegiance to his cause and they would serve him until they drew their last breaths. Still, the thought of going home brought smiles to their faces. Their boots clattering against the stone floor, they left the solar.

"News of the children?"

The question startled Durham. "Aye, but not the news I hoped. Saladin also searched for them, but it is unknown if they were found."

Henry sat down beside his brother-in-law. "Will you tell your lady?" he asked gently.

Durham shook his head. "She did not know I sent a messenger to the king. But damn, Henry, I would have thought Richard would be en route to England by now."

"The king," replied Henry, "finds no allure in his own lands. If he loses them to John, it will be his own doing."

"But the people support him."

"That support will last only as long as they see him as their champion. Should John and his cadre suddenly prove to be concerned with their welfare, they will follow him. For now, John is unpopular; we can only hope their distrust of him continues long enough for Richard to return."

"*If* Richard returns." Durham rose and stretched his long, lean frame. "I have given much thought to your words of yesterday, brother. You were right in saying I must return to my own lands. We will leave York tomorrow."

"So you told your men."

"So I did," admitted Durham. "If truth be known, I am anxious to return home. I find I miss it."

Henry slapped Durham on the back and chuckled when the tall man winced. "You need peace and quiet for a while, Gil. Go home and stay home. Get a son on your lady and settle down. T'would make your mother happy."

"Aye," he laughed, "that it would. And old Eleanor as well. She views us all as breeders of future liege lords. I should not mind, though. I am weary of a soldier's life."

Further comment died on Henry's lips when Margaret stormed into the solar. Her face was a stone mask, her blue eyes hard as sapphires as she marched directly up to Gilbert and slapped him full across the face. "You will come with me," she announced, not waiting for his protests.

With a hand to his reddened cheek, Gilbert followed his sister through the hall and out into the garden, his stride matched hers step for step. When they reached the gazebo, she ordered him to sit down. As soon as his buttocks hit the bench, she turned on him. "You are a barbarian, Gilbert of Durham. A brute! How could you simply take a girl without her consent? Count yourself fortunate that she hasn't run you through with your own sword, as well she could. That girl, that woman, has a greater sense of chivalry in her little finger than you have in your entire body! You speak of noble causes, yet you took her from her home without so much as a forethought to the consequence. I did not think knights were to behave in such a brutish manner, Gilbert. And you, based on your actions, are no knight!"

Her words stung far more than her slap and Durham's face was red, this time with shame. "I did what I had to do," he shouted, trying to cover his humiliation. "I thought I was saving her life! His life! For God's sake, Maggie, I thought she was a boy!"

"You thought…you *thought*? Obviously you did not think at all! Had you thought after she told you who she was, you should have turned around and delivered her back to a place from whence she could have found a way to rejoin her children. Instead, you have caused her great, unnecessary harm, not to mention what harm might have befallen the children. Thank the Holy Mother that Elizabeth has reason to believe they are safe. I cannot imagine what I would do in her position, but I doubt I would have suffered you to live."

"She told you everything?" he asked amazed.

"Yes."

"Then you know more than I," he grumbled. "She has never seen fit to tell me the whole story."

"Have you ever asked?"

"I have tried."

"No, you haven't, Gilbert. She would have told you had you asked."

"She said it would jeopardize our safety," he protested.

"Nonsense. There were many times you could have asked the question and received an honest answer. But you! You chose to bully your way along, never taking her into consideration at all."

"I have given her great consideration, Maggie! I've not touched her. I've let her have her way with things at Westminster. I've tried to help her heal her wounds."

"Did you ever bother to ask her about the little rug which came with the others?"

Durham thought for a moment and recalled she had seemed upset when the monkey rug arrived with the other, larger ones. "She said it pleased her."

"As well it should have, Gilbert. *It is her rug!*"

He stared at his sister. "What do you mean?"

"The rug was given to her before she was abducted from her caravan; 'twas a wedding gift from a merchant who knew her mother. When she saw it, she knew someone intentionally sent it with the others."

"She said nothing to me." Durham rose from his seat and went to the rail to stare out over the garden. "She never speaks of her past and I always thought it was too painful for her. I did not pursue the subject, lest she become upset."

"It would seem," said Margaret dryly, "everyone around you knows. Even the old lady with the jongleurs brought her a message…and she told you that. Right now, she is biding her time, certain someone will come to take her home."

"I sent another messenger to Richard when we arrived at Westminster," said Durham, turning to face his sister, "asking his help in finding the children. The two men who arrived today brought word that the children have not been found. I had hoped for better news." He paused for a painful moment. "They brought with them her lord's sword and cloak."

"Will you tell her," asked Margaret, her voice gentler than it had been.

He shook his head. "I cannot bear to."

"Do not keep these things from her, Gil," she said, "'tis not good policy."

"What would you have me do, Maggie? Do I take her south and find a ship to carry us to Alexandria? Or do I take her north and wait until she finally gives up hope?"

"Take her north. Our mother is expecting her, and the lady is expecting to go north. She believes that if she is meant to be found, she will be found. If not, she reserves the right to make her life here with you."

For the first time, Durham felt a glimmer of hope. "Does she consider that?" he asked cautiously, almost afraid of the answer.

Margaret nodded slowly, watching her brother's eyes as she did. There was no point in denying that the lady had given consideration to remaining in England, but Margaret felt she had to be honest. "She does. Despite your horrible behavior, she cares deeply for you and would not see you hurt. Or Anne. You must understand, Gil, her greatest desire is to return home if it is possible. Once you come to accept that, you may find yourself less at odds with Batsheva."

"How can I accept this when she holds my heart?" he asked in anguish. "'Tis folly to take her north when she may suddenly leave. And what of Anne? She has lost one mother already; can she bear to lose another?"

She was relieved to hear him mention his daughter; the girl had not been far from her thoughts. Anne was a cause for concern. During the earlier conversation, she had assiduously avoided mentioning the child. She was obviously attached to the lady and as far as she was concerned, this was her new mother. Only once there was some kind of resolution between the adults, could Anne's position be discussed. She told Durham what she thought, and he agreed. "Let our mother help in this, Gil. She is close to the child and once she is recovered from her illness, she will be able to take Anne in hand again."

She said it with such surety that he could not doubt her. He agreed despite his own misgivings regarding his mother's precarious health, at the same time knowing if his mother did not survive, Margaret could certainly step into the void. Temporarily. He bowed his head in assent. "I shall proceed with your counsel in mind, Maggie. In truth, I have no other choice."

PART VI

Durham 1192
The Earl Comes Home

CHAPTER 26

On the Road to Durham

MAY 1192

The trip north was slowed by rainstorms. On the fourth day, the coach was mired in mud on several occasions. To lighten the load, Batsheva insisted on riding Yaffa despite Durham's constant protests. Batsheva, however, did not complain; she was happy to feel the rain in her face and the wind in her hair. Rather than fret about the weather, she laughed as she opened her mouth to catch the drops. "'Tis wonderful," she told Durham again and again. "You cannot imagine how wonderful until you have lived in a desert!"

The soldiers escorting them snickered behind their cowls, but Durham silenced them with a stern look. Even dripping wet, with her hair plastered against her face where it escaped from her hood, she was easily the most exquisite woman he had ever known. Trotting his own mount close to hers, he couldn't help but smile at the radiant face beneath the sodden mantle. "You'll catch your death," he warned her for the 100th time.

"I'm not one to dissolve simply because it is raining, my lord." A loud clap of thunder echoed in the distance. "See, even the heavens agree with me!"

"I think they protest as much," he said dourly. "Another hour and we will stop."

"I would not mind two!" she laughed against the wind. She gently kicked Yaffa, urging her forward again.

The rain stopped just long enough for the sodden band to make the last two miles in relative ease. Durham, at the head of the column, signaled for them to turn off the main road. "We shall stay the night at Crompton Hall," he shouted to the company and from the ranks came a shout of approval.

"What is Crompton Hall?" she asked when she caught up with Durham.

"'Tis a small manor about a day's ride from the city proper, although we are already on Durham lands. 'Twas my mother's estate."

"Does anyone live there now?"

He shook his head. "In season, we use it as a hunting lodge, but the rest of the year, 'tis vacant. No one seems to want it."

The little hall came into view. Unlike the other fine houses at which they had stayed their journey, this was a small mud and plaster affair, its whitewash in need of renewal, its thatched roof in need of repair. The grounds untended, the garden gate hung open in the high stone wall around the property. To the left of the house, a short distance away, stood a stable topped with a slate roof. And beyond that, there were several ramshackle huts, all looking as if they would collapse in the first big wind.

"It looks so sad," commented Batsheva as they rode through the gate. "Why doesn't anyone tend the compound?"

One of the men-at-arms who had re-joined them at York answered for the earl. "I heard at York that when the earl died no one bothered with the private lands. The servants moved closer to Durham where there was protection from highwaymen." He glanced at his lord and added, "Now that his lordship is home, perhaps they will come back. I for one would settle here."

"Then 'tis yours, Will," announced Durham. "Find yourself some crofters and take it on. I am looking to make this land useful once more, this time with men who can stand up for themselves."

The soldier who had fought at Durham's side during the campaign and who had volunteered to return to the Holy Land on his master's mission, bowed at the waist. "Thank you, my lord."

"The thanks are mine, Will. You have earned a place of your own." He turned to the other soldier who had risked so much for his lord. "And you, Rob," he asked solemnly, "would you be willing to take on Bolston? I hear they are in need of a headman."

Batsheva watched the two men sit a little taller in the saddle. She guessed, from the way Durham treated these two soldiers, they had been with him throughout the campaign. Still, she could not help but wonder if they had been present when she was taken or when Khalil was cut down.

Mary and Lydia went to work setting the little hall to rights. Mary began putting together a meal for them all, grumbling as she hauled provisions from the cart to the hall. "Cheer up," one of the soldiers told her, taking a large kettle from her hands, "tomorrow we shall be in Durham, and you'll have the finest food and cooks in all England!"

"And not a moment too soon," she answered gruffly, "I've grown weary of rustic cookery."

Batsheva, overhearing the conversation, had to agree. Although they had stayed in fine manors on the journey northward, she had to admit she would be relieved to reach the final destination. It was time to settle down for a little while, at least. She was, she discovered, tired. Miriam kept her awake during the night; she seemed to always be hungry. And while they often had decent beds, she longed to call one her own. Margaret assured her Durham Castle was large, clean and comfortable, with spacious unused rooms that could be claimed for suites and nurseries. Even Anne, who would have preferred to stay at Westminster forever, admitted she was looking forward to sleeping in her own bed once more. Wet, exhausted, and feeling the need to nurse Miriam, Batsheva took the babe from the cradle now set in a quiet corner of the hall and secluded herself behind a divider screen they had found pushed up against the wall.

As usual, Miriam was hungry. Greedily she suckled at her mother's breast, making low smacking noises as she attempted to drain the last drop. Her little fingers clenched in a fist, she seemed to mark time tapping her mother at a constant rhythm. Batsheva smiled down at the little girl, each time amused by the way she devoured her meals. "I hope you learn more ladylike manners," she whispered against the tiny ear turned to her. Leaning back against the whitewashed wall, she closed her eyes. The bustle in the hall drifted into the background; she was so tired she felt herself slipping into a cat nap and would have let sleep overcome her had she not heard two voices nearby. They spoke in English and, although it was hard for her to catch every word, she found herself straining to listen. She recognized one of the of voices as Will's, the soldier who had joined them at York.

"Ye should have told him, Will," said the other one, his voice low and confidential.

"There was no proof. Rumor, that was all, and even then, a dozen stories for each act."

"But ye heard the same thing many times."

"I was there, Robbie, you were not. I saw him fall. The sword went through him. No man could live with wounds so great. He was covered in his own blood."

"And his horse's. Ye didn't tell him that ye saw them take his body."

"I wasn't certain 'twas his," protested the second voice. "It could have been any of the bodies on the field. We gave him what we found, Robbie! And ye didn't tell him they were looking for her. She's Saracen and ye know it."

There was a momentary pause before the one called Rob answered, "They'll not come to England for her. 'T'would be suicide."

"I'm not so certain of that, either. The Jew said they wanted her back at any price."

"But ye didn't take his coin."

"Nay, I would not do that. The lady is nothing but a pawn in a game that is over."

"Some say she has bewitched him."

"And there are dragons in Sherwood Forest," guffawed the one called Will. "Let it be, Robbie. There's no point in playing the fool."

There was a series of thumps, then the voices moved off. Her eyes wide open, Batsheva knew they were talking about her. She knew they were talking about Khalil. Suddenly, she realized Durham must have sent these two back to Palaestina to gather information. He had not bothered to tell her, and anger welled inside. Pushing it away, she concentrated on remaining calm for Miriam's sake. She closed her eyes again and willed herself to breathe steadily.

She moved through the remainder of the day with a listlessness even Durham noticed during supper. Batsheva picked at her food, barely eating so much as a morsel of the bread and avoiding the watered wine completely. No sooner had she finished pushing away her plate than she excused herself from the board and sought seclusion behind the screens set up to separate the lord's family from the others. Durham waited a while before following her to the sleeping area.

He found her lying on a crude pallet, Miriam beside her. "Are you not well, Bess?" he asked with serious concern.

"I am tired," she shrugged. "'Tis been a long day."

He squatted beside her and took her hand in his. "And tomorrow it will be over. You will feel better once we are at Durham."

"Yes, my lord." Her response was without any shade of emotion.

"Bess," said Durham, "are you worried about reaching Durham?" He saw her shake her head. "My mother will be pleased to have us home. She's a kindly lady, much like Maggie. You will like her, I'm certain."

"Yes, I'm sure I will." She hunkered down beneath the cover. "I would like to sleep now, my lord."

He leaned over to kiss her forehead. "Sleep well, my heart. You shall feel better in the morning."

Batsheva did not answer.

The sun was bright and the road beginning to dry when they resumed travel north to Durham. Batsheva rode Yaffa close to the coach, eschewing Durham's company although he tried to stay near. Anne was permitted to ride with her father on his great destrier and anxiously scanned the horizon to catch first glimpse of the castle. The nearer they came to Durham, the happier the child became despite her earlier sullenness about their return. Her newfound enthusiasm was infectious for Mary and Lydia; the two maids craned their necks out the opening to stare repeatedly at the landscape.

No one wanted to stop for luncheon, so the band kept going. It seemed even the horses were anxious to reach their final destination and when they spotted the last mile marker on the road, their pace quickened. Soon they were almost trotting up the long hill leading to the city.

Upon seeing their earl, people in the fields stopped their work to cheer his homecoming. The closer they came to the gates of Durham, the more men, women, and children joined the little parade. Batsheva, working hard to keep Yaffa in hand, was amazed at the outpouring of joy that greeted Gilbert of Durham and his retinue. When some children began tossing flowers, she thought she would burst out in tears.

Durham, his hood thrown back, raised his hand in greeting, calling to those he knew; graciously he acknowledged the warm welcome. Tall, fair-haired, and incredibly handsome, he looked every inch an earl, right down to his lovely young daughter sitting tall before him in the saddle. Batsheva could feel herself become an object of some curiosity as she rode beside them, wishing this was Islam where she could keep her face covered. She found their stares discomforting and did her best to keep a pleasant countenance while her innards were rapidly turning to jelly.

As they crossed the bridge over the River Wear and into the city, people poured out into the streets to welcome their earl home. The roar was almost deafening as Batsheva reined Yaffa tightly to keep the skittish mare under control. She could see the unabashed joy on Durham's face as he led them slowly through the streets toward the castle. Though the crowd impeded their progress, he seemed not to care. It gave her a chance to look about. Instead of the grime and filth she had come to expect in English cities, she saw a bright, prosperous town, with clean streets and well-built houses. As they passed through the market square, she noticed the wealth of goods ready for purchase in tidy stalls and sturdy carts. Banners and ribbons proclaimed this a market day, but Batsheva had the sense that the town always looked this well-tended. To one side, she could see the castle looming above its walls, on the other, another enormous building.

Durham skirted his mount close to hers and pointed toward the castle. "That is my home," he said proudly. Then he pointed to the other building, "And that is the cathedral."

"A church?" asked Batsheva, unsure of the right word.

"Aye," he answered in English, "a church. 'Tis a great seat of learning, Bess. You can have your fill of books there."

Batsheva wasn't so certain she wanted to read books from a church, but she smiled anyway. "I am certain I will find it all interesting, my lord."

Anne giggled at the exchange and added her own comment. "You will like the archbishop, Bess. He's a jolly good uncle and lots of fun."

"I've never thought of an archbishop as fun," Durham chuckled, "but I suppose if one could be, our Uncle Charles would be that." He noted the look of confusion on Batsheva's face. "Charles is my father's youngest brother and chose the church for his vocation. He is closest to Margaret in age, but we have had our times together as well." He wiggled his brows at her.

As if he heard his name, the archbishop appeared at the end of the castle bridge. Almost as tall as Durham, but wider in girth, the Archbishop of Durham was an impressive figure in his ornate clerical robes. Even from atop her mount, Batsheva could see the same blue eyes sported by Durham and his sister. His hair, however, was raven black with just a bit of grey at the sides and bushy brows to match. "Welcome home, my son!" he called to the earl as he stood in the gateway.

"Thank you, my lord Archbishop!" shouted Durham above the clatter of hooves against the cobbles. He stopped just short of the bridge and let Anne slide from the saddle. As soon as her feet touched the ground, she barreled toward the churchman with her arms extended.

Foregoing decorum, the archbishop knelt to gather the child into the protective circle of his embrace. He kissed her soundly on each cheek, then held her at arm's length. "You look fit and well, my little princess!" he told her happily. "How glad I am to see a smile on your face."

Anne stepped back and curtsied her cousin. "'Tis good to see you," she said, then she leaned forward and whispered, "Uncle Charlie!"

The archbishop roared with laughter as he scooped Anne up into his arms. "Are you to stand there all day, nephew, or are you going to come in?" he yelled to Durham. Without waiting for a reply, he turned and carried Anne into the castle courtyard.

They walked their horses over the bridge, but as soon as they were within the castle walls, the earl dismounted and went to assist Batsheva. "Welcome to your new home," he murmured as he lifted her down. "I hope you come to love this place as much as I do."

His voice was so filled with emotion, Batsheva could do no more than nod. Although she knew he had been loath to return, she understood now why his heart was in Durham. Letting him take her arm, he escorted her into the castle.

The archbishop was waiting for them outside the great hall. Through the arched doorway, Batsheva could see the huge, vaulted chamber with its banners hanging from enormous timbers. Her eyes widened at the size of the room, and she wanted to go in, but Durham's hand stayed her. She realized he was talking to her; she quickly recovered her attention. She heard him introduce the archbishop and she automatically curtsied. When he extended his hand to her, she glanced nervously at Durham. She saw his lips purse ever so slightly and she reached forward to kiss the proffered ring. It felt odd, but she managed to avoid a shudder, hoping the cleric took no notice of her lack of proper decorum.

But he did notice. Assigning it to nerves, he dismissed the rumor that she was Saracen; after all, she hardly looked like one with her coppery hair and grey eyes. She was, he admitted to himself, quite lovely, if somewhat young. "Welcome home to Durham, my lady," he said with a warm smile. "We are pleased to have a new countess in residence."

Batsheva swallowed hard and forced herself to return his smile. "Thank you, my lord Archbishop."

He noted the lilting accent of her English and thought it delightful. Turning his attention to his nephew he said, "Your mother awaits you in her chamber. She's not been well, Gil."

The smiles faded when Durham asked, "How ill is she?"

"Very," replied the archbishop gravely, "but your return may well be the medicine she needs to recover. Go to her…and take your lady. She is anxious to meet her."

Keeping her hand in his, Durham mounted the staircase to the upper floors of the castle. He said nothing, but the firm set of his mouth told Batsheva he was worried. As best she could, she kept up with his quick pace on the stairs.

The upper hallway was wide and well-lit with torches. Batsheva could see they needed trimming and noticed the hallway could use a thorough sweeping out. *The lady has not been well enough to tend to her household,* she thought sadly.

They reached a wide oak door at the end of the hall. Before Durham could knock, the door was opened by a portly woman in plain brown garb. The lady bowed deeply to the earl before she stepped aside.

At once, the fetid odor of the room assailed their nostrils. Dark and dank, the chamber had been closed for far too long. In the center, dominating the room, a huge, curtained bed stood alone, with a small, frail woman propped up against the pillows. "Gil," she cried weakly, barely able to raise her hand in greeting.

Durham crossed the space between them to kneel at his mother's bedside. Taking her hand, he pressed it to his lips. "Forgive my long absence, Mother," he said softly, brushing a lock of grey hair tenderly from her forehead.

"No matter," she breathed, "you are home now."

Batsheva stood rooted at the door, barely able to breathe the foul odors. Two servants hovered in a corner, watching her closely, their hands clasped before soiled aprons. Glancing away from their stares, Batsheva saw the matted rushes on the floor and willed herself not to gag. *No wonder the woman is ill,* she thought. And then, the tiniest scurrying sound caught her attention. Without waiting to be asked in, she suddenly marched across the room. "Gilbert, remove your mother from the bed immediately!" she commanded.

Durham stared up at her. "What?"

"Remove her to another chamber *now.*" Her gaze, filled with wrath, turned to the two servants. "You! Find charwomen with brooms and filled buckets." The women looked from one to another but remained where they were. "NOW!" shouted Batsheva. Immediately, they fled.

"Bess!" cried Durham, rising from the filthy floor, "what are you doing?"

"Do as I say, my lord," she snapped, then turned to the woman in the bed and curtsied deeply. "*Pardonnez-moi, madame la Comtesse*, but this is intolerable. If you are to get well, you cannot stay in this room. Gilbert, find another chamber for your mother, then send Mary to me. And Lydia."

Lady Matilda looked from the woman to her son, to the woman again. "I think, Gil, you should do as she says."

Gently, Durham lifted the featherweight that was his mother and carried her from the chamber.

"Remove these rushes, but do not replace them," ordered Batsheva when the charwomen arrived. "And this bedding, all of it, and burn it somewhere outside the castle." She went to the shutters and pushed them open. The breeze was strong, and she breathed the fresh air deeply. "You," she said, pointing to one of the women, "remove these chamber pots and do not bring them back until they are completely clean."

The woman started to protest, but quickly changed her mind when she saw the firm set of the lady's jaw; this new countess was not to be trifled with and she set about her task without a word. Passing two more servants as she left the room, she warned them of the harridan inside. "She's a tough one, Mae," she whispered, "don't give her any of your lip."

The newcomer frowned then steeled herself to enter the chamber. Batsheva immediately pounced on her. "Find clean bedding. And a layer of new wool. Make certain it is well carded. Then bring fresh linen." The maid scurried out the door.

Mary approached her mistress cautiously. "They are afraid of you, my lady," she said softly.

"As well they should be. They have left their mistress to lie in her own filth, with no concern for her health. We can mend fences later, Mary. For now, let us do what must be done…and quickly."

The portly woman who had been with Lady Matilda when they arrived was standing near the doorway. Batsheva wagged her finger in her direction and made her way across the room slowly. "What is your name?" she asked the maid.

"I am Rose," the woman replied as she curtsied shallowly.

"Are you Lady Matilda's maid?" She saw the woman nod, then continued. "Please take a fresh bed gown to the lady and help her to wash before she dresses again. Is there a bath available?"

The woman's eyes widened in shock. "Oh, no, my lady. We don't do that sort of thing here."

Batsheva frowned. Even Durham enjoyed a hot bath and to learn his mother did not do the same seemed improbable. "How does one wash oneself, Rose?"

"With a pitcher and bowl, my lady."

"Mar…"

Before she could finish her maid's name, Mary answered, "'Tis on its way up now, my lady. Shall I have them bring it here?"

"No, take it to the chamber where Lady Matilda is resting. Then arrange for hot water. Then, would you be so kind as to teach her maid the proper way to assist her?"

"Yes, my lady." Mary looked Rose up and down. "Do you not have a clean apron?" Without waiting for answer, Mary sailed past the maid. "Come with me."

Batsheva took one look at the way the charwomen were sweeping and took a broom from one of them. She began instructing her on the proper way to sweep. When she felt the progress was steady, Batsheva set off to find Durham and his mother. She found Mary on her way back and was assured the lady was properly washed and in a clean bed. Batsheva sent her on to the lady's chamber to supervise the restoration of order.

As soon as she walked into the chamber, she knew it was Durham's. The curtained bed was centered against the inner wall and he sat beside it, on a low stool, speaking softly with his mother. When she reached the bed, Batsheva curtsied, her head bowed, until the older woman spoke to her.

"You certainly are determined," she said in French. "I have not seen that much movement in my chamber since before I fell ill."

"They have taken advantage of your weakened state, Madame," replied Batsheva, "and they will do so no longer. Your recovery is of great importance; it will not be left to chance."

"I suspect my son underestimates your determination," she replied dryly. "He tells me you are from the Holy Land."

"I lived there for some time, Madame, but I am from Al-Andalus."

"Yet you speak French…and English well."

"I learned French as a child, but English is new to me. I am slow to understand."

The old woman started to laugh, but coughed instead, "Let them think you understand every word." Matilda touched her son's cheek. "Go now, Gil. Let me speak with your lady in private."

Durham looked uncomfortable, but he rose anyway. "I will return shortly, Mother."

"Not too shortly, I hope. Go see to your entourage."

He knew when he was being dismissed and he went, but not without shooting Batsheva a warning glance.

Lady Matilda took a long, critical look at the woman standing before her. She was young yet there was a certain oldness in her eyes which she instinctively knew came from a life hard lived. "I am glad my son has found someone to love again," she rasped. "I thought he would kill himself on crusade rather than return to the place where his wife lies buried." She waited for a comment, but when there was none, she asked, "Did Gilbert adequately prepare you for Durham?"

"As best he could, Madame. Words do not justice to the beauty of the countryside."

"No, I suppose not. But I doubt it is the countryside which brought you here," she said bluntly.

"My lord earl's concern for me is what brought me to England. He has seen to my welfare since…the day we first encountered each other."

An odd choice of expression, mused Matilda, but then, this was an unusual woman. She was poised, self-assured, yet demure, despite her earlier performance in her chamber. She suspected this woman was used to being in control of her situation and obviously had been well trained by someone. Curious, the lady asked about Batsheva's mother.

"My mother has died," admitted Batsheva with a twinge of sadness. "She was not of noble birth, but a fine gentlewoman. She ran a proper household and, hopefully, taught me to do the same."

"I would not doubt it," chortled the countess. "You behaved most remarkably when you encountered my condition. It grieves me, though, to have you see me in such a sorry state." Her remarks were punctuated by a fit of coughing and Batsheva immediately helped ease the woman into a more comfortable position. When the coughing stopped, she added, "You seem to have knowledge of the healing arts."

"No more than any other woman of homeland, my lady. There, it is expected the chatelaine tends the sick. Her role is to care for those in her charge."

"As well it should be," said Matilda with respect. "At times, we forget we have this august responsibility." Her eyes closed for a moment.

"I fear you are tired, Madame," murmured Batsheva with a last check on the covers. "Sleep now, and when you awaken, we shall return you to your own chamber."

The room was sufficiently aired out for Batsheva to permit the laying of fresh bedding. Beneath her watchful eye, she had the servants install a mattress of clean straw and fragrant herbs. Over the linen covering, she had a duvet filled with newly carded wool evenly spread. Only then did she allow the chambermaids to enclose it all in a sheeting of pristine linen of a fine weave. "Mary!" called Batsheva into the hallway where she knew her personal maid was supervising the porters, "have them bring in the blue."

The porters arrived with the rug balanced precariously on their broad shoulders. Hurrying to the bed, Batsheva pointed to the place where she wanted the rug to be unrolled.

"But my lady," protested one of the chambermaids when the rug was unrolled, "we've not yet laid the rushes!"

When the rug was in place, she waved the chambermaids over. "There will be no rushes in this room," answered Batsheva bluntly. "The countess cannot be exposed to rotting straw. From now on, you will sweep the chamber floor twice daily. This is called a rug," she explained in a patient voice. "It must be swept every day with a clean, stiff broom. On the first day of each month, it must be rolled and taken outside to hang over a wall for beating and airing. When the time comes, I will show you how it is to be done."

"Yes, ma'am," chorused the three chambermaids. They thought her a little mad, but they were not about to argue. Besides, this thing was as beautiful as anything they had ever seen.

Batsheva was not done. "Pots will be removed after each use and returned perfectly clean. Sheeting will be changed each morning when the lady rises for her toilette...."

"And her shift must be changed as well!"

Batsheva spun around at the sound of the new voice. "Jane!" she cried, rushing to greet her closest friend. She was about to embrace the chubby seamstress when she stopped in her tracks and stared, open-mouthed. "Have you grown rounder?" she asked.

Jane patted her belly. "'Tis not my good cooking if that is what you think, Bess. I'm with child!"

In what had been his father's private solar, Durham sat closeted with the archbishop, Jamie, and a man Batsheva did not recognize. Tapping lightly at the half-closed door, she waited for Durham to ask her to join them. When he did, the men, including Uncle Charles, rose. "Bess, this is Ned Bottom, my estate manager."

The man bowed low from the waist. "Welcome to Durham, my lady. We are all pleased to have you amongst us."

"Thank you, Master Bottom. And so good to see you looking so well, Jamie," she added a hint of a smile. Although Durham offered her a seat, she declined. "May I have a word with you in private, my lord?"

Durham excused himself, asking the men to stay while he stepped outside with Batsheva. "I am reviewing the accounts with them," he explained grimly. "Since my father's death, Charles has tried to manage as best he could, but frankly, he is unprepared to deal with the day-to-day decisions required for a large holding."

"I am sure you will soon have everything laid out according to your wishes, my lord."

"I hope," he snorted. "How is my mother?"

"Her chamber is ready to receive her. Am I right in guessing the room in which you placed her is your own?"

"Was my own, Bess. Now we will have the chambers in the west tower. Have you been there yet?"

"No, I'm afraid there's not been time."

Durham pointed to the staircase. "Go to the left, instead of the right. At the end of the passage, turn again and you will find our chambers. Anne's is the first door, Miriam's is beside Anne's, with a sitting room between them. The babe's chamber and yours are connected through a robing chamber. And mine," he looked at her hopefully, "is beside yours."

"Then I will see to our suite next. After that, I'm afraid I will be too tired for anything more than a tray tonight. I hope others won't be disappointed if I forego the meal at the high board."

"There has been no meal at the high board since my father's death, Bess," he frowned. "When you are ready, we will reinstate the custom."

She nodded, understanding the deeper meaning in what he was saying. "I shall be seeing to our installation, my lord," Batsheva told him.

He watched her mount the stairs and noticed she was not moving as quickly as she had earlier in the day. She was tired and he could see it not only in her step, but in her eyes as well. No doubt, she would sleep well on this first night in her new home.

When she opened the door to her room, Batsheva was relieved to find her trunk already at the foot of her bed. *Mary's been busy,* she thought as she stepped into the enormous wardrobe room to find her clothes folded on shelves and hung neatly on pegs. Her rugs were laid on the recently swept floor, and the monkey rug spread before the fireplace with two chairs placed just as she liked them. Looking about the room, she noticed the wide shutters had been pushed open, letting the late afternoon sun ignite the room with a ruddy glow. A simply carved window seat sat beneath the window, with its lid raised, and inside Batsheva found Mary had placed her sewing basket, embroidery frame, as well as the small chest in which she kept her packets of herbal remedies. Torches were ready for lighting in elegantly wrought iron sconces on the wall and candles stood waiting in silver holders on the table and nightstand. The bed was a large, canopied affair, with heavy crimson drapes held back with thick tasseled ropes. Opposite the bed stood a simple *prie-Dieu* beneath a large crucifix mounted on the wall. *That will have to go,* thought Batsheva as she stared at the tortured figure attached to the cross. Reaching up, she gently lifted it from its hook and placed it on the stand. Batsheva looked up and noticed the carved moldings around the edge of the ceiling. Someone had put a great deal of time and effort into the hundreds of fruits and flowers that encircled the chamber like an autumn garland.

Jane appeared at the door, in her arms a rainbow profusion of fabric. "Your wardrobe, my lady," she grinned as she entered. "Everything we made up in anticipation of your slender shape."

"I'd almost forgotten," laughed Batsheva as she helped Jane lay the gowns on the bed. "It will be good to have clothes that fit. I've grown tired of overfull skirts."

"And now I shall have the joy of wearing them." Jane sat down on the bed. "I could not believe how Miriam has grown, Bess. She is more beautiful than I remember."

Batsheva's hand automatically went to her breast. "If I do not feed her soon, I shall burst and then what will you do with all those lovely frocks?" Suddenly, the sound of a baby's wail filtered into the room. "Ah, my lady's voice. And not a moment too soon."

The cries grew louder, and Lydia appeared in the doorway. "She will wait no longer, my lady," said the nursemaid with no small frustration in her voice. "I am sorry."

Batsheva reached for Miriam and laughed. "'Tis all right, Lydia; it is well past the time I should have nursed her." Jane helped Batsheva to loosen her laces and watched Miriam throw her little self against the proffered nipple. "She is greedy; that is why she grows so fast. Just wait, Jane, and soon enough you, too, will know the constant demands of motherhood." She settled herself on the chair near the fireplace and beckoned Jane to join her. "Tell me all the news, my dear friend. I have missed your jolly tales."

"Not all jolly, but there are tales to tell," laughed the seamstress, joining Batsheva. But before she could begin even the first, Mary came bustling into the room.

"My lady, the Lady Matilda is racked by coughing. I thought you might have something we could give her."

Without rising, Batsheva pointed to the window seat. "Bring me the herbs, Mary." When Mary brought the little box, Batsheva picked out a small packet into which was folded a mixture of dried chamomile, willow bark, and lemon balm. "Prepare a tisane for the lady with this," she said, handing the packet to Mary. "Let it steep for a moment or two, then strain it. Certainly you can find a piece of cheesecloth in the kitchens. And if you can find some honey, add a large drop; it will ease her coughing."

"Yes, my lady." Mary dipped a little curtsey and scurried away.

Jane eyed her friend critically. "You look as though you could use a tisane yourself, Bess."

"No, I am just tired."

"I think you are more than tired, Bess. Your voice is scratchy, and you've rings beneath your eyes. You need a good night's rest."

She had to admit Jane was right. Her throat was scratchy, and her eyes were beginning to burn as though there were a smoky fire in the hearth. Then she sneezed. "I suppose," grumbled Batsheva, "riding in the rain was not the wisest thing I might have done."

Not bothering to ask the lady's permission, Jane got up and went to the wardrobe. She examined several shifts before she finally selected one. "Finish with Miriam and we shall get you into bed," she ordered sternly. "I'll take no nonsense from you, girl!"

Looking quite small in the chair, Batsheva laughed. "But only if, when you've got me tucked beneath the covers, you tell me how you've fared since you left Westminster."

The day was fading when Jane descended the stairs to go in search of her husband. She found him still closeted in the solar with the earl. "Your lady is asleep," she said with a frown. "I fear she's taken a chill."

"She is unwell?" asked Durham.

"Not yet, but if she doesn't get some rest, she will be. I've left Mary with her. She's taken some broth and bread, but that was all she would eat." Jane wagged an accusing finger at the earl. "Just like a man, my lord, to expect a woman just out of childbed to be able to sustain a difficult journey. You might have waited until she was fully recovered."

"But she said she was anxious to leave!" he protested, "She wanted to come to Durham."

"Would she have countered you? Would she have admitted she was still weak? You know her better than anyone and should know better than that."

Jamie saw the dark look in his earl's eyes and touched his wife's arm. "I think you've said enough, Jane."

She glared at him but did not argue. Instead, she started for the door.

It was Durham who stopped her. "Wait, Jane," he called, "tell me, what should be done for her?"

"Keep her quiet for a day or two; she needs to rest, or her milk will dry up." She thought for a moment before she added, "Your lady mother is weak; do not let Bess tend her until she is feeling well, lest your mother add this to her list of ailments."

Durham crossed the room to where she stood and lifted her hand to his lips. "Thank you, Mistress Jane, for being her friend. I know she is glad to have your company once more."

Blushing just a little, Jane looked up into Durham's blue eyes. "I know you care for her, my lord; you must have the patience of a saint."

He laughed softly. "Aye, there are times I think I do."

"Well, don't let it go to your head," she warned "or she will knock it right out of you."

"That she would, Mistress FitzHugh; that she would!"

Durham looked in on her before he retired to his own chamber. He noticed the placement of the rugs and chairs as well as the missing crucifix. He saw it lying on the prayer stand and simply removed the offending icon. In the morning, he would have the prie-dieu removed as well, with an explanation that the lady preferred to pray in the family chapel when the spirit moved her. No one would question him; his mother felt much the same way. As quietly as he could manage in his boots, he went to stand beside the bed. Gently, he brushed back an errant copper curl. Batsheva's eyes fluttered open, and he whispered, "Sleep well, sweet Bess."

"Mmmmmmmm," was the response as her eyes drifted closed once more. "'*Bonsoir, cher.*"

For a brief moment, he felt his heart soar. Perhaps there was hope.

CHAPTER 27

Durham

MAY 1192

By morning, Batsheva was feverish. When Mary arrived with her breakfast, she took one look at her lady and immediately summoned Durham. "Do not even consider rising from this bed, madam," he ordered sternly, concerned with her flushed face and glassy eyes. "You will remain here, with extra servants to tend you."

"Yes, my lord," she replied meekly. She did not have the strength to argue, nor did she want to. All she wanted to do was sleep. She asked Mary to fetch the herb chest and picked out two packets. "This one," she said, handing the first to the maid, "is for Lady Matilda. Brew it as you did yesterday. And this second one is for me." She paused to sneeze. "I think I am in need of my own medication."

Batsheva continued to nurse Miriam, but when the babe was not at her breast, she slept. Durham checked on her several times, but quietly; he was loath to awaken her. In the evening, however, it was the earl who arrived with a tray.

"I thought you might be hungry," he said, setting it on the stand beside the bed. He handed her a large, earthenware tankard filled with a steaming brew. "'Tis your own remedy, Bess," he chided when she tried to give it back.

Batsheva made a face, but sipped the tisane slowly, letting its aromatic steam fill her stuffed nose. "I feel wretched," she muttered right before she sneezed.

"You look wretched, my lady," Durham agreed. "A few days of rest and you'll be just fine." He sat on a stool beside her.

She sipped again, despite the fact it hurt to swallow. "How is your mother?"

"Much improved, thanks to your efforts. She rests comfortably in clean linen and looks better since her bath. Mary is overseeing her tiring women and, if they do not like it, they've not grumbled near me."

Batsheva managed a weak laugh. "Who would dare grumble near the earl?"

He scowled at her, but it was more to make her laugh again than to disagree with her assessment. "Jane called, but I sent her home; considering her condition, I thought it unwise to let her sit with you."

"Thank you, Gilbert; that was wise."

A tremor raced through him when she called him by name. She rarely did; the sound of the word always gave him hope. "Anne wishes you well again, Bess. She had hoped to show you the market tomorrow, but that will wait. There will be plenty of time to learn the city once you are well."

Batsheva was silent for a minute. She had planned to go to the shops today; there were things she needed to buy. She also had something else in mind. Surely there were Jews here, but she did not want to ask the earl. Instead, she asked if there was a goldsmith in the town.

"Two that I know of, Bess, perhaps more. I've been gone for some time." He chuckled at his own admission. "I need to learn the growth of my own city. When you are feeling right, we shall explore together."

"That would be nice," she sighed, setting the tisane aside. "Tell me, would it be possible to arrange a tutor for Anne through the offices of the archbishop?"

"A tutor?" asked Durham.

"Surely there must be a scholar willing to earn a little extra coin for teaching. Anne is a bright child and needs to learn. I fear I won't have enough time to do the job properly."

"I suppose," he replied with caution. "What would you have her learn that she cannot learn amongst the ladies?"

"My lord, she already reads. She needs to know numbers if she is to run a great household one day. Gone are the days when one can trust servants to see to these things. Look about you," she stopped to sneeze again into her handkerchief.

"God bless you, Bess. Perhaps you should rest now."

"Thank you and do not change the subject," she scolded lightly. "While your mother has been ill, the running of this castle has been lax. And probably you have found your accounts in poor condition, judging by the length of time you spent closeted with your manager. A lady should be able to run the accounts as well as decide menus, Gilbert. Where I lived, the ladies were all capable, and that allowed their husbands to attend to more important business while they ran the house and estate. While my father and uncles tended to affairs of trade, my mother and aunts supervised the households and saw to the management of any lands. It was done differently, of course, with women veiled and servants whose sole function was to act as go-betweens. It was obvious from your words yesterday that your own system has not properly functioned."

"Since my father's death, I fear nothing has functioned…as you put it."

"If your mother had been more familiar with the business of the county, she could have stepped into the breach more efficiently. Think what would have happened had your father died while you were young, and she was left with this august responsibility until you came of age! Could she have managed, or would she have been forced to trust someone to do it for her?"

She was right and he knew it. "Admittedly, Bess, I had not considered this."

She raised an eyebrow at him. "Anne's value as a wife will increase if she is well schooled."

Durham wasn't convinced that this was so, yet he saw merit in her suggestion. "I will ask my uncle for a recommendation, if that is what you wish."

"That is what…" she was cut off by another sneeze. "Oh, I do feel wretched," she mumbled, wiping her nose on the handkerchief.

"Then go to sleep, sweeting." He bent forward and kissed her brow. It felt warm to the touch of his lips. "You are feverish."

"I know." She took the tisane from the stand and drank a little more. "'Tis a bitter brew," she complained.

"Be a good girl and drink it down. After all, 'tis your own remedy."

"I know. I know." She sipped again, then handed him the cup. "Enough of this. I am going to sleep now." She hunkered down beneath the covers.

Durham tucked her in and kissed her again. "Sleep well, Bess; you'll feel better in the morning.

Batsheva felt worse in the morning. Her fever had risen, and her eyes burned. Despite the covers, she shook violently. When Lydia brought Miriam, she took one look at the lady and reluctantly handed her the child. "Let me call the earl, my lady," she pleaded with Batsheva. "You are not well."

Scowling, she agreed. "Do not alarm him, Lydia; I am not so ill as to be at death's door." But as soon as she put Miriam to breast, she reconsidered the last statement. Her skin seemed all the more tender because of the fever and Miriam's sucking was painful. She gritted her teeth and tried to ignore the burning sensation. By the time Durham arrived, Batsheva was ready to pass Miriam to Lydia. "Ask Mary to prepare a willow bark tisane," she croaked through dry lips. She looked up at Durham. "I feel worse."

Concern was etched on the angular lines of his face. If it were possible, she looked worse than the night before. Her face was terribly pale and huge dark circles around her eyes gave them a sunken look. "Can I get you something, Bess?" he asked.

"Jane." She closed her eyes. "Send for Jane."

Batsheva grew warmer with each passing hour. With Jane's help, Mary was able to rouse her enough to take some willow bark tea, only to have her throw it up almost immediately. Quickly, they removed her from the bed, changed the bedclothes and her shift before she realized what was happening. Jane sat beside her, sponging her forehead with a cool, damp cloth while Mary prepared a vapor pot for the fireplace. Soon the chamber was heavy with the aroma of herbs simmering over the fire and although the day was warm, the ladies rolled up their sleeves and kept the fire going. Toward noon, they were able to get Batsheva to take some tea again and, this time, she managed to keep most of it.

For a while, Batsheva slept, her breathing shallow despite the vapors misting the room. "She needs nourishment, my lord," Mary told Durham when he came late in the afternoon. "She'll take naught but the tea. When we brought her some broth, she pushed it away."

Suddenly, there came from the bed a cry so bloodcurdling that Mary dropped the bowl she had just refilled with cool water. Durham raced across the room to Batsheva.

She was thrashing in the bed; he wrapped his arms about her to cradle her against whatever terror haunted her. "What is it, Bess? What is wrong?" he asked over and over.

Her words were a jumble none could understand. Pushing against Durham, she fought his grasp. *"Ahrib ya 'atfal! 'Ujri bsre!"* she cried *"Arkud 'iilaa baba. Alan! Alana!"*

Durham looked to Jane. "I cannot understand her!"

"'Tis not a language I've ever heard, my lord."

The terror seemed to fade and Batsheva stopped fighting. When her breathing returned to normal, he gently laid her against the pillows. He motioned to Jane to follow him out of the chamber.

"I will return shortly," he told the seamstress quietly. "Should Bess awaken, give her more of the tisane; 'tis supposed to help the fever."

"Yes, my lord."

"And keep her quiet. It will not do to have the entire castle in a panic."

Without benefit of an escort, Durham skirted the streets of the city, eschewing the central square where men still sat outside the pub with a tankard of ale before heading home. Through the long shadows of the afternoon, he found his way along familiar streets. The few people he saw took little notice of the tall man in a grey cloak; he felt almost invisible and was glad for it. At last he reached the street of the cobblers. Counting the houses, he found the old oaken door he recalled from days long ago when his father took him here to meet the master of the house. Whatever his feelings were toward Jews, the late earl respected and liked this one. Durham remembered the Jew as an old man with a grizzled beard and sharp, dark eyes; he hoped he was still alive. Glancing about to make certain he was not seen, he rapped on the ironbound door.

A girl with luminous dark eyes answered his knock through a small opening in the center of the door. "Yes?" she asked with caution.

"I would see Isaac, if he is here."

"Are you His Lordship?" Her voice was soft but full of awe.

"Yes."

She closed the window and slowly the heavy door opened. "Follow me, my lord." She led him down a dark hallway and pointed to a small room. "I will fetch my grandfather, my lord. You may wait here." With a swish of somber brown skirts, she disappeared into the back of the house.

The room was filled floor to ceiling with books and ledgers. Durham marveled at the sight; other than the archbishop's library, he had never seen so many volumes in a private residence. A table littered with parchment sat in the center of the room, with two chairs, one on either side. Candles burned in simple iron holders; the scent of beeswax mingled with heartier aromas of cooking coming from elsewhere in the house. It made the earl's stomach rumble. Voices filtered down the hall; he could not make out what they were saying, but one was calm while the other seemed to be issuing a warning of some kind. At last, Durham heard slippered footfall on the wooden floor.

"Welcome to my home, my lord earl," smiled Isaac HaCohain. "It has been too long since you came to visit." He bowed slightly in acknowledgement of Durham's status. "I hope I may serve you as I served your father before you."

He felt very young, very green before the old man. "It is good to see you so well, Isaac," replied Durham formally.

"And you look quite fit, my lord, after your long absence. The journey was kind to you. How fares our king? Will he return to England soon?"

"King Richard fares well…or at least that is what the last messenger told Queen Eleanor. We all hope he comes home quickly." Durham shifted uncomfortably, then screwed up his courage to explain why he had come. "I am in need of a favor, Isaac. A very personal favor."

"If you need coin, my lord…"

Durham shook his head. "No, 'tis far more personal than that. I've come about my lady."

Puzzled, the old man took his chair at the table and waited for Durham to do the same. "Are you in some difficulty, my lord?"

"The lady is ill. In her fever, she speaks in a tongue I cannot understand. I thought perhaps you might come and hear her."

"May I ask why you have come to me?"

He swallowed hard. "She is a Jewess from Al-Andalus."

"Ah, I see," murmured Isaac. "It would be unwise for me to attend her, my lord. It might bring…speculation."

Durham frowned; he had not counted on Isaac's refusal. "Surely you could come to the castle."

This time, it was Isaac who shook his head. "Nay, my lord. It would be dangerous to have me attend the lady in her chamber. My daughter, however, is well known for the healing arts in our community. Let her attend your lady. If she speaks in our language, Rachel will understand."

Durham saw the wisdom in his words. "I will wait for her here."

Rachel was a slim woman, half his size, but her bearing made her seem taller. She curtsied to the earl when she entered the room. "I would bring my herbs," she said, showing him a small basket. "What are the lady's maladies?"

Durham listed the history and symptoms of the illness, noticing how her dark eyes followed his every move. "She has refused all nourishment, mistress," he explained, "and I fear it is because she believes the food to be unclean. She does not partake of pork and eats sparingly of all meats and fowl."

A small frown formed at the corners of Rachel's mouth. "'Tis not uncommon, my lord. If you will wait but a moment, I will bring food I think she will eat." She hurried from the room.

Isaac waited until she was gone before he spoke to the earl. "I would ask a favor in return, my lord."

"Anything in my power I would grant you, my friend," answered Durham.

"Rachel is an independent woman, but please, have her escorted home. I would not risk her safety alone in the streets." His voice was filled with fatherly concern, but his words went deeper.

"Are you in danger here?"

"All Jews are in danger, my lord. A woman alone is easy prey."

Durham nodded. "I will see her home myself, Isaac; and know now that I am back, I will make certain you and your people are safe in Durham."

Isaac bowed from the waist. "Thank you, my lord. You are your father's son."

Rachel returned with a larger basket on her arm that Durham insisted on carrying. "It would look odd otherwise," he told her as they left the house. Rachel did not answer, but handed over the basket before she followed him into the street.

The sentry greeted the earl with a salute as they passed the gate. Inside, all was quiet; Durhan led the way up the staircase and through the winding corridor until he reached Batsheva's chamber. The door was ajar, but he rapped softly. Jane answered his call.

"She drank a bit of the tisane, but her fever seems higher to the touch." She noticed Rachel. The young woman was unfamiliar to her, yet she had the sense Durham had specifically sought her out. "Is she a healer?"

"Yes."

When he did not elaborate, Jane simply stepped aside to allow them entry to the sickroom. "Mary will come to sit with her through the night, my lord, and I will return in the morning."

"Thank you, but that won't be necessary; we will stay the night," Durham replied. "She will be better tomorrow."

"Pray God that she is, my lord." Jane took her mantle and disappeared down the hallway.

Without waiting for instruction, Rachel took the stool Jane had vacated and drew it closer to the bed. She gently placed her palm on Batsheva's forehead and held it there for a moment. Then she picked up the cup sitting on the bedstead and sniffed its contents. "Willow bark?" she asked Durham.

"I believe so."

"Good. Her fever is high, but not so high as to cause *great* concern; I suspect the fever will rise again, but repeated doses of the tisane will keep it from consuming her."

"This is a common remedy?" asked Durham.

"Yes, my lord, very common." She fell silent for a moment and leaned close to listen to Batsheva's breathing. "Her lungs are congested," she murmured, then rose and went to the fireplace. With skillful hands, she stoked the logs before she added fresh water to the vapor pot hanging above the flame. Digging into the small pouch she carried around her waist, she removed a small bag of herbs and dropped them into the water. In a matter of moments, the scent of mint and chamomile drifted through the chamber. "My lord, if you would close the window?"

"She prefers it open in a sickroom," protested Durham quietly.

"As well she should, but for the moment, it is important that the steam reach her. Later, when her breathing is eased, I can open it again." Rachel prepared a fresh tisane and placed it on the nightstand before she resumed her place at the bed.

For lack of anything better to do, Durham paced the length of the chamber. Back and forth he strode, his hands clasped behind his back, his mouth set in a firm line, his eyes dark as ocean depths. Each time he neared the bed, he would pause, stare at Batsheva, then renew his steps. This went on until a log collapsed in the hearth, causing a shower of sparks to hiss against the vapor pot.

"My lord," sighed Rachel, when the steady footfall had become too irritating to ignore, "I mean no complaint, but could you cease?"

Durham stopped in his tracks and stared at the young woman. "I apologize," he replied curtly.

"Perhaps you would be wise to consider retiring for the night. There is nothing you can do here."

"I prefer to stay."

Rachel shrugged. "Then please, for the lady's sake, pace silently."

He glared at her but held back the comment on his tongue. He jerked one of the chairs near the fireplace until it faced the bed then sat down with a thud. Stretching his long legs before him, he rested his chin on his hand, all the while grumbling in a voice too low for Rachel to hear.

Rachel ignored him but smiled inwardly. She bent over the basket and removed a small volume, barely the size of her hands. She turned slightly to take full advantage of the candle burning on the table and opened the book. For a while, she tried to read, but Rachel could feel Durham's steady stare in her direction. From beneath lashes lowered demurely, she watched him, feeling a great relation to a mouse eyed by a cat. *A great, large cat,* she decided. Every girl in Durham came close to a swoon when he would appear; she easily recalled her sister's excited prattle each time she saw him. But he went off to the crusades and for a long time Rachel had forgotten his very existence. *What would David say if he knew I was here?* she thought, thinking of her husband away in London on family business. A little smile threatened to inch across her face, but she refused to let it appear. Casting her eyes back on the fine parchment page, she forced herself to read the beautiful Hebrew script.

The lady in the bed began to moan. Rachel replaced her book in the basket and leaned forward to feel the fevered brow. It was warmer now than it had been earlier. She took the cloth from the basin on the nightstand and applied it to the lady's forehead. Batsheva moaned and tried to twist away. Gently, Rachel brought her face around. "Be still, lady," she said in English, "You are safe."

"*Ahrib ya 'atfal! 'Ujri bsre!!*"

Durham was on his feet. "That is what she was saying. What does it mean?" he demanded.

"Shhhh!" commanded Rachel without looking up. "She is telling the children to run quickly."

"*Arkud 'iilaa baba, Daud! Arkud 'iilaa baba, Amina*!" cried Batsheva, twisting violently against Rachel's touch.

"*Kl shay' ealaa ma yuram*," murmured Rachel, close to her ear, hoping the lady would understand this as well.

Her response soft. "*'Ant aman*?"

"*Nem nem; 'ant baman ya sayidatan*." The words seemed to comfort her, and she quieted.

"What did you say?" asked Durham, relieved that the woman could understand and respond.

Rachel pressed the cloth against Batsheva's forehead before she replied, "I told her all is well, that she is safe." She glanced at Durham. "Who are Daud and Amina?"

"Her children." Durham paused, then added, "They remain in the Holy Land."

"Oh." Leaning close to the lady, Rachel began speaking softly to her. It did not matter what was said, only that the sounds were comforting to the ailing lady, and it seemed that they were.

Batsheva murmured something as she began to rouse herself. Slowly, her eyes opened, and she stared blankly at the stranger beside her. Her mouth was dry. She licked her lips as she tried to focus on this new face. Finally, she asked, "Who are you?"

"*Ani Rachayl*." She replied in Hebrew, hoping the lady would understand.

Batsheva managed a weak smile and croaked, "*Barucha ha'ba'a, Rachayl*."

Her eyes closed again, but Rachel would not let her lapse into sleep. She helped Batsheva sit up before she held the cup to her lips. "Drink this, my lady," she urged gently; "the willow bark must do its work. You have a fever that must come down."

Nodding, Batsheva sipped the tea and grimaced. She tried to push the cup away, but Rachel urged her to drink a little more. "Where is Miriam?" Batsheva asked in English when Rachel at last set the cup down.

Durham answered quickly, "She is asleep in her nursery; Lydia is with her."

With a sigh, Batsheva nodded and slid down the pillows. "I will nurse her in the morning," she mumbled as she closed her eyes.

Rachel adjusted the bedclothes, then went to prepare another tisane. Gliding about the room, she took notice of the rugs on the floor and the faint wall discoloration in the shape of a cross. *Someone has recently removed it,* she thought silently as she carried fresh herbs to the vapor pot. Satisfied she had done all she could for the moment, she settled herself on the stool and picked up her book once more.

"Tell me," said Durham from across the room, "what is it that you read?"

"The Psalms, my lord," Rachel answered in a whisper.

"Would you read to me in your language?"

She turned a few pages, found what she was seeking, and read:

> *Al naharot bâvel shâm yâshavnu gam-bâkhiynu bezâkherênu' et-Tziyyon*
> *\`al-\`arâbhiym betokhâh tâliynu kinnorotêynu*
> *Kiy sham she'êlunu shobhêynu divrêy-shiyr vetolâlêynu simchâh shiyru lânu mishiyr Tziyyon*
> *'Eykh nâshiyr 'eth-shiyr-Adonay \`al 'adhmat nêkhâr*
> *'im-'eshkâchêkh Yerushâlâim tishkach yemiyniy.*
> *Tidhbaq-leshoniy lechikkiy'im-lo' 'ezkerêkhiy 'im-lo' 'a\`aleh 'et-yerushâlaim \`al ro'sh simchâthiy*

"What does it mean?" he asked.

Rachel met his eyes straight on:

> *By the rivers of Babylon, we sat and we wept when we remembered Zion.*
> *We hung our lyres on the willow branches.*
> *There, our captors demanded songs; our torturers wanted joy, saying, Sing us one of the songs of Zion.*
> *How shall we sing the Lord's song in a strange land?*
> *If I forget you, O Jerusalem, let my right hand forget her cunning.*
> *If I do not remember you, let my tongue be chained to the roof of my mouth*
> *if I do not prefer Jerusalem above my chief joy.*

Her rebuke stung in so many ways; he knew the lady's message was directed at him, the one who had been in Jerusalem.

He changed the subject. "Do all your women read?"

Rachel shrugged. "Not all, but most. 'Tis no handicap to have an educated wife."

"Like my lady, you seem to think we prefer our women ignorant."

Her eyebrow rose questioningly. "Do you not?"

"Nay," replied Durham after a hesitation, "I do not consider it a handicap although many do; that my lady reads and writes is an asset. It sets her even farther above other women." His tone was so filled with admiration that it took Rachel by surprise. When Durham came to perch on the edge of the bed, she watched as he held the lady's hand in his, gently stroking her forearm, his eyes brimming with undisguised love for her. "The lady is from Al-Andalus, mistress. Her world is a world apart from ours. She has had a life of adventure and great tragedy." He paused, his breath almost ragged, "I love her too greatly to lose her to this."

"You will not lose her to this, my lord. What she needs now is rest to let her body heal itself. Listen." She cocked her ear toward Batsheva, "already her breathing eases."

"Then why does she cry out in her sleep if demons are not chasing her soul?"

Her laugh was as light as it was kind. "There are no demons, my lord. She is simply suffering from a rather bad cold. The lady is simply run down and pays the price. As for the restlessness…she relives parts of her life in her dreams. That is all; there are no demons, no evil spirits."

Durham sagged with relief. He replaced Batsheva's hand on the gently rising breast and sighed. "You are certain of all this?" he asked.

Rachel nodded. "If you wish to retire for the night, I will stay."

"Nay, I could not sleep." He got up from the edge of the bed and went to the fireplace. He poked at the logs then added two new ones from the pile. Rachel had given him relief where he saw naught but danger. She was much like Batsheva: the same practical tone in her voice, the same matter-of-fact analysis of a situation. Once, Durham would have found those attributes disturbing in a woman; now, however, he preferred them. Turning back to the woman sitting beside the bed, he asked, "Have you a family of your own?"

Rachel felt herself blush. "Yes, my lord; that was my daughter who answered your knock."

"And a husband?"

"That, too. My husband is David Vital, late of York, now of Durham." She said the last part without rancor, but again, the meaning was not lost on Durham.

"My deepest sympathies on your losses, mistress," he said gravely. "I heard what happened when I returned to England."

Rachel bowed her head in acknowledgment. "'Twas a great tragedy on all counts, my lord; we have done nothing to warrant such outrageous acts against us. We pay taxes, help build your castles, and support the king with loving fervor. We do not deserve to die at your hands."

Involuntarily, Durham looked down at his hands. "My sister, Margaret, Countess of York, and her husband were greatly grieved by the action."

"I heard," she replied flatly.

They lapsed into an uneasy silence. Something niggled at Durham's brain, though, and he tried to recall why the name Vital sounded so familiar to him. He thought about the night Edward told them about the burning at York and remembered. "Hannah," he suddenly said aloud. "Did you know Hannah?"

"Yes," Rachel answered slowly. "May I be so bold as to ask how you knew her?"

"I did not. My nephew did and spoke of her to me."

"Hannah was my husband's cousin. She was orphaned at a tender age and lived with her uncle, my David's father. I did not know her well, but she was a lovely child."

"She has a brother."

Rachel nodded, "Akiva."

The name struck Durham in the gut. "And your husband, does he work for the family as well?"

Rachel was bothered by his questions, yet she had no choice but to answer. "He factors for the family, but he has established his own trade with my father. Because I have no brother, he will inherit my father's holdings."

"Then Akiva Vital would have no cause to come here," stated Durham bluntly.

"No, my lord, he would not." She noticed the slightest bit of relaxation in his face as she puzzled over the questions.

Durham noticed the way the dark wings above her eyes furrowed as she thought. Swearing to himself, he cursed himself for saying too much. And then, he saw the dark eyes widen right before Rachel snapped her head around to stare at the lady in the bed. "Yes," he murmured before she could ask the question.

"But she is dead…or at least that is what we were told. Oh, my lord!" she cried, clutching the book to her bosom, "how did you find her?"

"'Tis not for me to answer, Mistress Vital; if she wants you to know, she will speak of it herself. But I beg you, as someone who cares greatly for the lady, say nothing to your husband or father. This is her affair; she will run it as she sees fit." He unexpectedly sighed. "I, for one, would dare not countermand her."

Rachel studied the earl for a moment: this was a man deeply in love. In the light of the fire, the lines and angles of his face were softened somewhat, but there was no denying he was handsome, like some statue left by the Romans. His eyes were the color of the bluebells in the fields and they watched her as carefully as she watched them. *Any woman could fall in love with him*, Rachel decided with a start, *even me. But Batsheva; she was a woman apart. She loves Akiva, she would never have betrayed him if there had been a way for her to return.* There were endless stories about Batsheva Hagiz, the flower of Málaga. Rumors circulated after her abduction; that she had survived and was living in a sara'i in Tunis. But then Yehuda had sent word his sister was dead. Still others reported her alive, but there was never any proof. Not until now. Tales told of coppery curls, storm grey eyes, and the uncommon beauty of her face. Rachel wondered why she hadn't immediately known this was Batsheva. And the way the earl gazed at her! It was enough to make a pragmatic woman like herself believe in chivalry! She would wait until Batsheva was well enough to speak for herself before she decided what and how much she would tell David.

The earl continued softly. "There is one more request I have of you, mistress. I would ask you not to tell her your husband's name."

"But, my lord, she would want to know," protested Rachel.

"Later perhaps, but for now, it would cause her great pain and I would spare her that. Her ties to her own family are…strained." Rachel would have responded, but he held up his hand to silence her. "The lady would be best served by peace until she recovers. She has been through much torment. Believe me when I tell you knowledge of your ties to her family would harm her."

"My lord," she started slowly, "that decision should rest with the lady. Unless she questions me directly herself, I will say nothing. I will not, however, lie to her."

Her words were so firm he dared not counter her with protest. "That is all I can ask, Rachel Vital. I am in your debt."

"Nay, my lord, you are not. I would do this for any living soul. There is no debt here."

"Then you have my thanks, my lady. You are a woman of valor."

Rachel blushed at the compliment and nodded her understanding. There was nothing more to say, so she picked up her book and found her place once more.

'"Here," said Durham, carrying one of the cushioned chairs from beside the hearth, "you need a more comfortable seat." She waited while he moved the small, three-legged stool, then placed the chair beside the bed. That done, he returned to his own chair and stretched out before he closed his tired eyes.

The candle was almost to the lip of its stick when Rachel realized that she, too, had been dozing. From across the room came the earl's soft snore. His head thrown back, his hands dangling over the chair arms, powerful legs extended onto a footstool, he slept soundly despite the uncomfortable-looking position. Rachel chided herself for staring at his body. Rubbing the sleep from her eyes, she checked Batsheva's forehead and frowned. The fever was still too high. She then set about the task of refilling the vapor pot, carefully sidestepping the sleeping lord; it would not serve to awaken him for the moment.

Pouring water from a ewer into the pot, she saw the pitcher was nearly empty. She checked the larger vessel nearby and saw that it, too, was dry. Hefting the earthen jar into her arms, she slipped from the room to go in search of water.

In her nightmare, Batsheva heard the clang of steel against steel. She was standing in her tent, the children of the camp crowded around her. "Why did you come here?" she asked the children. Theirs was a mute response of terror mirrored in their eyes. "We must go to the Well of Tears, children," she ordered, leading them outside a slit in the rear of the tent. When she turned to count their numbers, they disappeared one by one as she touched their heads. "Daud! Amina!" she cried, spinning, spinning, in search of her own children. She called them again, but there was no sound save the battle raging. The screams of the horses and the cries of the men came closer and closer until she could smell the blood in her nostrils.

She stood alone, outside the tent, a scimitar in her hand. She was dressed as a boy. Near her, Yaffa's whinny turned to a shrieking whine. With a single slash, she severed the rope that held Yaffa at the rail and she watched as the horse galloped away from her. "Come back!" she shouted, but the horse could not hear her cry. Suddenly, the pounding of hooves was coming toward her. She raised her sword when she saw Khalil ride over the ridge, followed by men in strange armor. Khalil wheeled his horse around to battle them off. Soon, he was knocked from the saddle, but he rose, sword in hand, the steel shaft a blur as he cut down as many soldiers as he touched.

Batsheva ran towards him, her own sword extended, her arm ready for battle. She tried to join Khalil in the fray, but as close as she came, they seemed to move off until she could run no further. Standing there breathless, she watched a lone knight ride along the ridge. From beneath his helmet he watched the battle until Khalil subdued the last warrior. Then, with sword raised against the deep blue azure sky, he barreled full tilt toward her amir. He engaged Khalil in single combat. The swords sang as they met again and again above the hard desert earth.

She saw Khalil draw first blood, yet the knight did not fall. He seemed not to care about the spurt of blood from his forearm; instead, the knight bellowed, his war cry curdling Batsheva's own blood. Khalil did not notice her screams; his blows continued to rain down on the knight's shield. Then he stumbled. With a single, swift movement, the knight's sword came at plane angle to Khalil's shoulders and Batsheva watched in horror as the blade reached his throat.

She was sitting up and screaming. Screaming at the tops of her lungs. Durham leapt from his chair to throw himself across the bed to rescue her. "Rachel!" he yelled as he flew. But there was no answer.

Her eyes wide open in terror, Batsheva fought him off. She screamed and screamed, her arms flailing at him, her hands arched as if to scratch his eyes out. He grabbed her hands and pulled them aside. "Bess!" he cried, "wake up! Wake up!"

Rachel burst into the room. She ran toward the bed and set the pitcher on the nightstand. "Release her," she ordered Durham, then took his place. Gathering Batsheva into her arms, she began rocking the feverish woman. "*Shhh, shhh, sayidati,*" she murmured into her ear. "*'Ant aman.*" Her arms wrapped around Batsheva, she slowly eased the woman into a more comfortable position. "A*latfal bi'aman. 'Ant aman.* " As far as she knew, the children were safe, and she felt it important to reassure the lady.

Batsheva wept though her eyes remained closed. Moaning against Rachel's breast, she quieted some, yet the sobbing continued. Durham stood, helpless, nearby. Finally, Rachel motioned to him. She gently extricated herself from Batsheva and indicated he should take her place. "I must refill the vapor pot," she said as she rose from the bed.

Durham said nothing, he simply held Batsheva in his arms.

She was so small, so warm against him. Her tears soaked through the linen of his shirt and felt hot on his skin. He stroked her hair, letting the tight copper curls brush his cheek. Even after a night of fever sweats, she stilled smelled of herbed soap and lilac water. As Rachel had done, he gently rocked her as though she were a babe in his arms. Holding her so close made his heart beat faster; he dared to kiss the top of her head. "Come back to me, Bess," he whispered into the delicate shell of her ear, "do not leave me."

Batsheva murmured something he could not understand. Motioning to Rachel, he asked, "What do I say, that she would understand?"

"Say *ana huna,* it means *I am here*. She will hear your voice through the fog of her fever." Rachel was holding a wet cloth in her hand. "I need more water. She is fine for the moment; I will return shortly." She did not wait for an answer; she simply left him alone with her.

For a long while, Batsheva was quiet. Her breathing seemed easier, and she rarely coughed. She nestled against Durham and in her sleep, her hand reached for his. When she began to murmur, again, Durham repeated the strange words Rachel had told him: "*Ana huna, Bess; ana huna.*"

This seemed to comfort her, and she pressed herself into the circle of his arms. She spoke again in the odd sounding language; he wished he understood. He held his cheek against hers and said the words again. This time, her hand reached up and touched his face. "*Khalil, habibi, Khalil.*"

Durham's heart froze in his chest. Arching his neck backward, he wailed a silent scream of anguish. He could not extricate himself from her, yet the pain she inflicted was as sharp as if she had cut him with a knife. No greater torture could he imagine than the pain which now ran white hot through the bowels of his soul. He fought back the urge to cry out and to weep. Inside, a piece of him died in that moment. As gently as he could, he removed his hand from her grasp and laid her on the pillows. Standing over her, he brushed a damp curl from her brow as he stared down at the deathly pale face. "I love you," he groaned; "I will always love you. But you are lost to me, Batsheva Hagiz. God give you the peace you deserve."

Durham almost collided with Rachel as she entered the chamber. "Are you leaving?" she asked, surprised to see him away from the bed.

He did not answer her question. "Care for her, Rachel Vital," he said gruffly as he swept past her.

Rachel watched him disappear into the dark hallway and wondered what had happened. Whatever it was, the event was obviously painful for the earl, and despite her sympathies for the patient, her heart ached for him.

CHAPTER 28

Durham

MAY 1192

Weak as a newborn kitten, Batsheva lay against the pillows and allowed the servants to bustle about with little complaint. She nursed Miriam, but other than that small diversion, she did little more than sleep and eat of the food Rachel brought along each day. Vaguely, she recalled Rachel's face from the depths of her fevered night, but when she was awake and more alert, she asked Rachel again who she was. Keeping to her part of the bargain, Rachel told her only she was the daughter of Isaac HaCohain of Durham.

Rachel came daily armed with her basket full of broth and bread, adding more solid food as the lady's appetite returned. She was thankful to see color once again grace the pale cheeks and was relieved when, on the fifth day, Batsheva was alone, sitting up with a book in her lap.

"Well, my lady, you are much improved today," pronounced Rachel as she hung her mantle on a hook beside the wardrobe. Following the servants lead, she always addressed her in English.

"All because you have the kindness to bring me food I will eat," laughed Batsheva. "I fear, however, soon I will be forced to dine from the kitchen. I do not know how long I can play at weak stomach."

Rachel replied, "We can make an arrangement, my lady, whereby Mistress FitzHugh can deliver that which is proper."

Batsheva closed her book and folded her hands on her lap. "Come sit with me and let us talk," she said, suddenly serious. "There is much I would know about you."

"What is there to know?" asked Rachel as she drew up a stool. "I am a simple woman who happens to live in Durham."

"Have you a husband? Children?"

"Yes," she answered slowly.

Batsheva wondered why the lady was so reticent. Surely Rachel saw no reason to distrust her. "I have more than just Miriam," she said quietly. "I have twins, a boy and a girl. They are with their father's people."

Rachel swallowed hard. "You must miss them terribly."

"I do. But to know that they are safe is most important to me. One day, with God's help, I shall be with them again."

"Cannot your husband bring them to you?"

Batsheva smiled sadly. "He is not my husband, Rachel. I have no husband."

She paled considerably. "But they call you his countess."

"I cannot stop what they say; but I would not wed him in a church, therefore, I would not wed him at all." Batsheva watched the color return to Rachel's face. "Nor was I wed to the father of my children, for much the same reasons."

"Perhaps it is best that we speak not of these matters, my lady."

Batsheva switched, unexpectedly, into the odd Castilian dialect she was confident her visitor spoke. "I do not know you, Rachel, but I fear if I do not speak of these things I will go mad. Durham's sister knows the truth and has promised to help me. I trust her, she is a good woman. But I need friends…allies here, in Durham. Will you be my friend, Rachel?"

The other woman slowly nodded. "*Comprendo.* Whatever you tell me shall remain between us and will go no further."

Batsheva put aside the book and smoothed the covers around her. "My name," she began in a soft voice, "is Batsheva Hagiz, daughter of Yosef and Miriam. We lived in Málaga and I was on my way to my wedding in Sfax when I was abducted from my caravan…."

Suddenly, Rachel cut her off. "*Yo sé*, Batsheva. I already know."

"How do you know?" gasped Batsheva. "Did Durham tell you?"

She shook her head. "He said nothing to me. I know because my husband is David Vital. We wept when you were taken; and hoped when we thought you were found. But Yehuda was the one who said you were dead. We had no reason not to believe him. And then the stories began."

"What stories?"

"All sorts of stories. First it was Benghazi, then it was Alexandria, then Akko; that you died in childbirth. Then we heard that your parents had letters. Akiva was ready to rush off but then Yehuda said the letters were not from you but someone posing as you. Next, we heard tales you were seen in Marseille, dressed as a boy who tore the collar of his shirt when he was told Yosef and Miriam were dead. We did not know what to believe until Yehuda sent word and told us it was false; that you were, in fact, dead; he claimed to have buried you himself. He said your captor killed you on the spot when you demanded to be released from slavery, when Yehuda offered ransom."

A slow anger burned inside Batsheva. "*I* refused to go with Yehuda when he came to Benghazi," she growled. "I was already huge with the twins. Khalil gave me my choice and I *chose* to stay with him." Her mouth snapped shut but her eyes grew soft. "I came to care for Khalil; I would no more leave him than cut the heart from my own body. And that was done for me when he was slain in battle." Shutting her eyes tightly, she fought back the tears she knew would come.

"How did you come to be here? This I do not understand."

"I was dressed as a boy. I was going to Nablus to find Khalil. Durham's troops attacked our camp. We were defenseless. I fought as hard as I could, but I fell in the battle. Durham found me beneath my horse, and thought I was a boy to be rescued. He took me and my horse, but discovered the deception on the ship. In London, posing as a boy was no longer possible."

Rachel took her hand. She was surprised by the strength of Batsheva's grasp. "The earl loves you, Batsheva," she offered sincerely. "You could make a life for yourself here, with him and the child."

"Miriam is not his child, Rachel; she, like her sister and brother, is Khalil's."

"But the earl accepts her as his own."

"To what end? To marry her off to some Christian for an alliance? I would not permit that."

"What of Akiva? He still mourns for you and has not married."

Batsheva shook her head. "I am not the same girl who left Málaga with stars in her eyes. I am hardened. I have lived a hard life in so many ways; I would be unable to sit with the women and pretend I am like them."

Rachel felt suddenly helpless. Within her own world, there would be remedies for such a thing. A religious court, for one, would declare her free to marry without consequence; there was no stigma of bastardry in

Jewish law for such a situation. A religious court would demand the lady be released. But there wasn't a Jewish court in England that would dare to intervene with an earl. She had not a single idea of how to extricate Batsheva from the mess in which she found herself. And now, she was party to it and it worried her. The earl's anger could be costly for her father and husband; what happened in York could happen in Durham. "I know not how to counsel you, my lady," admitted Rachel after a long silence, "but know that if there is some way in which I can help, I will."

"Have you told your husband of me?"

She shook her head. "He is in London; we hope he will return by the Sabbath."

"Do not tell him. For now. Let me think on this, Rachel," she said with gravity. "And while I do, learn discreetly from your father whether or not he has had recent contact with Avram Hagiz in Tiberias."

Nodding, Rachel fully understood the danger, not only to herself, but to her family as well. "You have my word, my lady."

There was something else bothering Batsheva as she lay back on the pillows. "Have you seen the earl these past few days?" she asked Rachel, reverting to English.

"No; I have not seen him since the night you lay in the fever." She dared not ask whether he had been to see her, but Batsheva answered the question for her.

"Nor have I. 'Tis strange he has not been here even once that I recall." Frowning, she dropped the subject. This was not something to be discussed with Rachel.

Mary rapped softly at the door. "My lady? Lydia says Miriam needs to nurse."

"Bring her to me, Mary," called Batsheva. Although she was exhausted by her conversation with Rachel, she had as much need to feed the babe as the babe had to eat. In a moment, Lydia came in with Miriam squirming in her arms. "Is she a handful?" asked Batsheva with a frown.

"More than a handful," giggled the nursemaid as she handed over the babe to her mother. "She is two armsful! We will have to get a cot for her, my lady; she rocks the cradle with frightful force in the morning!"

"When my lord earl comes, I will speak to him," said the lady, putting her daughter to breast.

"The earl, my lady? He is not here, and I fear we can wait no longer."

"Oh," said Batsheva, hiding her disappointment. "No matter." She called to Mary. "If the Lady Matilda is up to receiving, you may ask her about a proper cot for Miriam."

The two maids bobbed curtsies before they left the chamber. Before she could ask Rachel what she knew about the earl's departure, another knock caught her attention. "Anne!" cried Batsheva with a happy smile. "Come in, come in. I've not seen you for days! Where have you been?"

The little girl slowly approached the bed and executed a very proper curtsy to the lady. "Grandmama says I must practice," she announced gravely. "She thought my dip clumsy."

"Well, I do not think you are clumsy at all, Annie sweet. But perhaps your grandmother is right; it never hurts to practice. Come, sit by me and tell us everything you've been doing."

Anne glanced at Rachel before she perched herself on the edge of the high bed, her feet dangling several inches off the floor. "Is my lady improved today?" she asked the visitor.

"Yes, Lady Anne, she is doing quite well." Rachel gave the child a warm smile and was relieved to see the girl relax.

"I see you've been introduced to Anne," said Batsheva. "I've come to treasure her company since she came to us at Westminster." She squeezed the girl's hand. "And how fares your grandmama today?"

"Much better, Bess. She's been about her chamber and vows to leave it before week's end. She was very upset, though, when papa left."

"Oh?" inquired Batsheva.

"Oh, yes. She was terribly cross with him. She told him he must stay here and tend to the castle before he goes off to see his lands. She said there is much work to be done here. They had a frightful row, you know."

"I am afraid I did not know, Anne."

Rachel stood and curtsied deeply toward the ladies. "I think it is time I returned to my own home, my lady," she said tactfully. "I will come again tomorrow."

Batsheva thanked her for her company. "I look forward to our conversations, Rachel. If there is anything you need that we might supply...."

"Thank you, my lady, but we are well situated. Until tomorrow then." She picked up her basket and left them alone.

Batsheva patted the bed. "Slide up here and tell me about this frightful row, Anne. I am most curious."

Anne did as she was told and snuggled against Batsheva. As she talked, she played with Miriam's tiny fingers. "Papa went to see Granny the morning after you were so sick in the night. At first, it was very quiet in there, and then I heard Papa shouting and Grandmama shouting back. It was awful, Bess. Lots of banging about, too."

"And how did you come to hear all this, little lady?" asked Batsheva with one curiously raised eyebrow.

The little girl sighed, "I was on my way to see Granny when I heard all that noise. I couldn't very well go in, I stood outside the door. I couldn't help but overhear."

"What exactly did you hear?"

Anne squirmed, uncomfortable with the question. "Papa said he could not bear to stay here, that you would leave him in a moment if you had the chance and he could not stand to be broken-hearted like that. He said he was going to ride the countryside and with any luck, you might come to your senses while he was gone." She stopped, then stared at Batsheva. "You do love my father, do you not?"

It was Batsheva's turn to sigh. "I love your father very much, Anne, but it is very complicated. Too complicated for you to understand at your age."

"But I do understand," cried Anne. "I remember what happened when my mother died. I remember how papa cried and cried. He was so hurt; we could not help him. Are you going to do that to him? Make him hurt again so?"

"It is not my wish to hurt him, Anne, but in a great way, he has hurt me." She slipped her arm about the quivering shoulders and held Anne close. "You see, darling child, I did not choose to leave my home, your father took me. It was an accident and perhaps, had he not, I might be dead. But he did and here I am."

"You do want to stay?" she asked.

"Yes and no. If I thought it was the right thing to do, I would stay with your father forever; but this may not be the right thing." She touched her lips to Anne's fair head. "I will tell you this because you are old enough to understand." She sucked in her breath. "Miriam is not my only child,

Annie lamb. I have twins, a boy and a girl. They are five years old now and I miss them terribly."

"Where are they?"

Batsheva forced herself to smile, although it was a sad one. "I do not know for certain. I must believe they are safe with their father's people."

A little furrow creased Anne's brow. "Can they not come here?"

"No, sweetheart; they must stay where they are."

"Then you must go to them," she pronounced gravely.

Batsheva sighed. "That is the problem, Anne. I do not know if that is possible."

"Then stay with us, Bess. Stay here and be our mother. Miriam and I need you!"

Batsheva did not have the heart to tell Anne that Miriam was not her sister.

CHAPTER 29

Durham

MAY 1192

A much-improved Lady Matilda called on Batsheva. Unassisted but for an ornately carved walking stick, she entered the room and immediately dismissed Mary and Lydia. "Sit, Elizabeth," she commanded when the lady began to rise from her chair near the hearth. "It is high time we had a visit." Despite her diminutive size, the dowager countess's presence filled the large chamber. She took the other chair as her own and slowly eased herself onto the cushions. "I am sorry that your intervention on my behalf cost you your own health," she began in a firm voice. "I fear had you not arrived when you did, Gilbert would have come home to a funeral mass."

"Do not sell your own strength short, my lady," replied Batsheva. "Your quick recovery bespeaks your fortitude."

"Poppycock, child. The only reason I continue to live is because I simply refuse to die until I see Gilbert settled once more. I had hoped your presence here would allow me to rest at long last."

Batsheva was startled by her comment. "I am afraid I do not understand your meaning, my lady."

"I am neither addled nor stupid, Elizabeth. I have eyes in my head and ears as well. Of course, you might tell me whatever there is between you and my son is none of my business, but frankly, child, it is. In the event my son does not produce a son of his own, Durham will revert to my late husband's nephew, a rather selfish, unpleasant fellow who already casts his green eye on this castle at every opportunity. Another daughter simply will not do."

"Are you referring to Miriam?" asked Batsheva, shocked.

"Yes."

Batsheva was non-plussed. Whatever she had expected from the dowager countess, this was not it. "I am sorry, Lady Matilda, but I cannot control what I birth."

"Assuming, of course, that the child is indeed my grandchild, I would have to agree with you." Her crystalline blue eyes bore into Batsheva's. "I can count, my dear."

"And if the child is not his?" replied Batsheva waspishly, "then what?"

"Frankly, I do not care, so long as you succeed in giving him a son. In order to do that, Elizabeth, certain events must take place."

"Pray, Lady Matilda, inform me."

The old woman frowned. "Don't play me for a fool, child. You must have relations with him."

"I see."

"And," she continued without regard for Batsheva's icy glare, "from what my son told me prior to his departure, that seems to be a problem."

"Whatever problems there may be, Lady Matilda, are between your son and me."

She waved her hand as if to dismiss her objections. "What goes on in this castle is my business. And as for the matter of you and Gilbert, I find I must concern myself."

"I think, madam, you overestimate your ability to control your environs."

The dowager countess laughed, "You are one to comment, Elizabeth. You were not in this place a moment before you wrested control of my care, ordered the servants about and, in effect, established yourself as chatelaine in my place. Mind you, I am not complaining; you performed admirably, much the same as I would have done in your place. But you see, Elizabeth, this is but a beginning. You are young, untutored in managing a great house. You need my expertise unless, of course, you have experience which has not been made known to me."

Batsheva's head was beginning to pound; this was not how she envisioned Durham's mother. By Margaret's own description, she expected a kindly, loving woman who would at least understand the nature of her predicament. Rubbing her temples, she tried to formulate her response. "You are correct," she started slowly, "in assuming I have no experience with a great house such as this. I did, however, learn the art of management from my late mother. While I do have need of your knowledge and expertise, I found the discipline of your staff sorely lacking when we arrived. You were lying in your own filth, Madame. Either you were too weak to protest, or your ladies are unschooled in how to tend an invalid. Had I opted for polite silence, *you* would be dead."

"Now you are admitting that you saved my life," countered the dowager.

"No, madame, fresh air, a bath, and a clean chemise saved your life. I did nothing but open a window. Never did I intend to usurp your place as chatelaine; quite the contrary, my only desire was to ensure your continued good health in that position. I have not now, nor do I desire in the future, to take a place not rightfully mine. Therefore, Lady Matilda, I will beg your indulgence when I ask you to carry on as lady of the castle and allow me to remain here as your guest."

"Brava, Elizabeth, brava!" laughed Matilda. "Well said and quite cunning, too. You think that as my guest it would be in poor taste for me to ask personal questions and by God's bones, you are right. However," she waved her cane at Batsheva, "you are not a guest. This is your new home and I do believe you are worthy of being its mistress…eventually. Gilbert may be many things, but a fool is not one of them."

"Excuse me, Lady Matilda, but have not you just subjected me to a critical examination of my lack of worthiness to be his wife?"

"In a word, yes."

Gripping the arms of the chair, Batsheva rose. "How dare you come in here and behave this way, Madame? In my world, you have committed the most unconscionable of acts. I would much prefer to reside in a stable than be subjected to this manner of conversation as a price for a roof. I may not be born into your aristocracy, Madame, but at least I had the good graces to learn your manners before I arrived." Gathering the skirts of her robe, she left the lady sitting open mouthed beside the hearth and disappeared into the robing chamber.

With a twinkle in his Durham blue eyes, the archbishop could barely contain his amusement when Matilda recounted her conversation with the lady. "What say you to this, Matilda?" he sputtered, trying to catch his breath.

"I say it is high time we had someone here with a spine instead of aspic in her back. Honestly, Charles, I cannot imagine how Gilbert managed to keep her in check in Westminster. According to Isabella, the lady was positively mousey."

"And who wouldn't be, around that harridan?" countered the archbishop. "Isabella makes her position clear the moment she enters a room and brooks no contest from those around her. I am certain our Elizabeth read her like a book and chose to appear mousey."

"*Our* Elizabeth?" The lady arched an aristocratic eyebrow at her brother-in-law. "Be that as it may, she will give Gil quite a time. But tell me, what is this you heard from Westminster? Are they wed?"

"Not according to my clerical brother at the cathedral. He sends word the couple has not been churched and should do so immediately. It well might be they have waited until your blessing was given before proceeding with the nuptials."

Matilda snorted indelicately at him. "I hardly think Elizabeth would concern herself with something as inconsequential as my blessing if she were of a mind to wed Gilbert. No, I think there is something else here. And whatever this something else is, it has caused Gilbert to trot off to the hills." She shot the archbishop a sharp glance. "Perhaps it is time you paid a call on the lady. After all, she is recently recovered from an illness and might find a prayer or two with his grace, the archbishop, a welcome thing."

"Then again, she may not," countered Charles. He saw the grey eyebrow shoot upward. "'Tis said the lady is not one for church nor chapel."

"And what does that mean?"

The archbishop shrugged his broad shoulders. "I thought perhaps you might know."

She shook her head. "Perhaps a Spanish confessor, then?"

He shook with laughter. "Heavens no, Mattie. I wouldn't subject anyone to that without a specific request. I suppose I will have to go myself."

"A fine idea," agreed Matilda. "Do come to see me after you've interviewed the lady."

Nestled within the cocoon of her bed, Batsheva vacillated between seething anger and cold hatred of Matilda of Durham. Never had she been as humiliated as she had been by the dowager countess. Instead of finding an ally as Margaret had promised, Matilda was a *bruja,* a witch, of the worst order. Clenching her teeth, "No wonder he is like he is," she muttered beneath the blankets as she tried to put order to the jumble of her thoughts. At no other time had she felt so abandoned, so lonely, not even in during the first days of her captivity. She cried until the pillow was sodden, and then she flipped it over and proceeded to dampen the other side. Feeling weak and adrift, she closed her eyes against the day. *This is no night terror,* she told herself, *for I will awaken and everything will be the same.*

She slept for a short time, but when she woke, she was not alone. Sitting on a chair beside the bed was the large man Durham had identified as his uncle. She could not recall his name, but his position in the church was perfectly clear. She stared at him until he shifted uncomfortably and faced her.

"I am glad to see you back in the land of the living," he said with more conviviality than he felt. "I thought I would be sitting beside you through the night."

Batsheva narrowed her eyes and studied his face. It was a nice enough countenance, with those same sapphire blue eyes. But where Durham was angular, the archbishop was round, with a less pronounced nose and thinner lips. Still, he had not the look of a tyrant, although Batsheva was loath to trust anyone associated with that family. Without giving away one whit of her thoughts, she asked in French, "What do you want?"

"Actually, Lady Elizabeth, I've brought some of my own home-brewed remedy for what ails you." He lifted an earthenware jar from a basket beside his feet and poured its contents into a cup. "Shall I taste it to prove it is not poisoned, or will you trust my word as a priest? 'Tis nicely hot." His eyes twinkled merrily at the lady. When she did not move, he chided her as though she were a child. "Come now, my lady, surely you who are familiar with the healing arts are familiar with jasmine tisane?"

She eyed him with greater suspicion. "To what end?" she asked.

"What end?" He laughed heartily, "To improve your temper, I should think, my lady. I thought perhaps you would appreciate a taste more familiar to you."

The thought of a cup of hot jasmine tisane was appealing; it would certainly ease her aching head. Sitting up, but drawing the covers close around her, she accepted the drink. For a moment, she let the steamy vapors penetrate her still stuffed head. "Thank you," she murmured before she sipped.

Pleased she accepted his offering, he was not completely convinced she would not toss it in his face. "There, does that not feel better?" he asked when the cup was drained.

Batsheva did not answer directly. She set the cup on the nightstand and studied the archbishop. Then she asked, "Why are you here?"

Two red spots briefly appeared on his rounded cheeks. "I have come, Lady Elizabeth, to make amends for my aged relative with little common sense."

"Madame la comtesse," she frowned.

"The very same. Unfortunately, my sister-in-law is used to being… how might I put it…the queen bee in this particular hive. It is to my discredit that I have allowed her to…."

"You haven't allowed anything as I see it, my lord archbishop," Batsheva snapped peevishly. "She does what she wants because she is the countess; her age allows her to behave in a manner others would find intolerable." She glared at him. "There, have I convinced you I am the harridan she surely has described?"

"Hardly a harridan, my lady. You have yet to say anything either untrue or undeserved. A bit short-tempered, perhaps, but that is to be expected; you've been ill. I, for one, find myself short-tempered when kept indoors too long. A good long walk or ride in the country always sets my tempers to right."

"Harrumph," snorted Batsheva.

"I could not possibly have won a round with so easy an argument, Lady Elizabeth!" cried the archbishop. "I am disappointed. I was so eager for dueling wits!"

Batsheva sneezed, then wiped her nose on a handkerchief. "I am hardly in a condition to duel with anyone," she sulked.

"Poppycock! You coddle yourself. You think you are in no condition because you are peeved at Matilda. I wager that if I brought that magnificent mare of yours 'round to the castle gate, you'd be up in a blink of an eye."

"I do not think so," she sniffled. "And, if I may ask, what concern is it of yours what I do or do not do?"

"You are a stubborn one," chuckled the archbishop, "but I will not let that get in the way of our chat. Therefore, I shall change the subject." He stroked his smooth cheek for a moment or so before he said, "I hear you want a tutor for Anne."

"She needs a teacher better than me. My skills in English are limited, and she must be able to read and write in her own language."

"Is French your native tongue, Lady Elizabeth? I thought I detected a faint accent."

"You did and it is not."

The archbishop sighed; this was a far more difficult task than he had anticipated. "Gilbert tells me you speak several languages."

"I do."

"Perhaps, Lady Elizabeth, you would grace me with a personal favor." He saw her shrug, but she did not respond. "Would you read Hebrew with me?"

"Hebrew?"

"Yes. He tells me you are familiar with Greek and Arabic as well."

"I am no scholar, my lord archbishop; you would do better to consult one of your learned brethren."

"Exactly my point, dear Lady Elizabeth. You are not a scholar, yet you know the language as the spoken word. It is precisely this expertise I seek. Surely, you would help a poor cleric to better understand the word of God?"

Batsheva frowned deeply at him. She was certain he was trying to trick her into something, but she knew not what. Shaking her head, her copper curls bobbed her answer. "As I said, I am no scholar. I'm afraid you've been misinformed as to my abilities." She hunkered down under the covers again. "Thank you for the jasmine, my lord archbishop, but I fear I am exhausted now."

Charles rose from his seat and stood looking down at her. She was a beautiful woman, he had to admit, one who would tempt even him in the right circumstance. "Think it over, Lady Elizabeth," he said seriously, "and should you change your mind, I would be pleased to come read with you." He murmured a prayer for her recovery and made the sign of the cross over her. That done, he was gone.

Batsheva hoped he did not see her shudder.

Day by day, Batsheva grew stronger until she was forced to admit she could no longer hide in her chamber. Sooner or later, she would have to rejoin life in the castle. Mary reported daily that since their arrival, conditions were improving, most due to Lady Matilda's determination to take back control of her own home.

"She tours in the afternoons," explained Mary as she helped Batsheva to dress; "she marches about with her two maids, checking for grime and issuing orders. There is grumbling below stairs," she giggled, "because they've grown lazy during her prolonged illness."

"And after that?" Batsheva asked, trying to determine the best way to avoid the dowager countess.

"By then, she is tired and usually retires to her chamber. She is still weak, my lady."

She wanted to ask about Durham, but bit back the question. He was gone a fortnight without word and although she was curious as to where he might have gone, she did not want to give the appearance of concern. Batsheva steeled herself for her reentry into society.

With Mary at her side, Batsheva finally toured the entire castle. Beginning with the great hall, the maid led her through the labyrinth of rooms and corridors, pointing out the aspects of the castle she deemed important. But it was not until Batsheva stood on the crenellated battlement that she saw the width and breadth of Durham. Her breath left her as she gazed out over the landscape. To one direction, she could see fields already ripe with grain. Sheep dotted the hillsides, and in the distance, she saw a herd of cattle moving slowly along a country lane. The city of Durham encroached the castle walls on the other side, and Batsheva could see the bustle of a thriving city. The market square was busy; shouts of the vendors and the buzz of the customers reached her ears and for a moment she longed to be amongst them. Turning suddenly to Mary, she announced, "Let us go to the market. I have a need to buy a ribbon or two!"

They raced back to the chamber where Batsheva dug several silver coins from her stash in the window seat and showed them to Mary. "Do you think these are enough?"

Mary's eyes widened. "More than enough, my lady! We should be able to buy a hundred ribbons!"

"Let's find Anne; perhaps she will want to go, too."

With bubbling enthusiasm and two footmen just for good measure, the three ladies set off, arms linked, for the market square. Joining in the crowds, Batsheva and Anne stopped at every colorful stall to examine the goods. Peddlers hawked their wares at the passersby, their voices rising above the din of the crowd. There were potters and tinkers, carpenters and weavers, all anxious to engage a potential customer in barter. At a fruit seller, Batsheva demonstrated her expertise as she checked over a flat of fresh picked berries. Mary stood beside them, basket in hand, as the lady poured over the fruit until she had selected enough to fill the little container the farm wife was happy to provide for the lady. Next came the tinker's booth, where Anne insisted on buying a small spoon for Miriam, insisting the babe would soon need her very own implement. They chose a cleanly made silver spoon with a rose engraved on the handle. They were about to stop at a cobbler's stall when the jongleurs pranced into the square. Forgetting the array of fine kid slippers, they hurried over to watch the acrobats perform.

"Are these the same ones we saw at York?" Anne asked when two brightly clad dancers whirled past.

Batsheva admitted she wasn't certain, but then she pointed to their troubadour. "Perhaps they are," she answered, "I recall seeing him before."

"Oooh," sighed Anne as she listened to him weave a song about a beautiful lady who lost her one true love, "isn't he handsome!"

"Anne!" Batsheva laughed, "You are too young to notice such things!"

She rewarded the comment with an arched look. "I am old enough to know my father is already seeking a husband for me."

"What?"

"'Tis true, Bess. He told me himself he thought Robert, Viscount Newcastle would be a suitable choice. He is eldest son of Earl Newcastle and, " she added with her chin jutted out in pride, "a descendent of William himself."

"Have you met him?"

"No, but I hear he is quite nice to look at and is very kind."

Batsheva snorted her disapproval. "That is hardly enough information, Anne."

"But all marriages are made that way, Bess," she protested, "and you must trust my father to find a proper husband. I'll be old enough to marry, soon."

She eyed the child, then replied, "I suppose that is true enough, Annie dear. And if that is so, I have been remiss in your training. Someone must teach you to run a great house."

A smile crept across her face, turning her lips upward at the corners. "I am learning already, Bess," she boasted, "Gwyneth has been letting me help her."

Batsheva vaguely recalled Gwyneth as the stern-faced woman who was with Lady Matilda on the day they arrived at Durham. Since then, she had not seen the woman; she made a mental note to ask Mary about her later. "I am glad you've been busy, Anne, but now that I am back on my feet, we must resume your lessons."

Anne looked very pleased. "I was afraid you had forgotten, Bess."

"Forgotten?" she cried. "Heavens no, Anne. In truth, I mentioned your lessons to the archbishop. I thought perhaps he might recommend a tutor for you; you need to study English reading and writing, and I am not quite up to the task. I thought perhaps I would join your lessons."

"That would be great fun," Anne giggled, "I should like to learn with you."

Before she could say anything else, Batsheva heard a familiar voice calling her name. Spinning around, she caught sight of Jane scurrying toward them, a market basket swinging on her arm.

She reached them, breathless from her jog, her face bright with a broad, happy smile. "You are certainly looking better," she observed merrily, "and just in time! There's a foreign peddler come to Durham for just this week and he has the most wonderful things to sell. Come along, come along," she took Batsheva's arm, "before the others pick him clean."

Laughing, they let Jane cut a path through the crowds to where a brightly painted wagon stood off to the side of the square, a makeshift table beside it laden with a rainbow profusion of material, ribbons, and wools. The shrill voices of women haggling with the peddler filled the air but, when the lady's approach was noted, the cacophony gave way to curtsies and deferential greetings. Batsheva smiled and nodded, unused to the behavior, and with a quick glance for reassurance from Jane, she acknowledged the women before she turned her attention to the peddler.

He was a gaunt man, yet there was great strength in his narrow face. His skin was olive cast, and his eyes piercing black, but within them there was a sparkle which made him less formidable. His clothes were definitely Venetian in style and cut with great care. When he spoke, his English was heavily accented. "What treasures can I show my lady?"

"What treasures have you to show?" countered Batsheva with the merest hint of a smile. "Show me your most precious treasure, master peddler."

He waved his hand over the table. "I have silks from the east and spices to please the most discerning palate. Does my lady fancy silk thread for her needlework? Or perhaps some fine linen from Egypt for her babe's swaddling?" He pulled on the corner of a cloth hidden beneath the linen and with a snap, a magnificent square cloth of gold magically appeared. "Or perhaps this, from the weavers of the sultan himself!"

Oohs and aahs floated into the warm afternoon air as everyone pressed a little close to see the fabric. Batsheva was impressed, but she held herself in check. "This is all very fine, but surely you have something truly unique."

He regarded her carefully before he removed a pouch from the voluminous folds of his tunic. Smoothing a square of black velvet on the table, he untied the pouch and emptied its contents onto the cloth. "These, my lady," he said softly, looking directly into her eyes, "are precious only to those who know true quality."

There were gasps, including Batsheva's own. On the cloth lay a profusion of wonderful jewelry. There was a bracelet of braided gold and a strand of lustrous, creamy pearls; a pair of golden rams' head earbobs was tied together with silver thread, along with a second pair resembled roses with sapphire centers. Heavy chains of gold seemed to be knotted together. There were brooches and buckles, some with stones, others with elaborate filigree. But it was a small ring that caught Batsheva's attention. The peddler followed her glance and smiled. "'Tis a trifling trinket," he said carelessly, "I do not know why I carry it with me. Hardly worth your attention, my lady."

Unless you know what it is, thought Batsheva. She picked up the ring and let her finger linger over the engraved top. It was deceptively simple in shape, but the simple pomegranate engraved on the top was familiar… too familiar. "How came you by this, master peddler?" Batsheva asked suspiciously, then added, "I do like to know the history of things."

He shifted uncomfortably. "A sad story, my lady. I bought it from a fine lady. The ring had been a gift in happier times, but the recent loss of her…sister caused her to look upon the ring with sadness. The lady said she had no need of it any longer and thought perhaps another lady would find it…useful."

Batsheva's head snapped up and she stared at the peddler. From the back of the crowd, someone asked "Is it a magic ring?" Laughter followed the question.

"All rings are magic when slipped onto the right finger!" he called back with a deep-throated chuckle.

"Tell me, master peddler, will you ever see this lady again?"

The man shrugged, his palms open. "Who can say? If it is the will of...God, surely I will."

Batsheva opened the pouch she kept secreted in the girdle of her gown and pulled out a single silver coin. "I would say to you, master peddler, that the lady did not realize how much she would miss so tender a reminder of her...sister. Take this coin in exchange for the ring and swear to me you will return it to the lady whence you encounter her again." She was oblivious to the exchange of startled glances from the ladies about her as she gave him the coin and the ring.

The peddler accepted the coin without looking at its surface and slipped both coin and ring into his sash. "My lady is tender-hearted and generous," he murmured as he bowed. Surreptitiously, from within the deep folds of his gown, he removed a small object and palmed it. Shocking the ladies around her, the peddler took Batsheva's hand. "Your devoted servant, my lady." He bowed over her hand, touching it to his lips.

She felt something pressed into her palm and she thought she heard him say *Vashti*, but she could not be certain. Instinctively, however, she withdrew her hand and slipped the object into her open coin pouch.

Picking up his head, the peddler suddenly looked disturbed. "You must allow me to give you a gift, my lady. Something of value for your kindness."

"I could not accept a gift from you, master peddler," she said loud enough for the others to hear.

"Not a gift, then, but a token of my respect." He picked up the cloth of gold and let it flutter for a moment in the light breeze before he allowed it to flutter down over her own, plainer veil. "For a tender-hearted lady," he announced.

The ladies all clucked and urged her to accept the veil. "Do I dare?" she asked aloud.

"I think you'd better," warned Jane with a giggle, "lest they think you mad!"

Laughing, Batsheva dipped her head toward the peddler. "I thank you, master peddler. You, too, are most generous. But you must also allow me to purchase something."

"A bejeweled bauble, perhaps?" he asked, his eyes twinkling again.

"No, not a bauble." She rummaged through the bolts of cloth stacked on the table until she found one in an unusual shade of blue. "This, master peddler. Will you take a silver coin for this?"

"A silver coin?" laughed the peddler. "Surely, my lady, you know I must earn my way with these trifles. Eight silver coins…and that is a bargain."

"Eight!" hooted Batsheva, suddenly enjoying herself immensely. "Two and not a copper more."

"Two?" His eyes opened wide. "Ladies, who will offer me a reasonable price for this silk? Surely one of you has an eye for great quality!"

No one dared bid against their new countess, but it didn't stop the two principals from friendly haggling until they agreed on a price of five silver coins. Batsheva paid him and the peddler bowed low as he accepted. He wrapped up the bolt and tied it with a crimson ribbon. "There, my lady, now you need only a fine needlewoman to sew the perfect gown!"

Jane intercepted the bundle before he could hand it to Batsheva. "She's got the fine needlewoman, if you can see the cut of her gown with your eyes!" she groused with a teasing voice. "I'll just take that; master peddler indeed."

He laughed as he passed the bundle to the chubby seamstress. "Make certain it is the finest gown your nimble fingers have ever sewn, mistress!"

The rest of the market needed to be explored before Batsheva would agree to return to the castle. Jane left them after she purchased eggs and milk from the dairyman, claiming her expanding state made her more tired than usual. And even with Jamie off with the earl, she had more than enough to do to make their little house ready for the coming child. With a cheerful wave and the bolt tucked under her arm, Jane disappeared into the crowd.

"Where shall we go next?" asked Batsheva.

"I want to see the minstrels," Anne answered firmly. "I want to buy something to eat and to sit down. My feet are tired."

"Already? Anne, you would make a terrible adventurer," laughed Batsheva, grasping the girl's hand. "Well, come on then, let's find the baker's stall.

❁ ❁ ❁

The old gypsy woman crooked her bony finger at the peddler and bade him come closer to where she lay in her wagon. "The journey was profitable, little man?"

"Most profitable," agreed the peddler as he exchanged his nondescript brown mantle for an elegant black cloak with an ornate filigree closure.

"You saw her? For yourself, you saw her?"

"Yes, *jida*, I saw her at last. I had almost lost hope."

"She is the one," the old woman cackled gleefully. "Just as I said, she is she and no other."

The peddler drew the cloak over his shoulders and fastened the silver clasp with a snap. "It grows late, jida. Here," he dropped several coins into her withered palm, "our master says soon you will go home."

"To home, to home. Are you to home, little man?"

"No, not yet. My part in this is not finished."

"Then nor is ours. We will wait for the master of us all. Yes, little man, we will wait for our master. Then, perchance, will we go home."

He bowed graciously to the old woman. "Then I shall see you again, jida."

"Yes, yes, little man, you shall see me again."

Outside, he could hear her thin cackle as he made a last check of the hitch securing his borrowed wagon to that of the old woman's. He could see the men gathered around the fire nearby and as much as he would have liked to sit with them for one more night, he knew his own ship was waiting in Hartlepool. He untethered his horse and mounted in a single, fluid leap. Quietly, he walked the horse away from the camp before giving the stallion his head on the road leading eastward to the port.

CHAPTER 30

Alexandria

MAY 1192

Travel stained and weary, Kassim knelt before Khalil. "Praise be to Allah, my lord, for your continued return to good health."

"And praise be to Allah for your speedy return, my friend." Khalil indicated Kassim should sit beside him on the divan. "What news have you brought me?"

The younger man's dirty face was split by a wide smile, his white teeth flashed against his dark skin. "She is well, my lord, and was gladdened to learn that the children are safe." He tossed the gold coin to Khalil. "The old woman played her part well. We were wise to trust her."

"Does she know they are with me?" he asked intently.

"Of that I cannot be certain. She has been most secretive about her past, that much I learned from the gossips. No one knows for certain from whence she came, nor do they know anything about how she came to be in England."

"And the man Durham?"

"He seems to care deeply for her, but there is talk they are not wed. And…" his grin widened, "you have another daughter."

Khalil's dark eyes flashed and his mouth fell open. "A daughter? Are you certain?"

"Yes, my lord. The child was born less than eight months after her capture by the Franks. You may be certain the child is yours."

"Tell me, Kassim, have you seen her?"

"In the garden, near where the jongleurs made camp. I saw not her face, but she has a cap of red hair, like her sister's." He couldn't help but grin at his amir.

"And Batsheva? Did you see her? Did she see you?"

"I saw her briefly in the same garden. She looks well, but" he furrowed his brows, "skinny. Like when she first came to us. The servants say she does not eat well."

Khalil roared with laughter, his head thrown back. "That is my amira," he howled. "She is a picky eater and would starve rather than eat that which she does not like."

"I did not dare let her see me, my lord. There was no way to take her away from there and I would not risk her safety. Rashid met me in Marseille. He has gone to the place called Durham."

"He will deliver the locket and Devorah's ring?"

Kassim nodded. "He knows to tell her nothing but what he has been instructed to tell her no matter what question she asks. With Allah's will, she will understand the message. By now, he should be well on his way back to Paris. He still has his business to conduct for Avram Hagiz. I will send word to him when we reach Marseille, and he will meet us at Calais to cross the channel." Kassim smiled at his amir. "Now we must plan how to take her away from England."

Take her. Khalil did not like the thought of *taking* her from this place any more than he would have approved of taking her from her caravan the first time. But times had changed; he needed to see her again to ask if she wanted to come home. Khalil rose and walked about the chamber. While the children had been a source of comfort and strength for him, he wanted to hear their mother's sweet voice as she sang songs to them.

His reverie was cut short by shouts coming from the garden. Going to the archway, he watched as Daud tackled Amina, sending her sprawling into a flowerbed. Momentarily, he considered reprimanding the boy, but the thought vanished when Amina scrambled up and in a single leap, toppled her brother. "Wild things!" he called with as much gruffness as he could manage. "To me!"

Hiking up his wide pantaloons, Daud marched toward his father while Amina took a moment to attempt to straighten her soiled jacket. "Yes, Abu?" said Daud when he reached his father.

"It is unwise to tumble little girls, my son." He hid a smile as he thought of their mother and the square in Málaga. "Especially ones who can tumble you in retaliation."

"She started it, Abu. She said I was skinny." His chin jutted out just enough to point to his sister.

"You are skinny, Dudu. You're the skinniest boy in the palace," Amina tossed off.

Khalil squatted down to bring his face to their level. "Daud, you may be skinny, but this is not so bad. You are wiry; you tumble like a little monkey and can outrun all the other boys. Is that not so?" The little boy nodded gravely, for it was true. "If you were not so skinny, you would not be so fast."

"I am fast, too, Abu," Amina pouted.

Khalil tried to suppress another grin as he watched his daughter take a stance similar to that of Daud and in that moment, he saw that very young, very obstinate little girl in Málaga. Reaching out, he tugged her vest back into place. "Yes, little princess, you are fast, too, but it is not so important for a girl to be fast. A girl must be sharp sighted to see danger *before* she must run from it."

"See, Dudu," Amina announced proudly, "girls must be smarter than boys."

"Abu did not say that!"

"He did so!"

"He did not!"

Amina made a fist and waved it in her twin's face. "A girl has to be smarter than a boy, lest she be led down an evil path away from Allah's garden!"

"Amina!" roared Khalil, quickly staying the clenched ball that was her hand. "You are running away from Allah's garden very quickly on your own!"

Her little head dropped down as she replied, "Yes, Abu."

Khalil did not miss the smirk on Daud's face, nor the quick flick of the tongue Amina shot in his direction. "Continue, my little ones, and you will find yourselves counting the number of tiles in the corner." Both children seemed to deflate before his eyes and, for an instant, he was sorry to have chastised them. "Now you, Mina, run along to Sufiye Auntie and let her help you with your needlework. And you, Daud, you may take a map from my desk and study it near the pool. I will join you shortly." He watched them trudge off, their high spirits somewhat dampened by the rebuke. Turning to Kassim, he sighed. "I am both mother and father to them. It is not an easy task."

"Forgive me, my lord, but you were the one who insisted they remain with you and not go to live in the sara'i with Sufiye."

Khalil sighed again and ran his hands through his dark hair. "I did not want to separate from them; they still feel the loss of their mother keenly." Then he brightened a little. "I enjoy teaching Dudu; he is quick-witted and sharp. And Mina is just as quick, though more hot-tempered than he." He stopped talking to watch Daud turn upside down to walk on his hands. "He is a monkey," laughed Khalil.

Kassim watched the display. Suddenly, a smug smile tugged the corners of his mouth upward. "A monkey is just what we shall need, Khalil."

A rough plan devised, Khalil sent Kassim to the baths. Looking about his opulent surroundings, Khalil idly wondered what Batsheva would think when she saw their new home. Certainly, if his knowledge of Frankish castles was correct, she would find this infinitely more comfortable than a stone fortress in a land where snow fell.

A slight rustling caught his attention, bringing him out of his reverie. In the archway, a dark-eyed, dusky-skinned woman stood awaiting his command. "What is it?" he asked more gruffly than he intended. He tried to recall her name but could not.

The woman immediately dropped to her knees. "My lord," she murmured, "your slave has prepared your bath."

Sufiye surveyed the rumpled bed when she arrived to see her nephew. Clucking, she clapped her hands and two servants appeared. "Clean this up," she ordered before she went into the garden in search of Khalil. She found him, sword in hand, slashing at a crusader shield mounted on a thick pole. She could only imagine the clanging Khalil was going to hear if Batsheva returned to find a populated sara'i in her new home. "Batsheva will not tolerate other women in your chamber when you bring her home."

"She will learn to live with it." He continued his assault on the dummy.

"She won't and you will regret your actions, Khalil. You will lose her to your own stupidity."

He stopped swinging to stare at his aunt. "She will never leave me again."

"You have spent too much time in the sun, child." The old woman shook her head slowly. "Think with your head, not your lance."

Khalil stopped lunging at the dummy. "You go too far, Auntie."

"As do you. We are talking about Batsheva, not some doe-eyed slave girl who sees you as a path to high status. Batsheva has all the status she needs without you. If you want her to come home and stay home, consider your own actions." Sufiye spun on her heel and started for the door.

"You must already have a plan."

"You will leave this to me?"

"Do I have a choice?" He looked critically at his aunt. "There are times, Auntie, I think given a choice, you would keep Batsheva and send me to the infidels."

"So, now you are a mind reader?" she snapped as she turned toward the archway into the garden. She hid the smile behind her hijab because he was right.

"We leave in two days' time," he called after her.

Sufiye stopped and turned to face him. "Have you told the children?"

"Yes. Amina will stay here with you. Daud will ride with me."

Her eyes flew open. "No, Khalil! You cannot…you must not take Dudu!"

"He is old enough. He needs to be with his father on this journey."

"It is dangerous for a child, Khalil. You risk his life."

"No harm will come to him. I will protect him."

Sufiye saw there was no arguing with him. As she walked away, she heard the clanging of a sword against a metal-clad shield once held by an infidel.

CHAPTER 31

Durham

MAY 1192

When the ladies arrived home from the market, Batsheva asked Mary to arrange for supper to be served in her chambers and asked Anne to join her. The girl regretfully declined, explaining she had already promised her grandmother she would dine with her.

Left to her own devices, Batsheva was bored. She nursed Miriam when Lydia brought the babe, but too soon the nursemaid reappeared to take the child off to bed. When Mary brought in an overfull dinner tray, Batsheva asked her to stay and dine with her, rather than eat alone. "Besides, there is much I want to know about this place, and you seem to be the best one to illuminate my self-imposed darkness."

"Hardly self-imposed, my lady," clucked Mary as she set a second place at the table. "You've been far too ill to bother about the household."

"Still, there are things I must know." Batsheva, as was the custom, served herself first from the platter of salmon Mary had chosen for her. "Tell me about Gwyneth."

"The housekeeper? Oh, she is reasonable, my lady," said Mary, "although she thinks quite highly of herself."

"Too highly, Mary?"

"'Tis hard to say. She has been in charge of the castle for a long time. And in truth, she does know everything that goes on here."

"For example?"

"She knew about the row between the Lady Matilda and my lord earl. And when she found me in the kitchen preparing a tray for you, she warned me gossip from upstairs is not tolerated at the castle. Lady Matilda is harsh with those who break her rules."

"Obviously not harsh enough, considering how we found her," snorted Batsheva as she poked at the fish.

"In defense, my lady," said Mary gravely, "your way of healing is most different from the usual healing arts. Not everyone sees the benefits of fresh air and baths."

"Would," Batsheva grumbled, "that they did. They would surely smell more pleasant."

Mary was piqued by her attitude and felt a correction was in order. She had come to know the lady well over the months she had served her and knew any scold must be gentle. Clearing her throat, Mary said softly, "Forgive me, my lady, but I think grumbling is only going to make matters worse for you here." She saw a small frown formed at the corners of the lady's mouth. "I *know* being away from your own home, your own people, must be difficult. I've seen how the castle operates and the staff is more curious than frightened of you. Below stairs, the old servants credit you with saving Lady Matilda's life; they would express their thanks if they thought you approachable. But because of your own illness, they hang back. You see, my lady, they don't know you at all."

The frown deepened, but Batsheva was not angry; how could she be angry when all Mary did was tell the truth? This was no way to begin life in the castle where it might come to pass that she spent the rest of her days. She was silent for a long moment before she asked, "Can this be repaired?"

"I should think so," replied Mary, "but it must be done with deliberation. T'would seem strange if suddenly your demeanor changed."

Batsheva thought on this for a while. Certainly, there were things she could do to improve her image; she had been virtually invisible since she fell ill and that must change. Despite all the signs that she was being sought throughout England, it could be that knowledge of her whereabouts was desired, not Batsheva herself. As long as she knew the children were safe, she could live out her life in Durham and indeed marry Gilbert. *Gilbert*: the very thought of him made her terribly sad. She did not know what she had done to offend him, but surely it must have been horrible to cause him to leave as he did. "Tell me, Mary, is there news of the earl?"

"Precious little," replied the maid, "only that he is riding his lands reacquainting himself to his people. I suppose this is necessary; he's been gone a good long time and the people need to see their lord is alive and well."

"What do they think of him?"

"They care deeply about him, my lady. Here, in the town, he is well loved by everyone. They are happy to have him home again and Anne, too. The subject of your marriage to him, however, is cause of great speculation. Some say the queen forced him into it. Others say you bewitched him with your grey eyes."

"What nonsense."

Mary shrugged, "Nonsense it may be, my lady, but that is how they talk."

"And the remedy for this?"

"Action, my lady. When his lordship returns, you must take your place on the high board beside him. Whatever differences you have, they need be kept behind doors; you cannot let them see there is strife between you."

"A moment ago, you said this must be done slowly," said Batsheva with great gravity.

"And so it must. I do not suggest you march into the kitchen and begin changing their ways. No, I think you should begin with an expression of interest in what happens here and slowly win them over. It can be done, I am certain." Mary stifled a yawn. "Forgive me, my lady, but I confess I am tired. Today was too exciting by half."

"And I imagine there is someone you would bid goodnight," smiled Batsheva, "before the hour grows late."

The little maid blushed pretty pink. "John would speak to his lordship when he returns," she said quietly; "since I have no parents, 'tis the earl's permission he must seek before we can post banns."

"Oh, Mary, that's wonderful! I am so happy for you."

Mary began to gather the plates onto the tray. "I think, my lady, you need to rest as much as I do. John thinks his lordship will be home soon enough and you will have your hands full with the running of the castle."

Batsheva could not disagree. "I think I shall retire for the evening. As for tomorrow I shall set about righting the misconceptions about me. Let us begin with the housekeeper. As soon as Miriam is fed, let us meet her in the great hall."

Mary went to the door and summoned the footman. The boy cleared the tray and left quickly. When he was gone, Mary helped Batsheva with her laces.

"I can manage from here, Mary. You go find your young man, lest he thinks your eyes are roving toward another."

"Are you certain?" Mary asked.

"Most certain."

The girl dipped a curtsey and wished her lady good night.

Alone at last, Batsheva sat thinking. Durham had yet to tell her about the return of his messengers. He had not mentioned a single word about his search for the children. The men she heard talking at Crompton Hall were not certain the Iron Amir was dead. *Dead.* The word made her shudder. She closed her eyes to conjure up his face, but it would not come to her. Even in her dreams of late, his image faded. No one was searching for her; if they had been, surely, she would have been found by now. The gypsy fortune-teller was nothing more than an old hag repeating old gossip. *But the peddler,* she thought. *The ring looked like Devora's. No, not like it; it was the ring I gave Devora.* Batsheva did not believe for one moment Devora had sold the ring out of sadness. It was given to the peddler as a sign and by giving him the coin, she had acknowledged the message. Surely, the peddler had been sent. *But by whom?* Batsheva could not decide if the messenger was from Devora or from the sultan himself. There was no point in going back to the market to find him; whoever he was, he was long gone.

Suddenly, she remembered the trinket the peddler pressed into her palm was still tucked in the pouch in her girdle. Batsheva dug into the girdle still about her waist and when she had the object in her hand, she moved closer to the torchlight to study it.

It was a locket no larger than a sparrow's egg, but not as round. The gold case was simple yet exquisite in its execution. One side was engraved with a tiny pomegranate set between two scimitars. The other side was covered in miniscule Arabic script. Batsheva stared hard at the writing, desperate trying to make out the verse so minutely engraved into the gold. Her spoken Arabic was much better than her written skills and the elaborate script was difficult to decipher. She could make out but one word… *habibi,* my beloved, but the rest was too small, too ornate. Sighing in frustration, she turned her attention to the clasp. It seemed to be a latch, but when she tried to pry open, it remained locked against her fingers. Batsheva held it up to the light and then she noticed the way the hasp was hinged to the side. Using her fingernail, she pressed against it as she pushed the hasp to one side. It popped up and the locket opened.

The breath left her body; Batsheva sagged against the wall as she stared at the contents. Two locks of hair, one dark as night, one the color of polished copper, were fastened to the pale blue enameled interior. She did not need anyone to tell her from whose heads these fine curls had come. She closed her eyes and murmured a prayer of thanksgiving, then she opened her eyes again. She touched the dark curl and immediately felt the enamel move against her touch. Gently, she lifted the dark lock from its case and found, beneath it, a tiny portrait of Daud. When she lifted the coppery curl, Amina's face appeared. She stared at the two faces and a sense of relief flooded through her. The portraits had to have been painted after her abduction; no one in the Bedouin camp was skilled enough to reproduce the wide eyed, innocent faces of her children. They looked, to her mother's eye, older. *They are alive*, her heart cried out. *They are safe; they are safe; they are safe.*

She slipped the locket back into the pouch she had carried with her since the day she was taken from the Bedouin tent. "Sleep well, my darlings," she murmured as she replaced it in her trunk. "Your mother's heart flies out to you this night. I love you both." Nothing but the crackle of the torch in its iron holder answered her words. Shedding her clothes, she pulled on her night-rail, snuffed all the torches save one, and crawled into the bed. With the covers drawn up, she slipped into deep slumber, the smallest hint of a smile on her face.

True to her word, Batsheva rose early and was dressed before Lydia arrived with a fretful Miriam.

"She's been chewing her fist, my lady. I think she is terribly hungry."

"Or," laughed Batsheva, "she is beginning to teethe. The time is right." She wiped a gob of drool from Miriam's lip, then inserted her finger into the rosebud mouth. The babe immediately clamped down and began chewing. "Yes, I'm afraid she is teething. I will have to make a little willow bark salve to keep when it begins in earnest." She put the babe to her breast and leaned back against the pillows.

Mary arrived just as Miriam finished. She waited until Lydia had taken Miriam to the nursery and then asked, "Are you ready, my lady?"

Batsheva smoothed the blue tunic gown she had chosen for her meeting and retied the laces of the chemise. "I am ready as I shall ever be," she answered bravely. "Let us beard the lioness in her den."

With a grin, Mary led the way down the wide staircase and into the great hall. It was almost deserted but for a couple of servants clearing the remains of breakfast. As soon as they saw her, they curtsied before scurrying out the back toward the cookhouse.

Almost immediately, Gwyneth appeared in the door. She dipped perfunctorily, then declared bluntly, "Breakfast is served at sunup, my lady, but if you would care to eat, I shall send a tray to your chamber."

"Thank you, Gwyneth," replied Batsheva with a sweet smile, "but I have already broken my fast; I would have a word with you...if you have a moment to spare. I know how busy you must be caring for this enormous castle and its residents."

Gwyneth blinked several times; this was not at all what she expected. Although she had seen the lady only once or twice during her illness, she had seen her in action on the day she arrived. For so small a person, she was a presence to be reckoned with. "I have a moment or two, my lady," she managed to say more calmly than she was feeling; "how may I serve you?"

"Let me be honest with you, Gwyneth. I am afraid my arrival at Durham was most unnerving for your able staff. This was not intentional; my concern was for Lady Matilda's health. Had I myself not fallen ill, I'm certain we would have gotten off to a better start. Let us start afresh."

"As you wish, my lady," stuttered Gwyneth.

Batsheva smiled warmly at the housekeeper, glad to see her taken off guard. "As you must know by now, I come from Al-Andalus."

"You speak our tongue well, my lady," Gwyneth added in an effort to seem at ease with the new chatelaine.

"Thank you. I hope to improve as I learn about more about how you manage the household. I have no wish to lose you in this position; I only hope to understand the everyday business. In my home, a lady is expected to know all this."

"As well she should," agreed the housekeeper emphatically. "A lady should know exactly how her household runs."

"Then we agree, Mistress Gwyneth. Will you help me in my learning?"

"Yes, my lady."

"Thank you, Mistress Gwyneth." She glanced around the room and noticed an empty bench near the fireplace. "Let us sit while I ask my questions."

Gwyneth had never been asked to sit with a lady before and although she thought it a bit strange, she followed Batsheva to the bench. She noticed that, although Mary followed them, the maid remained standing near her mistress.

"First, how many souls are fed at the earl's table?"

For rest of the morning, Batsheva asked questions and Gwyneth answered them grudgingly at first, but her respect for the newcomer grew with each passing minute. Mary translated for both women when the need arose. Servants who entered the great hall and saw the three women deep in conversation quickly left to report the sight to others behind the scenes. Heads poked in and out, anxious to see such an unusual sight for themselves. Even the cook left his roasting pit, unwilling to believe his own ears.

Gwyneth had been at Durham since the birth of the present earl and loved him almost as much as if he been her own son. She watched little Lord Gil grow from a chubby baby to a powerful, handsome man. The housekeeper had bandaged his cuts and scrapes, taught him how to tell a good egg from a bad one, and fed him treats whenever he burst into her little cottage at the back of the garden. She supervised the wedding festivities when he married Lady Joan and attended at the birth of the little Lady Anne. When sweet Joan died, she felt the pain as acutely as anyone else in the family and prayed to the Holy Mother that Marquess Gil would find a wife as lovely as the lady had been. The arrival of this foreigner was a shock; her first impression of the diminutive lady had not been good. Still, she began to understand why his lordship had tumbled for the girl, for she seemed little more than a girl. This Lady Elizabeth was sharp as a tack, well-bred and, judging by the way she worked in Lady Matilda's chamber that afternoon, unafraid of hard work.

"Have we covered everything?" asked Batsheva when she felt she had exhausted all her questions.

Gwyneth was silent for a moment, then said, "While Durham is a fine city, my lady, it serves as county seat, therefore your concerns will need to go beyond the walls. You must ask his lordship to take you on a tour of all his lands so you might meet the people whose lives you will touch as their countess. "

"Is it common for a lady to ride out on her own?" she asked.

"Not alone, my lady. One always takes men-at-arms; his lordship will assign men to be your personal guard." She smiled tentatively at Batsheva. "The roads are generally safe, but one can never be too careful."

"I see. Then I shall wait until the earl returns before I venture beyond the walls of the city. In the meanwhile, I will continue to explore Durham."

"The people will like that, my lady. Lady Joan, may God rest her soul, was much beloved. They want to love you, too, but will need time to grow used to your ways."

"I do hope you are right, Mistress Gwyneth. I thank you for your encouragement," smiled Batsheva. "Now, before you resume your duties, I have but a single request."

Ah, here it comes, thought Gwyneth. She steeled herself for some impossible task. "Whatever your ladyship wants, we will endeavor to do."

"I am not certain when the earl is returning, but when he does, I want to have a feast. I will leave it to you to arrange but would ask that you bring the menu to me before the cook begins his preparations. His lordship's tastes have been altered by his travels and I would please him with presenting dishes he has grown to favor."

Gwyneth's round face broke into a wide smile. "Of course, my lady! We can do this with ease. We were only waiting for word from you to prepare a welcoming fête for his lordship."

"Good, then again we agree." Batsheva rose, signaling the end of the interview. "I shall leave you to you work and I look forward to when we meet again to discuss the fête."

Mary followed her into the earl's solar off the great hall. "Oh, my lady!" squealed the maid, "you had her eating right out of your hand."

"Let us hope she does not come to think I bewitched her!" laughed Batsheva with relief. "It did go well, did it not?"

"Very well. If Mistress Gwyneth becomes your ally, the rest are sure to follow."

"And right now, I guarantee she is on her way to Lady Matilda's chamber to give her the news."

"The dowager will come around, I warrant," said Mary. "She is too well liked by everyone here to be the harridan she presented to you. I think she has only her son's happiness at heart."

"Perhaps, but…."

"Do not give it another thought, my lady. Let nature takes its course and all will be well."

Batsheva sat down in the chair beside the earl's table. "I must go into the city today, but I wish to go unnoticed. Can it be done?"

"I think so. If you wear a simple cloak over your gown and a plain linen headscarf, we should be able to slip through the gate. Where do we go?"

"To Mistress Fitzhugh. But I would prefer to go alone."

"That might be unwise, my lady."

Batsheva sighed. "I cannot be caged up like a bird, Mary. I need to move about on my own…to have time to myself. Help me do this, Mary."

Swathed in Mary's light grey cloak, Batsheva slipped out of the castle, through the gate, and into the city. She found her way back to the market with ease and, from there, she had little trouble learning where the seamstress had her new establishment. When Jane opened the door and saw her friend standing there alone, she quickly ushered her inside.

"I cannot stay," said Batsheva, "but I need your help. I must find the house of Rachel Vital."

Jane was not surprised by the request. "It is nearby, Bess. Shall I go with you?"

"No." She smiled at Jane. "I shall be all right, Jane. I simply wish to repay my debt to her."

"Well, if you must…." Jane was uncomfortable with her refusal of an escort, but she understood Batsheva's need to do things on her own. She gave her directions and saw her out the door. "Will you come here before you go back?"

"If there is time." Batsheva pecked Jane's cheek, then hurried down the cobbled street.

Rachel was shocked to see Batsheva standing in the entry. "Why are you here?" she asked bluntly.

"We must talk."

She led her into the solar at the back of the house. "Are you not well?"

"I am much improved, thanks to you, Rachel. But I need to know what you've learned about my family."

The news was not good. Rachel did not know what to tell Batsheva and what to omit. Sitting on a bench in the tiny garden courtyard, she stared down at her hands in her lap for a long while. "My husband does have dealings with Avram Hagiz. But when I asked, he grew curious for the reason I asked. He pressed me for an answer, but the only thing I told him was that the new lady had heard of his skill as a goldsmith while in the Holy Land. I did not tell him who you are."

"What did he say?"

"He was pleasantly surprised and said that if there was something you wanted from Avram, he could arrange to have it sent." She paused. "The trade routes are difficult, Batsheva. Our people continue to suffer at the hands of the crusaders."

"Surely the sultan is protecting them as best he can."

"So we are told. But still, it does not make travel easy. Couriers are few and far between."

"Have there been couriers?"

Rachel paused again before she said, "Yes."

"Recently?"

She nodded. "Very recently."

The timbre of her voice filled Batsheva with dread. "Who was the courier, Rachel?"

Rachel swallowed hard. "Yehuda."

Batsheva blanched. "Is he here? Now?" she whispered.

"He is in London." She reached for Batsheva's hand. "Since my husband knew nothing when he left, he had nothing to tell Yehuda when he saw him. But he did ask whether or not a Spanish woman was recently come to Durham. My husband said there were rumors that our earl wed a Spanish lady, but this could hardly be the one in question. He asked about the color of your hair, but my husband could not answer; he has never seen you."

"Praise God for that," groaned Batsheva. "Will he come here do you think?"

"Perhaps. My husband does not want him to come north; he fears for Yehuda's state of mind. Even the last time, when he saw Yehuda in Antwerp, he said his behavior was strange."

"How so?"

"There is something not right in his head, Batsheva," Rachel said softly. "He speaks of revenge on those whose name he will not speak aloud. While in one breath he calls you a martyred saint, in the next his eyes burn with hatred for you. Whatever happened between you in Benghazi has scarred him badly. Although he never says as much outright, I think he is searching for you."

Batsheva shook her head. "It makes no sense, Rachel. He tells everyone I am dead, yet he looks for me. What does he want? Does he want to kill me himself?"

"David speculates, although I've not told him who you are, that Yehuda is seeking some sort of retribution from a Spanish family. We do not know for certain."

Batsheva was about to comment when a man stepped into the garden. "Rachel?" he called. When he saw them sitting there, he grinned at the ladies. "Forgive me, my love, I did not know you had a visitor." Rachel's husband came toward them, but as he did, the smile faded from his lips to be replaced by shock widening his dark eyes. He was seeing a ghost "Bashi?"

Her mouth fell open, but no words came out.

"Bashi?" he asked again.

Batsheva jumped up and threw herself at David. "I thought you were dead! They told me you were dead!"

"I was here, not in York," David said grimly. He held her at arm's length. "I cannot believe I am seeing you, Bashi."

"I am so very glad to see you." She hugged him again. She was crying.

"I did not know you knew her, David," said Rachel, wiping away her own tears. "I would have told you as soon as you came home."

David shrugged. "I suppose because I trained with Hagiz, I assumed you would have guessed I knew the whole family, not just Yehuda."

The name Yehuda hung in the air for a moment.

"What of my brother, David? Rachel says he is in London."

"He is. I will not be the one to tell him you are here. It would be dangerous for you. He is not right, Bashi. His mind is…twisted."

A thousand images flashed through her brain, but the one which remained was the rug given to her by Abdullah in the market; the one which now lay on the floor of her chamber. She swallowed hard. "He knows, David. He knows I am in England."

"How? No one has told him!"

"Someone did." She told them about the little rug. "Whoever shipped the rugs I ordered included my monkey rug in the parcel. They knew… someone knew it was my rug. It would have been returned to my parents' house with the rest of my dowry. Yehuda would have had access to it. And Yehuda knows I have it now." She stopped abruptly, then asked, "Did he say anything about my children or Khalil?"

"Only that he was glad your amir was dead." His voice grew soft. "How are you alive, Bashi? You were a slave in his household."

She shook her head. "I know how hurt Akiva would be if he knew. It is all so difficult to explain."

"You don't need to explain anything to me, Bashi."

"But I do! Khalil did not take me from the caravan; two rogues kidnapped me and gave me to him as tribute. I did not go to his bed willingly. In truth, David, he was the kindest man who ever lived. He loved me deeply. The day I learned he fell in battle I thought I would die. And Durham! He picked me up out of the dust believing I was a boy in need of help. I was already pregnant with my daughter; he sought only to protect me."

"You are wed to him." It was not a question.

Batsheva shook her head. "We are not wed."

David did not know if she shared the earl's bed, but he was not about to ask. "Akiva would marry you, Bashi. He still grieves for you."

She looked at Rachel and sighed. "So Rachel has told me. I could not marry him or anyone else. Until I have proof Khalil is truly dead…" her voice trailed off.

"And Durham? Do you love him?"

Batsheva felt her own tears on her cheeks. "I do. He has done nothing but shown me kindness and compassion."

There was a moment of intense silence. "Does the earl know any of this?" asked David.

"Some, but not all. I've not told him about Yehuda."

"You must tell him, Bashi."

"How? He is gone a fortnight now and I have no idea when he will return." Her face heated at the admission. "Rachel, you said he left the night I lay so ill. Have you seen him since?"

"No."

"Nor have I," added David, "although I heard he travels the district. Beyond that, there has been no word."

Batsheva thought for a moment. "I will tell him when he returns…if he returns."

CHAPTER 32

Durham

JUNE 1192

Durham spent the night with his father's oldest friend, Sir Thomas of Crichton Wood. The aged knight welcomed the young earl into his home and would have hosted a feast in his honor had Durham not insisted the visit remain private. They dined away from the high board, choosing instead the small room Sir Thomas used for his council meetings. There was much business to discuss and Durham felt time was too fleeting to be wasted on endless toasts to his good health. Catherine, the old man's granddaughter, saw to their comfort before leaving them closeted in the room.

"I encountered the dark knight on the road to York," Durham told him. "Since then, I have come to learn he roams the north at will, terrorizing travelers and threatening the villagers. They say he is the one who burned Greenwood Knoll."

"Aye, I heard that, and would believe it."

"Have you seen him?"

"Twice, but only from a distance. He stays clear of the cities, preying instead on the outlying villages."

"Who is he, Thomas? York could not put a name to him."

"With good reason; no one knows his name. They say he's a dark fellow, though none have seen his face. His ties are clearly to John or, rather, John's purse strings. Did your brother-in-law tell you he is seneschal to John?"

"Yes, but not much else."

The old man clenched his teeth. "He was here not four months past. Rode into Crichton Wood with 12 of his men, bold as brass, and demanded a levy on our spring wool! I may be old, Gil, but I'm not dead yet. I stood my ground and refused to give him a single copper. Told the bugger my taxes go to Richard and Richard alone. I'll not be intimidated by the likes of him."

"And he did nothing when you refused?"

"Nothing. I had 30 men-at-arms in my courtyard. I fear he will be back, though. I think he's not one to make idle threats."

"I'll put a garrison here, Thomas, if you think he is a threat to the peace."

"Put a garrison here and he will be," chuckled the old knight. "Nay, Gil, my men are capable. But there is a favor I would ask…as your liege man."

"You know I will grant anything you ask."

"It's not for me. 'Tis Catherine. Take her to Durham, Gil; she needs to be away from here. There's no future for her if she insists on caring for an old man in his dotage. She needs a husband, a family of her own."

"Are there no suitors?" asked Gil, rather surprised; he had known her since she was a child. Catherine was a comely girl and one any man would want for a wife. How she had been passed over seemed rather unlikely and he said so.

"She was betrothed to Henry of Middlesex when she was eight, and we all expected a marriage when she reached fourteen. He died two months before the wedding day, from the coughing sickness. She knew him well and loved him deeply; when he died, she went into mourning. Without a mother to counsel her or a father to arrange another match, she has devoted herself to seeing to my needs."

"What of your son, her uncle? Has he no say in this?"

Thomas looked at him strangely. "Laurence died last summer….

"I'm sorry, Thomas, I hadn't heard."

"Leaves me in a bit of a bind," said the knight sadly. "I have no other heir beside Catherine. Unless she marries and produces an heir, my lands revert to the Crown. Make her your ward, Gil. You could find her a suitable husband, one who would live at Crichton Woods gladly. A third son, perhaps. No one too important. She's not a frivolous girl nor so old as to be thought long in the tooth."

"Does she know this is what you want?"

"I suppose she must; she knows our predicament."

"Then talk to her, Thomas. If she agrees, bring her to Durham."

In the morning, Durham took his meal at the high board with Sir Thomas and his granddaughter. It gave him the opportunity to watch the girl as she saw to the meal before taking her place on his left. For all his experience, he could not understand how such a lovely English rose had been left alone when women of good family were in high demand. She was tall, but not too tall. Her slender figure was demurely clad in a simple, but well-tailored gown with a pretty embroidered girdle circling her slim waist. Catherine's fair complexion offset the deep hazel of her eyes and the auburn glints in her neatly plaited hair. When she spoke, her voice was gentle yet firm. In short, Durham found Catherine to be perfectly charming.

As if she could sense his study of her, the girl addressed him directly. "My lord," she stated quietly, "I was told the nature of your conversation with my grandfather."

Durham smiled at her. "Are you of a mind to heed his advice?"

"It would depend, my lord, on several factors." She saw his eyebrow slide upward and continued. "I would not be a burden on your household. If I come to Durham, I need to have an occupation. I'm not used to idle hands and I would be most unhappy to sit about and do nothing."

"I am certain there would be more than enough to keep you occupied at Durham, Lady Catherine," he smiled warmly. "My lady would be glad for your company."

"She would not object?"

He shook his head. "Bess is happiest in the company of intelligent women. As she is new to England, I fear she is lonely. She has no family here and few friends. I think she would welcome you happily."

"Lastly, my lord, I will have a say in whom I accept. I will not be foisted onto someone who wants me only for my grandfather's property."

"Aye, you will have more than a say, Lady Catherine," answered Durham, "your approval is required."

"Then I shall come to Durham, my lord, when the time is right. I thank you for your kindness and only hope your lady feels similarly."

Durham left Crichton Wood with no destination in mind. His men followed behind him at a short distance; they had no better idea of where they were going than their earl. Finally, when they had ridden south for half the day, Jamie felt it was time to direct his master homeward. Trotting up to him, he rode abreast of Durham for a while. Finally, he could hold his tongue no longer.

"'Tis time I went home to my wife, my lord," he said brusquely. "She's heavy with child and no doubt is wondering what has happened to her man."

Durham neither slowed his pace nor looked at his squire. "Are you planning to ride alone?"

"No, my lord."

"Are the men talking treason?"

"No, my lord."

Durham glanced at Jamie. "Are you telling me it is time to return to Durham?"

"Yes, my lord, I am." He waited for a moment, then cleared his throat. "Ye can't go on like this, Gil. 'Tis past the time ye went home and faced yer demons. Whatever happens between you and the lady is none of my business, but ye can't be riding the land forever. We need to go home."

They had reached a crossroad. Durham reigned in his horse and stood face-to-face with Jamie. "You are right when you say 'tis none of your business, FitzHugh," he said gruffly, "it is not."

He watched the earl's mouth set in a tight line across his hardened jaw. "Don't ye go pulling a face with me, Gilbert of Durham. I've been with ye since ye were nothing more than a stripling and I've bound yer wounds too many times to count. I'll not be bullied by ye, I tell ye." The mouth turned downward yet remained shut. Taking it as a good sign, he continued. "She's a fine lady, Gil. Headstrong but she cares deeply for ye. I need not be the one to tell ye that."

"What makes you so certain?" scoffed the earl.

This time, it was Jamie who frowned. "Ye know it in yer heart, my lord. She had plenty of chances to kill ye if she wanted, but she has never done anything but give ye respect. Did she not care for yer lady mother? Does she not dote on young Annie? She is finally on the mend from her own hurts and ye need to have patience."

"You know nothing about it!" roared Durham. His horse shied at the sudden loud noise.

Jamie narrowed his eyes at the earl as he leaned forward in the saddle. "Have it yer own way, my lord. But we've been gone more than a month; time to go home." He kicked his mount and cantered to where the others were waiting. "We are for Durham," he shouted.

"But his lordship?" called one of the men.

"He'll be along in a moment or two." Without a backward glance, Jamie led the troops onto the road that would lead to Durham.

Durham watched them disappear over a low rise then, unable to help himself, he began to laugh. Again, for the hundredth time, he understood why his father had appointed James FitzHugh his man-at-arms. There was uncanny wisdom in Jamie's words and, try as he might, he could not deny it. Jamie had let him run his anger out on the road, but he knew when it was time to quit running. Spurring his horse, he cantered in the direction of home.

Durham's return was heralded with a great flurry of activity. A single rider sent ahead announced the impending arrival, sending the entire household into motion. Lady Matilda emerged only to find the newcomer standing in the center of the great hall calmly issuing polite requests to the staff who, in turn, ran off to do her bidding. The old woman was caught between pleasant surprise and the uncomfortable sense she was no longer needed. Without making her presence known, she returned to her apartments.

When she was certain all was in order, Batsheva hurried to her own chamber. There was hardly enough time to bathe, but she managed to wash herself clean before letting her maid help her into a graceful, apple green bliaut Jane recently finished. Mary brushed her hair until it shone like a new copper penny then twisted the bottom into a tiny chignon before she fastened a buttery linen wimple over Batsheva's curls.

"Done," announced Mary as she handed her mistress the polished silver mirror. "You've never looked more lovely."

Batsheva had to admit she liked what she saw in the polished silver. Her cheeks had good color and her grey eyes sparkled. Her hair was finally growing out enough to manage; she touched the wisps of ringlets peeping out from beneath the linen. "Thank you, Mary," she smiled.

"No thanks needed, my lady. I'm happy just to see you looking fit. You gave us a terrible scare, you know."

Batsheva smoothed the line of her gown then stepped into a pair of soft kid slippers. "We must go down," she said to Mary. "Would you ask Anne to join me at the gate, please?"

Mary curtsied and went to fetch the girl.

Alone, Batsheva went to her trunk and opened the lid. She pulled back the layer of fabrics, then stared down at the dirty cloak she had been wearing the day Durham found her.

I was given to Khalil as a gift, she reminded herself, *and he took me as was his right according to his law. I did not love him, but I grew to care for him because he was a man above men. Gilbert has never touched me against my will...does that make him less of a man?* She dropped the fabric and closed the lid.

She had not reached the point where she longed for Gilbert's touch, but she found his closeness comforting. Had he not held her when she wept? Had he not put chivalry above his male needs when she was not prepared to let him into her bed? His tender regard for her feelings had wormed itself into her heart and now, as he approached his own castle, she considered how she would greet him.

From a place on the parapet from where the entire valley was laid out in a symphony of summer green, Batsheva watched the cloud of dust move closer to the castle walls. Anne, standing beside her, could barely contain her joy.

"Look, Bess, see the banner?" She pointed to what appeared to be a standard snapping smartly in the wind. "'Tis the lion and thistle! I love to see it fly. How glorious it must look in battle!"

Batsheva did not answer. She had seen that banner in battle...against a helpless band of old men. It was not a glorious sight. She sighed although a smile remained on her face; she would not let unpleasant memories mar this day for either her or him. *When he comes through the gate,* she decided, *I shall greet him as he deserves to be greeted.*

Now the hoofbeats could be heard on the dry road. Anne could wait no longer. Leaving Batsheva on the battlement, she raced down the outer stairway, her long hair flying out behind her. When the horses reached the final flat stretch of road before the great gate, Batsheva raised her arm and let her handkerchief catch the afternoon breeze.

Durham spied the slim figure framed against the brilliant blue of the sky and his heart fairly left his chest. Setting his spurs to his horse, he urged the beast faster. The sound of hooves against wooden bridge could not come soon enough for him.

Stable boys darted between the huge battle steeds as the earl and his men clattered into the courtyard. Every available hand was pressed into service to help the men from their mounts. The earl saw his animal led away by a groom then quickly dismissed his men. When he turned around again, he saw Batsheva standing at the top of the steps with Anne beside her. They made a genuinely lovely pair; he noticed the way Batsheva held Anne's hand tightly in her own. Slowly, he mounted the wide steps.

Her heart fluttered wildly, but Batsheva managed to keep her face serene as Durham approached. When he reached the step below where she stood, she sank into a low curtsy, at the same time pulling Anne to do the same. She could see the toe of his boot, but it was the warmth of his hand she felt when he took hers. "Welcome home, my lord," she murmured.

"Are you glad to see me, Bess?" The question was soft, almost tentative.

She looked up at him and he saw her eyes were bright. "Aye, Gilbert, I *am* glad to see you home at last."

Durham sat in the steaming tub with his eyes closed and his head against a soggy cushion. The hot water felt good against his skin; it had been far too long since he was clean. In his ear, he heard Batsheva humming as she moved about the outer chamber picking up his discarded garments and selecting fresh ones from his wardrobe. The song she hummed was strange to him; he had not heard it before, but it did not matter, so long as it was her voice creating the sound.

The humming stopped and Durham opened his eyes. He smiled when he saw her standing before him, a towel in her hands. "Are you planning to spend the night there, my lord, or will you join your household for the evening meal?"

He wanted to pull her into the tub with him but resisted temptation. "Unfortunately, I am famished. I need sustenance, woman."

"If you removed yourself from the tub, my lord earl, you would find an adequate meal awaiting you in the great hall."

"Adequate? Adequate! That is all you can offer me?" he bellowed.

"For the moment, it shall do." The serious set of her mouth did not reflect the smile in her eyes. She held the towel out to him.

Durham took it from her, but before he could rise, she turned and left him alone again. Sighing, he wrapped himself in the cloth as he stepped from the tub.

CHAPTER 33

Durham

JUNE 1192

Subtle changes in the great hall did not escape Durham's sharp eye. The banners hanging overhead were bright and clean, the trestle tables were freshly scrubbed. Even the huge fireplace looked as though it had been scoured down to the hearthstone. Gone were the haphazard rushes, replaced by new matting sweetened with herbs and clover. No dogs roamed the hall in search of the discarded bone. The old, scarred high board had been replaced by a long oaken trestle polished to high gloss. The traditional seat of the earl was the same chair his father had used, but Durham was pleased to see new brocade cushions in place of the old, worn ones. And throughout it all, the aroma of beeswax permeated the air.

"What other miracles have you wrought?" Durham asked Batsheva when she took her place beside him.

She flushed with pride at the compliment. "'Twas simply a matter of cooperation," she told him quietly. "Everyone was most happy to help." She nodded at Gwyneth and the meal was served.

Platter followed platter filled to overflowing with the bounty of Durham. Fish poached in white wine was served alongside braised veal and roasted duck. Two servants were needed to bring in a roast suckling pig, and although Batsheva did not touch the exquisitely prepared delicacy, Durham feasted on the crackling flesh. Beef and mutton pies were provided for each trestle along with baskets filled with bread still warm from the ovens. Pitchers of ale were passed from hand to hand.

"Forgive the simplicity of the meal, my lord," said Batsheva with mock humility, "but we had scant time to prepare."

"If this is simple, I am curious as to what you consider a feast," he chuckled as he refilled his tankard.

"If it is a grand feast you want, then you shall have one…tomorrow."

He stared at her. "Tomorrow?"

"Is that not soon enough?" she asked innocently batting her eyes.

"Too soon, Bess. Let us wait until the first harvest is in; then we will have a reason to truly celebrate."

"Whatever my lord wants...."

He pressed her hand to his lips. "What I want is to feast on you, my lady."

The dowager countess watched them surreptitiously from her place on Durham's left. She had to admit the woman performed remarkably once she set her mind to it and this was not a bad thing. Elizabeth had done well to consolidate her position within the household. Instead of hiding in her chambers, she worked hard alongside Gwyneth, reducing the normally taciturn Welshwoman to a gushing font of praise for the foreigner. If the dowager countess had been in a position to interview and select her successor, Elizabeth certainly would have been a strong candidate, despite her all too obvious shortcomings. However, the mother wanted to see her son married in church to a woman who would give her grandsons. Although the woman sat in the customary seat, she was not, as far as Matilda was concerned, countess.

The earl, however, seemed oblivious to his mother's concerns. He dutifully reported on his tour and assured her all was well. The farms were thriving, the towns bustled with commerce and, overall, the people seemed content. He made a brief mention of the dark knight and the threats apparently coming from John's man, but he assured his mother now that he was home, this would cease. The broad smile splitting his face was meant to convey the joy he felt at being at his own table, but the message it gave Lady Matilda was something far different. *They have reconciled,* she told herself silently; *would that I might feel the same happiness.* The matter of their marriage loomed ominously in her thoughts, and it was with great trepidation that she broached the subject with her son.

"Perhaps we can celebrate your marriage when the harvest has come in," she proposed casually.

His face remained calm, but the pain could not be more acute had she sliced him with a knife. "My marriage is not open for examination by you, madam, or anyone else."

"Is it a marriage, Gilbert?"

"I would suggest you have this conversation with your confessor in the privacy of the box. God's bones, Mother, take it up with Uncle Charles."

"I already have."

A palpable silence hung between them despite the noise of the hall. Durham faced his mother. "And what does the archbishop recommend?"

"That you should marry her here, quietly, in our chapel."

"I'll consider the request," he replied tersely, glancing at his uncle who sat beside his mother. The archbishop acknowledged the look and returned it with a bemused look, as if to say *I warned her already.* For the remainder of the meal, the earl ignored his mother.

Batsheva excused herself from the high board when Lydia sent word the babe needed to nurse. Durham promised to join her shortly; she could see portents of the night to come in the depths of his blue eyes.

Miriam was fussy. She nursed sporadically until her mother, frustrated by the child's lack of interest in the breast, asked Lydia to take her back to the nursery. "She's teething," sighed Batsheva. "Rub this on her gums, then give her a hard biscuit. That will help soothe her pain." She handed the maid a jar of salve made from willow bark and honey.

Alone in her chamber, Batsheva managed her laces and shed her gown. She changed into a linen night-rail and woolen robe before she went about the business of tidying up. Not unhappy to be alone for a few minutes, Batsheva sat down at her dressing table and began to brush out the tight chignon Mary created for the evening.

She caught her own reflection in the polished silver mirror. She touched her hands to her face. It was not an unpleasant face, although she thought she looked older of late. Still, after everything she lived through, all the troubles and the pain, she caught herself wondering if Khalil would still say she was the most beautiful woman in all Islam. Her thoughts turned to Khalil and she blushed when she recalled her first night with him. Her maidenhead was taken against her will on a pile of cushions in a tent in the desert. The blush turned to crimson as she recalled the pain, the confusion, the hatred of Khalil in that moment. *But I grew to care for him in my heart*, she remembered in the same breath. For a second, she could almost feel his hands against her flesh, and she trembled. Khalil made her body come alive; when he moved within her, she found the greatest of all physical pleasures. *Will I know this again? Will my soul ever cry out as it once did?* she wondered, suddenly afraid. Pushing herself away from the table, she hurried from the chamber.

Batsheva opened the door to Durham's chamber and peeked in. She saw the damp toweling lying across the bed and with a cluck of annoyance, she went to pick it up. The masculine scent of the cloth took her by surprise and for a moment, she stood frozen. Too many memories threatened to spill into her head. Forcing herself back to the present, she hung the towel on a peg in his wardrobe.

She tried to close the door, but something was caught. Batsheva stooped to dislodge the offending piece of cloth, then realized whatever it was, it was filthy. Pushing aside a pair of boots, she pulled out the cord-bound bundle. It was heavier than she expected. No sooner had she brought it into the torchlight, she knew what she was holding.

Her breath was shallow as she sunk to the floor clutching the bundle against her chest. She buried her face in the cloth. It was faint, but the scent of Khalil, the desert, and blood clung to the fabric. *Khalil's blood.* Blindly, her fingers tore at the knot.

She did not hear the door open. Durham stood quietly and watched her. "Bess," he rasped. Slowly, he went to her.

Her silence was deafening. When she finally looked up, her eyes were vacant. Slowly, she removed the rope with trembling fingers. The cloth was stained with too much blood. Batsheva swallowed hard, then forced her hands to unroll it. The cloth became a burnous and before she reached the end of the roll, she lovingly smoothed the stained, torn fabric. "'Tis Khalil's," she whispered as she fingered an embroidered band. "See the *tiraz?* I put it here." She closed her eyes and blindly felt for what was hidden inside the robe. Khalil's sword slid easily from within. Her hand slid lovingly over the blackened blade before she grasped the hilt. "Khalil would never permit his saif to be so soiled," she whispered. Slowly, she rose as her eyes met Durham's; when she spoke again, her voice was cold. "Did you kill him yourself?" She faced him, the sword balanced in her hand.

"No."

"I know how to use this. Should I run you through, Durham?"

"It would not bring him back."

Stepping toward Durham, she touched the tip of the blade against his chest. "You were there; by Allah's law, I am entitled to kill you."

"And kill yourself as well?"

She lowered the sword, then let it fall to the floor with a thud. *Like the dagger,* she remembered.

Durham grabbed her by the upper arms. "He is dead, Bess! He died in battle and naught you can do will bring him back. Is it not enough to have him in Miriam? You have his daughter. 'Tis time you got on with living!"

"Two daughters, monsieur, and a son…or have you conveniently forgotten them, too? I have not. They have lost both mother and father."

He released her arms. "'Tis true, but you have told me they are safe. Can you ask for more than that?"

"I can ask to go home."

There was another long silence. "There is nothing to go home to, Bess. You do not know where they are. Would you spend the rest of your life searching one desert after another? Have you given no thought to Miriam? Does she not deserve to have at least one living parent?"

Batsheva stared at him in disbelief. "You are one to talk, monsieur. Did you not choose to abandon your own daughter?"

"Aye and was a fool for it. But I knew exactly where she was and that she would be there when I returned. 'Tis not the same thing."

"How long have you had this?" asked Batsheva, suddenly quieter. "Did your spies give this to you in York?"

"I sent two messengers back to try to find the children. They returned with this."

A hard smile crossed her face. "You could not find them, could you, Durham?" she spat. "They are safe from your scheming."

"God's bones, woman, I wanted to bring them here…to you. I thought that would be the best way."

"They will never let Daud leave, even if you could find them. He is sheikh now." Her eyes glittered dangerously. "You have numbered your own days, Durham, for they will come looking for you."

"They will do no such thing. If all went according to plan, your sultan knows you are safe. His emissary made no offer of ransom when he learned where you had been taken."

"Is this true?" she gasped.

He nodded. "I swear by all that is holy. And I swear by all that is holy that I love you, Bess. I am alive and I love you more than you could imagine. Everything I do, I do for the simple joy of seeing your smile reach your eyes. Can you not accept that it is natural to want to go on living? Can you not understand that you are allowed to build a life for yourself? If what you believe is true, that the twins are safe and well, can you not find relief in that and allow Miriam to have her life here? I have promised to love her as my own. Had she been a boy, Bess, I would have named him my heir. Can that not be enough for you?"

He pricked the bubble of her existence and Batsheva felt the air rush from her body. She swayed and reached out, but before she could fall, Durham grabbed her and crushed her against his chest.

His mouth came down on hers, for the first time, taking possession of that which he long desired. Her lips were warm and sweet against his and she did not fight him off. He felt the swell of her breasts against him and he held her as tight as he dared. "Love me, Bess," he whispered into her ear, "love me just a little and I will be satisfied."

As a drowning woman clings to a tree limb, Batsheva held fast to Durham. She did not push away from his kiss; she yielded to him. Her hands wrapped around his body, and she pressed herself against him. She let her lips part as his tongue touched hers. Her mouth answered his question.

Finally, it was Durham who broke away. Gently, he held her face in his hands so he might study the stormy depths in her eyes. "Do you come to me freely?" he asked, almost afraid of the answer.

"I come of my own will, Gilbert. No one forces my decision." The words echoed strangely in her head...she had said the same thing to Khalil in another lifetime.

His mouth took hers again and this time her lips yielded to the pressure of his tongue. She tasted him, savored him, until she was completely certain he wanted her as much as she wanted him. With a feather's touch, he caressed her through the thin fabric of her robe. His thumbs brushed against her nipples, twin rosebuds puckered beneath her lawn gown. The ribbon closure caught beneath his fingers; he tugged gently as the knot released. Batsheva let the robe puddle at her feet. Nor did she protest when he slid the gown from her shoulders.

When he touched her bare flesh, she gasped. His hands slid along her curves. Her own fingers found life of their own as she unfastened his belt. He stood perfectly still when she untied the laces of his shirt. Gilbert pulled it from his body, tossed it aside, then swept her up into his arms to carry her to the bed.

She could not deny his touch aroused her. As his lips trailed down her throat, Batsheva moaned. Whether it was the heat of his caress or her own fears rising to the surface, she did not care. All that mattered was Khalil was dead and would not return to her. If Durham could exorcise his ghost, then so be it. She gave herself over to his ministrations and willed herself not to see Khalil's face in the darkness.

Although she was pliant as fresh clay in his hands, Durham felt her struggle within. He kept himself in check as he began a methodical exploration of all her defenses. As much as he wanted to feel her around him, he delayed; it was more important that she be ready than for him to satisfy the burning desire he long had for her. Beginning with the smooth column of her throat, he let his mouth slide over her skin, delivering light, teasing kisses as he discovered the most tender places on her body. Slowly, deliberately, he let the fire he lit grow within her.

Her flesh grew hot where he touched her. Batsheva, so still at first, began to move to accommodate his exploration. Tentatively, she answered the touch of his mouth with kisses of her own. He was persistent in his desire to share his passion and Batsheva slowly responded. "Love me just a little, Bess," he rasped against her ear.

Batsheva felt his uncertainty and his pain; she suddenly wanted that pain to end. It was as acute in her as it was in him. With a moan from deep within her, she began to explore him. She traced the line of several scars on his stomach and smiled when he groaned. As her hand ran along the hard ridge of his thigh, she enjoyed his response. When she found the straining source of his masculinity, she closed her hand over the length of him. The tip of her tongue touched the tip of his manhood. "Does this please you, my lord?" she breathed.

"Mother of God!" cried Gilbert as her tongue circled his shaft.

She ministered to his needs, making him lay back on the bed as she straddled him. Batsheva needed no instruction on how to arouse him; she needed only to find what drove him into the vortex of passion.

He bucked against her as he probed her most secret of places. His hands cupped her milk-filled breasts as she moved her hips in a way designed to drive him to the brink; the harder his thrust, the more powerful her downward motion. She kept him at the edge of the abyss forever, until the precise moment of union. "Now, Gilbert," she groaned, her head thrown back, her eyes closed against the fading torchlight, "Now!"

His exploded inside her as he arched to push himself completely into her. He cried out as her thighs squeezed his hips. Her skin, made slippery by their exertion, was hot and satin smooth when he ran his hand along her body. "I need you," he rasped, "I need you to be part of me."

"I am part of you, Gilbert of Durham. I will always be a part of you." *As Khalil is part of me, as Joan is part of you,* she thought silently. She would not let herself cry; tears would be misunderstood no matter how they were taken.

Still joined together, they slept.

The drapes around the bed fluttered with a light breeze coming from the open shutters. From somewhere in the castle garden, a lark began to herald the coming morn. Whether it was the breeze or the lark, what awakened Durham was unimportant. He seized the moment to study the rise and fall of the lady's breast as she slept still nestled against him. Gilbert propped his head on his hand and looked down at Batsheva's face. He noticed the way a curl fell haphazardly onto her forehead and how her incongruously dark lashes spread like fans against her cheek. Her nose, he noted, was quite straight, not at all like the gently curved noses he usually found pretty on ladies. And if the truth be told, she was indeed not pretty by common standards. Although her hair was coppery, her brows were darker and arched upward like the wings of a bird in flight. She was still too thin; when he held her in his arms, he could feel her bones through her skin, although her color was better than he had ever seen it. *She's eating better,* he thought idly as he let his free hand rest on the swell of her backside.

She stirred but did not awaken and Durham felt himself arouse as that impertinent little rump snuggled against his groin. He groaned but pushed back the temptation to make love to her again. She needed to sleep, and he needed to watch her just a little longer. It wasn't her face or the feel of her skin against his which captured his attention; it was the whole being that was Batsheva. He whispered the name in the semidarkness of dawn.

It sounded strange against his tongue, yet it was as exotic as she was. From the moment she regained consciousness aboard the ship, he was intrigued. True, she was tougher than any woman he had known, and equally true, she had gained that strength through living a less-than-ideal life. He knew she had been taken from a caravan against her will and been given to the amir, but what had Khalil done to earn the undying devotion she kept for him? He winced when he recalled the sheer agony in her eyes when she removed the amir's sword from the cloth, and worse, her vacant stare as she held the scimitar in her hands with no more effort than had it been a fruit knife. He did not doubt for one minute that she was skilled in its use; there was something perfectly natural about the way she gripped the hilt. She said she was coming to him of her own will, but when she eventually opened her eyes, he could not predict what he would see in them. He prayed it was not hate; if he was lucky, there might be the tiniest trace of love. It was the most he could hope for as he moved his lips in silent prayer to the Blessed Virgin. She, he was certain, would understand the fear in his heart.

"Are you unwell, Gilbert?"

Her voice caught him unprepared, and he startled. "What?" He looked down and saw her grey eyes looking up at him.

"Are you unwell?"

His smile was almost shy. "Nay, I am quite well. Are you?"

She didn't answer. Instead, she turned over and matched his pose with her face close to his. "I shall live."

He was disappointed, then chided himself for feeling so. "I would do nothing to harm you, Bess."

"Not intentionally. I know that. Tell me what your messengers learned."

Durham sighed and fell back against the pillows. "I sent them back to Richard when we reached Westminster. I did not tell you because with what little information I had, I did not want to raise your hopes."

"What did you tell them?"

"I gave them a description of you, that you had twins, and told them to return to the place we found you. They did that and more. They learned the amir's woman had come from Akko with the children, and they went there to see if anyone was searching for you."

Batsheva felt her heart stop. She clutched the ring she still wore on a chain about her neck. "What did they find?"

"There was a great search for the children, but not for you. They could not learn the fate of the children, but an emissary of Saladin approached them through Richard. The king summoned Will and Rob and they repeated what they had been told. The emissary made no mention of a ransom for you, but when the children were mentioned, he indicated they were safe."

"Indicated?" cried Batsheva. "What does that mean?"

Durham shook his head. "He would provide no information other than to say the children were in no danger. But you already knew that from the old woman at York."

"What of Khalil? Did they ask about him?"

"He is dead, Bess. There were stories that he lived, but the emissary denied it. He said he no longer walked amongst his men."

Batsheva laughed, but it was harsh. "That could mean anything; he denied nothing."

"You have his cloak and sword. They were taken from his body by Guy de Lusignan himself. Richard demanded they be turned over to my men."

"Did your men tell you they had conversation with a Jew about me?"

He stared at her. "What are you talking about?"

"I overheard their conversation at Crompton Hall. One made mention that a Jew was looking for me and wanted me back *at all costs.* "

"They did not tell me that."

"I will tell you then, Gilbert. I do not know with whom they spoke, but I would wager whomever it was came from my brother."

"Your brother?"

Her grey eyes turned to ice chips as she told him about Yehuda. "It had to have come from him, because my uncle in Tiberias would have gone to the sultan himself. He knew Yehuda was not right; Uncle Avram warned me about him more than once." Batsheva stopped talking and stared off into the distance for a while, then she sat up, cross-legged on the bed. "Gilbert, if you are to understand me…if we are to make a life together…I think it is time you knew all that I know."

Durham bolted upright in the bed. "Are you willing to tell me?"

When she smiled, her eyes warmed as she reached out to touch his cheek with her hand. "If I was not willing to tell you, Gilbert, it was because you never truly asked. Your sister was right; you must be bolder when you want something." The smile widened just a little. "Sit here; I will return in a moment." She slipped from the bed. When she returned, she wore a light robe over her shoulders and carried her pouch. She climbed back onto the bed and faced him. She pulled out the locket and handed it to him.

"From whence did it come, Bess?"

She told him about the peddler. "I have no doubt the ring belonged to my dearest friend Devora. Nor do I have any doubt that she gave it to the peddler in believing it would find me. I sent it back to her with a message that I am safe. What I do not understand is this." She took the locket from him and opened it. "These are my children, Gilbert." She gazed at the miniatures before she handed it back to him.

The faces were beautiful. "The girl looks like you, but the boy must resemble Khalil."

She nodded. "Now, close the portraits."

He did as he was told and found the two locks of hair. "The children's?"

She nodded again. "But what confounds me is how the peddler came to carry this, if not from the Sultan himself. Surely, he has the children with him."

"There is no way to be certain. But at least now you know they are indeed safe." He reached for her hand. "Perhaps that is what you are meant to know."

"They look older," she said softly.

"Then the portraits were made after…." He could not say *after I took you away from them.*

Batsheva nodded as she took the locket from him. "It seems strange, Gilbert, that someone would take such great pains yet make no offer for me."

"Use your head, Bess; think about what you said. You think someone knows where you are, yet you are not certain who it is."

"True."

"And if your uncle knows your brother is dangerous, would it not stand to reason the sultan knows the same thing?"

"I would think so."

"Would Saladin's agent, a man privy to his master's thoughts, be so careless as to tell an enemy stranger the whereabouts of the children? *Your* children?" There was a flash of understanding in the grey eyes. "Taking all this into account, Bess, perhaps Saladin believes you to be safer where you are."

"But Yehuda knows I am in England! How else would the rug have reached me? Besides, David saw him in London."

Durham was confused. "David?"

"Rachel's husband."

Durham grimaced.

"You were kind to bring Rachel to me while I was ill. I do not know why you left on that night, but it was Rachel who brought me back to the land of the living when I thought I would rather not return. I went to see her after I met the peddler in the market and, while I was there, David came in." Tears welled up in her eyes. "I thought he was dead, Gil. I thought they were all dead in York, but he was not there; he was here. You could not have known…David is…," she suddenly laughed and swiped at her eyes. "This must all be so strange for you! The world from which I came is a close, tight world and we all know each other! Akiva, the man I was to marry, is David's cousin; Hannah was with David's family. They are Vital. We are Hagiz. Our families have been trading partners for generations. Oh, how strange this must all seem!" She wiped her eyes again.

It was strange to Gilbert, and he was having a difficult time following all the ins and outs of his lady's tale. Still, it seemed she understood what was happening. "What of your brother? Vital says he is in London. Will he come here?"

"I do not know. David could not tell him I was in Durham since he did not know until after he returned."

"You are safe here, Bess. He cannot hurt you as long as you remain here."

"Here in the castle…or here, in your bed?"

"Both." He leaned forward to brush a kiss against her lips. "I will not let harm come to you."

"You cannot keep me caged like a bird."

"I thought you learned your lesson in York."

"And I thought you learned yours, my lord. Assign guards to me if you must, Gilbert, but Yaffa must be exercised."

"*You* must be exercised," he laughed. "Use not your poor nag as an excuse."

"Poor nag, indeed, my lord. You are plainly jealous."

"Nay, nor would I be if you rode me as you ride her!"

Batsheva's laugh was light and music to his ears. "We are but new to each other, Gilbert," she admonished. "Let us learn to please each other."

"I am willingly your pupil, Bess." He kissed her again, this time letting his lips linger on hers.

CHAPTER 34

Durham

JUNE 1192

A strange noise invaded Durham's dream. He was standing on a hill watching a lone horseman ride toward him, but instead of steady hoofbeats, he heard the sound of a cow with its hooves stuck in the mud. Shading his eyes against the bright sunlight, he tried to see the animal, but even the horse had disappeared. The noise grew louder and with a groan Durham opened his eyes. A low rumble of a chuckle escaped his smiling lips.

Batsheva was sitting up in bed, Miriam busy at her breast. She looked over the top of the babe's head and saw two sleepy blue eyes watching her. "We did not mean to awaken you, Gilbert," she whispered.

He turned to get a better view. "'Tis the greatest sight to see, Bess." He reached over and poked a finger at Miriam's tightly balled fist and smiled from ear to ear when the little hand opened and closed over his finger. "See, she knows me."

"Of course, she knows you," laughed Batsheva.

Sensing something had changed, Miriam stopped sucking to stare at Durham. He immediately laid her on his bare chest. "She is so smooth and warm."

"She is a babe. All babes are smooth and warm."

"I fear I had little experience with Anne. When she was young, I was…" he frowned at the memory, "gone much of the time. I was not…."

Batsheva placed a finger over his lips. "You were doing what was required of you. Few men here dandle babes on their knees."

"Did Khalil?"

"As often as he could," she laughed softly. "The twins were born in Akko just before the war began. His command kept him away from us once the battles started. Like you, Gilbert, Earl of Durham, Sheikh Khalil bin Mahmud did what was required of him."

Durham was stroking Miriam's back when she suddenly let loose a loud burp. He laughed, shaking the child, then laughed harder when she picked up her head to stare at him, looking all the world as if she had been deeply offended. "I apologize, Lady Miriam," he said gravely. And as if she understood, her head dropped back onto the broad expanse of his chest.

"I hope, my lord, you have nothing better to do today, for if she decides to sleep upon your chest, you'll not be able to move for several hours."

"Nay, I cannot think of anything I would rather do, my lady, except perhaps…."

With an indelicate snort, Batsheva rolled away from him and off the bed. "Then I shall leave you both and go about my business. Should you need one, there is a dry nappy on the table, my lord." Grabbing her robe, she hurried from the chamber.

The Archbishop of Durham was sitting with Anne at a trestle in the deserted great hall. As soon as Batsheva entered, Anne waved to her. "Oh, Bess," cried the child, "Uncle Charles has found me a tutor, just as you asked. He's coming tomorrow for my first lesson."

Batsheva eyed the churchman suspiciously. "Thank you, your grace. This is most kind."

"Not at all, Lady Elizabeth; not at all. I must confess, I found a great deal of wisdom in your request. Annie is most anxious to get on her with learning and pestered me until I found a scholar suitable for the position. I think you shall find him most competent."

"I am certain your judgment is sound, your grace."

"Good. I'm glad we are in agreement." The archbishop glanced around. "Tell me, Lady Elizabeth, did Gilbert ride off early this morning? I've not seen him."

Two pink spots rose on her cheeks. "I'm afraid, your grace, his lordship is still abed. Shall I have someone awaken him?"

"Heaven forbid!" roared the archbishop; "let him sleep. He's been on the road for weeks and surely deserves a day of rest. Nay, tell him I would speak with him at supper this evening." He rose from the bench he shared with Anne. "Be a good girl, sweet Annie, and find your grandmother. Tell her I will see her later."

The girl rose and curtsied, first to the archbishop and then to Batsheva. She was almost to the door when she turned, "Can we go to the market today, Bess?"

"We shall see, Annie. Lamb." Batsheva noted the little pout before the girl disappeared. She turned her attention back to the archbishop. "With your permission, your grace, I shall be off to see to the menus for today."

"Actually, Lady Elizabeth, I would have a word with you in private."

"I'm not certain that would be proper, your grace; I am no longer an invalid."

"I assure you, private conversation with a priest is highly proper. Come, let us use the earl's solar." Without waiting for a response, he led the way.

She was surprised when he did not take the chair behind Durham's large desk and indicated they should sit beside the hearth. She took a seat, her hands folded in her lap.

"There is a matter Lady Matilda wishes me to discuss with you," began the archbishop. "A rather delicate matter. Now that Gilbert has returned, we feel something must be said." When she remained silent, he cleared his throat and continued. "There is the issue of your marriage to the earl, my lady. Certain questions have arisen which have not been adequately answered."

"Are you asking if we have wed in church?" she asked calmly.

"Yes."

"The answer is no."

"But the child...."

"There is no bastardry here, your grace; the child had a loving father."

"Yet Gilbert acknowledges the babe as his own."

"That is his choice. I never asked him to do so. And frankly, your grace, since the child is female, the question of inheritance is a moot point."

The archbishop was surprised by her candor. "Then, you are not wed at all."

"I did not say I was. You did, as I recall."

He regarded her in silence for a long moment. "Do you play shatranj, my lady?" He saw her nod. "I think you must be a skilled tactician."

"I am."

His sudden laughter caught her off guard. "I do not think I would play against you, Lady Elizabeth! I fear I would have no chance to win."

"Do you play only if you are assured of victory, your grace?" she asked with the smallest hint of a smile.

"It depends on the game. I prefer to avoid unnecessary risks."

"And I take risks when presented with a good challenge. What risk would you have me take, Archbishop?"

The archbishop leaned as close to the woman as he dared. "I would have you take the greatest risk of all, Elizabeth. I would ask for your trust."

"My trust? I am afraid I do not understand."

"Exactly. You see, Elizabeth, there is nothing I want more than to see this family continue. I do not want to see some second-rate husband snatch Anne from Durham only to return to wrest control of this earldom upon Gilbert's death. I am far too fond of my family to see our name disappear because my nephew has not fathered a son."

"And you believe he can get that son on me?"

"Yes."

"I see. You put me in an awkward position, your grace."

"I am certain I do, but I'm willing to strike a bargain with you."

Batsheva chewed her lip thoughtfully, unsure of what he considered to be a bargain. Still, after the events of the last night, she found herself to be curious. "Go on, your grace; I shall listen to your proposal."

"I propose, as you put it, that you and Gilbert be married in my private chapel with the witnesses of your choice. The ceremony will be brief, yet official. That done, you will unquestionably be Countess Durham."

"Why are you doing this?" she asked.

"Because, Elizabeth, you are in grave danger. You have an enemy in Westminster, one who would see you unseated. Need I mention her name?"

Batsheva refused the bait; instead, she met his eyes boldly. "And what possible harm can Isabella do? Even Queen Eleanor dismisses her gossip as simply that, gossip."

"The queen is a wise woman, but she cannot control everything around her. Her hands are too full with problems left behind by her crusading son. She relies heavily on our learned brethren to attend to certain matters."

"Oh," sighed Batsheva with obvious annoyance, " do get to the point, your grace. What has Isabella done now?"

He liked this arrogant, feisty woman who had no taste for prevarication. "Isabella has applied to my brother in Christ, the Archdeacon of Canterbury, to appoint an examiner for an investigation into your marriage."

"They will find nothing."

"Precisely my point. You told Eleanor you followed a different rite in our church, but Isabella believes you follow no rite at all. She told Canterbury she suspects you of witchcraft.

"Do you believe her?"

"Should I?" The flash of anger in the lady's eyes was brief. The archbishop chuckled softly as he said, "Nay, lady, I do not believe her. Still, 'tis a dangerous allegation under any circumstance."

"What do *you* want, your grace?"

"As I told you, nothing more than for you to wed Gil. Properly. But I sense there is an impediment to that marriage you are reluctant to discuss with me. So, my lady, I shall discuss it with you."

Batsheva leaned back in her chair and regarded him carefully. There was something so comforting about him, something so reassuring that she did indeed want to trust him. Still, he was a servant of a church that would sooner see her people burn in hell than to let them live as they wanted. He was asking her to lower her natural defenses and she was not certain she wanted to do that quite yet. Khalil, his image flashed in her memory, once told her always do more than listen to the enemy, watch them. They reveal more in the manner in which they move than in the words themselves. *Had not that been the case in Akko, when the two men came for Devora?* Batsheva steeled herself inwardly while keeping her outward appearance calm. "Go on, your grace."

"Good. Hear me out. I think you are no daughter of Christ. You may be from Al-Andalus, and you may have traveled with crusaders to the Holy Land, but you are not one of us. Nor I do not think, although some do, that you are Saracen. Nay, I think you are of an ancient and honorable people, the people of our Lord, Jesus Christ." Her face remained an immutable mask. "The truth of how you came to be with Gil is unknown to me, but I hope one day you will tell me the story. That, however, is unimportant at this moment. I would ask your forgiveness if, in my desire to see you recover, I offended you with my prayers; I hope you know no harm was meant. Therefore, I will repeat my offer: marry Gil in the privacy of my chapel and I will pledge to keep your secret."

"At what price?"

"That the children from this union be raised in the bosom of the Holy Mother Church."

*From this union…*it would not necessarily include Miriam. "You ask a great deal, my lord Archbishop. If I refuse?"

"Then I will be unable to protect you when the time comes…and it will, Elizabeth. It will."

"Will you answer a question honestly for me, your grace?"

"I fear you would ferret out any deceit before the words left my lips, my lady."

"Why would you do this for me when your people ride the world forcing us to abandon our ways? Surely, there is something else you want."

"I told you. I want peace in this household. If you do not agree to this, Matilda will be on me to pressure you until such time as Canterbury declares you either witch or heretic. You will not be permitted to just ride away, Elizabeth. They will try you, convict you, and your life and the life of your daughter will be forfeit. Let me help you, and by helping you, help Gil. He loves you; that much is clear, and I believe you care for him. Do you care enough to protect not only Gil but your innocent daughter as well?"

Batsheva was at a loss of words. He had maneuvered her to the place where he wanted her, and while she saw a great deal of wisdom in his words, she also saw an enormous risk. She had refused to marry Khalil, but in Islam, that was not such a great issue. Thus far, she had managed not to wed Durham, but this was not Islam, and it was becoming a bigger problem than she had anticipated. She was in a corner and the archbishop was offering her a way out. "When do you require an answer?" she asked, her voice barely above a whisper.

"As soon as you have one." His voice was warm when he said, "To be frank, Elizabeth, I like you. You are fresh air in this place, and I would be unhappy to see it made stale again. Think hard on this and send word when we can talk again. No one will think it strange if you visit me in the cathedral."

"I shall consider your offer carefully, your grace." She rose from her chair and walked to the door. Then she turned. "Thank you, my lord archbishop, for your candor. I appreciate your honesty."

He watched her as she left the little solar. *I hope you have the good sense to listen,* he thought as he pushed himself from the chair. There was little more he could do if she refused his offer. It was only a matter of time before Canterbury sent an emissary to investigate Isabella's allegations.

Batsheva found Gwyneth in a corner of the great hall, the cook, red faced and upset, beside her. The housekeeper curtsied and the cook bowed as soon as Batsheva approached. "My lady," they started in unison; until Batsheva held up her hands to make them stop the stream of rapid-fire English. When they stopped talking long enough to breathe, Batsheva took advantage of the break to inquire as to the problem.

Gwyneth shot the portly chef a hard glance before she said, "My lady, Lady Matilda has ordered a menu for this evening which *he* says is in contradiction to the menu you have requested."

"Her ladyship wants suckling pig and baked swan," countered the cook, "while you have already requested a side of beef and capons. I have already ordered the slaughter and the pit is ready to take a side of beef."

"Can you not accommodate both, master chef?"

"Not easily, my lady. There is only so much time and space in which to work. We are not prepared for so extensive a menu on such short notice."

"But surely you can find room for a small pig?"

"Not if we are to keep the fat from coming together as you have requested." The chef gave her a sympathetic smile. "When my wife bore our children, she, too, had a delicate constitution and could not eat some things without…," he patted his ample stomach, "troubles."

"You are most kind to consider my health, master chef, but I must defer to Lady Matilda. If it is pig she desires, then pig will be served. As for swan…." She looked to Gwyneth, "Do you think the lady would object to capon?"

"I…I…I…cannot say," stuttered the cook. "I've never gone against her."

Batsheva turned to the housekeeper. "Mistress Gwyneth?"

She frowned but nodded. "I shall delicately inquire, my lady."

"Good, then this is a crisis averted. If the lady feels swan must be served, then we shall manage somehow to serve swan. If she agrees to capon, then that is what will appear at table."

The cook bowed before he barreled back to his domain. Gwyneth curtsied and started toward the stairs. Batsheva remained in the hall, thinking about what to do next.

"A veritable Solomon," called Durham from the archway.

Batsheva spun around to see the earl, a grin stretched across his face, Miriam propped up against his shoulder. The infant seemed perfectly content to view the world from this new height.

"Hardly worthy of Solomon, my lord. 'Twas simply a cookhouse dilemma," she laughed. When her mother reached out to relieve Durham of his burden, Miriam tightened her grip around his neck.

"I fear you've been replaced, my lady," chuckled Durham as he nuzzled the babe's cheek.

"For the moment," Batsheva countered with a grin to match his. "Wait until her belly rumbles and then see how quickly she calls for her mama."

Durham extended his free hand to Batsheva. "Come, Bess, let's enjoy the morning. I would show you the gardens."

From her window, Lady Matilda watched her son and his lady strolling amongst the early summer flowers. She noticed how Lady Elizabeth kept her arm tucked securely in Gilbert's and she was convinced whatever rift was between them had been traversed. Despite her misgivings about this foreign lady, the dowager countess suspected the woman was a good match for her son. If Charles could convince them to be wed, she would be much relieved. It was the mixture of emotions that bothered Matilda most; she wanted nothing but Gilbert's happiness in marriage for that was what she had shared with his father.

CHAPTER 35

Canterbury-Windsor-York

JUNE 1192

The august Archdeacon of Canterbury, Herbert Poore, carefully observed every motion, every expression, every hesitation in the posture of his lovely visitor. This was not their first conversation on the matter of Durham's purported marriage; it was their third. It wasn't that he disliked Isabella; he was wary of her words.

"Is it possible, my daughter," the archdeacon asked Isabella, "that she does indeed follow another Christian rite? As you well know, the distance ruled by the Holy See is vast and not all congregations behave identically."

"No, Archdeacon, she follows no rite known to anyone. She is clearly un-shriven and refused communion at Easter mass."

He pressed his palms together. Some women preferred to make their confessions in private and if the lady was unfamiliar with the priests of Westminster, she might have been shy about sending for one. There was still the matter of rumors about the lady; everything from her being a witch to being a Saracen, although Archdeacon Poore could not decide which would be worse. "What would you have me do?"

He waited until the door closed behind her before summoning his secretary. "Did you hear?"

"Yes, Archdeacon."

"And?"

The cleric shrugged his shoulders. "I do not know what to think. The Lady Elizabeth's deportment is impeccable, and she has done nothing to earn anything but honest admiration from those who have encountered her. You, yourself, commented how lovely she was."

"True, true," mused the archdeacon. "I think, Father Thomas, there is more behind the request than simple sisterly concern for Durham." He saw the young priest stifle a laugh. "Go on, laugh if you must. I would, too, if I were not so concerned for the damage that blonde baggage can do if left to her own devices. If she gets no satisfaction from me, she will try Rouen. Or worse, Geoffrey at York."

"Shall we send an inquisitor, your grace?"

"I suppose we shall have to send someone to Durham…if the queen consents." He smiled at the young priest. "Thomas, would you like leave to visit your mother in Guisborough?"

With almost indecent haste, Isabella rode to Windsor. She bypassed her usual social stops in an attempt to reach Eleanor before she left for her summer progress. She wanted the queen in Durham when Lady Elizabeth met her downfall. Isabella was certain Gilbert would turn to her for consolation; should the queen be in residence, her place as Countess Durham would be assured.

Eleanor was informed the moment Isabella arrived and summoned her immediately. "God's boots, Isabella, have you joined a convent?" cried Eleanor. "Has someone died?"

Sweeping into a deep curtsy, Isabella shook her head. "Your Majesty, I did not take time with dressing, my desire to speak with you so great."

"Oh, do sit down, Isabella. I have precious little time for your domestic intrigues. Tell me, where have you been?"

Isabella was certain the queen already knew. Still, the question demanded an answer and Isabella provided it with appropriate murmurs of concern. "You cannot imagine how dearly I care for them," she sighed.

"I am sure I can, Isabella," replied the queen dryly. "We simply hope you understand in full measure exactly what you have done. We would not be pleased to have a minor crisis on our hands if Durham bridles at your interference in his private life."

"But *you* understand, Your Majesty. Surely you can understand how my heart aches for them all! I pray to the Holy Mother that my fears are groundless. I do not want to see him hurt."

"You want to see him in your bed, I'll warrant," Eleanor chortled. "Isabella, you are a troublesome wench. It would be better for all if you would pick some available swain and declare a match. You've already rejected a dozen, including Sir Roderick, and we are running low on applicants. Have you given any consideration of the offer from the Comte de Beaulieu?"

Isabella shuddered. "I would not leave England, Your Majesty."

"'Tis a pity; he's quite wealthy."

"And quite plump. I fear I would be crushed."

"Isabella!"

She flashed a coquettish smile. "I cannot help myself, ma'am. I have loved the best and will not settle for less."

Eleanor changed the subject. "Will you accompany us to Leicestershire? We are planning to visit Castle Belvoir and we know how you love it there."

"I had planned to return to Lincoln."

"We plan to travel as far north as York." Eleanor waited for the next salvo.

"Not Durham, Your Majesty?"

"No."

"Perhaps you might reconsider. A visit to Durham is long overdue and it would help solidify the king's position in the northern districts."

"Since when are you so interested in our politics, Isabella? Or is it that you would have us provide you with an excuse to visit Gilbert?"

Isabella's face flushed red. "I meant only that the crown has not toured the counties above York in some time."

"Your concern is noted, my dear. We shall consider the possibility. In the meanwhile, we think you should reconsider Beaulieu's offer. It is well within our power to marry you to whomever we see fit."

"Yes, Your Majesty."

"I'm glad we understand each other, Isabella."

The interview was over. Isabella rose and curtsied. "Thank you, Your Majesty," she murmured.

Eleanor sat quietly alone for a moment before she called for her secretary. "Edward, we wish to send a letter to Canterbury. And we are relying on your oath of loyalty to our person to keep this to yourself. Do you understand?"

Edward of York took his place at the table opposite his queen and prepared to write. When the letter was finished, he wished to God he had sworn no oath.

Henry, Earl of York paced the battlements with a scowl firmly implanted on his otherwise pleasant face. His wife watched his repetitious movements in silence; there was little she could say which would soothe his turmoil. It was bad enough the queen was coming to York; that she was going on to Durham was simply too upsetting to consider. The plans made to travel north were now in an uproar. "I cannot wait, Henry. I will go to Durham tomorrow and return in a fortnight, in time for Eleanor's arrival. What choice do I have?"

"You are not going to Durham!" Henry thundered at Margaret. Although he rarely shouted at anyone, his patience was sorely tried. "You will remain here until the queen leaves. You cannot go running to your mother with Eleanor a fortnight away."

"My mother is not the issue, Henry. Elizabeth cannot possibly understand what is about to happen. If Isabella holds true to fashion, she will closet herself with the archbishop. I am not about to sit idly by and let that bitch in heat go after Gil and Bess."

"Why can't you trust Archdeacon Poore to keep her at bay? He has promised to look into the matter of their marriage and he's a level-headed sort. He's not about to burn anyone on Isabella's word. Besides, Maggie, if there were any real danger, would not Edward have written?"

"Edward may not realize the depths of her depravity, Henry. He's a boy."

"He's a man in service to the queen. Edward is neither blind, nor is he stupid, madam. If he thought his hero uncle in danger, he would move heaven and earth to help him."

"He may not be aware." She looked over the wall toward where Father Thomas's black figure made a dark splotch in the middle of her colorful garden. "What exactly did Canterbury write?"

"He said Isabella had been to see him again and was pressing for an inquisitor to be sent to Durham. Young Father Thomas was to serve in that capacity and anything we could do to help him would be appreciated. Archdeacon Poore knows us both, Maggie. He knew, when he wrote the letter, we would send word to Gil. The man is cunning; he obviously wants to keep this from becoming a scandal. Let us follow his lead and send Father Thomas on with a letter to your Uncle Charles. He can handle everything without your presence."

Margaret chewed her lip in thought for a moment. "All right. Send a letter to my uncle. I hope you know what you are doing."

Henry smiled and brushed a kiss on his wife's flushed cheek. "There now, that's better, Maggie. Let the Church handle its own."

CHAPTER 36

Durham

JUNE 1192

Durham sat in the archbishop's office listening to his uncle's sonorous voice outline the details of his agreement with the lady. The decision had been made, but Batsheva left the explanations to the churchman. Durham's jaw dropped when Charles explained Elizabeth had agreed to the marriage.

"You must understand, Gil, she is justifiably nervous. In her mind, marrying you in church goes against everything she holds holy."

"She told you this?" he asked, amazed.

"She's told me very little. 'Twas the appearance of Rachel Vital at her bedside which convinced me she, too, is a Jewess. Under normal circumstances, I would not perform this marriage without the baptism of the lady. But these are extraordinary times, and I would see you married to her." A wry twist of his lips threatened his somber appearance. "Gil, you must marry her soon lest I try to woo her away!"

Durham's laughter exploded across the room. "You are a reprobate, Uncle!"

"I am a man despite these purple trappings, my son. And she is a delectable morsel. Your Elizabeth needs no witchcraft to bewitch; she does it with a flash of those mourning dove eyes. A man could get lost in them… just as you have done. Shall I tell you how enamored I am of her wit and wisdom?"

"'Tis true, Uncle. From the moment she opened them aboard ship, I was lost. She is stubborn, arrogant, difficult, and unbending, but…," his voice trailed softly off.

"No need to enumerate the lady's attributes, Gil. Just keep her happy and full of babes."

Babes. The word brought Durham's chin up sharply. "Will she allow you to baptize Miriam?"

He shook his head. "She has forbidden it. I think the lady has it in her mind to return the child to her father's people at the proper time." He saw the shock in Durham's eyes. "She did not say as much, but you might gently broach the subject with her. Do it delicately, Gil; she is unsettled on what is right for little Miriam. If she changes her mind, the babe can be christened as quietly as you will be married."

In an uncharacteristic gesture, Durham knelt and kissed the archbishop's ring. "Thank you, Uncle, for interceding."

"Nonsense, Gil," he said, waving his hand. Then he made the sign of the cross and blessed his nephew. "Go with God, my son, but say nothing to your mother. I will handle my sister-in-law."

He found Batsheva in the stable with Yaffa. She was so small compared to the horse, yet he knew well she was made of the hardest Toledo steel. For a moment, Durham kept his distance so he could watch her as she spoke to the mare; he could almost imagine the soft, strange sound of the language. Suddenly, Batsheva glanced up and saw his silhouette framed in the doorway. She smiled and his heart thumped against his chest. "Let us take a ride, Bess."

Her smile widened. "I was hoping you would come. Yaffa needs the exercise."

The three men-at-arms who rode out with them kept a respectable distance. For a moment, Batsheva could almost imagine they were alone, but she knew better. Since the earl chose to ride without benefit of mail, she was glad to know they had some protection. Even his position as earl did not mean he was immortal.

They rode heading north; Durham wanted her to see a little more of his lands. Along the way, they were greeted exuberantly by workers in the fields; at each village, they were entreated to take a bit of ale or cider. Batsheva was most impressed at the sheer number of names Durham could remember; try as she might, she could not memorize all the people to whom she was introduced.

"I will make a terrible countess," groaned Batsheva as they started back. "How will I ever know who comes from which village?"

"You will learn," Durham laughed. "And they know you cannot remember everyone on sight. I've a lifetime with them!"

"A proper lady knows her people, though I must confess, in Islam, I was required only to remember the women. My contact with men other than my lord was quite…limited."

"Then take your lessons from Queen Eleanor. She is as bold as any man and certainly as cunning. There is not a man alive in England who could fence words with her and win."

"No woman either, I should think. She has a way of cutting through the fat straight to the bone of a matter."

"Aye, that she does. And she likes you, Bess, for the same reason. She found you guileless and direct; she admitted that was a refreshing quality." Durham took a deep breath. "There is rumor that she will visit Durham soon."

Batsheva jerked Yaffa to a sudden halt. "The queen is coming here?"

"Possibly. It was not on her progress itinerary, but…" he replied, trotting back to her.

"When were you planning to tell me, my lord," she snapped. "On the night before her arrival?"

"The consideration arrived this morning."

"She travels with a retinue?"

"Aye."

"How on earth shall we house them all? And feed them? Can we feed that many people for so long? We shall need another cookhouse to handle just the servants! And entertainment? How shall I find singers and dancers and acrobats? Musicians! Are there musicians in Durham who can…."

"Stop!" cried Durham. "You run ahead of yourself, Bess. We've hosted the royal progress before and we can do it again with ease. My mother shall help you learn what you need to know."

Batsheva slumped in her saddle. "Your mother will give me precious little help. She shall feign recurrent illness and leave me to humiliate myself."

He could not help but laugh and instantly regretted it when he saw the look of anguish in her grey eyes. "My mother will come 'round, Bess. She won't allow Eleanor to find anything less than perfection at our home."

"I hope…." The words died in her mouth as she spotted a rider coming toward them at breakneck speed. "Look, Gil!" She pointed down the road.

Durham wheeled his horse around to follow her finger and saw the same thing. He spurred his horse to meet the rider, Batsheva and his men-at-arms close behind.

As the rider closed the distance, they all realized it was a woman in the saddle. Durham recognized her immediately. "Catherine! What is wrong?"

She gasped to catch her breath. "My lord, the dark knight returned. He's torched Crichton Woods. My grandfather is dead."

"When?" demanded Durham.

"This morning. I escaped only because I was out tending to a crofter."

"You are certain it was the same knight Thomas described?"

"Aye, my lord. I saw him for a brief moment on the road. His shield is blank. Is that not the same one?"

Durham nodded. "In what direction does he ride?"

"To the east, my lord."

They flew back to Durham as fast as the horses could manage. Once there, Durham donned his mail as his men assembled in the courtyard. In a matter of minutes, a small army moved quickly across the bridge. The two women watched them go and when they were no longer visible, Batsheva put her arm about Catherine's shoulder and led her into the castle.

A room was hastily prepared for Catherine in the west tower. Batsheva accompanied her to the chamber, then left her to rest while she went in search of clean clothing for Catherine. "We can send for your things later," she told her.

"There is nothing to send for, my lady. Everything was in the hall."

"Then we shall visit my friend Jane. She is a seamstress, and she can begin sewing for you."

Catherine curtsied deeply to Batsheva. "Thank you, my lady."

"Do not thank me, Catherine; one must always do what is necessary to survive. You have done that today and we must all help to set things to right."

"Things will never be right, my lady. Never." She began to cry.

"They will be put right again. Perhaps different, but you are alive and you have a responsibility to your grandfather to continue living so his name is not forgotten. These are the things one does. You will do them with honor. You will strive, you will accomplish, and you will be stronger for it. His memory will be your blessing."

In her own chamber, Batsheva felt suddenly very old. Her own heart ached for the woman; she wished she had a magic potion to fix the hurt. There was no magic potion, but she had the experience to tell Catherine honestly that she could and would survive.

Lady Matilda's arrival cut short her deliberation. The old woman tapped her way into the chamber with little more than a sharp rap at the door. Without waiting for an invitation to enter, she brushed past Batsheva and parked herself in the chair beside the fireplace. "Sit down, Elizabeth," she commanded.

Batsheva shook her head in disbelief but did as she was told.

"My brother-in-law tells me you and Gil are to be wed in his private chapel. He also tells me there will be no celebration. Is that correct?"

"*Oui, Madame,* " replied Batsheva.

"Speak English, child. You must force yourself to converse in English at all times…unless, of course, you are addressing Eleanor. Then you should speak French, for she prefers it. Otherwise, it is pompous."

"Yes, my lady."

"That's better. As for the lack of celebration, that is just as well. Let everyone else believe you were married before you arrived here. However, Eleanor will wish to give the crown's stamp of approval. Expect to be installed officially as countess by the Queen…if she comes." She waved her cane at Batsheva. "Do not think for one moment I am loath to relinquish the position! I am not. I am far too old to be playing hostess in this castle. I have no taste for it. While my husband was alive…that was a separate matter. As for hosting the queen and her entourage, I will remain here long enough to do that should she decide to favor us with a visit. Come the autumn, I shall retire to York where I intend to remain until they return me enshrouded in a coffin."

Batsheva stared at her.

The old woman chuckled at the astounded look on the lady's face. "You did not think to be rid of me so soon, did you, Elizabeth?"

"I did not think to be rid of you at all, my lady! I am certain my lord will object."

"Gilbert has been objecting to me most of his life. He can object to this, too, for all I care. I am going to York."

"Does Margaret know?"

"I will not live with Margaret. I will take up residence at Conisburgh Castle with my sister."

"What will Margaret say? Will she not feel deserted?"

"Deserted? Why on earth would she think that? If anything, she will be relieved. I did not want my mother hanging about when I had a household of my own."

"But, my lady, what of your grandchildren?"

"They can come to see me when they feel the need. Not that they will, mind you."

"I think you underestimate your own importance, my lady," stated Batsheva. "If you were my mother, I should want to have you near. I would worry about you."

"I am not your mother, Elizabeth, nor do I have any wish to serve in that capacity. I simply wish to see Eleanor leave this place in a happy mood and then get on with my own affairs." When Batsheva remained in stunned silence, she continued. "Now, as to the matter of Catherine. Did Gilbert tell you she is to be his ward?"

"He mentioned it briefly. What does that mean?"

"It means he is to find her a suitable husband. She's a bit long in the tooth, and now, with the manor gone, she is certainly less desirable, but she retains the lands until she either marries or dies. It would be preferable to marry her off. While the court is here, you will need to keep a sharp eye on her and those who would woo her for the sake of her lands. We cannot have Thomas's granddaughter allied with some oaf who will be of no service to us. Gilbert will make the decision, but you must use your intuition to manage his choice. Do you understand?"

"Yes, my lady."

"Good. Now, let us discuss hosting the Queen and her entourage."

She felt as though she should have written everything down for when Lady Matilda was at last finished, Batsheva's head was swimming with details. The dowager countess assured her the staff could handle the preparations with little supervision save the daily tour. As for the extra cookhouse, there was one behind the main kitchen. If Eleanor's retinue numbered over two hundred as it usually did, the soldiers would make camp outside the walls while the nobility would expect housing inside the castle itself.

She and Gilbert would remain in her chamber, but the queen would take the earl's. The girls would stay in the nursery along with any other young children who arrived for the festivities. High-ranking ladies would take over the large chambers in the west wing while the gentlemen would be housed wherever there was room. Some would use the battle tents. Lady Matilda promised it would be cramped, but they would manage.

Summoning Gwyneth and Mary to her chamber, Batsheva outlined what needed to be done. Gwyneth's eyes grew bright with excitement while Mary looked as though she was about to faint. "Do not worry about a thing, my lady," announced Gwyneth at the end of the interview; "it sounds worse than it is."

Batsheva continued to hope the queen would decide not to come after all.

Durham had not returned to the castle by the time Batsheva found she could no longer keep her eyes open. Mary helped her into her night-rail and Lydia brought Miriam to nurse before the exhausted lady crawled gratefully into bed. She slept fitfully but no dreams argued against her slumber.

In the morning, Batsheva met Mary and Gwyneth in the great hall. Together, they divided the work of the day before each set off on individual projects. First on Batsheva's list of things to accomplish was to see to Catherine's wardrobe, but before she could find the lady, a messenger arrived from what was left of Crichton Wood. Arrangements were being made for Sir Thomas' funeral and the news had to be delivered to his granddaughter.

Batsheva found Catherine on her knees in the chapel. "Your grandfather has been taken to the Church of St. Brandon," she told her gently. "The priest has sent word a mass will be said as soon as you are ready."

"I shall never be ready, my lady," murmured Catherine, fighting back tears.

"The mass can wait a day or two, Catherine. Right now, I would take you to my friend Jane. There are things that need doing and only you can do them. I understand your sadness and your pain, but you are alive and must continue to walk in the land of the living." She smiled softly. "And you cannot walk anywhere without any clothing."

"I suppose you are right." She made the sign of the cross and rose from the prie-dieu.

"Oh, you poor, poor dear!" cried Jane when she heard the story. "Now, do not worry about a thing, my lady, I'll get started right away." She hurried into the back of her little house and emerged a moment later with a bolt of black wool. "It shall have to be a simple tunic gown, Bess, if it's to be ready so quickly. I shall measure for cotes now, but they can be sewn at the castle." Jane whipped a length of yarn from her pocket.

If Catherine was amazed at the way the two women worked in perfect harmony, she said nothing. Instead, she moved when she was told to move and stood still when told to do that. The measuring didn't take long; Jane's skillful fingers soon had the wool rough cut and draped enough to pin. "There," she announced with a satisfied grunt as she struggled up from her knees. "I'll send a simple cote late tomorrow. In the meanwhile, you can take this with you." She pulled two folded bundles from a shelf near her worktable. "I made these some time ago, but I never had use for them. With a quick nip and a tuck, they should help get you through the week. Now, go in there and put on the dark blue."

When she was gone, Batsheva whispered, "Durham will pay for the wardrobe, Jane. Catherine is without means at present."

"I was not concerned," she sniffed.

Batsheva hugged Jane and whispered, "If you are not concerned about your outlay, Mistress FitzHugh, I shall be the first to tell Jamie you are careless with his coin." She pecked Jane's cheek.

They stopped at the market square on their way back to the castle. As much as she hated being followed by her personal guard, Batsheva found them useful for carrying her parcels. The men seemed to be used to the procedure and accepted their burdens with nothing more than a polite nod and a tolerant smile.

Catherine found herself being drawn into the shopping expedition. Batsheva asked her dozens of questions about local craftsmen and listened carefully to the answers. They stopped at the cobbler long enough to order slippers and then at the silversmith to purchase combs and simple brooches to replace the ones lost in the fire.

"I have not enough coin for something so grand," whispered Catherine when Batsheva picked a heavy silver chatelaine. "I can purchase only the necessities."

"You are Durham's ward, Catherine," countered the lady; "your bills are paid by the earl."

She shook her head. "Still, my lady, I cannot be extravagant."

"This is not extravagant, Catherine. You cannot appear as a pauper at the mass. Your grandfather's crofters must believe you are well dowered despite the fire. They must see you properly attired so they feel *they* are safe. If you appear any less, they will fear for themselves and Durham would not be pleased."

"I understand."

"Good." Batsheva turned to the craftsman who waited patiently to the side. "Master Smith, we shall have this chain along with the other trifles. Present the bill at the castle for payment," instructed Batsheva. She waited while the craftsman wrapped their purchases. "There, now. Was that not easy?" she asked Catherine.

CHAPTER 37

Durham

JUNE 1192

There was no trace of the dark knight nor his men. When they reached the outskirts of Hartlepool, Durham concluded the trail was cold. No one had seen strange men in the area and although they all heard the tale of the dark knight, not a villager could recall seeing one. Disheartened, Durham and his troops turned back along a different route, but the result was the same.

They went directly to Crichton Wood to view the remains of the hall. Sir Thomas's men worked within the burned-out shell of the house, rakes in hand, looking for anything of value to salvage. When the earl arrived, they ceased their labors and stood quietly as the lord examined the ruins.

"What of our Kate?" asked one sad-looking face blackened by soot and ashes. "She rode to Durham."

"Aye," confirmed the earl, "she is safe within the walls of the castle. She'll be well cared for there."

Another man came forward. "What of us, yer lordship? Sir Thomas was a good laird to us."

"And I'll not send ye someone less fit. Ye've got my solemn oath on that." His words had their desired effect; the men seemed to breathe easier. "When Catherine marries, her husband will be the new master. I'll not marry her to someone who will not care for ye all."

As soon as the earl was spied from the battlements, Batsheva ordered a bath prepared in his chamber. She hurried to exchange her own tunic for a fresh one and went to wait on the steps.

The sight of her made Durham smile in spite of the bone-aching weariness he felt. He was tired and dirty, but he could not wait to kiss away the concern clearly etched around her mouth. He dismounted quickly and crossed the courtyard to her open arms.

"Did you find him?" she asked, still a little breathless from the intensity of his kiss.

"Nay. There was no sign of him. 'Tis as though he's a spectre in the mists."

Catherine came down the stairs and curtsied low to the earl. "Thank you, my lord, for everything you've done," she murmured softly.

"I have not done enough, my lady. Your grandfather's murderer still roams the countryside." He motioned to the women to follow him into the castle and led them to his solar. "The mass will be tomorrow at noon, Catherine, with your approval. We shall ride to church in the morning. Your grandfather's crofters found his sword and shield; the monks sit vigil."

She could not answer; she wept silently but managed to nod.

Batsheva put her hand on Catherine's arm. "You will stay with us, sweet Catherine. There is nothing you can do for your grandfather now."

She nodded again, then rose, curtsied, and fled the room.

"How is she, Bess?" asked Durham when she was gone.

"Hard put, but she will improve with time. I took her to Jane yesterday and a wardrobe is underway." She told him about their foray into the market. "All bills are to be sent here."

"Of course," replied Durham. "I am responsible for her now, and I expect you to see to whatever she needs."

Batsheva smiled warmly at him when she agreed. "As if she were your own, Gilbert. I know you will do the right thing for her." She took his hand in his to pull him toward the door. "Your bath grows cold, my lord."

"Bath?" His eyes brightened a little. "'Tis a good idea, my sweet. I stink like the horses."

"Aye, that you do."

"Will you wash my back?" he asked with a smirk.

"If you so order, my lord." She sighed when he pulled her close for another kiss. The heat of his lips burned right through her, but she pushed him off. "You do stink, my lord earl."

Durham sat in the steaming tub and listened to Batsheva as she listed the things needed to be done at the castle before the arrival of the queen.

With eyes closed and head resting on a folded towel, he tried to concentrate on her words rather than on the melodious sound of her voice. It was difficult; he found her accented English a delight to his ear. She still sought words, mispronounced a few, but in general, her English was vastly better than most of society. He thought about the way she whispered in his ear, and it tickled him. Durham smiled lazily as he anticipated the coming night.

"Gil?" There was no response. "Gil?" repeated Batsheva.

He opened one eye. "Hmmmmmm?"

"Are you listening to me?" She was standing at the foot of the tub with a ewer balanced against her hip.

For a moment, he could envision her standing at the well near the Bedouin encampment. "Yes, my love. I am listening."

"What do you think, Gil?"

"Whatever you want is fine."

A smirk inched its way across her face. "Then I shall summon the workmen immediately and have the stables torn out by morning."

Durham bolted upright, sending water sloshing over the sides of the tub. "What?" he roared.

The grin widened. "See, you were not listening." With a lightening motion, she dumped the pitcher of water over his head.

He roared again as he snapped out his arm. He missed hers but managed to grab a handful of gown. With a single jerk, he caught her off balance and pulled her into the tub. The pitcher bounced harmlessly on the rug.

"Gil!" she gasped. "The servants!"

"The door is barred, wench." He pinned her arms against her sides. "Now, pay for your sins, woman."

Batsheva did not need much prodding. With the solemn-eyed look of a penitent, she brushed his lips with hers.

"'Tis not enough, I want more."

She kissed him again, this time lingering just a little longer.

Durham was not satisfied. He pulled her closer and brought his mouth down on hers. His tongue teased the half-parted lips until they opened to receive him. "I would have all of you, Bess." He released her arms and set his fingers to work on the wet laces.

The great hall was strangely empty when Durham and Batsheva descended the staircase to take dinner. "Do you suppose they grew impatient with us?" she whispered as she glanced about the deserted room.

"Are we so late?"

"I think so, my lord," blushed Batsheva. "Perhaps we could find Gwyneth."

The housekeeper came barreling through the archway on the opposite side of the hall. "Oh, my lord!" she cried as she bobbed a curtsey. "Forgive me, my lord, but your lady mother said you were too exhausted to take dinner in the hall. She, Anne, and Lady Catherine dined in her chamber."

"'Tis just as well. I was overlong in the bath.

The lady's damp tendrils gave them both away and the housekeeper turned pink. "Shall I send a tray to your chamber, my lord?"

Durham caught his lady's reddening and chuckled. "Shall we dine in my solar, Bess? There are matters to discuss."

Batsheva settled herself in a chair while Durham read several documents Ned left for the master's perusal. "I am sore out of practice, Bess," he sighed as he read the first parchment.

"I thought you did quite well, Gil."

He shot her a wry frown. "'Tis not what I meant. I am out of touch with my holdings. There is so much to do that I fear I shall be buried by detail."

"Is not your manager competent?"

"Very, but as earl there is much I must do myself. At the same time, I feel an obligation to continue personal patrol of the county. This dark knight will not be gone for long. He preys on the weakest links in my chain and disappears. I cannot help but wonder what he seeks in Durham."

"He spreads fear, Gil. And it would be worse if you had stayed in the Holy Land with the king. Your presence, no doubt, will make him reconsider his targets."

Durham was intrigued. "What makes you think so?"

"With no earl in residence and the archbishop the only government, he knew defense was scant. Your return, while important, was lacking in armed force, thereby letting him believe your defenses were lacking as well. How many men did you take on crusade?"

"Three dozen."

"How many returned?"

Durham scowled; his losses had been heavy. "Six. Twelve stayed with Richard. The others died in the name of the Cross." He snorted. "You killed at least one or two of them yourself, my lady."

"We were attacked unprovoked, Durham," retorted Batsheva sharply. "You were my enemy; I acted as any soldier. I killed because there was no choice."

"Let us not have words about this, Bess."

"Then do not throw it in my face." She went to stand beside him. "Tell me, Gilbert, if Joan had lived, would she have taken on the business of Durham when your father died?"

"Aye, she would have used Charles to guide her. Joan could not read as you do."

"And when you returned? Would she relinquish her duties?"

"Most, but perhaps not all."

Batsheva chewed her lip as she picked up the document Durham discarded. She read it slowly, but she understood what was written. "This is your tax roll, is it not?"

He nodded.

"It says there are two villages behind in their taxes. Are these, perhaps, the villages who lost men in the crusade?"

Durham took the parchment from her and scanned. "Aye. Three from Bowes and six from Brancepeth."

"Do you think it fair to penalize them for supporting your cause?"

"Bess!"

"Answer the question, my lord earl. Is it fair?"

"Nay, if that is the reason."

"What other reason could there be?"

"A dozen reasons, Bess. Any one of them could be true."

She didn't answer. Instead, she picked up another parchment. "This is a petition for land division. Will you grant it?"

"Ned does not think it necessary. 'Tis a large section though, too big for one man."

"Would not two brothers benefit working each his own parcel? There would be less friction between families and the land would be better managed. In addition, two households would ultimately provide more work and more work would attract more workers. More workers would mean more taxes, and more taxes…."

"Enough!" shouted Durham. "I yield to your logic."

Batsheva dropped the sheaf and watched as it floated to the table. "Which only proves women can make decisions."

"I did not know that was the issue."

"'Tis always the issue, Gilbert." She perched herself on the edge of the table. "I am offering to take on some of the business. You need someone you can trust, and I need something to do."

"Haven't you enough to do with the queen's visit almost upon us?"

"In truth, the staff is able to manage this all with little direction from me. Your mother and Gwyneth work well together and, whilst I can learn from her, it is not enough just to trail after her skirts. Queen Eleanor will ask me how I fare as the new chatelaine, and I would answer her honestly that I perform those tasks. Do not relegate me to boredom."

Durham stared at her. "Boredom?" he echoed.

"Had I married Akiva, Gil, I would be expected to help with ledgers and participate in running our family business. I was not educated to be idle; I was educated to enable me to work with my husband. In our world, I would be the one to visit the ladies in their quarters since men could not. Every woman loves to shop, and I would be, in essence, the merchant."

Without comment, Durham dragged a chair close beside his. "Then sit you down, Bess," he ordered as he handed her a quill. "Let us read these together."

So engrossed in their work, they did not hear the scrape of the heavy door when Lady Matilda pushed it open. She saw them, heads together, reading together. A dinner tray with a few leftover scraps was pushed to one corner of the table. "So, this is where you hide, my son!" she scolded. "I thought you would have the decency to call on me when you returned."

He grinned sheepishly. "I apologize, Mother. I was anxious to bathe." He pointed to Batsheva. "Bess claimed I was unfit for society."

"He smelled, my lady," added Batsheva solemnly. "You would have been offended."

"I have smelled him much worse I assure you, Elizabeth." She approached the table. "What is it that occupies you so, Gil?"

Durham stretched his powerful arms over his head and sighed. "The crops are good this year, Mother, but there will be a shortage of men at the harvest. The population has diminished these last few years."

Lady Matilda raised an eyebrow. "What would cause this? We have never lacked able bodies before."

"Father's death, together with last year's ague, has hit the county hard. We lost more than a few hardy souls to the disease…just as we almost lost you."

"And the solution, Gil?"

He glanced at Batsheva. "My lady has made an observation which bears closer examination."

Suddenly, his mother cut him off. "Your lady cannot be your lady unless you stand before Charles, Gilbert."

"Is this the reason for your visit?"

"In truth, yes. I will not permit you to cavort with your…lady… under my roof. The servants have been scandalized enough; they speak in whispers of how you are not wed. You are both becoming a source of gossip in the town. You, Gilbert, for bringing a foreigner home posing as your countess, and you, Elizabeth, for parading yourself in the streets of Durham while accumulating endless bills to be paid by the earl."

"Endless bills?" echoed Batsheva. "What are you talking about?"

"Your little excursion yesterday has sent tongues a-wagging!"

"That little excursion, Madame, was to purchase clothing and necessities for Catherine, your son's ward. Or have you not heard she was burned out of her home with nothing but the clothes on her back?"

"What of your exchange with that strange peddler while my son was away? Did you not think that would come back to me?"

"What I purchased that day, Madame, was purchased with *my own coin.* I did not come to Durham without means of my own."

"Whatever coin you have, Elizabeth, should have been turned over to the earl as part of your dowry. Not that you have a dowry. After all, *you* arrived in England with nothing but the clothes on *your* back."

"Not by my own choice, Madame, but not without coin." Batsheva's voice was steel edged.

"I'm sure you worked it to your own advantage, Elizabeth, just as I am equally certain you used my son's sense of chivalry in your posture as a damsel in distress. You must have been a fetching sight in your boy's attire."

Batsheva turned on Durham with fury in her eyes. "If you do not put a stop to this, my lord," she snapped, "I will."

His hand slammed down on the table, knocking over a goblet. "I will have no discord in *my* home. Mother, hold your tongue. Bess, keep your temper in check." He waited until both women were still. "As for the problem of the wedding, come Friday, it will be a problem no longer. Uncle Charles will marry us in his chapel. Mother, if you wish to be witness, you may attend.

"Bess, I have told you before, your coin is your own to do with as you see fit; I will not allow you to use it as dowry. You need bring nothing into this marriage but yourself and our daughter.

"As for bills sent to the castle, Mother, tend to your own business. Catherine is my responsibility. She needs the proper accouterments for a lady and so she shall have them. Her grandfather entrusted her care to me, and I will live up to my oath."

"Isn't she a bit old to require a guardian?" snipped Lady Matilda.

"She is unwed and alone. Until she is wed, I will see to it that she has a roof over her head and tender care from us. All of us, Mother. Do not test me on this."

"I am not testing you, Gilbert. I am merely pointing out this is a most odd predicament in which you find yourself. You cannot expect to shelter every orphan you encounter. At her age, I hardly consider her an orphan. Find Catherine a husband and be done with it."

Batsheva jumped up from her seat. "Madame!" she cried in French, horrified. "How can you be so…so…so callous? The lady has lost her grandfather, a laird, through an act of murder. He is not yet buried and already you are throwing her out. Your own daughter told me you were a lady of compassion and wisdom. I can see she does not know her own mother. *Pathétique!* What a shame that Margaret is blind to you. I, for one, am not." Batsheva stormed from the solar.

"Are you happy now, Madame?" asked the earl, his voice tight. "Have you spewed enough of your venom for one night? Or have you reserved more for my ears?"

Lady Matilda sat down and deliberately smoothed the heavy fabric of her gown. "You are a fool, Gilbert, an overgrown fool. What has she done to you that you would sit there and allow anyone to go on as I have? Has she so emasculated you that you cannot stand up to your own mother? As a child, you did that regularly enough!"

"What game do you play?" asked Durham.

"Your father, may God assoil him, despaired your ever remarrying, Gilbert. He feared you would never find a woman as kind and beautiful as Joan. Her smile, he would say, could chase thunder from the sky. I used to wonder if he were not a bit in love with her himself." She paused, cherishing the memory, then waved it away. "But I had faith, child. I believed you would find another, equally suitable, wife. I had not, however, bargained for *that.*"

Durham was incensed. "What fault have you found with Elizabeth, Mother? Has she done you grievous harm while I was gone? Has she usurped your place? Has she banished you to some crumbling corner of the hall to share scraps with the dogs?"

"Don't be absurd, Gilbert. She has done none of those things."

"Then what is it you want of her?"

Lady Matilda's eyes flashed steel blue fury. "She is not one of us, Gilbert. I know not what she is, but she is not one of us!"

"And thank God that she is not, if you are to be held as a shining example of what we are!" He realized he was bellowing; his mouth snapped shut. "The discussion is ended, Madame. If you have something to add, I would suggest you take it to the confessional." He followed Batsheva's footsteps out the door.

He found Batsheva not in her chamber, but on the battlement, staring up at the half-moon centered in the black, diamond-studded sky. Wordlessly, he slipped his arm about her shoulders and was relieved when she nestled against him. After a while, he spoke softly to her. "I am sorry, Bess."

"Do not apologize for her, Gil. She has reached a conclusion about me for which you are not responsible."

"She is my mother…."

Batsheva pressed her forefinger against his lips to silence him. "The Bible tells us we must honor our parents; we are neither required to agree with them nor accept what they say as perfect truth." She smiled up at him. "I think my own parents would have said much the same about you, my lord."

"They would not accept me as your husband?"

"No, they would not. They would have declared me dead…as my brother has done."

"But they accepted…."

"No, they did not. But they also knew we were not wed and held hope that I would return to them with the children." Her brow knitted into a furrow. "'Tis complex, Gilbert. I cannot explain it to you any more than I can make you understand the world from whence I came. Let it go; your mother will fight me until the moment we are wed and then, grudgingly, she will leave us in peace. She only loves you and wants what is best for you."

He held her a little closer. "What makes you think kindly of her when I cannot?"

"Unlike you, I am a mother." She shivered a little and pressed against him. "*Zeh ya'avor,* Gilbert. This will pass."

For a long while, they stood together and watched the moon.

CHAPTER 38

En Route to Durham

JUNE 1192

The garments acquired in Mallorca were different from anything Khalil had ever worn. Daud liked the breeches and short tunic; he paraded around the deck of the ship enjoying the freedom of movement the garments afforded him. The ship's barber trimmed his hair in the manner of the Franks and this, too, he liked. Although his features strongly resembled his father's, his skin was lighter, and Khalil was thankful for it; the boy would be inconspicuous once they landed in England.

The winds and the currents were favorable as they made excellent progress toward Marseille sailing under the Castilian flag. The weather held fair after they disembarked in the port city, but they did not linger. Daud rode with Khalil. Kassim and three men carefully chosen from the sultan's household, all of whom looked more European than Muslim and spoke at least passable French traveled with them to Calais. Only one of the three, a slave named Yusef, spoke English and would cross the channel with them.

Yusef was Saxon. His father's farm near Ipswich was too small to divide amongst his four sons. Yusef, the youngest, once known as Joseph Williams set out to seek his fortune as a sailor. His career was cut short when his ship was attacked by pirates; rather than throw himself in the sea, he made the best of this adventure. Bought by one of Salah ad-Din's captains, he soon discovered his talent for language could take him far. While Yusef remained a slave, he learned this was no impediment to upward progress. His reputation as an interpreter grew, and he found himself in the center of the sultan's court. Life was far more pleasurable as a favored slave than as a poor farmer. He was on loan to the court of the sultan's emissary in Alexandria when Kassim approached him about joining Khalil's expedition. From the moment he joined them, his job had been to teach rudimentary English and French to the amir and his son.

The boy was bright and quickly surpassed his father in speaking the new tongues. At night, while Daud slept, Yusef coached his new master in the words needed for polite conversation as well as possible confrontation. By the time they reached the northwestern coast France, Khalil was ready to face whatever lay across the channel…with an accent he could not hide.

Rashid appeared at their campsite at dawn the day they were to depart for England. He knelt before the amir and touched his head to Khalil's boot. "Allah be praised, my lord," he murmured. "The ship awaits in the harbor."

Khalil nodded; his stomach was so knotted he could barely speak. In all his years as sheikh to his people, general in the sultan's army, and now amir, he was not prepared for the harsh, jangled nervousness he felt knowing England was on the other side of the water. Turning, he took Daud's hand and brought him forward. "This is my son," he said at last. "Will he cause eyes to stare?"

Rashid raised his head. But for his eyes, the boy was, to him, clearly Ayyub. Even so, he would not seem at all strange in England. "No, my lord, he will not attract attention."

"Good," said Khalil gruffly. "Let us break camp and go."

They did not sail straight across to Dover; instead, the captain steered the ship northward, skirting the coast of England while maintaining a safe distance from shore. Daud stood on the prow, letting the salt spray and wind buffet his face. Only when nightfall was close upon them did Khalil join his son. He dropped a heavy cloak over the thin shoulders. "The weather turns cold, even in summer, my son. You must stay warm."

"Yes, Abu," replied the boy as his fingers tied the woolen strings. "Is this how English boys dress?"

"So I am told. We will see for ourselves in a day or so."

"When will we find my mother, Abu?" he asked for the millionth time, looking up at his father.

"Soon, little prince." His stomach lurched; the knot seemed to gnaw more at his innards the closer they came to the place called Durham. He touched Daud's shoulder. "Come, let us eat now. The hour grows late."

"May I sleep on deck?"

Khalil chuckled and ruffled the boy's short hair. "Yes, Dudu, you may sleep on deck."

On the second day, the captain announced they would make landfall at the next dawn. "We shall put in near Scarborough; there, my lord, you will find a man called Devereaux. He is employed by the House of Hagiz as an agent. Much like Rashid."

"Is he a Jew?"

"I do not believe so, my lord, but he is to be trusted. He will take you to a safe house where you will encounter the jongleurs. They are faithful children of Allah and loyal to our lord, Salah ad-Din. Can the boy sing?"

"Yes," replied Khalil.

"They will teach him songs which will allow him to slip easily into the castle with the others."

"You have planned this well, captain. You will be amply paid for your services."

He swept a low bow. "My only reward is to serve our master. His kindness to me is boundless."

"Then you will not refuse my coin, for it comes from the hand of the sultan himself. The safety of the lady is close to his heart."

"As you wish, my lord Amir." The captain looked out over the prow of his ship. "Do you see the hump jutting out into the sea?"

Khalil shaded his eyes against the sun and followed the captain's gaze. "Yes. There is a house atop the hump."

"On the far side of that, there is a cove. The place is called Flamborough Head. When you have the lady, send word there, then ride south. We shall meet at the place called Hornsea."

Khalil repeated the names; they were strange on his tongue, yet he committed them to memory. "Again, captain, I thank you. Know you will always have a place in my household."

The captain laughed, his white teeth flashing against his dark beard. "May Allah's will be that I never need it, master! But I will rest easier knowing it is there."

As promised, Devereaux was waiting for them when the skiffs carrying Khalil, Daud and their men slipped through the early morning fog and onto England's shore. "*As-salāmu 'alaykum*!" he called softly when Khalil disembarked, his son in his arms.

"*Wa-'alaykum salaam*," replied Khalil just as softly. "You are Devereaux?"

"Yes, my lord, Marcel Devereaux, agent for the House of Hagiz in Paris at your service." He nodded to Rashid who smiled back at his French counterpart.

In the pale morning light, Khalil studied the man. He was a spare figure, dressed in a plain brown tunic and cape. His skin was fair, but his short beard quite dark, yet shot through with grey. When he extended his hand to Khalil, his grip was firm in the style Khalil had been warned about. He returned the greeting with similar strength.

Following a trail toward the road, the little band hiked the short distance to a manor house tucked safely behind a thick stone wall. Devereaux unbarred the gate, then led the procession in securing the gate behind them.

"In the stable, my lord, you'll find the finest horses coin could procure," said Devereaux in his heavily accented Arabic. "I have purchased Norman saddles. I told the stablemaster you are Spanish, but you would do well to treat him with disdain. The less he hears your voice, the better he will keep his own counsel. It is not uncommon for a servant to speak for the master here."

"A strange place, this England," commented Khalil. He followed Devereaux into the house. "How long until the jongleurs arrive?"

"In two days' time. Until then, you must practice riding with the new saddles; they are heavier than what you are used to."

"Is there a mount for my son?"

"Yes, my lord. I've picked a good pony for him. She is small but sturdy. When he travels with the jongleurs, however, he will be expected to ride in the wagon with the other children."

Khalil grinned. "He will protest, but not too loudly."

Devereaux returned the smile. "The other children are not unaware of who he is, but they will welcome him." He bowed and left Khalil and Kassim with Rashid.

"You trust this man?" asked Kassim.

"Implicitly. He has much at stake here; he says her brother is mad."

Khalil stared at Rashid. "Yehudah?"

Rashid nodded. "The brother is in England and he does harm to their business. Like me, Devereaux seeks only the return of the woman if, for no other reason, than to support the rightful claim of Asher Hagiz, the lady's oldest brother, to remain head of the trading house."

"I understand, Rashid. You have done well."

The jongleurs were late in getting to the little manor, but when they arrived, it was with bells, ribbons and song. However, as soon as they entered the stable yard, their eyes were cast downward as they waited in silence to be addressed by the favored of the sultan. Only when Khalil had greeted them, did Alonso, leader of the troop, come forward. Tall and swarthy, his dark eyes missed nothing as they passed over the newcomers.

"We have done your bidding these last months and will continue to aid you in the land of infidel, sire." Their leader touched his fingers to his heart and bowed; the others followed suit. He then went to the boxed wagon to help the old woman descend the few steps to the ground.

She pushed him aside and hobbled toward Khalil leaning heavily on a thick, wooden cane. "So, I see you again at last, little boy," she cackled.

Khalil hid his smile and touched his heart as he bowed low to her. "You are well, old grandmother? Our master will be pleased to know."

"Bah! If he cared for this old *jida* he would call her home to die. Our master is a silly boy with a big head."

"Only you could speak such words and live, old grandmother," said Khalil gravely.

"Bah. Where is the boy, boy? I would see the boy."

Daud stepped close to his father, his small hand seeking out Khalil's large one.

"Is this the child? This is the first of two?" She peered at him through her clouded eyes. "Yes, yes, his eyes are her eyes. I have seen her, little boy, and I have seen her eyes brighten when told you and your sister are safe. Yes, yes, little boy, her heart misses you and longs to see you. And the other. Yes, the other as well. The girl is not here, is she? It does not matter; she will see her mama soon enough." The old woman leaned close to Daud and tapped a bony finger against his chest. "Are you worth all this, little boy? Are you worth the trouble?"

The boy sucked in his breath and puffed out his chest. "Yes, old grandmother; *we* are worth the trouble."

"Aieee!" laughed the crone. "You are definitely your father's son. And your grandfather's grandson. Yes, you will do." Still cackling, she turned her back to them and hobbled away.

"Who is she, father?" whispered Daud when she was almost to the wagon."

Khalil bent close to his son's ear. "She is a great lady. Once, long before even my father was born, she was nursemaid to the sultan himself. As a reward for her service, he freed her to return to her own people. Since then, my son, she has wandered the world as the eyes of her beloved boy."

Daud's eyes widened. "Oh, Abu, she must be very old."

"Very," chuckled Khalil. "When I was your age, she was old. My father told me she was favored by Allah, and I will tell you the same thing: you must do whatever she tells you to do. Never question her wisdom."

For a fortnight, the jongleurs camped within the walls of the manor as they taught Daud everything he would need to know before they began the journey northward. The boy was an apt pupil; he mastered the tumbles and tricks as well as the songs the troubadours sang. Daud's voice was sweet, and it was decided a song would be the best way to reach his mother's heart. Each night, he tumbled, exhausted, onto his pallet, only to be awakened at dawn for prayers and another day of training.

"I have written the words for his song," Khalil told Alonso one night when Daud was already on his pallet. "You must translate it into French." He handed him a parchment.

The jongleur nodded as he read the poem the amir had penned. "I will write him a sweet, sad ballad for your words. There will not be a dry eye when he sings."

Khalil sighed; this was hard for him. There was so much unknown that could not possibly be anticipated. He looked closely at Alonso and said, in English, "Thank you."

A market fair was planned in nearby Scarborough; Alonso decided they would take Daud for his first performance. "He must have experience, my lord; the people must see him and word of him must spread if we are to be invited to play midsummer fair at Durham. His voice is sweet and his face pretty; he will do well with the ladies."

Khalil agreed to let them take Daud, but privately, he told Rashid they would follow and watch from the crowd. "It is not that I do not trust them, my friend, but I would see them perform for myself."

"As you wish, master. We can leave after they leave and still arrive in the city before them. The fair will be crowded; we should have no trouble melting into the masses."

The market square in Scarborough was teeming with people. No sooner had the jongleurs reached the city, than Alonso began singing an old French song. The boys stood on the wagon bed to join the chorus, their bright costumes vivid against the drab city. The sea of people parted to make way for the performers; behind them, children ran after the wagons shouting for tricks and tumbles.

In the main square, the boys jumped from the cart and began their first routine. They all performed a host of tricks, including Daud who walked about on his hands, all the while singing a little ditty taught to him by Alonso. He found he liked the attention; he liked the way people clapped at every trick and when they tossed coppers at him, he scrambled to gather them as he had been instructed. In the heat of early summer, Daud worked as hard as the other boys and he had a pouch full of coins to prove it.

The dancing girls performed next; their bright ribbon skirts twirled in the sun as they tapped tambourines above their heads. With hair flying, they danced and sang for all who would stop to watch and listen. Only when they had collected the coins scattered on the hard ground, did they disappear through the crowd to where the wagons were tethered.

Alonso motioned to Daud to join him as he perched on the edge of a wagon stage set in place while the boys tumbled, and the women danced. He strummed his lute to check the tune then nodded to Daud. "Sing the winter song," Alonso whispered. The boy clambered up onto the stage and, as he had been instructed, he waited until the crowd grew quiet. Then, Daud heard the familiar chords, cleared his throat, closed his eyes, and began to sing.

At first, the sound was reed thin, barely loud enough to be heard above the noise of the square. But as he warmed to the melody, the sound grew louder, bolder, and when he dared to open his storm grey eyes, he saw everyone staring at him. Somehow, he managed to smile just a little as he sang. His knees had been shaking, but now they were steady. His arms started rigid at his sides, yet they soon had life of their own as his hands came up to add expression to his song. He was almost sorry when he reached the last verse. And then, too soon, it was over.

The crowd was deafeningly silent. Frightened, Daud looked to Alonso and saw the man motion for him to take a bow. Woodenly, he bowed from the waist. Then it began. The shouts and the cheers were thunderous in Daud's ears. He rose, his face bright red, then bowed again, this time a more elegant, sweeping bow before he scrambled to pick up the coins pelting him.

"You must sing again, boy," called Alonso. "A merrier tune this time." He strummed his lute with a flourish and paused while Daud took his place center stage once more. The song was an easy, little ditty and he had no trouble at all sending it out. Again, the applause was loud and the coins plentiful. Feeling full of himself, he tumbled about as he swept up the offerings.

The rest of the afternoon passed in a haze for Daud. When he gave his coins to Antonio, the master jongleur returned several coppers to him. "Explore the market, little prince," he chuckled when the boy's eyes widened at his good fortune. Grabbing the coins, he dashed off to join the other boys.

As he ducked around the wagon, two hands reached out and grabbed Daud. He twisted and turned, but his feet were off the ground and when he tried to shout, a hand pushed his hood over his eyes and clamped over his mouth. Instinctively, he tried to bite the offending hand. He felt his attacker begin to move; he went limp. He heard a deep rumble of a laugh. Instead of being afraid, Daud twisted again, and his feet touched the ground. He pushed back his hood.

"Abu!" he nearly shouted when he saw his father's face. "Why did you do that?"

Khalil squatted to bring his face close to his precious son's. "To teach you caution, David," he said, using the Castilian name Daud knew was his. "This time, it was me who captured you. Next time, it could be someone else. And you must speak Castilian or English or even French; our language is unknown here and may be dangerous to use."

"*Sí, papa.*"

"*Bueno.*" He grinned at his son. "You did well today, *hijo*. I was a proud papa."

"Do you think my mother will know it is me when I sing for her?"

Khalil grasped Daud's shoulders. "I think, my son, in her heart she will know as soon as she sees you. A mother always knows her own child."

Daud pursed his lips. "I am afraid, Papa. What if she does not want to be found?"

"In *my* heart, I believe she does." Khalil held Daud close for a moment. "But we shall know soon enough. Now, keep your hood out of your eyes and go join your friends. I will see you when you return to the manor."

Daud hugged his father and ran off. Khalil watched him go then turned to where Kassim waited in the shadows. "I pray to Allah that I am right, my friend."

"Do not fear the outcome, Khalil," said Kassim, slapping him on the back. "Rashid said her eyes spoke volumes to him. She wants to be found."

Khalil sighed, "I will not be whole until she is with me again." He managed a wry smile. "Let us find Rashid and go to the tournament."

The three men walked to the open field outside the walls of the city. Standing in the crowd, they watched two knights joust in the lists. It was important to them both to see the manner in which the knights held themselves, as well as the way they challenged each other. Dressed in simple, peasant garb, they attracted no attention as they observed the local nobility. The presence of women, their faces and hair exposed for all to see, amused the Muslim men. "I cannot understand why they let their women parade in such a state of undress," commented Kassim. "Do they enjoy the bold stares of other men?"

Rashid laughed; his experiences in England and France had taught him much about their habits. "The women enjoy the stares, and the men enjoy staring. The married women are not always as faithful as we think proper, and the unmarried women do not value chastity as we do. They go to their priest each week for absolution from their sins, only to go sin again." His flashed in a smile. "Sometimes, one may find this…pleasurable."

"I believe you've taken advantage of this, Rashid." Khalil was not surprised.

"Why not? The women are hot and juicy; they welcome a skilled lover."

"And you've provided your services at every opportunity?"

"On occasion. A man has needs. Is that not so?"

"Which is why I prefer a sara'i full of beauties anxious to attend my needs," said Kassim, looking at Khalil. "Their practice of one wife must surely lead to chaos."

Khalil was silent. He had women waiting to be summoned, yet he desired only one woman. While it was true that in Batsheva's absence he had lain with others, it was her face he saw at the moment of climax. When he returned to Alexandria, he knew there would be no other women in his bed; he doubted she would tolerate sharing him. And in truth, after this was over, he doubted he would want to be shared. "Turn your attention to the knights," he said gruffly, "and learn what needs to be learned."

A new knight was taking up his position at the end of the list. Khalil watched him with great interest; he was dressed differently from the other knights. His helmet was almost black and his shield without decoration of any kind. Even the chain mail of his hauberk was dark as was his overlaying tunic. Khalil noticed his horse was impatient and the knight had some difficulty keeping the steed steady as he waited for the signal from the master of the joust.

When at last the charge began, the dark knight remained upright until the last possible moment. Then he leaned forward in the saddle, tilted his lance upward, and caught his opponent high on the chest. The crowd gasped and roared as the opposing knight was lifted from his saddle before he was thrown completely away from his horse. Pages and squires rushed out onto the field to attend the fallen knight..

The sun was setting when the tournament drew to a close. The dark knight had dispatched six opponents to take the day. He received his prizes from the nobleman. Then, in what Khalil surmised to be an odd gesture, he did not remove his helmet when he saluted the spectators. And instead of accepting the nobleman's invitation to attend the banquet, the knight rode off with his men.

Khalil could not understand much of the language about him, but Rashid translated for him. The local folk seemed disturbed by the knight's refusal to dine with the lord almost as much as his refusal to remove his helmet to show his face. No one recognized him. It was obvious the people were angered by the blatant lack of respect displayed by the knight.

On the ride back to the manor, Khalil questioned Rashid about what they had seen. "He is unrecognized, but not unknown," he told Khalil. "There are rumors about him. Some say he is in the service of Prince John, brother to Malik Rik. Others claim he is simply a rogue knight. All that is known about him is that wherever he rides with him comes trouble."

"No one stops him?" asked Kassim.

"They are afraid of him. It is said he burns villages for sport."

"Strange that the lords do nothing," Khalil mused. "Are they so weak here?"

"Not weak, master; wary. With no king in the land and no direction from Eleanor who rules in his place, they are loath to confront him."

"Eleanor," repeated Khalil. "This is the mother of the king?"

"Yes."

"And she rules in his place?"

"Queen Eleanor keeps the throne safe for her son. She is well respected by the nobles and her word is strong. She summons councils in the king's name and they assemble at her bidding. She is a wise woman."

Khalil shook his head in disbelief. A woman behind the throne was one thing; a woman on the throne was something completely alien to him. "How long will *Malik Rik* allow this to continue? I cannot understand how a king can leave his people in such disarray."

"Did you not leave your people, master?" asked Rashid.

"I left my people in a place where they were safe, with a leader who would tend to their needs."

"And now? Are you not Amir in Alexandria?"

"Mustafa sits in the amir's seat while I am gone. I will succeed him when the time is right. It is not the same thing."

Rashid shrugged. "Perhaps not. But then again, our sultan controls his territory in a way which is different from these people."

"That," snorted Khalil, "is obvious. There would be no empire without those who follow the word of Salah ad-Din. These petty lords could learn much from us."

"To each his own, my lord Khalil. Whatever disarray, they are formidable adversaries on the battlefield."

The sun was long gone when they reached the manor. Khalil called for Daud, but when the boy did not come, he turned suspicious eyes on Alonso.

"He is asleep, master. The day proved too much for his young spirit." Alonso led Khalil to where Daud was curled up on a pallet in a corner of the hall.

The father looked down at the peaceful face of his son and smiled. After all the boy had accomplished on this day, it was no wonder he was exhausted. He pulled the cover over the little body and left Dudu to his dreams.

Outside, Alonso was waiting for him with a bowl of hot stew. "Tomorrow, Master, we shall begin our journey to Durham. Tonight, we sing. Join us at the fire. Dance with us, master. It will do you good to let yourself be free."

He stared at Alonso for a moment. Khalil had not danced since the night of his wedding to Hafsah. He extended his arm. "Let us dabke like village men," he laughed, "Let us all be free of care for a night."

When the songs had ended and they had exhausted themselves dancing, Khalil stayed outside, not ready to seek his pallet. Staring up at the half-moon hanging in a star-filled sky, he took comfort in knowing Batsheva could look up at that moment and see the very same jewel. Tonight, his heart was warmer than it had been in a year; he felt her presence near to him and he knew that at that same moment, her eyes were sharing the sight with him. He could feel his heart still dancing.

CHAPTER 39

Durham

JUNE 1192

Batsheva stood on the rampart staring into the sky. She was restless this night and had slipped away from the warmth of her bed to walk the battlement. There was so much to think about, so much to consider that she thought her brains would burst screaming from her head. Looking up at the moon, she was unexpectedly infused with warmth; peace dropped over her like a warm abaya. *This must be the right thing to do,* her head reassured her; her heart, however, said nothing.

The wedding to which she finally agreed was postponed indefinitely when word reached them that Canterbury was sending an investigator. For two long weeks they waited for him. In that time, as Batsheva went about the task of learning about the castle and its environs, nothing could lift the sense of impending doom from her. Gilbert's uncle tried to still her fears, but he could do little more than implore her to remain calm. Now that he had finally arrived, the Archdeacon of Canterbury's personal representative had been closeted with the Archbishop of Durham most of the day. No one dared disturb them, not even Matilda who called on her brother-in-law shortly after the noon meal. Late in the afternoon Gilbert was summoned to the residence.

Charles made the introductions, then sat back to let young Father Thomas explain the reason for his visit. He watched as his nephew's face went from white with shock to red with outrage, all the while keeping his own counsel.

"Though impediments to the marriage are many," said Father Thomas calmly, "they are not insurmountable. His grace wishes only that the problems be resolved before the sacrament of marriage can be administered… privately. We have no wish to make a public scandal in Durham. While his grace fully understands your lordship's desire to put this behind you, as your spiritual leader, he wishes you to understand his position."

"I fully understand his position," replied Durham through tight lips. "And I would tell him to his face it is none of his concern. The Archbishop of Durham, is well qualified to see to my spiritual health. I do not need Canterbury's meddling."

"This is not meddling, your lordship; this is canon law. You cannot be wed to the woman unless she, too, receives the sacrament. A marriage any other way would be invalid. Surely you realize this would present a problem in the line of inheritance for your lands and title?"

"I see no problem, save the one invented for me. I can well imagine who invented it."

"Gil," warned the archbishop quietly.

He waved away his uncle's concern. "We all know there are differences in rites from one place to another. Can we not just accept this as fact and get on with it?"

"Are you questioning the wisdom of the Holy Father in Rome?"

"No," spat Gilbert, "just the wisdom of the Archdeacon of Canterbury. Need I apply to the pope himself for this wedding to take place?"

Father Thomas was perfectly calm when he answered, "Yes, it may come to that if your lady refuses the sacraments from the hand of Archbishop Durham."

Durham rose from his chair and paced the length of the chamber. "I cannot answer for my lady; she is of independent mind and will not be coerced into doing what she does not want to do." He glanced at his uncle and saw the slightest hint of a smile. "If you choose to speak with her on this, be forewarned; she will not take kindly to it."

"I have no choice, your lordship. When can I see her?"

"Take supper with us at the castle this evening, Father. Afterwards, you may speak with her."

Only when Father Thomas had retired to his cell, did Charles hand his nephew the letter the priest delivered from York. Durham scanned the contents quickly: Eleanor was traveling to Durham directly after York. "What say you, Uncle?" he asked.

The archbishop shrugged his wide shoulders. "Your sister, God preserve her, is too clever by half for a woman. She is right in one thing, Gil. Bess already knows she may come, but do not speculate on the date of her arrival until after the priest has had his interview; it would serve no good purpose but to make her more anxious than she already is. I will tell you when the time is right. A day or two will make no difference. And there is always the possibility Eleanor will choose to send a messenger of her own with the news of her arrival in York."

Durham scowled, "I cannot think of this as timely."

"Nor can I, Gil, but there is nothing either of us can do about it. She's made up her mind and, with any luck, Margaret will travel north with Eleanor; that should soothe your mother."

"I am not particularly concerned about my mother, Uncle," he growled, "although Bess does get on well with my aunt."

"Then put it from your mind for now. You have far more important things to occupy it."

Durham returned in a black mood. He went directly to his solar and slammed the door behind him. Facing Bess was not what he wanted to do most in the world. When he heard her call to him from outside the door, he asked her to join him. In a tone kept barely in check, he explained what had happened.

Her response surprised him. "Of course, I will speak with him, Gil," she said without anger. "If the queen has concerns, they must be addressed."

"What makes you think 'tis Eleanor who has instigated this inquiry?"

"'Tis well known that Canterbury does nothing without her approval, Gil. But I did not say I believed she is at the root. I am neither stupid nor naive." She smiled at him. "You know who is at the bottom."

"Isabella."

"Your sister warned me when we were still in York."

"I could wring her scrawny neck."

"And what good would that do?"

"I would feel better."

"I am certain you would. I, of course, would then be left in England without a protector. No, Gil, wringing her neck is not an option."

He could not help but laugh. "I admire your ability to remain unperturbed, Bess. I am not so calm."

"Then tell yourself you are until you believe it. Getting into a lather about Father Thomas serves no purpose but Isabella's. If we anger this priest, we have everything to lose and Isabella has everything to gain." Batsheva patted his cheek. "Go and bathe, Gil; you always feel better after a good soak."

"Will you join me?" he asked hopefully.

"I think not; I think I shall visit Gwyneth in her lair and ensure the menu for this evening is modest yet impressive."

The priest was duly impressed with the hospitality offered at Durham Castle. Afterward, when the earl escorted him to his solar where the lady awaited them, Father Thomas noted the cheerful greetings offered by servants and guests alike. A house in turmoil, he knew, was not so warm and pleasant.

He had seen the lady from his place at below the high board where he sat with his brethren in Christ. She was more beautiful than he anticipated, and although their eyes met but once, her gaze was neither aggressive nor submissive. It was simply curious, and he met it with a steady gaze of his own. In that brief encounter, he could see, despite his clerical robe, why Isabella of Lincoln viewed this woman as a danger. Why, if other women of England were to follow her example, surely anarchy would prevail. With a simple inclination of her head toward the earl, she captured and held the attention of everyone gathered in the hall, even Archbishop Durham seemed to be completely captivated. Added to that, the men seated with him, while unaware of the true purpose of his visit, had naught but kind words for the lady.

The door to the solar was open. There, standing serenely beside the earl's table, stood the Lady Elizabeth. She smiled at the two men then asked Father Thomas if he would care for a sherry. "My lord earl brought home several casks when he returned," she explained in her lilting English.

"Thank you," replied the priest, then he added, "if you would prefer to converse in French…."

She stopped him with an elegant gesture. "My English, while still slow at times, is competent enough to serve. I think English might be most comfortable for you, since you are from Guilesford, are you not?" She poured an ample amount of amber liquid into a goblet and handed it to the priest. Then she turned her steady grey eyes on the earl. "As much as I would like you to stay my lord, your steward, asked if you would seek him out. I believe he is in the granary."

Durham did not smile although he wanted to; she had dismissed him. He dipped his head in agreement. "I shall leave you alone…for now. There are some matters which require my attention." He quietly closed the heavy door behind him.

"Please, Father, let us sit. I am certain you have many questions for me."

"Aye, my lady, I do." He sipped his sherry while he tried to compose his first question.

She could sense his discomfort. "Let me begin for you, Father Thomas. I was born in the south of Al-Andalus…."

Without ever stating that she was a Jewess, Batsheva gave him a brief, carefully edited version of how she came to be in England. Nor did she lie when she admitted that she did, indeed, believe in *God, the Father*.

"An interesting statement, Lady Elizabeth," mused the priest, impressed with her composure. "Tell me about the rite which you practice."

Batsheva experienced a sudden attack of nerves; this was the moment she dreaded. "The rite which I practice, Father Thomas, is rooted in a most ancient path. My people devoutly believe in God and His power. We accept the Holy Scripture as the irrefutable Word of God and practice the teachings of the Bible most faithfully. Would the Blessed Virgin walk the earth today, I think she would not find fault with our rite."

He could not help but smile; she knew exactly what she was saying, and in truth, he could not argue with her. Still, there was the matter of the sacraments. "Yet, you do not take communion, my lady."

"I do not take communion as you perform the rite, Father. I do, however, observe the ritual according to the rite of my people. You must understand we lived apart from what you now call the Holy Mother Church. In itself, that does not prevent one from following in the footsteps of the Teacher."

But which teacher? he wondered silently. "Do you accept the words of the Gospel?"

"I accept them as the words of the Apostles, if that is what you ask. I also believe that the prophets of the Bible prepared us to understand their words."

"You seem well versed in scripture, my lady. Is this so?"

She nodded. "My parents believed strongly that a daughter should be well taught. Is it not true that the first responsibility of the mother is to be the first teacher of the child? If a mother is unschooled, how is she able to transmit the word of the Lord to her children?"

"Well said, Lady Elizabeth! You make a strong case for teaching women, however, 'tis the exception rather than the rule that a woman is educated. The Holy Mother Church teaches us a woman with too much learning becomes restless in the home."

"I should think quite the opposite is true. There are times, Father Thomas, to sit with a book is a most peaceful thing. I cannot imagine how poor my world would be without reading."

"How many languages can you read, Lady Elizabeth?"

"Several."

"May I ask which ones?"

Batsheva swallowed hard, but her composure held. "French, Occitan, Castilian, Greek and some Latin. I am but beginning to master English, but it is difficult. You use letters strangely."

"Ah, 'tis true. His grace, Archbishop Durham, said you also read and write in Hebrew."

"I am able to make out the letters," she replied.

"And the language of the Moors?"

She nodded again. "My people are traders; 'tis useful to be able to read and write a document in that language."

"'Tis hard to imagine," he said, impressed with the breadth of her knowledge, "that a woman would be used for such tasks."

"Does not our Queen Eleanor rule in the king's stead? Could she be the great queen that she is if she were unable to read dispatches from her council?"

"She is a queen; her station requires it."

Batsheva flashed a smile that, in her mind, signaled impending victory. "In her own home, every woman must be queen. She must rule wisely and with good temper if her husband is to be king of his own domain.

Even the poorest vassal needs the respect of his family. Does not scripture command us to honor our parents? A parent without respect is a parent without honor."

"This would explain why your stepdaughter is being taught by a brother monk. The arrangement was regarded as..." he paused to seek the right word, "unusual...in Canterbury."

"Perhaps, but I do not think her value as a wife will be diminished because of it. Do you, Father Thomas?" she asked sweetly. Her victory was complete; he could not argue the point with her.

He burst out laughing. "Nay, Lady Elizabeth, I do not. If you are the one who guides her education, I daresay she will be a jewel in any man's household." He rose and took her hand in his. Boldly, he touched it to his lips. "The hour grows late, my lady. I thank you for your hospitality and your conversation. This has been a most enlightening evening."

She wanted to ask him what he would tell Canterbury, but she refrained. In the end, she suspected it would not matter; their archbishop would do whatever he felt was right. Instead, she smiled warmly at the youthful cleric. "I hope, Father Thomas, you will enjoy your stay in Durham, but I would ask a favor of you."

"If I can grant it, I shall." He braced himself for the request.

"Please take time before your return to Canterbury to visit your mother. Although Mistress Martha is much improved after her recent tumble in the cottage, a visit from her son would surely speed her full recovery."

Father Thomas's mouth dropped open. He knew his mother had taken a fall and been confined to bed for a brief time. "Of course, my lady, I had planned to ride there tomorrow." He did not dare ask how she knew about his mother.

Now, as she stood looking out over the sleeping valley, she regretted not being bolder with her own questions. *Surely, he would have told me his recommendation*, she told herself as she drew her mantle close about her. In the same breath, she had to admit she rather liked him; he was not at all what she expected to be sent up from Canterbury. Her innate woman's sense told her the archdeacon there was humoring Isabella more than he was holding her slanted opinion as truth. "Then why am I not relieved?" she asked aloud.

"Perhaps," murmured a voice behind her, "because you haven't settled this within yourself." Durham put his arms about her and drew her close. "When will you make peace with yourself, Bess?" he asked softly.

Batsheva did not have a ready answer for his question. "I do not know, Gil. Every night I go to sleep hoping to awaken with a lighter heart, but…." She nestled against him, letting his warmth flow into her. "Do you think they see the same face of the moon in the Holy Land?"

"Aye. In all my travels, the moon and the stars followed the same paths they follow here in England. If your children were to look up, they would see the moon just as you see it."

"I take comfort in that," she whispered.

Durham said nothing; he simply held her a little tighter.

There was no word from Charles the following day, nor the day after. Batsheva could barely go about the daily business of the castle. Durham, unable to stand the tension, took 10 men-at-arms and rode down to Crichton Wood to check on the hamlet. Catherine asked to go, but Durham refused to let her accompany him, citing the recent reports of highwaymen raiding to the south. Left to her own devices, Catherine spent her day trailing after Batsheva until the lady finally begged her to find something else to do. Anne, coming out of the great hall, caught the exchange and stepped in to rescue Batsheva. "Let us take Miriam and have a picnic in the kitchen garden," she said in a most mature voice. "'Tis too lovely a day to waste inside." Taking Catherine's hand, she guided her back into the hall to ask Gwyneth to prepare a basket.

Alone at last, Batsheva ran quickly up the stairs and down the hall to her chamber. She picked up her light cloak and a small basket, then went down the stairs again. Finding the guard who traveled with her when she went outside the castle walls, she hurried him out the door. "I would go to see my friend, Mistress FitzHugh," she told him as they passed through the gate.

Jane was at home, a pretty piece of fabric spread before her on the table. She greeted her friend joyously, then sent the guard around to the kitchen where her newly hired cook would feed him while the ladies visited. No sooner had he disappeared, than Batsheva took Jane's grey cloak from its peg and swung it over her shoulders.

"How long will you be gone?" whispered Jane, knowing full well where Bess was going.

"Not very long. I need only speak with Rachel for a moment."

Jane opened the door and looked out. "Be careful and come back soon," she warned with a wagging finger.

Batsheva nodded and hurried down the quiet little street. It was not far to Rachel's house, but she kept the hood of the cloak pulled low over her brow. There was no point in being recognized running about the city unescorted.

She reached the house, knocked softly, and was admitted almost immediately. "Is your mother home?" she asked the little boy who opened the door.

"She is in the garden, my lady." He did not bother to show the way; he merely stepped aside to let her pass.

"Is everything all right?" asked Rachel with alarm as soon as she saw Batsheva.

"I do not know…is everything all right?"

Rachel breathed a sigh of relief. "Yes, as far as we know. Come, sit with me and I shall tell you the news from London."

Shedding the borrowed cloak, Batsheva sat down on the bench beside Rachel. "Where is my brother?"

"He is not in London. David hopes he has crossed the channel, for he has not been seen in several weeks."

"Has there been word from my uncle in Tiberias?"

"'Tis still too soon, Batsheva. The ship from Venice is not expected for another fortnight at least. However, we have heard from Paris."

"And?"

"No one knows anything about the locket. The drawing we sent has gone on to Marseille. If they do not recognize it, they will send it on to Venice and so on until we know who crafted it."

"That will take a lifetime," Batsheva complained. "I do not know if I can wait that long."

"You will wait that long and longer still, if need be." She held Batsheva's hand in hers. "There is good news from Toledo. Your cousin Yakov's wife Tzipporah has delivered a healthy baby boy."

"Baruch ha'Shem!" cried Batsheva with delight. "This is indeed good news."

"We are all happy for them. They have named him Yosef for your father."

"I am glad; my father would have been pleased. What else, Rachel?" she asked eagerly.

"There is one other thing David asked that I tell you." She took a deep breath. "He thinks it unwise to acknowledge the babe." She regretted the words immediately when she saw the stricken look on Batsheva's face. "He thinks it would be safer for you if they do not know you are here. Until the matter of Yehuda can be resolved…."

"Am I to be his prisoner forever? How long will he punish me?"

"He is dangerous, Batsheva. You cannot underestimate his madness. David hopes he is in Normandy or Paris, but he cannot be certain. There is every possibility he continues to look for you here in England."

Batsheva stared at Rachel for a long while. "You know something else. I can see it in your eyes."

"There is nothing else."

"Rachel."

"There is nothing I can tell you, Batsheva…except perhaps this. Marry the earl in whatever way the archbishop will permit it. If you are the countess, you will have protection. He will not be able to harm you. For the sake of your daughter, marry him."

"He is here, isn't he, Rachel. He is somewhere close to Durham."

"I do not know."

Batsheva paced narrow garden. "The Archdeacon of Canterbury sent an investigator." She told Rachel of her meeting with Father Thomas. "Until Gilbert's uncle makes a decision one way or the other, we will not be wed. I think perhaps this is a sign from the Holy One. What choice do I have? I cannot go back to Akko, nor can I return to Al-Andalus. I am trapped here."

"Even my grandfather thinks you would be wise to marry the earl."

"An act of desperation…."

"You care for him; you have said so yourself."

"I do, but…."

"One can do extraordinary things to preserve life, Batsheva. It is not simply your life in jeopardy; it is Miriam's. Would you risk hers as well?"

"Why can I not just ride away from here and live my life alone in some village?"

"Simply because you cannot. You have no one else to shelter you. We cannot take you in for we are in Durham. No, Batsheva, you must do what you must do. God will understand."

"That is where you are wrong; God will not understand." She picked up her cloak. "I will send word to you when the decision is made. Be well, Rachel."

As quickly as she came, Batsheva was gone.

PART VII

Durham
Eleanor's Visit

SUMMER 1192

CHAPTER 40

Durham

JULY 1192

Despite silence from Archbishop, there was work to be done. Miriam was quickly outgrowing her gowns while her mother seemed to be swimming in hers. Jane's nimble fingers could only stitch so fast and when the pile of garments on her worktable grew to unreasonable proportions, Batsheva insisted that she, Catherine, and Mary take on some of the work. Now their mornings were spent together in Batsheva's reception chamber, mounds of garments around them.

Batsheva did not mind the work; it took her mind off other things. She was perfectly content to sit with Jane and Mary and sew while she practiced her English. And when she was not needed elsewhere, Anne would come to read to them as they sewed.

Durham happened on the little circle of stitching ladies on the third day after Father Thomas's inquisition. He stood in the doorway and marveled at the charming peacefulness which hung about them as they worked. He could hear their light laughter and see their smiles. Most of all, he could hear Anne's voice reading French poems with surety. And he could not believe this was his daughter. The girl was light of heart and it showed in her eyes. All his doubts about the benefits of educating a daughter disappeared in the face of her progress and the joy that came with it. And as much as he hated to disrupt their morning, he rapped gently at the door.

"Do not move on my account," he said genially.

Batsheva set aside the little gown she was working on and went to him. Slipping her arm through his, she guided him toward the far end of the chamber. "Has your uncle sent for you?"

"Aye, he has; I am to the cathedral now."

"Shall I go with you?"

"Nay, stay here. I will come directly when we have finished our business." He touched her cheek. "Do not fret, Bess; I am certain all is well with him."

She looked up into his blue eyes and read worry in their crystalline depths. "Whatever happens, Gil, we will weather this together."

"I know, Bess, I know. I just want it to be ended."

There was little to do but wait. In her chamber, Batsheva sat beside the window and, between stitches and nursing, looked toward the gatehouse in hopes of seeing Durham striding through the archway.

The day was quite warm. Even in her light tunic, Batsheva felt herself perspiring as she sat with Miriam at her breast. With nothing to distract her, she remembered other sunny days, when she sat on the rooftop in Akko nursing the twins, or in the desert when, despite the intense heat, she worked alongside Bedouin women drawing water from the well. *'Tis the same sun,* she thought idly. She noticed the old fear for the twins' safety had abated somewhat since the peddler had slipped the locket into her palm. Automatically, she felt for the golden chain she still wore about her throat but now, instead of just one object, two, nestled between her breasts. She sighed when Miriam's little fingers twined themselves around the chain. "Your brother and sister," she told the babe. "One day, my little princess, one day you will meet them." Miriam gurgled; Batsheva laughed softly and brushed a kiss against the wispy, copper curls. Turning her face toward the window, she spied Durham and her smile broadened; his step was light, the news must be good.

Good. She caught herself. Would giving in to the marriage be good for her…or would it chain her to England for the rest of her life? Did she really want to stay here? *Have I relinquished all hope of returning to my children?* she asked silently. She shook her head and her own copper curls bounced. She had lost her sense of what was good and what was not good. She realized she no longer knew the difference when it came to her own life. *Good is being at peace with the world around me*, she told herself. *And if I keep telling this to myself, then perhaps one day I shall believe it.*

She listened for the familiar footfall on the stone of the passageway. When Durham came through the door, she called, "What news?" before he could even greet her.

"Good news and bad," he replied as he pulled a stool close to where she sat. "Which would you have first?"

Judging by the light in his eye, she deduced the bad was not terrible. "Good news first, Gil."

"Father Thomas was most impressed by you and although he would be happier if you agreed to take sacraments from the hand of a priest, Charles thinks he will report favorably to Canterbury. Charles tells me he argued against the priest's insistence you be baptized before the wedding; that is a sticking point. However, Father Thomas found your defense to be without heresy and admitted he could find no fault with your logic."

"I should've told him I've been to a mikvah," she grumbled. She saw the question. "A ritual bath we women attend each month. The process, I hear, is the same." The corners of her mouth turned upward. "I said naught but the truth, Gil. If I am guilty of anything, 'tis the sin of omission."

"He appears quite convinced you practice a Byzantine rite of some sort; he said he will explain this to Canterbury."

"When we will we know?"

"As soon as Canterbury renders an opinion, he will send a messenger." His eyebrows knitted together for a moment. "Charles has a request of us, however."

"Is this the bad news?"

Durham's laugh was wry. "No, if we recall our own history. He asks that while our fate lies with the Pope's council in England, we lie apart."

"Did you tell him we lie together now?" she gasped, alarmed.

"No, Bess, but he is a man. He did not need to be told." He grinned when she blushed.

"You agreed?" She saw his nod. "Then I shall abide by his wish. If he believes this is best, I will not argue."

"Good, then it is settled for now. Although I confess, I will be hard pressed to sleep alone now that I am accustomed to having you beside me in the night."

"You will live, my lord earl. And no doubt, you will be strengthened by it. Is not the honey sweeter after long abstinence?" she replied.

"Aye, 'tis true." He did, however, lean over and briefly kissed her lips. Miriam stopped sucking and giggled at him. He placed another kiss atop her head and let her grasp his large finger in her tiny hand as he took her from her mother.

"And the bad news?" asked Batsheva as she closed her chemise.

Durham took the babe from her arms. "Brace yourself, Bess."

She stared at him. "What has happened now?"

"Eleanor will come to Durham by month's end."

"God's bones!" exploded Batsheva, using Durham's favorite oath. "When will we know the date that she arrives?"

"She is to York next week."

"And how long will she stay with us?"

He shrugged. "Her progress is never questioned, but most likely she will stay a week. Two at the most." Miriam released a loud belch. "See, Bess, even our babe is excited by the news."

"Excited? Nay, already her stomach is in distress. As is mine. Have you told your mother?"

"I thought I would leave that to you."

"You are not amusing, Gilbert, Earl of Durham."

Miriam giggled against his shoulder. "My daughter thinks I am."

"What does she know?" snorted Batsheva. "She is not the one who has to manage your mother. I would suggest you find Lady Matilda. She, no doubt, will be thrilled."

"As you wish, my lady," chuckled the earl as he strode purposefully to the door.

"Where are you going with Miriam?"

"To find my mother. 'Tis past the time she grew used to seeing me with our daughter."

Batsheva sat at the table in her receiving chamber, quill in hand, composing a list of things that needed doing before the arrival of Queen Eleanor. First on the list was the reassignment of sleeping chambers to accommodate the guests. Some, she was certain, could be housed in the archbishop's palace, while others of less noble stature could be roomed together in the larger castle chambers on the ground floor. Sighing, she almost wished there were a women's quarters where all ladies could sleep, en masse, around a pleasant pool, just as they had done at her aunt's house in Tunis. The memory, faded as it was, made her stop writing and smile.

Just as she thought of that most happy of nights, Lady Matilda's sharp voice pierced her reverie.

"Why are you sitting idly when there is work to be done, Elizabeth?"

Batsheva glanced up and gasped. In Matilda's arms, Miriam was sound asleep. She jumped up from her chair and rushed to take the babe, but the old woman waved her away.

"She sleeps perfectly well with me, Elizabeth."

Batsheva thought she noticed the slightest bit of warmth in Matilda's voice, but she could not be sure. "I was listing the number of possible sleeping chambers, my lady. I understand her majesty's retinue is quite large."

"Anne and Miriam will share your chamber. Anne's chamber is large enough to hold six ladies-in-waiting and the nursery can be furnished to hold at least four more. Eleanor will use the earl's chambers."

"Where will the earl sleep?" asked Batsheva.

"Not with you, obviously. He will be in his childhood chambers in the west tower where other ranking noblemen will be housed." She saw the look of surprise on the lady's face. "This is common practice, Elizabeth. Gilbert will not feel displaced; no one will think anything of it." Matilda brushed past her and took the chair at the table. "Now, read me your list."

"Yes, madame." Still amazed, Batsheva pulled a stool to the table, sat beside the dowager countess, and began reading her notes aloud.

From the hallway, Durham heard Batsheva's voice. He was about to enter but heard his mother's voice and stopped. Without being seen, he poked his head as far in as he dared, then stifled the laugh threatening to expose his presence. He could not believe his eyes: there was his lady and his mother, still holding the sleeping babe, having a civil conversation. *Will wonders never cease?* he asked himself. Chuckling, he ambled down the hall, a feeling of optimism and relief washing over him.

"Assuming she arrives midday, Elizabeth," said Matilda when they had finished with the sleeping arrangements, "it is customary to hold a banquet on the first night."

"There will be banquets every night, will there not?" asked Batsheva.

"Yes, but the first is most important. We will have no more than three days' notice of her exact arrival, which means messengers must be sent out to inform the local gentry of which night to come to Durham."

"Isn't that rather short notice?"

"No, the first messengers go out tomorrow. Word that she is coming will travel quickly, but there are those who must have word directly from us. They, in turn, will inform the others. It is an old chain, one that has served us well in the past. You must learn its workings so you may employ it at will." She set about dictating who was to be told what and in which order.

As fast as her quill could move, Batsheva covered parchment. For the sake of speed, she wrote in French, but once, when Matilda stopped to consider a point, Batsheva wished she could be writing in another, more flowing hand. *How much easier it would be!* she laughed to herself. When Matilda had finished off the chain of invitation, Batsheva asked what was next.

"The feast, of course. I will set the menu."

"Forgive me, my lady, but I was hoping to…," she searched for the words, "…participate in the planning."

"Oh?"

"While we were at Westminster, I prepared a luncheon for her majesty. Queen Eleanor enjoyed the dishes and I thought she would be pleased with a feast that was…a little different from what she usually tastes when visiting."

"Her majesty brings her own cook."

"I understand, but I thought we could also prepare some interesting delicacies for her."

Matilda eyed her carefully. "This luncheon…you prepared the dishes yourself?"

"Yes, my lady; I spent the morning with her cook; he knows me well."

"You cooked food yourself?"

"Yes, my lady."

"This is most irregular, Elizabeth."

"In my world, a lady is expected to know how to do these things. We take great pride in our ability to personally supervise a banquet."

"It seems your people take great pride in a number of things, Elizabeth," she replied dourly. "Well, if you wish to do that, I will not stop you. But after the first banquet, please leave the kitchens to the cooks. You will have more than enough to do while the queen is in residence."

"Thank you, my lady."

She waved away the gratitude. "Do not thank me, Elizabeth; simply pray your strange victuals do not upset the royal constitution."

Throughout the entire conversation, Lady Matilda held Miriam. Batsheva, although wary of this new interest in her daughter, saw nothing but tenderness in the way the old woman stroked the chubby cheek and nestled her against her breast. When Miriam finally did open her eyes, she babbled and cooed at Matilda, as though she was used to seeing the aged blue eyes smiling down at her.

"You see, Elizabeth, Miriam does not find me repulsive," she said dryly.

"Nor do I, Madame;" replied Batsheva with perfect calm, "I find you a concerned woman with a great deal of responsibility on her shoulders. Some might find the gravity of that position makes you seem harsh and unbending but I, for one, do not."

"I would have thought you did, Elizabeth. After all, we do not see eye to eye on many subjects, my son being one of them."

"*Au contraire, Madame*. We see his lordship in much the same way. He is a man devoted to king and country, with a great deal of honor. Home and hearth are important to him, as is the well-being of those whom he views as in his charge. Had he not that sense about him, my lady, he would not have returned to England with the haste that he did; he would have remained with King Richard."

"And you would not be where you are now."

"That is true."

"Yet you claim you do not resent him for removing you from your home. I find that difficult to believe."

Batsheva stared at the old woman. "Is that the source of your discomfiture with me? That I have hidden my hatred only to take my revenge later?"

"It would make sense, Elizabeth. You, yourself, admitted you did not come willingly."

"I was unconscious; the decision was not mine to make." She managed a wry smile. "Had the decision been mine, you know I would have stayed with my children. But I also believe I have a responsibility to survive for the sake of this child in your arms. She deserves to have a loving mother for as long as God permits her to have one. My son and daughter, I truly believe, are safe where they are and if God sees fit to reunite me with them, then so be it. For now, Lady Matilda, my life is here…with your son and his people. You may either choose to accept that or reject it, but if you reject it, understand you will always have a home under this roof. You will be given the respect and the honor due as both mother and dowager countess. But I think, Lady Matilda, you will find it unbearable to live without the love of your son."

"Your own mother taught you well, Elizabeth; you are clever with words and know how to cut to the heart of the situation. I admire that in you."

"Thank you."

"Do not thank me yet, Elizabeth; I have not finished. I also think you are cunning and manipulative. You have Gilbert tied around your finger, but this shall pass. Eventually, he will awaken to your machinations and will tire of them. It would be unfortunate if Eleanor found disharmony in Durham. I would present to her a picture of domestic bliss. Are you agreed?"

"Yes."

"Good. I hope we understand each other, Elizabeth."

"I believe we do."

Almost reluctantly, Matilda handed Miriam to her mother. "She is a sweet child." She did not wait for Batsheva to respond. Instead, she strode majestically from the chamber.

Too stunned to comment, Batsheva sat with Miriam in her lap for a long while. *'Tis a first step,* she thought, *perhaps there are more to come.*

CHAPTER 41

Durham

JULY 1192

The castle was in an uproar; constant hammering reverberated through the great hall as workmen installed a bigger, better dais to hold the queen's chair and a larger high board. Batsheva ordered the walls stripped of armor, shields, and banners before a fresh coat of whitewash was applied. Maids, aided by an army of strapping young men, beat dust from tapestries and bed drapes. Women were hired from nearby villages to stuff new mattresses as Batsheva instructed. Anyone not directly involved with an occupation was summoned to the castle where extra hands were needed for a myriad of tasks. In the middle of it all stood Batsheva with her list.

From sunrise to sunset, she marshaled the forces of cleanliness to scour the castle from top to bottom. Only when the corners and crevices were completely clean did she allow buckets of clean water dumped on the stone floors. With rags, mops, and brushes, the floors were scrubbed until not a speck of soot or dust remained. Fresh rushes would be laid the day before the queen's arrival.

At night, she tumbled into her bed with nothing but a chaste kiss on the brow from Durham. As much as she would have preferred to snuggle up against him, she refused to let him even stretch out atop the covers beside her. And Durham, for his part, accepted his banishment gracefully.

"Lady Anne! Lady Anne!" called Gwyneth to the little girl sitting beneath the apple tree in the kitchen garden. The child, unable to resist a perfect day, had taken her lunch and her slate outside to wait for her teacher. "Your tutor has come."

Anne glanced up from her slate. "Ask if he would like to sit outside today; 'tis too nice to be indoors."

"Aye, that it is!" laughed the housekeeper as she turned around.

A moment later, an unfamiliar figure in brown friar's robes was strolling through the garden to where Anne still sat. "*Bonjour, mademoiselle!*"

She rose, bobbed a little curtsey, and asked in the same language, "Where is Brother Ben today?" She was disappointed her regular tutor had not come; she dearly loved the jolly little monk. And this one had a funny accent. "I hope he is not unwell."

"Brother Benjamin is perfectly well, my lady," said the monk, "but his grace has need of his fine hand on this morning. He has sent me in his place. I hope you will accept his apologies."

"I suppose if Uncle Charles needs him," she pouted. She waited for him to sit on the stool beside hers. "Who are you?"

"I am Fra' Giovanni, little lady. I come from Venezia."

"Oooh, Venice. They have canals there instead of streets and roads. Is it very pretty?"

"*Si, signorina*, very pretty."

"How came you to be here?"

"I am on pilgrimage to holy shrines in the west. I am newly come to Durham, but I have been in England for some time. His grace thought you might enjoy my teaching for a day or so." He smiled at the girl. "But tell me, signorina, what have you been writing on your slate?"

"Numbers. My lady stepmother is teaching me sums. Every lady needs to know this so she may run an honest household."

"Your stepmother is very wise; a good lady tends carefully to her lord's coin. When the lord of the manor is away, it is she who must look after the estate. If she cannot do sums, the lord can be cheated by those who would take advantage of him."

"You sound like my lady stepmother," giggled Anne.

"Does she have an accent, too?" asked Fra' Giovanni.

"Yes, she does."

"Ah, perhaps she, too, is from Venezia!"

"Oh, no. She is from Al-Andalus." Anne studied the new tutor; he was younger than Brother Ben and certainly much more handsome. His skin was dark and his hair very black, but his eyes were light, not quite blue, more like the color of a dove, but not as grey as Bess's. "Have you had adventures, Fra' Giovanni?"

"Some, but not so many as to take me from my sacred task. Let us make a bargain; if you study hard, I shall reward you with a story. Yes?"

"Oh, yes, Fra' Giovanni. I would like that very much!"

"*Buono! Buono!* Let us begin then with your sums."

At the end of the lesson, Fra' Giovanni walked back to the chapel house where visiting monks were housed. There was much to do, and he found his resolve to be wavering in the face of a little girl. A bright little girl. For a moment his mind's eye flashed on another little girl beneath a tree in a very different garden calculating sums faster than he could. That memory served its purpose; the anger was back in place.

Standing on the battlement supervising the beating of rugs, Batsheva noticed a slim monk striding toward the gate. "Hmmm, that is not Brother Benjamin," she mused aloud. There was something about the monk that reminded her of someone else. At first, she couldn't put a name to the slight swagger in his step, but then a picture flashed in her memory and, in spite of everything she knew, she smiled. "Yehuda," she murmured, thinking kindly of her brother for a moment, "he swaggers like Yehuda."

Five days before Eleanor's suspected arrival, Jamie rode onto the castle grounds and went in search of the lady. He found her in the cookhouse supervising the preparation of huge vats of fruits to be cooked into jellies. He chortled when she glanced up, her face red from the heat of the fire, her hair escaping from the ash-stained kerchief she wore. "If I didn't know ye, my lady, I'd think ye were a scullery maid," he laughed.

"I feel dirty enough to be one, Jamie," she answered in kind. "What is the news?"

"We found them, my lady. The jongleurs are indeed heading north. They will cost a pretty penny to divert them from their destination, but they will come."

"When?"

"They will arrive in five days' time."

"That is the same day we may expect the queen!"

"Aye, but not to worry, my lady. They will come."

"You haven't paid them in advance?" she cried, alarmed.

"Nay, but they know the value of the queen's presence."

Batsheva rubbed her forearm against her sweaty brow. "I hope you are right; 'twill be a poor banquet without jongleurs."

"And what entertainment they will be! They have added a new boy since we met them in York. His voice is said to be so sweet even the most sour crone is moved to tears at his songs."

"Let us hope they are timely and well prepared; this visit is too important to ruin with so simple a thing as amusements." She pushed an errant hair from her eyes. "Thank you, Jamie."

He swept a deep, courtly bow. "For you, my lady, all things are possible. But now, I am off to join his lordship at the tourney field."

Batsheva smiled as she watched him leave. Of all of Durham's men, Jamie FitzHugh was her favorite. Without his cheerful countenance, she thought life would not be nearly as pleasant. It was Jamie, after all, who brought Jane into her life.

Jane was waiting when Batsheva finally managed to break away. Standing amidst a profusion of silk and fine linen, the rapidly expanding seamstress was barking orders at two maids trying to make order from chaos.

"What are you doing?" laughed Batsheva as she stripped the filthy scarf from her head.

"Your wardrobe, my lady," Jane replied with a wave of her hand. "You now have enough gowns, bliauts, and tunics to see you through the queen's visit."

Batsheva moved slowly through the sea of fabric, stopping to inspect a piece here and there. "You managed to finish this all?" she asked, amazed. "How did you do it?"

"Extra hands. I found two nimble-fingered women to aid in the impossible," Jane yawned. "There was no choice, Bess. With the babe soon to be along and the queen coming sooner, it had to be done now. Besides, once the babe is delivered…"

Batsheva finished the sentence for her. "I will lose the services of my best needlewoman."

"I admit I think about it. We have enough from his lordship to keep us comfortably."

"I do not blame you for a moment, Jane. I would be of much the same mind. I shall not argue."

"Harrumph," snorted Jane rather indelicately. "I thought you'd at least protest a little."

"Will I lose my friend? Will I be without her good company?"

"No."

"Then why should I argue? As long as we can spend our afternoons sitting companionably by a winter's fire or in a summer's garden, I have no complaint."

"Oh, you are an easy one, aren't you, Bess!" giggled Jane with a pretty pink blush.

"Perhaps."

The giggle became a hearty laugh. "You are the least easy woman I know…and you know it, too."

Batsheva glanced at the two maids gaping at them from the door of the dressing chamber. "'Tis good they speak no French, lest they think ill of us both." She scooped up a pale blue gown embellished with tiny silver and gold pomegranates embroidered along the neck, sleeves, and hem and shook it out. "This, Mistress FitzHugh, will make the queen take notice of your work. I think I shall wear it for the first night banquet."

"Then you'd better try it on now," scolded Jane, "and let me check the length one last time. It would not suit to have you tripping on the hem." She turned on the maids. "Heat water and fill the tub," she ordered in English, "and do it quickly…please."

Feeling infinitely better after a bath, Batsheva stood patiently as Jane and Mary put the final touches to a dozen gowns. Jane showed Mary how help the lady, and the girl quickly mastered the most intricate fastenings. Once that was done, Batsheva dressed in a simple tunic and chemise, then sat at her dressing table while they went to work on her hair.

Longer now but still in tight curls, her coppery hair was becoming more manageable. Mary experimented with a new braid which began at the crown of the head and plaited tightly against the skull. When it was tied off, Jane draped a gossamer veil over Batsheva's fitted cap so the leaf circlet appeared to be floating on a bank of clouds. Batsheva looked in her mirror, turning her head this way and that to see how the new creation looked.

"'Tis different," she said, pleased with the result.

"Aye, it still hides your lack of hair. Those who do not know it is not there will never guess," said Jane smugly. "Who knows, perhaps you will begin a new fashion."

"Ladies cutting off their hair?" asked Mary with shock in her widened eyes.

"Nay, Mary," Jane frowned, "the cap. If the queen likes it…."

"If her majesty likes what?" Lady Matilda's voice sliced the air and all three heads turned toward the door where she stood. "Leave us," she commanded.

Batsheva nodded at Jane and Mary and the two women bobbed quick curtsies to the dowager countess before they bolted from the chamber. Batsheva rose from her seat at the dressing table and also dipped toward the lady. "To what do I owe the pleasure, my lady?" she asked with a smile.

"Do not patronize me, Elizabeth." She moved across the chamber until she stood face to face with Batsheva. "I am here to examine your wardrobe."

"How kind, my lady."

Matilda shot her a sharp glance. "You are relatively new to England, Elizabeth; there are rules and conventions which much be observed. What on earth is on your head?"

"'Tis a cap and veil, my lady."

"With *my* circlet."

Batsheva sighed. She removed the circlet and handed it to Lady Matilda. "Forgive me, my lady; my lord presented it to me whilst we were in residence at Westminster. I did not know it belonged to you."

"It belongs to the current countess of Durham."

"Then it does indeed belong to you. Again, my apologies."

Matilda dropped the circlet on the table. "Wear it if you wish." She walked into the wardrobe and began examining the gowns hanging there one by one without comment. When she finished, she returned to where Batsheva still stood. "They will do. Be certain none of your personal ornamentation outshines her majesty's. Eleanor does not take well to competition; she is the queen."

"Yes, Madame." Despite the smile in place, Batsheva was gritting her teeth.

"Are Anne's gowns prepared for the visit?"

"Yes, Madame."

"I shall leave the choice for the first night to you; you seem to have a way with the child." She glided to the door, then stopped. "Oh, Elizabeth?"

"Yes, Madame?"

"If you insist on grinding your teeth whilst your hair is so tightly braided, you will no doubt begin a headache." Lady Matilda flashed a cold smile at the stunned woman and left.

"Grrrrrr," growled Batsheva when she was gone, and then laughed.

Supper, as usual, would be served in the great hall. Batsheva went down early enough to check on progress made in the re-hanging of the armaments on newly whitewashed walls. Although she knew Gwyneth had supervised the order, she wanted to make certain nothing was inadvertently omitted from the display. She stood in the center of the hall and counted first, the number of shields, then the swords and maces and, finally, the banners. She rather liked the profusion of color hanging in the dark timbers above her head and she liked knowing what each represented. One banner, however, was new; it replaced one which, when taken down, had been badly tattered. Batsheva stared up at it and shielded her eyes as she tried to make out the design; it was definitely not what she ordered. She gathered her skirts in her hands and hurried off to find Durham.

She found him sitting in his solar with Anne. The girl was reading to her father as he sat stretched out, eyes closed, in his favorite chair. "Gil!" she called as she trotted into the room."

He opened one eye. "Is anything amiss?"

"No, but there is a strange new banner."

"Did you like it?" he asked with a tiny smile tugging at the corners of his mouth.

"I saw it only partly unfurled but 'tis not what I expected. I ordered the new one to replicate the old."

"I know." He sat up and leaned toward the desk. He rifled through several parchments before he found the one he wanted. "If you do not like the design, Bess, we can have it changed." He handed her the sheaf.

"*Mon Dieu!*" breathed Batsheva when she saw the rough sketch. Between two crossed scimitars sat a single pomegranate.

Anne came around the table to look over Batsheva's shoulder. "Do you like it, Bess?"

"I do not know what to say!"

"Say you like it," laughed Durham.

"It will cause gossip, Gil!"

"But it fits you well."

"The banner will warrant explanation. Have you one prepared?" she demanded.

Durham took the parchment from her. "The pomegranate, Bess, is your emblem; Eleanor decreed it so. The crossed scimitars show you rose above the battle. That is all; very simple."

"Not so simple, is it, Gilbert? The shape of the sword will cause comment."

"What comment?" asked Anne.

They both stared at the girl, then laughed. "The comments, my curious little lady, will be centered on the shape of the sword," replied Batsheva honestly. "They resemble the swords used by the soldiers of Islam in the Holy Land."

"Infidels' swords!" grinned Anne, pleased to show she had learned her lessons well." She was not prepared for the look of horror on Batsheva's face. "Have I said something wrong?" she asked with grave concern.

Batsheva knelt down to be face to face with the child. "Never let me hear you call the soldiers of Islam infidels, Anne," she said gently. "They believe in God just as we do."

"But they fight against our good Christian knights."

"They fight for their land just as we would fight if England were invaded."

"But…," she looked to her father.

Durham joined Batsheva as he told the child: "We have a difference of opinion with those in the Holy Land. But never doubt, for one moment, that they believe in God with any less devotion than we."

"That is not what Fra' Giovanni has told me."

The adults looked to each other, both puzzled. "Who is Fra' Giovanni?" asked Durham.

"My new tutor. Brother Benjamin is scribing for Uncle Charles. He's terribly nice."

"What exactly has the good friar told you, Anne?" Batsheva inquired calmly.

"That the infidels are despised by God and will all burn in hell. He says they hurt innocent women and keep them as slaves."

"Men do strange things in war," muttered Durham. "Not just those who follow the banner of Islam."

The comment was not lost on Batsheva and she put her hand on his arm. "I am certain, Anne, Fra' Giovanni has reason to say these things, but I sincerely doubt he has ever been in the Holy Land or has made the acquaintance of any who follow Islam. I think it most unfair to condemn an entire people based on rumor and innuendo."

"Did you know any of them?" asked Anne.

"Yes," replied Batsheva. "And those I know are very kind and loving people." She glanced up at Durham and her glance was not lost on him. "We cannot say all Muslims are kind and loving, just as we cannot say all Christians are kind and loving. We may only hope the ones we know are."

Anne's brows knit together in thought. "Did Fra' Giovanni lie to me, Papa?"

"Not intentionally, sweeting. He repeats only what he has been told."

"Then I shall correct him on the morrow when he comes. I should not like him saying evil things that are not true."

Batsheva's grey eyes flared in Durham's direction, and he caught the meaning quickly. "It is not for you to correct him, Annie lamb. Leave that to Uncle Charles. I will personally explain your concern and he will correct Fra' Giovanni."

"Yes, Papa."

"Until then, my sweet, say nothing of this to the friar. It would be rude," added Batsheva with a tender smile and a reassuring pat. "Now, be a good girl and go change your tunic before supper is served."

Anne glanced down saw it was white with chalk dust. She scrambled from her stool, bobbed a quick curtsey, and went to the door. "And Bess…I do like the new banner."

"As do I, sweetheart."

When the door closed behind the child, Durham let loose a long whistle. "What are we teaching her? It could be thought of as heresy."

"If that is heresy, Gil, we would serve her best by taking her out of England. You could not possibly want a child to grow up believing all those who differ from her are evil."

"There are those who profess that very idea, Bess."

Stormy eyes flashed with anger. "And you would not disabuse her of the notion?"

"Aye, I would."

"And Charles, your uncle? Is he of the same mind as this Fra' Giovanni?"

"I do not know, but I would think not. Has he not agreed to marry us?"

She eyed him suspiciously. "Has he changed his mind?"

"No, he has not. We are still awaiting word from Canterbury."

"Canterbury!" spat Batsheva. "I have never so much as seen the man, yet he believes it is his right to determine what I shall or shall not do. I cannot understand your fealty to a church that governs so heavily from afar. Surely, this is madness!"

"I cannot argue with you, Bess," sighed Durham in frustration. "I do not know what other way to turn. Charles has always seen to our spiritual well-being; I have never before felt the need to question him."

"Perhaps now would be the proper time to begin." With a swish of her skirt, she started for the door.

"One last thing," called Durham before she could leave. She turned. "Do you truly like the banner?"

"Yes, Gilbert, I like the banner very much."

"I am much relieved." He picked up a small box and held it out for her. "I am hoping you will like this as well."

Opening the box, Batsheva gasped. A gold pomegranate atop a ring whose sides were in the shape of scimitars was nestled in silk. It reminded her of the ring Khalil's mother had given Sufiye to hold for a granddaughter. "Oh, Gil! I don't know what to say!"

"It is made by the House of Hagiz in Paris. Say you will wear it when we wed, Bess."

"Yes, Gilbert of Durham; I will wear it when we are wed." *If,* the thought silently. Batsheva briefly wondered if this was yet another message.

CHAPTER 42

Durham

JULY 1192

Messengers announced the queen's progress three days before her arrival. Batsheva and Lady Matilda immediately toured the castle and grounds for imperfections. Together they went from room to room checking for anything that might cause some wellborn lord or lady to comment unfavorably on Durham's hospitality. Batsheva found the dowager countess uncommonly civil during the tour; she attributed this new attitude to Lady Matilda's desire to have the queen remain outside family squabbles. Even Batsheva had been exposed to Eleanor's meddlesome nature, although the queen viewed the behavior as devoutly maternal on a grand scale. Not one to push aside a truce, Batsheva simply made up her mind to enjoy the peace while it lasted.

Two days before the royal entourage was to make its appearance, Durham prepared to ride out. "The dark knight," he told Batsheva with a grimace, "has been seen near to Darlington; I would secure the road lest Eleanor encounters him."

"Has anyone been hurt?" she asked, mindful of Catherine's plight. She handed him a new chemise she had just finished for him.

"Nay, not that I have heard." He slipped the shirt over his head. "'Tis strange, Bess; he burned Crichton Wood with no more excuse than a whim, and according to Uncle Charles, he has done much the same to the north. I thought we were well rid of him when we chased him off, but now it seems he has returned."

"Perhaps he wishes to confront the queen?"

"I would prefer proper circumstance, not on a road." He straightened the shirt and tied it to his braes. "I can ill afford to be embarrassed before the court; he must be stopped before he threatens their progress."

"And still you do not know who he is."

"Aye, that much is true. He carries John's warrant and uses it at will. I will not permit that on my lands, nor will any other lord around me." He let Batsheva tie the side-laces of his tunic. "I'll not need a valet if you keep on, Bess," he teased lightly.

"You need a valet, Gilbert, not an old man who can no longer walk up the steps to your chamber." She caught his sigh. "I know you are fond of Old Thomas. At the very least get him a second, someone he can train. Someone who might shave your face without the nicks."

He kissed her mouth to silence her. "Yes, my love, after Eleanor departs, I will find a man to press into service." He went about the business of tying his cross garters. That done, he donned his hauberk and tugged it into place before he bent to let Batsheva drop his formal tabard over his head. The white lion rampant stood out brightly against the cobalt blue field. Durham tied a narrow belt around his waist, then added the heavier sword baldric. "One day, Bess, this will no longer be needed," he said as he slid his sword into place.

"Your mouth to God's ear, Gil," murmured Batsheva.

Batsheva handed him his earl's gold circlet. "My father detested this thing," he muttered as he took it, "and so do I."

"That may be, my lord earl, but you are obliged to wear it, especially now. You must appear as an earl; being one is simply not good enough."

"And you, my lady, have been spending too much time with my mother." He kissed her again.

"Do not wear it until you are to meet the queen," she shrugged.

Durham sighed and glanced about his chamber. "Where will my belongings be stored, Bess?" he asked suddenly.

"In my robing chamber, but your bed will be in your old room in the north tower. Mary will tend to your linen daily. Do not give it a thought, Gil; we have it all arranged."

"Except that I might lie at night beside you."

She raised her eyebrow. "You made a promise, Gilbert, and I will hold you to it."

"I do not have to care for the arrangement."

"You do not; you simply must abide by it."

He slipped his arm about her waist and drew her close. His lips lingered on hers for a moment. "I cannot wait, Bess," he groaned.

"You can and you will." Batsheva stroked his smooth cheek. "It will make our coming together again that much sweeter."

"I shall hold your words in my heart, sweet Bess." He kissed her yet again. "And know I am counting the days until Charles summons us to his chapel."

As they rode out, Durham caught sight of a small, slender figure standing on the battlement with a blue kerchief snapping at arm's length. It was a sight that thrilled him to the marrow; only reluctantly he turned his eyes back to the road.

All was quiet as the earl and his men rode toward the southern border of Durham's lands. Hamlets along the way had prepared for the queen's tour by cleaning their squares, whitewashing their buildings, and replacing old thatch with new. As their earl rode through the little towns, the people stopped long enough to greet his lordship and offer refreshment. If Durham thought this a waste of precious time, he made no frown, no sour face at his people. Instead, he smiled anew with each speech and gladly accepted tankards of watered ale to quench his thirst. He was glad to see their apparent joy in the impeding royal visit and equally gladdened by their reception of him.

As they neared the village of Trimdon, Durham spied a small band of travelers coming north toward his city. Judging by the brightly painted wagons and the beribboned horses, he rightly decided these must be the jongleurs. His men slowed their pace as they neared the wanderers. A tall, dark haired, dark eyed man stood upon the buckboard of a wagon full of odd pieces and children. When the earl approached, Alonso swept a deep, courtly bow, "Good day to you, my lord!"

Durham wheeled his horse to a stop. "Are you to Durham?"

"Aye, my lord, we are. We are the entertainers summoned by the lady." He added a little flourish for effect. From the corner of his eye, Alonso saw Kassim move closer to where Daud sat in the wagon.

"We look forward to your amusements, *monsieur le jongleur,*" replied Durham as he quickly looked them over. "Tell me, are you the same we saw play in York after Easter?"

The leader bowed again. "Aye, my lord, so we are."

The earl surprised them with a hearty laugh. "We liked what we saw there. My lady is anxious to have you within her sight, so were I you, I would hurry to Durham!"

"Then on our way we shall be, my lord!" He swept another bow and remained low until he heard the horses move off. Only then did he look up.

❀ ❀ ❀

"Was that him?" asked a small boy standing in the wagon.

"Yes, little prince, that is him."

"My mother is his lady?"

"That, too, is true."

Daud sat down with a thud. The man on the horse was very big, almost as big as his own father. But he was not at all the cruel barbarian Daud imagined; instead, he was jolly and most brave looking. Just the kind of man he would want to know. Daud wished his father still rode with them, but Alonso had insisted it would seem odd a knight traveled with the jongleurs. Shading his eyes against the sun and staring off down the road, Daud wondered if his father had seen the knight.

As if he could read the boy's mind, Alonso beckoned him with a finger. "Worry not about your father, boy; think more about the words of your song."

Daud did not respond; his eyes were focused on the road ahead.

Durham had little time to think about the jongleurs, but he was glad to know they were close; it was one less thing to worry about. They seemed to be jovial enough and the children he saw in the wagon were respectfully silent while their leader spoke. Some jongleurs, he knew from experience, were a rowdy lot, but this band, even in York, was different. It was something he could not put a name to, yet he decided he preferred his entertainers like this. *Perhaps I should offer them protection so they would come here often. Or perhaps a place which they could call a home; surely even jongleurs have homes.*

As if he could read his earl's thoughts, Jamie trotted up beside him. "If they perform well, my lord, you might offer them shelter for the winter; 'twould be nice to have jongleurs in the bleak times."

Durham laughed aloud. "I thought much the same thing a moment ago. I shall mention it to the lady and see what she thinks. Bess knows more about these things than I." Smiling, he urged his destrier into a trot. "Come, let us reach Aycliffe before they send out a search party!"

The jongleurs camped that night near a stream. Satisfied everyone was well prepared for the coming days, he settled himself against a log and, lute in hand, began singing songs of their homeland. The children, wrapped in their cloaks and positioned as close to the fire as they dared, were lulled by the low sweetness of his voice. Soon, the little eyes were closed and even the adults found themselves drowsing. Alonso finished his song and stretched. He called to one of the men still sitting upright near the fire. "Take the first watch, Diego. Wake me when the logs fall." He did not wait for an answer; he simply drew his cloak about him and closed his eyes.

He had been asleep for what seemed to be only moments when Diego shook him gently. Alonso opened his eyes and immediately saw Diego's fingers against his lips. "*¿Qué pasa*?" he whispered.

"Horsemen, Alonso. Not ours."

"Where?"

"North. On the hill above the bend in the stream."

"How many?"

"Four, perhaps five; I could not tell."

"Are they armed?"

"One is a knight; the others, henchmen. They carry no banner."

Alonso rose silently, woke Kassim and they both followed Diego to the point where he first heard the strangers. Crawling along on his belly, Alonso crept as close as he dared to the encampment, then listened as best he could to their conversation. The voices carried in the night air, but even so, Alonso had to work hard to understand their guttural Norman expressions. Although he spoke French with ease, this dialect was difficult to decipher at his safe distance. When he dared to look down into the camp, he counted five men at arms and a smaller, thinner figure in a long, dark robe. "A priest?" he asked Diego and saw his comrade nod.

"You are well paid for your intelligence," the dark knight growled at the monk. "You have no complaint."

"And you will have no land if you do not dispatch him to hell before the queen arrives," countered the monk. "If you let Durham live long enough to entertain Eleanor, you are assuring his continued popularity. Get rid of him now."

"What do you know about it, Roman clerk? You are not English yourself."

"But I am skilled in the maneuverings of men. Mark my words, Gaston d'Artois; you will have nothing if you do not move against him before the court crosses onto Durham land. Kill him when he is alone, and then play the hero. You do know how to do that, do you not?"

The knight's face was mottled in the firelight. "What are you implying?"

"I imply nothing; you are experienced in treachery. Your history is not as well hidden as you would believe. You were seen injuring your own foot."

"I should kill you in Durham's stead."

"And if I die, my parchments will be read by the archbishop when they clean out my cell. That would not help your cause," spat the monk. You will do what is necessary to consolidate your position on behalf of John."

"There is more to this than you are saying, brother. What is it that you want?"

The monk's eyes narrowed dangerously as he replied. "I want the woman."

"Ha! You are a monk. Where are your vows of chastity?"

His voice was a whisper in the darkness. "Do not be a fool, d'Artois. I do not want the whore in my bed. I want her in the ground."

Kassim heard enough and motioned to Diego to follow him back to the camp. "How much did you understand?"

"Enough to know a wise word needs be put in the right ear."

Kassim nodded in agreement. "How far is the master from here?" He was certain Diego would know the location of Khalil's camp.

"A half-league to the south."

"Can you find your way there?" Kassim asked Diego.

Diego nodded as he cast his eyes upward toward the moon. "It will not be difficult." He tucked his knife in his belt and pulled his hood over his head. "I shall be back before first light."

The moon was still high when the dark-robed man remounted his donkey and set off into the night. He was not afraid of the night; he preferred it. At night, he would meet no parishioner in need of sacraments; he could ride in solitude. And on this night, time was most important. He must reach Durham before dawn, before he was missed. Slapping the little donkey's rump, he urged him into a trot. It mattered not to him the method of Durham's undoing, only that he be undone before the queen arrived. It was enough to know Durham would be dispatched to hell and the whore would follow him. She had no right to live; it was her desertion that brought the plague to their house. It was her selfishness that caused his parents to lose the will to live. And if he died in the act, it would be the sanctification of God's name.

Gaston d'Artois lay apart from the others. Hands locked behind his head, he stared up at the canopy of stars in the sky. As a boy, he used to try to count the stars, but that task was no more possible than reaching up to grab one. Dispatching Durham to hell was not his idea; it was Prince John's. The prince wanted him away from his mother and out of the way.

He left Artois with the intention of returning as a knight, with all the power and prestige that came with the title. He intended to replace his brother and succeed his father as Comte d'Artois. He succeeded in ridding himself of his weak elder brother on the battlefield outside Akko. Upon returning, however, his succession was no longer guaranteed. The late Comte d'Artois led an ill-fated attempt to wrest Burgundy from the current duke and failed. Disinherited, discredited, and disenchanted, Gaston d'Artois left his former home with every intention of returning in power to demand restitution of family land.

Intentions, however, were no more reliable than clouds and now, instead of crusading against the infidel in the Holy Land, he was sowing fear and distrust amongst nobility and peasantry alike, smoothing the way for Lackland's ascension to the English throne. He understood the position of younger son and disliked it as much as the Prince. If he were to succeed in his own quest, he had best toss his lot in with he who could sympathize as well as bestow. Prince John, for all his shortcomings, was just such a man. John intimated if Durham was dispatched, Durham would be his. The new information provided by the strange foreign monk was unexpected.

Perhaps I shall kill the monk and keep her for myself, he thought; *she is said to be a saucy piece, at that.* If all went according to plan…if all the pieces in the puzzle fit…if nothing went wrong…. Closing his eyes, he allowed himself to sleep.

Gilbert chose to camp with his men on Aycliffe's land. Even as a boy, he never minded sleeping on the ground; he loved looking up into a star-studded sky, picking out the few constellations he knew. Now, he squatted beside the fire and poked the dying embers with a stick. Sparks flew into the air, little stars flying up into a sky full of little diamond specks and he wondered for a moment if they had once been part of a divine fire. All around him his men lay sleeping; the cacophony of snores was loud enough to keep the birds awake in their nests. In the waning moonlight, he spied his two sentries exchange greetings before moving in separate directions. Durham knew he should be sleeping, but he could not close his eyes.

Much weighed on his mind, not the least of which was Eleanor's impending arrival. Every other time the royal caravan sojourned at Durham it was his father who sat beside the crown. He recalled the times when Eleanor would come with Henry and then the times when Henry would come without his queen. He was young, but not so young as to be unaware of the strife between the royal couple; still, young Gilbert was partial to the steel-spined queen. All he wanted now was for Eleanor to come, not as the queen, but as his great-aunt, and give her blessings to his union with the Lady Elizabeth. If Eleanor spoke on their behalf, he was certain his mother would cease her objections.

He poked the fire again, sending a second column of sparks into the night sky. Tossing the stick into the embers, he went to lie down.

Wrapped in his cloak, Khalil leaned against a boulder and stared out over the rolling hills cast grey by the moonlight. Near him, Rashid knelt on a small rug quietly chanting verses from the Qur'an. In this strange place, the singsong recitation warmed the amir. He could not deny that England was lush and beautiful, yet it was alien in landscape to his world. If this chill was summer, he could barely imagine winter in such a place. He wondered if they took water for granted.

A rustle caught in his ear and Khalil silently slid his sword from its sheath. He saw Rashid do the same. The rustle grew louder. Before he could move, Rashid sprung from his rug and lunged toward the sound… then laughed. From the tall grass, two men emerged.

Diego touched his fingers to his heart, his lips, and bowed. "*As-salāmu ʿalaykum.*"

"*Wa-'alaykum salaam,*" replied Khalil. "Is there news?"

Diego related what he and Alonso had seen and heard. "We do not know what real danger they pose to Amirat Batsheva, but we both felt you need to know of their presence."

"This queen who approaches…she allows him free movement in her lands?"

"No one seems to have control over him, my lord," Diego shrugged; "his master is the displaced son who is not in England."

"Who rules this place?" snapped the amir. "Are they so disorganized that one hand knows not what the other does?"

"When you are at the front with Lord Salah, are you able to know what takes place in every wadi? You hope your sheikhs and sharifs do as they are instructed to keep the peace. It is no different here."

"There is some wisdom in removing one's brothers," he growled.

"That may be, my lord, but it is not the way here. A younger son may be settled with smaller lands and retain a position of power within the council."

Khalil rubbed his chin thoughtfully. "There is too much strife and dishonor in this place." Khalil's wry smile was white in the darkness. "Perhaps we should look to England for our next conquest."

"And stay through winter?" laughed Rashid. "Besides, who would want to civilize these people? I have no stomach for their habits."

Khalil agreed. "I will be happy to board a ship home."

Diego remained for a while longer then, when the moon had disappeared from the sky, he rode as fast as he dared; he wanted whatever sleep he might be able to snatch. And as he rode, he wondered if perhaps he was wrong not to tell Khalil of their encounter with Gilbert, Earl of Durham.

Batsheva awoke with a jolt. The room was dark but for the moonlight filtering through the open shutters. Whatever had awakened her had been in her dream and like most of her dreams of late, this one was hazy and foggy with no real definition. She saw Khalil's shadow, she heard his voice calling for her, but she could not see his face. That his image might be slipping from her heart dismayed her.

Foregoing the warm comfort of the bed, she padded across the thick rugs to stare out the window. The sky was still filled with stars, but she could see the tiniest rim of grey on the eastern horizon. She stared in that direction and idly wondered if her children were getting ready for *Farj,* the first prayers of the day. Was Daud rolling out his prayer rug? Who was teaching him *Al Fatihah*? What verses was he learning? A breeze rustled her nightgown and she shivered. Murmuring a prayer for the continued safety of her children, Batsheva crawled back into her bed and pulled up the covers. There was still time for sleeping before the long day would begin.

CHAPTER 43

Durham

JULY 1192

On some mornings, fog and mist wrapped around the English countryside like thick woolen stockings, but on this morning, the sun burst into the sky to push back the night and illuminate the day. Batsheva bustled from room to room overseeing the last small details before ending her tour in the cookhouse. There, she checked on the victuals being made ahead, and reviewed the roasting schedule with the cooks. Everyone was working hard, yet smiles greeted Batsheva wherever she went. They liked the lady who knew their names, rolled up her sleeves, and set to work with them even past the point when sweat soaked her dress. No lady had ever been shoulder-to-shoulder with them, and they loved her for it.

Outriders met Durham and his men early in the day. "The queen rides north at a quick pace, my lord," announced the captain. "They should cross onto Durham land by midday. Your lordship's sister rides at the side of Her Majesty."

This was the first he heard of it. "Margaret?" roared Durham with unexpected ferocity. "What in God's bones is Margaret doing with the queen? Henry's last letter said she would remain in York!"

The man looked perplexed. "I am sorry, my lord, I do not know. She left York with us."

Durham swore none too softly. "Who else rides with the queen?"

"Not as large a company as in the past, my lord; only about four score or so. They will break the journey at Ciltonia as planned. Lady Margaret and Lady Isabella are both mounted. A dozen more ladies follow in coaches."

The swearing increased in intensity; he had not counted on Isabella's appearance, but that would account for Margaret's. Still muttering, he dismissed the rider. "Ride on to Durham Castle to alert my lady." Spurring his horse, he and his men continued south.

The men of Durham stopped to break their fast at Crompton Hall. The earl was delighted by the progress Sir William made in his short tenure as the new laird The hall itself was much improved; the thatch was thick and fresh, and the walls bright with whitewash. The knight's wife had joined him there; just as the land was ripening with new growth, so was the lady. She welcomed the riders with warm bread and pitchers of ale served on trestles in the yard. Beneath a stand of apple trees, the Earl of Durham toasted his host.

"My lord," said Will when the men were eating their fill, "a word with you in private." He led Durham away from the table. "The dark knight, the one we saw near York, has been seen close to here."

"How close?"

"As late as two days ago, my lord, he was thought to be taking shelter at Barnard."

"Are you certain, Will?"

"Aye, as certain as I could be without seeing him for myself. Two of my crofters were to Barnard's market; there they spied a dark-clad knight with no mark on his shield. Although he did not molest them, they were unnerved. 'Tis unnatural to ride with no mark."

"'Tis unnatural to ride without leave of the lord," mused Durham. "But he has stayed clear of Crompton and the surrounds?"

"Aye."

"Then he is for something else. He burned Crichton Wood without a second thought. I cannot fathom what plan he has."

"Nor can I. He is out there somewhere and not to be ignored.

"I agree, Will. I would demand answers myself were I to find him on my lands. My men and I have combed the countryside, still he eludes us. He is almost as a phantom."

"He is flesh and blood, that much is known; he has a scar on his left cheek and a nasty one at that. He favors one leg. He's been touched by someone's sword although not handily enough if ye ask me."

Durham laughed and clapped Will on the back. "Again, old friend, I agree. Let us see if we cannot dispatch him today. I have an odd sense that we shall see him on the road."

"I would join with ye if ye would have me, my lord," said the knight. "'Tis not every day the queen comes to Durham lands."

"Then saddle your best horse and come along. I would be glad to have your skillful sword arm at my side once more, but leave your best here for defense."

The two returned to where the men now stood swiping the crumbs from their tunics and the last drops of ale from their lips. At the word from their lord, the men mounted their horses and left Crompton Hall.

The old queen enjoyed nothing as much as a ride through her realm and, on this day, she was content with the appearance of the lands around her. As they passed through villages and hamlets, the people greeted her lovingly, something she never took for granted. With Margaret by her side, she even paused now and again to receive posies proffered by freshly scrubbed children.

Margaret, Countess of York, received a warm welcome home once she was recognized. As they approached Durham's holdings, the eldest daughter of the late earl was cheered by those who remembered her from her youth.

"Would that your own people greeted you, Isabella," commented the queen dryly to the lady on her other side. "You would do well to ask Margaret how she has managed to retain her popularity."

"Yes, madame," Isabella grimaced as she managed to force a smile. When the queen trotted ahead, Isabella drew closer to Margaret. "Did you attend the sick and dying, Margaret," she queried, "or do they simply recall the days you rode bareback through the countryside with your skirts flying over your hips?"

Margaret checked her annoyance as she answered, "What they remember, Isabella, is an earl and countess who cared for them with honesty and without guile. They recall my father's insistence that his children know our people and how they fare. Perhaps if you took an interest in your late husband's people, you would ensure your son's continued good health in Lincoln." She did not wait for a rebuttal; Margaret simply tapped her mount and moved up to join the queen.

"Has she piqued you, Margaret?" Eleanor asked curiously.

"Not really, although I confess I would prefer not to be left alone with her. I find her conversation…inappropriate."

"What you find, my dear niece, is her conversation is trivial and lacking merit. Do stop being so serious, Margaret. Surely, Henry must find it tiring."

"I am not so serious at home, ma'am," she protested, then, she laughed at the sound. "'Tis true, I am serious by nature, but my children will tell you we have a jolly household. I grow more serious near to you, Your Majesty, because you, yourself, are like-minded."

"That may be, but we still enjoy a good bit of gossip. We do laugh now and then."

Margaret reddened. "Should I be listening more to Isabella's prattle, ma'am?" she asked.

"Far be it from us to instruct you, dear Margaret, but we have learned over a lifetime that interesting information may be passed in most unusual ways. If it were our brother who was the quarry, we might spend a little more time listening so that we may be prepared for whatever cunning she has in mind." Eleanor smiled knowingly.

Margaret sighed. "Thank you, Aunt Eleanor, for your wise guidance."

"Do not thank me until after your brother is safely wed to the lady of *his* choice." Again, the queen smiled. "I am neither so old nor so blind as to be unaware of the intrigue which plagues Durham with or without his knowledge. Gilbert has always been close to my heart, much as your Edward is now. I care greatly for both uncle and nephew and 'twould pain me to see either of them caught unwittingly in a net. I would rather see them wed according to the conventions of the crown," she sighed before she added, "and each according to his heart."

"But what of Elizabeth, Your Majesty? Surely she would not be your choice for Gil?"

"She is a fine match for him." Eleanor turned her head just as Isabella drew her mare close to the queen. "Wouldn't you agree, Isabella?"

"Agree to what, Your Majesty? I'm afraid I have not heard the proposition."

Margaret saw the queen's brow rise slightly and she hid her own grimace when Eleanor asked Isabella whether or not she thought Lady Elizabeth to be a good match for Durham. And she bit back her laughter when Isabella's face flamed red.

"Elizabeth *is* a lovely child, Your Majesty, but her age is so…tender. I fear the demands of Durham may be beyond her…experience."

"Oh?" breathed Eleanor. "Many a tender-aged lady marries into an august position. If the lady is intelligent and sweet tempered, there is no reason why she would not grow, as it were, into the job. And, after all, Elizabeth does have the benefit of Lady Matilda's wisdom." She glanced briefly at Margaret. "Your lady mother must be much relieved to have Elizabeth at Durham."

Before Margaret could comment, Isabella gushed, "Oh, but Lady Matilda is much concerned over Elizabeth, Your Majesty. She thinks the girl rather…headstrong."

"How came you by this intelligence, Isabella?" the queen asked quietly. "We have not heard this."

"From the Archdeacon of Canterbury, ma'am. He inquired about the girl."

"Why would he ask you?" demanded Margaret.

"Because I am well acquainted with her," she wasped. "You are not the only one who has spent time with her, Margaret."

Margaret's mouth, poised to say something, snapped shut.

Not blind to the animosity between them, Eleanor allowed a small, indulgent smile and gently changed the subject. "Tell me, Margaret, has Edward spoken to you of Rochford's daughter, Alice?"

CHAPTER 44

Durham

JULY 1192

From a wood-covered hill, Khalil watched the road stretching to the south. Directly to the east, he saw a clutch of buildings and a troop moving away from the cluster. At the first crossroads, the troop paused before six of them continued west, leaving two knights alone. They cantered up a grassy hill and stopped, giving them an unobstructed view of all four roads.

"The one in the blue tabard, master, is Durham," Rashid said to Khalil. "He sits atop the hill and watches."

"Why does he not ride with his men?" asked Kassim.

"He is awaiting the queen. His men will ride ahead to announce his presence nearby. Seems an odd protocol, but it is proper by their standard."

"Even though she acts for King Richard," added Yusef with authority, "Durham as sheikh will invite her onto his lands at the border."

Khalil smiled at his little Englishman. "They are most polite, these English lords. They seem to put much stock in decorous behavior."

"It is more than that, my lord," Yusef explained. "Her Majesty puts much importance on this."

"I learned as much from the prisoners we took in Palaestina. I cannot say I comprehend their ways, but they are interesting to observe. For now, we shall stay here; the vantage is good."

Durham shaded his eyes against the bright sun and scanned the open road for the first sight of Eleanor's banner. "She moves too slowly," he groused to Sir William beside him. He wanted her on Durham lands the sooner the better.

"She is old and traveling with too many ladies, no doubt," chuckled the knight. "And we already heard she is on horseback."

Durham laughed aloud, "Not even God could hurry Eleanor if she is of a mind to dawdle. I shall wait here; you go on to the south, but at first sight of her entourage, ride back to me. I'll meet her at Scotch Corner."

"As you wish, my lord," agreed Will. He left the earl on the hilltop and cantered off.

Exhausted and more than ready to nurse Miriam, Batsheva made her way to her own chamber that she would soon be sharing with the children, Mary, and Lydia. Not that she minded, especially since Anne was so excited to have them all together. She opened the door to find Anne sitting at the dressing table while Mary was braiding her hair in an intricate design.

Anne's face was immobile, but she did not complain at all. "We are trying a new style, Bess," she said through tight lips. "I do not dare move."

"You look so grown up, Annie!" She brushed a kiss on the top of her head as she flew by. "I shall just wash a bit before I feed the babe. Where is she?

"With Lydia in the garden," said Mary, never taking her eyes off Anne's hair.

She beckoned to one of the chambermaids hovering near the door. "Fetch Lydia and Miriam, please," she ordered sweetly, "then bring the basket of herbs I left in his lordship's solar. You'll find it on the table."

"Yes, ma'am," replied the girl, bobbing a curtsey before she scurried from the chamber.

Batsheva joined Anne at the dressing table. "I think, sweet Anne, you have the most beautiful hair in all England."

"Grandmother says it will darken as I get older."

"You father's hair is the color of wheat in the autumn. Perhaps yours will be like his."

"Oh, I do hope so, Bess," blushed the girl. "I think he is very handsome."

"Aye, that he is; he is a very handsome man," she admitted as she went to strip off her dress in favor of a robe.

"Was your late lord handsome like Papa?"

A question asked in innocence, caused a pang in Batsheva's heart. She stood in silence for a moment as she composed her answer. "My lord was very handsome, as dark as your father is fair. If two men could be night and day, then they would be your father and my late lord. The poets say that beauty is in the eye of the beholder, and I think we each see beauty in those we love."

"Charlotte says her mother preens like a peacock because she wants to be pretty. I think she has a hard look about her."

The astonishing statement caught Batsheva off-guard. "Perhaps the lady's life has not been easy."

"Yours has been terribly difficult and sad, yet you do not look hard. Nay, I think her meanness makes her brittle."

"Annie! How came you to that thought?"

"My tutor says a lady is judged by her inner beauty as seen through the window of her eyes," answered Anne, her eyes still trained on the polished silver mirror. "If a woman's eyes are dull and lifeless, then her soul is timid and she fears her own mortality. If her eyes are warm and full of kindness, then she is inspired by the Holy Mother herself. But if her eyes glitter like ice, then her soul is lost to the devil because she is a cruel woman who thinks only of wealth and power. Since life is a fragile thing, she will break from her hardness. Brittle, you see."

"I see. I also see this new tutor is teaching you a wide range of subjects other than numbers and letters."

"Fra' Giovanni says a woman needs to know of these other things to run a good Christian household, Bess. Did you not learn these things from your mother?"

"I learned tolerance from my mother," replied Batsheva dryly, "and would hope you shall learn the same from me. One cannot judge others by what one thinks one sees. There are times the eyes may glitter like ice, as you say, when one suffers from a fever. Does that mean the lady is evil?" When Anne did not answer, Batsheva went on. "I fear Fra' Giovanni is very young and full of exuberance for his ideas." Batsheva sat down in her favorite chair. "I hope your tutor will honor us with his presence at the banquet for her majesty."

"I have asked him if he will come and he answered he would be honored to simply be in the same city as Queen Eleanor. He is most anxious to behold her majesty from afar; he says he would be blinded if he came too close."

"I am anxious to meet him, Annie sweet. If he is one tenth as illuminating as you say, he will be a welcome addition to the company." Lydia arrived with Miriam, and Batsheva happily took the squealing infant. "And now, let us all have a moment of peace and quiet before we walk with your grandmother."

D'Artois knew the land well enough to know there were places from which he could observe Durham without being seen. He sent his men on to Nottingham; he did not trust their ability to remain silent and hidden. Their constant noise alone would jeopardize the mission, and he was not willing to do that. Keeping to the edge of the forest where he could see out while still hidden, he remained in the forest, slowly making his way toward Scotch Crossroad where he was certain Durham would greet the queen as she entered his lands. The faster he dispatched Durham, the faster he could be declared the hero and be on his way to Nottingham where the bailiff would attest to the deed in the name of Prince John. If the old queen didn't reward him with Durham straight away, John, when he became king, would.

The crossroad was deserted when D'Artois arrived, leaving a clear view in all directions. Helmet on and shield up, he remained hidden in the tall undergrowth, the canopy of trees further shading his presence until he felt confident that he had command of the crossroad. He did not see Durham on the hill behind him.

But Durham saw him. Moving out of the line of vision, he let his horse pick his way halfway down the grassy knoll. He waited until the knight was exposed at the center of the cross before he hailed him from a position of advantage on the hill. "Identify yourself!" he called to the dark knight, rising in his stirrups.

The dark knight saw Durham and swore as he raised his visor. "Must we play that game again, Durham? You know who I am and what my business is."

"You ride my lands now, sir."

"I ride the king's lands, Durham. Yours is but temporary stewardship and soon to be relieved of that. When John is king…and know you that he will be so crowned…I shall have Durham and you, my dear earl, will already be dead."

Durham's fingers gripped the sword until his knuckles turned white. He would not be baited into beginning swordplay, but he was prepared to separate the knight's head from his shoulders if attacked. "State your business, sir."

The dark knight weighed the options in answering the question. "I have business with the queen."

"In the middle of the road? Her Majesty does not transact the business of state with strangers on a road."

"Perhaps you would prefer I come to Durham?" he asked, his voice dripping with malevolence. "Or would that upset your little red-haired infidel whore?"

Durham rode into the crossroad as he raised the hilt of his sword. "I know not who you are, but you are unworthy of the title of knight."

"Do you challenge me, Durham?" he sneered.

"Do not tempt me, for you will lose."

"You leave me no choice, Durham, but to challenge you," d'Artois shouted. "Prepare to die, Gilbert of Durham, for that is what you shall do on this day," before he dropped his visor.

Lowering his own visor, Durham drew his sword as he wheeled his horse around. Without missing a beat, he charged the other knight. The clang of metal against metal shattered the stillness of the summer's day.

From his vantage point on the opposite hill, Khalil watched as the knights battled. The two seemed evenly matched, but the amir did not like the way the dark knight aimed low towards Durham's horse on several maneuvers. Whatever feelings he had toward Durham, he was not about to let him die. Slowly, he began to move into a better position, keeping his eye on the action. He signaled to Kassim and Yusef to remain hidden but close enough to enter the battle if necessary.

Gilbert drew first blood, but it was not enough to stay the other knight's powerful swing. He heard d'Artois laugh and saw him draw the broadsword back in preparation for the next strike. Reining his destrier in a tight circle, Gilbert moved to avoid the blow, but the edge of the sword sliced into the thick padding over his mount's neck. The animal screamed as he faltered, nearly unseating his rider as his leg muscles spasmed below the wound.

Rearing up despite the weight on his back, the horse shook off the pain as he leapt forward, his hooves coming down precariously close to the dark knight's mount. Gilbert's sword made contact with his adversary's shield, sending waves of vibrations through his body. D'Artois pushed back as he raised his sword; the side slammed into Gilbert's helmet before the blade sliced through his mail hauberk. The earl slipped dangerously in the saddle.

A shout in the distance caused d'Artois to twist around, giving Gilbert the moment he needed to right himself in the saddle. But it was too late. His destrier, losing ground, stumbled; Gilbert leapt from the saddle and barely escaped being caught beneath the huge animal. On foot, he charged the dark knight, thrusting his shield upward into the oncoming horse's neck. Durham jumped backward when the animal reared but was not quick enough. Hit in the shoulder by the raised hooves, he was knocked to the ground. Only a quick roll away from the horse saved him. Then he saw the second knight charging toward him.

Spurring his horse, Khalil raced toward the crossroad, his shield now raised and his sword out of its scabbard. With a roar, he charged the dark knight. Khalil's sword whirled above his head once, twice, three times before he was close enough to the dark knight to make contact. Without giving him time to recover from his mount's rear, Khalil crashed into him, throwing the dark knight from the saddle. Khalil rode past the place where the dark knight lay sprawled on the ground. As he came around for a second attack, he saw Durham on his feet heading for the dark knight.

The dark knight rose and recovered his sword. He saw Durham rushing toward him, sword in position for combat. Standing his ground, he steeled himself for Durham's attack. Metal clanged against metal as two swords met again and again. Durham's wound was costing him both strength and mobility. D'Artois had Durham at a disadvantage; he was pushing the earl hard and Durham was losing ground. As he maneuvered Durham so that his face was to the sun, he saw the red stain spreading across the earl's tunic. A few more parries and the earl would be dead. He could see the trench behind Durham, and he continued to push Durham toward the edge.

Khalil saw Durham's boots dangerously close to the trench. Without a second thought, Khalil leapt from his horse to push himself between the dark knight and Durham just as the earl fell.

Durham felt himself falling slowly backward and prepared for the bite of the knight's sword through his entrails. When he realized the sounds of the battle continued without him, he painfully raised his helmet as he struggled to regain his stance. In the road he saw the dark knight battling another knight; through the cloud of pain behind his eyes, Durham tried to discern who had come to his rescue. He did not recognize the armor nor the shield. Grabbing at the dirt and weeds, he pulled himself to the edge of the trench before he succumbed to the pain and his world was swallowed by darkness.

Khalil had the advantage: he was not injured. His opponent was tiring, and the amir considered disarming him in order to capture him for Durham's pleasure. The thought disappeared from his brain when a well-placed blow turned the helmet and forced the dark knight to yank it off. Khalil to stared intently into a pair of cold, black eyes. "You!" he shouted, almost unwilling to believe what he saw.

Recognition came to d'Artois at the same moment. "I thought you were dead." He circled slowly, his sword ready to strike at the first opportunity.

"Your master wished me dead. Allah does not grant the wishes of fools."

"Your wife is Durham's whore. She spreads her legs for anyone who asks. Better to join with me and take your revenge."

He was being baited; to lose his temper was folly. "Foolish words from a foolish man. You should have stayed in Palaestina and died feigning honor for your family. You bring nothing but shame on your house."

"What do you know about it, Saracen?" he snarled.

"I know you are a traitor to the English king. But then, you were a traitor to your own lord as well. You killed another knight from behind in battle, then turned your sword on yourself. Whatever glory it is you seek, it will not come to you, for you are a coward." Khalil spat at his feet. "Your blood is not worthy of my saif."

D'Artois lunged at Khalil, but the amir moved gracefully aside. Ever the practical one, Khalil saw no reason to toy with the vicious stranger and, without so much as a warning shout, he spun around and neatly separated d'Artois' head from his shoulders.

Taking a moment to fill his lungs with air, Khalil looked up to see Kassim and Yusef riding toward him. Not knowing Durham's condition, he waved them off. Khalil approached the earl and squatted, a painful but necessary position, as he held his hand beneath the earl's nose. The warmth of breath was still coming from him. As gently as he could, he turned the body to examine the wound. It was oozing blood from beneath the mail shirt; using his knife, Khalil sliced through the laces, pulled the sleeve off, the opened the side of the shirt to see the second wound. He cut a strip of cloth from the bottom of the stained tabard and tied it tight around Durham's arm just above the wound. Then he returned to his horse for his kit bag and water skin.

With another strip of cloth taken from the edge of the tabard, Khalil washed both wounds, clearing the dirt as best he could. He pulled a small clay vial from his kit and pressed salve into each cut. Durham groaned yet his eyes remained closed. Khalil dribbled a little water onto the earl's lips and watched as they moved slightly. Satisfied he had done as much as he could, he left Durham alone for the moment.

Durham's huge battle steed was skittish. Khalil spoke softly to the horse as he crept close to the frightened animal who sidled away, but not too far. Extending his hand, he let the horse sniff at him before he dared approach. Once the animal was satisfied this stranger was not out to harm him, he let Khalil lift the quilted blanket. Thick padding had prevented the injury from being fatal, but Khalil knew if he did not clean the cut and apply salve to staunch the bleeding, the horse might die. Using the blanket, he pressed against the cut as hard as he dared, slowly increasing the pressure until the horse ceased moving. With his free hand, he scooped more of the salve from the vial and applied it. The horse startled at the slight burning sensation, but Khalil's continual smooth talk seemed to calm the beast.

"Is he all right?"

Khalil's head snapped up at the sound of a voice, but the horse only nickered. "Again?" asked Khalil as he turned to face Durham, who now sat upright in the ditch.

"Is he hurt?"

Khalil thought for a moment before he answered, "Yes, he is hurt. It is not...important."

Durham looked at Khalil strangely; he did not quite understand what he meant. "Will he die?"

"*Non.*"

Durham managed a smile that seemed more of a grimace…anything else hurt too much. "*¿Parlez-vous français?*"

"*Un peu,*" replied Khalil as he limped toward Durham.

"Are you hurt?" Durham asked as he managed to pull himself up to standing. He saw Khalil shake his head, then he saw the helmetless head sitting across the road from the knight's body. "I would know who you are."

"*Je suis,*" pronounced Khalil slowly, "Don Carlos de Granada."

"I am Gilbert, Earl of Durham. I owe you my life, Don Carlos." He studied the dark, bearded man for a moment. He knew Spaniards to be swarthy and this one certainly was that, but there was something about him that Durham could not name, an odd familiarity. "Have we met?"

"I do not think so, Gilbert, Earl of Durham."

Durham took a tentative step toward his rescuer; he stumbled, only to be caught up by the man's powerful grip. "I fear I am weaker than I thought."

"We rest here," announced Khalil. "Your men…come?" He helped Durham to a grassy spot beside the road.

"My men?" asked Durham warily as he sat down again. "You know then I am not alone?"

White teeth flashed in a quick smile. "You await your queen."

Durham's glance betrayed his surprise. "How know you this?"

"This is known, Gilbert, Earl of Durham."

"Are you seeking audience with her?"

Khalil, unsure of the question, he asked Durham to repeat it. "My command of your language is poor," he recited as Yusef had taught him.

"You speak French well enough. My lady speaks your tongue. She can translate for you. Come to Durham as my honored guest."

A tight smile crossed the amir's face. "I am honored, Gilbert, Earl of Durham." The last thing he wanted was to like this man.

CHAPTER 45

Durham

JULY 1192

Hoofbeats were in the distance. "Outriders," groaned Durham, trying to stand.

Sir William was the first to reach the crossroad. "My God, Gil! What has happened?" He jumped from his horse and ran to the earl.

"I was attacked. This man, Don Carlos de Granada, slew my adversary when I fell."

Sir William walked over to the body and stared down at it. "'Tis the dark knight. Did he name his purpose?"

"No. Only that he meant to kill me."

"Gaston d'Artois," said Khalil, picking up the head by the shock of black hair. "He is traitor to his king. He is for the brother prince."

"John," spat Durham. "That much we knew."

Sir William was staring at Khalil. "Have we met, my lord?" he asked suddenly. "You look familiar to me."

Khalil stroked his beard thoughtfully for a moment; all the English looked alike. "No. I have not been in England long."

"Perhaps in the Holy Land? Did you fight for our Lord, Jesus Christ?"

"No. I have not had that…honor." He may have fought, but certainly not for their god.

The knight shook his head. "I must then be mistaken. No matter, I am thankful to God Himself that you happened along. I would lose not only my lord with his death, but my friend as well." Sir William extended an arm to Durham and helped him up. "The queen is but a league behind me. Are you fit enough to meet her?"

"Have I a choice?" chuckled Durham. He glanced down at his blood-stained hauberk. "She will understand, I should think."

Sir William laughed aloud, "Perhaps the queen will, but will Lady Elizabeth?"

"Elizabeth?" echoed Khalil. He wanted to know more, but this needed to be accomplished with delicacy.

There was a definite reddening to Durham's fair cheek. "The Lady Elizabeth is my…fiancée," he mumbled. "She will be distressed when I return in this condition."

"The lady must love you gravely," said Khalil.

"She does. She is a widow, and hard won," managed the earl with a pained look, "and worth the effort. You'll likely agree when you've met her."

"I look forward," said Khalil, his face an impassive mask. He risked neither a smile nor frown that might be misunderstood. "I must leave now."

"Will you not stay to greet her majesty?" the earl asked.

"Tomorrow, Gilbert, Earl of Durham. You are safe now." He bowed toward the earl.

They watched him ride away. "I swear, Gil, I've seen him before," mused Sir William. "Does he not seem familiar to you?"

"Yes, but I cannot place the face. It does not matter. Tomorrow, when Don Carlos de Granada comes to Durham, he shall receive a hero's welcome."

Eleanor was outraged, Isabella swooned, and Margaret trundled her brother into the coach. Assured the wound was more superficial than it appeared, the queen joined them in the coach, where she continued her diatribe against her youngest son and his henchmen. For a while, Margaret and Durham listened in respectful silence but it was clear to Eleanor that neither felt empowered to tell her to cease and desist. At long last, she stopped shouting.

"Has your temper run its course, Your Majesty?" chided Durham gently.

"No, but I think you have both heard enough. I am being forced to take a stand I do not wish to take." She settled back against the seat, her arms folded tightly across her chest.

"Often you have taken this same stand, Your Majesty," frowned Margaret, "and it has little effect. Only Richard will put an end to this treason. When will he return to England?"

Eleanor stared at Margaret. "Do you think I have not sent message after message to him?"

"He needs reminding that he is King of England!" grimaced Durham.

The royal mouth flapped open, then closed abruptly. Through clenched teeth, she said, "We are obviously unable to make the case for his return. If you have any suggestions, Gilbert, we would listen."

"I told him before I left the Holy Land that he was needed at home."

"And did he listen to you any more than me, his mother?" countered Eleanor.

Durham shook his head. "He is stubborn."

"He comes by it honestly enough," snapped the queen. She looked hard at Durham. "You are all stubborn. There isn't a single child in this family who is spared that trait. And you, Gilbert, you are the most stubborn of all." She smiled at him. "I suspect you've met your match in Elizabeth."

He could not help but laugh. "Aye, Auntie, that I have."

With Durham wounded, Eleanor ordered her captain to increase the pace to arrive by nightfall. The jolting coach was not the most comfortable conveyance and soon the queen left for the relative ease of her saddle. Alone with her brother, Margaret quizzed him about their mother.

"She has been brutal toward Elizabeth," he sighed, "but they seem to have reached a stalemate."

"And I suppose Elizabeth has taken a firm stand on her own. Our mother will come 'round, Gil; give her time."

"Bess has been the picture of decorum, all things considered," he admitted, "she's contained her anger and lashed out only at me."

"And you do not mind, do you, Gil?"

"Nay, I think it is good. She's out of her mourning."

"Any word of the children?"

He shook his head. "Only that they are safe." He paused and stared down at the floor of the coach. "I was given her late lord's sword and cape. I meant to give them to her myself, but she found them before I thought the time ripe."

"Oh, the poor thing. 'Twas real confirmation for her that he is indeed dead?"

"Aye, but I think the wound still aches. I never paid mind to women and their musings, Maggie, but with Bess, I find myself more concerned with her thoughts than all others. She will never cease longing for her children but takes comfort in Miriam's presence. I am glad, though, the child is fair. If she were dark…."

"Stop, Gil!" admonished his sister. "You cannot blame the child for the complexion of the father. Besides, you yourself said he was a great leader. She will never know any father but you. Are you man enough to be her father?"

"I do love Miriam," he protested angrily. "I will dower her as my own and see her wed to a man befitting her station as my daughter. Just as I will for Anne. There is no difference between them in my eyes."

"Make certain Bess knows this well, Gilbert, or it will be your undoing." Margaret lapsed into thoughtful silence for a moment. Then she said, "And watch yourself around Isabella. She continues to design for you. You and Bess are not yet wed."

"Thank you for the warning," he growled, "'tis unnecessary. I am well acquainted with her…fantasies." He closed his eyes and leaned back against the leather seat.

The outriders reached Durham Castle as the sun was nearing the horizon. Batsheva threw everyone into a frenzy of activity as they prepared for the arrival of the queen a full day early. Once the wheels were in motion, she ran to her chamber to nurse Miriam and help Anne before she changed.

When the last ribbon was tied in Anne's braid, Batsheva and Anne went to Lady Matilda's chamber. The dowager countess was standing in the center of her bedroom with Rose bustling about her. "Is it proper, my lady, to await the queen here or at the city gate?" she asked politely.

"Here. We shall stand on the steps with Charles and the other ranking members of the household. Have you seen to supper?"

"Yes, my lady. The trenchers are being laid now, but it will be a far simpler meal than what we plan for tomorrow. I would think her majesty will be exhausted after so hard a ride."

"Have the riders explained their early appearance, Elizabeth?"

"No; they merely said her majesty wished to reach Durham tonight. Perhaps she is unwell."

"I doubt it," snorted Lady Matilda. "She is most likely bored with her company." She turned to her maid. "Are you quite finished?"

Rose bobbed her head up and down. "The seams are straight and the ribbons tightly tied."

"Good, then we can go." She swept past Batsheva. She reached for Anne's hand. "Come along, Anne." She stopped at the door but did not turn. "Are you coming or are you standing, Elizabeth?"

"Coming, my lady," sighed Batsheva as she gathered up her skirts. "I am coming."

"I do not see my lord," said Batsheva to the archbishop as the first riders entered the castle.

"Perhaps he rides with the queen," he replied in a calming voice although he already made the same observation. Then he saw Eleanor on her palfrey. He immediately began down the stairs to greet her. "Welcome to Durham, Your Majesty," he said, sweeping into a courtly bow. He crossed the short space between them and reached up to help her from her horse.

"Never mind me, Charles; Gil's been hurt."

Batsheva was close enough to hear her words and her hand flew to her mouth.

"He is in my coach with Margaret, Elizabeth," continued the queen. "He's not mortally wounded, but he does need attention." She waved her hand, dispensing with the formalities.

Batsheva curtsied, then ran past Eleanor to where the coach was rumbling to a halt, leaving Lady Matilda to see to the queen. Without waiting for the footman, she wrenched open the door. "Gil?" she cried.

He managed a lopsided smile. "A minor incident on the road, my love, but you'll be relieved to know the dark knight has been dispatched to eternal damnation."

"You killed him?"

He shook his head. "Nay, not me, but another knight who happened onto our battle. You will meet him on the morrow." Holding onto the frame of the coach, he maneuvered himself out. "See, Bess, I am quite in one piece."

"What I see, my lord, is that you are bleeding through your mail. Jamie!" she called to his squire, "Come help his lordship to my chamber."

Jamie pushed his way through the crowd and slid his arm around the injured earl. "I knew I should nae have let ye go without me," grumbled the squire as he helped Durham up the stairs past his mother and the queen.

Batsheva stopped before Eleanor just long enough to make her apologies, but the queen merely kissed her on both cheeks and sent her on her way before turning to Lady Matilda. "We hope you've treated her well," smiled the queen; "we find her to be an absolute treasure."

"Hrrumph," grumbled the old woman. "I'm most certain, Aunt Eleanor, your opinion would be quite different if it were Richard with whom she had taken up."

"Matilda, that is most unkind; let me assure you, if any of my sons brought home a wife like that, I would be overjoyed. As it is, I cannot say I care for any of my daughters-in-law." She slipped her arm into Lady Matilda's. "Now, let us go have a little sherry in the solar. There is much we need to discuss." She turned to the archbishop. "As for you, my lord archbishop, we shall converse with you later…in private."

Charles grinned as he swept another deep bow. "As you wish, Your Majesty." The grin widened as he watched Margaret step into the breach as hostess to the entourage.

"Margaret will see to the arrival," Durham assured Batsheva as she and Jamie carefully removed the bloodied garments. "She is perfectly able to handle everything."

"I don't recall saying I was concerned," Batsheva snapped as she gently peeled away the shreds of fabric threatening the wound. "Can you raise your arm?"

Durham did as he was told, wincing with pain as he slowly lifted his arm out of the hauberk.

"Who salved and tied your arm?" she asked when she noticed the linen.

"The Spanish knight. He tied it, then spread a balm. He also treated my destrier. I thought that kind."

Batsheva's eyebrow slid up. "Is that unusual…that he would treat the horse?" The only people she knew who did that were Imazighen.

"Yes, I suppose. Perhaps that's their custom. Is there much damage?"

"The wound is not deep."

"I meant to the hauberk," he chuckled.

Batsheva's head snapped up. "I do not give a fig for your armor, my lord." She stormed off to prepare a washing solution of fresh water and herbs. "You are in need of stitching, Gilbert. Lie down."

"I think the lady is annoyed," commented Jamie as he helped Durham over to the bed.

"With good reason!" she shouted from her commode. She tossed a length of toweling at the earl. "Remove all his lordship's bloody clothing, Jamie, then find him a clean nightshirt."

"Yes, my lady," said the squire with gravity. He pulled off Durham's boots then began unlacing his hose.

Supper in the great hall was a subdued affair despite the queen's presence in the castle. At her majesty's request, Lady Matilda arranged for a table to be laid in the queen's outer chamber. There, she and Margaret, along with several other ranking ladies of the retinue took their evening meal with Eleanor. If anyone was surprised when the Lady Elizabeth did not join them, they had the good sense not to mention it; Eleanor saw no need to inquire.

Isabella, however, bided her time while she tasted the dishes set before them. While the other women voiced their approval at Elizabeth's hand in the kitchen, Isabella remained silent, and this sullen silence was noted by both the queen and Margaret.

When a bowl of early berries was served with dollops of clotted cream, Isabella committed her first error. "I had hoped for something more… more…exciting," she commented as she plunged a fat blackberry into the mound of cream set before her.

"And what, Isabella, is the problem with this?" asked Margaret.

"I see nothing wrong with the dish, Lady Margaret, only that it is so…simple."

Eleanor's sigh was long and belabored before she said, "We find a simple fruit to be more conducive to the digestion, Isabella, rather than a more complicated confections we are often forced to endure."

Isabella's mouth opened to respond, but it suddenly snapped shut when Batsheva flew into the room. She curtsied low to the queen. "Forgive me, Your Majesty," she said quietly.

"No need for apologies, my dear Bess," Eleanor smiled warmly. "I trust Gilbert is comfortable now."

"Oh, yes, ma'am. His wounds are properly cleaned and bound; he has gone to his chamber. He begs your forgiveness, but he is not quite up to eating at the moment." She did not mention that he had devoured a good-sized haunch of lamb before Jamie helped him to his boyhood quarters. "He will rejoin the company on the morrow, after a good night's sleep."

No one dared comment on the phrase *his chamber*, but it did not pass unnoticed; especially by Isabella. "Perhaps if I brought him a little sweet cream and berries; when we were children that was always his favorite."

"A kind thought, Lady Isabella," replied Batsheva with a very sweet smile, "but his lordship has taken a sleeping draught and should be asleep by now. I am certain he will be pleased by your tender concern when I relay it in the morning." She turned the smile on Lady Matilda and the queen. "The knight who aided my lord will come tomorrow for the banquet. Is there some proper way to express our gratitude? I am uncertain what the custom would be here in England."

Fascinated, Eleanor asked, "What would be done in your land?"

The smile turned impish when Batsheva replied, "Most likely he would be offered a beautiful girl to add to his household…as well as a chest of gold coin and other valued gifts."

"Barbaric!" cried Isabella. "One cannot *give* a girl!"

"But you do it all the time, Lady Isabella" laughed Batsheva, "under the guise of marriage. This is not so different. The girl can be a politically advantageous match, just as a princess may be to a prince. After all, Lady Isabella, were not you married to a man of your father's choosing to increase his own position?"

Isabella's face mottled visibly. "I loved my husband deeply," she began, but Eleanor cut her off.

"That, Isabella, is a fantasy better saved for your children. You were bound to Lincoln because it suited your father and the crown. Bess, you are correct, however, offering the knight a lady or even gold, for that matter, may well offend. We may offer him lodging, food, provisions and perhaps a gift or two of value, but we do not offer coin in that way. Our hero might take offense. Let us offer him something meaningful…we would certainly decorate him in the name of the Crown. And," mused the queen, "I know of a certain manor in need of a laird. Perhaps our Spanish knight would care to make his home in England and pledge his fealty to this crown." There were murmurs of approval from the ladies. "Yes, that is what we shall do. Of course, if he is unwed, we could offer him a wife to secure the bargain." She looked to Isabella and saw the woman flush red as there began a series of delicate titters from the other ladies.

"Your Majesty, you wouldn't!" she whispered.

Eleanor waved a bejeweled hand. "Who knows, Isabella; he may be very…handsome!"

Before she retired for the night, Batsheva went to check on Durham. When she touched his brow, it was cool; he stirred slightly when her hand caressed his stubbly cheek. His eyes opened slowly. "I am sore, but do not feel ill," he mumbled groggily through dry lips. "Some water."

She held a goblet to his lips. "You shall live in spite of yourself, Gil," she whispered.

"Are you glad?"

"Of course, I am glad."

"How is the queen?" He made room for her to sit on the edge of the narrow bed.

Batsheva quickly told him of the exchange concerning the Spanish knight. "What manor does she mean, Gil?"

"Probably Crichton Wood. Sits empty now."

"And Catherine, what of her?"

"Marry her…to him…if he is without lady." Durham closed his eyes. "Do not fret, Bess. Kiss me and I shall sleep."

She leaned over and touched her lips to his forehead. "Sleep well, Gilbert." He was asleep before she left the room.

Sleep for Batsheva, however, was long in coming. She lay in the big bed, Anne beside her, unable sleep for more than a few moments. Each time she drifted off, her mind filled with images of the twins and Khalil. She would reach out to touch them and they would vanish, and she would awaken. *It is Gil's brush with death,* she told herself, *I fear losing him, too.*

Up with the sun, Batsheva supervised the morning meal before running back upstairs to change into clothes more suitable for a day with the queen. Eleanor had expressed an interest in visiting the archbishop and Batsheva knew she would be required to attend her majesty throughout the day. When she returned to her chambers, Anne and Miriam were just beginning to stir and she immediately put the babe to breast. Lydia helped Anne to dress while Miriam nursed and then, as soon as she could be taken from her mother, she took the babe. Mary had Batsheva's clothes brushed and ready for her mistress. She was lacing the long sleeves when Durham entered.

"Good morning, ladies," greeted the earl as he brushed a kiss on Batsheva's upturned, smiling lips. "All is well here?"

"You are certainly cheerful, my lord," laughed his lady. She noticed his arm was tucked in a sling. "Any pain?"

"Some, although not enough to be bothersome."

"Hunting, however, is out of the question, Gilbert, so do not even think about riding out today."

He looked sheepishly at her. "I had given it some thought."

"Do not. I will tell the queen to forbid it. They can manage very well without you."

"But…."

"Do not contradict me; I will not have you dying of your own stupidity. You were wounded, stitched, and must have some time to heal. If you insist on hunting, you will only open the wound again and probably bleed to death if you did not kill yourself falling from your horse. There is more than enough for you to do here."

"Aye, there is," he sighed dramatically. "I need closet myself with Her Majesty's men to discuss taxation."

"An activity far better suited to your condition."

"And where are you today, my lady?"

"With Her Majesty. We will attend the archbishop this morning and in the afternoon we shall have a picnic near the river. Gwyneth is seeing to the details."

He kissed her again. "Then I shall break my fast in the great hall with the members of the household before I see them off to hunt."

"Make certain that is all you do, my lord," admonished Batsheva with a waggle of her finger. "And I shall make certain you are in your solar with the queen's men."

In a clearing outside the walls of the city, the jongleurs broke their fast and took advantage of the river to bathe and wash clothes. Kassim, Rashid,

Yusef, and Alonso sat apart from the others and listened to Khalil outline his plans for the coming day.

"You are to keep Daud out of the city," he warned. "I would not have her see him before tonight. Rashid, you will go to the market; let us know if anything is amiss."

Rashid smiled, "You are too anxious, master. By the time the moon has risen, you will be with your lady again." He pointed at the river. "Swim, my lord, it will soothe you."

"Later. For now, I would go somewhere now to meditate. I am in need of spiritual refreshment." He saw Daud's look of disappointment that he would not be permitted to go into the market. "Then we shall swim," Khalil added with a tousle of his son's dark curls.

CHAPTER 46

Durham

JULY 1192

Wagons carrying picnic provisions left the castle early in the morning, but the queen and her party did not begin the short journey to the site beside the river until the sun had almost reached its zenith. Batsheva rode Yaffa, causing much comment amongst the ladies.

"She is the most beautiful horse I have ever seen," admitted the queen candidly admiring Yaffa. "How did you come by her?"

"She was a gift from…" Batsheva paused to choose her words carefully, "friends of my late lord. In English, she would be called Beauty."

"A fitting name for her. She seems most devoted to you, Bess."

"She is, Your Majesty. She has saved me more than once." Batsheva leaned forward to pat the mare's graceful neck. "She is a good companion and a good reminder of my home."

There was a wistful quality to her last words and Eleanor, as much as she would have liked to ask another question, sensed the topic would be a painful one for the young woman. Instead, she asked about the strange-looking saddle.

"'Tis a Saracen saddle, ma'am," replied Batsheva. "I confess, I have never mastered the way you and your ladies sit. Is it very uncomfortable?"

"Not once one is used to it," the queen laughed, "although I prefer astride if it were not so…incommodious according to our habit."

Batsheva glanced down at her own position and blushed. "Perhaps I should learn…."

Eleanor cut her off. "There is no need for that! Perhaps you will begin a new fashion. Soon, all the ladies would demand Saracen saddles." In the corner of her eye, she saw Isabella frown. "Come, Bess, show us the path to the river."

At a gentle trot, the ladies left the city of Durham and picked their way down the sloping trail to the spot Batsheva had selected for the royal outing. The place boasted a wide, sandy edge backed with a wider expanse of grass, mown just that morning by several local farmers pressed into temporary service. As the ladies dismounted, grooms led the horses safely away, lest their presence too close bring flies and foul odor. A canopy was set up on the grass, beneath it, a trestle was laden with all manner of foods appropriate for the occasion. Nearby, other smaller tables and chairs were set out. The ladies, led by the queen, admired the repast before Eleanor selected several choice morsels to indicate the picnic could begin.

Queen Eleanor surprised everyone by sitting down in the grass to remove her boots and hose. Hoisting her long skirts up to her knees, she waded into the cool water. Batsheva was the first to follow.

"I can think of nothing more delightful, my dear," whispered the queen to her hostess, "than to stand in the water and watch the fish swim between my toes. It makes me feel positively young again."

"Do you swim, Your Majesty?" asked Batsheva.

"Heaven's no! At least not since I was a child. Then, of course, I would paddle about with my brothers. Do you, Bess?"

"Most assuredly, ma'am. I grew up on the sea's edge and we all loved to play in the salty surf. When we camped near a city, the ladies swim in the public baths. Not to swim would be odd amongst my people."

"I have heard of the baths. There used to be baths such as those here in England, built by the Romans. I cannot image bathing like that now; it seems barbaric!"

"And I think not bathing is barbaric," replied Batsheva lightly. "I miss the baths. They were a place a lady could go to relax with other ladies. One always met one's friends at the baths."

The queen shook her head in disbelief. "Unthinkable. How is it you all did not die of the ague?"

"I do not know, Your Majesty. We were a healthy lot!" She stared out over the water and for a moment, she wondered where Daud and Amina would be swimming on a hot summer day.

The queen's voice brought her out of her reverie. "Let us return to the others, lest they think we have gone mad."

The ladies ate, sang, and played lawn games beside the river. Batsheva sat with Margaret, listening to her tales of growing up in Durham while the queen and Lady Matilda sat on chairs beneath a tree, so deep in conversation that the others were loath to join them. Several of the children dashed along the shore, their laughter splitting the otherwise gentle summer silence.

Margaret shielded her eyes against the sun and watched as Anne played with children her own age from the local gentry. "'Tis good to hear her laugh again," she said.

"She is a solemn child, 'tis true, but she seems to have gained some gaiety since we've been at Durham. I think having her father again is the cause."

"And having a mother, I'll warrant," smiled Margaret. "You've done wonders with her. More than I could have done."

"I suspect she was overwhelmed by your household. She is more used to quiet living…or was until recently. Our own household becomes livelier with every passing day."

It pleased Margaret to hear her refer to Durham as *our own household*; it meant the lady was setting down roots, roots which she might not readily abandon. But still, the subject required discussion, and this seemed the best time to begin. "Have you changed your mind about leaving England?" she asked gently.

Batsheva's sigh came from deep within her heart. "Each night I murmur a prayer for my children, yet each morning I awaken eager to face life at Durham. I have agreed to marry Gil; your uncle says he will perform the ceremony for us as soon as we have permission from the queen and his brother archbishop to the south. You know I have been investigated."

"So I heard. Eleanor wishes to see you married and what she wants, in many ways, is law. Perhaps she will ask Charles to marry you to Gilbert in her presence. There is no greater honor and then, of course, she will expect to stand as godmother to your first child."

The thought made Batsheva shiver. "I had not thought of that." She fell silent for a moment. "There are many things I cannot relinquish. I cannot see…." She dared not voice her next thought.

"You cannot think of baptizing a child, is that not so?" She saw Batsheva's nod. "There are things, Bess, which we must do because we have no choice. Your choices are somewhat limited here. Do you love Gilbert?"

"Yes, I do. Yet, there is something I cannot name nor can I express."

"Gil tells me you know for certain your amir is dead and that the children are safe. But, do you *believe* that?"

She nodded again. "I was sent this." She pulled the chain from beneath her chemise and showed Margaret the locket. "The portraits show me the children as I left them, except Daud's curls have been cut off. If they were not in safe hands, this would not have reached me. I think the sultan knows where I am, and this is his way of telling me all is well."

"But he has not called you home."

"No."

"Then your life is to be here?"

"I believe this might be the intent of the message."

Margaret reached out and took Batsheva's hand in hers. "Then marry Gil, Bess. Make a home for yourself here. You cannot doubt that he loves you."

She shrugged her shoulders. "I think, Margaret, I am waiting for a sign." Before she could continue, Batsheva heard her name being called and saw Anne racing toward her. "You are completely wet, Annie lamb!" she cried. "Have you fallen in again?"

"Oh, no, Bess. We were splashing. I told them you can swim, and they did not believe me. Won't you show us?" she pleaded.

Margaret looked at Batsheva. "You can swim?"

"Of course; cannot you?"

"Not since I was a child."

Batsheva looked toward the river. "'Tis hot. The water does look to be refreshing." She suddenly stood up. With deft fingers, she untied the ribbons on her sleeve and quickly shucked her cote. Her wimple followed in short order. "At least come get your toes wet, Margaret!" she laughed as she took Anne's hand and started for the river.

The other ladies lounging on the grass gasped in shock as they saw the chemise-clad figure dashing toward the river. They saw the Lady Elizabeth stop only long enough to twist tie her skirt before she waded into the water.

"She will drown!" cried one lady.

"We think not!" shouted the queen as she quickly moved toward the bank. Raising her own skirt, she waded into the water again. Behind her, all the ladies were gathering on the shore. A few were shedding hose to join the queen.

Batsheva's head was now above the water as she swam back to where the queen stood. "Forgive me, Your Majesty," she laughed heartily, "I could not resist!"

"Would that we were younger!" the queen retorted with a laugh. The ladies now standing around her suddenly joined in her laughter.

Isabella watched from beneath the awning where Lady Matilda still sat. "She makes a spectacle of herself," she wasped to the older woman.

"Nonsense, Isabella. You would do the same if you had the courage. 'Tis a hot day."

Isabella saw Lady Matilda's smug smile and winced; she had been counting on her support.

Batsheva cavorted with the children for as long as she dared before she finally emerged. Mary was standing nearby with a length of toweling. "Get my cote, Mary," she instructed as she looked about for a place in which she could towel off in privacy. On light feet, she hurried toward a clump of bushes. There, she stripped off her chemise and wrung it out before she began blotting herself with the cloth.

A splash in the distance caught Batsheva's ear. She turned toward the sound and there, at the place where the river bent, she saw a man and boy in the water. The man raised the child in his arms before launching him into the water. She heard the child's giggle and, for a moment, she stood transfixed. The man was swarthy and bearded; the child was dark headed like the man, but even in the distance, the skin was lighter in color. They played happily, oblivious to the presence of the royal party. Then, the man started toward the bank. Batsheva noticed he limped, but it did not seem to hamper his movement. Suddenly, Mary's voice was calling to her. The man stopped and looked in her direction. Batsheva ducked down into the bushes, lest he see her. When she peeked out again, they were gone. But the image of the man and the child coming out of the water stuck in her mind's eye and, for a moment, she almost believed the unbelievable.

The remainder of the afternoon passed in a haze for Batsheva. She was glad when Eleanor announced it was time to return to the castle.

Batsheva found Durham sitting in the solar with several of the queen's councillors discussing the levy. No sooner than the lady appeared at the door, the earl rose from his seat and excused himself from the room. "You are damp," he murmured as he kissed her cheek.

"I swam with the children," she answered with a light laugh.

"I am sorry I missed the sight of you in the water. Did my mother object?"

Batsheva shook her head. "She seemed not to mind, especially since the queen waded into the water after me. But this is of no import. How is your arm?"

"Sore, but I swear, Bess, you have the healer's touch." He raised his arm to show her the range of motion. "Even the side pains me far less than I would expect."

"'Tis the salve, but do not over tax it, my lord Durham, lest you being to bleed again. I would have you rest before the festivities this night."

"With you, my love?"

"Nay, Durham, by yourself. I must check the progress in the kitchens and then I shall nurse Miriam. I shall see you when it is time to attend the banquet."

He frowned but kissed her again. "I shall rest, my love, but 'twould be better in your arms."

She frowned at him. "See that you do rest, Gil. I would not have you falling asleep during the entertainment!" With a wag of her finger, she was gone.

There was barely time enough to dress before the ladies of Durham gathered to attend to last-minute details. Standing at the balustrade above the great hall, Batsheva stole a glance at the dowager countess to gauge her reaction to preparations for tonight.

Torches burned brightly in sconces polished to a high gloss. The banners, colorful emblems of Durham and those families linked to the castle and its master, fairly burst against the newly whitened walls. Above their heads, the enormous iron chandelier was ablaze with 100 wrist-thick beeswax candles. Below, servants scurried to and from the cookhouse, their arms stretched wide with crockery, trays, and plates. On the dais, two women were laying out the queen's personal plate, cup and utensils before the royal seat brought from Westminster. Durham's seat was to her right and Lady Matilda's to her left. The archbishop was to Matilda's left with Margaret on his left. Batsheva would sit on Durham's right with Henry beside her. The seating arrangements, explained Lady Matilda, were dictated more by the queen's whim than by protocol. Batsheva, concerned about the lower tables, asked numerous questions about their arrangement.

"Do not worry so, Elizabeth," instructed Lady Matilda. "They all know where they should sit; the only one new to this is you, and you have dined with her majesty before."

"And the trestles will be cleared before the jongleurs, as it was done at York?" she pressed.

"After the meal is served, there will be a brief promenade in the cool of the evening. In summer, the queen expects a short constitutional. When we return, the trestles will be gone, the benches replaced, and the entertainment shall commence. Gwyneth is well experienced and will direct the change."

Margaret, standing beside Batsheva, rested her hand on the young woman's arm. "All will go smoothly, Bess. Your job will be to smile and nod and converse with my Henry. You know he is affable and will amuse you greatly."

"I hope you are right, Margaret," sighed Batsheva, feeling less than assured.

"I am right, Bess. Wait and you will see; all will go well."

The hall was filled to overflowing with the queen's court, the ranking gentry of Durham, and members of the archbishop's staff when heralds announced the entrance of the earl and his family. Durham entered the hall with his lady on his arm. Behind him, Margaret followed with Henry. Archbishop Durham escorted Lady Matilda. They progressed slowly through the hall, acknowledging friends and vassals alike with small nods of their heads. No sooner had they taken their places at the high board than the heralds' trumpets blew again, and Queen Eleanor appeared at the doorway. Ladies curtsied and men bowed low as the queen moved majestically toward the high board. She stood at her throne for a moment before she gracefully lowered herself into the cushioned chair. Although no one spoke, there was a moment filled with the sounds of wood scraping against the floor as the others took their seats.

Eleanor leaned toward Durham. "We do not see your Spanish friend, Gil."

"Perhaps he changed his mind."

"Or their custom is different from ours," she replied. "He will come when he is ready…and I am ready for him."

Gil raised an eyebrow at the queen. "Dare I ask what you have in mind, Your Majesty?"

"I thought to offer him Crichton; perhaps he would look favorably on Catherine." She looked directly at the woman seated at a trestle table near the wall. "She is a handsome woman and needs to be well married. The Spaniard may be the perfect match."

"That assumes he is not already married...or betrothed at the very least."

"True. Did he tell you his purpose in coming here?"

"To see you, ma'am."

She smiled at him. "Then I anxiously await his arrival." She turned her attention to Lady Matilda.

The banquet progressed without delay; platter after fantastic platter of succulent meats and savories were presented to the queen. Batsheva marveled at the old woman's prodigious appetite as she kept a careful eye on those seated below the salt. From the high level of conversation and laughter, she could only conclude the meal portion of the evening was a success. Still, too nervous to eat, Batsheva barely touched even a morsel of the food that Durham insisted be put on her plate. Henry kept her as entertained as best he could, distracting her as Margaret had promised.

With a nod of her head, Batsheva ordered the remains of the main course cleared. Wine and ale flowed unceasingly as an army of servants removed the enormous platters now reduced to a pile of bones and gristle. There seemed no pause in the conversation until those same servants began to carry huge trays of sweets into the great hall. Custards and pies, towering mountains of fruits and cheese were paraded through the hall before the choicest and most perfect selections were presented to the queen. Eleanor, thoroughly delighted by the display, rose to speak to the assembly.

"We are most pleased by your welcome and your great show of loyalty to our son, King Richard. In this time, when our king battles the infidel on foreign shores for the restoration of the Holy City of Jerusalem, we cannot be more thankful to you, his people, for your outpouring of love and support for our holy cause. We know well the trials and tribulations of war and we take great comfort in knowing you are behind him in his sacred quest. Richard will be heartened to learn that Durham remains a chief jewel in his crown."

The veiled reference to John's attempted coup was not lost on the people seated in the great hall. There were murmurs of approval, and the queen smiled her recognition.

"In that same light, we are also honored to be here, with you and your earl. We count Gilbert, Earl of Durham, as liegeman of great importance. You can only benefit by his recent return from the Holy Land, made earlier by his unflagging loyalty to you, his people. His elevation to earl was confirmed in the Holy Land by our son, King Richard, and now we reaffirm this in your presence." She turned slightly as Durham rose from his seat. "People of Durham, we present Gilbert, Earl of Durham. Long may he live!" She raised her cup and drank deeply of the burgundy brought for the occasion. Her toast was answered with shouts of "Hear, Hear!"

Batsheva sat back in her chair and smiled with smug satisfaction as the meal drew to a close. She allowed herself a few precious minutes of quiet observation; this was her first real banquet, and she was greatly relieved it was a resounding success. In a few moments, the queen would signal the promenade through the gardens while the trestles were removed for the entertainment. Gwyneth had already informed her the jongleurs were on the castle grounds and would begin tumbling on the lawn during the brief interlude. Closing her eyes, Batsheva quickly whispered a prayer of thanks to God for letting her survive this far.

Near the stables, the jongleurs were making final adjustments to their costumes and props. Alonso sat in a quiet corner with Daud, as the boy rehearsed his song. His costume was a parti-colored tabard in red and gold, with bright blue leggings and a cap to match. On his face, he wore a cloth mask that tied in the back, covering only the top of his face. Alonso helped him adjust the eyeholes so he would be able to easily see his surroundings.

When one of the castle servants hurried out to announce the immediate commencement of the promenade, Alonso turned his young charge over to Diego and went to gather the tumbling boys. Daud sat down on a bale of hay beside the older man and sighed.

"Do not be frightened, little prince," whispered Diego. "Soon enough you will be with your mama and all will be right in the world."

"What if she does not know me?" he asked.

"A mother always knows her son, my prince. She will know you."

"What if she does not wish to come home with us? Then we shall leave her here and I shall never see her again."

Diego slid his arm about Daud's shoulders and held him close. "You mother wants to go home. I have this on the very best authority."

Daud looked up at him. "You are certain?"

"Absolutely." Diego saw the little lower lip tremble and the big eyes grow bright with unshed tears. He let Daud nestle against his chest and his heart was filled with tender love for the child. "You have been so brave these last weeks, little prince. Just a few more moments and it will all be over."

Snuffling just a little, Daud tried to smile. "What if I forget the words?"

"You won't, little prince. You won't."

Khalil, Kassim, and Yusef rode unchallenged through the gates of the city. The amir could not help but be impressed by the solid fortifications and, as they rode, he tried to memorize aspects he could bring back to his own city.

Rashid was waiting for them at the deserted marketplace. "You are expected at the castle, my lord. We can leave the horses there. Yusef, you will stay with the animals. They should not be unsaddled, lest we need them quickly. Find the lady's mare and, if possible, arrange to have our horses near the white."

"She would not leave Yaffa behind," chuckled Khalil.

"You will need her to have a mount, since she will be carrying your daughter."

Khalil's eyes grew warm at the thought. "I long to hold my daughter in my arms," he admitted softly. "My children are my greatest joy."

"Beside their mother," Kassim added with a wink. Kassim had not forgotten the night the lady killed his father. His father was a traitor; the amira had his unwavering devotion.

"Yes, my friend, beside their mother." Khalil remounted and, slowly, they made their way back to the castle.

CHAPTER 47

Durham

JULY 1192

Ladies in colorful gowns floated about the courtyard as knights and gentlemen punctuated the scene with more somber hues. Bits of laughter and conversation wafted into the evening air. Archbishop Durham, the queen's arm safely tucked into the crook of his elbow, escorted Eleanor through the well-tended garden. Batsheva took advantage of the crowd to seek out Jane and Rachel who walked with their husbands. Although they had been relegated to a trestle toward the back of the great hall, Batsheva had seen to it that the Vitals had foods they could eat. Rachel, never before in attendance at a royal banquet, chatted excitedly with Jane and Batsheva as they strolled.

When the talk turned to children, Batsheva asked, "Are you feeling ready?"

"Oh, yes. Not much longer, I hope," sighed the dressmaker dramatically. I've not slept in a week."

"She's not slept in a week sewing her frock for tonight," grumbled Jamie with a good-natured chuckle. "She kept making it bigger and bigger."

"To accommodate your son, squire," Jane shot back. "Ooh, this babe is a fierce one. I pray 'tis a boy, for it is most unladylike in its kicking."

Rachel was not to be left out. "And soon enough, I shall join you in the nursery," she said with a loving glance at David. "We shall have another mouth to feed by winter."

There were squeals of delight as Batsheva and Jane hugged Rachel; Jamie simply congratulated his new friend.

"Tell the earl," he instructed David gravely; "he'll see to it that the babe is well founded."

"I need nothing from him," replied David just as gravely, "only a peaceful existence for my family."

"And that you shall have," Batsheva assured them. "Gilbert knows the value of your loyalty and your friendship, David. No matter what happens to me, you are safe."

Jane and Rachel stared at Batsheva. "What could happen to you?" asked Jane.

"Nothing," Batsheva hastened to reply, "I simply meant that your fate is not tied to mine."

Rachel touched Batsheva's arm and instinctively understood. The question, however, could not be asked until they were alone. "David," she said, "I see my father speaking with Sir William. Would you ask him if he will stay for the jongleurs?"

"I think we've been dismissed, squire," laughed David. "Come, let me introduce you to my father-in-law. He is a man well worth knowing well." He steered Jamie toward where the older man was deep in conversation with the new lord of Crompton Hall.

Rachel immediately turned to Batsheva. "Have you a premonition?" she asked.

Batsheva looked at Jane, then at Rachel. "I cannot put a name to it, Rachel, but there is...movement in my soul I cannot describe. It is as though...," her voice trailed off. "Never mind. I am being silly."

The sudden pallor of her face did not impress either Jane or Rachel that it was silly. "Perhaps it is the excitement of the day, Bess," offered Jane.

"And I'm certain you did not eat a thing," added Rachel knowingly.

Someone was calling her name. Batsheva looked up to see Anne barreling toward her, her hair flying. "Anne! Walk!" she scolded when the girl almost crashed into her.

"The jongleurs are here, Bess! They are tumbling on the grass! Come watch them with us. Papa sent me to find you." She tugged at Batsheva's hand.

"I think I must go, ladies," laughed Batsheva.

When she had disappeared into the crowd, Jane said, "Rachel, you know more of these things than I. Is she all right?"

"Yes, I would think so. 'Tis just her imagination playing tricks. Once she and the earl are wed, she will be able to put to rest her pain and get on with living her life completely. So long as she knows her twins are safe, she will be able to live on here, in Durham."

"I hope you are right. There are times I think Bess would bolt if given the opportunity."

Bess would bolt given the opportunity. Isabella was standing just close enough to hear the words. *Why not give her the opportunity?* she thought silently. She spied Archbishop Durham standing near the garden wall talking with a thin monk draped in dull brown. As casually as she could manage, she sashayed her way toward them.

The archbishop greeted her warmly. "Isabella! How goes it?"

The lady dipped a deep curtsey and kissed his proffered ring. "I have come to pay my respects, Your Grace. 'Tis been too long since we've met."

"Far too long, my dear Isabella."

The monk cleared his throat. "If you will excuse me, Your Grace, I would return to the cathedral."

"Heaven's no, brother. Stay and enjoy the jongleurs! Even you need amusement now and again, Fra' Giovanni."

"Are you from Rome?" inquired Isabella politely.

"Venezia, my lady," he replied.

"Fra' Giovanni was just telling me how he's concerned for Gil's immortal soul. He thinks our Lady Elizabeth is too frivolous."

"Elizabeth frivolous?" laughed Isabella. "I should think she is too serious-minded." She wondered if perhaps she had an unwitting ally in the monk. " She turned her great blue eyes on the monk. "Have you had conversation with her, Fra' Giovanni? I do believe she speaks your language as well."

"I have not had the privilege."

"Then how can you say she is frivolous?"

Fra' Giovanni swallowed hard. "She fills the head of Lady Anne with strange notions."

"Oh?" fluttered Isabella, anxious to hear more.

The archbishop, on the other hand, had heard enough. "I shall leave you two to your discussion. Perhaps you will favor me with your company during the entertainment, Isabella."

"I would be honored, Your Grace." She curtsied again.

"Until later, then. And brother, please reconsider and remain for the jongleurs. I'm certain you'll find them amusing."

"Then I shall remain, Your Grace," replied the monk with a bow.

"Good, good." Archbishop Durham left them at the garden wall.

Isabella turned all her charm toward Fra' Giovanni. "Tell me, what does she say to little Anne?"

"She teaches the child to ask questions when a good Christian child should accept her catechism as it is taught. She tells her that belief in God is not enough for grace. This is not so and could easily lead the child from the true path. The Lady Elizabeth does not see the danger in this."

"What is your remedy, Fra' Giovanni?"

"I would prefer not to say, Madonna Isabella."

She put great sympathy into her words. "You may be frank with me, Fra' Giovanni. I have only Lady Anne's best interest at heart; the child is very dear to me and I would be remiss in my Christian duty if I allowed something untoward to happen."

"The child should give thanks to the Blessed Mother for so loving a guardian of her immortal soul, Madonna Isabella," murmured the monk.

"Then tell me what I may do to help."

"The lady's influence should be diminished, if not excised completely."

Isabella thought for a moment. "Has his grace received permission for the marriage?"

Fra' Giovanni's eyebrow shot up as he sputtered, "You…how….?"

"I am privy to a great many things, Fra' Giovanni. I have friends in a great many places and my words are heard in some very important ears."

Fra' Giovanni attempted a tentative smile. "I can see you are a woman of high moral standard, Madonna Isabella."

"And I see we share certain…beliefs."

"This may be true, Madonna."

"I cannot help but think that you would be able to do something about the Lady Elizabeth. After all, you seem to be in good standing with his grace, the archbishop."

He gestured palms upward, "I am merely a guest at the cathedral."

"More than a guest, I'll warrant, Fra' Giovanni; he seems to put some faith in your words."

"True; he has asked my opinion on several matters."

"Why not proffer your opinion to the earl, himself?"

"Oh, Madonna, I could never do that!" he protested.

"The earl would listen to your concerns. He would see there are those who are simply worried for his spiritual well-being. Surely there is no harm in that!"

"Perhaps not, but it would be overly bold for this humble monk to speak on so intimate a subject to his lordship. No, Madonna, I could not do that."

"Then would you speak to Lady Elizabeth directly? I could secure a place for you near to her. Someplace where you might have her ear for a moment."

This was an unexpected opening for the monk. He had been unable to get close to the lady and he knew he would need someone to provide that moment. "Yes," he said slowly, "that might be a way."

"Good, then it's done. Look for me tonight and I will make certain you have your moment alone with her." Isabella smiled at the monk and noticed, for the first time, his eyes were a most penetrating shade of grey. Like hers. "You know, Fra' Giovanni, you resemble her in just the slightest way. 'Tis the color of your eyes, I think."

The slender monk reddened beneath his cowl. "The color of my eyes is common in my part of the world, Madonna."

"Of course, of course." Isabella gathered up her skirts. "Look to me and all will be well."

Fra' Giovanni bowed deeply from the waist. "I am forever in your debt, Madonna. God bless you." He made the sign of the cross.

"Until later, Fra' Giovanni." She gave him a last, very warm smile, and strolled toward where Durham was standing with Sir William.

"Have you seen Elizabeth?" she sweetly asked the earl.

Durham glanced around and spied his lady near the herb beds. "There she is. What mischief are you up to, Isabella?" he growled in return.

"No mischief, my lord. I would simply bend her ear for a moment." Isabella smiled at the two gentlemen with the earl and walked toward Batsheva.

Batsheva saw her coming and groaned inwardly before forcing the corners of her lips upward. "Isabella, are you enjoying the evening?"

"Your banquet was a marvel, dear Elizabeth. I look forward to seeing the jongleurs. But," she pulled Batsheva away from Anne's earshot, "I just met a most fascinating monk and I would beg a favor of you."

"If it is something I could do tomor..."

Isabella cut her off. "It would seem Fra' Giovanni is a troubled man and would seek a word with you in private." She leaned close to Batsheva. "He voiced concern to me about Anne."

"Anne?" echoed Batsheva. "What could he possibly say to you about Anne?"

Her voice dropped to a whisper. "He fears for her immortal soul. Fra' Giovanni says you are filling her young head with...questionable thoughts."

A million sharp retorts flashed across Batsheva's mind, but she bit them back. "I fear there is little I can do for the moment."

"He begs just a word with you, Elizabeth. Won't you take a moment to reassure him?"

"Now?"

"It would just take a moment."

"Perhaps after the jongleurs conclude their performance." Batsheva eyed Isabella suspiciously, but nodded despite her misgivings. "When the guests have departed, I shall meet him in the earl's solar."

The jongleurs twisted and tumbled amongst the gentry, delighting them with feats of acrobatic daring. The boys, all masked, all in brightly striped costumes, moved with alarming speed from trick to trick. Pedro, the littlest tumbler, was tossed from boy to boy like a spinning sack of flour. There were *oohs* and *aahs* as the small body flipped and rolled as he flew through the air. Even Eleanor was applauding enthusiastically.

As twilight faded, servants bearing torches appeared to stand at strategic locations. Soon, however, the jongleurs began to skillfully maneuver the guests back toward the castle. The queen was lured to follow Pedro as he tumbled his way toward the great doors. Batsheva stayed with the queen long enough to be certain she would lead the way back into the hall, then ducked around to go through the kitchen entryway. Skirts in hand, with Mary and Gwyneth scurrying beside her, she hurried through the kitchen, stopping only long enough to shout her thanks for a meal well executed to the cooks. Passing into the hall, she skidded to a stop.

The great hall had been transformed into a carnival tent complete with a myriad of bright banners and ribbons strung from the chandeliers.

Maypoles wrapped with red and gold ribbons stood at the four corners of the playing ground, and a matching canopy had been set over the dais. More ribbons were looped from sconce to blazing sconce, and every bench was festooned with colored cloth.

"Oh, Gwyneth!" cried Batsheva, "it all came together so well!"

"Aye, my lady, 'tis a wonderland! The earl will be well pleased with you."

"With you, Gwyneth!" She squeezed the housekeeper's hand. "I cannot believe how magical it all looks."

The first tumbler was rolling into the hall. He took no notice of the decoration, only of the distance between himself and the playing ground. With a quick glance over his shoulder to check the queen's progress, he flew into a series of flips and rolls. No sooner had he reached the center of the room than the jongleur women seem to materialize from nowhere, their tambourines tinkling as they began to entice gasping gentry into the hall.

Durham escorted Queen Eleanor to the dais. The queen took her seat, Durham on her right and the archbishop on her left. Batsheva sat beside the earl, watching with great personal satisfaction as her guests openly admired the transformation of the hall.

"You're a wonder, Bess," whispered Durham. "I cannot remember a more magnificent banquet."

"Thank you, my lord," she replied. "Let us hope your lady mother is equally pleased."

Suddenly, the leader of the jongleurs leapt into the center of the arena and clapped his hands for attention. The crowd quieted to hear him.

"*Mesdames et Messieurs*," he began with a great, flourishing bow, "we humbly offer an evening's entertainment." There was a rattling of tambourines and the beating of drums. "We are simple travelers, brought here by our gracious host to amuse you all with tricks and tumbles, songs and dances, perhaps a ballad or two." From within his sleeve, Alonso magically produced a huge bouquet of wildflowers and presented them to Queen Eleanor. "With your permission, great and noble queen, we shall commence!"

"Permission granted!" cried the queen and those close enough to see her cheeks spotted a definite blush as she accepted the bouquet from the dashing jongleur.

Alonso bowed again then suddenly sprung backwards, his huge sleeves flying, to herald the start of the entertainment.

The jongleur girls skipped out and began their first dance. They sang and clapped through the complicated flamenco steps, their skirts becoming naught but a whirl of bright color while three of the jongleur men strummed hard against their lutes. The crowd cheered the girls and quieted again when the dancers slowed. Into the flurry stepped Gregor, the jongleurs' best male dancer. With sinuous movements, he danced through the ranks of the women until he selected one, seemingly at random, to dance as his partner. Their arms rose in parallel motion and their bodies moved in synchronous rhythm. The obvious eroticism of their dance was not lost on their audience. All chatter ceased as the dance progressed leaving only the sound of their castanets. All eyes were riveted to the two as they twisted and turned, never touching yet seeming to make love with every fiber of their being.

Unconsciously, Durham reached for Batsheva's hand and squeezed it. "You have set the bar high, Bess," he teased "Others will covet your success forever."

Batsheva rolled her eyes as she leaned toward him, her finger waggling at him. "I fear you make too much of this, Gil. It's only an entertainment." Beyond him, she saw Eleanor clapping her hands and laughing. "I will be happy when it is all behind me," laughed Batsheva. "Very happy."

In the far corner, a knight newly arrived gritted his teeth until his jaw ached. He could see the roll of her eyes from where he stood, and the smile that went with it. He wanted to reach out to capture the wagging finger only to bring it to his lips as he had done so many other times. Instead, he clenched his hands into fists.

"Keep calm," murmured Kassim, sliding close to Khalil. "The moment is almost here. Do nothing." He accepted the amir's silent nod as agreement and moved off.

Daud waited outside the great hall. He did not like all the ribbons of his costume, nor did he like the hat. He hopped from one foot to the other until Diego's broad hand reached out to cease the incessant movement. Daud stood still for a moment then began fidgeting again.

"A prince does not fidget," whispered Diego in Arabic. "Do you need to relieve yourself?"

"No. I cannot help it," complained the boy. "I am bored."

"Be patient, little prince. Before you know it, you will be called to sing."

Daud frowned. "I do not know how much longer I can wait."

The brown-robed monk standing in the shadows was close enough to overhear the brief conversation. *Little prince.* He inched forward to get a good look at the child; instinctively he knew he was looking at his nephew. *If the child was here, the father was nearby.* Moving slowly, he made his way back into the great hall; if he were to reach the whore before Khalil, he needed to be in just the right position.

Batsheva's eyes scanned the assemblage for Rachel and David. She was especially pleased with the Spanish flavor of the jongleurs' dances and hoped they would enjoy them as much as she did. As her glance moved along the back of the room, her eyes encountered a face which looked familiar yet strange. Briefly their eyes met. Tapping Durham on the arm, she quietly indicated where the stranger stood but when the earl looked up, he was gone.

"Perhaps it was Don Carlos," said Durham hopefully. "I wondered if he would come."

Batsheva did not respond; there was something about the way he looked at her which made her feel as though mice were running up and down her spine. Shaking it off, she turned her attention back to the performance.

A magician made doves appear out of air and turned blue kerchiefs bright red. More tumblers performed feats even more amazing than those in the gardens and the dancers frolicked a merry caper to the accompaniment of pipes and drums followed by a fire-eater who swallowed a flaming sword while the ladies shrieked and giggled. When everyone was convinced there could not possibly be anything else, the chief jongleur stepped into the center once more.

"And now, Mesdames et Messieurs, I offer for your enjoyment a change of pace…a child whose voice is so sweet it will warm even the coldest heart in the deepest winter." Alonso stepped aside and Daud approached the dais. He bowed low to the queen, then stood upon a small box set out for him. In the corner, Alonso took up his lute and began strumming softly. Daud waited for his cue, then he began his song.

Upon my lady mother, I have fixed my heart.
My lady mother, the sweetest pomegranate of my father's garden,
Most cherished and beloved, keeps close in my heart
I miss her every day.
Where she walked more flowers bloomed
Oh, my mother, are you lost to us?
Our hands reach out to you.

Daud's eyes met his mother's, and he watched the smile fade from her face. He watched her raise her hand slightly as if to stop him, but he kept singing, kept staring at her.

My lady mother, there is no day we do not weep
Our hearts are heavy with longing for your kisses.
In my heart, I hear your laugh; I see your eyes.
In my heart I see her, my lady mother,
The pomegranate of my father's garden,
As I pray she sees me now.

Not a sound could be heard in the great hall, save the occasional sniffle as the music faded away. Then all eyes turned toward the dais as the lady of the castle rose unsteadily to her feet. Slowly, woodenly, Batsheva moved down the steps of the dais, then stopped. "Dudu?" she called softly. She stared at the boy through the haze of tears what seemed to be an eternity before her arms opened to him.

"*Om!*" he cried as he pulled the mask from his face and bolted toward her open arms.

Durham leapt from his seat. The queen rose to follow him.

As Batsheva wrapped her arms about her son, there was a commotion at the back of the hall. Her head snapped up and she saw the stranger yet not a stranger pushing his way through the crowd. "Khalil!" she cried.

Suddenly, someone shouted "A blade! Stop him!" There were more shouts. Batsheva heard someone shout "*Puta*!!" and then, from out of the throng on the other side a brown robe came hurtling toward her. She saw the glint of metal in the torchlight. Twisting herself over Daud, Batsheva presented her side to the attacker. The knife came down; she felt it slice into her.

Women screamed. The queen's guard closed ranks around Eleanor. Batsheva turned to see Yehuda standing over her, her blood spattered on his face and hands. "Hudi?" she asked, her arms still clutching Daud. "*¿Por qué?*"

"Puta!" he hissed, "*Zonah*! Whore! You shame us!" His mouth was still spewing poison when Durham's sword pierced his heart.

"No!" screamed Batsheva; "No! No! NOOOOOOO!" She looked at Durham. "*¡Mi hermano!"* she cried, "*¡Mi hermano!"* The light faded; her grip on Daud was broken, and she started to crumple.

Khalil almost toppled Durham as he reached to grab Batsheva. He scooped her up into his arms.

"Follow me," ordered Durham as he picked up the shaking Daud.

Khalil did not argue. He followed the earl out of the hall and up the stairs two at a time. Jane, Anne's hand clutched in hers, and Rachel hurried behind them.

CHAPTER 48

Durham

JULY 1192

Durham led the way to Batsheva's chamber. He handed Daud to Mary who took the sobbing child off to the side with Anne. As soon as Khalil laid Batsheva on the bed, Rachel ordered him aside and set to work on locating the wound. Quickly, she pulled off the cote and tore open the cut in the chemise at the same time ordering clean cloth and water. Jane was already coming toward the bed with a pitcher and basin while Durham pulled clean chemises from Batsheva's wardrobe and immediately tore one into strips.

"Jane, the box," ordered Rachel as she pressed against the wound to stop the bleeding.

Jane was back with Batsheva's box of remedies and began picking out the jars she knew Rachel would need. She laid them on the little table close to the bed, then stepped back to let the other woman work unimpeded.

The wound was longer than it was deep. Rachel continued to apply pressure with one hand as she dipped her other hand into a pot of salve. "This will staunch the bleeding," she said as she pressed the cloth against the wound. Then she laid her head against Batsheva's breast. "Her lungs seem clear, my lords, I do not think the knife pierced them. The cut is deep but it can be closed."

"¿Vivirá la dama?" asked Khalil, standing helplessly to the side.

"*Creo que sí.* We will know by morning," Rachel answered in the same language. "Jane," she said in English, "fetch her sewing basket."

"You need silk." Jane went back to the trunk and returned with the basket.

Rachel asked Jane to thread a needle. "I shall sew closed the wound," she told the men. "You will have to hold her."

Durham's eyes narrowed as they met Khalil's, but he said nothing. Instead, he fastened his hands on her ankles while Khalil pinned her shoulders to the bed.

Batsheva groaned, then cried out when the needle pierced her skin. Durham and Khalil maintained their grip on her while Rachel plied fine stitches along the length of the cut. When she had finished, she gently patted more salve onto the wound then pressed a clean cloth strip against it. She stood up and faced Durham and Khalil. "The wound may seep a little blood, but I think the worst is over."

Queen Eleanor swept into the room, Margaret, Isabella and her other ladies pressing close behind her. "Is she alive?"

Rachel sunk into a deep curtsey. "Yes, Your Majesty."

The queen approached the bed and looked down at the pale figure lying amidst bloodstained clothes. "Has she lost much blood?"

"No, Your Majesty. I have stitched the wound closed." Rachel lifted the linen strip. "See, already the bleeding has slowed. I do not believe the wound is mortal."

Eleanor closed her eyes and swallowed. "We are thankful to God for that." She opened her eyes again. "Who are you, child?"

Rachel flushed pink and curtsied as she replied, "Rachel Vital, Your Majesty."

"You seem to be a skilled practitioner of the healing arts, Rachel Vital. We are lucky you were in attendance. I doubt if my own physician could have done as well."

"'Tis a practical thing, ma'am," said Rachel, meeting the queen's eyes with her own. "One must be able to care for one's own."

The message was clear to Eleanor, and she nodded. Then, her eyes found Khalil leaning against the wall on the far side of the bed, Daud clinging to him. Their eyes locked for a long moment; Eleanor instinctively knew he was no simple knight. Turning to the others now crowding the room, she ordered, "Everyone out! You, Gilbert and Margaret; remain." She saw Isabella lingering at the door. "Out, Isabella!"

Once the room was clear, Eleanor faced the stranger. "You, sir, are the one called Don Carlos. Yes?" she asked in French.

"Oui."

"Is that your son?"

"Oui."

"And our Elizabeth is his mother?"

"She is Batsheva Hagiz al'Amirat bint Yusef bin Ayyub, beloved adopted daughter of Salah ad-Din," he answered slowly in French.

"Well, this is a fascinating turn of events. And you are…?"

Khalil drew himself up to his full height; he looked down at the most powerful woman in Europe. "I am Khalil bin Mahmud, Amir of Alexandria, Sheikh of el-Ayyub Al-Andalus, and Lord General of Salah ad-Din's army."

"Am I in personal danger, Sire?" asked Eleanor.

Khalil laughed. "No, Malika, you are in no danger from me. Am I in danger from *you*?"

"No." She furrowed her brow. "How fares my son in the Holy Land?" She was certain he would give her a fair assessment.

"Your son, Malik Rik, is a strong warrior. At last word, he was still astride his horse."

"Thank you for that. A mother does worry." She glanced at Batsheva, "Much as this one has worried. I thank you for your timely arrival at the crossroads. I would have been greatly grieved to lose my nephew." She looked at Durham who stood glowering near the bed. "Gil," said the queen softly, "this is terribly difficult for you. But I think we need wait until the lady awakens before decisions are made. Margaret has told me much about her circumstance. Too many decisions have been made *for* Elizabeth. This one will be hers alone." Eleanor started toward the door then turned back to the two men. "I do not envy her the choice. Come along, Margaret; we'd best find your mother to soothe her vapors." Margaret, her mouth set in a firm line, followed the queen.

Daud clutched his father's hand. Together, they looked at Durham. "We shall wait here. Together." Without speaking, Khalil picked up Daud and sat him beside his mother. He helped the boy remove his boots, then covered him with the same light blanket that now covered Batsheva. "Sleep, Dudu," he said softly in Arabic before he leaned over and kissed his brow. The boy's hand reached for his mother's, then his eyes closed. In a moment he was asleep.

Durham dragged a chair over to the bed and sat down. He watched his adversary do the same. For a very long while, both men sat in sullen silence, blue English eyes locked with dark Ayyub ones, each man wrapped in thought. Each grappled with the ramifications of the decision yet to be made. When a gentle knock broke the silence, Durham went to the door.

Rachel, Miriam in her arms, stepped into the room. She walked slowly past Durham to Khalil. "*Su hija, señor,*" she murmured as she presented the child to him.

The hardened planes of Khalil's face melted as he opened his arms. "*Gracias, señora, muchas gracias.*" He looked down at the little red curls and the grey eyes that met his boldly. "*Maryam*," he murmured as he nuzzled the babe. When his finger touched her nose, Miriam immediately grabbed it and pulled it toward her mouth. "See, she knows her abu."

Durham felt as if a knife had been plunged through the center of his heart. This was *his* daughter; he was the one who carried her about and made her giggle and squeal. He was the one who sat up with her when she cut her first tooth. Miriam went to him when she cried, and it was on his chest she slept after she had nursed in the night. *He cannot have her!* screamed Durham silently. And then the awful truth crashed down on him: *this* man is Miriam's father, and with a stab of painful truth, *this* man loved her before he even knew her, just as he, himself, had loved Anne. *This* man's complete acceptance of the child, without question, pained Durham most.

Khalil, lifting his head to look at Durham, felt the other man's pain as acutely as if it had been his own. The Englishman had stood as father to Miriam and, if what he already knew about him was true, he loved her as his own. There was no anger in Khalil's heart; he felt incredibly grateful. Reluctantly, he handed Miriam back to Rachel. "Take her to her own bed, señora. She needs to sleep."

"As you wish, señor," murmured Rachel as she took the babe. As quietly as she came, she left the chamber.

There was a moment of silence before Khalil addressed Durham slowly in French. "You have my gratitude, Gilbert, Earl of Durham, for the care you have given Batsheva and our daughter. I am forever in your debt."

"We believed you were dead."

"I was," replied Khalil with a rueful smile. "I was left for dead on the battlefield. Someone took my sword and burnous so I could not be named. It was Allah's will I was found in time."

Durham rose from his seat and went to the large chest beneath the window. He removed the bloodstained bundle from where Batsheva kept it and presented it to Khalil. "These are yours."

"My burnous?" Khalil accepted the bundle, surprised by the weight until he thrust his hand into the center and withdrew the sword. He surprised Durham when he smiled broadly. "My father's saif," he chuckled. "I thought it gone forever."

"'Tis a good weapon."

"The finest made in Toledo. It served me well…to a point. Thank you." He looked at the earl. "Gilbert, Earl of Durham, we are both honorable men. In another place, we might be friends."

The admission caught Durham off guard. It was not what he expected to hear from the fearsome Iron Amir. "I suppose," he grunted.

A slow smile crossed Khalil's face. "Has she behaved?" he asked.

"At times. Not always."

"She is difficult."

"Yes, she is."

"And stubborn."

"And…," Durham had to find just the right word, "…arrogant."

Khalil nodded; the word was close enough to Castilian to be understood. He spied the chessboard on the table. "Does she play shatranj with you?" He saw Durham nod, and shook his head. "Her father taught her. She is a master. Did you ever win?"

"Only when she let me." Both men allowed soft chuckles.

They lapsed into silence. Then Khalil asked, "How did you find her? I thought they were well hidden."

Durham recounted the story of the unsanctioned raid, giving Khalil details he could not possibly have known before. "I thought her a boy; her hair was cut short, and she was wearing boy's clothing. She later told me she was leaving to find you at Nablus." Taking pains as he went to make certain Khalil could follow his French, Durham described their journey to England.

There were times in the story that they both laughed and other times when Khalil's face tightened noticeably. Gilbert made clear that Batsheva had remained faithful to him until after she had his sword and truly believed he was dead. Khalil could not be angry; Durham obviously loved her. He had sheltered her and his child, searched for the twins, and indeed, Durham would have made a fine match if he had been dead. And there was the matter of how he, himself, came to love her. Khalil was certain that if he displayed any untoward hostility towards the Englishman, Batsheva would, with a vengeance, skewer him with their own beginnings.

The men had been talking quietly for what seemed hours when Batsheva stirred in the bed. Both froze. Her head was turned and when her eyes opened slowly the first thing she saw was Daud's head. " *Mi hijo,*" she rasped as she tried to kiss the dark curls, "Dudu. *Un sueño. Un sueño.*"

Her eyes traveled upward until she saw the dark, bearded face filled with concern staring down at her. "Khalil," she murmured as her eyes closed. *"'Ant mit." You are dead.*

"La, habibi; 'ana last maytana," Khalil knelt beside the bed. He touched his lips briefly to hers. "*Ma ismik, ya fatah?"*

"Majhula," she murmured.

Khalil snorted. "Bashi, open your eyes," he commanded softly. Relief flooded his face when the grey eyes fluttered open and stared into his.

"Don't call me that, dirty boy," she rasped, and then she managed the tiniest smile. She touched his cheek. "The beard. I saw the beard in my dream. Are you a dream? Am I dead?"

"*La, habibi.*" He took her hand and pressed it to his chest. "I am real, Batsheva; as real as our son beside you."

"I saw you toss Dudu in the river. You limped."

He did not know he had been seen. "I was wounded; I am still healing."

She turned her head toward Daud. "Mina?"

"At home with Sufiye."

"Home?"

"Alexandria."

"Ah." The grey eyes slid closed once more and silence filled the room.

After a while, Durham stood and stretched. "I am thirsty, and you must be, too." Walking to the door, he opened it, spoke to someone outside then returned. "I've sent for refreshment." He resumed his seat beside the bed. Suddenly, he looked up at Khalil. "Who was that monk?"

"Her brother."

This made no sense to Durham. "Her brother? A monk?"

"A…trick. He was…" Khalil touched his finger to his temple "…insane."

"You knew him?"

"He came to Benghazi. Batsheva was…big." He gestured the shape of her pregnancy. "She refused him. Her Uncle Avram said he searched for her with hate. More, I do not know."

"Are the jongleurs your people?"

Khalil shook his head. "They are their own people." He would not tell Durham more, lest their existence be jeopardized. "They travel the world freely."

A servant arrived with a large tray filled with fruits and cheese, along with a jug of wine and one of water. The amir refused the wine but partook of fruit and cheese. They ate in relative silence; afterward, they returned to their seats on opposite sides of the bed.

Both were snoring softly when Batsheva awakened again. Her mouth was dry; she looked for something to drink. Without disturbing Daud, she managed to reach Durham's goblet sitting on the table beside the bed. Slowly, she drained the contents of the cup, not caring what it was, but was glad when she tasted wine. Moving again, she pulled herself upright enough to see the strip of linen stuck to her side. Gently, she peeled it back to examine the wound as best she could. The fine stitches told her Rachel had tended her. On the bed table sat the jar of salve, and she gingerly reached for that. She reapplied ointment, took another piece of linen from the mound of the stuff left on the bed, then pressed it against the wound. "Ouch!" she muttered as pain sliced though her side. She was relieved, however, that the pain faded quickly. "I shall live," she uttered matter-of-factly, but softly.

Pulling herself into a more comfortable position, she glanced from Khalil to Durham and had to suppress a laugh: both sound asleep, heads thrown back. She cast her eyes on Daud and, with her finger, played with a lock of hair that had fallen onto his brow. In his sleep he murmured "*Umi,*" and she smiled as she whispered, "*Ana huna,*" into his ear. That soothed him, and he snuggled against the length of her leg.

Batsheva realized her chemise was in tatters. Looking about, she saw a clean chemise beside the other linen left on the bed. She used her toe to draw it closer. As quickly as she could muster, she managed to discard the torn, bloodstained garment and slip the clean one over her head. It was painful work, but she felt much better for having done it. *At least I am modestly covered again,* she thought. Sliding down, Batsheva closed her eyes and drifted back to sleep.

When she next opened them, it was early morning and both Durham and Khalil were staring at her. She looked from one to the other then back again. Daud was gone. "Where is Dudu?"

"Lydia has taken him to break his fast. Are you all right, Bess?" prodded Durham gently.

"As well as can be expected. Where is Yehuda?"

"He is dead. I am sorry; I did not know he was your brother."

"Do not apologize, Gilbert. I know he is dead. Where has he been taken?"

"David Vital claimed his body."

"Good. Pick up your arm. Are you bleeding again?"

Durham shook his head but lifted his arm anyway. "I would have asked Rachel for help if I was."

She turned to Khalil and asked in Arabic, "Did you follow Yehuda here?"

"*La*; it was fated to happen this way." He paused. "I have come to take you and our daughter home."

"Have I no say in this, Khalil?" she countered sharply in the same language.

"Do you not want to come home?"

"I did not say that."

"Then what is the difficulty, Batsheva? As soon as you are well enough to travel, we shall leave."

"You cannot simply ride into this castle and expect me to ride out with you. You who are supposed to be dead."

"I was left for dead; I was injured."

"So you said. But you managed to send enough cryptic messages!"

"I did not know what danger you were in! By the beard of the Prophet, woman," he roared, "I am the enemy here!"

"So you placed our son in danger?" she shouted back.

"He was in no danger."

"And when you knew the first message was received, you could not just send a letter? You have forgotten how to dip a reed in an inkpot? By the beard of the Prophet, Khalil, you have enough spies here!"

"*Aljasus*?" snapped Durham, sitting up a little straighter. It was a word he recognized.

"Not military spies," dismissed Batsheva in French with a wave of her hand. "The peddler with the blue samite in London? The old woman in York? The jongleurs? The rug merchant in London?"

"Rug merchant?" echoed Khalil. "I know of no rug merchant."

"That must have been Yehuda's doing. Never mind. And that…that peddler from Venice?"

"Rashid." Khalil chuckled. "He, in truth, works for your Uncle Avram."

But there was no hint of mirth about the corners of her mouth as she pointed a finger at him. "Do not laugh, Khalil. You take too much for granted."

"I thought you would want to come home."

"And if I do not?"

"Then I shall take Daud and Maryam and leave you here."

"You will do no such thing, Khalil bin Mahmud."

"I will do what must be done, Batsheva Hagiz!" he shouted.

"You will not dictate to me, Khalil bin Mahmud."

"You will do as I see fit!"

"I certainly will not!"

Durham's laughter made both heads snap around. He didn't have to know the language to understand the argument. "Is she always like this?" he asked Khalil holding up his hands in mock horror.

"Always. She is difficult…and arrogant. Do you want to keep her?"

"I am not so certain. She is a bit of a shrew."

"Shrew?" repeated Khalil. "I do not know this word."

"*'Limr'atan salayta*," snapped Batsheva automatically. "I am not!"

Khalil ignored her. "Yes, that is Batsheva. Perhaps we should just sell her to slavers."

"I am not amused!" shouted the lady.

"I think, Princess," Durham snorted, "we are."

Batsheva stared from one to the other, her face aflame with anger. "How can you make light of this? What if I tell you I would prefer to go home to Málaga?"

The smiles faded and were replaced by more serious faces. Durham spoke first. "In my heart, Bess, I know you never ceased believing this man still walked amongst the living. I am not so much a fool as to believe you will stay here with me and Annie."

"I care deeply for you, Gil, and for Annie, too."

"But you do not love me."

"That is not true, Gilbert." Tears threatened to dissolve her composure, "I do love you, but he holds my heart in his."

Durham rose from his chair. He leaned over and kissed Batsheva's forehead. "I will always hold you in my heart, Bess."

Only when the door had closed behind him, did Khalil gather Batsheva into his arms to hold her as tightly as he dared. No words were spoken because no words were needed. It was enough that his arms were around her, his warm body pressed against hers as she wept.

CHAPTER 49

Durham

JULY 1192

Gossip and speculation ran rampant through Durham by midmorning. The events of the previous night were discussed, dissected, and reconstructed by everyone from the lowliest scullery wench to the highest court chamberlains.

Propped up on pillows, Khalil sitting beside the bed, and Daud snuggled against her, Batsheva was wreathed in smiles. Daud told her everything she had missed in the last year. She could not stop touching him, holding his hand, and hugging him close. There was much to tell: from the day they went to the Well of Tears until he was standing outside the great hall waiting to sing. Batsheva learned how the sultan himself sheltered them in his tent until Abu could safely be taken aboard a ship bound for Alexandria. He told her about the physician, Mussa bin Maymon and how he came every day when everyone thought Abu was dying. With a child's eye, he described the wonders of their new home in Alexandria, with its pools and gardens. When he talked about his twin sister, he lit up with pride tempered by sibling annoyance. He told his mother Amina was a silly girl and that Abu said so himself more than once. Only when he described the *other ladies* in Abu's chamber did Batsheva raise a single eyebrow at Khalil who reddened ever so slightly, but that topic was best addressed when she had Khalil alone.

When Mary arrived with a message inviting the amir to go falconing with Queen Eleanor, Batsheva insisted he go. "You cannot just sit here, Khalil. You will go mad with tedium while at the same time you will try what little patience I have left." With a kiss, he was gone, only to return a moment later to ask Daud if he wanted to come along. The boy bounded off the bed, then stopped.

"I cannot go in these. They will laugh at me!" he moaned, looking down at the blood-spattered costume.

Mary came to the rescue. "Come with me, Prince Daud," she smiled at the boy, "I think we can find something for you to wear." In a flash, they were gone.

Rachel arrived just as they were leaving; she was more than pleased to find Batsheva had changed her own bandage not to mention chemise. The patient teased her friend about leaving her in a state of undress.

"I had no choice, Bashi," frowned Rachel. "I could not countermand the queen and when I returned, I was not about to stay in that room with them. Besides," she leaned closer, "you are…having courses. I could not tend to that with them in the room. I just covered you as best I could.

"Thank you for caring for me. Just as well that I am having my courses now," she sighed, relieved she was not carrying Durham's child. "I am so sorry you were trapped between them, Rachel. Was it awful?"

"The tension was so thick one could slice it with a knife! When I brought Miriam to him, I thought the amir would just dissolve into a puddle, but my lord earl looked as though I stabbed him through the heart. You must take time to talk to Lady Anne as well. She is most confused and upset."

"Where is she now?"

"She has gone falconing with the others."

Batsheva chewed on her lip for a moment. "Perhaps when she returns." Before she could say anything else, there was sharp rap at the door and Lady Matilda swept into the room.

"We are in your debt, Mistress Vital, but I would speak to the lady in private," she said in the kindest voice Batsheva had ever heard her use.

Rachel curtsied and fled the chamber.

Lady Matilda took the seat the other woman had vacated. "I see you are well on the road to recovery, Elizabeth…or perhaps you would prefer if I used your proper title?"

Batsheva shook her head. "Elizabeth is very close to my own name, my lady."

Lady Matilda was quiet for a moment then said, "Have you made a decision?"

"I think, my lady, there is no question that I will return to my home. My duties lie there, with my children."

"I understand you are not wed to him, either."

"That is true, but…."

Lady Matilda cut her off. "You could remain here and marry Gilbert."

The statement shocked Batsheva. "You *want* me to stay?"

"What I want is not as important as what my son wants. Although he told me he is prepared for your departure, I want *you* to understand there is a choice. You were taken twice against your will, but I will not allow you to be removed a third time without your absolute consent. Eleanor and I are in full agreement. I, for one, do not believe women should be forced into any marriage bed, let alone be kidnapped. Had I understood more about your history, Elizabeth, I might not have been so quick to judge you."

Batsheva stared at the dowager countess for a long moment. "I came to Durham believing you to be a kind and welcoming lady because Gilbert and Margaret assured me you were, yet from the start, you set out to rid your son of my presence. You faulted my intentions when I tended to your illness, you drew conclusions that were ridiculous at best, and you strained your ties to your own son. I cannot pretend to understand why you would behave in so hostile a manner to a stranger, much less one who was to marry your son." She paused to see if Matilda would say something; she did not, so Batsheva went on.

"'Tis a pity you do not know the man who is your son; I imagine his father would be proud, because I am sure he learned well at his own father's knee as well as from his brother-in-law Henry. Gilbert is a man of honor and integrity. He may have taken me from my home, but he believed he was being kind to a child. Since then, he has done everything possible to help me heal. He gave me the most precious gift of all…time. Time to heal, time to learn, time to stop being afraid. No man could be kinder. But now you know I am of elevated rank and I am not a penniless adventuress, you are asking me to stay, to marry Gilbert. I am touched by your new-found concern, my lady; let me assure you that had my lord amir indeed been dead as we all believed, I would wed Gilbert with or without your blessing. I would have been proud to be his wife. But Khalil is alive, and I can say with perfect candor that he is my spouse. That I also have come to deeply love Gilbert cannot be discounted. I am torn in two and, when this is behind me, I will grieve the loss of that love, and equally, the loss of Annie. However, my pledge is to Khalil, and I have no wish to renege on this."

Lady Matilda was silent for a moment. "I was unkind and unfeeling. I cannot undo what has been done, but I can tell you I am truly contrite. If you hate me, it would not be unexpected."

Batsheva sighed. "I do not hate you, my lady. I have learned much from you, even though you never set out to teach me. I will carry those lessons back to Alexandria, and I hope my household and my children will benefit."

"When you go home, you will be a queen. That must be an attractive thought."

"Amira in our world is not the same as a queen here. I will not have the same position as her majesty. Any influence I have will come through Khalil and, when he is truly gone, through our son…if I live long enough to see our son ascend to the seat of the amir; it is not guaranteed. Women are sequestered in Alexandria." She smiled, albeit sadly, "That will be new to me. I have never lived within a sara'i."

Lady Matilda surprised Batsheva with an indelicate snort. "Somehow, Elizabeth, I believe you will manage to adjust as you wrest control." She paused for a moment. "There is something else of a more delicate matter I would discuss with you."

"If there is anything I can do for you, my lady, please, tell me."

The dowager countess adjusted herself in her chair. "I am concerned for Gilbert's state of mind. He is putting on a good face in the light of this turmoil, yet I know my son well enough to know his heart is breaking a second time. Therefore, I would ask a great favor of you." She took a deep breath. "I would ask that you speak to Eleanor about Gilbert's future."

"His future?" echoed Batsheva

"Yes. He needs to be married…and *not* to Isabella. I will not have that harridan under my roof as daughter-in-law."

It was Batsheva's turn to snort. "I cannot see fault in that. Do you think speaking to the queen will help?"

"Most assuredly. Eleanor respects you, Elizabeth; you have her ear. If you were to express concern to her, she would listen."

"Then I shall speak to the queen." Batsheva had no idea what she would say, but she was certain she would come up with something before the moment arrived.

"Thank you, Elizabeth. I appreciate your candor."

"And I, yours, my lady."

Lady Matilda stood up. "One last question, Bess." She paused for another long moment. "Are you carrying my grandchild?"

Batsheva sighed and shook her head. "Decisions would be far more complicated if I were, but no, I am certain I am not."

The lady smiled sadly. "I would have loved that child, Bess, because he would have been loved at the moment of creation." She paused again. "I am afraid I have tired you. Do try to sleep a bit." She left Batsheva alone.

For the short time she had before Rachel would be back, she thought seriously about Durham's future. Her conclusion was drawn the moment Catherine entered with Miriam in her arms. A smug smile inched across Batsheva's face and she knew she was looking at the answer to Durham's problem.

Miriam squealed when she saw her mother, and Batsheva, reaching for the squirming child, winced when the babe was set on her lap. Despite the pain, she opened her chemise to allow Miriam access to her too full breasts. "I thought I would explode," she laughed as the babe suckled with her usual enthusiasm.

"Miriam was most eager to join you, my lady," agreed Catherine as she moved about the room tidying up.

Batsheva decided she had better take advantage of the moment to talk to Catherine and called her over. "Sit with me a moment, I have something I would discuss with you."

She looked puzzled but sat down on the chair beside the bed. "Is something amiss?"

"No, not at all, Catherine. I would ask you a serious question and hope you would answer me honestly. Much depends on it." She saw Catherine nod, then proceeded. "Would you...could you find it in your heart to love Gilbert?"

"What?"

"I am leaving Durham, Catherine. Lady Matilda and I are of a mind to prevent Isabella from sinking her talons into Gilbert. She has asked me to speak against this to the queen. Not that I believe Eleanor would agree to such a match, but the lady believes I have the queen's ear and she would listen to me. I would propose you as a vastly more suitable match for Durham."

Catherine's hands flew to her face to cover the red stain blossoming on her cheeks. "But his lordship cannot possibly want me! I am…I am…I am…," she stuttered.

"You are perfect. You're lovely, kind and, most of all, you are known here. You would make a fine countess for Durham; I am certain that, given a little time to heal, he will be a devoted and loving husband. I can think of no better plan than to propose your marriage to Gil to the queen."

"Lady Matilda will never agree. I am not high enough born."

"Lady Matilda would accept you readily, Catherine. After everything that has happened, she will welcome you with open arms." *And I will make sure of that,* decided Batsheva.

"I am not so certain."

"I will speak with the queen first, then with Durham if the match is acceptable to her majesty." Batsheva reached for Catherine's hand. "I can tell you from experience, Catherine, there is no finer man than Gilbert of Durham; he is kind, gentle, and loyal. Together, you will build a fine life."

"I could not replace you, my lady."

"Do not replace me, Catherine, succeed me. You will do it in such a way that my memory will quickly fade as he comes to love you more than he ever could have loved me. You share much already; it is simply a matter of allowing nature to take its course."

"I would not agree if he does not want me," she said firmly.

"I understand, but I think he will."

Catherine agreed to allow the match be proposed and, when she took Miriam back to Lydia, Batsheva thought she detected just the slightest spring in the lady's step. "What woman could help but love Gilbert?" she whispered as the door closed behind Catherine.

Isabella sat upon her palfrey and watched not the falcons as they took flight but, rather, Gilbert of Durham. She could not be happier at the turn of events, although she could understand why the witch would want to keep the outrageously handsome Saracen for herself. Had the witch chosen Durham, Isabella would have offered herself as a replacement. She could barely contain her imagination at what lay beneath the close-fitting hose. Isabella had to push back thoughts of carnal bliss lest her face turn as crimson as her gown. She took the opportunity to trot over to Durham sitting apart from the others, watching birds in training. "A penny for your thoughts, my lord earl," she said lightly.

"Go away, Isabella," he growled. "I am not of a mood to banter with you."

"I would hardly call this banter, Gil. We have serious business to discuss."

"I have no business with you, madam."

Isabella would not be put off. "With Elizabeth leaving, Gilbert, the queen will marry you off to whomever she pleases. Why not go to her and announce our engagement before every hopeful mother begins petitioning for your hand."

Durham stared at her through narrowed slits. "What makes you think I would have you, Isabella?"

"Before you left for crusade, we had an agreement."

"*You* thought you had an agreement; I made no promise."

"Gil," she wheedled.

With a scowl, Durham kicked his horse and went to rejoin the others.

Isabella knew Eleanor well enough to know the queen often acted on impulse, especially when high romance was the game. Taking a moment to smooth her hair and adjust her skirts, Isabella trotted over to the small rise where the queen and her falconer were watching her new bird.

"She hesitates," commented Eleanor to her falconer. "She will lose her quarry." The bird swooped down, only to rise again with her talons empty. "See, she has missed it."

"Give her time, ma'am," chided the falconer. Just then, the bird dove into the brush and this time, she emerged with a small animal clutched in her sharp talons. In seconds, she brought her prey back to the falconer. He rewarded her with a chunk of raw meat when she released the rabbit she carried. "Sweet girl," he cooed, "good girl."

The queen grunted her begrudging approval. "A good sign, Hal, but keep working her." She turned slightly in her saddle to face Isabella. "We see you've been out hunting, too, Isabella," she smiled. "How is our nephew?"

"Surprisingly clear-headed, under the circumstances, Your Majesty. Forgive my boldness, but I would propose something to you."

"And that is?"

"Announce our engagement as soon as possible. Gil needs a woman in his castle as much as he needs a woman in his bed."

"What he needs is time to heal. This is a terrible blow."

"Your Majesty, he needs to have his mind taken from his grief. Why not go on as we had planned before he returned with Elizabeth?"

"Have you spoken to him?"

Isabella allowed herself to blush. "Yes, ma'am, we have spoken of it."

"Does Durham agree?"

"He does not disagree."

"Let us consider this carefully, Isabella; but in truth, we see no real obstacle…*if* you can convince my nephew he wants to marry you. "

Isabella's eyelashes batted as she smiled prettily at the queen. "Thank you, Madame."

"Save your guiles for Gilbert, Isabella," she replied as she trotted off, silently adding, *you will need them.* She watched Isabella trot off in the direction of the castle; she was afraid to think what havoc she would wreak next.

Durham joined Khalil watching Anne and Daud as they learned from Durham's falconer. In appearance, the children were night and day, yet there was an easy manner between them Durham had not expected. Anne knew and fully understood what was to happen when Bess was well enough to travel. In the hours she had spent with Daud, however, she had discovered, as best as he could tell, some kind of natural ally. When the children giggled at something the falconer told them, Durham felt himself wince.

Khalil observed the same scene and noticed the same things. Clearing his throat, he caught the earl's attention. "They get on well," he said slowly. "We can learn from them."

Durham's blue eyes met Khalil's dark ones straight on. "Their hearts are not about to be torn out. I cannot fault you in your efforts to find her, my lord amir. I would have moved heaven and earth had I been in your place."

"I find you less my enemy and more my brother, Gilbert of Durham." He glanced toward where Isabella was talking to the queen. "Will the yellow-haired one move to take Batsheva's place?"

Durham grunted. "She will try, but I will not have her. Isabella is far too…," he hesitated to find the right word, "…ambitious."

Khalil considered the word for a moment. "She has the ear of your queen."

"That she does, but I think Eleanor will not put Isabella in my bed if I speak against it."

Khalil looked strangely at Durham. "Your queen makes marriages for you?"

"She has that power but wields it wisely." The earl laughed wryly, "I pray she wields it wisely."

"I do not understand you English," admitted Khalil. "In my world, royal women remain behind the screen. A woman's task is the education of her children and, through them, she gains her power."

"Eleanor has done just that. Her power is in the name of her son… *Malik Rik*. She carries his warrant through his justiciar, a man called de Coutances, and through that, her word is his law. Without that, she is powerless."

The amir shook his head. "I prefer my woman behind the screen. I fear what chaos Batsheva makes if she sat in council!

"Do not underestimate your lady," chuckled Durham. "She knows well how to make her wishes known in a variety of languages. I fear for your safety should you try to restrain her."

"Has she become more difficult, Gilbert?"

"Perhaps more experienced, Khalil, but no more difficult than usual."

Eleanor spied the two men laughing together. *Would that my own sons got on that well.*

In her chamber, Batsheva rested comfortably propped up on a stack of feather pillows. Rachel had gone home, Catherine was in the garden with Lydia and the baby, and Mary was off to Jane's with several garments in need of mending. Blissfully alone, Batsheva considered the recent kindness of the fates and decided she had earned a little peace. She was glad that Khalil and Gilbert met face to face; she could never have explained the earl to the amir. She only hoped their outing would give the two men a chance to speak in private. A small, sly smile settled on Batsheva's face; the thought of Catherine marrying Gilbert pleased her immensely. She could think of no one better suited to be his countess. "A better countess than I could ever hope to be," she said aloud. Closing her eyes, she snuggled into the bed and drowsed.

The door opened none too quietly. Batsheva opened one eye to see who disturbed her rest and frowned. "What do you want, Isabella?" she asked curtly.

"Have I awakened you?"

"Yes." Batsheva was unwilling to fence words with the woman and kept her eyes closed.

"I thought we might have a private word."

"Why?" The need for politeness had dissipated with Khalil's arrival.

Isabella was not deterred. "There is a matter on which you should be advised; I think it best you know now, before you are in the throes of your departure."

My departure from Durham or from this earth? thought Batsheva in annoyed silence. She heard the scraping of a chair as Isabella brought it closer to the bed. *Did I ask you to sit?* she muttered silently. "Say what you will and leave, Isabella. I am tired and of no mood to argue."

Isabella settled herself in the chair and waited for Batsheva to open her eyes. When the grey eyes met hers, she said, "I have just now come from Eleanor's side. Her majesty has decided Gil and I shall marry as soon as possible." She braced herself for Batsheva's reaction.

"Has she spoken to Gilbert?"

"Yes," she lied.

"And Gilbert has agreed to do this?" Batsheva asked calmly.

"Yes."

Batsheva struggled to sit up in the bed, then she looked placidly at Isabella. "I think, madam, I would see you in hell long before I would see you walk down the aisle of a church with Earl Durham as your groom."

"Then you would be dead, Elizabeth."

Batsheva rolled her eyes heavenward and began laughing. "You must think we are all fools to be played by you, Isabella. Let me assure you, we are not. Gilbert would no sooner marry you than he would cut off his sword arm."

"Then he shall be a groom without a sword arm. 'Tis a *fâit accompli*, Elizabeth. The decision has been made."

"Do you know," asked Batsheva evenly, "what happens to liars?"

"I do not lie, Elizabeth."

She continued as if Isabella had said nothing. "They are found out. And when they are, the price extracted is usually far more than that they are willing to pay. But since your late husband left you well-dowered perhaps, then, you can afford the price. Be assured, Isabella, he will not marry you. Not before, not now, not ever. You may spread your legs for him from now until the cockerel crows in the morning, but he will not so much as *entertain* the thought of touching you."

"He will not go against Eleanor's wishes," she said tightly.

"Do not presume to know Eleanor's wishes, Isabella. Whatever has passed between you and the queen will be meaningless in light of the earl's decision." Her grey eyes never wavered from Isabella's face. "I would not, were I you, put all my hopes and aspirations into Durham's basket."

Batsheva decided she felt well enough to get up.

She was already angry that Durham had ignored her express order not to hunt. When Mary returned, she had her fashion a wrap for her torso to prevent any untoward movement of the newly stitched wound and dressed in her least restrictive tunic. Standing on the battlement, she saw the hunting party moving leisurely toward the castle. "At least he's not at full gallop," snorted Batsheva. She watched for a while before she started slowly down the stairs.

No sooner had Durham entered the yard than Batsheva saw the dark splotch on his tabard. Grumbling, she marched toward him. Khalil started to say something, but she waved him away. "My Lord Durham, come with me," she ordered, and Durham, despite the chuckles around him, complied. She led him to his solar, ordered Mary to get her box of salves, and waited none too patiently while Jamie removed his master's tabard and tunic. Blood was seeping out of the wound and there appeared to be new separation in the stitching. "God's bones, Gil!" she muttered as she dabbed the cut, 'Whatever were you thinking? Have you no good sense, or did it bleed out of you?"

"Do you really care, Bess?" he growled. "Or is this a noblewoman's duty?"

"Of course, I care, Gil. I care deeply. I cannot just stop even if Khalil is alive. We have made a history between us, and whilst I will go home, it does not make our time together disappear or become less precious to me." Mary arrived with the box and was promptly dismissed. As Batsheva laid out linen and jars of salve, she continued. "Do not think this is without heartbreak. I am not simply leaving *you*; I am leaving Anne whom I love as my own child, as well as dear, dear friends."

"And me? Is leaving me hard?"

Batsheva stopped and stared at him. "Harder than you can ever imagine, Gil. I love you. I was willing to wed you; I am not willing to wed Khalil. You were determined to right all the wrongs, and I will forever love you for that. You are precious to me."

He took her hand. "Then don't leave. Stay. Stay and marry me."

Her heart was broken anew. "I am torn in two, Gilbert, but I know where my heart needs to be and that is where it should be. I cannot undo what has been done. Yes, I was given as a gift to Khalil, but over time my hatred turned to respect. I could not return to the girl I once was, so I chose to make a life with Khalil and our children. He is a good amir and a loving, doting father, and we share kindness and compassion between us. What you don't know is that he had been wed before. His two wives, his son, and his unborn child were slaughtered in a raid on their village in Al-Andalus. Like you, he grieved." Her eyes were filling and there was little she could do to keep the tears from spilling over. "You are so much alike in so many ways." She resumed tending the wound with salve and fresh linen strips.

"I will grieve again," he said, taking her hand, "for you."

"You will love, again, of this I have no doubt." She took her hand back.

"Not Isabella," he snorted.

"God forbid, not Isabella." Batsheva took both his hands in hers. "Catherine. You will marry Catherine, and I know you will love her as she already loves you." He stared at her. "Gilbert, I do not say this lightly nor without great forethought, but you must marry Catherine. She is devoted to Anne, she is kind, and most of all, she is strong. She will stand up to you when you need it. And your mother, too," she added with a tiny grin. "Your mother asked me to speak to the queen to keep Isabella at bay. And then I saw Catherine and I knew this is best for you and Anne."

"*You* made this decision *for* me, Bess?" he growled, more than a hint of annoyance in his voice.

"Yes. It is my last gift of love for you, Gilbert. Eleanor will approve, as will your mother. It serves many purposes, the least of which is keeping Isabella out of your bed." She raised a single eyebrow at him. "What say you?"

"You are a cunning one, Princess Batsheva." He pulled her hands to his lips and kissed them. "You know I will think of you when I bed her."

"For a while, but not for long. She comes to you a maid, and you will come to love her deeply. She will become the heart of you, Gilbert, I promise. I will, God willing, be forgotten in time."

The queen spent her days closeted with her nephew and Khalil, acknowledging that the amir was, in truth, her enemy, but pleased to have the opportunity to know him. Long evenings, Batsheva translating as needed, were filled with serious discussion countered with generous laughter. Khalil found his footing in French, and Eleanor found him progressively easier to understand. Even Durham's smattering of Arabic was hauled into use. But it was Batsheva's translations, sprinkled with her own commentary, that made it all so entertaining.

They debated the rights of Crusaders in the Holy Land, and Eleanor had to concede that the same invasion of her lands would yield the same result. "'Tis a matter of perspective, my lord Amir," she told him one evening at twilight as she stood on the battlements of Durham Castle with Gilbert and Khalil. "And there is little one can do to change one's natural perspective. I imagine we are all born predisposed to something."

"Once, majesty, I would have agreed, but I am not so certain now." He pointed toward two small figures racing in the courtyard. "If Daud were born to hate Christians, would he play with Anne? I think no. He would be here, at my side, with the only other person like himself."

"Is that intentional? That you taught him not to hate?" asked Durham, thinking about the things Anne had been recently told about Muslims.

"His mother is not of Islam; that is a beginning. Blood feuds run deep in my people. I want change. There must be ways to resolve differences without harm. There must be a way for everyone to live in Al-Quds without armies. Can you tell this to your brother kings? Can you tell them to leave if they are promised safe transit to visit their shrines?"

Eleanor continued to watch the children. "I think their faith urges them on. I do not think, though I am a Christian queen, that I have power to change that." She turned to Khalil. "I am also of the thought that if women ran the world, we would have far less war."

The amir threw his head back and laughed. "Batsheva would agree, majesty, but she has not spent time in a sara'i. More time with women might change her idea."

It was Eleanor's turn to laugh. "Oh, my lord amir, we are of one mind there. I have spent a lifetime avoiding close quarters with unoccupied women. Take Isabella as an example…."

He cut her off with a wave of his hand. "*La shukran*, majesty. I do not want her at all."

Durham commented with a snort. "On that, we are in complete agreement."

"And speaking of Isabella," sighed Eleanor as she poked a finger at the amir, "your sudden appearance has caused me a world of difficulty."

"Apologies, majesty. It is not my intent to cause harm."

"Oh, do not be so serious about it. 'Tis but a tempest contained in a cup. However, I do so detest slopping cups."

Khalil leaned against the parapet with his arms folded against his chest. "Shall I tell you what I would do?"

"Does it have anything to do with sacks and high walls at the edge of the sea?" Durham asked with a disarming smile.

Khalil returned the smile. "There are some who like that method. I prefer more …," he struggled for the word, then his smile broadened, "… subtle solutions."

Eleanor was curious. "Do go on, my lord amir."

"I would find a sheikh of good rank, but young, to fill her with a dozen babes. I would give him a district on the far edges of our land to govern. When she returned to the city for gathering, I would put her in the finest apartments…away from other women…treated with respect and…deference…so she would have nothing of consequence to say."

"Hmmm. Give her to a stallion as brood mare. 'Tis cunning, my lord amir, and certainly worthy of consideration; I know just the stallion to do the job." Eleanor studied him for a long moment. "I like you, Khalil bin

Mahmud. Would that you were one of my liege lords." *Would that you were my son,* she thought; *I could die in peace.*

Daud called to his father from the courtyard. "With permission, majesty, my master calls," Khalil bowed to Eleanor before he went to join the children, leaving the queen and Durham on the battlement. When he had gone, Eleanor turned to her great-nephew. "Are you settled on Catherine, then?" she asked gently.

He nodded. "Bess is right. I need a wife and Anne needs a mother. We have spoken to Anne together, and she resolved to the idea. She will miss Bess, but Annie likes Catherine very much."

"Do you?"

Durham's brow furrowed over his eyes. "I do. I have liked her as long as I've known her, which is most of our lives. She is a fine woman, a good daughter to her father and to her grandfather."

"You are not buying a horse, Gil; we are discussing your marriage bed."

"I look at Bess and her amir and I see the silent language between them. A raised brow, pursed lips, a single glance, and a bond I have not seen even in my own parents," murmured Gilbert softly. "In my heart, I want what they have, Aunt Eleanor."

"They have had years of hardship and joys to arrive at this place, Gil. I had that once, long ago, with Henry, and you are right, it is the most precious part of loving someone. What is said in the silences can make or break a marriage. Catherine is much like our Batsheva. She is strong and practical. She has already managed a holding and a household so she will find this one only larger. If you are open with her, if you are honest with her, you and Catherine will have your own unspoken language." Eleanor sighed and put her hand on his shoulder. "Have you resolved the question with Catherine, herself?"

He nodded. "We are agreed that we should be quietly married after Bess leaves. Wedding Catherine is right and proper."

"With all the commotion about our Elizabeth and her amir, *can* this be quietly managed?" With a raised brow and a hint of mischief, she added, "Isabella will be most anguished when she finds out. As wicked as it sounds, child, I do hope to be present when she does."

Batsheva and Khalil remained in Durham long enough to welcome Peter Gilbert FitzHugh into the world. While Batsheva was busy with the new mother, Gilbert taught Khalil some of the practical ins and outs of being laird with a large land holding, things he would find useful when he fully assumed the seat of the amir in Alexandria. Khalil, in turn, used the chessboard to impart new battle strategies to Gilbert. Kassim and Jamie found themselves in similar roles and spent their time learning from each other. Anne and Daud were joined at the hip, exploring every part of the castle and the town that their parents would allow. Behind closed doors, Matilda and Margaret discreetly schooled Catherine in her new role as Countess Durham.

Eleanor was delighted to be the one to tell Isabella that Gilbert and Catherine would marry immediately after the amir and amira left Durham. That same afternoon, Isabella announced she was needed in Lincoln. From the battlement, Catherine and Batsheva watched her ride over the bridge with her escort. Arms around each other, they sighed their relief together.

With everything in an uproar, Batsheva spent as much time as she could alone with Anne. On the surface, the girl was adjusting well to all the changes, but underneath there was a certain amount of turmoil that Batsheva quickly recognized. She made it a point to take her on one excursion or another each day in hopes that Anne would open up about her fears.

When Batsheva asked Anne if she would like to ride Yaffa before they left, the girl was ecstatic. With three men-at-arms riding safely behind them, the lady and the girl trotted toward the place they often picnicked. When they reached the little stream, Batsheva helped Anne from Yaffa's back, and they quickly shucked their hose. Sitting side-by-side, hand-in-hand on the bank, their feet just touching the lapping water, Batsheva waited for Anne to say something.

"Remember the day you saved me?" she asked.

"I do. Holding you in my arms as I swam to shore made me believe I could be your mother if you would let me."

"Oh, Bess, I wanted you to be my mother. You were so patient with me when I came to Westminster, but I was so afraid you would go away. And then I thought you would be here forever. But you *are* going away." Tears were beginning to trickle down her cheeks.

"I thought I would be here forever, sweet Annie. I truly believed Khalil was dead." She turned Anne's face toward hers. "When I opened my eyes and saw Khalil, I thought I was dead."

"But you weren't," smiled the little girl. "I thought Fra' Giovanni killed you. I was so frightened."

"I was frightened, too. And then, I could not believe I was seeing Khalil and your father in the same room. I could not possibly be alive to do that. But I was!"

"Did you truly love my father as you said?"

Batsheva nodded. "I love your father very much. I still do, and I will always carry him - and you - in my heart. But I also carry my children in my heart. You know Dudu now."

"I like him very much."

"You would love his sister, Amina. She is strong like you, and brooks no nonsense from her twin," grinned Batsheva. "You would be more than friends; you would be like sisters. And I will tell her how you are a big sister to Miriam. She will know you through my stories, and I shall make sure Miriam never forgets she has a fair-haired sister in England."

Anne threw her arms around Batsheva. "I will miss you so very much," she sobbed, "but I will have Catherine to help me remember. We will remember you every day."

Holding fast to the little girl, Batsheva felt her own tears slide down her cheeks. "And I will remember you all the days of my life."

On the morning of their departure, there were tears and embraces all 'round. Rachel and David came to see them off with a basket of food they knew Batsheva would happily eat. Jane and Jamie brought little Peter for a last farewell. Catherine and Batsheva hugged and wept. Promises to send messages via Hagiz and Vital were solemnly made. Even Anne and Daud hugged and called each other *sibling.*

Khalil and Gilbert embraced, brothers, if not in-arms, but in the spirit of loving the lady. When Batsheva embraced Gilbert for the last time, he held her close, and whispered, "when the time is right, I shall give the pomegranate ring to Anne."

Tears slipped from her eyes. "Thank you." She held him close for another moment, then stepped back to join Khalil and Daud.

Lady Matilda stood to one side with Margaret, but when Batsheva turned to take her leave she curtsied low to the old woman. Matilda nodded in silence, but Margaret smiled her appreciation. Archbishop Durham informally blessed the journey but managed, with an impish grin, to refrain from making the sign of the cross over the travelers.

Eleanor spoke last. "Your devotion to your lady and your people is beyond admiration, my lord Amir Khalil bin Mahmud; you have my greatest respect. If the stars are in our favor, we shall meet again, but if not, I shall forever think of you, Khalil, as the son I wish I had."

Khalil took the queen's hand and raised it to his lips. "*Insh'Allah*, Malika Eleanor, we shall meet again. I have learned much these last weeks; I shall think of you as a mother I wish I had." His voice was solemn, but his smile was warm.

Finally, Queen Eleanor embraced Batsheva, kissing her on both cheeks. "As much as I would have been pleased to have you as niece, Amirat Batsheva, I embrace you as a sister queen. You will be good for your amir, and you will be good for your people." Leaning closer, the queen whispered, "And wed that poor boy. *I* would feel better if you did!"

Batsheva hugged the queen, a most uncommon gesture that was surprisingly returned as the two women laughed together one last time.

Eleanor dispatched a company of her own guard to see the travelers safely to Hartlepool where their ship was now waiting. Two of her own ships would escort them south as far as Lisboa. Traveling on horseback with but a single coach for Mary, Miriam, and Lydia, and a wagon for the trunks, they reached the port by dusk.

Standing dockside, Batsheva and Khalil, Maryam asleep against his shoulder, kept parental eyes on Daud as he stood on deck watching the trunks being lowered into the hold. Batsheva was anxious to get underway, but there was something she had to do before she walked Yaffa up the gangway. "Khalil?" she said softly as she looked up at him.

"Your eyes tell me something is bothering you, habibi," he answered.

She could not help but smile just a little. "There is something I must say before I board this ship." The crease between his eyes deepened and she could tell he was concerned. She turned to face him. "Khalil, I want you to always remember that while I did not choose to come to you or come into your tent, *I* chose to stay with you in Benghazi, and that *I* choose to go back to wherever you call home now. *I* have chosen, not you, not anyone else. Do you understand what I am saying?"

Khalil placed his hand on her shoulder and matched her stare. "You are a freewoman. You are in charge of your own destiny. You have made important choices, ones that I have yet to learn about, but they are *your* choices. I am honored you have chosen to live your life with me, Batsheva."

Standing on tiptoe, she brushed a kiss on his lips. "It is time for me to take Yaffa aboard."

When Yaffa was safely in her stall, the amir and amira took their final leave of England. Together at the stern, they watched England fade into the distance. Khalil could tell by her pursed lips and furrowed brow, Batsheva was deep in thought. He watched her surreptitiously, loath to intrude. There was so much to talk about, so much to decide. But with his daughter nestled snugly in the crook of one arm, Daud between his parents, and the other arm around his amira, Khalil was at peace.

Batsheva let the feel of him, the scent of him, the strength of him, flow into her. She wanted the sensations to fill all the troubled and empty spaces that remained in her soul. She wanted to explain how hard leaving was, yet how natural it felt. She wanted Khalil to understand how her dreams were always filled with him and the twins, but her life had taken a path she now had to reconcile in her heart. *We will have years to talk*, she reassured herself.

Once the shore disappeared and Daud scampered off to watch the sailors trim the sails, Khalil waited for her to look at him; he was not certain how she would answer his question. When she finally looked up, he asked, "Would it please you to stop in Málaga for a day or two? We carry cargo destined for the port."

Her grey eyes widened. "I don't know," she whispered. "I don't know if I would be welcome there."

"Asher and Esther are hoping we will come."

"Asher? You have news of Asher? Why did you not tell me?"

He handed her a small, folded parchment. "This arrived this morning from the hand of Ezra Torres to Rashid. He gave it to me whilst you were seeing to Yaffa."

With trembling fingers, she read her brother's invitation to come home. Batsheva handed it back to him and smiled. "We will break the journey for a day or two, and then we will go home. My son assures me my elder daughter is in need of her mother."

EPILOGUE

Málaga 1214

As much as she loved Alexandria and understood hers was a position of power as mother of the new amir, once Khalil was laid in his tomb and her own thirty days of mourning were over, Batsheva knew it was time to go home. Daud arranged for his mother and five younger siblings to join Maryam in Málaga where she lived with her husband and children. Uncle Asher was there and he, too, would keep an eye his widowed sister. Amina, not too far away in Sevilla, would be able to visit frequently and that made everyone happy.

Batsheva sat beneath a pomegranate tree, her newest grandchild asleep on her shoulder. Maryam's twins sat on low stools, their eyes intent upon their *Aljidat Bashi* as she told how *Aljidu Khalil* came to rescue her from the English castle when their mother was a tiny baby. It was an oft-told tale, one missing some of the more difficult moments, but one in which their grandfather was the hero and Amir Gilbert, the treasured friend. Any story about Abu was a good story.

Just as things were getting exciting, Maryam bustled into the courtyard. "Mama," she called softly as not to wake the baby, "there's a gentleman to see you."

"Oh?" Batsheva gently handed little Sofia to her mother. "Who is he and why is he here?"

"I do believe he is here about a match for my little sister. You do not know about this?"

"Yasmina? I had not thought…."

"Well, she has, Mama." Maryam shooed the children from the courtyard.

The gentleman was richly dressed, with a silk turban the color of a pomegranate. His beard was dark but shot through with silver. He approached with great dignity and stopped at a respectful distance. "*As-salaam, Amira.* I am here…."

Batsheva looked hard at him. "Akiva?" she whispered as she rose from her chair.

He nodded. "Amirat Batsheva," he started again. "I am here for two reasons. My son and your youngest daughter seem to have found each other…attractive."

"She has not said anything to me." Yasmina was too busy with her friends to pay much attention to anything, let alone tell her mother she found a boy.

"From Binyamin's description, she sounds like a new version of you." There was the tiniest hint of a smile.

Batsheva sighed, "That's what her father always said. He said she was dangerous on her best days, but she is truly her father's daughter. Does your son know *what* he's getting?"

"She's *your* daughter. She can be no more dangerous than you at that age."

That age. The same age she was when she left Málaga for Sfax. "I will talk to her. I would be amenable to such a match."

"Binyamin will be glad." He looked down at the ground and took a deep breath. "But there is another reason I have come, Amirat Batsheva." He picked up his head.

Batsheva's eyes met his. She could not understand why tears were threatening her composure. "I am listening, Akiva."

He did not move closer to her when he said, "I am a widower, Bashi. Neither of us has ties to bind us to anyone. I am thinking we're not terribly old and…."

Batsheva did not wait for him to finish. "Yes, Akiva. The answer is yes."

GLOSSARY

LANGUAGE	PHRASE	ENGLISH
Arabic	abaya	cape-like robe
	abu	father
	agal	rope-like band to hold akufiya in place
	ahrib ya 'atfal! 'ujri bsre! alan! alan! arkud 'iilaa baba!	Run, Children! Run fast! Now! Now! Run to Papa
	Al-Quds	Arabic name for Jerusalem
	Alatfal bi'aman. 'Ant aman	The children are safe, you are safe
	Aljasus	Spies
	Amirat	wife of an Amir
	ana huna	I am here
	ant mit	You are dead
	djellaba	outer robe
	djinn	Genie or sprite
	eurus saghira	Little bride
	ghusil janabat	Ritual washing after sexual intercourse
	habibi	beloved
	hijab	Head covering that many Muslim women wear
	Imazighen	the peoples of North Africa.
	Insha Allah, Khalil. Insha Allah	God willing
	Jida	Grandmother
	jizyah	ransom
	Kli shay' ealaa ma yaram. Kulu shay' ealaa ma yaram	All is well. All is very well
	kufiya	square head covering
	la	no
	la kurat	no balls
	la shukran	No thanks
	La, habibi; 'ana last maytana	No, my love, I am alive
	Limr'atan salayta	Shrew
	Ma ismik, ya fatah	What is your name, girl?
	madraga	voluminous outer garment worn by Bedu women
	Maghreb	North Africa from Morocco to Libya
	majhula. Sayidat majhula	Unknown; nameless. Nameless lady.
	Malik Rik	King Richard

	nem	yes
	num jayidaan	Sleep well
	qubila	tribe
	Risala fi'l-Ishq	A mystical treatise on love by Ibn Sina
	saif	sword
	Salaam and variations	Peace be with you. A greeting.
	sara'i	Enclosed quarters for women
	sayadat bidun aism	Nameless Lady
	Sayida/Sayidi	My lady/my lord
	Shatranj	Chess
	shibreeyeh	camel saddle for women
	shuk	market area in a city
	sirwal	pantaloons
	thobe	Ankle length garment with long sleeves
	tahadath bialearabia	Speak Arabic!
	tiraz	an embroidered band set into the sleeve of a burnous
	umi	My mother
Hebrew	Baruch ha'ba, Barucha ha'ba'a	Welcome
	Baruch ha'Dayan Emet	God Is a righteous judge (said upon hearing of a death
	dodah	aunt
	Ha'Kodesh Baruch Hu	The Holy One (God)
	Hineini	Here I am
	kallah	bride
	ketuba	marriage contract
	mikvah	Ritual bath
	shiva	7 days of mourning
	ten'aim	betrothal contract
	zeh ya'avor	this will pass
	zonah	
Spanish	¿Vivirá la dama?	Will the lady live?
	Bueno, bueno, mamacita	Good, good, little mother
	Como desees	As you wish
	Creo que sí	I believe so
	Es muy importante, Infanta	It is very important, Princess
	Granadita	Little Pomegranate
	No es importante	It is not important.

	No llores, mi pequeño tesoro	Don't cry, my little treasure
	No más, no más	No more, no more.
	Por qué	Why
French	De boeuf? Ce n'est pas de bœuf, mon garçon	Beef? This is not beef, my boy.
	Mais bien sûr	But of course
	meurtrier	murderer
	Mon nom ce n'est pas garçon	My name is not boy
	Pardonnez-moi, monsieur	Forgive me, sir
	peliçon	A women's robe usually lined with fur
	prie-Dieu	kneeling stand used for personal Catholic prayer
	Qu'est-ce que c'est	What is
	sauvage	Savage, wild, untamed
	sucre	sugar
	Toi, petit garçon; viens ici	You, little boy, come here
	Votre Altesse	Your Highness
	Vous ne ferez rien de tel, garçon	You will do no such thing, boy
Greek	Óla eínai óso kalá anaménontai, xadélfia.	All is as well as can be expected, cousins

Made in United States
North Haven, CT
14 April 2024